P9-EFJ-425

Also by Karleen Koen

THROUGH A GLASS DARKLY

Now Face to Face

KARLEEN KOEN

NOW FACE TO FACE

RANDOM HOUSE NEW YORK

This is a work of fiction. The characters, incidents, and dialogues are products of the author's imagination and are not to be construed as real. Where the names of actual persons, living or dead, are used, the situations, incidents, and dialogues concerning those persons are entirely fictional and are not intended to depict any actual events or change the entirely fictional character of the work.

Copyright © 1995 by Karleen Koen

All rights reserved under International and Pan-American Copyright Conventions. Published in the United States by Random House, Inc., New York, and simultaneously in Canada by Random House of Canada Limited, Toronto.

Library of Congress Cataloging-in-Publication Data

Koen, Karleen.
Now face to face / Karleen Koen.—1st ed.
p.   cm.
Sequel to: Through a glass darkly.
ISBN 0-394-56929-6
1. Virginia—History—Colonial period, ca. 1600–1775—Fiction.
2. Great Britain—History—18th century—Fiction. I. Title.
PS3561.0334N69 1996
813′.54—dc20   95-8584

Manufactured in the United States of America
24689753
First Edition

Dedicated to my dear sister,
Carmen Marie Smith Rawlinson.
She made the life of everyone who knew her special.
I am grateful that she lived long enough
to read this manuscript.

WHEN I WAS A CHILD, I SPAKE AS A CHILD, I UNDERSTOOD AS A CHILD, I THOUGHT AS A CHILD: BUT WHEN I BECAME A MAN, I PUT AWAY CHILDISH THINGS.

FOR NOW WE SEE THROUGH A GLASS, DARKLY; BUT THEN FACE TO FACE: NOW I KNOW IN PART; BUT THEN SHALL I KNOW EVEN AS ALSO I AM KNOWN.

AND NOW ABIDETH FAITH, HOPE, CHARITY, THESE THREE; BUT THE GREATEST OF THESE IS CHARITY.

—I CORINTHIANS 13: 11–13.

Now Face to Face

Historical Note

Spies, treachery, financial disaster, ambition, romance—elements of fiction and elements of history weave themselves like silver threads into the setting of *Now Face to Face*.

This book is, of course, first and foremost a novel, and it recounts the loves, losses, and adventurous life of a fictional character, Barbara, Lady Devane. Yet the historical period in which Barbara's story unfolds is important, too, to the action, as human lives are always affected by the times in which they are lived.

Now Face to Face takes place in the early eighteenth century, when two men, cousins, claim the right to wear the crown of England, and each has just cause. A tangled web of events preceded the rival claims. By the time the Elector of Hanover, George, crossed the English Channel in 1714 to be crowned King of England, division was deep within the minds of many of his English subjects. Who was the right and proper king? Was it George, who had never set foot in England, but crossed over now from Hanover? Or was it James III, he who had been born twenty-six years earlier in London, and was a direct descendant of the Scottish House of Stuart, and of a king of England, James I?

George or James?

James was the third of his line to bear that name, and the two Jameses before him had both been kings of England. One, James I, was his great-grandfather; the other, James II, was his father.

To tangle the knot further, this man, this James III—or the Pretender, as he was known among those loyal to George I—was half-brother of Anne, the English queen who had just died in 1714. Years earlier, in 1688, Anne and her sister, Mary, who was queen before Anne, had turned their backs on this little half-brother born late in life to their father and his second wife. Many said that in the last years of Queen Anne's reign, as one after another of her children had died, and it became clear that there would be no heirs to the throne through her, Anne regretted her earlier betrayal and wished the crown to go to the man she'd seen only as a tiny baby. He was a grown man now, a half-brother, but a brother she had betrayed. And certainly courtiers and ministers in her court intrigued—whether out of guilt over past deeds or from simple expediency—to have the crown return to him who owned it by right of birth: James III.

But there was a law, passed in 1702, that the one who wore the English crown must be Protestant. Bloody religious and civil wars marked the years between Queen Elizabeth's reign and Queen Anne's. James III was Catholic. George of Hanover was the closest living relation to the House of Stuart who was also Protestant.

In 1688, James III, while yet a baby, was removed from London by his mother and father, then King and Queen of England, who feared for their lives. They lived to see the King's own grown daughters, Mary and Anne, declare open rebellion against their father and assume, one after another, the English throne. Mary's husband, the Dutchman William of Orange, invaded England in 1688, at the invitation of most of its nobility. And for the rest of his life, King James intrigued to be returned to his throne; he led two invasions to try to accomplish this. His son, James III—the Pretender who figures in the story of *Now Face to Face*—also plotted, also invaded.

Intrigue, espionage, betrayal, lies, not to mention true love—these are the stuff of history, and of fiction. Welcome to *Now Face to Face*.

LIST OF CHARACTERS

Saylor Family and Friends

BARBARA MONTGEOFFRY, COUNTESS DEVANE—WIDOW OF ROGER, EARL DEVANE, AND GRANDDAUGHTER OF THE DUCHESS OF TAMWORTH

THÉRÈSE FUSEAU—DEVOTED SERVANT OF BARBARA

HYACINTHE—A TEN-YEAR-OLD SLAVE, SERVANT OF BARBARA

ALICE SAYLOR, DUCHESS OF TAMWORTH—BARBARA'S GRANDMOTHER AND THE WIDOW OF ENGLAND'S FAMOUS GENERAL RICHARD SAYLOR

ANTHONY RICHARD SAYLOR ("TONY"), THE SECOND DUKE OF TAMWORTH—GRANDSON OF THE DUCHESS OF TAMWORTH, AND INHERITOR OF HIS GRANDFATHER'S TITLE AND LAND; COUSIN OF BARBARA

MARY, LADY RUSSEL—TONY'S SISTER; BARBARA'S COUSIN

CHARLES, LORD RUSSEL—HUSBAND OF MARY, AND FORMER LOVER OF BARBARA

❧

Abigail, Lady Saylor—Tony's mother; daughter-in-law of the Duchess of Tamworth

❧

Diana, Lady Alderley—the Duchess of Tamworth's daughter; mother of Barbara

❧

Clemmie—servant of Diana, Lady Alderley

❧

Louisa, Lady Shrewsborough ("Aunt Shrew")—sister-in-law of the Duchess of Tamworth; great-aunt of Tony and Barbara

❧

Sir Alexander Pendarves—friend of Louisa, Lady Shrewsborough

❧

Sir John Ashford—neighbor and oldest friend of the Duchess of Tamworth

❧

Jane Cromwell—daughter of Sir John Ashford; Barbara's childhood friend

❧

The Reverend Augustus Cromwell ("Gussy")—husband of Jane; secretary to the Bishop of Rochester

❧

Philip, Duke of Wharton ("Wart")—friend of Barbara

❧

Philippe, Prince de Soissons—cousin to the royal family of France; friend of the late Roger, Lord Devane

❧

Annie, Perryman, Tim—servants of the Duchess of Tamworth in her country residence, Tamworth Hall

House of Hanover

GEORGE I—KING OF ENGLAND, AS WELL AS ELECTOR OF HANOVER; BORN IN HANOVER

❧

GEORGE, PRINCE OF WALES—HEIR TO THE THRONE THROUGH HIS FATHER, GEORGE I

❧

CAROLINE, PRINCESS OF WALES

❧

TOMMY CARLYLE—A COURTIER IN THE COURT OF GEORGE I

❧

ROBERT WALPOLE ("ROBIN")—MINISTER OF GEORGE I

❧

LORD TOWNSHEND—MINISTER OF GEORGE I; BROTHER-IN-LAW OF ROBERT WALPOLE

❧

LORD SUNDERLAND—MINISTER OF GEORGE I, AND RIVAL OF WALPOLE AND OF LORD TOWNSHEND FOR THE KING'S FAVOR

❧

DUCHESS OF KENDALL—MISTRESS OF GEORGE I

House of Stuart and Jacobite Followers

JAMES III ("JAMIE")—KNOWN AS THE PRETENDER, BORN HEIR TO THE THRONE OF ENGLAND; COUSIN OF GEORGE. HIS FOLLOWERS WERE CALLED JACOBITES.

❧

LAURENCE SLANE (ALIAS OF LUCIUS, VISCOUNT DUNCANNON)—DEVOTED FRIEND OF AND SPY FOR JAMES III

❧

THE BISHOP OF ROCHESTER—BISHOP OF THE CHURCH OF EN-GLAND; SECRET AGENT FOR JAMES III IN ENGLAND

❧

CHRISTOPHER LAYER—AGENT FOR JAMES III IN ENGLAND

❧

PHILIP NEYOE—AGENT FOR JAMES III IN ENGLAND

Virginians

SIR ALEXANDER SPOTSWOOD—DEPUTY GOVERNOR OF THE COLONY OF VIRGINIA

❧

COLONEL VALENTINE BOLLING—LANDOWNER WHOSE NEPH-EW'S ESTATE, FIRST CURLE, WAS LOST TO BARBARA'S BROTHER IN A GAME OF CARDS

❧

KLAUS VON ROTHBACH—BOLLING'S NEPHEW BY MARRIAGE; CAPTAIN OF BOLLING'S SHIP

❧

COLONEL EDWARD PERRY—LANDOWNER; NEIGHBOR OF BAR-BARA

❧

BETH PERRY—COLONEL PERRY'S DAUGHTER

❧

MAJOR JOHN CUSTIS—LANDOWNER; KNOWLEDGEABLE ON GARDENS AND TOBACCO SEED

❧

JOHN BLACKSTONE—SERVANT INDENTURED FOR HIS PART IN THE JACOBITE INVASION OF 1715 AND OVERSEER FOR BARBARA

❧

ODELL SMITH—OVERSEER FOR BARBARA ON FIRST CURLE

❧

MARGARET COX; MAJOR JOHN RANDOLPH—NEIGHBORS OF BARBARA IN VIRGINIA

❧

KANO, SINSIN, BELLE, MAMA ZOU, JACK CHRISTMAS, MOODY, GREEN, CUFFY, QUASH—SLAVES ON FIRST CURLE

FALL

WHEN I WAS A CHILD, I SPAKE AS A CHILD,
I UNDERSTOOD AS A CHILD, I THOUGHT AS
A CHILD: BUT WHEN I BECAME A MAN, I
PUT AWAY CHILDISH THINGS.

CHAPTER 1

On the first day of September in the year of 1721, a galley with a center mast and one sail glided through the waters of the James River in His Majesty King George I's Royal Colony of Virginia. It was manned by slaves on oars, and in its middle, as if to emphasize her importance, sat its principal passenger, Barbara Montgeoffry, widow to an earl, and therefore a countess: the Countess Devane. She was young to be widowed already, only one-and-twenty, like the century. She sat small, exquisite yet fragile-looking in her widow's weeds—clothes solidly black as the manners of the time demanded.

Other passengers included the Deputy Governor of the colony and the Countess's servants, a young French maid and a page boy, a slave himself. Two pug dogs, a cow, and six willow baskets with chickens inside were wedged in and around trunks, wooden boxes, barrels, and furniture wrapped in oilcloth.

The river was wide, the sky blue-white. Birds chirped in trees that stood like ancient sentinels on the banks. For some time now, from the east, from the direction of Williamsburg—the principal town and capital of the colony—clouds had been gathering, rolling over and into each other. At this bend in the river, there were no houses, only fields and trees, a forest of trees, huge trees, primeval trees, as old possibly as the land itself, certainly older than the colony, which had existed upon the shores of this river and three others to the north only since 1607.

"Governor Spotswood, how much farther?" asked Barbara impatiently.

She was the reason the Governor had taken time from his duties to man a galley up the James River.

"We are not half the way yet. Are you unwell again? Shall we land? Perry's Grove is an hour or so ahead," Sir Alexander Spotswood answered. An older man, in his fifties, he was deputy governor of the colony. As he spoke, a sudden wind came up to shake the fringe on his buckskin coat and pull at the sides of his wig, a full, formal, dark wig, in the style that the late king of France, Louis XIV, had made fashionable. It was parted in the middle to hang down majestically around the face.

"I'm quite well, just impatient to reach First Curle."

She'd come to Virginia from England to look over her grandmother's plantation, but there had been a delay of a week while she recovered from a fever. Her arrival was completely unexpected, as was her fever; to the Governor, it was as if a shimmering butterfly had landed unexpectedly in his colony, a butterfly with the most impressive of ancestors. The Countess's grandfather Richard Saylor had been a renowned and beloved general in the long war with France that had taken up the Governor's young manhood—and that of so many others—in the 1680s and '90s and into the beginning of this century. Richard Saylor's military exploits had earned him a dukedom. The Governor had served under him once upon a time.

Is there going to be rain? thought the Governor, staring at the sky. The clouds were suddenly closer; he'd swear they had moved at least a mile since the last time he checked them. He looked at the shore, estimating where they were, where to take shelter should it begin to rain.

He looked over to the young Countess, his fragile black butterfly. He did not imagine her responding kindly to a storm of rain, though she had displayed nothing but beautiful manners so far, beautiful manners that matched a beautiful face the precise shape of a heart, a fair and sweet face.

The Lionheart's granddaughter, thought the Governor, for a moment taking time to wonder at the world, at its smallness. Richard

Saylor had been called the Lionheart by his soldiers. To imagine that he took the Lionheart's granddaughter to a river plantation that belonged to the family. What honor. And what obligation. He glanced once more at the sky. The clouds were above them now. It was going to rain.

Do I land or keep going? he thought. Will she be more angry to be wet or to be delayed? She's been ill. She's in mourning. She is not used to our roughness—only look at the entourage she's brought with her: a French lady's maid, a page boy, and two pug dogs. Her dogs, her servants, were the talk of Williamsburg. I'd better seek shelter and see that she is protected, he thought.

Large, determined drops of rain splattered the oilcloth covering the table and chairs, the barrels and trunks. The waters of the river stirred underneath the galley, as if something large and menacing had turned over. Wind rattled the ropes and iron rings on the sail, and the galley rocked back and forth in spite of the steady, powerful rhythm of the rowers. The cow, wedged among boxes and barrels, stretched out her neck toward land and lowed.

At that moment, the wind struck like a fist, and a basket of chickens fell over, the chickens in them escaping, clucking, squawking, flying into everyone. The dogs began to bark, and the young page boy, Hyacinthe, leaped up to lean dangerously over the side after a chicken.

"Hyacinthe! Sit down! Never mind the chickens! What is happening, Governor Spotswood? Thérèse! For God's sake, shut those dogs up!"

It was the fragile black butterfly, Barbara, who spoke, yanking her page boy back down on the plank seat beside her as she did so.

Spotswood did not answer, for he was maneuvering his way through the cargo to get to the center mast and let down the sail, which was whipping in its rigging like something desperate to be free. A squawking chicken flew straight into his face. It screamed. But not any louder than he did.

"Damnation and blast and confounded hands of Jesus Christ! A storm, that is what is happening, Lady Devane. A large one!"

He sent the chicken whirling overboard. Over them, the sky was rolling, ominous, cresting clouds. The day was, in a moment, dark, as if evening had come. Barbara watched yet another chicken cluck and cry and run amok until it flew into the water and disappeared, squawking and screaming to the last, under water that was now foaming and cresting dangerously.

"Oh, no," said Hyacinthe in French, "your grandmother the Duchess—" He did not finish. But then, he did not have to. Barbara's grandmother, the Duchess of Tamworth, Richard Saylor's fierce and indomitable widow, was quite proud of her chickens and cows, wanting them on her plantation in Virginia. She had been specific in her instruction.

"Never mind," Barbara said, also in French. "The chickens have no importance as long as we are safe."

She raised her face to the rain, to the dark sky, exhilarated rather than frightened by this sudden wildness coming up from nothing around her. During the week she had lain impatiently in the best bed in the best bedchamber in the Governor's house in Williamsburg, ill with an ague, or fever, which was one of the hazards of coming to this colony, they had warned her of these sudden storms. They'd described ferocious lightning and deafening thunder as part of the storms.

Carters, Burwells, Lees, Pages, Fitzhughs, Ludwells. They were among the biggest landowners, the Governor had told her, the gentry of this colony, and she was wise enough in her fever to smile upon them as they buzzed around her sickbed like bees, buzzing colonial bees, attracted by her title and family, the surprise of her crossing the ocean to join them. They rode in from their plantations, the Governor said, to see her. They brought her flowers, wines, cooling fever waters; they were profusely apologetic that she should be sick, as if it were their fault she had the ague. They chattered to her of their colony—the vastness of its bay, the size of its rivers, the deadliness of its snakes—as proud of its flaws as they were of its beauties.

They begged her to visit their plantations, and she could feel the curiosity burning in them as deeply as the fever burned in her. She was exotic, a novelty. A countess. A young widow. Someone seemingly rich and secure, above them in all ways. The granddaughter of one of England's most famous generals. Why was she here, they had to be wondering, when the world was hers in London?

Because the world was not hers in London. But, of course, she did not say so.

There was a sudden zigzag of blue-white lightning, and on shore, before her amazed eyes, a tree crackled, sizzled, and fell over, fire hissing in what was left. Now there came the accompanying rolling crack of thunder, so loud, so startling, so near, that she jumped, and her servant Thérèse looked ready to weep.

"Head for shore," Barbara was glad to hear Spotswood command the slaves. She glanced at the boy beside her. Hyacinthe was looking afraid. Of course he's afraid, she thought. He's only ten.

"An adventure," she said to him, to comfort him. She spoiled him, but he was quick and lively, easy to spoil. She loved him.

"You have no nerves, either of you," snapped Thérèse. Rain had ruined her starched white cap, which was collapsed and limp about her pretty face. "We should have waited another day." Thérèse's words spilled out in hissing French. She clutched a growling, nervous pug to each breast. "You will catch the fever again, and then where will we be?"

"The chickens," said Hyacinthe. "The Duchess said I must take care of her chickens, that you would be too busy with other things."

There was another flashing, jagged blue-white streak of lightning, again very close, and Barbara thought: This is too much adventure. Are we going to drown on this colonial river? I didn't come here to drown.

Loved ones came to mind. Roger, she thought, I may drown in a river and see you again, soon, after all. Harry, are you laughing at me, here in this storm, here in Virginia, in your place? Roger was her husband. He had died at Christmas. Harry was her brother. He had died in the summer a year ago. It was for them that she wore black, for them and for vanished dreams. The death of dreams. Nothing harder to overcome, so said her grandmother.

Lightning made another slash across the sky, the vibrating ear-splitting thunder following in an endless roar. Rain was falling in sheets now. Grandmama, thought Barbara, counting off people she loved, Tony, Jane. The slaves had rowed into a creek opening onto the river.

"Abandon ship!" the Governor shouted, but Barbara didn't need his command to be galvanized. We really are in danger, she thought. And when in danger, one fled. She'd known that since girlhood.

Scrambling out in the rain and wind, she stumbled in shallow water and fell to her knees, but another lightning bolt, another rolling crack of thunder, had her up in seconds and running through rain that fell in pellets, stinging the skin where it touched. The slaves were heaving bundles and baggage ashore—her trunks and barrels from England, her tables and chairs, her remaining baskets of chickens. The cow, eyes rolling back white in its head, strained and pulled at the rope that held it in the galley.

Barbara kept moving upward, kept urging Hyacinthe and Thérèse to follow, the three of them scrabbling in the dirt of the hilly bank, toward a grove of trees above them, giants: pines, oaks, maples, silverbells, cedars. She found herself half crawling on hands and knees upward as the rain pelted her. Underbrush scratched her face and arms, stabbed into her chest and belly. The wind rattled the trees above her as if they were thin saplings instead of oaks and pines hundreds of years old. It was a fierce storm. The colonials did not lie.

Barbara looked back to see the Governor. He was still inside the galley, where a slave was chopping at the mast with an ax. She heard the crack as it fell over like a tree. Then, the Governor and the slaves were out of the galley. They were all straining to turn it over on itself. Why? thought Barbara. The cow had either torn loose of her rope or been cut loose; she leaped out of the galley the moment it tipped over. Then the cow—Grandmama's finest, thought Barbara; oh, well—was gone, splashing down the shore and away through the underbrush.

"Come back!"

The Governor was shouting, pointing to the heavens.

Come back to what? thought Barbara. Is he mad? Then, to her horror, she was blinded by flash and flames as a tree somewhere above them split open to its roots, and branches went flying everywhere, over her head, behind her, to the sides of her. There was the terrifying stench of scorched earth and tree, of fire and brimstone, of hell, as a deafening roll of thunder cracked on and on around them, making their ears ache with its sound. No more need be said.

Barbara turned around at once, sliding back down the bank, half carrying, half dragging Hyacinthe with her, back to the galley. Spotswood pointed beneath it. She scooted under, dragging Hyacinthe every inch of the way, somehow avoiding impaling herself on jagged edges of broken center mast. Thérèse was just behind them.

"The dogs?" Barbara said, ready to go back in the storm for them if she had to.

Thérèse unfurled her grimy, clenched apron, and there they were, their eyes bulging even more than normally with terror.

Good. Everyone was here, her family—Thérèse, Hyacinthe, the dogs. Spotswood was crawling in, on his belly.

The slaves were crowded at one end between the planks that served as benches. Among them were some of the chickens. Barbara could still smell the lightning, the scorch of the burned tree, could still see the explosion of tree and branches, hear the thunder in her ears. Rain pounded on the hull over them. Rivulets of water eddied under them, cutting deeper channels. At the point where the side of the galley did not meet sand, the storm's dark was split with continual flashes of light, as thunder cracked and roared, like a monster prowling around, searching to eat them.

"Summer storms," Spotswood said, after a moment, as if some explanation were necessary.

"It is not summer!" Thérèse snapped, in French, forgetting to speak English, forgetting the courtesy due the Governor of one of His Majesty King George's colonies.

It was clear she had been pushed beyond endurance: traveling for weeks aboard a crowded ship whose sway made her ill, arriving in a colony whose inelegance took them all by surprise; her mistress catching a fever but, too impatient to wait to be fully well, insisting they journey to her grandmother's plantation at once, all of them drenched now because of Lady Devane's impetuosity, and frightened, under a galley in a dreadful storm.

Thérèse's starched, white, lace-trimmed cap was gone, and her dark hair was plastered around her pretty, soft face, a face covered with mud and scratches and beaded blood. A chicken peered over one shoulder, silent, blinking. Barbara began to laugh. She could not help it. They could not have begun to imagine this in England. She held her hands over her mouth to stop herself, but that just made it worse.

Crouched beside her—they could not have been any closer if they were lying together in love—Spotswood, his official wig gone in the storm, water eddying down his face, his buckskin coat smelling like an old goat, gave a snort, suddenly amused himself. He was also relieved. He'd expected to face another storm under this galley, one of tears or rage. Fragile butterfly, indeed.

There was a smear of dirt across her cheek, as well as several scratches. Her gown was soaking, ruined, torn. Had she ever been so wet before, so bedraggled and dirty? So, he thought, you have your grandfather's courage—and more, I think: something of your grandmother's stamina and firmness. Good. If ever you will need them, it will be here.

"Have I welcomed you to Virginia?" he asked, testing a jest, still not absolutely certain whether she would decide to take offense.

Barbara laughed harder than ever.

That afternoon, Spotswood called orders to the slaves rescuing baggage and whatever else they could find now that the rain had stopped. The sky was as clear, as hard a blue as if there had never been a storm. Barbara's page, Hyacinthe, had disappeared into the woods above the bank. Thérèse searched through an open trunk for dry clothing.

Barbara sat on the incline of the bank, watching, trying to take it all in, but she could not stop shivering. I must learn all of this, she was thinking, how to salvage oneself, make do, repair loss. It was clear there was going to be much making do here. But she needed to stop shivering first.

She looked up, and Spotswood was standing over her. Without his wig, he seemed sterner; his face was sun-lined, disciplined, the face of the soldier he had once been. He served under your grandfather, her grandmother had said. I'll write him a letter that reminds him in no uncertain terms of his duty. The Governor looked both angry and concerned. What was in that letter? wondered Barbara. With her grandmother, there was no telling.

"Mademoiselle Fuseau," he said to Barbara's servant, "find the Peruvian bark." This was a fever water that made the fever stop. He knelt and took Barbara by the arm.

"Here, now, come along, Lady Devane, and we will just walk around this little curve of the creek. She needs to be put into dry clothing at once," he said to Thérèse, who was following. "That's it. Come along, Lady Devane, a few more steps. There we are. Mademoiselle Fuseau, if you please."

He left them alone. Barbara opened her mouth to take the bitter mixture, held out her arms so that Thérèse could begin to unfasten and unhook things.

I am ill again, damn it, Barbara thought, shrugging and moving impatiently out of this and that. Take it all off, she thought, all the garments of mourning: black leather gloves, like another skin; black gown, once tight at the waist and sleeves but loose now; black undergown; whalebone hoop; stays, their ribbons and laces black; chemise; the garters tying her black stockings; black shoes. All of them off, the required dark garments of mourning, signifying loss. Her brother was dead, and her husband. Within the last year, both had died.

"I knew it. I knew it," Thérèse was murmuring in French. "You were out of bed too soon. Anyone could see it. 'Stay another few days,' I said, but no, we must go to the plantation. As if the plantation will not wait. Barbarous place. Barbarous river. What are we going to? Have you thought of that? Their principal town is little more than a village, and I am kind to call it that. Plantation. What does that mean?"

"Our paper about it says house and barn and cookhouse. Slaves. There's a well. There are fields for growing tobacco. And many acres, Thérèse, some two thousand needing three men, three overseers, to see to them."

"Acres of what, I ask you? The house I grew up in in France as a girl was better than some of these I saw from the river this morning. You are soaking wet. Wet to the skin, madame. Those chickens. Did you see? Drowned in a moment. We might have been drowned, too. I shiver every time I think of it. Drowned or burnt to nothing by lightning. We will not put on a hoop. What can a hoop matter in this wild place? Who will know? Who will see? Savage. Barbarous. I am going to pray for us tonight."

"Good—do that, Thérèse. I depend upon your prayers."

Laced up in fresh stays, those unyielding undergarments every lady must wear to pull her waist in as small as possible, to push up breasts, to make the body, whether it wished to or not, conform to fashion, Barbara held up her arms for a dry gown to be pulled over her. Black, of course. I will be glad when I no longer wear black, she thought. I will be glad when I no longer feel loss. Surely there comes a day when you no longer feel loss. It's because I'm ill that I feel it so terribly this moment. Surely, it's that.

She leaned against Thérèse as they walked back around the curve, where she sat down, abruptly, in a patch of sunlight, raising her face to the hot sun. Over her Thérèse piled gowns and shawls and cloaks, anything dry she could find. Her dogs huddled into her lap, and Thérèse began unpinning her hair. It was red-gold, curling, one of her beauties, but then there was very little about Barbara that was not beautiful, as she was well aware.

"You are wet yourself," she tried to say, but the effort made her head ache terribly, so she simply allowed Thérèse to have her way, to untangle her hair, to dry it with a shawl, to brush it. It was soothing to have her hair brushed; when she was a girl, her grandmother had always brushed it for her. The dogs were warm in her lap, and the shivering seemed a bit less; after all, she was nearly over the fever. Her eyelids felt heavy, and the sun was warm on her, and she snuggled into the sand with the dogs, like one of them, and fell asleep.

It was a good, long nap. When she opened her eyes, her dogs were gone and it was late afternoon. She sat up. The fever seemed to be gone, too, but her heart was aching. It was the sudden, unexpected, coming-from-nowhere missing that was part of grief. She was more than familiar with it by now. Some days on the crossing over—nothing to see but sky and sea—she'd thought she'd go mad from it. She missed Roger. She missed her brother. She missed home. What on earth am I doing here? she thought. Insane, her mother had said, raging at Barbara as only her mother could do. I cannot believe you do this idiot thing.

Barbara looked around. The Governor had made camp with the decisive action of a born soldier. She approved. Wet clothes—gowns, chemises, stockings, hoops, shawls, breeches, cloaks—were spread over the bushes everywhere. Her table and chairs, still in their oilcloth, propped up the back of a shelter made of the boat's sail. She counted the baskets of chickens that had survived the storm. One . . . two . . . yes, three. She felt better.

"I captured some of the others."

It was Hyacinthe, who had come up behind her. "See, madame."

She did see. There they were, captured chickens on their sides, silent, defeated by storm and boy, for Hyacinthe had tied their legs together with rope.

"Very clever."

"Are you well now, madame?"

No, darling, I am not well. My heart hurts for all I've lost and feels as if it will never heal. And I think I may have been a fool to come here.

"Much better now. Thank you."

"The cow is still gone."

If she remembered correctly, she had fallen asleep listening to Thérèse lament chickens. Really, it was too much of her grandmother to instill a sense of obligation into two servants who were not even her own. When she went back to England, she'd tell her so.

Spotswood walked down the bank from the trees above, holding a dead rabbit by its long ears. He marched to where she sat, pleased with himself.

"Supper," he said.

"However did you manage that?"

"The slaves can snare rabbits and birds and anything else in these woods. Help me, boy."

He knelt at the fire and began to skin the rabbit. Barbara watched. When she'd been a girl, her brother, Harry, had taught her how to skin game he'd caught. And just as Hyacinthe was doing, she and Harry and Jane had hacked branches into a rough spit, and the three of them had cooked Harry's kill in Tamworth's woods.

There was a shout from near the galley, and a slave in the creek held up a line. At its end was a wiggling, silvery fish.

"More supper," Spotswood said to her.

"Delightful."

The sky had begun to streak itself with evening. A wind rustled the trees, like a woman running fingers through her hair, and a few leaves, still green with summer even on the first day of September, floated down and settled on the bank, on her. She held out her hand to capture one, a game she and Jane had always played as girls. It was a sign of good fortune to catch a leaf. As one floated into her hand, she closed her fingers around it carefully and smiled to herself. It was a dazzling smile, another legacy from her grandfather.

Spotswood, watching her, blinked. With her hair down and dried into unruly curls, with those large eyes the color of sky, with that smile showing small, pearly teeth, she was the loveliest woman he had ever seen. Valentine Bolling might even be moved. Certainly, Bolling's nephew, Klaus, a man with an eye for a pretty woman, would be. Good. Anything to make her arrival at First Curle easier. He had not prepared her properly for First Curle. He must do so.

Suddenly, he realized she was staring back, head lowered, brows drawn together, expression haughty, challenging him as if he were some footman who'd transgressed, and he was at once aware of the gap between them, he an old soldier for her grandfather and she a countess, granddaughter of a great duke. He'd forgotten it when they'd been under the galley, but now she reminded him. To think he'd thought of her as fragile. Perhaps someone ought to warn Bolling.

He made much ado of producing from his baggage an iron skillet with little iron legs on it, like a trivet.

"This iron is from a mine in the northern part of the colony." He tapped the skillet. "I brought the miners over myself. This colony depends overmuch on tobacco. Not that anyone will listen to my theories. Everyone continues to plant as much tobacco as possible, and the price is down again. I think the South Sea Bubble is touching us here, the way a rock thrown into water makes ripples that expand outward. You had it all of last year. Now it comes to us."

Barbara shivered. It was as if a ghost had walked over her grave.

"We hear such stories; are things still bad back in England?"

"Yes."

Families ruined, fortunes in shreds because of the fall of South Sea Company stock, a dizzying, terrifying fall that seemed to have no end. Everyone affected—every company, every banking house. For a time of months, there had seemed no bottom to the fall of the price of everything in all of England: land, carriages, cattle, corn, other stock. Her brother, Harry, had killed himself over his losses. And her husband, Roger, had died trying to deal with his obligations as a director in the company. He'd lost everything, leaving her not only without him, but without an estate. South Sea. She hated the words.

"I hear they are fining the directors in the South Sea Company. To my mind, they ought to hang them," said the Governor, beginning to scale the trout.

She was silent. Even though he was dead, Parliament had fined Roger for being a director. She'd had to dismantle his great house, Devane House, in London, sell furniture and art, even the paving stones of the gardens, toward the fine Parliament levied. She dug her fingers into the sand in which she sat, angry, her throat swelling with grief she did not speak. Grief over dreams. What might have been, but was not, would never be. Roger, his fine house, his dream—he dreamed, too—little left now but the land upon which it rested.

"Parliament was in the process of deciding the final amount of each fine when I left." She spoke slowly, carefully, not wishing the Governor to see her distress.

"It is not good for the kingdom when something like this happens. I heard the King's mistress took enormous bribes of stock, yet lost little when everyone else did. I heard the same of the King's ministers. People wanted to impeach them, I hear. I tell you, Lady Devane, the Pretender should have invaded last year. It was the perfect time. As an old soldier, I know these things."

"Are you a Jacobite?" she asked him.

She was curious, intrigued. Jacobites were followers of James III, called the Pretender. They believed James was the rightful king, rather than George, the cousin from Hanover who was on the throne now. Her brother, Harry, had been a Jacobite; so had her father.

"My father always believed James II was betrayed by his own Parliament," he replied. "I'm Scotch, Lady Devane. We Scotch keep a soft place in our hearts for the royal House of Stuart. No, I am not a Jacobite. The law says George of Hanover is King, and I follow the law. But you've a Jacobite on one of your quarters—"

"Quarter? What is that?"

As he explained, the Governor neatly gutted the trout, placed it in the skillet, and moved the skillet to the fire over which the rabbit was roasting.

"The land belonging to your grandmother spreads across the river. It is divided up into sections called quarters. This storm has shown that you must never take anything for granted out here, Lady Devane. I meant to speak of it to you sooner." And now he was off on another track, lecturing her about the colony. Whenever she traveled it must be with extra provisions, an ax and a knife, and flint and steel and a blanket and a musket and other things, so that she could survive if there should be an accident and she was stranded, as they were now. The closest plantation was several hours' walk away through forest and underbrush, and anyone who did not know the way would become lost.

"That is why I insisted upon coming with you." He frowned at her. "This is not the world you are used to, Lady Devane."

The world I am used to, Barbara thought, and in her mind, she saw that world, moved like a doll among its inhabitants, the King, his son, the Prince of Wales, the Princess, the courtiers. What would the Frog say if he saw me now, she thought, in my crumpled gown, with my hair hanging in my eyes, my belongings spread out like a Gypsy's camp?

The evening dusk was soft as a velvet mask on her cheek, a dusk made clean from the storm, like a slate wiped fresh to begin again. She was beginning again, too. Go on to Virginia and remove yourself for a time from this mess Roger has left you, her grandmother had said. Go and tell me the lay of the land, its gains, its losses. Tell me if I should sell this plantation back to the country bumpkins who formerly owned it.

"Show me how far we are from my grandmother's plantation."

"Your grandmother's plantation. I am very glad you bring it up. The river narrows and curls back on itself another half day's journey from here. Your grandmother's plantation is in one of those curls, the first one."

"And where are the Bollings?" It was a Bolling who had written her grandmother asking to buy the plantation back.

"Past you on the river, farther west. Your plantation is the last place on the river deep enough to take tobacco ships. It has value as a loading place; at its dock there is also a storehouse where tobacco from other plantations is stored."

That would explain why Bolling wanted the plantation back, thought Barbara.

"I've been meaning to speak to you of Valentine Bolling—" he said.

"Valentine. What a promising name."

"Do not be misled by it. Valentine Bolling is the only one left now, though he has a nephew by marriage. The niece is dead, but Bolling remains close to the nephew, Klaus Von Rothbach, Lady Devane . . ."

The Governor was staring at her in a concerned way.

"I've been wishing to speak to you of Valentine Bolling. He's of a certain sort, here—older, having carved a place for himself from nothing, from forest and creek and swamp and Indians' hunting grounds. Such men are not soft men. They cannot be."

I've dismantled Roger's house, a beloved house, a beautiful house, and sold it down to the last brick and stone to survive; I face a huge debt; I've buried both my dear brother and the only man I ever really loved, my husband. Your Bolling cannot frighten me, Governor, Barbara thought.

"You could sell the plantation back easily," the Governor was saying. "I must say I think once you've seen it, you won't want to stay. It is not what you're used to. I've been thinking of that since you arrived. Once you've seen it, come right back to Williamsburg with me, or remain upon it a few weeks, if you must, and I'll send my galley back for you; you have only to send word. From Williamsburg, I will find you a ship back to England."

He had it all planned, did he? "The fish is burning," she said.

He moved to pull the skillet from the hot ashes, burned his hand as he did so, cursed, begged her pardon. The smell of browned fish mingled with roasting meat. I'm starving, thought Barbara.

He was distressed, she could see it. What distressed him now? What other warnings, other advice, had he for her?

"I have no plates, Lady Devane."

She smiled. "Once I was a wild girl who ran through the woods with my brother and a friend. I know how to eat with my hands, Governor."

He speared fish into her hands, and she tossed the crumbling, hot pieces back and forth until they were cool enough to eat, shared them with Hyacinthe and Thérèse. Night had fallen, like a cloak, over them. Juice dribbled down her chin as she ate. No supper in a royal drawing room had ever tasted so good as this supper on a creek, she thought, remembering suppers as a girl, with Harry and Jane—those suppers, too, in the woods, with only a fire; those suppers, too, delicious and satisfying.

Her dogs whined and cried and did flips in the air as Hyacinthe threw them scraps.

"Where are the slaves, Governor?" asked Barbara.

"At the galley. They have their own fire, their own supper."

Spotswood produced a bottle of wine from his baggage, opened it and presented it, with a flourish, to Barbara.

"To the storm," she said. "To survival."

One after the other they drank from it.

"You are a man after my grandmother's heart," said Barbara, "prepared for anything." She saw that these words pleased him. "My grandmother dislikes disorder, will not have it."

There was a rhythm and a sense of purpose to her grandmother's life, comforting, like this fire. Order holds back chaos, thought Barbara, the way fire holds back dark.

The sky blazed with stars, like hundreds of diamonds sparkling and white, laid out on a black velvet gown. Everywhere were the sounds of night: crickets, frogs, water lapping, small rustles in the underbrush. There was a far-off howl, like a dog's, but not a dog's. Her pugs, in her lap now, lifted their heads. The short fur on the back of their necks rose.

"Wolves," Spotswood said.

Thérèse, who was sitting near the fire with them, bare toes peeking out from her gown as she wiggled them in sand, looked up. She was French and had lived on a farm; stories of wolves, slavering monsters who ate children alive, were something she had ingested as regularly as black bread and sour wine.

"No danger," said Spotswood. "It is only in winter that they might be hungry enough to attack."

Thérèse made a face as if to say, See, what a barbarous place. Barbara smiled. Hyacinthe was playing with a turtle he had found along the bank. She called his name, patting the sand near her; he left his turtle, curled himself against her stretched-out leg like a small animal, and was instantly asleep, as she'd known he would be.

One of her dogs, the male one, named Harry after her brother, jumped from her lap and trotted away, but she did not call him. Thérèse was in the shelter now, rummaging through her portmanteau, an ancient, faded bag of leather, setting it to rights. Order out of chaos, thought Barbara. Doubtless she was also searching for a charm against wolves. Spotswood stretched out on the sand to smoke a long Dutch pipe of tobacco. Barbara heard her dog barking.

"Perhaps he has found the cow," said Barbara. She'd rather not write to her grandmother that she'd lost the cow. The chickens lost would be bad enough.

"I sent two slaves off to search for your cow. They have not returned. They have more than likely run away. Some slaves try it over and over again. If they make it to the mountains, the Seneca—a fierce Indian tribe—find them and bring them back. If they can get to Carolina, to the south of us, they live there among the runaway indentured servants. I have asked the Board of Trade in England to limit the number of slaves allowed here, but they do nothing. We need another import duty to stop their coming. There are too many of them here. . . . If they were to all rise up . . ."

He did not finish. Barbara was silent, trying to put straight in her mind the sight of those silent rowers today, the sight of all the dark faces she had seen since her arrival, cooking, cleaning, weeding gardens, repairing fences, carrying water, with rebellion and fear, but she could not.

"What will happen to the slaves when you find them?"

"They'll be whipped. The incorrigibles have their toes chopped off." There was nothing apologetic in his voice. Barbara was silent, digesting his words.

The pug ran toward them with something dark and hairy in his mouth. Oh no, thought Barbara. The pug was shaking it back and forth, and it hung limply, obviously dead.

"What's he caught?" Spotswood said, interested, rising to his feet. "I had no idea pugs could hunt. Here, boy. Here!"

Harry laid his trophy at Spotswood's feet and sat back on his haunches, panting, pleased with himself. Spotswood bent down and picked up his own wig.

Barbara laughed and clapped her hands for the dog to come to her.

"Good dog!" she said to him. "Mighty hunter. Savage one."

Spotswood pushed a stick into the ground near the fire and set the wig upon it to dry. It reminded Barbara of the rotted heads of traitors hanging above the city gate of Temple Bar in London. The heads that hung there now belonged to the nobles who had supported the Pretender's invasion attempt in 1715—a frightening year, that, with the old Queen dead; a new, foreign King, disliked; and invasion.

"The Seneca rip off the crown and hair of the head of an enemy and wear it on a thong at their side," Spotswood said. "The trophy is called a scalp. It looks rather like that wig. More dried blood and loose skin, of course." He extended his arm. "Feel this."

She rubbed two fingers over the soft sleeve of his coat. The coat was ornately embroidered with peak shells, purple and white.

"A buck's skin, softened and dried over smoke by a Seneca Indian maiden. You insult a man here by calling him buckskin. It means he is an oaf, an ignorant, a man of the backwoods, half savage."

I must send Grandmama a buckskin gown, all worked in these pieces of shell, she thought, and Tony a coat like this, and something for Jane's children. Jane was her closest, her dearest friend. Tony was her cousin, the present Duke of Tamworth. He loved her. She sighed, and the Governor heard.

"You must be exhausted, Lady Devane, after this day we've had. Your maidservant has made a bed for you in the shelter. We'd best sleep, for we'll make an early start in the morning. Good night."

"Pleasant dreams, Governor."

On the other side of the fire, he wrapped himself in a blanket and, with his back to her, lay down on the ground, as if it were a feather bed. She considered him. Yesterday, he'd worn a satin coat and white stockings, had silver buckles on his shoes; there had even been a black silk patch shaped like a quarter moon on his cheek. One must be ready for anything here, she thought.

There was a sound. A rustle. A slave in ragged breeches, on the other side of the fire, glanced at her and then quickly away, pointing to the fire. He was adding wood to it. That must be his task, thought Barbara, to add wood all the night. In another moment, he was gone. It seemed to her she heard music. She settled the dogs, sleeping themselves, against Hyacinthe, and walked along the bank of the creek until she saw the slaves' fire. They were around it, and one of them held something to his mouth. It made a light, flutelike sound. She took a step forward, and the slaves stood, one after another. The music stopped.

"May I join you?" she said. "The music you make is so beautiful."

They made a place for her among them. She sat down, bunching her skirts in about her knees. The slave played a short pipe, cut carefully from wood, hollowed out, holes for sound carved. It must be dear to him, she thought, to have survived the storm. A craftsman, she thought, a musician, here in Virginia's wilds. There was something haunting and piercing about the tune he played. She looked up to the sky and its hundreds of bright, shining stars, little pinpoints of light in the darkness, order in the chaos.

Go, and catch a falling star, she thought; Get with child a mandrake root. The lines were from Roger's favorite poet. Tell me where all past years are, / Or who cleft the Devil's foot. Tell me, God, she thought, where Roger went, or how to live without him.

The wind came through the trees, rubbing branches together, making them creak and moan and cry, like grieving women. The slave piped his sweet song. His friends listened gravely. There were twigs and sticks in their braids, and scars upon their faces, scars that looked as if they had been deliberately made. When? By whom? thought Barbara.

How beautiful this night, this fire, these men with their scarred faces and twisted hair were; so beautiful, hurt was almost eased. This place was tamed only in places. Savage, as Thérèse said, dangerous, barbarous. Good. It suited her heart.

Tobacco. Barbara thought of the Governor's words this evening, of the words she'd heard from those who came to visit in Williamsburg. They'd been talking tobacco, too. It was this colony's most important crop.

When I grow it, thought Barbara, it will have to be the best.

CHAPTER 2

It was the following night on the plantation of First Curle, and six slaves gathered at the small kitchen building, settled back on their heels, and at long last, ate. They had been in the fields until past dark. Tobacco leaves were being harvested. It was nothing but labor for the slaves until the leaves were casked in the big barrels called hogsheads, until winter came and its cold gave them respite from the tobacco plant everyone grew here.

Light came from the kitchen's fire, a glow they could see reflected through the kitchen's opened door. The oldest of them by many years sat on the steps. With reverence, the other slaves called her Old Grandmother. She was cook, now that she was too old for the fields. She looked like something carved from petrified wood, all hollows, wrinkles, bone, her hair a thin, white, grizzled halo on her skull, her legs brittle twigs.

Squatting down before the others, his fingers dipping into their communal bowl of cornmeal and hog's meat, one of the slaves told of the new mistress who had come to them this day. She was young. The slave, always a wit, pointed to the youngest slave among them, a girl. Not that young. He pointed to Old Grandmother. Not that old. She came with another woman—a servant—and a boy, a slave like them, but not like them either. The Governor's galley slaves, who ate with the plantation slaves, agreed.

He has fine clothes, said the witty one, the teller of this story. Soft clothes. His voice in the darkness conveyed those clothes Hyacinthe wore, warm and whole, a master's clothes on a boy like them. He described the shine of the buckles on the boy's shoes, the sweep of the feather in his hat, the glow of the silver collar around his neck.

There were two dogs, also—such dogs! Never had he seen such dogs. Uglier than the overseer—a comment that was much enjoyed. The teller of tales went to the steps, where the glow from the kitchen's fire made a backdrop for him, bulged out his eyes to show the way those dogs' eyes bulged, curved out his arms to show the way their legs bowed out. He stooped over and held his hand over the step to show how small they were. And so worthless, so useless, they had not even smelled him when he'd peered in the window of the house earlier to see what there was to be seen.

"Overseer."

The word dropped into their eating, their talking, like a stone into water, and they became mute. The only sounds now were the wind in the trees, and fingers scraping the wooden bowl.

Odell Smith, the head overseer of First Curle, walked up. He had been making the rounds, locking the basement, the corn house, the smokehouse, the barn, upset by this day, upset by the arrival of Barbara and her entourage.

"Finish eating," he ordered them, roughly. "There's work tomorrow. Much work. We have to get the leaves in the tobacco barns. You all know that. Sinsin, take the galley slaves with you to the slave house. A new mistress has come. Lady Devane she is called, from across the sea, from England, where the king of us all lives. You are to obey her as you did Master Bolling. That's all."

Scratching at his freckled hands, which burned always from sun, Odell walked to his own cabin, by the slave house, near the first of the two deep creeks that made this plantation worth what it was. This afternoon he had been summoned from the fields by a slave boy dressed as finely as he had ever seen a man dressed; he could hardly believe his eyes. Or his ears: The boy told him that his new mistress was here and wished to see him.

New mistress? What new mistress? His thoughts awhirl, he had gone to the kitchen house to talk to the slave there, old Mama Zou, who knew everything she shouldn't, but there were two young women with her, preparing a supper for themselves and the Governor of this colony. The Governor. Governor Spotswood himself had come all the way up the river to First Curle. Odell Smith had never seen the Governor, had heard of him only.

One of the young women was a countess. Odell had never seen a countess, either. She was the one with hair a lighter shade than his, but with red in it nonetheless, with big eyes and a face shaped like a heart. He had been too surprised to stutter more than a few words and scratch at his hands helplessly.

The Countess had been full of questions for him: Where were the slaves? When could she explore the plantation and the other quarters of it across the river? Was he drying tobacco? When could she see that? Would he join her and the Governor for supper? He would not.

What was Colonel Bolling going to say? That was the question in Odell's mind now as he walked up the plank steps of his cabin. It was bad enough for that duchess in England to send someone over from England to look over them, but to send a woman? And here he was with a storehouse filling higher with barrels of Colonel Bolling's contraband tobacco, tobacco they did not send to England, as was the law, but sold in islands south of here for a better price.

Why, this countess owned the creek out of which they'd ship those barrels; she owned the storehouse in which they sat. What if she discovered their smuggling? What were they going to do?

Odell was not much of a scholar. He knew enough to write his name, order goods, figure hogsheads, read bills of lading from the tobacco ships. How would he put everything into a note? He did not even have paper. All the paper was in the house, where she was. On second thought, after he had locked the slaves in, he would ride over and tell Colonel Bolling in person. That way, it became not his problem, but Colonel Bolling's. Colonel Bolling would see to it, the way he saw to everything.

In the early morning, in the attic bedchamber in the small main house of First Curle, Barbara lay dreaming in bed. She dreamed of Devane House, dreamed she was walking from one ornate chamber to the next, all about her polished marble, mirrors, gilded paint, intricate carving, inlaid floors. The furnishings were exquisite, the finest men made: footstools, chests, armoires, cabinets; Chinese vases as tall as she was. On the footstools and chairs were stiff crewel, colored threads, satins, velvets, striped silk, tassels.

She searched for Roger, walked through room after room, through echoing galleries and large parlors, searching. She knew he was here, just ahead of her, just a chamber beyond. She could feel it. She had to speak to him. It was imperative that she speak to him. In one of the chambers was Jane, her childhood friend, with her children. Barbara picked up a little girl who grabbed the necklace she wore, a necklace of rubies and diamonds. Be careful of your necklace, Jane said.

Necklaces I have by the dozens, Barbara replied, but no beautiful babies like yours.

Barbara set down the child. She opened doors that led to wide terraces that overlooked expansive gardens that were the talk of London. There was the landscape pool, long and sleek, with swans afloat on its surface. There was Roger, standing with another man. Marry in green, afraid to be seen, she heard Jane chanting to her children. Marry in red, wish yourself dead. The chants of girlhood. If in October you do marry, love will come, but riches tarry.

How glad she was to see him. Her heart felt like a bird rising to the sky. Impatient, impetuous, the way she could be, she picked up the soft material of her gown and began to run to him in her ivory-heeled satin slippers.

Roger, she called. I have to speak with you. The man standing with him turned to face her. It was Philippe.

Barbara woke, her heart beating, Philippe still vivid in her mind, standing before her in all his solid hauteur; that dueling scar across one cheek. Dangerous Philippe, her enemy, her foe, a snake. She hated him. It was hard to wake to hatred.

She sat up, taking in her surroundings. She was in the attic of the house on First Curle, a room that spread across the two chambers below. She touched her left breast. Her heart was aching, a literal ache. Philippe hurt her, even here.

She stepped over Hyacinthe, who slept bundled in a blanket on the floor beside the bed. The dogs had abandoned her in the night and slept with him. Harry raised his head. She shook her head and put her finger to her lips.

She found a shawl, wrapped it around her shoulders, opened the door, and slipped down the stairs. Trunks and barrels crowded the hall. She could hear the Governor snoring. His bed was in one of the two chambers that made up the downstairs of this house, a simple house, sturdy, solid, like a cottage on one of her grandmother's farms.

Lifting the latch to the door, she stepped out into cool dawn, as a dog went running past her. Harry. As impetuous as her own dear brother, thus his name. Charlotte was the lazy dog, who would sleep as long as Hyacinthe did. Barbara stood on the steps of the house.

Four huge pine trees, so large she could not have encircled their trunks with her arms, were before her in the house yard. Beyond, a road ran through a meadow that became woods. To her left, behind a fence of rails, was an orchard. A chicken landed in the yard from nowhere. Then she saw that there were chickens in the trees. There they had roosted for the night; with the sun's light, they were waking.

Back in the house, she walked down the hall to the door at the other end and stepped out into this yard. This side of the house faced a creek, but the creek could not be seen, nor could the river up which they'd traveled. That made the house seem like a secret, like an afterthought set in woods and fields. There was a picket fence here, with tobacco fields on its other side. A garden here took the whole yard, a garden cut into rectangles outlined with oyster shell. In one corner of the yard was the privy house. Barbara went to it and opened the door, the smell a familiar, privy smell. So. The kitchen and well, smokehouse and woodpile were to her right.

She knelt at a rectangle of neglected garden, moving leaves and debris to see what there was. Some herbs: straggling marigold and lavender and marjoram, a cabbage head, lamb's lettuce, and a vine. A wave of homesickness spread over her, so strong she thought she might die from it.

Grandmama, she thought, it is not as we imagined. There is forest all around. There is neither lawn nor landscape pool nor fountain. In her mind was Tamworth Hall, the home of her girlhood, its twisted chimney stacks, the grape arbor, the terrace, the fish ponds, the deer park, the woods she walked through to reach Jane's house, the lane to church. She could see Devane House in its splendor—the marble from Italy, the paintings by Verrio, a green silk bedchamber. The dog Harry appeared to sniff among the herbs, and she shooed him away, stood, wearily, feeling far older than her one-and-twenty years.

Who'd planted the daffodils and lilies whose dark green leaves grew along the fence? she wondered. Jordan Bolling was the name on the deed to this plantation, but the sight of the lilies, the daffodils, made her wonder if this Jordan had had a wife. And what had happened to her when she learned her husband had died? No wife, but rather this Valentine Bolling, had written to her grandmother asking to buy back the plantation.

The Governor would row away today to return to his duties and Williamsburg. He wanted her to return with him. For the first time, standing here in what was farm cut out of forest, Barbara seriously considered it.

She tilted her head to listen to the morning silence, which was not silence, but, like Tamworth's, a country quiet in which one heard birds calling one another, small creatures rustling, the wind in the tops of the trees, and finally, if one was attentive, oneself.

I hate weak, whining women, Bab; I have no patience for them, said her grandmother in her mind.

Neither, Grandmama, do I.

Years, my Bab, it takes years—not days, not months, but years—to recover if the grief is deep enough.

How many years, Grandmama?

Don't look at me with that impatient expression upon your face. Two, perhaps three, more.

Bah.

Bah, yourself, Bab. You've lost everything—husband, brother, home, fortune, dreams, all you thought to have. Give yourself the time to heal from those losings. There will be other dreams.

Other dreams? Other loves? Here? Barbara looked around, taking in the small, sturdy house, its clearing, the barn in the distance, the fields all around, the thick woods.

On her fingers was the soil of the garden, rich and crumbling. Tobacco tires land, she remembered a Major Custis saying in Williamsburg, so that more land is always necessary. She turned in a circle, slowly, trying to decide what she'd do.

Barbara stood with the Governor at the first creek that cut through her plantation. His slaves were in the galley, waiting to pole it out into the river.

"I only leave because I have no other choice. I have a meeting with my council that I may not miss. But I don't like this," said Spotswood. "It is settled then, you will come to Williamsburg a month from now, in October, during our village fair, and I will give a fête for you, to introduce you to the colony as you should be introduced. I will send this galley from Williamsburg for you, and you can ride back down the river in style."

Can you last until October? he was thinking, remembering the expression upon her face as she'd walked up from the creek yesterday, toward an empty house engulfed by woods and fields. You've pride, he thought; perhaps too much. He'd stop by Perry's Grove, tell Edward Perry to see to her. That thought made him feel better. The Lionheart would have approved of Edward Perry. There wasn't a better man in all Virginia. She is quite courageous, he'd tell Perry, wishing to do her duty to her grandmother, to learn the plantation, but I wouldn't leave my daughter alone in such a forsaken place; no, I would not.

Barbara held out her hand.

"Thank you for seeing me to my journey's end. I will write to my grandmother and my cousin, the Duke of Tamworth, of your many kindnesses to me—and they were kindnesses. Safe journey, sir."

"Remember, Lady Devane, if you need anything, Colonel Perry is at Perry's Grove, and you can reach your closest neighbors by foot within an hour."

"Yes." Her grandmother's solicitor in Williamsburg had drawn a map. It was in the house.

"Remember if you ride out alone to take a blanket and knife with you, and something to start a fire."

"Yes, yes, I remember. Good-bye."

Spotswood stepped into the galley and gestured for the slaves to begin poling out of the creek and into the river. "Mind you make sure there is plenty of firewood cut. The weather here can change abruptly once autumn comes."

He called various other reminders as she followed along the bank of the creek, stepping through clumps of small bushes and around saplings, her boots sinking into leaves and mud. The galley slipped into the river. She and Hyacinthe ran to the riverbank.

Spotswood cupped his hands around his mouth to shout. "You are not as alone as you think. The Randolphs are down the river—"

Waving, the chant the slaves rowed to floating across the water to her, she shaded her eyes to watch until the galley rounded a bend in the river, a curl. Well, she thought, I am on my own. She looked around herself, at trees, river, fields. Not as alone as you think, the Governor had said, but at this moment, the strangeness of her surroundings felt overwhelming. You are leaving everything you know, leaving people who love you, leaving position and court, her mother had shouted. Once you arrive there, it won't be as you imagine. Nothing ever is.

Never run away from the truth, because it sits upon your shoulder. When you least expect it to, it will put its ugly face into yours and say, Boo. A saying of her grandmother's. What have I taken on? thought Barbara. What do I know of running a plantation? Why did I not simply return with the Governor? Boo.

Barbara glanced down at Hyacinthe's face. He looked forlorn. What have I brought my beloved servants to? she thought. She squeezed Hyacinthe's hand, and they began to walk back through the fields to the house.

We ought not to plant this field again, she thought, but let it grow to grass so that the house has a wide lawn running to the river.

Upstairs, in the house, a clothing trunk had been opened; out of it spilled a welter of ribbons, laces and feathers, shoes, stockings, gloves, stays, garters, chemises, the accoutrements of a woman of birth and name. Shawls, cloaks, lace caps, scarves, muffs, fans. They looked odd here, out of place. Thérèse knelt on the floor, sorting through satin ribbons, cherry, silver tissue, cinnamon, sky, colors Barbara had worn before mourning. There, among a pile of stark black widow's gowns, were others peeping out: dove, daffodil, primrose. For use when her mourning was over. At Christmas, Roger would have been dead a year. Would they last here that long? What was she to do? How did she begin?

She sat down, thinking that Jordan Bolling must have sent to London for this big bed, with its high, carved bedposts; across the room stood a matching chest on tall legs.

How to begin? said her grandmother in her mind. By beginning. Order out of chaos.

"We must make bed curtains, Thérèse, before winter comes, so that we can close them around the bed against cold. Hyacinthe, I must begin to sort myself out. Find paper and pen. They might be in the parlor—"

"Parlor? Where in this tiny cottage is a parlor?" Thérèse was scornful.

Better than weeping, thought Barbara. "The chamber with my chairs and table is now the parlor. See if there is paper and pen and ink there, Hyacinthe."

"There are those narrow beds downstairs, Thérèse. If we were to put one up here in that corner, and pull the big chest before it, Hyacinthe would have his own place."

What must I do? thought Barbara. Explore the whole plantation, ride across the river to see the other quarters, meet the two other overseers, introduce myself to neighbors. Neighbors were important here, the Governor had said. People depended upon one another here, he said. This house needed scrubbing and polishing. They must see what stores, what food was in the basement. She needed a counting of cattle and hogs and household goods. She needed an accounting of the tobacco being harvested.

There was a storehouse on the second creek. The tobacco ships took on the tobacco there. She would need to look it over. At Tamworth Hall, in autumn, fruit was picked from the orchards for the making of wines and cordials and for cooking; hogs were killed, and sausages and puddings made; wood was cut and stored; nuts were picked from under the trees; candles were poured, seeds and herbs preserved, meat salted. Wasn't it the same everywhere, the provisioning for winter? They'd provision for winter, then.

Suddenly she saw the small wooden box among her ribbons and scarves. Thérèse tried to cover it with a scarf, but too late. Barbara knelt among the ribbons and opened it. Inside were plans and drawings, all that was left of the great house Roger had built in London, Devane House. And there was a pair of leather gloves—hers, kept by Roger in this box. Keep thy heart with all diligence; for out of it are the issues of life, her grandmother had read to her from the Bible. Roger, thought Barbara, you were my heart. How do I forget you?

The attic door swung open. It was Hyacinthe, and from the expression upon his face, it was clear that excitement had come to First Curle.

"Monsieur Bolling is here."

Bolling? The infamous Valentine Bolling?

"A visitor, Thérèse," Barbara said, suddenly as excited as Hyacinthe. "Our first visitor." She put her hands to her hair. "Hyacinthe, you go and tell him that I will be with him soon. Beg his forgiveness and give him something to drink. What, Thérèse? What will we give him to drink, other than water from the well? Well, you go to the old kitchen slave and ask her where things are, Hyacinthe. Do what you can until I appear. Quickly, Thérèse, I don't want to be rude to my first guest."

Even as the door was closing, Barbara was untying ties on her gown; in a moment she was in another—black, of course—and as Thérèse tied and buttoned it, she repinned her hair. In another moment, Thérèse had opened a jar of rouge and was patting it into Barbara's cheeks. Another moment, and patches were found, those tiny, soft, dark shapes of silk, glued to the face with mastic, that were so fashionable in London.

"By my brow and my mouth, only," Barbara commanded. "Give me the rouge, and that piece of mirror. Hurry, hurry, Thérèse."

Deftly, too impatient to wait for Thérèse, she put rouge on her lips, combed her lashes and brows with lead combs, and went down the stairs to meet her first guest.

How kind of him to call, she was thinking, and there was a sudden pang as Roger came into her mind, his manners so polished there was no imperfection to them. He would have called upon a new neighbor, would have welcomed her in every way. In the hall, she moved swiftly into the parlor, expecting to see a man sitting in one of her French chairs. There was no one, not even Hyacinthe. She could hear the dogs barking from behind a closed door, but when she opened the door to the other chamber across the hall, only the dogs looked back at her. She went to the window and looked out. No one there either.

For a moment, she was as disappointed as a child. She went to the garden yard. No one. Well, she thought, he will soon show himself again, I'm sure. There was a pen and an inkpot and paper gathered for her by her obedient Hyacinthe, and she sat down and began to make a list of all she needed to do. If these colonials thought her grandmother's precious chickens were going to roost at night in trees, they had another thought coming. "Chicken coop," she wrote firmly, boldly, thinking suddenly that she'd make a notebook for her grandmother about the plantation. It was her dogs barking, a good half-hour later, that made her raise her head and go to the window again.

Two men had ridden up under the pines. The older was Bolling, she guessed, and the younger Klaus Von Rothbach, the nephew by marriage. Greatly excited to have guests, she touched her hair, smoothed the front of her gown, and walked down the steps into the yard—but her dogs ran out ahead of her and charged at the stallion upon which Bolling sat.

The stallion pawed the ground and tried to rear, so that Bolling had to work to keep himself in the saddle. Barbara managed to call the pugs off, to run with them back into the house and close them away into a chamber. Awful, she thought, awful dogs.

Back outside, she walked forward, not minding the nervous, dancing stallion.

"I am Lady Devane." She was abrupt, boyish, without artifice, and therefore at her most charming. "Those were my dreadful dogs. I do apologize for them. You handle a horse wonderfully. I did not mean to keep you waiting before, but I had to change my gown. You are my first guest, you see, and I wanted to receive you properly. I hope you forgive me, both of you."

God's eyes, thought Klaus Von Rothbach, taking in the tiny star-shaped patch at her left eye, the thick red-gold hair, held in place by pins with pearls upon their heads but some of it escaping, curling about her face, with its lovely shape; she is beautiful as they said she was. That voice of hers, it has the texture of dark velvet.

"I am Valentine Bolling," said the man atop the stallion, "and this is my nephew, Klaus Von Rothbach."

"Won't you come inside?"

"No, I won't. How do you find the plantation, madam?"

Startled by his refusal and abrupt question, Barbara was not quite certain what was in his voice and in his face.

"Disordered."

"It has been without a master for over a year. A year and four months, to be precise. You see, Lady Devane, that we still grieve."

The young man, this Jordan, her grandmother said, had killed himself. He'd lost his plantation in a game of cards with her brother, Harry, and later killed himself. That had meant little to her, then, but of course it meant everything here. His uncle would be angry and grieved. It was truly dreadful. She herself had yet to be recovered from Harry's death. They must mourn their losses together, must discuss wild young men and how much one could love them.

"Yes, the circumstances were tragic—" she began.

"The circumstances, madam, were disgraceful."

And with those words, the stallion came too near Barbara, moving directly at her shoulder, forcing her to stagger back. If she had not been experienced at handling horses, she would have been frightened. As it was, she nearly fell.

"Uncle, stop at once!" cried Von Rothbach.

Bolling handled a horse too well. He did this deliberately, Barbara had time to think before Hyacinthe came running from somewhere, screeching like a savage. He ran headlong into the belly of the stallion, causing the horse to rear and dance backward on two legs, Bolling wrestling to control him.

"Hyacinthe!" Barbara's breath caught at the sight of him under those flailing hooves, but the other man, Von Rothbach, had ridden forward, was nudging the stallion away with his own horse, leaning over and grabbing Hyacinthe up.

"Little fool," Barbara heard him saying, and he was speaking in French, flawless French. "Calm yourself. This is not England. A slave can be killed for striking out at a master, even a boy dressed up like you. Settle down. No one will hurt your mistress."

"Give him to me," Barbara said, her voice shaking with anger. How dare Bolling behave so. You watch your temper, her grandmother said in her mind. I am watching it, she thought. Temper was one of her flaws.

"I have made your grandmother a fair offer for this place," Bolling was grim and solid atop his stallion. "My brother and I built it. My father and mother are buried here. My brother, my niece. I will add one hundred pounds to the amount of purchase. I am good for it.

You may have my bill of exchange upon Micajah Perry or William Dawson, both merchants in London, or I will give you the amount in my best tobacco, whichever you wish."

His audacity was amazing. "You take my breath away, Mr. Bolling."

"Colonel."

"I beg your pardon."

"Colonel Bolling."

"Colonel? You are a military man, then? So was my grandfather. In which campaigns did you fight during the French wars? Blenheim, with Marlborough? Lille, with Tamworth? My grandfather, the first Duke of Tamworth, was called the hero of Lille. My late husband, too, was once a soldier, a soldier and a gentleman. Rudeness was unknown to him or to my grandfather."

"I am a lieutenant colonel of the Virginia militia."

"The militia . . . a jest, yes?"

Klaus Von Rothbach, watching, thought, My uncle has not frightened her at all. There was strength beneath that beauty. And anger. Such anger. You intrigue me, Countess.

"My offer, Lady Devane."

"I will write to my grandmother of it."

"Seven years; it takes seven years to make a good tobacco man. And even then, the rain, the worm, the stupidity of one's slaves may interfere. Will you whip the slaves, Lady Devane, when they refuse to work? Will you ride the fields to watch over the tobacco as it grows? Will you know when the leaf is cured? There is a certain texture, a spotting. A good tobacco man knows it. In seven years he has the feel, if he is fortunate. And the hogsheads, Lady Devane. There's a trick. Too much leaf inside, and the staves break open. Not enough, and the tobacco crumbles away to dust. And if the rain doesn't rot your crops or the slaves ruin it or the hogsheads break, there is still the merchant in London with whom to deal. Charges for freight, Lady Devane, which you pay. Duties at customs, which you pay, cheats upon the drawbacks, which likely you will never discover. They go to line someone's pockets. No rest for the weary, Lady Devane. No letting up, ever. Not for a good tobacco man."

Odious, burly, bearish man, thought Barbara, do you think I cannot do it? I can do anything I set my mind to. This last year has taught me that, if little else. I would like to knock you off that horse. How dare you come here and try to bully and frighten me? The muscles of her face set, showing themselves through the soft flesh. Those in England would have seen that she resembled, not her famous grandfather, as everyone so often observed, but her grandmother.

"I will write my grandmother. I will report your offer." She said the words very slowly, very deliberately.

Like a hundred small slaps, thought Klaus.

Bolling snorted, a contemptuous, impatient noise that made Barbara even angrier.

"Amuse yourself, then. It makes little matter to me. But not for too long, or this plantation won't be worth my first offer. I assure you, I never pay more for something than it is worth. Good day to you, madam."

He spurred his horse, and before she could speak he had galloped from under the giant pines and out onto the road.

"Pig!" Hyacinthe called after him, in French. "Bully! Barbarian! I saw, madame. I followed. He would not come into the house. I went out to him with cider—I told him you would be with him, very soon, that you begged his pardon, but he would not come into the house. He told me to go away and leave him be. 'Let's see what damage she's done,' he said, and he and this man"—Hyacinthe pointed to Klaus, who sat atop his horse a respectful distance away but close enough to hear every word—"they went to your fields. I had to run so hard to follow, but I did run, and they talked with the overseer. *Your* overseer, now. I saw them."

Hyacinthe was angry enough for both of them. Barbara saw him whirling out of the house, running into the stallion for her sake. He might have been hurt. Hero.

"Please forgive my uncle."

Klaus had dismounted and was walking forward slowly, hands extended in a gesture of peace, as both Barbara and Hyacinthe watched him warily. There was not a penny's worth of difference in their expressions.

"I must apologize for him. His behavior becomes worse with each passing year. He quarrels with everyone. For his sake, let me say he was quite fond of his nephew Jordan, and he has no children of his own, so that Jordan was his child. It was a shock to him, both Jordan's death and the loss of this plantation. He has been fretting over it since it happened. For all his harsh words, he really would not harm you."

"No, he would only allow his horse to trample me, and my servant, too. No real harm in that. Who are you?"

"Jordan Bolling was my brother-in-law. I married his sister, may she rest in peace. Klaus Von Rothbach, madam."

Barbara was bristling still, furious that Bolling should have walked his horse into her, should have acted and spoken as he had. He had made an enemy of her before she had time to decide whether to be one.

"And you, unlike your uncle, are not angry with me? Why not, sir?"

"Did you know Jordan?"

"I never met him."

"Then you did not urge him to gamble, did you? Or risk his plantation on the play of a hand of cards? Jordan did a foolish thing of his own."

Barbara considered him, his calm reasonableness.

"I came in peace. I wish you no harm. I apologize a thousand times, and that is still not enough, for my uncle's behavior."

His courtesy, in such contrast to his uncle's rudeness, was calming her a little, as did the fact that they conversed in French, the language of all that was civilized. She looked him over more carefully. He must be at least thirty. He had a Gypsy, impish face, flat cheekbones to it. The sun had browned that face a warm color.

"You're correct; a thousand apologies are not enough, Mr. Von Rothbach."

" 'Captain'—I am captain of a sloop for my uncle, and so I am known as Captain Von Rothbach here," and he smiled, acknowledging her earlier angry scoffing at colonial titles. The smile transfigured his face making it a wonderful triangle of mouth and cheekbones. Barbara found her interest in him piqued. He had intelligence and wit.

"Warn your boy, please, that he must behave himself here. The laws concerning slaves are very strict."

"I don't know the laws about slaves."

He had pulled himself up into the saddle; now he looked down at her from atop his horse. "Then, if I may, I will ride over one day and instruct you."

Barbara cocked her head, smiled a small smile. Flirting was another of her flaws. You mind yourself, Bab, her grandmother said, in her mind. I am minding, Grandmama. It does no harm to flirt with an attractive man.

He remained where he was. "May I ride over one day, Lady Devane?"

"I don't know."

"Without my uncle. I come as a neighbor and friend."

At this moment, a neighbor and friend sounded delightful. "Perhaps."

"I'll take that as a yes."

He was riding away, through the yard, into the high grass of the meadow, his back rising straight up from the saddle.

"Pig," said Hyacinthe.

"He is not a pig, I don't think."

"The other one is."

"Yes, he is."

Klaus found his uncle squatting with his back against a tree in the woods near the first creek. His horse grazed nearby. Klaus dismounted.

"Your behavior was inexcusable, unforgivable. I thought I was going to have to strike you myself. What possessed you?"

"I could see nothing but her standing in what was Jordan's yard, her with her patches and painted face. She doesn't belong here, and Jordan does—only Jordan is dead, buried at an English crossroads, not even allowed the sanctity of a graveyard, because he killed himself. What word do you have on the sloop?"

"Your sloop can't be repaired for almost two months. What shall we do? The carpenter hasn't the cured wood he needs, but must send to Maryland for it. Odell is as nervous as an old woman about the barrels."

They smuggled tobacco to the Dutch West Indies in barrels branded "Flour" and "Pork." Klaus sailed the sloop into the second creek, and they loaded the barrels from the storehouse there.

"We'll do as we always have."

"We can't."

"This one last time we can."

"How will you keep her from noting it?"

"I'll leave that to you. Take her riding. Keep her distracted."

"I have your permission to call on her, then?" Klaus was ironic.

"You have my permission to do anything you please, until the barrels are loaded."

"And once the barrels are loaded?"

"I don't know, Klaus."

Even though he was angry with him, Klaus put his hand on his uncle's shoulder, for there was grief in Bolling's face, resignation in his voice. Klaus was going to say, Yes, I miss Jordan, too.

"It is a good creek I've lost," said Bolling, "a good, deep creek, and the last decent place on the river that ships can sail to without going aground. What the devil does she think she is going to do? Manage a two-thousand-acre plantation with two worthless dogs and a French maid to help?"

Bolling laughed, genuinely, darkly, amused, and the laughter was so spontaneous, and so unexpected, that Klaus, in spite of himself, began to laugh, too.

Barbara and Hyacinthe picked peaches. Gone were the patches on her face, the beautiful gown and hoop, the stockings of silk. She'd borrowed a gown from Thérèse, for she possessed nothing plain enough, unless Thérèse took intricate laces off and laboriously unpicked embroideries. She wore a large straw hat with fluttering ribbons down the back, one she'd worn to fêtes on the grounds of Richmond House, outside London. There the Prince and Princess of Wales summered; there they would be at this very moment.

Her mind was on Bolling. He looked like one of those beefy overfed merchants who drove up in their coaches to call upon her in her grief. How sorry we are, madam, they had said, for your loss of Lord Devane, madam. They had soft faces and softer hands, but hard eyes, to assess loss. Theirs, not hers. Our deepest condolences, madam, they said, but there is the fact of Lord Devane's debt.

The shafts of grief were silver-white and sleek, stabbing her. If she closed her eyes, it was a year ago, and she sat in a garden; Roger was still alive, so hope that they would at last make things right between themselves was still alive, dancing in her like a candle's flame. Devane House was being finished, equaling the South Sea stock speculation in excitement, rising stone by stone to keep all awed and gossiping. He builds it for you, Barbara, friends said.

It was love, Philippe had told her. Roger loved me. And I him.

Barbara shook her head and looked around the orchard, as if she might see Philippe stepping out from behind a peach tree. But Philippe was in England, and she was in Virginia, wasn't she?

"You might have been hurt, running under that horse the way you did," she said to Hyacinthe, thinking, How tired grief makes one feel.

"You might have been hurt, also, madame. The Duchess said I was to look after you."

Grandmama, overseeing from England. Barbara smiled. "Tell me what you saw and heard."

Hyacinthe was just waiting for her command. "They went to the overseer. I don't like that man, madame, and he doesn't like me, this Mr. Odell Smith."

"How do you know?"

"His eyes. It is in his eyes. The overseer was talking about us, describing us. And they were talking about barrels."

"Barrels? What kind of barrels?"

"I don't know. Barrels."

"What did he say about us?"

"Just that we were here."

"So we are."

Her feeling of desolation was lessening somewhat in the late afternoon's sun, in the movements of reaching up to pick, bending over to put away, in the satisfaction of seeing peaches begin to fill the basket. The trees in this orchard had not been pruned or grafted or cared for properly in a long time, longer than a year and four months. Jordan had been careless about more than cards.

She would send her grandmother peach brandy made from these very peaches. I'm homesick, she said sternly to herself. I'm far away from all that is familiar, and in a wild place. This will become home with time. There will be friends here, with time, won't there?

"I am a slave, yes, like those here?"

Like those here? No and no, again. Never would he be locked into a house at night to sleep, never would he eat out of a communal bowl like an animal at a trough, or be chained to his place in a galley.

"You are my most treasured servant."

"Yes, but I am a slave. Please answer, madame."

Roger had given Hyacinthe to her in Paris six years ago. It had been, was still, the height of all that was fashionable to have a small black page to carry one's train or fan, to bring one's wine, except that this boy was far more than a page, just as Thérèse was more than a lady's maid. Hyacinthe would ask until she answered. He was a child such as she had been, willful, curious, not easily put off or fooled.

"Yes, you are a slave. My slave. But much, much more. Now hush."

Seven years to make a tobacco man, Bolling had said. In seven years, she would be eight-and-twenty, quite old. There was commotion on the road cutting through her meadow. Someone else was coming. Many people were coming. Her dogs began to bark.

A two-wheeled cart, hitched to a horse, pulled in under her pines. Men and a young woman dismounted from horses. Dogs, which had come with them, barked. Her own dogs ran out to challenge.

A woman, quite large, as round as one of the great barrels of tobacco called hogsheads, was helped down from the cart by two of the men.

"Hush those dogs up," she told them and gave her hand to an older man, much older. His face was seamed, his silver-white hair worn long and loose, like a woman's, like that of the cavaliers and courtiers of Charles I's day, odd and out of fashion these days. Like Tony's, thought Barbara.

The dogs, snarling at hers, nevertheless obeyed the whistle of one of the young men and jumped into the cart one after another. Her own dogs went wild, thinking themselves the reason. The lone young woman laughed, bent down to the pugs, held out her hands.

"Call them," said Barbara; Hyacinthe clapped his hands, and the pugs ran to the orchard.

"There is Rosie, madame."

There, tied to the back of the cart, was her grandmother's cow, the storm's victim, rescued, it seemed, by these people. Barbara walked out from under the peach trees, stopping under one of the pines. There must be at least seven people in her yard, not to mention half a dozen dogs.

"I am Lady Devane," she said, her husky voice, her mother's voice, a stark contrast to her angelic face under the big hat.

"I am Margaret Cox, your neighbor," said the round woman, her eyes, bright, dark buttons, lost in her plump face. "These are my grandsons, Bowler, James, and Brazure. This is Colonel Edward Perry, another neighbor of yours and mine, and this is his daughter, Beth. Colonel Perry found this cow, Lady Devane, and thought it might belong to you. Now, we have brought you some supper, and a little something extra to settle you in and welcome you. James, Brazure, take it out of the cart before the dogs eat it."

"I am delighted—*we* are delighted—to make your acquaintance, Lady Devane," said Edward Perry, his voice calm, peaceful, like the sound of reeds in a river. The bow he made was quaint and old-fashioned, and the eyes in his seamed face were lively and kind. Barbara liked him at once. He was dressed all in black, plainly, like the Quakers of London.

Barbara watched as the young men shyly brought forward three hams, two unplucked geese, sacks of something, and a basket of candles.

"Cornmeal in those sacks. One of my sons-in-law owns a grist mill," said Mrs. Cox. "Those candles have been made with bay myrtle. They smell sweet when you burn them."

"All for me?" Barbara smiled, her grandfather's smile, charming, dazzling. That smile's a gift, said her grandmother, none of your doing at all, numbing those who see it, so mind how you use it, Bab. I am minding, Grandmama.

"Come into the house. I can't take supper alone. I won't take supper alone. You must all join me."

She remembered this, country kindness, neighbor looking after neighbor. It was a good thing, a far better end than Colonel Bolling would have made to her first full day at First Curle. Kindness begat kindness. She could feel her heart open again. How kind they were to make her first evening alone here less lonely.

"Please," she said, meaning every word she spoke, "it would make me so happy."

"Well, then," said Mrs. Cox, "it will have to be done, won't it?"

"Tell me," said Barbara to them all as they entered the house, "how difficult is it to grow tobacco?"

Colonel Edward Perry took a heavy silver goblet from the silver tray Hyacinthe held before him. He surveyed the parlor, which was still in disarray but already changed by the fine table and chairs, by a painting brought from England and set upon the plain mantel. Plump, naked nymphs with deliciously rounded flesh lolled in some dark garden. The lushness of the pose, the skill and craft of the brushstrokes, fed his soul.

I was unaware my soul needed feeding, he thought, but it clearly does. His lively, kind eyes went to Barbara, who was speaking to her page boy in rapid French, then moved to serving dishes of silver—plates, goblets, trays, unpacked but not yet put away, upon the table. Though he possessed some rich things himself, he had not been able to keep himself from touching these plates, this tray, could not help but run his fingers along the design, feeling the heaviness of the metal, marveling at the craft of the silversmith who made the intricate design of grapes and leaves over which his fingers played.

Lady Devane was singing to them, now, some French nonsense song, her maidservant harmonizing with her, and he, like the others in the chamber, was struck silent at the beauty and liveliness here in Jordan's plain parlor.

Jordan's parlor no more, thought Colonel Perry; her presence already vibrates through it. She has the shining patina of that silver I cannot keep my eyes from—and, I wager, the solid inside, the strength that bends but won't break easily. She must have graced the court. Why did she leave it to come among us?

When he'd gone to England as a younger man, he'd heard an Italian opera for the first time, and had found himself weeping, because the beauty of the music, the voices, was so unexpected, so fiercely fine and perfect. There was something of that emotion in him now, here in this simple parlor transformed by paintings and French chairs, by silver goblets and the sure and certain grace of the young woman singing to them. What is there here that I am so touched, so moved within? he thought, as another song began.

"Tell me of this," he said to Barbara later, when the singing was finished and she sat near him, fanning herself with an exquisite fan. He pointed to it, and she handed it over.

He examined the scene painted on its furled-out sections: a rose garden, and yew trees beyond.

"It is Tamworth Hall, where I grew up. This is the rose garden my grandfather planted."

"The famous Duke of Tamworth?"

"Yes. He planted it in the last years he lived, when he was frail and unwell. My brother gave this fan to me as a gift for my sixteenth birthday."

What sadness in that lovely face, thought Perry. "Your brother?" he prodded gently.

"Harry. He's dead now. All my brothers and sisters are dead." She changed the subject abruptly. "What is the best tobacco seed?"

"Digges seed, from the Digges plantation on the York River, but the man to ask is Major John Custis in Williamsburg, not I. You're thinking of planting a crop of tobacco?"

"This is a tobacco plantation."

"Let me tell you that my tobacco merchant in London writes me a melancholy story, Lady Devane, of the ruinous effect of the South Sea Bubble—"

I cannot escape you, Bubble, thought Barbara. She clenched her hands around her drawn-in fan.

"—and its consequences to trade. I think tobacco will sell low again. We endured ten years of sales worth little or nothing the last time prices fell. I think we may be coming to such a time again. A wise man or woman would pull in his—or her—horns and live small."

"Would she?" Barbara smiled at him. He was kind to warn her. "Thank you for your advice."

"Not my advice, simply my opinion. Tobacco grows best on virgin land. We grow perhaps three years of crops upon a field before moving on to clear others, leaving old fields to rest. That is why only a portion of this plantation is planted. Jordan was looking to his tomorrow, to the tobacco he would need to raise four and five years from now. Tell me the news of England. Are the South Sea directors fined yet?"

"Parliament was determining the final amounts of the fines when I left England."

"I read a great hatred of Robert Walpole in my letters. Do you think he will last as a minister to the King?"

"He was my late husband's dear friend, and my husband always said that Robert is a rock around which the water must flow."

"Even with his defense of the King's ministers over this South Sea debacle? The writers of my letters say the people despise him, that King George must eventually dismiss him."

Barbara shrugged.

"Will the Pretender invade?" he asked.

This was the second time within days that this question had been voiced. Surely this was just old men playing soldier, yet Colonel Perry's words disturbed her now, as the Governor's had not. The clans had risen in Scotland at the end of 1714. James had landed and been declared king. Would he attempt invasion again?

"He had not done so when I left."

"I see from your face you think he will not. Yet my letters from England are filled with nothing but talk of how unhappy all are with King George and his ministers. It would be the perfect time."

"Do not say so."

"You are for King George?"

"I am for no one I love being hurt by war."

"Very wise."

Later, Barbara stood out in the yard, seeing them off. It was quite a sight: restless horses, barking dogs, lanterns being lighted, Mrs. Cox being helped into the cart. She said to Barbara, "You won't find a better neighbor or finer friend than Edward Perry, Lady Devane."

A moment later, Colonel Perry looked down at Barbara from his horse.

"You won't find a better neighbor or finer friend than Margaret Cox," he said. "I will call upon you tomorrow to see how you do."

The cart was moving off in the dark, its entourage with it.

"If you don't have enough meat in your smokehouse," called Mrs. Cox, "you let us know. My boys can kill anything moving."

Walking into the house, Barbara said to Thérèse, "Who is it Colonel Perry reminds me of? I cannot put my finger upon it."

Thérèse looked at her in surprise and didn't answer.

"You know. Tell me."

"Lord Devane."

Roger? Roger had been the handsomest man who ever lived, time doing nothing more than frost and refine that which was already beautiful. Everybody had said that he was ageless.

"The color of the eyes, the shape of the mouth, his gestures, his manners," said Thérèse. "If Lord Devane were seventy-and-something—I think so, madame."

The eyes, thought Barbara. His eyes are like Roger's, that same color of faded sapphire. Her heart ached its familiar ache. There would never be someone like Roger again. How could there be?

"Digges seed," she said, aloud.

"What?" said Thérèse.

"Nothing, just something I was thinking." She'd grow tobacco to get over Roger.

Were they safe at home? They must be. They were her talismans, her dears. Were they in danger?

Of course not. Spotswood's talk, Colonel Perry's: just old men playing soldier. Yet in her mind was a memory of Italy, of the Jacobite court there with its backbiting and ennui, the fatal flaws of a court in exile. Yet within that milieu had been bold and committed men who could take back a throne. She'd flirted with one of them in a garden, and thought, If there were ten thousand like you, King George would sail back to Hanover tomorrow.

CHAPTER 3

In London, backstage in a crowded theater, Laurence Slane, an actor all the rage in the city, moved the oil over his face that would take the paint and rouge from it. Behind him, down the corridor, he could still hear the applause from the audience, still hear the name Laurence Slane being called.

"They are throwing fans and orange peels," said Colley Cibber, who owned this theater and wrote the plays for the troupe. "Go back onstage and let them have another look at you." Cibber was excited. It had been a while since anything had livened up audiences the way this Laurence Slane did.

Slane moved past stacks of painted scenes—of castles, drawing rooms, forests—past the ropes that brought the curtain down, past his fellow actors and actresses, and stepped out onto the stage, ignoring the ladies' fans that littered it.

Directly to his right and his left were the best seats in the house, in boxes rising one above the other, those inside all but onstage themselves. Sometimes, depending on how well tickets sold, the audience sat in chairs directly upon the stage. In these boxes this evening, standing, applauding him, were a group of the King's ministers and their wives, also some members of the famous Tamworth family, including the present young Duke and one of his aunts.

Candles in lanterns were flickering at the stage's end; just beyond,

Slane could see the pit—the cheapest tickets, because the audience stood—and past it were the benches and then behind them the galleries, holding yet more people, footmen and servants in the upper ones. The clapping had increased at the sight of him, and he stood a moment, allowing it, the smell of orange peel sharp in his nostrils.

From the pit, someone held up a rough bouquet of white roses. The signal at last. Slane felt his heart swell open with an emotion like blood lust, like the moment when a man takes his first step toward a seen enemy in battle.

The signal meant the Bishop of Rochester would see him.

He leaned over to take the roses and held them aloft a moment, over his head like a trophy—indeed they were a trophy—before walking off to the sound of his name called over and over again, to the clatter of more ladies' fans hitting the stage, the stamping of feet upon the floor.

"I am going to extend the play," Cibber said, blinking like the rabbit of a man he was. "Four—no, five more days."

Most plays enjoyed only a brief life before the audience tired of them and began to throw things at the actors and actresses. "You are performing bears, like the ones baited by dogs across the river," Cibber told the actors. "Keep them entertained, or they will turn on you."

Standing before a bit of chipped mirror, holding the roses crooked in his elbow, Slane removed the rest of the paint on his face. Though the face that stared back at him was calm, the mind behind it was leaping.

He had received the signal. The Bishop of Rochester would see him.

Weeks of the most careful maneuver and intrigue lay behind these white roses. Rochester, a bishop of the Church of England, was a leader in the Tory party, a faction of the English Parliament that King George chose to ignore—to his peril. Slane was a gosling, part of an elite corps of spies for King James III. He'd been here in London since June, to make an identity for himself, and to see Rochester, who trusted no one—and with good reason.

They had been planning an invasion since word of the magnitude of the South Sea Bubble reached them. Jamie, the Pretender, King James III, son of James II, nephew of Charles II, brother to the traitor queens, Mary and Anne, had been crowned in 1715 in Scotland as King of England, Scotland, Ireland, and Wales. But Scotland was as far as Jamie had advanced toward his crown. His generals had lost the battles to the generals of George of Hanover, already here.

"The South Sea Bubble has burst too many dreams," wrote Rochester to Jamie, who was in Italy. Rochester was the most cautious, most wily of the undiscovered Jacobites, nominal head of all Jacobites in England. "The Hanoverian and his ministers"—Whigs, the other party of Parliament—"are hated as never before. Come at once and claim your throne," he wrote. So they were.

Outside, Slane saw King George's ministers waiting for their carriages. One of the wives among them beckoned to Slane.

"Let me introduce you," she said. "Robert Walpole, Lord Townshend, Newcastle, this is Laurence Slane."

Slane bowed to the men, listened to the women compliment his performance, their voices high, like those of excited young girls, their eyes soft, admiring. He pretended not to hear how handsome they declared him.

"Lovely roses," said one of them. "Are they from an admirer?"

"I'm sure you have nothing but admirers," gushed another one.

Slane divided the roses among the women present, smiling into the eyes of each as he gave over her share. Amused, feeling predestined, he kept one apart and presented it with a bow to Robert Walpole, the minister who had managed to save King George's ministers from dismissal for their parts in the South Sea Bubble. There was much hatred against Robert Walpole for that. It was on the streets, written in the broadsheets that dripped gossip, sung in the street-corner ballads.

It was good, this hatred, reminding people that there was another king for the asking. Thank you, round Robin, Slane thought.

Plump, heavy-lidded, a great maneuverer of men, Walpole stared at the white rose, then at Slane.

"For His Majesty, King George," Slane said, "with all my compliments. Tell him that tonight he is in this lowly actor's thoughts as never before."

"Come and seize your throne," Rochester had written Jamie and his advisers as the public cried out for the heads of King George's ministers to be delivered upon platters. Invade, now.

Spring, Slane would tell the Bishop of Rochester when he saw him.

We invade in the spring.

CHAPTER 4

Barbara kicked at her horse's side with her boot heels, urging it forward along the edge of a fence. The fences these Virginians made were called worm fences because they undulated like a worm moving upon the ground. She had drawn a picture for her grandmother in the notebook, showing how the fence timbers met and angled first one way, then, at the next meeting, another. Her grandmother would be amused to have a worm fence, would likely want one made upon Tamworth. She was several miles from the house, at one of the fields in which slaves were harvesting tobacco. Hyacinthe sat silently behind her on the horse. This place consisted in the house in its clearing; then, scattered through cleared woods, fields. Across the river was more land, more fields, watched over by two more overseers.

Here, in this field, slaves were cutting down tobacco stalks, leaving each stalk atop the small hilled mound on which it had grown, moving on to the next stalk and the next.

"Not all the tobacco is ready at the same time, ma'am," said Odell Smith, her reluctant guide in this. "I spend much time riding from field to field judging what should grow a few days, a week more. The weather is my enemy. The tobacco must grow as long as we can allow, but autumn rains, due in another few weeks, or an early frost might ruin what is not yet cut."

"So that you have to rely on your instinct," said Barbara.

"Instinct and good fortune. If we had more slaves, I could gather in more tobacco."

A girl was gathering the scythed stalks by the armful and carrying them to the edge of the fields. Barbara moved her horse to a rough scaffolding there; from it hung drying stalks from yesterday and the day before. She stared at the leaves, only just beginning to dry. This was what Virginians depended upon. This was made into the snuff that all fashionable men inhaled in London and Paris and every city and town of Europe.

"We air the stalks a few days before taking them to the barn," said Smith. "Then comes the drying, Lady Devane, which is most important of all."

"Why is that?"

"Well, if the weather is damp—and it usually rains in September—we have to light fires in the barns to help dry the leaves. You'll know the tobacco barn when you see it. It has planks missing to better air tobacco. If the leaves aren't dried just right, they catch the mold, and ruin in the hogsheads. The merchants find rot."

"And what do they do then?"

"They throw the tobacco out, but you've still paid freight for it to cross to England. And a duty when it arrived in London."

"Thank you, Mr. Smith. I'm going to ride on, explore a little."

Every day, she tried to ride out farther and farther, learn the boundaries of the plantation. When she knew every horse path, every tree, every field, then she would know First Curle and be its mistress in the truest sense of the word.

"If you'll wait a bit, Lady Devane, I'll saddle a horse and come with you. I don't like you to be out alone."

"No, thank you. What you do here is far more important to me."

"Suit yourself."

For some reason, his words made her temper flare. He was rough, unlettered, a man who knew nothing but these woods and creeks—so Colonel Perry had explained. "So I shall suit myself, Mr. Smith, at every opportunity."

He's a good tobacco man, Colonel Perry had said. She could feel Odell's eyes on her as she rode away. She didn't like him, good tobacco man or not. Neither did Hyacinthe. Once they were out of the overseer's sight, she stopped.

"I have no idea where we are, Hyacinthe. Give me the map."

Behind her, he reached into his jacket and pulled it out. She opened up the crude map and looked at it, tracing her route from the house today. She was at some kind of spring. It ran out of the ground and through grass, which became high reeds.

"Do you see a spring on this map?" she asked Hyacinthe, irritated at being so at the mercy of her ignorance.

He shook his head.

She followed along the outermost edge of the reeds, careful not to let her horse stumble in the marshy ground. Eventually the ground cut away to water.

"Is this the first creek or the second?"

"I don't know, madame. Look, madame, there is a path there, through the trees."

It was little more than a footpath; with the limbs of trees on each side brushing her shoulders, she followed it until it gave onto a clearing in which stood two crude houses, one large, one small, nothing to them—weathered, unpainted boards, a roof, no porch, no grace or amenity of any kind. The ground around was clear of grass. Looking at the map, she saw that a slave quarter was marked on the other side of the first creek. The two tiny inked rectangles on the map might be these houses. If it's so, thought Barbara, I must remember to mark the spring on it when I am back at the house.

She trotted around the smaller house. A garden. A wooden chair propped against the house. Hyacinthe pointed, and she urged the horse toward a whipping post. There was a crude pillory near—two boards fastened to posts, the boards cut to make holes to imprison a person's head and arms.

Breaknecks, these were called in England, for if the person inside fainted, his neck might snap against the wood. It was one of the sights of London: someone carted to a pillory, the condemned following a cart to which he was tied, while inside the cart stood a man who whipped him; if he survived the carting, he was then imprisoned in the pillory. She had seen such a thing when she'd first gone to London. She and Jane had seen it, and Jane had cried. How cruel, she had said, weeping.

"Look, madame," said Hyacinthe. "What is that?"

There was a narrow box lying on the ground, the size of a man, hardly larger than a coffin. Crude breathing holes punctured its top.

Barbara dismounted, went to the box, put her hand to the closed lid, opened it. The hinges clanged in the silence all around them. No birds are singing, thought Barbara. She let the lid bang shut. Thank God there was no one inside. What would she have done if someone had been inside?

"What is it for?" asked Hyacinthe.

"I don't know." But she did. Odell must lock unruly slaves inside that box, until they were unruly no more.

There was a collection of harnesses and shackles hanging on the outside of the house.

Were those for rebellious slaves also? wondered Barbara.

One of them looked as if it locked over a head. New ones have to be tamed, Odell had said the other morning. It is up to them how easy the taming is. Sometimes old ones have to be punished.

You'll need to buy slaves, Colonel Perry had told her. There is a ship due in our part of the river in another few weeks that will have slaves on it. Buy them now, and by spring, they'll be tamed to work your fields. If tobacco sells low, you need more plants to harvest, more tobacco to dry and sell to stay even with yourself. Thus you need more slaves.

She stood before the slave house, one long, crude rectangle. Barbara peered into the doorway, Hyacinthe off the horse, right beside her, her partner in this. The house was built up off the ground, and the floorboards did not all join.

They stepped into the silence. There was little here to mark a life: bed boxes or woven mats for sleeping, a blanket folded neatly, a homemade broom, shirts hanging from a peg, a broken clay jar holding a leafy arm of forest ivy, an iron pot or two at the fireplace, some baskets.

On one wall were drawings, some kind of wild deer with two long horns spraying upward, and figures of men hunting, the men shaded dark, drawn too long for real men, but their length somehow made the sense of the hunt, of motion and death, come alive. Was this their world, before?

Outside, she shivered and rubbed her arms. What a dark feeling this clearing gave her.

"They stare at me, madame."

"Who does?"

"The slaves. At night, when I go to sleep, in my dreams, they stare still, as they did in Williamsburg. When you were ill, madame, and lay in the bed, they came up to me, and they talked to me in their language. I could not understand what they said, but I saw what was in their eyes. The same that is in the eyes here."

"And what was that?"

"Hatred, madame, for you, for all like you, masters."

"Hush, Hyacinthe. Give me the map. Let us see how to leave this place."

At the creek, she let the filly drink, leaning over to pat her neck, thinking of Hyacinthe's words. What would those at home think of what she had just seen? Dark, that was how she felt inside, dark and suddenly despairing.

It would be hot soon. The afternoons here were unbearable, but that would be changed in another few weeks, said Colonel Perry. Then you will see the beauty of our autumn. Tomorrow, or the day following, she would go across the river to the two quarters there, to meet the two overseers, see the fields, the slaves.

The filly had finished her drink. Barbara urged her along the bank through the thick trees growing there, until she saw a plank wharf jutting out from the opposite bank.

This was where they'd landed day before yesterday. I know where I am, she thought. First Curle, I begin to know you.

"Look, madame, Captain Von Rothbach," Hyacinthe said.

He was walking onto the plank wharf. In the water was the dinghy Hyacinthe had found yesterday in the barn.

"Come across, Lady Devane," Klaus Von Rothbach called, waving to her. "Come for a sail."

Barbara splashed the filly across the creek; for a moment, as the water rose past her waist, before the filly began to swim, she thought, This creek is deeper than I thought. Hyacinthe made a frightened sound.

"Hold tight to my waist," she said. "Don't be afraid. The filly will swim us across, you'll see."

That was the treasure of the second creek, that it was deep and wide enough for a small sloop to sail into. It had given the Bollings their own, small port, Colonel Perry had said last night, tapping the unfurled map with his finger. The river was too shallow and dangerous farther up. Tobacco ships couldn't sail it. She had the last safe place to anchor and load tobacco. Planters farther inland would come to her landing and leave their tobacco to be loaded, and she was allowed to charge them a small fee for it.

"I didn't think to see you again so soon," said Barbara. I'm glad to see you, she thought, a little more glad than I thought I'd be.

"But I said I would call. Where did you find that filly?"

"Colonel Perry loaned her to me."

"You haven't been here three days, and Colonel Perry loans you one of his famous horses? You've charmed him—but then, I would imagine you charm anyone you set your mind to."

He's Swiss, said Mrs. Cox. From Hanover, I think, said Colonel Perry. A bastard, whispered Mrs. Cox, a Swiss nobleman's son who came over with Swiss miners to hunt gold on some land the Governor owns. He ended up sailing for Bolling, ended up captaining his sloop, ended up marrying Bolling's niece.

"Ride the horse to the house," Barbara said to Hyacinthe irritably, the dark from the slave quarter still in her. Why not spend the afternoon sailing? Why not?

"I want to sail with you, madame."

Good. The mood she was in, she needed a chaperone. There was no telling what she might do. She hadn't felt this way in a long time, this dark, this headstrong and ripe for trouble. What's happened, she thought, to make me feel this way again?

As Klaus rowed the dinghy out into the river, Barbara unpinned her hat and raised her face to the sun. The warmth of it was like having her face cupped in a lover's hands. A lover's hands. It has been a long time since I've had a lover, she thought. Not since Charles.

"So," he said, speaking now in French, "how have these first days been?"

"Interesting."

She'd begun a letter to her grandmother, the Duchess.

"Dearest Grandmama," she'd written, "you possess a small house and an orchard and three overseers, two of whom I have yet to meet, but will, and fourteen slaves, not all of whom I have seen, for a few of them are upon other sections of the plantation, where the two other overseers are. The slaves' names are Kano and Sinsin and Belle. The men have marks on their faces, Grandmama, scars across their face and chest. It is frightening to see, but I am told it is their way; it is a mark of their tribe. Their hair is braided, and carved twigs are twisted into the braids. They have holes in their ears or in their noses, where once they wore jewelry.

"The slaves toil half naked in the fields or at the tobacco barn, like engravings of savages in books. The women, an old slave and a girl, wear a simple blouse, a short skirt. The men wear a cloth wound over and around their thighs and buttocks or ragged breeches. They have names like Green, Grandmama, and Mama Zou, Cuffy, Jack Christmas, Moody, Quash. Tomorrow night, I give a supper for them. The overseer says I must wait until tomorrow, because it will be expected that I give them rum, and they will dance all night in my honor; Sunday they do not have to work, anyway, so I save him a day of having to force them to work when they've danced all the night before. Colonel Perry says I must buy more slaves if I mean to plant more tobacco next spring."

"Have you any idea how beautiful you are?"

Klaus wasn't rowing anymore, but leaning at his ease against the rudder, watching her, not the least bothered that her servant was with her. There was open admiration in his eyes.

"The day before we met," he said, "I was at the Harrisons' seeing about my sloop, which has a hole in her keel, and Philip Ludwell came to visit. He'd seen you in Williamsburg, and all he could talk about was how beautiful you were. I thought he exaggerated, the way men will, but he didn't. He did not describe you vividly enough. Your hair glows like gold. Your skin is like fresh cream. Put your hat back on so that you don't burn. I should hate to see you burned."

She could feel something rise up inside herself. Lazily, provocatively, meeting his eyes directly, her stare bold, challenging, Barbara tied the hat back upon her head, before turning away, trailing her hand in the water. Those in England would have said, at this moment, that she resembled her notorious mother.

Yes, I know how beautiful I am, she thought. I know how to make men think they love me, how to make them crow and dance and fight over me. It was one of the reasons she'd left England, not to begin an affair again with Charles.

Moody, restless, brooding, she leaned over the edge of the dinghy. They wouldn't love you, you know, her brother Harry had said once, if they knew what was behind your face.

Yes, they would, she'd answered back, and Harry had kissed her, surprising her with that sweet, swift brother's gesture. You're right, he said, they would, they'd be wild in love.

Well, now, Grandmama, do I write to you of the spark that just leaped from this man to me and back again? Do I write of the despair in my heart at this moment, as if life has no meaning, no purpose, and therefore, what can dallying hurt? I want to forget the dark of the slave quarter. I want to forget the dark of Roger's dying. What better place than in a man's arms? There is no forgetting like that forgetting. A Virginia flirtation? Why not?

The woman reflected in the river stared back up at her with a girl's eyes. No, the girl said. Barbara knew this girl, her fifteen-year-old self, another self, strong in what she wanted, strong in what life meant, believing in virtue and truth and honor.

It was love, said Philippe.

She put her hand in the water and made her image disappear. I shall do what I shall do what I shall do, she thought.

The dark was back inside her, that dark of a year ago, a dark she'd fought to put behind her. It was back, and it was deeper.

Those in England would have shaken their heads.

CHAPTER 5

"Stay here," Barbara told Hyacinthe, and he, remaining in the dinghy, watched her climb up the rope ladder of a large ship. It was October. They'd been here in Virginia a little over a month.

I hate it here, thought Hyacinthe. The dinghy in which he sat lurched against the hull of the large ship beside which it was anchored.

There was a sound; Hyacinthe, who was sitting on the plank that served as the dinghy's seat, made a startled movement and immediately stood to look in every direction, but there was nothing to see except the ship and the river and the wild, untamed, distant shore.

He leaned out dangerously over the water that separated the dinghy from the tall slaver. "Slaver" was what the colonials called these ships that appeared in the river; their cargo, their trade, was slaves from Africa. He tried to put his ear against the hull, but the dinghy moved as he leaned, and he nearly fell into the river. Still, he held his breath, listening.

Through the gentle lapping of the water, he heard a groan. The sound again; the inside of the hull was its source. Moving back as far as he could, as fast as he could, to the stern of the dinghy, Hyacinthe fell. The sun beat down strongly and made the ache in his head worse, but he didn't care. Around his neck was a silver collar, the crest of the Earl Devane engraved in it, and under that was a necklace with a saint's medal at the end of it. Clutching the medal in one hand, he closed his eyes and prayed the prayers Thérèse had taught him.

"Hurry, madame," he said between prayers, "hurry. This is not a good thing."

Barbara was aboard the slaver, on the middle deck. Some ten slaves stood apart from her on deck, naked, their skin shining. They would likely be rubbed with oil, Colonel Perry had warned, a slaver's trick to make them look their best. Chains looped around the slaves' legs from one to the next, so that if one fell, all must fall. On other portions of the deck, behind the mizzenmast, near the bowsprit, were more slaves, in smaller groupings, similarly chained, watched by sailors. There were no children among them, and few women.

"Only look here, Lady Devane," the captain was saying, "here are some fine samples for you, in their prime, young and strong. They will work well for what you desire." The slaves drew back as the captain and Barbara approached. Their ankle chains scraped the wood of the deck.

"Here, now, this one"—the captain touched his finger to the round arm of a woman—"she'll make a fine breeder. She had two little ones hanging on her legs in the slave market at El Mina, so I can swear to her fecundity."

Where are her children now? Barbara thought.

Her mind went to Hyacinthe. He came from the slave market in Paris, was one of the offspring of the market's stable of French slaves who bore children to be sold. I was reared to be sold, he'd told her once. I always knew it. I always knew I would leave my mother. Other than pity for him, she'd never thought what that had meant to the woman who bore him. She'd never really thought what such, in turn, must mean to him.

"Lady Devane is interested in field slaves," said Colonel Perry. He had insisted upon accompanying her. He and two other planters had taken an interest in this ship, which meant that besides sharing in the gains or losses, they sent word to select planters, ones who could be counted upon to be able to pay, that the ship was in the river and might be boarded. Coins were little used here, there being no mint to make them and not enough of them to do anyway, so the slaver's captain would be paid in bills of exchange, made good by tobacco merchants in London, or in tobacco itself, or in the promise of tobacco. Colonel Perry had personally vouched for Barbara, who now watched as the captain opened the mouth of a slave by pulling back hard on the man's hair and wedging the slim end of a wooden club into the man's mouth.

"I'm an honest man who does not try to sell old slaves for young. Be still, black devil, let the lady look you over," the captain was saying. "They ought to thank me for not taking them to the West Indies. There we dispose of them by what is called a scramble. We agree on a common price beforehand with the planters, land the slaves, place them in a large yard, and throw open the gates of the yard to those who wish to take them. You've never seen such a sight, Lady Devane, as planters seizing anyone they can, the confusion, the shouting. The poor devils are astonished and terrified. No, indeed, you don't realize my kindness, do you?" he said to the slave in whose mouth the club rested.

There was an interminable moment in which Barbara found herself looking into the slave's eyes. Then she turned around and walked away. She went to the side of the ship, close to the opening of the hole, which was covered with a crisscross hatch of wood. The crisscrossings made air openings. A smell came from the hole. She took a step or two closer and peered down. It was too dark to see anything, but the smell was too strong to be ignored. It was not a mere smell, but a stench, of death and disease. This was where the slaves were kept when they were not on deck—in the hull, a slaver's hull, especially built to hold as many as possible, she'd been told.

Barbara gripped the ship's railing, breathing shallowly to keep herself from retching. She made herself listen to the river, to try to calm herself. The view of shore was lovely: Colonel Perry had been correct. Autumn was beautiful here. Vines as thick as her wrist hung from branches; red-orange berries bunched along the stems of the wild hollies growing under the trees. In the weeks she'd been here, leaves had cleverly turned crimson and gold among the green, like the promise of a coming festival, except that the festival was winter.

Autumn arrives more slowly here than in England, she thought. Anything not to think about where she was, what she was doing. The heat of summer was fiercer and lingered longer. It was hot today. Hyacinthe had complained of the heat as they sailed along the river this morning. He had been complaining for some days. . . . Where she was, what she was doing intruded. Never run away from the truth, because you carry it on your shoulder. And someday it will put its ugly face into yours and say, Boo.

She turned to face the truth and saw that Colonel Perry had taken command for her; he was examining slaves' mouths, kneeling down to feel their legs, his seamed, aged face intent, nothing in his expression to indicate that what he did was anything other than ordinary. "Of all to whom I have been introduced," Barbara had written to her grandmother, "I find a distant neighbor, Colonel Edward Perry, the most kind, the most knowledgeable. He has lived upon this river where I am for almost eight decades, Grandmama, and he is kind enough to treat me as if I were one of his family."

He's fond of you, said Mrs. Cox, more than fond. Edward Perry is a friend to nearly everyone, but it's clear he has a special regard for you. And Barbara had a special regard for him. She felt beloved when she was with him, as beloved as she did in her grandmother's presence. He might have been her grandfather, or an angel—Yes, she'd said to Hyacinthe, my Virginia angel, sent by Grandmama to watch over me. That would be like her. God, she would say, now I've sent Barbara to Virginia, but there is no telling what she will do there, so assign an angel to her, if you please, and not just any angel either, but a good strong one.

"These two will do," Perry said. A sound went up from among the slaves as he pointed, a sound that lost itself in the masts and rigging and clear Virginia sky. Barbara's ears rang with it. It struck her to her soul. It's too cruel, Jane had said, weeping, about London's punishment of criminals. Too cruel. Yes, this was.

"They think we buy them to eat them," the captain said.

Sailors began to unlock the chains on the two Colonel Perry had selected. Fierce movement erupted among their fellow slaves. Some clung to them, others shouted and tried to attack the sailors, who beat at heads and shoulders with wooden clubs, the same kind as that the captain carried.

"I've changed my mind," Barbara said.

"Those are the best among the lot," Perry said. His tone was reasonable, kind; there was no judgment of any kind in it at her abrupt words. He hadn't wished her to come aboard this ship, but she wouldn't listen. Send your overseer Smith, he had told her, for you won't like it.

"They'll make good hands in six months. You need slaves to open up new fields of tobacco. Let me handle the buying of the slaves for you. It is not necessary that you have the worry of it. It isn't a task for you, and it may be easily done without your having any further distress of it. I will have one of my men bring the slaves over later to your overseer, who will know what to do from there. You never have to see these men again until they are field broken, and by then you will have forgotten—"

"No."

"Does she think I'll come down on my price?"

The captain had crossed the deck to them, had been listening to Perry with an impatient frown. "This is prime buying time. I can sail up the York River and be done with it in a month."

"Lady Devane needs more time to make up her mind—"

"You've come a distance this morning, Lady Devane," said the captain, his tone changing when he saw that she was, indeed, leaving. Barbara, skirts bunched in one hand, had nimbly perched on the railing and was now maneuvering herself, skirts and all, down the rope ladder that had been thrown over the side to take her aboard. Below Barbara, one hand clutching the ladder as if it had grown there, Hyacinthe was staring up at her, his face strained and perspiring.

"Pull up the anchor," she said to Hyacinthe, stepping into the dinghy.

Hearing what sounded like groans, she looked at the tall bulk of the ship.

It is groaning, she thought, her hands on an oar. Sweet Jesus. It was the groans of the ones too ill to show but not yet dead. Terrible fish called sharks followed slavers, Mrs. Cox had told her. Sharks ate flesh, and a slaver gave them good meals as it crossed the ocean, for many a slave would die on the way over.

"Row," she commanded Hyacinthe, "hard. Keep up with me if you can."

The wind for sailing was gone. Earlier she and Hyacinthe had sailed in daringly, looking as if they had captured a bright butterfly with a single white wing and were riding it upon the water.

Aboard the slaver, Perry watched her, watched the resolute dip of the oars in and out of the water, the uprightness of her back, of the boy's, as they rowed away. They rowed as if they were pursued by devils. Edward Perry, onetime member of the Governor's Council, owner of much land, traveler to other colonies and watcher of the river, found himself quoting softly, in Latin, a phrase that floated up into his mind:

" 'Man is wolf to man.' "

Yes, he'd felt the same—the disgust, the horror—the first time he'd boarded a slaver. Now he was used to it. Is that a good thing? he wondered to himself, to have become used to this, to no longer regard it with horror?

The captain had glanced quizzically at Perry on hearing him speak Latin.

"I'll purchase the slaves," Perry said.

That the captain understood.

Barbara and Hyacinthe rowed for a long time, Barbara taking comfort in the steady, monotonous movement of the oars, in the lift and strain of the muscles in arms and shoulders, in the growing ache there and in her hands. She did not look back at the slaver once, but rather ahead at some distant point of water, which she rowed toward but never reached. Finally, the pain in her shoulders and hands was enough to force her to stop.

Her gown was wet under the arms and at her neck and bosom. Her hair had fallen from its pins and clung to her perspiring face and neck. Beside her, Hyacinthe breathed in and out, rapidly, shallowly, like a small bellows she'd set to work too hard. The pace of rowing had been too difficult for him, she could see, but he had not complained. He was as damp with their exertions as she was. More so.

Hero, stalwart companion, she thought, gazing at him affectionately. He was with her in all her explorations here; he was master of the left dinghy oar; he was the only one brave enough, other than Klaus Von Rothbach, to go with her while she practiced sailing. Even Colonel Perry said he'd rather stay on shore and watch.

She heard a faint honking and looked up; in the distance was a vast, wavering series of formations, dark dots, birds, geese or ducks, hundreds of them, more than she had ever seen together in her life. Colonel Perry had warned her to be on the lookout for them: A certain sign of autumn, a certain sign of God's grace to us, he said. How beautiful, she thought. The abundance of them was amazing. There must have been hundreds. The abundance of everything here was amazing. Graceful, winged caravan, she thought, they would never believe your numbers in England, never.

"What did you see there . . . on the slaver, madame?" Hyacinthe seemed barely able to push the words past his breathing.

The other side of this place and its beauty. "Nothing. I saw nothing."

They were out of the current of the river, near the bank, a wild, untamed bank, some wildflowers blooming like tiny stars everywhere. Colonel Perry's daughter, Beth, had showed her some pressed flowers she'd found on the riverbank during the spring; the flowers resembled pansies, with small brown marks on their petals, like the slaves' scars. Barbara shuddered again, the way she had on the slaver. The sound of the river filled her ears.

Evil, Hyacinthe. I saw the clear shape of evil, and it frightened me to my soul. Never run away from the truth, because it sits always upon your shoulder. What am I going to do?

In her mind was the supper she'd given for the slaves. She had worn a black gown of watered silk, and emeralds in her ears. There was ham and rum for the slaves; her coming here was to be the cause for celebration. She had stood on the house steps as Odell Smith introduced the slaves to her one by one. What a sight the scene would have made to anyone looking on; how she had wished that Jane, or her grandmother, or Tony, or even the Prince and Princess of Wales themselves might have seen it—the silent people, the dark night enveloping all: Lanterns and candles were nothing to the darkness. She in her finery, glittering and smiling, they in what could only be described as bits and pieces of clothing. They need little, said Odell. They are used to nothing.

She'd made them a speech, her heart pulsing high in her throat because everything—she, they, the forest clearly seen from the steps of this house that was scarcely larger than a cottage—seemed fantastic to her, out of time and place, as if she had been whirled into the dark night sky and placed upon the moon. One of the slaves had limped forward awkwardly as his name was called, and in the lantern light she saw that toes were missing from his right foot. For a moment, she had felt faint at seeing that which was real put to what had been only words before, the Governor's, Klaus Von Rothbach's words, explaining to her certain laws, necessary laws, they said, such as: Incorrigible runaways have their toes chopped off. And standing beside her in the night had been Hyacinthe, who would not hush, but repeated over and over in French, His foot, madame! Look, see his foot.

"My head aches. It ached when I was waiting for you," Hyacinthe whispered.

He was trembling. Barbara put her cheek against his forehead. It was burning hot. He had a fever. The ague. Thérèse was only just over it.

"Put your head in my lap."

She untied her hat and put it over his face as he laid his head on her knees.

"I'll row us home. We're nearly there. You'll feel better once we're out of this sun. Why did you not tell me? What? You did tell me? Well, I didn't listen, and I am sorry for that."

He was worse by the time she'd rowed the dinghy to First Curle. "Can you walk, my sweet?"

Leaves touched with bronze and yellow floated down around her silently as she pulled the dinghy securely onto the bank. Hyacinthe lay slumped across the plank seat, not answering.

Of course he cannot walk, cannot even push himself up from the plank to stand, or he would have done so, thought Barbara, furious with herself. She picked him up, noticing that his legs dangled past her knees. Children grow so quickly, Jane always said. Hyacinthe had grown in the month they'd been here, she would swear it. She half ran, half walked with him down the path.

There was the house now. Good, for she was beginning to be out of breath. She felt Hyacinthe's tears, hot with fever, on her neck. In her mind was what he had asked her after they had crossed the river to explore the other quarters of the plantation. Would you beat me? he had asked.

Have I ever beaten you? she had replied, astounded. It was because the overseer, not Odell, but the one who oversaw the quarter they went to see, had asked, in all innocence, if she wished her servant boy locked up for the night with the other slaves in the slave house.

"Thérèse!"

Barbara kicked at the gate of the picket fence with her boot.

The dogs came bounding out of the house, their paws scattering broken pieces of shell from the oyster shell paths, and then there was Thérèse, running down the house steps once she saw Barbara carrying Hyacinthe, the dogs yelping and leaping up, trying to lick his hands.

"What has happened? How is he hurt? Did he fall out of the dinghy? I knew he would."

"He's caught the fever. Help me carry him."

Hyacinthe moaned as they shifted him between them. It was no help that the dogs wove themselves in and out at every footstep, licking at Hyacinthe's hands whenever they could and barking too much. In the house, she and Thérèse put him in the bed in the downstairs chamber.

"The ague," said Thérèse, her hand against Hyacinthe's head. "Shoo, dogs, leave him be." The dogs had jumped up into the bed to be with him, ignoring her. "What of Williamsburg?"

"I won't . . . stay here," Hyacinthe said.

"It hurts you to speak." Barbara took his hand. "Hush."

In two days, the three of them were to go to Williamsburg, where the Governor was holding a fête to introduce her to the gentry of the colony. They were coming in from counties close and far, she was told, as if they had been called for an assembly of their governing body, their House of Burgesses. Except that wives and daughters were coming in, too. It's a rare thing for us to assemble together so, said Colonel Perry. It's become the talk of the colony. Some of the women are angry because the Governor did not allow time enough for them to order gowns from England.

"Don't . . . leave me, madame—they'll . . . eat me. They . . . groaned, I heard . . . them . . . The birds fly too close . . . they peck my eyes. . . ."

"He does not know what he's saying," said Thérèse. She compressed her lips, and Barbara saw how upset she was. Yes, Hyacinthe was child to them both.

Barbara ran up the stairs to fetch the Peruvian bark she had been given for her own fever. She, in turn, had dosed Thérèse with it. Holding the bottle, unevenly blown and colored brown, up to afternoon light, she saw there was only a little left. She stared a moment at a pile of gowns. There was no place to put them save folded back into her trunks, and so Thérèse had laid them out like bodies, one atop another, that they might air.

What fools she and her grandmother had been, to be packing gowns and French chairs, when what was needed here was clothing for the slaves, tools—and remedies, like her grandmother's aqua mirabilis, a cooling fever water smelling of cloves and nutmeg, balm and red roses, smelling of home.

Barbara had already decided that she would return to England on the first ship of the spring; there was so much to discuss with Grandmama, far more than any letter could hold. If her grandmother wished to make First Curle all Barbara believed it could be, coins needed to be spent, and Barbara had none. Asking another for money, even a grandmother, was something that needed to be done face to face. Just where are you going to put those coins, her grandmother would say, and how is that to my advantage? Everything she thought and saw here went into the notebook.

It would be time to return, anyway, and see what was being done about her own estate. This had been in her mind more and more as she studied First Curle: that she, too, had an estate, even if it was only land and debt now. As she thought about tobacco and fields and overseers, about the foodstuffs, the wood, that must be put away to see them all through the winter, she thought about Devane Square. Might it rise again under her hand, rather than Roger's?

Halfway down the steps, she heard a voice and recognized it at once, that pleasant voice, speaking French.

"Make a large fire and put more blankets on him. The more he perspires with the fever, the better. I know. One or another of my crew always has it. You'll have to bathe him often, every hour at least, so that the fever doesn't go too high."

Barbara put her hand to her hair, which still hung about her face, and sat down at once on a step to pin it into some kind of order. The movement of her arms was entirely graceful, like lilies bending in a garden. Her hands fluttered whitely against the thick red-gold of her hair. Her neck, too, was white, long and sleek, like a swan's.

Beautiful, Klaus said each time she saw him, the man she'd not yet written of in any letters, the man who came to see her two, even three times a week now, the man whom she was a step away from bedding.

In the chamber, she saw that Klaus stood over the narrow bed, holding Hyacinthe down by the shoulders as Thérèse tried to cover him with blankets he had kicked off.

"Don't fight the blankets, but lie still if you can. Let the fever take you—Ah, Lady Devane." He smiled, a light coming into his face and eyes.

"Can you help me give him this Peruvian bark water, Captain?"

"Of course. But you know how bitter it is."

She sent Thérèse for rum and sugar in the basement under this house, fetched the water herself at the well, pulling up the bucket by a rope.

As Thérèse mixed rum, water, and sugar to give Hyacinthe after he took the bark water, Klaus wrapped Hyacinthe tightly in a blanket, as if in swaddling cloth.

"He will take it better from you," said Thérèse to Barbara. There were circles under Thérèse's dark eyes, and she was too thin. She herself was still recovering from the ague—the fever—part of coming to this colony, it seemed, to catch the ague.

"Open your mouth," said Klaus, "so your mistress may give you your medicine. It will make you well. It will taste bitter, but swallow it all, as bitter as it is. . . . That's it, swallow. Good boy. Again. Now drink this, which Mademoiselle Fuseau has mixed for you. Good boy, you're a brave boy. What do you say? Yes, I know. Your head hurts."

He laid Hyacinthe down again, deftly pulling out his arms from under the blanket.

"We must cover him with the bearskin," said Thérèse. "It made my fever break faster."

"We put it back upstairs," said Barbara, and Thérèse went off to fetch it.

Barbara found some cloths, wet them, ran them gently over Hyacinthe's face. Klaus knelt at the fireplace, and put in some dry branches to start a fire.

"Hush-a-bye, don't you cry, all the pretty little horses . . . When you wake, I will buy all the pretty little horses," Barbara sang to Hyacinthe, her voice low and husky, like smoke.

Klaus closed his eyes a moment, to savor that voice. It made a man catch his breath, first hearing it. He was a sensual man whom pleasure did not frighten. Pleasure did not frighten her, either. They saw that in each other. It was like a promise between them.

He brought in more wood for the fire and placed it so that the logs would catch and burn. He stood, wiped his hands on his breeches, noticing, as he had not before, two miniatures upon the mantel. Their frames were exquisite, the gold work intricate, small amethysts and seed pearls set among the gold. Each man painted on the tiny canvas was more wig than man, though one bore some resemblance to Barbara, something about the eyes. One must be her husband. Klaus had heard that her husband had been much older than she. She seldom spoke of him. He realized now, standing here, looking at the miniatures, that though they spoke of sailing and of this colony, of himself, they seldom spoke of her.

Who was she? I've seen Saylor House, said Colonel Perry. Her grandfather built it. It is one of the sights of London. To live in one of the sights of London, and now to dwell in this small, plain house and yet not complain or cry or leave. Why did she stay? Had she past deeds to flee from? A man—he would imagine there was a man involved. With her sensuality and bold deliberateness, how could there not be? He watched her and her maidservant settle the bearskin about the boy, watched the dogs leap to the bed, turn themselves around and around to sleep by him.

"Good dogs," said Thérèse.

"Clever dogs," said Barbara. "You watch over our Hyacinthe."

They'd made this house pleasant again, these women. Wildflowers and lilies were set into goblets; forest ivies in jars twined down mantels; cushions covered chairs, bright shawls were draped across tables and trunks, pictures hung upon the walls; the odor of beeswax and bay myrtle was everywhere. They had made it a home.

Odell was complaining. He was afraid of her. He said that she went everyplace, that she wanted the outbuildings painted before winter, that she'd ordered a chicken house built, the slave house repaired. The storehouse, said Odell. She's been asking questions, wanting to make an accounting of its contents. She's angry that Colonel Bolling hasn't sent the key. The barrels are heavy on my mind, Klaus. I will be glad when they are gone.

I will be glad when they are gone, too, thought Klaus. I wish they were not between her and me. Suddenly he disliked himself, disliked this role of spy and admirer—which was not a role, either. "I'll take my leave of you," he said, abruptly, clicking his heels together, the slightest of smiles making his face slant upward.

"I'll walk you to your horse," Barbara said. Outside, she kicked at some oyster shell. He could see she was distracted, concentrated on the boy. "We haven't enough bark water. Is there any in the storehouse? I haven't a key, you know; your uncle has yet to give me one."

She must at all costs be kept from there. In another few days, the barrels of contraband tobacco would be gone. While she was in Williamsburg, he would sail in his sloop and load them. Then the masquerade would be over. Why did I not insist my uncle move them? he thought. Why did I think we could play out this deception so long?

"Your neighbor Captain Randolph has some bark water, I know," he heard himself saying smoothly, and he disliked the charm, the smoothness. "Let me escort you, there. I know a forest path over which the trees tower like giants. It is dark and cool. We might stop and walk awhile; perhaps we can find some wild mint. Hyacinthe would like his face bathed with mint water. We can be back here again before an hour has passed, and you will have enough Peruvian bark water to mend your servant so that you may leave for Williamsburg and your fête without worry for him."

"I don't think I'm going."

"Not go? Impossible. You will break half the hearts in the colony, and force the other half to weep from curiosity. Of course you must go. I have looked forward to nothing but dancing with you since I learned of it. All the Governor's Council will be there, and most of the burgesses and their wives. Men are leaving their tobacco drying and casking for your sake. You have no idea what an honor that is."

"I cannot leave him alone."

"We speak of a servant boy of ten or more years, a slave. We'll find someone to see to him while you're away. Otherwise you insult the Governor and the most important men in the colony, the men who grow the best tobacco. You've said over and over how much you want to talk with them about tobacco."

He snapped his fingers.

"Mrs. Cox! Mrs. Cox could come to stay with him; she won't be going to Williamsburg, the journey fatigues her too much. She's too round," he whispered, making Barbara laugh, as if Mrs. Cox's extreme roundness were a secret. "You have only to ask her. She is fond of you, and you are a neighbor. We take care of one another here. All we have is one another."

"You have all the answers, it seems. You tempt me, Captain."

He looked at her straight in the eyes a moment, because her words struck him to the heart, because he had never expected to like her the way he did. Desire, yes; but like, no.

"Do I?"

"Yes," she said, looking back at him. There it was, he thought, that bold vitality of hers, that directness, that made him think about her for hours.

"I'll go and saddle a horse for you," he said.

As he stepped over the fence and went toward the paddock at the edge of the house clearing, Barbara watched. Then she walked up and down the oyster-shell paths, so as not to watch him anymore.

I'm in mourning; I won't be dancing, she thought. She'd noticed in the house that he'd looked at the miniatures. One of the miniatures was of her grandfather. If you decide on any wildness, you just look at that miniature, Bab, her grandmother had said, and remember who your grandfather was, the finest man I ever knew. Barbara sighed. I am only flesh and blood, Grandmama, not a saint.

The other miniature was of Roger. She touched the toe of her boot to some straggling marigold, thinking to herself: Marigold is for grief. She touched at vervain, whose meaning she could not remember, then reached down and snapped a leaf of rosemary, for remembrance. She held it to her nose.

Remembrance. Roger, I am flirting quite seriously with a sloop's captain, a colonial. His face intrigues me, the moods and thoughts passing over it. He is not simple, like so many others here. His birth in another land, his schooling, his life of adventure, shows. He is not married, like Charles, nor a shy boy, like Mrs. Cox's grandsons, who ride over to see me but can think of nothing to say once they are here. I am lonely, Roger. I miss a man's arms around me, a man's presence in my bed. And the dark is in me again, that old darkness I hate.

Wind moved in the pine trees that were on the other side of the house, and at the sound, lonely, mournful, Barbara crushed the leaf of rosemary between her fingers, looking out at the tobacco fields visible from where she was.

Had Roger ever really known her, known the girl behind her eyes? Toward the last, she'd thought he had—and thought he loved her even more for the knowing.

Her cousin Tony knew her, the girl inside, and Tony loved her. Mrs. Cox's grandsons made her think of Tony with their grave silence, their tall shadows. Marry me, Bab, Tony had said. But she hadn't.

Will I ever marry again? she wondered. And does it matter, if I need not do it for family or policy—indeed, cannot, since I have nothing at this moment to offer, and would give a man who marries me an impossible debt.

What harm did it do to follow her whims, to feel alive again in a way that only lying with a man brought? It meant nothing to either of them. The Captain was leading a horse toward a stump that served as a mounting block.

There is a widow, said Mrs. Cox, over in the next county, whom Klaus Von Rothbach has been courting for a year now. It would be a good match for him; she has much land. Mrs. Cox had smiled, the smile a crease in her plump, knowing face. A land-wealthy widow is a find here, she said. Marrying Lettice Bolling was a clever maneuver. On her death, he received her parcel of land. But it isn't much, said Mrs. Cox. This widow has much.

Klaus had not mentioned his widow. That's a lie, thought Barbara, not to mention her, when it is so clear what is between us. Her lover, Charles, stood in the plantation yard with her now, among the marigolds, frowning evenly at her as he so often did. You're a tease and a liar, Barbara, he'd said.

Well, she had been a tease, but Charles was the liar. She hated liars. Roger lied, whispered the girl inside her, and Barbara shook her head to that. No, not really. Yes, really, said the girl. Klaus had not mentioned the widow. Did it matter?

Yes, it did.

Latching the gate behind herself, she stepped up onto the stump, pulling herself into the sidesaddle, avoiding Klaus's hands held out to help. She tucked her skirts about her. The gown she wore today belonged to Beth Perry. Thérèse was even now stitching up others for her, plain ones, useful ones, the cloth brought from Colonel Perry's storehouse. She wore no hoop, which upset Thérèse, but what was the purpose of a hoop to bell out skirts when one might go sailing in a dinghy or ride through tobacco fields? She'd wear a hoop in Williamsburg, and patch her face again, and be all that was expected of a countess from London, as she asked about tobacco.

"I'll race you to the road," she said with that abrupt willfulness that so charmed, and she turned the filly's head in that direction.

She remembered later, while she watched Klaus tease Mrs. Randolph, watched him make her serious-minded neighbor, Captain Randolph, smile, and then remembered it again on the way home with him, as he picked mint and presented it to her with a three-cornered smile. He was teaching her the constellations in the night sky. "I'll be back at dark," he said, "to show you Orion." She remembered vervain was for enchantment.

CHAPTER 6

Barbara had been in Williamsburg five days. Tonight there was to be a grand, final fête in her honor at the Governor's house. Tonight, she would see Klaus. Now, she and Colonel Perry were walking through the garden of John Custis, Colonel Perry's cousin, at the edge of the village. It was a delicious day, cool, clear, the day before her last here in the village. She was pleased with her time spent here; she'd met council members, burgesses, wives and daughters, made friends, asked a hundred questions about tobacco, and now, happy, she was buying plants.

A ship headed for England lay in one of the creeks that bordered the village; the letter to her grandmother was already in the captain's hands. But there must be more; she must send gifts to everyone she loved.

The Custis garden sprawled over several acres. Some of it was made up of clipped hedges, flowers in precise formation, young trees planted in orderly lines. Across a ravine, however, the garden became wilderness, its native trees—cedars, pines, oaks—left in all their splendor, smaller trees under them, as well as shrubs and wildflowers. The trees themselves, here and across the ravine, were very nearly a riot of golds, scarlets, clear butter yellows. Once in a while a leaf-strewn gust came up to whip her skirts and try for her hat.

"A dogwood, perhaps, Lady Devane?"

Custis walked her down one of his brick walks.

"Your grandmother the Duchess will want a dogwood for her garden. They bloom in the spring, Lady Devane, and are our loveliest of flowering trees, with white blossoms the size of your face, and a fragrance beyond compare. The Indians make a potion from the bark for fevers. I have sent several fine specimens to the Royal Society. Myself, I prefer lilacs. I am cultivating as many of them as I am given. They do not do as well here as they might in other places, but I have a weakness for them. I search all the woods, you know, like the village idiot, dig up what I like, watch it grow. My friends allow me the run of their woods, indulge my follies, think me mad. They send me things from far and wide—seeds, roots, young trees."

"Do not allow this man to fool you. He knows more of plants than anyone in the colony, Lady Devane," said Colonel Perry.

Custis pointed to shrubs at the edge of the ravine; bright red berries clustered like drops of blood on their branches. "Swamp holly. Those berries will be there until spring. You could send your grandmother a swamp holly and some of our jasmine. And some of our mountain cowslips, pretty things, Lady Devane, just what a woman would like, with clusters of trumpet-shaped blue flowers. I have them planted in my flower beds here. Beautiful in the spring, beautiful. Oh, and a pomegranate, she will have to have a pomegranate tree, with scarlet flowers in the summer and a red fruit later. Our cousin, Will Byrd, who's in England now, gave one to the King."

"Lady Devane brought rosebushes with her," Perry said.

Custis's nose quivered. He might have been smelling a delicious dish for dinner. "Not the Tamworth rose—"

"And spinach seeds," continued Perry. "Her grandmother's spinach is equally famous."

Barbara smiled. Colonel Perry's gentle teasing of his cousin was as beautiful, as bracing, as the day. "Will you take me across the bridge, Major Custis, and show me your wild garden?"

She began to walk down the side of the ravine. Stepping stones had been set in the side, then led to a wooden bridge, which crossed over the water of a stream at the bottom of the ravine. Already the mood of the garden was changing. The formality was gone. The skirts of her gown brushed against pine cones, acorns, piles of bright leaves. "I would like to send a dear friend of mine a dogwood, such as you spoke of, and I know my grandmother would be delighted with one," she said. "Would you sell me two from your garden?"

"I might. What would you pay me with?"

Be forewarned, Colonel Perry had said, John Custis would just as soon snap off your head as look at you. He likes people less and less the older he becomes. But if he takes a liking to you, there's no firmer friend.

"English shillings, a rose cutting, a spinach seed, a French fan, a hogshead of tobacco, a chick or two hatched from Tamworth chickens, fine cream from my cow, who survived one of your storms, a French song sung just for you. What else might you wish?"

A smile moved quickly across his face and was just as quickly gone. He liked her answer.

He pointed to a tree. "Waxy white, fragrant flowers in the spring, Lady Devane, as large as a cabbage. We call it swamp laurel. And this is a mulberry. Our savages here weave the bark into cloaks." He bent down and picked a branch from the ground. At its tip was a cone of crimson seeds. "From the swamp laurel," he told her, presenting it to her as if it were frankincense and myrrh—and for him, as Colonel Perry told her later, it was. "Send this cone of seeds to your grandmother with Major John Custis's compliments, and tell her in seventy years she'll have the finest trees in all England."

Barbara followed him across the little bridge. The water under it was crowded with leaves swirling away to their destiny. "Everyone says there are two varieties of tobacco grown here, orinoco and sweet-scented."

"Your land is best suited for sweet-scented. Count your blessings, Lady Devane, for it brings the highest prices. Though Jordan Bolling grew a good orinoco, too. The Dutch like the stronger tobacco—that's the orinoco—as do the French and Spanish. The trouble is that orinoco won't keep in storage over a year and has to be sold quickly, while sweet-scented loses weight in the hogsheads, so that packing it can be difficult. Too much and it might catch the mold. Too little and it rattles to nothing."

"What would be the very best tobacco seed?"

"Your overseer should have seed, but since you ask, the Diggeses on the York River, north of here, have a famous sweet-scented, known in London, fetching the highest prices."

Everyone said the same, Digges seed.

Major Custis pointed out a tree with leaves that shimmered like a gauze gown. "Silver maple. Exquisite. The leaves are green on one side, silver upon the other, so that when the wind moves through them, they shimmer. Your grandmother would like a silver maple. I know it. They please my heart, Lady Devane, and as Edward here will tell you, I'm a crusty soul with a difficult heart."

"Then my grandmother must have a silver maple. How would I purchase Digges tobacco seed?"

"You'd ask mad old John Custis what he desired for it."

"Every rose cutting I've brought is yours for your kindness in indulging me this morning, and I have to tell you, the lilacs at Tamworth Hall are among the finest ever I've seen. My grandmother might be persuaded to part with some cuttings . . . if someone dear to her asked."

"Bribery, pure and simple. Edward, you are witness to it. Two rose cuttings, a portion of the spinach seed, a lilac, and it's done. The seed is yours. I'll tell you what else mad old John Custis has for a lady like yourself: a secret in which no one believes. The best tobacco is grown from drained marshland. I've a friend from England, mad for plants, like me, who came to live among us for a few years. While here, he played with the art of growing tobacco, leased some land, drained a marsh, gave it a year to dry. And a year from that, there were plants twice the size of another man's, and the prettiest tobacco leaves from them you've ever seen. Not a man here can be persuaded to listen to me, to do likewise. They don't want the bother of it, you see, because there is always land over the next horizon."

Finished with her buying, she and Colonel Perry walked down the long green laid out before the Governor's house.

"When I was in England, I saw Saylor House," said Colonel Perry. "Your grandfather was still alive then. It was spring, and I went into the gardens; there must have been two hundred Dutch tulips planted. Red, I remember, as true a crimson as I have ever seen."

"You've been to Saylor House? I didn't know. The House of Orange sent tulips every year to him because my grandfather and William of Orange were colleagues in war and because Grandfather supported William when he came over to replace King James. My cousin Tony still keeps the gardens open, and every winter the tulips arrive, for my grandfather is not forgotten by the Dutch."

Perry moved in front of her so that she had to stop, took one of her hands in his, kneaded the flesh, gently, kindly.

"Have you any idea how kind you've been this last week, surrounded always by people? I know our horse race in your honor, our picnics and dinners, grand to us, must have seemed small to you, perhaps even ridiculous. But you have been all that is gracious, when you might have mocked us. You've made many a friend this week, Lady Devane. And you've just charmed John Custis. I assure you, that is no easy task. Everyone is talking of your kindness. They're glad, and proud, that you have come to be among us."

His eyes were alive and beautiful in his face, like matched stones; Barbara thought, Roger's eyes were just that shade.

"Why are you here?" he asked.

There was no reason she should satisfy his curiosity. You are an honorable man, thought Barbara. Impulsively, she said, "I have a great debt against me. My husband was a South Sea director, and the fine against his estate is large. He owed other monies, for a house he built and stock and land he bought. And when the Bubble burst—well, our estate burst with it. I guess you might say I ran away."

"Do you think to make your fortune here?"

"I think to do my duty to my grandmother. She wanted to know about First Curle, what it was, what it might be. I needed a time away from all the loss. But I think my fortune is in England. The cards there—the fine against my estate, the debt—are not played out yet. The longer I am here, the more I think about that. I'm going back in the spring, to report to my grandmother on what I've found here, on what I've begun here, and to see to my estate."

"Will you return to Virginia?"

"The river, the trees, the sky, certain people are growing into my heart. I would imagine I'll always be coming back."

They were at the Governor's house, a large, solid, three-story square of brick, with windows set into its roof, and a white cupola as crown.

Inside its hall, he said to her, "What you've just told me will remain between us, Lady Devane—"

"Of course it will. I knew that before I spoke."

A slight flush came to his cheeks. "I am honored by your confidence." He spoke stiffly, quite unlike himself. "Farewell, until this evening."

A servant appeared. "Mr. Randolph is here to see you, Lady Devane. He is in the garden."

Walking out into the gardens, Barbara saw Randolph, her grandmother's solicitor, at the edge of a small landscape canal the Governor had built in his gardens.

"Do you have it?" Barbara said, walking up to him.

"I do, but I must warn you that your neighbors will not be pleased. It unsettles slaves, madam, to see one of their brothers freed."

Barbara took the paper from him and opened it. "I don't think freeing one small boy is going to unsettle the colony." There it was, the paper that gave Hyacinthe his freedom.

There was a longtime law, this young man had told her, stipulating that freed slaves had to leave the colony within six months of receiving their freedom, but it had not been put back into the revisions of the slave laws in 1705. Thank goodness. Perhaps, when she gave Hyacinthe this paper and explained to him what it meant, he would stop fretting.

"There is just a bit more of business," Barbara said to him. "Come with me into the house."

Randolph was an earnest, serious young man, rather like the man who had been Roger's clerk of the household. "How might I purchase land, not in my name, but mine all the same?"

"You designate someone as silent trustee and put the land in that name. Where are we going, Lady Devane?"

"To my bedchamber," she answered, lifting her skirts and half running up the stairs, as he followed hesitantly. "Thérèse," she said as she entered the bedchamber. "I've brought Mr. Randolph up."

He stood uncertainly in the frame of the door.

"The meeting of the Governor's Council was very interesting to me, particularly the discussion of the granting of land. 'To Jeremiah Clower, four thousand acres; to Edmund Jennings, ten thousand; to Drury Stith, three thousand.' "

To Randolph's surprise, she lifted a pillow from the bed, and there were jewels, diamonds, pearls, emeralds, in earrings, in necklaces, in brooches and bracelets. Slowly, eyes wide, Randolph walked toward them.

"We keep them in the hem of Thérèse's gown. I want you to take a portion of them, toward buying land. I am a fool for gambling." Barbara smiled, but Randolph's eyes were on the jewels. "And I want to gamble in land."

Tobacco needs land. She'd heard it said over and over since she'd come here. Colonel Perry, Captain Randolph, and Colonel Bolling owned all the land around First Curle for miles—or so said Margaret Cox—land they didn't use now, but would.

"And there is a letter from His Majesty." She went to a table, rummaged among some papers, and handed Randolph the letter that had been waiting for her when she arrived in Williamsburg. "His Majesty is kind enough to say that I have to pay no quitrent at all."

"S-so he does," stammered Randolph. It was the law that quitrents, a tax, be paid to His Majesty upon any land bought, because the land was his. This letter, with its signature and seal of George I, freed Barbara from that tax.

"I will wear a portion of these tonight—the pearls, yes, Thérèse? But these"—she swept up emeralds and some of the diamonds as if they were nothing, and put them into his hands—"I give to you to safekeep and to use in purchasing land. Now, I really must say good-bye, Mr. Randolph. We'll talk again tomorrow before I leave, for I have an idea of where we might buy land, and I know you will, too. Good-bye, for now, Mr. Randolph."

Somehow, he was outside the bedchamber door. He stood a moment looking down at the jewels before carefully putting them in his pocket. He must give her a receipt for them. He would give her a receipt for them! His brother, her neighbor, had described her visits, the dogs her slave boy made do tricks, her singing of French nonsense songs to the children, who laughed in delight, she in gowns that a queen might wear. She is quite extraordinary, his brother had said, asking me one question after another about tobacco, about running a plantation.

Indeed, thought Randolph, she was extraordinary, and exhausting. At the idea of the amount of land he would be able to purchase with these jewels, at the idea of making the best purchase for the amount, at guessing at the future, a challenge he enjoyed, he thought: And she's exhilarating.

❧

Colonel Edward Perry did not go back to his cousin's house as he had planned, but walked to the side of the Governor's house, outside the gardens, the wall surrounding them, to a tall and spreading oak. From there, he looked up toward the windows of the room in which she stayed. He was deeply moved that she had confided so freely in him. A hundred men must have loved you for your face. Did any love you for your heart? I'm like a boy, he thought, besotted.

What is there that I remain so touched, so moved within, by you? It was as if, after all this time, he had stumbled upon something familiar, something he had long ago surrendered as gone, never knowing of the surrender until what had been lost was found again. Home was the river, whose sullen flow he'd watched for all these years. Home was the thick woods, the horse trails cut through them, the heavy heat of summer, the isolation winter storms brought, the simple, rough kindness of people whom he'd known all his life; yet all that seemed a dream now, faded beside the fact of Barbara's presence at First Curle.

Up until now, he had been content, particularly in these recent years of his life, living in a serenity that made him feel he flowed as beautifully, as powerfully, as the river. It was as if God had blessed him in every possible way, and he, aware of those blessings, had tried to return them. She touches my heart in a way I do not understand, he thought, and I am frightened by the depth of my emotion.

He would go to the church just down the green. It would be quiet inside; no one would be there. He would sit down upon a pew and pray about this, yet again. Prayer was his habit now, though he'd come to it late, only some fifteen years ago, when his son had died. The boy, like his daughter, Beth, had entered his life late, from a younger wife, a woman he'd loved, who had died bearing Beth. Prayer had changed his life, had saved him from the madness the grief of his son's dying brought. It would save him, now, from being a fool, or if it didn't save him from that, he would be guided, as always he was, to what it was he had to do with her; for somehow, some way, he and she were inextricably linked. All that being near her did was draw them closer, and so he must accept it. He must ask, until he was answered. It was almost as if they were pieces of a soul, split in two and found again. A poet's thought—which, again, frightened him, coming up from some place deep within him, a place he'd not explored before, indeed had not known existed.

"A law that tobacco must go to England, a law that the hogshead must be a certain size, a law that a planter must be fined if he casks the sprouts growing on the stalks after the leaves are cut—what a number of laws they have for tobacco," Barbara said to Thérèse.

Nicotiana is its Latin name, she thought as Thérèse unlaced her gown, repeating in her mind Major Custis's words: There is a native species here, grown by the Indians before the first one of us ever landed. It was sacred to them, and still is, despite us. When you smoke a pipe of tobacco with an Indian, you do not do so for enjoyment, but rather to sanctify a pact or treaty or deed. They offer it to the water to ensure good fishing, scatter it in fields to ensure good harvest. Sacred, you see. They are not prodigal with it, as we are.

She would cultivate fewer plants, grow less tobacco, but the best. Sort, it was called: tobacco, grown by certain planters, that could be counted upon for quality. Colonel Perry had a sort; so did Captain Randolph. So would she, beginning with Digges seed. There were no records of Bolling's tobacco to look at, no account book about his tobacco-growing. Doubtless his uncle had taken them. So be it. She'd write to Jordan's London merchants; better yet, she'd visit them when she went back to England.

She'd make her own sort, the best sort, from the best seed. She pictured Tony, Wart, Charles, all the fashionable young men she knew, holding snuff to their nostrils, sneezing, the snuff made from her sort. She could make her sort fashionable; she knew she could. Those at court thrived upon being in fashion, spent days and nights fretting that a gown might not be the latest style or worrying over the placement of a patch. She would send a hogshead to the Prince of Wales's favorite tobaccoist, with her compliments.

She heard the sound of a harp and sighed. Musicians practicing for tonight. In another couple of hours or so, the downstairs would be filled. She raised milk-white, slender arms over her head and thought about a sweet, mild tobacco. Could a tobacconist mix lavender in among the crushed leaves? Or mint. Lady D, the snuff they made might be called. Or perhaps—even better—The Duchess, for her grandmother.

Thérèse had laid her gown for this evening across the bed. There were the jewels and feathers, the ribbons and laces, the stays that would pull in her waist and push up her breasts and so constrict her that she would not be able to run ten steps without losing her breath. There were the patch box, the rouge puff, the accoutrements of a lady.

She went to the window. It overlooked the gardens. The Governor had built this house and planted these gardens. He patented land for himself, explored, had a plantation near the mountains, was always occupied. He left his mark.

I go to Williamsburg at the Governor's command to represent the people of this county as a burgess, Colonel Perry said, and I have the honor to serve on county court. It is my duty to know as much as I can about those I serve. My neighbors' needs are what I take to Williamsburg when the Governor calls an assembly to make laws; their troubles are what I listen to and decide about on county court day. How can I make a fair decision if I do not know my neighbor and his needs?

Or his lies and deceits, said Mrs. Cox. The Colonel is the fairest of men, she'd said. He is customs officer of the river, was once on the Governor's Council before quarrels lost him the position and he was too proud and honorable to fight back. And he can survey land, if need be, as well as write up a good, clean will. Colonel Perry left marks, too.

What marks had she made upon life?

"You must rest," said Thérèse, "so that you look beautiful tonight."

Barbara frowned down at the gardens.

Do I buy slaves? Can I buy slaves? Can I do as do the others, here, and simply close my eyes to its cruelty? Have I a choice? How else will I grow the tobacco I want? She would see Klaus tonight. He had promised to come to her fête. Something was going to happen between them before he sailed away. She could feel it. She drummed restless fingers on a windowsill.

Hyacinthe, what are you doing? Are you behaving? No. He'd been furious that they left him, but too feverish to accompany them.

That question made her think of others, at home, of her friend Wart, of her lover, Charles. Were they behaving? No. Court was too boring, the routines too stultifying. One had to amuse oneself or die. They never behaved. Tony did, dear cousin, solid and dependable.

Perhaps that's why I didn't love you, thought Barbara, you were too respectable for me.

CHAPTER 7

What's happening? thought Laurence Slane. It was late, very late, past midnight, not yet dawn, and he was in a small tavern in one of London's great squares, amidst noblemen and hangers-on and whores, most of them the worse for wine. It was the time of night when trouble happened, and it surely was.

"I would never allow any cousin of mine to be spoken of in such a manner," said the Duke of Wharton.

"I will not allow it," said Charles, Lord Russel. He stood up, knocking over his chair. "Repeat yourself, sir."

"Trouble?" Tommy Carlyle said to Slane. "Let us go and see. I do delight in trouble."

The tavern was quieting, laughter and loud talk dying back, as if others around the quarrel, beginning to sense something was astir, did not want to miss it.

"I said—" A man rose clumsily from his chair. He was loud, drunk, almost shouting out the words.

Who is that man? thought Slane. He recognized the others at the table—Tony, the young Duke of Tamworth; Tamworth's brother-in-law, Charles; Charles's friend, the Duke of Wharton. They represented great and proud families; Tamworth and Wharton had been young in 1715, when George came to the throne. The world was theirs, and they had all the time, all the encouragement, all the precedent, to while away lives and estates drinking and gambling and chasing whores. There was no war to challenge them, to cool the passions of youth and maleness. They made do with debauchery.

"I said that the Prince of Wales's bed may be cold this winter, but some Virginian's will be warm," said the man, Tom Masham.

You fool, thought Slane. There will be a duel over this, and before his thought was even finished, Tony stood and hit the man squarely in the face.

Slane was surprised, he had been expecting such action from Charles, already on his feet, not from Tamworth.

Everything then became pandemonium. Tom Masham fell back into Slane's companion Tommy Carlyle, who screamed like a woman. Masham's whore of the evening screamed louder than Carlyle and jumped on the Duke of Tamworth's back, beating at him with her fists. Charles fell on Masham, sitting up on the floor, as if, thought Slane derisively, Charles would finish what Tamworth began. The pair rolled in the sawdust and spilled wine like wrestling boys.

The Duke of Wharton laughed, a demented sound. He was out of the fray, but encouraging it.

"Hit Masham again, Charles!" Wharton was saying. "Tony, don't allow that woman to touch you. Slap her."

"I'll call the watch."

The tavernkeeper had out his club, but was fearful to use it upon noble patrons. The watch, thought Slane. What help will they be? They were old men whose duties were to walk through the streets and call out the hour and to round up rowdies and drunks. Except that their age made them less than effective, and so did their own predilection for liquor. I should just walk away from this, thought Slane, but he found himself taking hold of the whore by her waist and pulling her off the Duke of Tamworth. She kicked and scratched, but Slane held her arms tight and whispered in her ear cajolingly, confusing her.

"There, there. No need to fight. Come and sit here and let these rude men finish this without your help."

He saw that Sir Gideon Andreas, who was the King's banker—soon to be made an earl, it was said—had separated Charles and Masham; Andreas was forceful, broad, tall enough to do it, his stature and age—he was their senior by fifteen or more years—giving him an authority that was obeyed.

Slane left the whore weeping drunkenly and stepped outside, breathing in the night air, clearer by far than that in the tavern. Barbara, he thought, staring up at a lone star or two, you've likely caused a duel, and you're not even here. Are you still as beautiful as when last I saw you? Apparently so.

He turned at the sound of someone stepping out of the tavern. The Duke of Wharton.

"There will be a duel, I know it," said the Duke.

"You did your best to encourage it. I thought Tamworth was your friend."

"He is."

"With friends like you, he does not need enemies."

"You will use this," said the Duke—and for a moment, before Wharton went back into the tavern, it seemed to Slane that his eyes gleamed with an unholy light.

Yes. The scandal of this could be used to their advantage to keep discontent against George high. Slane began to walk. The Bishop of Rochester needed something to vent himself on. A wicked, vicious broadsheet about this would be just the thing. Duels were illegal. It would look as though the King could not keep order among his own people. The plan for invasion is on its way, Slane had told Rochester. King James was in Italy; his most trusted advisers—one of them a general in the French army—were in France; therefore, plans had to come from Paris. Rome to Paris to London takes time, said Slane.

Too long a time, replied Rochester. Irascible. Impossible. Impatient. So Slane had been warned of Rochester before coming to England. The warnings were not wrong. In another life, Slane's given name was Lucius. Keep him to me, Lucius, Jamie said.

Beloved Blackbird, thought Slane, I miss you. I miss Italy. King

James III had dark eyes, like a blackbird's, and a brown complexion, like a Gypsy's; he was called Blackbird by his closest friends. In another life, Slane was among those most trusted friends. Lucius, Viscount Duncannon, held vast estates in Ireland, estates he'd never seen, for his family had fled in the early 1690s, when old James II had tried to take back his throne by invasion through Ireland, and the English—victorious—retaliated by beggaring the island. So that in truth, he was viscount of nothing.

Hordes of Irish and Scots soldiers, nobles, and relatives had descended upon Europe, upon the various courts, to make their way as well as they could, once it was clear that James II would do no more, that William of Orange had defeated him in battle and in spirit, and that they must wait upon his son, Jamie the Blackbird, to take the crown.

Barbara, thought Slane, why do they slander you? I don't remember you as wicked. And now your cousin Tony may die over you. What havoc you wreak from so far away.

The next day, the second Duke of Tamworth, Anthony Richard Saylor—the middle name came from his famous grandfather and betrayed his mother's ambitions—walked into White's Coffeehouse. Opening the door was like stepping into haze, from the pipes smoked by the men who had been here all of the morning. Tony nodded to the woman who collected the fees for tea or coffee, and sat down at a table near the windows, which looked out onto the street. It was too late in the afternoon for many to be inside with him; now was the time when men who had spent morning and early afternoon in the coffeehouses that were everywhere in London, conversing, smoking pipes, reading the news sheets and letters of shipping news, the advertisements for elixirs, pills, snuff, and rejuvenating waters, posted on the walls, went home for an hour or two to their wives, and dinner.

Following dinner came a walk down the long double row of trees that was the Mall of St. James Park. The purpose of this stroll was to see and be seen. Then, as the sun set, a man went to a play or an opera, or to court if the King should be receiving guests. Or he began the inevitable evening round of taverns, to gamble and drink and talk once more, until late evening, when serious drinking and serious whoring began. The gambling never stopped. Tony had seen friends begin a morning game of cards at a coffeehouse and emerge only the following day. His cousin Harry had won a plantation in such a bout, the plantation where Barbara now was. Tony had been present when Harry had won it.

Tony touched the place on his temple that throbbed persistently. This whole summer had been a nightmare. He could not sleep. He could not eat. He could not think. He had had to look at Virginia upon a map of the world to try to make some sense of Barbara's unexpected, secret departure. No word from Barbara to him, no letter to explain or ask his blessing or even to say farewell, just the heart-stoppingly harsh fact—she was gone—staring him in the face at the end of a long journey to Tamworth.

First love, they said. Calf love. Least said, soonest mended. But what is a man profited, if he shall gain the whole world, and lose his own soul? Barbara was his soul. She had been since he was sixteen. He drummed his fingers impatiently on the table and stared out the window, waiting. He had the long legs of his father and grandfather and their fair hair, which he wore to his shoulders, like a woman's, but held back with a ribbon, unfashionable in this era of shaved heads and wigs. As a duke, he was allowed this eccentricity; as a duke, he was allowed much—anything, in fact, that he wished. His face was ordinary, neither handsome nor plain. A dimple appeared in one cheek when he smiled, and the smile was grave, shy, so that people who knew him well found themselves watching for it, always surprised, always.

Tony's brother-in-law, Charles, walked into the coffeehouse. For a moment, Tony could not breathe. Charles, his trusted friend, was his second in what was very likely to be a duel; Charles would have been to see his opponent.

Charles was dressed for a London evening, in satin coat, lace from the shirt underneath showing at the sleeves, a full periwig upon his head, and a black silk patch shaped like a circle on one even cheekbone. If you do not fight him, I will, Charles had said last night, the evenness gone then.

"Masham won't apologize." Charles pulled out a chair and sat, sprawling his legs out under the table. "He has chosen pistols. Do you own a pair of dueling pistols?"

"No—yes. My father—I have a pair of my father's. When is it, exactly, Charles?"

"Four-thirty. Tomorrow morning. Hyde Park. By the two oaks near the road to Piccadilly."

"He is still out there, I thought he was waiting for one of the orange girls or one of our actresses, but when Polly went out to him to see, he was not interested."

"Perhaps he is ill," said Slane. He put on his coat, then said impatiently, because he knew what Cibber was waiting for, "I will see about him."

"Thank you, Slane. I don't pay you enough, Slane," said Cibber, following the actor past scenery, past the actresses pulling on their gowns behind stacks of furniture.

"There he is," Cibber whispered.

The Duke of Tamworth had come for the afternoon play and remained where he was through the evening play. Now it was past nine, and still he sat, the only one left in what had been their audience.

Slane, compact, small, lithe, leaped nimbly off the end of the stage, took the lantern Cibber handed him, and walked into the darkness.

He was used to reading men, and in the flickering lantern's light it was clear the young Duke was in a state of shock. Slane had seen it before, the blank, bereft expression of men on the battlefield after a battle, when they were wounded but not certain where or how badly. How old is he? thought Slane, his eyes moving over the extreme whiteness of Tony's face. It was a good face, strong, offset by eyes the shade of summer sky. Twenty-and-two or so?

Though Slane himself was twenty-eight, he'd been in his first battle at the age of fourteen, fighting this man's relatives—this man's father and grandfather—in the French wars. And then, too, he had grown to manhood in exile, belonging to no one, to no place, to no home, his family estates in Ireland given to those who had chosen William of Orange over James II. Belonging nowhere brought out a man's instincts for survival, and it made him old before his time.

He felt little but contempt for these young noblemen of George I's, who had never fought a battle or done without anything. It was said that Robert Walpole, one of the King's ministers, bragged that every man has his price. In this world, under this reign, it was true. The South Sea Bubble had proved it.

"Your Grace, the play is over," Slane said. "We need to lock our doors and go home for the night."

Out of the corner of his eye, Slane could see Cibber wringing his hands nervously, not wanting to offend so noble a patron, but wanting, like everyone else, to be out of the theater and into bed.

Tony stood up. He doesn't even know where he is, Slane thought.

"Come with me, Your Grace, it's time to leave," Slane said cheerfully, thinking: The duel must be set.

It will end in a duel, that mincing hulk of a courtier Tommy Carlyle had said today. You mark my words, Slane.

This was likely the Duke's first duel. There was in Slane's mind the memory of his first battle. He had scarcely slept the night before it, and his hands had been shaking so before the cry of battle began, that he had dropped his sword and nearly cut off his foot.

Once they were out on the street, Slane wished the Duke well, said good-bye, and, whistling, began the walk to his lodgings, which were near. He was thinking about Rochester's glee over this quarrel. Young dogs, Rochester had said, impious and godless, just like this present reign.

Keep discontent stirred until I come: Those were his orders from Jamie. The broadsheet Rochester was writing about this duel over a

South Sea director's widow would do that. But now Slane made a mistake; he looked back and saw that the Duke of Tamworth was still standing where he'd left him, with that same hushed, stunned expression on his face. Cursing himself even as he turned around—he had a weakness for hurt creatures, birds with broken wings, dogs whose ribs showed through their fur—he walked back.

"What day is it, Slane?"

"The seventh of October." And then, when the Duke said nothing else: "My lodgings are near. You can rest there awhile."

Slane stopped at the pie shop below his room and bought a meat pie and a jug of ale. Inside his chamber, he lit a candle and put down the food.

"Sit down." He waved his hand toward the single chair that came with this lodging.

"Hello, darling," he said to the finch in the birdcage on the table that also came with this lodging. "Did you miss me?" He opened the door of the cage. The finch hopped out, and Slane crumbled some of the crust from the pie for her; she hopped over to eat it.

"Her wing was broken." He stroked the finch's tiny back with a finger. "I got her for nothing at the Sunday market nearby."

Slane whistled and held out his hand, and the finch hopped up on it. He raised his hand, and at another whistle the finch flew to his shoulder. "Brave girl," Slane said. "I love you." After a moment, as if secure with Slane's shoulder as a launching-post, the finch took flight and flew around and around the chamber, finally perching atop a post of the bed, cocking her head to one side, and singing. Tony smiled then, a grave smile, the smile like an unexpected good deed, and at the sight of it, Slane found he had to stand up abruptly, move to the opened window, and sit in it, to be anywhere but somewhere where he could see this man's face, and thus his pain.

"From my window, Your Grace, I've looked down more than once to wave at thieves and highwaymen on their way to Tyburn gallows. The carts pass from Wych Street into Drury Lane on their way to Tyburn Road. There's a whore's parade out here at dusk, but I regret to say you've missed it. Have some of the pie, Your Grace.

Here is a knife; just cut yourself a small piece and eat. Now, have a swallow from that jug. Good. You'll feel more yourself with your belly full."

One leg swinging out easily, Slane began to talk of the theater—of Cibber and his miserliness; of the actress who had come in drunk this afternoon, so that all of them had had to act around her, and how she had fallen asleep in the midst of saying her most important line. He talked easily, yet all the while he was thinking of Rochester. This reign does not control the passions of its young men, said Rochester, and it does its best to break the back of the Church of England. It's why I became Jacobite, Slane, because I saw that George of Hanover is no friend to the Mother Church, but buys our bishops and prelates the same way he buys the loyalty of the Whigs. The authority of the Church is besmirched, compromised time after time. Everything is for sale these days, Slane, even God.

As he spoke, Slane noticed a child holding a candle in the street below. She set the candle into the mud of the street and ran off, her form just visible for a moment in the light. The candle was a signal to him. Thank God, Slane thought.

"Your Grace, I must take my leave of you. I have a lady whom I've promised to see this evening, and I mustn't make her angry by keeping her waiting. Stay here as long as you like."

The candle signaled that there was a letter in from France, or possibly Italy, an important letter that only he and a few others would see. Let it be the plan for invasion, he thought, moving to stare at himself before a piece of chipped mirror, as if he did, indeed, go to see a ladylove. In a way he did though Rochester would blanch at being called such. But the Bishop was certainly someone Slane must keep wooed.

The face in the mirror was a face a woman would look at twice, and many did. There were dark brows above widely spaced and equally dark eyes. The nose was broad, as was the mouth. Handsome, people called him. Lady Shrewsborough had said, You're the handsomest thing I laid eyes upon in many a day. She was an ancient relative to the Duke, who sat right now in Slane's only chair. If your manners match your face, she'd said, come call upon me, and we'll play a game of cards. I can tell much about a person by the way he plays cards.

And now, thanks to her, Slane was becoming as fashionable in the drawing rooms of London as he was upon the stage. All to the good. The deeper he burrowed into the heart of this court, the more he could aid Jamie.

The Bishop of Rochester was impatient. Slane saw Rochester rather than himself in the mirror. Where is our invasion plan? the Bishop would ask. Upon its way, Slane would assure him. He would talk to Rochester for hours, settling him the way one settled a restive hawk: We invade in the spring, as you advised; during the election, as you advised.

Rochester would rub his hands together. Seven years, he'd say, as he always did. It has been seven years since there was an election of men to the House of Commons. All of England will be quarreling over votes. More than one man will be thinking to himself of the old days when there was a Stuart upon the throne, rather than this foreigner.

The Swedes would supply troops, or the Spanish. There would be risings here, among all those who would have risen in 1715, who had been waiting. Slane and Rochester had cut England into military districts, setting loyal Jacobites back into place, setting them to plot again, to secretly collect arms and coins.

I can feel the fever, Slane, Rochester said. Can you? It's our fever still racking us from the South Sea Bubble, for the way King George and his ministers tricked us. The hue and cry over final fines given to South Sea directors remained. No one thought the fines were high enough. So many had lost fortunes in speculation in South Sea stock that there was no fine, no punishment large enough to repair the sense of outrage and damage. People had lost trust in King George, saw his ministers as greedy and corrupt, as benefiting when South Sea stock had been rising but refusing to do what must be done once it began to fall. One of the King's ministers, Robert Walpole, had been burned in effigy in August. It was said he would be dismissed because people hated him so.

Slane could see the Duke of Tamworth's stillness reflected in the mirror, and while a part of him had sympathy for the man, there was another part that was cold, remote. Tony was the enemy, a man who could be hated in particular on account of his grandfather, Richard Saylor, if for nothing else. Saylor had supported William of Orange. King James II had said of him, a famous soldier, famous in every court for his tactical skill and his handsome manners, "He has the courage of a lion and the kindness of a saint." Lionheart, Richard Saylor had been called, after another famous warrior of English history. And so, Slane could look at his grandson Tony and feel both sympathy and scorn.

Once, he would have felt only scorn. Have I not the edge I should? he wondered. The years of intrigue were telling on him, years of going from court to court, of begging arms and money for Jamie, of seeing plans fail, one after another, to invade here and conquer. It wore on him to deal with an irascible man like the Bishop of Rochester, who would as soon curse a man as bless him; it wore on him to hear Rochester's doubts and fears echo his own. God save me, thought Slane; God save the Blackbird and me.

Farewell, young Duke. You're off to duel and perhaps die, and I'm off to plot, and perhaps die for that, too, in the end. We have more in common than you imagine. If your grandfather had stayed loyal to James II, the pair of us might be here, together, plotting. Or we might never have had to plot at all, for we would have won if your grandfather, and others like him, had stayed loyal.

Outside, in the dark, Slane thought of Barbara. He must use this duel to his own ends, and besmirch her name. He did not like it. He thought of Charles, Lord Russel, who had been her lover, and that made the doing of it easier. He did not like Charles, his temper and pride. If it were not for Charles, the young man sitting in Slane's chair might not be facing death. Would Barbara grieve if her cousin Tony died? He loved her, but did she love him?

Once upon a time—in Italy, and as Viscount Duncannon—Slane had courted Barbara for a brief moment. She had been capricious, charming, estranged from her husband, and oddly—and to Slane's mind, very sweetly—chaste. She was teasing, but was never won; she was not what people imagined at all. It seemed she had eventually abandoned chastity. I would have been better for her than Charles, he reflected.

When he accepted this mission to London he'd thought she would be here, and that since she knew him he'd have to stay burrowed out of sight, far behind the scenes of the action, the danger, the cleverness and daring that would be necessary intriguing to him. What was it his mother had accused him of? That he needed danger to feel alive. There had been a kiss between Barbara and him, a kiss they'd begun, once upon a time, in a garden; he was Viscount Duncannon, and she was, well, Barbara, Lady Devane, sister to Harry, a committed Jacobite. Now there was irony all around: One of Richard Saylor's grandsons, Harry, had been a Jacobite. The wrong grandson died, thought Slane, but perhaps that is going to be rectified in the next few hours.

Then all of Richard Saylor's grandsons would be, at last, dead.

Dark. It was so dark in the street that Tony stumbled over nothing from the sheer blackness of it. He held out his hands before him and woke, not knowing where he was for a second. There were some candles burning. In their light, he saw a birdcage, its door open, a finch in it. So. He was in Laurence Slane's lodging, and he was to fight a duel. The darkness was no dream; he was living it.

In another few hours he was going to face a man across a morning's mist. In his mind, he saw Hyde Park, heard the silence there, the breathless quiet that was early morning. In his mind's eye, he saw two men pacing off, turning, and firing at each other. One of them fell.

He walked to a window and looked out, wondering what time it was, but this part of London, shabby now, its time of fashion past, had no lighting, no lanterns on the buildings, and he could see nothing, though he could hear talk, laughter, songs, quarreling from the customers of the taverns and alehouses below. To be near the theater at which he performed, Slane lived in one of the side streets off

Covent Garden, an open plaza in London's very center where vendors sold fruit, vegetables, herbs.

He had not meant to fall asleep. After Slane had left, he meant only to sit awhile longer in the chair. But he had lain down upon the bed and closed his eyes, and that was the end of that.

He must leave. Surely the hour of the duel was close. What is the time? he thought, walking out into the street, toward the plaza of Covent Garden. All the stalls under the arcades that surrounded two of the sides of the plaza were closed, but faint light could be seen through the open windows and doors of three shacks, built haphazardly in the plaza, like stray thoughts the original architect would have hated. Inside, the revelers drank and sang; the whores would be picking pockets, the patrons would be too stupefied to care. These taverns stayed open all the night; it was in one of them that he'd quarreled with Tom Masham.

In his mind's eye, Tony saw Charles rise from his chair. If you don't fight him, Tony, Charles had said, I will. Tony glanced up at the sky. Stars. Night had dissipated clouds and haze from coal smoke to leave stars visible. They had never seemed so bright, so clear. A beam of light from a lantern bobbed up and down. It was a beadle, a parish officer who patrolled the streets at night with lantern and club. Tony asked him the time.

"Two of the clock in the morning, sir."

For a coin, the beadle accompanied him down the darkness that was Half Moon Alley, past puddles of water, past waste and sleeping beggars, until they came to the Strand, the only straight thoroughfare in the old part of London, a crowded London filled with narrow, twisting lanes that had names like Cornhill Street and Threadneedle Row. The buildings here had lanterns hanging from them, giving out enough light to make one's way. Down the Strand, toward older London, a church sat in the middle of the street. When Tony was younger, he and his sisters had watched the May Day dancing there, for there was a maypole near the church. It had been returned to its place of honor at Charles II's restoration, as a symbol that Puritan domination was over and the old days were restored again. But the maypole had become unsettled in its foundation, too insecure to weave the streaming ribbons around, and three years ago Sir Isaac Newton, who was president of the Royal Society, had bought it to send to a friend in Wanstead to use as a telescope pole. London's last maypole was gone. It was a sign of the times, said Tommy Carlyle, who said things like that, that the maypole had become part of a telescope.

There was no traffic on the Strand, as there always was during the day, as there had been earlier, after he'd heard from Charles that the duel was set, and he had walked down this street, not knowing where he went or why, but only that he must walk. Gone were coaches at this hour; there were no porters; even the linkboys, who held torches to light the way at night for carriages and pedestrians, had gone home.

I would never allow any cousin of mine to be spoken of in such a manner, Wart had said last night at Tom King's tavern, those keen, hooded eyes of his bright with malice and wine. I will not allow it, said Charles, standing up, knocking over a chair. In the slow and drunken confusion within himself, Tony had known one thing: Charles must not duel again, not over Barbara.

Tony was passing the massive front of Northumberland House, still lived in by Howards and Percys, one of the last big houses left upon this street. In his grandmother's girlhood, there had been a line of great houses from one end to the other, Essex House and Arundel, Somerset, Savoy, Salisbury. The houses had stretched in extensive splendor from entrances on the Strand all the way back to gardens and terraces that overlooked the Thames. After the great fire of 1666, when much of the city of London had burned to the ground, the nobility had moved on further west—Covent Garden had been in its heyday—and speculators had bought the enormous mansions and their intricate gardens and torn everything down to begin again. His grandmother's father had been such a speculator, nearly bankrupting himself in the process, but his grandfather had profited from it, and now, so did he. He owned half the tangled property and lodgings and buildings on the Thames side of the Strand. He was heir to twin legacies of wealth and personal courage.

Now he was at Charing Cross, the Strand's end, where it joined two other streets to make one of the busiest junctions of the city. There was a popular saying that anyone who wanted to know what was going on in London had only to go to Charing Cross and stand at the railing surrounding the statue of Charles I in the center of the crossroads to see everyone and hear everything. There was a public pillory here, but Tony did not notice it nor the figure sagging in it; the sight was too common.

When he had passed this way this afternoon, there had been an apple woman standing at the statue of Charles I, her basket of apples at her bare feet, along with a pan of live charcoal and a plate of tin on which to roast apples for customers. Tell your fortune, kind sir, she'd said, if you buy an apple, but he'd only half heard her. Now, he wished to know his fortune, but she was nowhere to be seen.

I may be dead by dawn, he thought. He tried to envision again the scene he'd taken so for granted this afternoon, the sound of the carriages and wagons and carts carrying hay, the curses of the coachmen and wagoners mingling with the street vendors' cries:

"Buy my fat chickens!"

"Long thread laces, long and strong!"

"Buy my four ropes of hard onions!"

"Green walnuts!"

"Knives, scissors to grind!"

There had been a babble of sound from hurdy-gurdy players, ballad singers, water carriers, pie men, bellows menders, London street life at its most vocal, anything and everything for sale. A man could walk up to another man or woman and buy cherries, early peas, spiced gingerbread, milk, eels, watercress, muffins, rabbits. He could buy lavender, brooms, chairs, old clothing. Each season had its vendors: Spring was flowers and herbs; June meant tubs of mackerels; autumn was plums and pears and walnuts; Christmas was wheelbarrows of rosemary, bay, holly, laurel, mistletoe. If he died tomorrow, he would die without ever hearing or seeing or smelling any of this again. He must make certain this duel was kept as secret as possible, must make certain that everyone promised not to speak of it nor admit to it, so that Barbara's name was protected as much as possible. I hate duels. He remembered her saying that, remembered her telling of how a duel had changed Harry. He remembered the scandal surrounding the duel over her last year, how, oddly enough, the participants in it were not blamed and reviled as much as she was.

The street in which he lived was not far from here. It, too, was quiet. There were candles burning for him in the entrance hall of his house, and the footman who normally escorted him to bed sat sagging in a chair, snoring. The heels of Tony's shoes seemed to click loudly against the black-and-white marble squares of the large hall, but the footman slept on.

His grandfather had built this house at the height of his fame and glory as a warrior, when it seemed to all the world that Louis XIV of France might do as he pleased, except that Louis's generals had had to face Richard Saylor, made first Duke of Tamworth. The house contained the required elaborate Baroque trimmings of those times, intricate plastered ceilings with priceless paintings from Italian and French artists among the plaster insets and also inside gilded ovals above every door.

This house, Saylor House, was one of the sights of London, filled as it was with marble busts of great men, Marlborough and Godolphin, Prince Eugene and King William, men who had been friends of his grandfather; French and Dutch furniture stood in its many formal rooms, as did collections of porcelains and medals, cameos and paintings. In the great parlor well-known tapestries hung on the walls, their scenes celebrating the first duke's military victories. It had been thought at one time that Tony's grandfather would replace Marlborough as Captain General of Her Majesty Queen Anne's armies.

There was a huge portrait of his grandfather in the hall; magnificent stairs climbed up on two sides to meet overhead in a wide landing, and portraits were hung under each ascending stair, one of

Tony's grandfather and one of his grandmother, the creators of this house. And the creators of a legacy it was Tony's duty to uphold and add to, as he had done most properly by the possessions and land and rents his bride-to-be would bring—possession and lands and rents now in jeopardy, whether he lived or died.

You are a good boy, Tony. My boy. The man who had said those words had become, in the years before his death, no longer the mighty general of this portrait, but rather a travesty of it, frail, forgetful, trembling, old, and mad as a March hare. Yet the gentleness, the sense of goodness had remained. No madness could vanquish that. The quality of mercy is not strained, thought Tony. It droppeth as the gentle rain from heaven.

Despite the illness, or, as some said, the devil, or whatever took his grandfather's mind in those last years, there had been no one like him. Tony continued to look up at the portrait. Placed near was another, smaller portrait, a portrait of Tony's father, a soldier also, who would have been duke before Tony, but had died in the marshlands of Flanders, cut to pieces by French soldiers, taking revenge against Tony's grandfather, it was said, revenge against Richard, the general, the Lionheart, whom the French feared so. Tony's father had died fighting, they said, screaming his scorn to the last at the enemies who surrounded and killed him. The character of hero, the stuff of legend.

Was I in my father's thoughts? he had asked his mother when the news of the death had come to them. Do not be ridiculous, his mother had said; there was no time. Of course he thought of you, said his grandfather, tall and golden, the madness unmanifest yet, sweeping the boy, Tony, up into his lap—in those days his grandfather had seemed larger than life in all ways. There is a second of time, Tony, no more than a blink, before death, when a dying man's mind flies faster than any bird to what is beloved in his life. Therefore, Tony, he thought of you. . . . I see your father in you. But the great soldier who spoke was now a broken, old man. Come here and give this old madman a hug, the old soldier said, as the boy to whom he spoke threw himself into his grandfather's arms. Memories of his grandfather possessed a mellow tint in Tony's mind, like old gold, like treasure put away, buried. His times with his grandfather had been golden, always.

He began to climb the stairs; the light from the candle did not quite reach the marble busts in their niches or the intricate carvings of the stair's balustrade and handrail, details of finest craftsmanship, among which he had lived most of his life. He did not stop at his bedchamber, but went on up to the next floor, where his grandfather's library was. The library contained Latin and Greek and French and Italian and English leatherbound books, many of them rare, printed in Amsterdam. Their pages were thin, crinkling when turned, and the print was tiny and difficult to read. All the knowledge of the men of science and philosophy in the western world was in them, from Plato and Aristotle to Cicero and La Rochefoucauld to Spinoza and Newton and Locke, men who had spent their lives searching for the meaning of existence, for the truth of the link between them and their Creator. "Reason is God's crowning gift to man," they wrote. Or: "I think, therefore I am." "There is nothing in the mind except what was first in the senses," they wrote. Or "No man is an island." "The nature of God is incomprehensible." Tony had spent much time in here these last months, searching for some answer, some sense to the world, some peace to his heart, but he had found nothing to satisfy the ache that was Barbara's absence.

There was a writing table, attached by hinges among the carved bookcases, and there would be pen and paper. He set his candle down and pulled forward a chair, dipping his pen in ink and scratching out the words to his grandmother, the Duchess. If she received this letter, he would have died, and so he asked her to do what she could to comfort his mother. His grandmother would never forgive him if he died, which made them even, for he found that he was unable, even with death hanging over his head, to write that he forgave his grandmother for sending Barbara away.

The Duchess possessed a hard mind. It moved like quicksilver. She had known how much he loved Barbara, had likely calculated down to the last penny what marrying Barbara would have done to his estate—it would have destroyed it—and so she had taken matters into her own hands. No conversation with him, no request to factor his passion against Barbara's debt, to think of his duty to the family, to put that duty above love—just the deed of sending Barbara away. The betrayal had been staggering. He ended the letter with an abrupt signature.

He took another sheet of paper to write a letter to Barbara, but he no more than scratched her name, then held the pen motionless until the ink dripped from it into a blot.

Propped against a wall was a portrait, a portrait of Barbara, one he had taken from the stored inventory of her estate. It had been painted when she was fifteen and newly married. She smiled at the viewer, and her smile was lovely, and she was lovely, beauty already evident in large eyes and heart-shaped face. Two pug dogs lay at her feet. A small black page boy held her fan. She wore diamonds and a flowing satin gown. Tony had taken the portrait like a thief and hidden it away here. I love you, he thought. I will never love anyone the way I love you. He could not eat. He could not sleep. He could not think. Because of her.

He scratched out a note to his mother and sister, telling them of his love and regard—Perhaps there will be no need for them to read these, he kept thinking—then scattered sand on the paper to dry the ink. He rummaged through a drawer for his seal and sealing wax, but could find neither, so he folded the letters and wrote out the names. He would leave it to a servant or his mother to send them should the news be fatal. Fatal. He could feel ice coalesce around his heart, and he tried to steady his breathing, which had become uneven. The sound of his heart was loud in his ears. He was tired from the rush of emotions, aware that time was passing.

What if my hand trembles when I fire the gun? Tony thought. How could my hand not tremble when I fire the gun?

He stood. He must go and find dueling pistols. He began to rummage through the drawers of the ornate armoire in his chamber, scattering shirts and gloves, cravats and waistcoats, stockings and shoe buckles, but he could not find the dueling pistols. Finally, he did not try, but sat down upon the bed.

Time was passing, perhaps his last moments on earth. Who would grieve for him if he died? His sister, Mary; his mother; his grandmother—but in her grief would be fury at him for dying. Your duty, she would say, likely over his grave, was to live, not die. His greataunt Shrew. To whom, by the way, he owed twenty pounds. She would likely dun his estate for it. Charles, his sister's husband. He moved away from the thought of Charles. Wart—who truly knew what Wart felt? The Princess of Wales. She was one of the most learned women he knew, and she would find this action of his, a duel, singularly stupid, particularly if he died. Who else? A servant or two. And Barbara: She would grieve for him. She loved him—not in the way he wished, perhaps, but she did love, and when Barbara loved, one knew it. He was considered the unworthy Tamworth, no swan such as Barbara was and her brother, Harry, had been. Silent, people said of him. A bit slow, they said. Eccentric, they whispered. So he was. So he was not. Which Barbara also knew.

He heard the call of the watch. "Four of the clock, and all is well."

Not true, not true, at all.

It was as if he stood outside himself and watched. It was as if he were not a participant, a principal participant, at all.

Charles was standing by a carriage, did not see him, was startled when Tony came up and said his name. He heard himself tell Charles that he could not find his dueling pistols, and Charles produced his own in their wooden box, as if he had known Tony would not find his. Tony went to stand under the two oaks, listening to the faint sounds of night. No birds were yet awake. He thought of Slane's finch hopping on the table.

He heard the horses' hooves on the ground, clopping, before he saw the carriage. His opponent, Thomas Masham, climbed down from the carriage, along with his second, who turned out to be, to Tony's surprise, the banker Sir Gideon Andreas. Andreas walked over to them. Large, beefy, older, he might have been Tony's father.

"I came to stop this if I can. Blame the wine, the phase of the moon, anything, but ask pardon and I will speak on your behalf, Tamworth."

"I have already spoken to Masham." Charles interposed himself into the conversation. "Yesterday."

"It is not yours to decide," said Andreas.

"The Duke of Tamworth cannot draw back with honor," said Charles.

Honor. A man must show willingness to fight at the first sign of insult, must follow through even if he died, or else he was not a man, but rather a coward. It was the standard of the times. Tony was the grandson of a mighty general. The son of a valiant warrior. The character of heroes. The stuff of legend. Richard Saylor's grandson.

"Tony," said Charles, "he insulted your cousin—my cousin, too, by marriage."

"I will not draw back now," Tony heard himself say. He was surprised he could speak at all. "I want to insist that Masham understand, that you understand, Sir Gideon, that this duel must remain an absolute secret, even if one of us is hurt. Not for the sake of what may happen to us if the duel is found out, but for the sake of the lady in question, who is innocent of any wrongdoing. I want Masham's word, and yours, on this."

"It is understood," said Andreas. Again, it was the standard, the code, that duels be secret—because they were against the law, and so the participants might be arrested; and because, quite often, they were over a woman.

"Nonetheless, will you speak to him again?" Tony said.

The banker nodded.

Tony watched Andreas do so, watched Charles and Andreas inspect the pistols, begin to load them. The smell of gunpowder was harsh in his nostrils for a moment. They poured the gunpowder down the barrels, tamping it with the special metal rod, inserting the small lead balls—too small to kill a man; how could anything that small kill a man? Then they inspected the barrels again. Tony felt a coldness come over himself, a clarity. There was nothing, nothing else in this world, but this moment, and though he had dreaded that he would tremble like a woman when it finally came and so expose all his secret weaknesses, he now felt nothing but a sense of coldness. It was as if the icy winds of a storm whirled and settled in his mind, chilling it to absolute clarity. There was nothing but the now, no emotion, no memory. There was now, and afterward, there would be something else.

He was walking out into the open, toward the other men. He was bowing to Masham, he was bowing his head as Andreas said a prayer, he was taking a pistol, closing his fingers over it. It was heavy; the handle fit his hand as if made for it. He was going out into the park, where the sky overhead was just beginning to color, faint, lovely tinges on the horizon. Charles was beside him, talking to him: He must not panic; he must take aim before he fired; he must keep his mind clear and cold; Masham was no expert with a pistol. The pistol was heavy in Tony's hand.

There were years of friendship between himself and Charles—but all Tony could see was Charles rising from his chair, saying "If you do not fight him, I will."

Masham came forward, bowed, his face showing nothing. Tony did the same. Now he had his back to Masham, and he could feel the warmth of the man's body, but it did not warm the ice in his mind. Someone was counting off, and he was walking forward, a loud humming in his ears, almost covering the counting. He would walk forever, until the number twenty was heard, and then there it was, sooner than he had expected. He was turning around, and all the blood in his body rushed to his head, and he raised his arm, just as Masham was doing. He squeezed his finger against the trigger. There was a boom, which hurt his ears. Smoke issued from the barrel of his gun as something went singing by him, and when the smoke cleared, he saw men running toward a fallen body, and he lowered his arm. Somewhere was the first mournful, morning cry of a dove.

Charles was bellowing like a savage, hugging him, half carrying him forward, and he thought, slowly, for the blood was draining away and he felt sick, I am not dead. . . . He would have fallen, if Charles had not been there, holding him up.

"You must leave at once, before a watchman comes," Charles was saying. In his face was a joy, a wild, manic zest, as if they had played a successful boys' prank or stormed the Tower of London. Charles's groom was bringing up his horse, and Tony put his foot in the stirrup. He could see from where he was that Andreas was at Masham's body, which did not move.

"Go and see to Masham, Charles. Make certain a physician sees him. At once. I will pay for it. Just get him a physician."

Charles glanced toward the carriage; Andreas and a servant were lifting Masham's body and putting it inside. The horses shied and the carriage jerked forward; there was a trail of darker crimson, of blood, as Masham's arms and legs swung back and forth loosely.

"Yes, I will. Have you a place to go?"

All must be brazened out now, everything denied. Everyone must act as if nothing had happened.

"Stay with Masham, Charles. See that he has everything he needs."

The sun was up, in a bright, clean morning, which was cold on his face and hands. Tony trotted his mount through Green Park, past the great house and gardens of the Duchess of Buckingham, into St. James's Park, maneuvering his horse along one of the long allées of trees. Milkmaids were herding cows toward a pond. They smiled, offering mugs of fresh milk if he would only stop and wait. He recognized the empty space of the Parade and Horse Guards building behind.

His great-aunt Shrew, or Lady Shrewsborough, as the world knew her, lived among the maze of houses and gardens that had been built on the grounds and against the remains of the burned palace of Whitehall, which had once stretched half a mile along the Thames, and—if Aunt Shrew's word was to be trusted—possessed some two thousand rooms. He was trotting across the Parade, the sound of his horse's hooves loud against the cobbles. He dismounted to lead his horse through an alley and across the street and then into the old privy garden of the former palace. He tied the horse to a tree and climbed over a fence, his long legs making it easy. There was the back of Aunt Shrew's house.

He sat down against her garden wall, to rest a moment. He kept seeing Masham raise his pistol, kept seeing the smoke curl from the barrel, kept hearing the strange, fatal song of the leaded ball going past; it was his life going past. *Give me a kiss and to that kiss a score, then to that twenty, add a hundred more* went some bit of poetry in his mind. He'd never kissed Barbara in passion. Calf love, they said. He had wanted to teach Barbara of his love, its depth and tenderness.

To the victor belong the spoils. I came. I saw. I conquered. They never found all the pieces of his father's body. *You're a good boy, Tony, my boy. I did it for the best; I sent Barbara away for the best,* said his grandmother, weeping. *Someday you will see.*

Ridiculous to have thought an hour ago that he would never forgive his grandmother. He was alive and might have been dead. He forgave her everything. If Masham did not die, life would be perfect, even without Barbara, because he was alive. The very air he drew into his nostrils was sweet. Tony closed his eyes. *I shall never duel again,* he thought. *Never. Nothing is worth it.*

Inside the house, Tony's great-aunt slapped a card down on the table. "After the election in the spring, there will be more Tories again in the House of Commons—"

Her lover, Sir Alexander Pendarves, shook his head no, but she ignored him, speaking to Slane. The three of them had begun to gamble late, when Slane called on them after midnight, knowing they'd be awake. None of them had yet been to bed.

"—and His Majesty will have to offer Tories places in his cabinet, Slane. He is under the dominion of rogues now, a highwayman's band of Whig rogues who gave us the South Sea Bubble. Lumpy is the only Whig I can abide." Lumpy was her name for Pendarves.

"Robert Walpole never supported the South Sea Company," said Pendarves.

"Which makes him no less of a rogue. He shielded those who did, men who have impoverished half the nation with their greed and money tricks. Robert Walpole is the savior of cheats and swindlers, within the King's cabinet and outside it, too. Of course, things have fallen to pieces anyway when the King of England does not even speak English."

"Now, Lou, no Jacobite talk," Pendarves said.

" 'Jacobite,' 'Jacobite'—you Whigs are always labeling everything you do not like Jacobite. It isn't Jacobite to say the truth. The House of Guelph rules over us. Now, I ask you, Slane, what kind of name is 'Guelph'? Not English, to my mind. —Aha, my trick! I've won the game!" She raked coins toward herself, cackling like a stage witch, a witch wearing a short, pink quilted jacket over a loose embroidered-cotton nightgown. She also wore a red wig and a lace cap; powder was caked into every crevice and wrinkle on her face, which bore three patches, as if she were two-and-twenty, instead of many times that. In her heyday, Louisa, Lady Shrewsborough had been one of the beauties of Charles II's court; she had retained her small-boned delicacy, which had charmed many a man who later found she had the constitution of an iron bar.

Slane shook his head at her good fortune. She was said to be the best player of cards in London, other than the Princess of Wales.

"You will have that fifteen thousand pounds out of my own pocket!" said Pendarves.

"Fifteen thousand?" Slane said.

"I lost a good quarter of my fortune when South Sea stock fell," said Aunt Shrew. "You cannot believe the madhouse London became, as people saw the stock dropping. There was a time when if you withdrew five pounds on a goldsmith's paper, it had dropped to three by the time you had crossed town. I had ten thousand pounds with a goldsmith. He slipped away to Brussels one dark night, taking my funds and others' with him, and never returned. May he catch the pox from a Belgian whore. I tell you, Slane, I've never seen anything like it, and I grew to womanhood in the aftermath of a civil war. What I have seen in my time! Name it—unrest, riot, plotting, treason, as well as prosperity, calm, and plenty. I've seen five kings or queens sit upon the throne of England. I was in London when William of Orange crossed over to invade and King James II fled. But I've seen nothing to equal the frenzy of panic which gripped us when the stock of the South Sea Company began its fall."

"Too true," said Pendarves.

"Goldsmiths fled into the night with gold others had entrusted to them. Banks in Amsterdam ordered London agents to sell stock. Established companies, with firm foundations—the Bank of England; the East India Company—saw the prices for their stock fall. Monies froze where they were—or worse, disappeared. One could not send twenty-five pounds from London to Dublin by bill of exchange."

Slane, so restless he thought he might explode, had to stand up. Word had come to Italy of the South Sea trouble in England; word had come to invade, but they were caught unprepared, no plan, no coin, no troops supplied from an enemy of Hanover George's. "Wait, then," wrote the Bishop of Rochester, "until Parliament is dissolved and we have our election in the spring of 1722." The letter that had come to Slane last night informed him that the plan of invasion was to arrive from Jamie in a few days.

"Another hand?" said Slane.

"You can't afford it, man. I'll have to loan you coin for your dinner today as it is."

"I can't afford another hand, either," said Pendarves, the tassel at the top of his stiff four-cornered nightcap shaking along with his head.

"Nonsense, Lumpy. You ought to have a bath. We'll play on that. If I win the next game, you bathe tomorrow." She dealt the cards expertly, and she and Pendarves began to play silently, ferociously, speaking only to ask for another card or call out points to Slane. After a time, her household steward appeared in the doorway, an odd look on his face.

"His Grace, the Duke of Tamworth," said the servant. So, thought Slane, Tamworth survived. I find I'm glad.

"Well, send him up."

Tony often came in the early-morning hours to play cards with her and Pendarves. You ought to be in bed with your whore or at White's with the bucks, she would tell Tony every so often, and he always answered that her company was better than any at White's and certainly better than any whore's, which never failed to please her.

"That's not possible, ma'am."

"What do you mean, 'not possible'? My point, Lumpy."

The servant went to the window, raised it, and pointed; Aunt Shrew made a motion with her head to Slane, who got up from his chair and joined the steward at the window.

"I think you'd better see this," he said to her.

She put down her cards, and, low-heeled mules slapping against her feet, joined Slane at the window, peering out to her garden below; she might be old, but she still had the eyesight of a hawk. She shook her head and gave out orders to the servant.

"Fetch His Grace upstairs at once and tell Lucy and Betty to make the bed ready in the blue bedchamber."

She settled herself again at the card table, which was a delicate thing, made early in the reign of Queen Anne when card playing had become very popular. The cards she and Pendarves gambled with were very small, very thin rectangles, depicting the various companies, bubbles that burst, springing from nowhere the summer before last, when speculating in stocks had reached such heights. There had been companies for, among other things, importing large jackasses from Spain, insuring marriages against despair, and making salt water fresh.

"Tony," she told Pendarves, "is asleep out by my garden wall. In his cups, drunk as a beggar, I wager."

She picked up her cards, laid down two. "I've won."

Pendarves stared down at the cards that had betrayed him. It was not as though he did not need a bath. Particles of snuff pressed themselves into the corners of his mouth, vying with liver spots and wrinkles on his face. There was dirt under his fingernails and all across whatever parts of his feet were visible in their slippers. The servant appeared in the doorway again.

"His Grace won't come up, ma'am."

"What do you mean, he won't come up?"

Aunt Shrew went to the window.

"Tony!" she called down. "Come up here and play me a hand of cards if you won't come and sleep. You owe me twenty pounds, you know. I ought to have you arrested for debt." There was silence from her as Tony called something back, something that neither Slane nor Pendarves could make out.

She sat down again at the card table, frowned, shuffled the cards, and began to deal them out, but only to herself. She pursed her lips and stared at the cards, moved one here, one there, dealt herself some more, staring at each one as she turned it over.

"Are we not to sleep today?"

Pendarves was undressing, motioning for Slane to help him, as if Slane were a valet. Who knows? he had said to Aunt Shrew. Slane may have been a valet in his time. Those dark eyes have secrets in them.

"She's forgotten the bath," he said in a low voice to Slane. Naked now, in the bed, Pendarves was not a pretty sight. "We'll leave it that way, heh?"

"Something's happened. It's in the cards." She tapped one of them. "Tell me, Slane—you know everything that goes on in this town. Why was my nephew sleeping out by my garden wall, if he's not drunk, and why was he not drunk at this hour of the morning, when he has been so all the summer? And why does he not come up-stairs to join us now?"

"You give me more credit than I deserve. I don't know."

She tapped another card with a fingernail. "See this. Scandal." Some of the powder caked in the wrinkles on her face flaked off onto the table. She flicked it away impatiently. "I see scandal in the cards. My sister-in-law the Duchess is upset. She's in the cards, too. And Barbara—Barbara's turned up, which surprises me."

"I hate it when she does this," Pendarves said to Slane.

"October is a scarlet month, the Duchess always says," said Aunt Shrew. "Scarlet for the leaves on the trees. Don't try to tell me you know nothing about this. Everything that happens in this town somehow comes to your ears. Tell me what you know."

The broadsheet was being written in great glee by men who were happy to slander and slight the Hanovers. It would be printed today or the next, so that in another few days the duel would be common knowledge.

"There was an argument," Slane said.

"Late at night and in a tavern, no doubt."

"And an insult made, and His Grace, the Duke, had to defend his honor."

"His honor? Someone insulted Tony? No one would do that. There is nothing to insult."

"They insulted a member of the family."

"What member? Who spoke the insult?"

"Tom Masham."

"A duel—there has been a duel, with Tony as one of the principals."

She moved from card table to dressing table. It was covered with pots of rouge—carmine, French, china wool—and pots of powder: plain, French brown, and orris for the hair; orange flower, à la reine, and maréchale for the face. There were curling papers for hair and wigs, and ribbons and feathers and jewels tossed about as carelessly upon its surface as if they were made of paste, although they were not. She rooted through the debris of her dressing-table top with the thoroughness of an expert as Slane came to her, took her hand, bent his head to kiss it in farewell. This was a breach of etiquette—he ought not to kiss her hand, only bow over it—but she encouraged his forwardness. She peeled off the patches, smacked a powder puff against the table to loosen powder before flouring her face with it. Preparing herself for war, thought Slane.

"Where are you going?" Pendarves asked her plaintively.

"Out."

Now that her face was stark white, with fresh layers of powder caked into every wrinkle and crevice, Aunt Shrew pursed her lips to spread more crimson rouge across them, never minding that much of it eased up into the myriad of wrinkles around her mouth, too.

"Tony Saylor is too even-tempered to fight another man over an insult, even when he is drunk," she said. "Someone must have said something about Barbara. My great-niece, Slane, in Virginia, now, as great a beauty as she is a hoyden—"

"Like her aunt," put in Pendarves, softly, to Slane.

"—and Tony is wild for her. If this duel becomes public knowledge, it will put a crimp in that marriage his mother is so proud to have arranged. It nearly broke my heart to learn that Abigail had allied him with that Holles clan. Whigs"—she said the word as if she were speaking of infidels or devils—"to the core. There's nothing worse. Tory I have always been, and Tory I stay. This may give me time to find a nice Tory girl for Tony. Lord Oxford ought to have a niece or something somewhere. After the election in the spring, there will be more Tories again in the House of Commons—"

Pendarves shook his head—no—at Slane.

"—and His Majesty will have to offer us places in his ministry." She stared critically at the ancient, ravaged, grotesquely painted woman in her mirror. "I was a beauty in my day." She tossed her head like a filly to the mirror and to Pendarves, watching.

"Still are, Lou." Pendarves winked lasciviously from the bed.

Her high cackles filled the bedchamber. She reached up and pinched one of Slane's cheeks—he was still standing by her—hard enough to bring tears to his eyes. Fingers dug into his cheek, she pulled his head down so that it rested upon one of her scrawny shoulders. They stared at their reflection in the mirror—she, ancient, lively, painted, and patched, he, dark-eyed, young, untouched, yet, by time.

"You'd have been wild for me, Laurence Slane," she said to him. "Nothing would have done but that you would have had to have me."

"I am wild for you," Slane answered, and he meant it.

"The plan is on its way," he said, very softly. She was a Jacobite, one of the most loyal. In the mirror, their eyes locked, and they smiled at one another.

CHAPTER 8

Dusk had arrived at First Curle. Smoke from the kitchen-house chimney swirled upward, then broke apart in the evening sky. Slaves had been driving wedges of wood, called gluts, into the trunk of a fallen tree; and when Odell Smith called to them to stop, they put down their wooden mallets and began to walk toward the kitchen house. From now until dawn, their time was mostly their own.

"Finish up, Belle," Odell Smith called to the half-grown girl who had the task of chopping the branches of the fallen tree into kindling. Somewhere in the distance, dogs were barking; as the girl finished a last bit of branch, he glanced in the direction from which the sound seemed to come.

"Bring the ax to me," he said. When she laid it at his feet, he reached out, putting his hand to her shoulder, a round shoulder, taut with young, worked muscle. His hand stayed there until the girl, stepping back, turned and ran, leaping over the fallen tree, her youth and something else making her fleet. Smith, his face slack, stared after her for a time before he reached down to pick up the ax. The barking of the dogs was louder, and again he looked for them but didn't see them.

Like the slaves, he began the walk to the kitchen house, to his supper, thinking, so her boy is near. Damn him for the trouble he gives us, running away. When I find him—but Odell didn't allow himself to finish the thought, because when he found the boy, there was nothing he could do.

In a tree above, Hyacinthe remained still, the sound of the wind and his own heartbeat loud in his ears. Certain the overseer was now far enough away, he climbed down, whistled for the dogs, wove his way in and out of trees, past fields, toward the clearing in which the house sat. He carefully skirted the kitchen house and burrowed into the cave he'd made behind the wood piled high in the woodshed. The dogs burrowed in with him.

"Hush," he commanded, "no more barking."

He shared with the dogs the food he had stolen from the kitchen house. His head was hurting a little, but he had the barkwater here, and the small brown bottle of the rum. The rum tasted bad, made him light-headed, happy, sleepy. He didn't miss Thérèse and Madame so much when he drank it. There were other things here that he had stolen: Smith's whip, the man's pillow, a blanket. He and the dogs slept on the pillow and blanket.

Soon Mrs. Cox would appear with her enormous bulk in the doorway of the house, and she'd call for him over and over. Last night, she'd sent for her grandsons to ride over to search for him. She sat in Madame's fine chairs, luckily armless so that her girth had a place to go. She smoked a pipe. He didn't want her here. He didn't want anybody here. Go away, he had told her rudely, but she had laughed at him. I am going nowhere, she said, and neither are you. So he ran away.

Last night, they'd talked of locking him in the cellar when they found him. He'd heard them. She won't like it, he'd heard Mrs. Cox say to a grandson, but what else can I do? He's been gone since this afternoon. Give him to me when you find him, Smith had said. I'll teach him how slaves must behave. Imbeciles. Idiots. Barbarians. He knew how to behave.

Hyacinthe thought about walking to Williamsburg, but these stupid colonials might think he was a runaway slave and put him in the county gaol. Well, they weren't going to find him. He was going to live here in the woodpile and spy and spy and spy until Madame was home again. Then he would tell her all the bad things her servants did while she was gone, how Smith made the girl, Belle, afraid. Mrs. Cox caressed the dogs but frowned at him. Then she crept up the stairs to look at Madame's gowns, to touch them with her hands. She didn't care if he lived or died. She liked the dogs better than she liked him.

She would give him to Odell Smith if she found him, he knew she would, and Smith would whip him with this whip he'd stolen. Smith did not like him, it was in the overseer's eyes. He would whip Hyacinthe until the flesh of his back fell down in ribbons. Kano, who was a slave here, had been whipped that way. His back showed it, the scars ugly and thick, like rope corded under the skin. It was true, and Hyacinthe was going to tell Madame that, too.

He shivered. The night was here. It dropped suddenly, taking all the light. This was when he was afraid, when he wanted to walk back to the house and stay there, maybe even in the basement if he had to. He pushed the dogs over and crept under the blanket, making himself as small as possible. The thing about running away was, it was hard to go back. He could not go back, not now, not until Madame was home, because she would understand. Pride, she would say to him, pride will make you trouble every time, Hyacinthe. And, later, after she had scolded him, she'd tell him something she'd done as a girl, like the time she ran away with Monsieur Harry to Maidstone, or when she and Jane gave the pigs the brandy. I was punished severely, she would say, as you should be, but she wouldn't punish him much, because she knew that half the punishment for bad behavior was facing up to it.

He closed his eyes to the night, which inked all the woods, the fields, the creeks, like so many small fingers of the river, inked marshes and swamps. The river was narrower here at First Curle, curling back on itself, but broader farther south, so broad near the village of Williamsburg that it stretched several miles across. It was friend, enemy, provider, deep enough that ships sailed far up its waters, in search of what had defined this colony, its settlements, its laws, its increase, its cruelty to others: tobacco.

CHAPTER 9

"She is wearing pearls tonight. They are in her hair, in her ears, everywhere."

"I wish her slave boy and the dogs had come with her. They say the slave speaks French. They say he has a suit finer than the Governor's. I wanted so to see the dogs. . . ."

The large hall of the Governor's house was crowded, and the two parlors on the east side of the house were already so filled that it was becoming impossible for people to find a place to stand comfortably. Every woman was in her best gown, every man in his finest coat and wig, for this occasion, the finale in the Governor's introduction of their famous visitor from England. The village of Williamsburg was at bursting point; people crowded in with any cousin or friend who lived or kept a house here; the rest parceled out at the few taverns or among those who lived on nearby plantations. Tonight was the final extravagance, a fête with an orchestra—two violins, an hautboy, three flutes, and a harp especially shipped in from the colony of Maryland.

Outside, on the grassy terraces stepping down to the landscape canel, Colonel Bolling and Klaus Von Rothbach had begun to quarrel.

"I didn't expect to see you here," Bolling said. "I expected you to be gone."

"I would not miss this. I've come to dance," Klaus said. Bolling swiveled and saw where Klaus's eyes went to Lady Devane, to Barbara, who was walking with the Governor and Colonel Perry. She rustled and shimmered like a slight young tree moved by wind. She wore a gown of shining black tabby—a watered silk—with heavier sleeves, stitched in a diamond pattern with silver thread. At one shoulder was a knot of silver and black ribbons, also at her bodice, where the gown made a V to show the swell of her breasts. There was a long necklace of pearls wound round her neck. Her hair was powdered, her cheeks rouged; there were patches at her mouth and brows, brows darkened with lead combs, as were her lashes. She smiled right and left at the people who greeted her. There were heavy pearl drops in her ears. Her pearl-headed hairpins held trailing black and gray feathers in place. She wore white stockings, black brocade shoes with ivory heels and ivory buckles, a pearl bracelet over long gloves, a heavy pearl ring. Bolling's eyes narrowed.

"You've a voyage to make, as I remember," Bolling said. "One hundred barrels of tobacco, as much tobacco as possible pressed into them this last month, the word 'pork' burned into every barrel. It puts me on edge that you are still here."

"And make the voyage I will. The sloop is ready. I sailed her up from the Harrisons' yesterday. She sits even now in the creek. The Countess's creek."

"And the barrels?"

"In the storehouse. I return tonight, and we will load the barrels and be off by afternoon tomorrow. No one will ever be the wiser."

"It would be better to be sailing tonight. It's what I pay you for, to be better. You came to see her." Bolling, squat, solid, unrestrained, jabbed his finger in Barbara's direction. "Don't be a fool, Klaus. She is a duke's granddaughter. She does nothing more than toy with the likes of you. You've got a widow in your pocket with a fine plantation, land, relatives on half the council. Don't ruin that over her."

"You told me to keep her occupied. If it weren't for my visits to First Curle, she might not be here tonight. It was in her mind not to come to Williamsburg at all, because her boy's sick. Go away, Uncle. Leave me alone." I am the one who will be at sea for weeks on end, thought Klaus. I am the one who will be hanged for smuggling.

"You go away—go back to the creek, load those barrels, go. I don't like it that you're here. I don't like it at all."

Klaus didn't answer, and after staring at him a moment, Bolling walked angrily away.

Barbara, sitting under the garden's trees, watched the moths that fluttered all about the lanterns. Every now and again, she could not keep herself from rising to try and wave a moth away, but the gesture was useless. The candles flaming inside lanterns lured them irresistibly, and on the ground under each lantern were tens of dead or dying moths.

"A man from the convict ships is overseer of one of my quarters across the river," Barbara was saying to the Governor and Colonel Perry. "His name is John Blackstone and his indenture is for ten years. How often do these convict ships land?"

"One can expect them several times a year."

"His Majesty dumps the undesirables—thieves and murderers—from his prisons among us, as if we were a closestool," said Colonel Perry. "I do not like it."

"There is room enough here for all," said Governor Spotswood.

Barbara had crossed the river, ridden over to the quarter clearing there, a crude cabin in a field of tobacco stubble, to meet the third of the overseers, John Blackstone, who dressed in rags, with a wild, unkempt beard, his hair long and tied back with a rag. He said he soothed the Africans by playing his bagpipes to them at night: They are Jacobites like me now, he said. A cousin of his was a factor, or agent, of a tobacco firm in Glasgow and lived somewhere on the river so that he might more easily buy tobacco for the firm. The cousin had had the bagpipes sent to Blackstone, who piped Barbara a farewell as she rode off, Hyacinthe behind her on the horse. She thought, as the odd, harsh sounds of the bagpipe filled all the woods; I must tell them at home of this, of this half-wild Scot living among my grandmother's slaves, who dance to the wail of bagpipe. Blackstone's quarter produced much tobacco.

"Blackstone is neither thief nor a murderer," said Barbara. "He came to us compliments of the battle of Sheriffmuir." At Sheriffmuir, James III had vied with George of Hanover for the English crown after Queen Anne died. But James had gotten no farther than Scotland, had ended sailing away again, leaving Scots clansmen to fight English, Hanoverian, and Dutch troops.

"Yes," answered the Governor. "In 1716 His Majesty sent a ship of captured traitors to us here."

"You've a Jacobite, have you?" said Perry. "I'd forgotten Blackstone was Jacobite."

"Jacobite, from the Latin *Jacobus*, for James," said Spotswood.

"We call a man Pretender," said Perry, "who is the son of James II, the nephew of Charles II, the grandson of Charles I, and the great-grandson of James I—and James I was Queen Elizabeth's chosen heir."

"We do it because to do otherwise is now treason," said Spotswood, heavily.

God bless the Church; God bless the King, the Church's defender; God bless, there is no harm in blessing, the Pretender. But who is that Pretender, and who that King, God bless us all, is quite another thing.

What would Governor Spotswood do now if I should recite that to him? Barbara wondered. Farewell Old Year, for thou with Broomstick Hard had drove poor Tory from St. James's Yard. Farewell Old Year, Old Monarch, and old Tory; farewell Old England, thou hast lost thy Glory—so they were saying up and down England in 1715 and 1716, as one after another of the great, noble Tories left, afraid of threatened treason trials, as elections for the House of Commons were held, and the Tories were beaten by Whigs as never before. It had been an ugly, perilous time. By law, the throne went to a cousin, George of Hanover, because he was Protestant and Jamie was Catholic. Yet many felt James was the rightful king. It was said that in the last year of her life, when she was so ill, even Queen Anne wished the throne to go to her half-brother, whom she had betrayed years before. Certain Tories had gambled she'd see it happen. The broomstick had reached Barbara's family. Without saying good-bye or even sending a note, her father had vanished, leaving her mother, like a scalded cat, to survive his branding as a Jacobite.

John Blackstone had fallen to his knees in disbelief, and then mock worship, when she'd repeated those verses to him. Treason, Hyacinthe had hissed at her, wedged as he was into the saddle behind her.

And what would Governor Spotswood say, Barbara wondered, if I told him my father was a Jacobite and had to flee England to save his head, that he died in service of the Pretender? No; in fact, by the time my father died, he had no loyalty left, not even to himself. He'd wasted it away.

She looked to the moths and their dangerous desire for light, thinking of her father, whom she and Harry had seen buried in Italy. Your father's a fool, her grandmother had once said, in a terrible temper because the Hanovers had come to the throne more easily than anyone had predicted and her father's disloyalty now threatened the entire family and all they had attained. I curse the day your mother married him, her grandmother had said, though marriage to your mother is curse enough.

Music drifted out of the Governor's house. People strolled the walks, their conversations a soft murmur. Thinking of my father has made me sad, thought Barbara, that we pursue so passionately the wrong things.

"You owe me a dance, I believe. I've come down the river to dance with every pretty woman in sight, and I must begin with you."

Barbara unfurled her fan and looked over its edge at Klaus. Was he the wrong thing to be pursuing?

"I'm in mourning, Captain Von Rothbach. I won't be dancing tonight."

"Not even once?"

"Not even once."

"That is my great misfortune. And when does your mourning end?"

"Christmas Day."

"I'll call the day after. Governor; Colonel Perry." He bowed and smiled and strode away.

"The dancing will be beginning," said Spotswood. "Come and see it. There is not an ill dancer in my colony, and Captain Von Rothbach is among the best." From the Governor's house came a joyous whoop, then shouts, as if some performance was stirring up the crowd.

"Go on with the Governor," Perry said. "I wish to stay outside awhile, but I will come and sit by you later, if I may."

In the hall, a circle had formed, in the midst of which Klaus danced. No one else—and they were all good dancers—displayed his vigor and zest. His partner, a plump, dark-haired woman, was shrieking as he lifted her high in the air, a movement from a dance that went back to the time of King Henry VIII. People stood against the wall clapping and calling out Klaus's name every time he performed an intricate step. His face shone with perspiration; he'd taken off his wig and thrown it to one side. Barbara watched. Is that his widow? she wondered. From across the room she saw Bolling standing in a doorway, watching also, a frown on his face.

She walked over to him and said, "Let there be peace between us. My brother cut his throat with a razor. There's been one death given for another, my precious brother's for your Jordan's. An eye for an eye. The score between us is even."

He stared at her, then said, "Only, madam, if the razor was dull."

She would have struck him then with her fan, but he caught her arm, held it low. "You play with my nephew. He has a fine plump widow dancing with him right now, a widow who would walk away from him if she knew how he flirted with you. You've taken my plantation, and now you meddle in what is none of your affair. There is nothing a woman like you can give a man like my nephew but heartache. You know it, and I know it. And of the two of us, Lady Devane, I, at least, am honest enough to say it."

Barbara stepped back, turned, and walked away from the hall, down a narrow corridor, going quickly up the stairs, not to the bed-chamber given her, but rather up the narrow steps to the third story of the house. Around a dark corner was the circular stair leading up into the roof's cupola, a narrow space, windowed all around. Barbara pushed up a window and stepped out onto the roof—it was flat here, with a railing on all four sides—and took a deep breath.

The night was soft around her and chill. The sky blazed with stars. Words filled her head. Klaus saying, "You owe me a dance, I believe." Owe? What did she owe anyone? Words Roger had written in his love letters, stealing the words of his favorite poet, John Donne, for his own ends, filled her mind, her clever Roger—but not clever enough for his ambitions; too clever; and then he died: Come live with me, and be my love, / And we will some new pleasures prove.

She rubbed her arms. All summer you've been playing a dangerous game, Charles had once said to her, and said again now in her mind. I could not keep myself from loving you in spite of it—which only makes me a fool. But what does this summer make you, Barbara?

Someone was coming into the cupola; Barbara stepped back into the darker shadow a chimney made. But the ivory heel of one of her shoes made a sound, as Klaus stepped through the window she had opened.

"It isn't Christmas Day, but I'm come to claim a dance anyway," he said. "What's that upon your face? Are you—were you weeping?"

"No. No, I never cry."

He reached out then and touched her cheek with a finger, and it told him she lied. He held out his hands in the gesture that began a dance. The music from below spilled through the open windows, drifted up softly to them. One dance, on a rooftop, where no one could see—what would it hurt? And so she put her hand in his.

Something shivering, vital leaped from him to her at that moment, and she thought, I shouldn't have done this. She saw that he was as affected by it as she. But by then she was in his arms. She felt his lips touch her forehead, then her cheeks, her neck, her mouth.

You are far too gentle, Captain, she thought, and she wrapped her arms around his neck. They kissed, and she thought, I want this, I want all of it, I do. His hands were at her breasts, which were pushing out now almost completely from her gown, and there were kisses upon her neck, on the tops of her breasts, and she thought, We will couple, right here under the stars. Good. It is settled between us, at last.

"I cannot stop thinking of you," he said. "There is a woman, a widow— Someone is coming." And quickly he pulled her back into the deep shadow of the chimney.

Inside the cupola, another couple appeared, then kissed, as Klaus and Barbara had done; but their kisses were interspersed with vows and with pledges of love. It was like having her face dashed with cold water, to watch their passion, to hear them pledge devotion, loyalty. It was a sweet thing, bittersweet to her. The mood of moments earlier, when she would have lain with this man beside her under the stars, vanished.

The couple went below again; it seemed to her in the moonlight that Klaus's eyes gleamed as a wolf's might. "They have left," he said.

"And so must you."

"What is it? What is wrong?"

"Go away, please."

"I don't understand."

"When you come back from your voyage, Captain, we'll see then."

"Do you promise?"

"I promise." He didn't want to go. Barbara saw it and leaned against the chimney, staring up at the stars, listening to the sound of him crossing the rooftop, and then to the silence.

Words tumbled through her mind, words Roger had written her, the words of John Donne: Come live with me, and be my love, / And we will some new pleasures prove / Of golden sands, and crystal brooks, / With silken lines, and silver hooks. / There will the river whispering run, / Warm'd by thy eyes, more than the Sun. / And there the enamor'd fish will stay, / Begging themselves they may betray. / . . . Let others freeze with angling reeds, / And cut their legs, with shells and weeds, / Or treacherously poor fish beset, / With strangling snare, or windowy net: / . . . For thee, thou needst no such deceit, / For thou thy self art thine own bait; / That fish, that is not catch'd thereby, / Alas, is wiser far than I.

Roger, she thought, I am not wise.

Bolling's words were awful, but also honest. What would happen if she and Klaus became lovers? She had no wish to break apart his favorable alliance. The purpose of marriage was to increase property and standing; she understood it well. Her own marriage had done so, had helped to pull her family back into favor, for Roger was loved by the Hanovers. If she began with Klaus, would she be satisfied with bits of time here and there? Wouldn't she—if she began to love him—want more?

She lifted dark, full skirts and swung herself into the cupola, going down the stairs in her ivory-heeled shoes, feeling thwarted, irritable, confused, and underneath it all, sad.

At the bottom of the stairs, staring up at her, was Colonel Perry.

It was almost as if he was waiting for her, and the angle of his face as he stared up at her, the way candlelight softened the seams, highlighted the bones, made her stop mid-step. His eyes were rare, perfect, matched stones in his face; they were the color of Roger's eyes, and it seemed to her for one moment that Roger looked at her out of them, looked out and offered solace. Her heel caught, and she stumbled, but he was up the stairs in an instant, catching her.

"My dear, are you hurt? Can you walk?"

"Yes, I can walk." And yes, I hurt.

"The Iroquois have arrived," he said. "They will all dance in your honor." He led her down to the hall, and she was aware of other things, too many bodies, too many candles burning, too much noise. It was as if the scene above with Klaus, the brief thought that she had seen Roger, had heightened all her senses. Then she saw them, the

Iroquois delegates, here to negotiate a treaty with the Governor, and honoring her fête with their presence, by special arrangement of the Governor. They stood at the fireplace, above their heads the arms of Queen Anne gilded in the chimneypiece. There was a circle of space around them, as if no one dared stand too close. She stopped where she was.

They were half naked, with ornate feather headdresses upon their heads, paint upon their faces and bare chests, bear claws clacking around their necks and hanging from their ears, long cloaks of fur and feathers trailing off their shoulders. Upon their feet were soft, heelless shoes studded with shells and beads.

"They have dressed in your honor and in honor of the King from whom I've told them you arrived." The Governor was now at her side, leading her to a chair, talking all the while. "Those shells on their dress are called peak. They are used also for wampum, their currency. Those are moccasins on their feet, made of buckskin. Their women soften and dry a buck's skin over smoke." The Iroquois held elaborately carved sticks with a hard ball of wood at one end.

"War clubs, tomahawks," said Spotswood.

The Iroquois had inscrutable eyes, sunken cheeks, dark skin; the paint reminded Barbara of scars upon their faces. Suddenly, she could see the slaves on First Curle dressed thus. Then their scars would blend with what they wore, be part of who they were, have meaning in a way they now did not.

"Mohawk, Oneida, Onondaga, Cayuga, Seneca: the five tribes of the Iroquois." Spotswood was telling her how the Indians could journey for a hundred miles on foot to stalk their enemies, their only nourishment a thing called rockahominy, which was Indian corn parched and reduced to a powder. "Nation of snakes, they are called."

"They honor the bravery of their opponent by making him die in great suffering if they should capture him," said Perry. "The chant of a warrior's death song is as important as his deeds. A warrior sings as he dies, tells the tale of his life, of his bravery."

Barbara sank into a low curtsy, a curtsy suitable for kings or their emissaries; these men—their wildness, their unexpected, painted, beaded, magnificent savagery—seemed one with all she had felt inside herself, and all she had seen here in Virginia so far, the wide rivers, the primeval trees, the sight of half naked, night-colored slaves toiling in fields under wide, blue skies; it all seemed one with the anger Bolling had made her feel, the desire Klaus had aroused, the anger and grief, not conquered even now, after almost a year's time, but instead rolling and surging in her, so that she felt wild with it, so that she imagined Edward Perry as an older Roger.

The two delegates from the Iroquois were as impressive in their finery as any foreign delegation come to King George's court. They owned the mountains, Colonel Perry had told her: "It is well for us that at last they agree to a treaty with us, because the French are settled on the other side of the mountains."

Such men should own mountains, Barbara thought, as she sat down in the chair held for her to listen to the eerie, strange songs. They sounded like nothing she had ever heard before. Wild chants from wild priests, she thought, which mock the finished and careful grandeur of this hall, aping its English counterpart across the sea.

There was a moment when she looked at those around her and was startled by what she saw. Pride that she should be entertained by these wild men, but fear in the pride, mixed with hate, masked with politeness. Hatred, said Hyacinthe, I see hatred in their eyes. The Iroquois are fools to make a treaty with us, thought Barbara. How will there ever be enough land for these men, and for the tobacco that eats it so quickly? We will dishonor our treaties with them, as we've dishonored agreements with other Indians, with the savages on our borders.

Colonel Perry had described it to her, how those whose land this once was had found themselves paying tribute to those who stole from them; the tribes became thin of men and women, a shadow of themselves from rum, smallpox, tribal war, death. How had Colonel Perry put it? Virginians were greedy for land, greedy for titles of honor, for sinecure, to be named sheriff and colonel, councillor and clerk. I have been ruthless in my time, as ruthless as Valentine Bolling, he said.

She knew greed; it was the currency of court and London. The South Sea Bubble had broken on greed's sharp edge. Her husband and brother had died of it. How did one live wisely in a world of greed? If the Iroquois were to declare war on us, the Governor had said the day she attended his council, not even the King's army could defeat them. Push us into the sea, you Iroquois, she thought, for we will take your land. The tobacco eats it, and always we must have more.

They sang to her, and danced a slow, fierce dance to the rhythm of their own voices, just as she'd seen the slaves at First Curle do on certain moonlit nights. And there was not another sound in the hall, and her heart swelled. Wildest grief for all that was gone filled it to the brim, but that was all right, a good thing; the grief was properly appeased by their songs, for it was as if they read her heart and sang the words to honor its fullness.

When they finished, she stood and walked to them proudly, handed them silently her fan with its ivory endsticks. One of them unfurled it so that he might see the scene painted on it, of Tamworth. She carefully unscrewed the heavy earrings from her ears, pulled from her hair both the feathers and the brooch that held them in place, and, curtsying deeply, held them up as tribute in her outstretched hands.

"Wonderful!" cried Colonel Perry, his words ringing up into the ceiling.

"Yes!" Spotswood echoed, and suddenly there was the sound of clapping in her ears and more shouts, as one man or woman after another took up a cheer.

Later, she sat watching the dancing, which had resumed, in a more sedate manner, once the Iroquois had left the hall. It had been quite an evening. The Governor, caught up in the spirit she'd begun, had ended by giving the Indians his own coat and wig.

"They'll keep maroon settlements from forming. They've agreed to it—any of our slave runaways they come upon in the mountains will be returned to us," Spotswood said to her, his soldier's face flushed, pleased at the success of her gesture, the success of this evening of which everyone was talking. "Excuse me, Lady Devane, I must see to the fireworks."

" 'Maroon'? What does it mean?" Barbara asked Perry, at her side.

"It came from a Spanish word meaning wild, untamed," answered Perry, slowly. Barbara saw that he was watching his daughter, Beth, who was dancing with Klaus. "Maroons are slaves who have escaped their bondage. In Spanish Florida and in the islands of the West Indies below us there are settlements of former slaves who have run away from their masters. The settlers have not enough numbers to defeat them and so must live at peace with them. What distressed you so before?"

"Colonel Bolling said something that hurt me. I asked him for peace between us; I said that both our loved ones were dead, that my brother had cut his throat with a razor, that the score between us was even. And he replied, that was possible only if the razor was dull." She didn't tell the rest, of Klaus and the rooftop kiss. "The deed I have includes the rolling house and storehouse on the second creek, so that I might, if I wished, take all the goods in the storehouse for mine."

"Never deal with a man when your foremost emotion is anger. Bolling would issue suit against you in county court, and there the jury would be made up of men who owe him for what they've bought from him. They would find against you, if you insisted upon all, because your claim would seem too much to them. He is known to them, and you are not. To say half the goods in the storehouse are yours is better, a fair portion acknowledging Colonel Bolling's labor of past years. I was a hard trader in my time, Lady Devane—"

"I don't believe you."

"No man got the better of me. But I've learned patience and wisdom."

"And what wisdom do you offer me?"

"That another man's gain may also be my own." He stood, frowned.

"What is it?" Barbara asked, seeing his expression.

"My daughter enjoys her dance with Captain Von Rothbach a little too much."

"You don't like him?"

"I like him very much. But time on the same piece of ground for more than a generation gives a man notions of gentility. My grandfather, like the Captain, left a warm bed across the sea somewhere and came here for a better life. I respect my grandfather for it; I thank him for it, for his hard work was the beginning of my inheritance. But I want something more for Beth."

The dance had ended, and Beth was walking toward them, her fine eyes—her father's eyes—alight and happy. And with her was Klaus. Joining them, too, now was the plump, dark-eyed older woman he had danced with before. His widow, Barbara thought.

"I hear you have a voyage to make within the morrow," Perry said to him.

"Yes. I'll sail back up the river this very night, board my sloop, and be gone."

"He came down to dance with me," said the older woman, and Klaus looked at Barbara, who lowered her eyes before what was in his. I intend to play straight and fair, and so must you, she thought, but she could feel again the kiss between them, taste it, and regret not pursuing it.

"You make me too aware of how old I am," Perry said, making a gesture that brought his daughter to his side.

"The fireworks are beginning," someone said, and they walked outside. The first explosion was wonderful, a pinwheel whirling out sparks. Everyone clapped, and in the light, Barbara saw the Iroquois staring up at the sky.

"Will you go with me tomorrow, before we leave, to the Iroquois camp?" she said to Colonel Perry. "I want to bargain for some things."

"Swamp myrtle, dogwoods—what else will you send your loved ones in England?" he said, smiling.

Moccasins for Jane, a buckskin gown for Grandmama, a tomahawk for Tony. I am glad this night is ending.

"So your brother, Harry, cut his throat with a razor," Perry said softly, as fiery designs above them outdid the stars. "What grief for you."

"How did you know my brother's name was Harry?"

"You told me."

"No, I never said his name."

"You did, you must have. Or someone else mentioned it."

"No one would know."

"Your maidservant knows, your boy. One of them said it. What is it? You look so distraught. How have I distressed you?"

"You haven't distressed me. I've distressed myself." The darkness in me again, the kiss, pain for Roger are all tangled in my heart. I saw him in your eyes when I came down from the rooftop. I felt quite wild in that moment, topsy-turvy, as if he were not dead, and all the grief, the devastation, the coming here, were a dream.

"I am tired, Colonel Perry, so tired. Will you excuse me?"

Later, when she lay in her bed, she thought, Roger is never coming back. That part of my life is over. I have to acknowledge it. It was hard to let go of that which you loved. There had been too much letting go in her life. Since she was fourteen, she had been losing those she loved: her father, her brothers and sisters, Harry, Roger. She pounded her fists into the bedcovers. Hard, hard to see them die. I begin to lack trust in life, she thought. Diversion, there is that in my dalliance with Klaus. If I begin with him, I do not have to look at my losses. I use him the way I used Charles, and before Charles, Richelieu.

It was love, said Philippe.

Roger, she thought, you betrayed me. And then you tried to woo me back, but you died before you could make a life between us come true. I hate you for dying. I hate you for leaving me with debt and despair. I wished I'd lain with Klaus; anything other than to feel what I am feeling now.

She floated down into dreams of Venice in winter, of the time of Carnival, when all dressed in disguise. She saw mist drifting up from canals, saw revelers dressed as Pantaloon and Columbine, two characters in Italian comedy, capering in the narrow streets. There was in her ears the sound of dream heels tapping over arched stone bridges, in her eyes the sight of dream snow falling on the shoulders of black capes, capes that swept the stones of the piazzas. While on every head, male and female, was the large, dark, tricorn hat tipped forward, attached to a black or white mask, which left only the mouth to be seen. There stood Roger, in a long cape, in tricorn hat and in black mask, beckoning. She ran as fast as her skirts would allow, ran with all her heart and all her soul to him, and once reaching him, she could do nothing more than stare at his white glove, the tiny pearl buttons fastening it, before taking the hand so enclosed and bringing it to her mouth to kiss tenderly, for he was her beloved. You left me alone, she said. I thought I would die from it.

The mouth visible under the Carnival mask smiled its beguiling smile. The fish that is not catched thereby, alas is wiser far than I. I left Virginia, she told him. I had to. They wanted to eat Hyacinthe.

Never mind it, he said. Come and dance the gavotte with me.

CHAPTER 10

The second creek at First Curle cut a deep mark in the landscape of trees and underbrush, and in it a sloop lay at anchor, its sails furled. The trees made a frame of green and brown shadow, dappled with gold and orange; the sloop's raffish bow was blue, and built to cut through the waters at a rapid pace, a necessity in the waters of the Caribbean, where pirates were as common as sharks. It was the blue that caught Hyacinthe's eye. Mrs. Cox had not yet found him, and he was glad, but tired, too, almost ready to be found. The dogs were somewhere behind him, sniffing and marking trees, as he stood inside his haven of woods to watch.

A man appeared from below the deck. It was Odell Smith, whom he hated, talking with Captain Von Rothbach, who had followed Smith up from the bowels of the sloop, and gestured with his hands as he spoke.

"Are you as glad as I am to have those barrels loaded?" Klaus was saying.

"God, yes—"

Just then, the dogs, panting and breathless from their exploration, came up behind Hyacinthe. Harry's ears pointed at the sight of the sloop. He lifted a paw and barked. Smith's head turned, an abrupt, surprised turning, as did Klaus's.

Hyacinthe would never know what told him to run: something in the way Smith's face changed, something in the way the skin at the back of his neck and along his arms prickled, something in the way his heart gave a sudden, pumping, mighty pulse. Smith did not call to him, but at once pulled himself up over the sloop's side to run down the plank to the creek's sandy bank.

It was the dogs that made Hyacinthe stop. They had been running with him, the three of them mindlessly crashing through underbrush, leaping over tree roots, dodging low-hanging branches, as he urged them and himself on. Then, somehow, they were no longer together, and he was both trying to run and looking around him to see where they had gone, his breath rising like a fist in his throat. Behind him was the sound of Smith, running, as he was, and Klaus calling to them both; and it was this silent, desperate race between him and Smith that told him, even as his mind denied it, that this was no game or foolish fear, but instead something dangerous, dark, deadly, unknown. He heard barking and growling, and then Smith's voice cursing.

Oh, no, he thought, please Harry, please Charlotte, run! He screamed the words in his mind. Then he heard the yelps. They pierced through the drumming in his ears, through the breath rising like bellows in his throat, through the burning in his lungs. One of the dogs was hurt. Do not turn back, the voice in him told him. Run. Run as far away as you can.

But he could hear a dog crying now, piteous, begging, hurt cries, while the other one growled and barked, high, yapping, ferocious. He stood a moment, fighting the fear that rose like water drowning him. He almost wept with the enormity of the decision he was making. And he ran back, dazed and unseeing, full of angry and despairing valor, the boy in him dying, dead, as if he already foresaw his destiny.

CHAPTER 11

Sir John Ashford, on horseback, trotted down the road to Tamworth Hall, a sprawling, wonderful Tudor and baroque edifice that was the principal house of the surrounding countryside. On either side of him were the fields belonging to Tamworth Hall, and he stopped a moment to look at them. Like his, they were scythed of grain and already gleaned.

By tradition, what was left in harvested fields went to those who had no fields of their own. The gleaners, mostly women, sang snatches of old country tunes and talked among themselves as they filled ragcloth sacks and willow baskets. Those who worked diligently collected enough grain, when ground, to last their families the winter.

Children had been everywhere, as much a part of the afterharvest as the field stubble in which the women worked. Playing with blades of grass or trying to eat unripened brambleberries, smaller children had sat under trees, within sight of their mothers. Babies had lain in baskets, their view the few loose silver-white clouds against the vast translucent blue that was an end-of-summer Tamworth sky.

Now, those same babies lay in their baskets under great oaks and hazels, among the leaves and ferns of Tamworth's woods, as their older brothers and sisters went a-nutting, picking the acorns and hazelnuts that had fallen to the ground. The Duchess of Tamworth, who owned Tamworth Hall and surrounding fields, allowed them also the too-ripe apples, plums, and pears her servants disdained to gather in her orchards.

Thinking of this—that part of the tradition of Tamworth Hall, of Ladybeth, his own nearby farm, and of others, was to provide for the less fortunate—Sir John felt a peace within himself, a sense of rightness and balance that he'd lost when he was in London—that, in fact, he'd not felt since the South Sea Bubble. Like others, he had lost funds in the fall of stock, seen bankruptcy and ruin stare him squarely in the face.

Perhaps, he thought, now all will be right again. We've made it through another year, another harvest. His farm, the rituals of the countryside, the rites of harvest and sowing, of seasons and nature, all unvarying, folding one into another, made a firm, bright, continual thread in his life from which he took comfort and derived supreme steadfastness.

Sir John began to hum an ancient harvest song, "Harvest Home," as he nudged at the sides of his horse with his spurs. The lane to Tamworth Hall was just ahead. The hall, with its great octagonal bays, twisted chimney stacks, and rambling size, was as much a part of the landscape as the lane to church or the hawthorn that bloomed every May. It had been there in his father's time, and his grandfathers', and he could no more imagine life without the great house— it watched over them all; it was a place of recourse should need arise—than he could imagine awaking one morning to find there was no sun in the sky.

Autumn, thought Sir John. Burning leaves. Frost on the grass in the mornings. Brambleberries to pick. All is right with the world.

"We have plowed, we have sowed, we have reaped, we have mowed, we have brought home every load": It was a tune older than he was, older than his father and grandfathers, part of ritual, part of tradition, part of life itself. He rode under the lime trees in the avenue that led to the big house of Tamworth Hall, the home of his dear friend the Duchess of Tamworth; he was singing out the words, his voice rising up in a rumble to mingle with autumn sky.

" 'Grapes grow wild there in an incredible Plenty and Variety—' "

Annie, tirewoman to the Duchess of Tamworth, read aloud to lull her mistress, who was in a difficult and prickly mood.

The book told of Virginia and was written by a colonial; since Barbara had left, it was the only thing the Duchess ever wanted to hear.

I've sent my precious Barbara to a paradise, thought the Duchess, thinking the thoughts she thought every day now; I have, except that it is so far away. It will be months yet before a single letter arrives, and ships wrecked themselves upon treacherous shoals, and storms turned them over into the sea, and lovely young granddaughters like Barbara drowned. Pirates—she'd lately heard there were pirates along the colonial coast. What if pirates had captured the ship Barbara was upon?

" '—some of which are very sweet, and pleasant to the Taste, others rough and harsh, and, perhaps, fitter for Wine or Brandy.' "

"I had a thought of pirates," said the Duchess.

"There is no mention of pirates here."

Thin, brown, impatient, Annie tapped the page of the book, a book she was tired of reading. By now, she knew more about Virginia than a body ought to know. Yesterday, it had been the colonial savages the Duchess fretted over.

"It's your stomach, isn't it? You've got wind again. If you had drunk savory tea this morning as I asked you to, you would be calm even now."

I have sent my dearest soul to a paradise of grapes, will not know for months if she has even arrived safely, thought the Duchess, and all my servant can do is babble of savory tea. Annie is a stubborn old stick. "I do not want tea." The Duchess spoke with the terrible dignity of the impossible-to-please. My servants ought to be more patient, more considerate of the old, the infirm, she thought.

A servant had come into the long, echoing gallery in which they sat, a favorite room because all of its many windows viewed gardens:

lawn, terrace, the maze, the woods. Both women turned to glare at him.

"Sir John Ashford is here," the servant announced.

"Is he? Things have come to a pretty pass when my oldest friend must be announced like a peddler come to sell his wares. Where is your mind, Perryman? Admit him at once. You ought to have known to do so."

And as the servant moved to do as he was told, the Duchess said to the view of the gardens, "My servants are impossible and ought all to be dismissed. I am old and too soft-hearted—"

"Old, yes. But soft-hearted? Never."

Sir John strode down the length of the Duchess's gallery, his boots heavy, dull, solid-sounding on the wood floors. Annie, the Duchess's guardian and keeper, her confessor and goad, thought: Good; she can torture him awhile and allow the rest of us a respite.

The Duchess held out her hands to Sir John, and he kissed her cheek, making a hearty, smacking sound as he did so.

"I've quarreled with my beemaster today. I want to send bees to Barbara in Virginia," she said.

"Impossible."

"Precisely what he said. I might have known you'd be no help."

"There were letters for you in the village, and I thought I would bring them by. This one is from the Holleses, and seeing how proud you are of the marriage the young Duke is making, I thought you'd want to see it at once."

Dropping letters in the Duchess's lap, Sir John pulled close a chair and sat down heavily in it, his eyes moving over her.

The Duchess appeared tiny settled back in her chair, and so she was. Time had reduced her, had long ago peeled away any trace of youth. In the passing, it had exposed her, the way water exposes shells upon a beach, so her essence was there for all to see in dark, snapping eyes, in the bones of her elegant, finely drawn face, as slim as a greyhound's.

Strength was in that thin face, and impatience, and sharp intelligence, but also, since her grandson Harry's death last year, a new frailness, as if she was, before everyone's eyes, drying up to nothing, and the next strong wind would whirl her away. She was carried everywhere by a footman because her legs were too weak, too brittle, to hold her.

Sir John was, by contrast, bluff and hale, as sturdy as one of her oaks outside. He had been her neighbor for thirty years, her friend for even longer.

She had opened her letter from the Holleses.

"They write to tell me they invite me to come and visit."

"Very proper, since you are their future relative. . . . I have decided I am returning for the autumn session of Parliament. I stay at Ladybeth only a few days." Sir John was half shamefaced, as if he were confessing a crime.

"Well!" exclaimed the Duchess.

Sir John never returned to London for the autumn session. He meandered in sometime after Christmas and considered the House of Commons fortunate to have his presence. But the setting of the South Sea fines had everyone stirred. Sir John had spent all the summer in London, fighting the amounts Walpole and the other ministers wished to exact from directors. It was all he had talked of when he'd first returned home, was talking of even now.

"Word is Walpole does not wish the King to dissolve Parliament; word is there may be no election come spring. This, when they've put it off for seven years! Word is Walpole is telling the King times are too unsettled for an election, that Whigs will lose too many places."

He had begun to glower, to puff up, ready for battle. He and she usually quarreled over such things.

"I do not trust that bastard Walpole—forgive my language, Alice, but if you could have seen his maneuvers to protect the king and the ministers and South Sea directors—"

"Did he succeed?"

"You know very well he did."

The war between the factions of Whigs and Tories for power with the King was as old as the Duchess. She was unimpressed.

"Well, then, that is his task, is it not? As a king's minister himself? Whether a minister is a Whig or a Tory, he is still a servant to the King and must do his bidding."

"His task," said Sir John, becoming very red in the face, "is to bring those who deserve punishment before the public to take their punishment for lying and cheating rather than screening them from harm! 'Skreen Master' is what Walpole is now called, and Skreen Master he is!"

"Bah," said the Duchess. It was a favorite expression of hers. "Tories have done nothing but fall over their own feet since King George came to the throne. Never mind Walpole. You must stop fighting among yourselves and pull yourselves together to make this coming election count for something. If there are enough of you elected to Parliament, the King will have to make some of you ministers again."

"Are you telling me how to make policy?"

"I certainly am. There was no one better than I in my time."

"Your time has passed, Alice. Things are different now."

"Are they? Do people no longer claw over one another for survival when the stakes are high and the losses immense? Do people no longer betray those who help them, if betrayal will serve better?"

"Why do I put myself to the task of visiting you?"

He grabbed for his hat. Her assessment of court, of life, always upset him. "I deliver your letters like a footman, and you lecture me as if I were a green boy who had never seen London. I'll take no more of it. And for your information, we have pulled ourselves together. We are going to put aside our differences and thwart every act the King's ministers attempt to pass. So there!"

Bowing, folding over like a stiff wooden puppet, he was furious and stuttering.

The quarrel would not last; it was simply a picking up of where they had left off. They'd be talking again by tomorrow—quarreling again, too. Quarreling with him adds years to my life, the Duchess always told Barbara.

Invigorated, she looked down at the letters he'd brought her. Though she lived quietly here in the country, rather than in the hustle and bustle of London and court, she kept up an enormous correspondence and delighted in it. Opening one letter after another, she saw that they were filled with talk of Robert Walpole, King's minister, made First Lord of the Treasury last spring as reward for his handling of the South Sea Bubble.

"Walpole is the champion of cheats and swindlers," wrote one.

"The King does not like or trust him," claimed another. "Walpole will not last six more months as minister."

She looked over to a portrait hanging among the many others in this long rectangle of a room. Her dead Richard gazed out serenely from inside his painted world.

I remember these skirmishes in the highest reaches of power where Walpole now is, the Duchess thought. Betrayal, often by the very men who had maneuvered you into the circle of power, came with the honor of serving the King; one survived, or one didn't.

"Will you visit the Holleses?" asked Annie.

"No."

"Is there a letter from the Duke?" asked Annie.

"No." The Duchess answered tersely. Richard, she thought—it was her habit to converse with her dead husband, usually aloud—Tony is even more stubborn than I am. I cannot bear it. I love him. Why does he not forgive me?

"Why does he not write?" she said to Annie. "I am old. I might die at any moment."

"He will write. Allow it time. He will forgive you. I feel it in my bones. He is the best of the lot."

The Duchess looked at her.

"As sweet as his father, God rest his soul," said Annie. "Sweeter. Kind. As bright as his uncle Master Giles was. Quiet. It is all hidden away. He will be the best of them, it will turn out, when all is said and done. Mark my words."

Sweet Jesus, thought the Duchess, the rest of them had died. Who knew how they might have turned out? In the gallery in which she sat, a huge clock began to drone the hour. It was five in the afternoon.

One, chimed the clock.

Tony, thought the Duchess. Word was he had spent the summer in London drinking, drowning his lover's sorrow at the unexpected departure of Barbara, whom he thought he loved.

Two, chimed the clock.

Tony had been so angry when he discovered Barbara was gone. How dare you, he'd said to the Duchess. The truth was you thought I was not good enough for her, Grandmama, but I am.

He did not forgive her her deceitfulness in the manner of Barbara's quiet leavetaking, unknown to anyone until too late. He had estranged himself from her. He, whom once she had considered most unworthy to inherit Richard's title, had come, over the last years, to mean much to her. There were within him certain signs of his grandfather's mettle.

We are not pieces upon a chessboard, Grandmama, he had said to her. We are living, breathing creatures with a heart and a soul. He was no fool. He saw at once that she had maneuvered Barbara away from him.

Three, went the clock.

A wanton woman, some called Barbara. There were missteps in her past, errors of judgment and impulse, but was she wanton? Ah, Barbara, I will not have you become like your mother—and here the Duchess's thoughts were as cold as a river running in winter, as if Barbara's mother, Diana, were not her only daughter, her only surviving child. Once the fairest woman at any court, Diana was still beautiful, as Barbara, Diana's daughter, was. Beauty is as much a curse as a blessing to a woman, thought the Duchess. Grandmama, I mean to do better, Barbara had said. Do you? Can you, when the gift of your face and young body may bring you so much with so little effort?

Four.

Your fault, Roger. Your fault she was wild, your fault she is bankrupt, and what good does it do either of us to say so? You are as dead as Richard.

Five.

Family, family was all. She and Richard had built a fortune upon ashes, had made their name as honorable, as known as any in the land. Tony must safeguard it, must now add to it. It was his duty. He might love a hundred women, but marry only one, the one who most added to family fortune and name. And this he was doing, it seemed, despite his drinking and debauchery. He had made an alliance to marry the Holleses' oldest girl. It was a triumph; they were a good, strong family with much land and in favor with this court.

Gloire, as the French phrased it, which meant service above all else to pride of name, of family, of house, which meant putting duty foremost, something one of the Saylors' rank must always do.

"Tony does what he should," the Duchess said. "I am pleased."

Her eyes went from one to the other of the different portraits in the gallery. Richard's importance, his position and hers, the distance they had climbed, were here for all to see in the painted faces of the great. Charles II was here, and his brother, the fool James II, who had abandoned England.

James II's daughters were here, ruling queens after their father, Queen Mary and Queen Anne, as well as Mary's husband, the Dutchman, King William. A family no better than mine, estranged and broken apart like mine, thought the Duchess. It happens to us all, doesn't it? Even in the highest reaches.

"His Grace will write," said Annie. "I feel it in my bones."

"Your bones have been known to be wrong."

"I am going to brew savory tea," said Annie.

"I don't want savory tea—" But Annie was gone. Annie never listened. She was a stubborn old stick who had to have her way, who bossed and bullied. And she herself was old, infirm, apt to lapse into daydreams. Her servants knew that. They ought to be more obedient, as ought her family, accepting that she acted for the best, always.

You and I, James, thought the Duchess, looking at the portrait of that foolish king. How sharper than a serpent's tooth it was to have thankless children. Her family did not appreciate her diligence and work. They thought her interfering and deceitful. There was not a deceitful bone in her body.

Her eyes were closing. She was dozing. Annie would walk all the way from the kitchen, hurrying so that the tea would be warm, and find her asleep. Well, she could not help it. She was old.

Like the kingdom, she had survived a dreadful year of death, anger, loss, estrangement. She needed her rest.

Witch, you sent Barbara away, said her daughter, Diana, a dream Diana, dark and vivid in her beauty. As a jewel of gold in a swine's snout, so is a fair woman which is without discretion. In Diana's nose was a jewel of gold.

It's a paradise, answered the Duchess, a veritable paradise.

Nothing is paradise, said Diana.

Take that jewel from your nose, the Duchess snapped. There's a pirate behind you who will kill you for it.

Charles, Lord Russel and the Duke of Wharton stood at Blackfriars Stairs, where Londoners hired small rowboats to cross the Thames, London's watery heart and river road. The stairs were located between the landmark of St. Paul's Cathedral, its dome towering over all the city in spreading majesty, and Fleet Ditch, a tributary of the Thames, down which now floated a continual, sluggish stream of butcher's offal and blood from an open square at which cattle were sold and around which the butchers had settled. A woman pushed between the two, intent on taking the boat they had just summoned.

"That is our boat, madam," began Charles, but on seeing who it was, he smiled. "Lady Alderley, it's been far too long."

Diana, Lady Alderley, Barbara's mother, looked the man up and down.

"My dear Charles," she purred, holding out her hand to him, her voice low and husky, as provocative as the look she gave him. "Where is Tony? Is he not with you?"

"No, not today. You know, of course, my friend, the Duke of Wharton—"

Diana spoke over Charles's words, ignoring the man he tried to introduce. "It's been too long since we've seen each other, Charles. We must remedy that. I am going to insist that you call on me some morning this week. Have I your promise? Wonderful. I've had no word from Barbara. Have you? No? Well, letters from Virginia can take many months to arrive, I've been told. I'm going home to change and then I'm off to the theater. I must see this actor everyone is talking of, this Laurence Slane. Why don't you join me? Bring Tony with you."

She completely ignored Wharton.

"What is all this crowd?" she went on. "I had to push my way through them."

Wharton moved forward and answered her. "Convicts are to be transported from Newgate." The prison of Newgate was near Blackfriars Stairs. "And the rabble gather to see the sight. Look there, in the river. There are the boats that will take them to the ships."

"Make way!"

There was a shift and murmur among the crowd as some hundred men, chains around ankles and wrists, shuffled down the broad, slippery steps, their guards shouting out for the crowd to move. Boats had come to cluster at the lowest steps like so many ducks come to feed. Those men in the front inched down the steps and climbed into the boats as well as they could. The boats would take them to the ships anchored on the other side of London Bridge, whose low arches kept large vessels from sailing so far east. Several carts from the prison waited, full of men who had gaol fever but were being transported anyway.

There was a sudden commotion: A man had fallen on the slime and mud of the lowest steps and pulled three others chained to him into the water of the Thames. Diana saw it and laughed, the laugh sounding like a small silver bell, her ruby-colored mouth open to show teeth with no gaps among them. That was unusual in a woman of middle age; but then, nothing about Diana was usual.

A magistrate and constable jumped into the water to pull up the men, who thrashed and struggled lest their leg chains sink them.

"I thought that one would drown. Too bad. Where do they go, Charles?" Diana's famous eyes, an odd violet shade, were shining.

"The York River," Wharton answered before Charles could. "I see your ignorance is as great as your bad manners, Lady Alderley. The York is a river in the colony of Virginia, madam. Shall we ask one of them to convey a loving message to Barbara before he slits her throat?"

The man who could completely abash Diana was not yet known in London and would have been offered a hundred toasts if he had been, but she was briefly silenced. After a moment she asked Charles to escort her to a rowboat; there was one waiting off to one side of the steps apart from these boats for the convicts.

"Why do you associate with Wharton?" she asked as he handed her into the boat. "He is half mad. I never liked him, never. Come with me to the theater tonight, and we'll talk about Barbara."

"Wharton is a friend."

"A dangerous friend. Ask Harry. Try to join me this evening."

"Perhaps."

"How is Tony? One hears such rumors about him these days."

Charles looked away to the river, the even pleasantness fading from his face. "He drinks too much, does what any man does when the woman he loves goes away."

"Take care of him, Charles. He admires you. I thought he might board a tobacco ship and go chasing after Barbara."

"I thought I might board a tobacco ship and go after her, myself."

Diana patted his arm. "We'll get her back, Charles. You'll see. It isn't the York River she is going to, is it? No, of course it isn't, it is the James River. Yes, because I remember thinking at the time I learned she was gone how like my mother it was to send Barbara to a river on the other side of the sea and named after such a foolish king. My father always said King James would not have lost his kingdom if he had stayed on English soil and fought William of Orange for it."

"I think the river is named after his grandfather James I, and not King James II," Charles said, but the rowboat was already moving into the river; Diana, settling her long skirts, didn't hear him, and would not have cared if she had.

When Wharton and Charles were in a boat themselves, the waterman rowing them toward Westminster, that portion of the city in which stood the royal palace of St. James and the stone townhouses and squares of King George's noblemen, Charles said, "You were quite cruel to Lady Alderley, Wart. It's said she's taken Barbara's leaving far harder than one might imagine."

"False tears. She has no true regard for anyone but herself."

"Why do you dislike her so?"

Gambler, whoremonger, Jacobite, she had called Wharton at the time of her son Harry's death—as if he had made Harry game too much or run up debt; as if her late husband, whom she had divorced once his ambitions became inconvenient, had not been a Jacobite, a gambler, and a famed whoremonger, himself. "She called me a Jacobite."

Charles laughed. Wharton stood up in the boat. He was awkwardly lean, with scrawny elbows sticking out; his arms ended in hands with oddly long fingers, his thin legs in long narrow feet. He had a narrow face and brooding eyes. Unlike Charles, he had nothing handsome about him—except his eyes. His keen mind shows through them, Barbara said to people who would listen.

His movement made the boat tilt to one side, but the waterman was skilled, used to rowdy passengers, to young noblemen with too much drink in them.

"God bless the Church; God bless the King, the Church's defender!" Wharton shouted for all the world to hear. "God bless, there is no harm in blessing, the Pretender. But who is that Pretender and who that King, God bless us all, is quite another thing."

"Amen," said the waterman, and Wharton tossed him a coin, which the waterman caught without missing an oar's stroke.

"There, haven't I told you?" Wharton said to Charles. "Touch a Londoner, touch a Jacobite."

CHAPTER 12

Barbara was traveling back from Williamsburg in Colonel Perry's coach, and they were nearly to his plantation. Her neighbors the Randolphs traveled with them, in their own coach.

"The Randolphs' carriage has stopped," said Perry. "Surely they have not lost a wheel. I will go and see."

I want to walk awhile, thought Barbara, and she stepped down from the carriage and stood in the road. As far as she could see, there was no problem with the carriage in front of theirs. Margaret Cox's grandson Bowler was there, on horseback, talking with Colonel Perry and Captain Randolph. She waved at Bowler and walked toward the men. As she came up, they stopped talking.

"Have you come to escort us home?" she asked Bowler, teasing him because he was so easy to tease. He simply stared at her.

"Lady Devane," said Perry, reaching out and taking her arm. "There has been a mishap at First Curle."

"Mishap?"

"Hyacinthe has disappeared."

"Get off your horse," she said to Bowler.

"Lady Devane," said Perry, "you cannot—"

"Get off your horse, Bowler Cox. At once!"

She pulled at his stirrup with both hands, and Bowler dismounted. Captain Randolph began to remonstrate with her, but Barbara put one foot in the stirrup and heaved herself up, allowing all the men a startled look at dark stocking and white thigh before she tucked down her rebellious hoop, kicked at the horse's sides hard with her heels, and galloped off down the road.

Beth Perry and Thérèse had gotten out of the coach, and Beth ran to the men, saying, "Father, we must do something—"

"We can go through the east field, find her somewhere near your plantation," said Bowler to Colonel Perry, still a little dazed at the way Barbara had comandeered his horse, at the way he had allowed it.

"The river would have taken her to First Curle faster. Why did you not tell her? Why did you allow her to ride away like that!" Captain Randolph's wife, leaning out of the carriage, was furious with everyone.

"I tried to stop her," said Captain Randolph.

"Nonsense! You were all of you useless! Breaking the news to her like that—"

"We will go on," said Perry, taking over. "You ride through the east field and see if you can catch her on the road, Will. If you catch her in time, bring her to my plantation, and we will take her up the river from there."

"Did the boy run away?" asked Mrs. Randolph.

"He is gone, that is all anyone knows," said Bowler. "Everyone who didn't go to Williamsburg is looking. They're talking of dragging the creek near the house—" It took him a moment to go on past the horrified sounds from the women. "Odell Smith thinks he may have drowned."

"Merciful Lord Jesus," said Mrs. Randolph.

"Beth," said Perry. He nodded toward the second carriage, toward Thérèse, who had not followed Beth all the way, but stopped at the horses of the second carriage. She stood there, small, fragile, dark-haired against the bulk of the carriage horses.

Barbara leaned down low on the horse's neck, urging him on, whispering encouragement, her mind racing, asking the same questions over and over: How long had he been gone? Had he wandered away and become lost in the woods? He might have fallen and hurt himself and be unable to walk, might be waiting for them to find him. Had they mapped out the plantation, pulled the slaves from the fields, sent them in gangs to search through woods and pastures? Were they using Harry and Charlotte? The three of them had slept together since the dogs were puppies and Hyacinthe a small boy— since Paris, when Roger had given them all to her. For fashion, but also, as she later understood, to keep her company, so that she would not complain when he was gone from her too often.

She'd always thought that if there had been a child—even a lover's—she would not have done all the foolish, wasteful, hurtful things she had done after Roger's betrayal. But there had been no child. There would never be a child, and so Hyacinthe was her child.

She bent her head to dodge a tree branch and kicked at the horse's sides. Faster, horse, faster, she thought. She would ride until the horse dropped under her; then she would walk until she could find another.

After a while, she became aware of the sound of another set of hooves. She looked behind her: Captain Randolph was on horseback, riding full gallop to catch her. She pulled on the horse's reins, slowing him to a canter, but not stopping.

"The river!" he shouted as his horse pulled alongside hers. "It will be faster than this road. Follow me."

He turned his horse in a wide circle, and she urged hers back to a gallop to match his. She had no idea exactly where she was in relation to First Curle; she knew only that if she followed the road she would eventually get there, and that Will Randolph had a faster way. After a while, they left the road to turn down a smaller one, passing fields and pastures bound by fences, passing tobacco barns with leaves curing, passing finally a stable and huge dovecot. It was Perry's Grove; she knew it by the dovecot. They trotted past the outbuildings, beyond the house, over the lawn, and to the river's landing pier, where a small sailboat lay.

Colonel Perry had come out of the house with his daughter. Barbara patted the horse's neck, and he shook his mane and blew through his nose in weariness. Randolph helped her dismount.

"You ride like the devil," he said, "and I mean that as a compliment."

"Do you want to come inside a moment, Lady Devane?" asked Beth.

"Thérèse?" said Barbara.

"She is in the house now, resting. She became ill in the carriage."

"Do you want to wait here?" asked Colonel Perry.

"No, I want to go to First Curle."

He took her elbow, walking her to the river, explaining that the sailboat was his best, his fastest, that he and Captain Randolph would take her to First Curle. He spoke very simply, very kindly. Bowler Cox was in the boat, holding out his hand to help her board, his young face anxious and concerned. She made her way to the bow, past a slave, and her face turned toward First Curle; she stayed huddled in the bow, away from the others, who let her be. The sail seemed terribly long.

Perry's slave maneuvered the sailboat skillfully into the first creek, and Barbara lifted her skirts and stepped up and out before anyone could help her. She ran up the bank, down the path to the house, but her stays were too tight, and she finally had to walk, holding her side, past the fields to the picketed yard of the house. The pug Harry came running out.

Barbara knelt. "Harry, where is Hyacinthe?"

Margaret Cox emerged, a grandson behind her, her face swollen with crying. At the sight of Barbara, she began to cry yet again, holding a handkerchief to her face.

"Come upstairs with me, if you would be so kind," said Barbara to her, "and help me to change."

In the attic bedroom, Barbara knelt at a trunk, tossing aside delicate laces and stockings and gloves as she looked for a gown in which she could search for Hyacinthe.

"He just never came back," said Mrs. Cox. "I missed him four afternoons ago."

Barbara stood. *"Four days?* He's been gone *four days?"*

She felt as if someone had slapped her a hundred times across the face, so that her head was fuzzy and ringing.

"That first afternoon, I didn't worry so much. I knew he was tired of being in the house; I thought it all right that he'd left. But when dusk came, he didn't come back. I called for him, and when there was no answer, I sent over for my grandsons and they hunted for me. I told Odell Smith. The next day, my grandsons looked for him, and Mr. Smith heard the dogs barking, and there was some food stolen from the kitchen. We all thought he was on the plantation, thought that he—" She stopped.

"Unlace me, please. Go on. You thought he was somewhere around and wouldn't come in to you."

"Yes. On the third day, I was beside myself. I went to Mr. Smith and said we must tell Lady Devane. We must bring her back from Williamsburg. But Mr. Smith said to wait one more day. He said he would take all of the afternoon and search with the slaves, and so we did. And then, this morning, we sent word out to neighbors to come over to help, and Bowler set out to find you. Hyacinthe didn't like me being with him, Lady Devane. I tried not to mind it, but he wasn't happy."

"He didn't like being left behind. It wouldn't have mattered who was with him. Where is Charlotte?"

"No sign of her, Lady Devane. Only his dog appeared, on the third day. Covered in mud. Briars and twigs in his fur."

Downstairs, Colonel Perry and Captain Randolph and Bowler were in her parlor. Perry looked at her hard. "You are not going out yourself?"

"There is no need, Lady Devane," Captain Randolph put in. "Others are looking—your neighbors, your overseer, some of the slaves. They will find him if he is to be found."

"And he is," Perry said. "I've spoken with Bowler here. They are searching everywhere, along the road, on other plantations; they even sent word to your other quarters. You must not trouble your-self. You must sit here and wait. Come, sit down. Play a hand of cards with me. Mann Page said you won seventeen shillings from his nephew in Williamsburg."

She sat down, accepted the cards he dealt, played card after card; then, somewhere in the game she stopped, stood up abruptly.

"If you become lost, searching," said Perry, "it will only complicate matters." He gathered up the cards and began to shuffle them again.

She did not look at him, or at the others. She went outside to the yard and stood there.

"She must have something to do," Perry said to Randolph. "Let her be."

Food and drink. The searchers would come in tired and hungry. Here was something she could do. Barbara walked out of the yard to the kitchen, thinking of all that must be done, but there on the table were huge hams and loaves of bread, dishes of pie and beans, wooden bowls of figs and nuts. They had been brought from nearby plantations, from wives and mothers and daughters, who could not come to search, but sent their men and their plenty. It was kind, more than kind, but at this moment, it reminded her too strongly of a funeral feast.

"What do you know, Mama Zou?" asked Barbara, but the old slave shook her head.

She went back to the house and made Bowler help her bring up from the cellar brown bottles of rum, a cone of sugar, jugs of cider for a punch.

She lit the fires in the fireplaces, moved from parlor to parlor lighting candles, had Bowler help her bring the food from the kitchen into the house; finally she went outside to walk the perimeter of the yard restlessly until finally she heard the sound of horses, men, dogs. Running to the barn, she searched for Hyacinthe among the men and horses.

"You did not find him?" she said to no one in particular. "Please," she told the dismounting men, "please come to the house and have a cup of punch and some supper."

She went to each man, repeating her invitation and introducing herself if she'd not met him before, thanking him for his time and trouble. She had to walk around the yard again, seeking command of herself, before she could walk into the house.

There, at the door on the other end in the hall, beyond the stair, stood Valentine Bolling and Colonel Perry.

"Your maidservant is here," said Perry. "She is upstairs."

"What are you doing here?" Barbara said to Bolling. "Have you come to gloat?"

He glowered at her. "I've only just heard the news. I came to help."

"He isn't to be found," said Perry gently.

"I want one more day," said Barbara. She lifted her chin, ready to argue, plead, or cry, whatever it would take to get her way.

"If you list him as a runaway, the sheriff will post the description at the county courthouse," said Bolling.

"He is not a runaway."

"You would need to word the notice carefully," Perry said. "Sometimes, runaway slaves are killed in capture. There is no punishment of those who do the killing."

"He isn't a slave anymore. I've given him his freedom. He has been kidnapped. Pirates. Governor Spotswood said there were pirates all along the coast."

"Pirates seldom sail this far upriver," Bolling said. "And they are not usually interested in slave boys—excuse me: servant boys who were formerly slaves."

"A Seneca, a Cherokee, a Tuscarora," said Perry, slowly, as if Barbara had started him thinking along a new path. "If he got across the river, he might have wandered onto a hunting trail, been taken."

"I will offer a reward. A diamond necklace."

"He is not worth a diamond necklace," said Bolling.

"A diamond necklace and a pair of earrings."

"List your reward at thirty pounds, and if he is to be found, he will be brought in," said Bolling.

Merchant, thought Barbara, some things have no price.

"You may have heard that the Privy Council and Parliament in their wisdom dump convicts from Newgate upon us." Bolling was looking at her as if she were an idiot. "News of a diamond necklace would be up and down the river in days. You might find yourself the hostess of most unwelcome visitors. Even more unwelcome than I."

"Captain Randolph has a brother who lives above the falls in the river. There are trails there the Indian traders use. We can make sure word of the boy's disappearance is passed along. The Governor might inform his rangers," said Perry.

"Rangers?" She pounced upon the word, which had a hopeful sound.

"They scout along the frontiers, past the heads of the rivers—"

"The boy is a sl—a servant," Bolling said impatiently. "The Governor will hardly call out the rangers for him. She has to understand. Lies will do her no good."

He will call out the rangers if Robert Walpole so orders, thought Barbara. Or His Majesty. You have no idea of my friends in England, Colonel Bolling. And then she thought, despairing, that it would take months to hear from them.

"It's settled then: one more day of searching. And we will inform the Governor. If you will excuse me." She went up the stairs before either of them could answer.

Bolling walked into the parlor, nodded to various men there, saw Margaret Cox sitting off by herself, and went over to her.

"Lost him, did you?" he said.

She didn't answer. He left her and went across the hall to the other parlor.

Upstairs, Barbara and Thérèse talked.

"What if he is dead?" said Thérèse. "How will we bear it?" Her face was swollen from crying.

"Until we find him, he isn't, Thérèse. Listen to me. I can't stay in this house. I'm going to go and hunt for him. Do you want to come with me?"

"Yes."

"Good. You go downstairs first. Just go quietly around the stairs and out the door that is on that end of the hall. Here, take Harry. Wrap this cloak around him so no one sees him. Wait for me."

Barbara rifled though a trunk, picked out a shirt, pulled a cloak from a peg, and then counted to a hundred. It was all she could do to wait. Stay here, they'd told her. These woods are thick. But she didn't want to stay here. She was going to do what she was going to do, and not a man was going to stop her. She walked down the stairs, paused a moment on the last step. She could hear voices in both parlors. She turned quickly, walked past the stairs to the door at the end of the hall, and stepped outside. She waited a moment, fastening her cloak at her neck. No one followed. No moon tonight, she thought, looking up. No moon for Hyacinthe. Thérèse stepped from behind a pine tree.

"You have Harry?"

"Yes."

"Good. There will be a lantern in the kitchen. I'll fetch it."

That done, she leaned down and gave the dog Hyacinthe's shirt to smell. "Good boy. Good dog. Find Hyacinthe. Where's Hyacinthe, Harry?"

The pug barked and ran into the night, and she and Thérèse followed.

❦

"What's that?" said Margaret Cox. "Do you hear it?"

She opened the door, and the sound was clearer, a lilting, mourning wail that grew stronger and stronger. Finally, men came into view, led by a giant, bearded, who marched into the yard of First Curle, some five slaves behind him, and gave a final squeeze to the bagpipes he played.

"It's John Blackstone," said Bolling, who had come outside. Indeed, everyone in the house had come outside as the sounds from the bagpipes had grown louder.

"We heard about the boy and came to help find him," Blackstone said. "They can find anything." He tilted his large and heavy head backward to indicate the slaves with him.

"You're across the river on another quarter, aren't you?" said Perry.

"I owe the ferryman for crossing us, but I figure Lady Devane will pay it if we find the boy," Blackstone answered.

"Well, come inside, Mr. Blackstone," said Mrs. Cox, "while I fetch her."

"I'm tired," Barbara said. "How long do you think we've been walking, Thérèse?"

"An hour or more. Harry! I don't see him, madame. Madame!"

Barbara stumbled, and her cry of surprise turned to a scream as she fell down a bank she'd not known was there. She fell into water; at the sound of the splash, Thérèse cried out her name.

The shock of water closing over her head made Barbara lash out. Her head above the water now, she saw the light of the lantern, heard Thérèse calling her, and moved herself in that direction. The bank was close, but so steep she almost could not climb up it. But Thérèse was there, on her knees, hand extended down to help her, and Barbara crawled back up, the ties of her cloak nearly choking her, her heavy skirts fighting her every inch of the way. She coughed and sputtered and cried once she had gained the top, which was fine, because Thérèse was crying, too.

"We're a pair of fools," Barbara said. "Give me that lantern." She stood, but all she could see was trees. She sat down, trying not to shiver.

It wasn't so much that she was cold. It was more that she had really frightened herself. If this happened to Hyacinthe, she thought, did he survive? If there was no one to help him? I must not think of it. I must believe he is alive.

"Let's just stay here," she said, "until morning."

You'll become lost, Colonel Perry had said. You don't know the woods well enough. She knew them well enough to find the second creek: She had just fallen into it. Thérèse sat down beside her. Barbara took her hand. "Hyacinthe has Charlotte with him. He won't feel so alone with Charlotte."

After a time, they fell asleep, waking to scream, one after the other, when Harry leaped out of the darkness and into Barbara's lap.

Barbara woke. She heard a bagpipe and stood. "Here!" she cried over its sound, "over here! Wake up, Thérèse, we're rescued."

And there in the distance was the wonderful sight of lighted lanterns bobbing, as the sound of the bagpipes grew stronger.

"Thank God," said Perry, when he saw the two of them.

Barbara ran to him, her skirts tangling around her legs. "I got lost."

"Well, now you're found."

She stood in the misting rain, at a place where the second creek joined the river. They had given her her second day, but the rain had been falling for an hour, and any child of the country knew it would erase tracks, eliminate scents. She had been riding along the river in both directions all morning, looking for some sign, following Harry's erratic lead, when Colonel Perry had ridden up to tell her they had found something farther upriver. She stood now on the bank, watching.

Across the river, a rowboat was grounded upon a small sandbar set close to the other shore. For several minutes now, the heads of slaves had been bobbing in and out of the water. Blackstone was there, too, swimming among the slaves. There was sudden activity in the rowboat as those inside it bent over to work with the slaves and Blackstone in the water. She pushed back the hood of her cloak and shaded her eyes from the rain with her hands. They had pulled something into the boat.

Perry put his arm around her. She held up her face, white and set, to the rain for a moment or two, eyes closed, and when she opened them again, the boat was rowing across the current toward them. Tony, she thought, where are you? I need you, now. When Roger had died, Tony had ridden through snow and ice to come to Tamworth, to comfort her. She had not appreciated, until this moment, his gesture.

They were having trouble landing the boat. Blackstone leaped out; the water reached to his shoulders, but he pushed the boat to the bank. A slave handed him something small, wrapped in a bit of blanket. It was too small to be a boy, Barbara saw. Blackstone walked up the bank, and it seemed to Barbara that three-quarters of him was leg. She wiped the rain out of her face, straining to read his expression. He seemed to want to say something, but all he did was kneel and gently unfold the blanket. Charlotte lay there, tangled in slimy weed. At once, Harry sniffed her body up and down and whined and pawed at her.

"Her back's been broken," he said. He pointed to her head, to a small hole and the puckered, whitened flesh around it. "Mercy killing," he said. Barbara knelt to touch her. She pushed Harry aside, folded the blanket back around her dog, and picked her up.

"I'll want to go home now," she said.

She rode toward the house, Harry at a trot behind her, and Perry behind them both. At the barn, she dismounted. At the gate to the yard Harry ran past her, barking. She looked up and saw Thérèse standing in the doorway.

"He isn't found," she said. "But Charlotte is."

Thérèse looked at the blanket-covered lump in Barbara's arms.

"Hyacinthe isn't dead," Barbara said, pulling up strength, pulling up a ferocious determination from someplace deep inside her, "until he's found."

CHAPTER 13

Some miles up the river from Aunt Shrew's, the Princess of Wales stepped onto the royal barge. The barge was draped with cloth of crimson and gold, its flags flying in honor of the occasion. She nodded her head graciously toward the oarsmen and their leader. She and the Prince of Wales were to spend several days at Hampton Court, and they were going there by river.

The visit was an impulsive thing—and therefore, an unusual thing, for Prince George was almost never impulsive. He was a creature of habit; one could set one's watch by the unvarying routine of his days: audiences; official business in the morning; a drive in the carriage or a long walk in the afternoon; his nap; backgammon or basset at night; at nine in the evening, an hour or so alone with Mrs. Howard, his mistress. Not at eight-thirty, or a quarter until nine, but at nine sharp. Day after day after day, the same routines followed, the same paths in the gardens walked, the same partners chosen in cards or dance or bed.

The Princess made her way back to her chair under the gilded, painted wooden canopy, smiling to her ladies, who were excited to be making the journey and who chattered among themselves like birds, the skirts of their long gowns belling under their cloaks like the cups of so many flowers.

Yesterday afternoon, as she strolled with him through the gardens of Richmond House, the Prince had said to her, "Let us go to Hampton tomorrow." And then, as she showed her surprise, he said, "We will have a fête. Yes, a small fête. Lady Alderley would like that. She is taking her daughter's absence so hard." And he had smiled in a satisfied, pleased way to himself, and afterward bragged to one and all of his plans.

The Princess allowed one of her ladies to settle a soft woolen lap robe about her. She smiled at one of her favorites—a young maid of honor, as the young, unmarried women who served in her household were called. She smiled at Harriet, who would marry the young Duke of Tamworth. It was a good match, the joining of the strong Whig Holles family with a family whose fame was legend—including scandals and disloyalties, but that was another story. The others watching (someone was always watching) she ignored as she waited for her husband, who was at the other end of the barge with the musicians. She could hear his voice, always too loud, and now and then the murmurs of a quite different voice, a woman's voice, low, husky, unmistakable. The voice of Lady Alderley, of Diana, aptly named for the huntress of myth.

Courtiers leaped to the right and left as the Prince walked in to join the Princess under the barge's canopy. On his arm was Diana. She curtsied to the Princess.

"Please, my dear," said the Princess, looking directly into Diana's famous violet eyes. They had snared many a man, including the one most disliked in London at the moment: Robert Walpole. Diana and Walpole had been lovers for some years. She had survived being tied by marriage to Alderley, an infamous Jacobite, to become lovers with Walpole, a man whose loyalty to the Hanovers was unquestioned. She always landed upon her feet, like a cat.

"Sit here, beside me. We would enjoy your company. . . . I'm told there is no word from Lady Devane in Virginia. How you must fret," said the Princess. She made it her business to know everything, all the gossip, all the scandal, all the happenings of those who served court.

"I pray to God, my daughter is well." Diana, her low voice sending a shiver up even the Princess's spine, looked away, out to the river, as if she could not bear her sorrow, allowing the Prince and Princess the sight of her profile, somehow poignant in its imperfections, the sags and lines overlying what had once been matchless beauty. It was still an extraordinary face.

Laurence Slane could do no better than the way she plays this role of tragic mother, thought the Princess: the sadness in the eyes, that throbbing undertone of grief in the voice. Diana had somehow managed to turn the Prince's rage at Barbara's leaving to her advantage. Lady Alderley is looking unwell today, he told her. Or, Lady Alderley seems sad. He put his own emotions upon Diana. Clever huntress. Manipulator of men.

There was a lurch, as the barge was pushed away from the bank. The oars were uniform in their straightness against the sky. Then came a barking command, and the oars dipped down in unison, like weathered brown birds, into the water. The breeze from the river lifted the edges of the ladies' small lace caps and played with the long curls of the men's wigs. There was a murmur of talk as the musicians began to play.

Tommy Carlyle, an immense, hulking man with rouge on his cheeks and a diamond in one ear, said, "I shall not give you my opinion of the French because I am very often taken for one of them, and several have paid me the highest compliment they think it in their power to bestow, which is, 'Sir, you are just like ourselves—' "

"So . . ." said the Prince, slapping his hands together. "We are on our way." He spoke with a Hanoverian accent, which courtiers mocked behind his back; the "w"s were "v"s and the "p"s were "b"s; his most famous remark had become "I hate all boets and bainters." But at least he spoke English, unlike his father, who conversed with his English subjects in Latin or French.

"I shall only tell you," continued Carlyle, "that I am insolent; I talk a great deal; I am loud and peremptory; I sing and dance as I walk along; and above all, I spend an immense sum in hair-powder, feathers, and white gloves." There was laughter from those who had heard him.

The Prince smiled, thinking the laughter was for him, for the excursion he had caused to come into effect. He was as happy as an overgrown boy today. They had not been on an excursion in months, and Hampton was one of their favorite palaces.

It was a beautiful palace, a grand Tudor spectacle of red brick and twisting chimney stacks and mullioned windows and stone gateways. It contained three large interior courtyards, the last of which had been redesigned by Sir Christopher Wren. Wren had torn down the Tudor facings and created a formal, baroque series of state rooms, their classical façades even and perfect, window matching window. The Wren courtyard looked out on the gardens. If one came to Hampton Court by river, it looked as if it had been built yesterday. But entering by coach or horseback through its front, one was transported back a century and a half to the Tudors, to Henry VIII and Elizabeth and Bloody Mary.

"The ghost of poor little Queen Catherine runs along the gallery of the state apartments," the Prince said, telling his favorite ghost's tale of the palace. A few seats from him, his mistress, Mrs. Howard, smiled sweetly as she tried to hear over the music, but her sweetness paled and died against the dark drama of Diana.

"Queen Catherine screamed, 'Forgive me, hear me, my lord!'" the Prince was saying. "But the guards dragged her back to her rooms. Her husband, Henry VIII, in the Chapel Royal, must have heard her, but there was no forgiveness in him. Off came her head—" The Prince made an abrupt, chopping motion with his hand, and several ladies squealed and clutched the arm of the man nearest them.

The Princess thought: She ought to have learned the lesson of her predecessor Anne Boleyn. Anne's badges and initials could be seen in the carvings of the vast great hall of Hampton.

"The moral:"—the Prince held up a pedantic finger—"Put not your trust in princes." Then he burst into one of his maniacal brays of laughter.

Everyone laughed with him, even those who had heard the tale before. Even those who had not heard the tale but had been listening to the music.

On the shore, people stopped to watch the royal barge, stately as a swan in its progress through the river. The men doffed their hats. The women curtsied, the white of their aprons bright against the sun. But there were no cheers. Not anymore. Once there had been—for the Princess if not for the Prince or his father. But now no faces were wreathed in smiles and goodwill. The names of those gone, disgraced, or dead this last year rolled through the Princess's mind: Aislabie; Craggs; Stanhope; Knight; Devane, her oh-so-charming Roger.

All of the royal family was tainted with the smudge of scandal: the Prince, as a former governor of the South Sea Company; the King, as governor of the company; the King's mistress, the Duchess of Kendall; and his ministers for bribes and special favors. "If we manage through the winter and spring," Robert Walpole had said to them—how they all hung on his words at St. James's Palace—"your house will survive."

Walpole was a large, clumsy, hearty caricature of an English squire, with a ridiculous moon face and dark, overgrown eyebrows and a big belly. He had bluffed and cajoled and threatened and compromised, and somehow—by talk, by intricate parliamentary procedure, by knowing when to give and when to stand fast—kept the Commons, that dangerous English breeding ground of trouble, from outright rebellion. There had been talk of rebellion everywhere this last year. The kingdom was trembling and spent, angry at the wrong it considered the South Sea Bubble, and blaming those who ruled, partly because they were foreign. Rebellion. The Princess shivered.

The English, the King said, shaking his head. They cut off Charles I's head. They asked his son, Charles II, to return from exile to rule them, but disliked his brother, James, so they invited William of Orange to invade, to rid themselves of James when his policies frightened them. The English are capable of great treachery.

Walpole will not last six months as minister to my father, he is that despised by the people of England, the Prince had told her just the other day. The Prince despised Walpole, too. My father will dismiss him to make the people happy. Put not your trust in princes, even when you save them.

The barge had landed. Two gentlemen of the Princess's household leaped out as it bumped into the bank near the small stone banqueting house that had been William of Orange's Baroque addition to Hampton Court. The musicians continued to play as everyone rose from their benches and chairs. The Prince helped Diana to her feet, as his official mistress, Mrs. Howard—not to mention his wife—sat just yards away.

John Hervey was offering his hand to the Princess. She smiled at him and allowed him to escort her into the summerhouse, where she sat down upon a gilded, embroidered armchair. Everything was noise and bustle as the Prince's equerry called out orders, and servants rushed forward, and ladies and bedchamber women and gentlemen of the household hurried off to see all was ready to receive them.

The walls and ceiling of the banqueting house had been painted by Verrio in an enticing, lush series of scenes of the arts and of the god Jupiter and his lovers. The Princess stared at naked arms and legs, flowers and clouds, swans and bulls, mounds of bellies and breasts, thin, trailing scarves and gowns that left more uncovered than covered. She stared at one of Jupiter's loves, a blonde who looked as she herself had looked not so many years ago, pretty and pink and plump. The Princess was still pink and plump; the prettiness had waned a bit, as prettiness was wont to do, but her cleverness had not. That had stayed, and was made sharper by this coming to England, to rule a people who hated, mocked, slandered, who were divisive and quarrelsome.

Someone was bringing her a glass of wine. Her dear Mary, sister to the Duke of Tamworth and married now to that handsome rogue Charles, Lord Russel. Mary wore a sack gown—the latest French style, which Barbara, Lady Devane, had made fashionable. The gown's front had no waist, but merely dropped from the bodice to the floor. Mary's hairstyle, a soft, curling around her face, was French too, after the figures in Watteau's paintings. Roger, Lord

Devane, patron of all that was beautiful, had introduced the art of the Frenchman Watteau to England. The pictures had hung for all to admire in his Temple of Arts, built beside Devane House. Magnificent Devane House, gone now—Devane House and Roger and the Temple of Arts, all gone, the buildings dismantled—a crime in itself—and lumber, marble, paving bricks sold to pay Lord Devane's fine. The South Sea, ruining so much, so many; and ruining the calm they had thought they'd finally achieved, after six years on the throne.

"Where is Lady Alderley?" the Princess asked.

"The Prince is walking with her in the gardens," Mary said.

"Yes, well. . . . Tell Mrs. Clayton that I want to play basset." She would not fret about Diana, the clever huntress who continued to prowl in the royal garden, still hoping to bag a royal prince for her daughter. Why fret when the daughter was not here? Anyone who played basset, or any game, with the Princess must be willing to risk high stakes; it was a sign of her character that many overlooked.

Laurence Slane walked down a narrow street, one of several that made a small pocket of ugliness and poverty, with leaning tumbledown houses and muddy yards in the large and grand shadow of the church of Westminster Abbey. He was on the westernmost edge of the city; houses ended here, at a great marsh called Tothill Fields. In the distance, beyond the marsh, were farms, fields, orchards, a path that led to the village of Chelsea.

Slane unlocked a door set into the brick wall of one of the private yards of the Abbey and walked quickly through to let himself into the buildings in which the Abbey's dean and clergy lived or worked. Walking down a corridor, he saw a man coming forward, and his mind went whirling. He put his hand to a door, but the door was locked; he was trapped. Brazen it out, he thought; the man is likely a servant, and will not remember seeing me, unless I do something to make him remember.

But it was Gussy—Augustus Cromwell, clerk to the Bishop of

Rochester. And a Jacobite. Gussy copied the letters Rochester sent abroad, so that Rochester's handwriting might not be recognized if the letters should be intercepted. Slane and Gussy, among others, had been up all the other night composing the broadsheet about the Duke of Tamworth. Gussy was passing him by without a word, as if he hadn't seen him. Good man, thought Slane.

"Make sure these doors are unlocked," Slane said as Gussy, tall and thin, like a drooping angel, moved by him, "so that I may hide in these chambers should I need to." And then, to tease: "There is ink on your chin."

"And yours."

It wasn't like Gussy to jest. He was a serious man, kind and gentle. Gussy must be particularly pleased with the broadsheet. It was out, on the streets at last.

"Red rover, red rover, let Jamie come over. . . ." Slane whispered a Jacobite rhyme, then smiled at the upset that registered on Gussy's face. Though there was no one in the corridor, there were rules, weren't there, that men like Gussy, hundreds of them, priests and carpenters, lords and merchants, kept; rules of secrecy, of never acknowledging true thoughts, so that one day, Jamie could indeed come over.

Safe inside a plainly furnished chamber in the upper floors, Slane crossed himself before the figure of the bleeding Christ on a handsome ivory crucifix fixed on the wall, then lit a candle and put it in the third of the arching windows along one wall. This done he walked behind the room screen that was at one end of the chamber.

Here was yet another window—his escape route if need be, yet a perilous one, a climb down a drain into the courtyard below, into which the sun never shone; but escape nonetheless. Signals, signs, secret words, avenues of escape, lies to cover deeds or where one had been, continual vigilance—these things made up the code by which he lived.

How do you even know who you are anymore? his mother asked. As he made certain the window pushed out easily, silently, as it was supposed to do, Slane allowed himself to think of his mother, seeing her vivid, expressive face, the vigor with which she moved and lived. She wanted him to leave Jamie's service. You have given enough, she said. Come to me and let me help you make a real life. He stretched out on the cot. Though he had sent word for Rochester to meet him at a certain time, he might have to wait a number of hours.

A French Jesuit had taught him a series of prayers that quieted the mind to watchful dozing, and made waiting endurable; and waiting was much of what he did. Letters had to be written, usually by a third party, so that an important man's handwriting could not be used against him should the letters be discovered. That took time. Then, the Blackbird's most trusted advisers were in Paris, so the letters had to be routed there, but the Blackbird himself was in Italy, so that news and orders must travel several places before they finally reached England. Slane was fortunate that he had been born with the gift of patience.

Yet he found that today he could not still his mind so easily. It took all his discipline, which was considerable, not to leave the se-crecy the screen provided and pace up and down. The news he brought was too exciting.

After a time, there was the sound of the door opening, the sound of slow, shuffling movement, of someone who moved himself with crutches: the Bishop of Rochester.

"Sing aloud unto God our strength: make a joyful noise unto the God of Jacob," said Rochester.

"Blow up the trumpet in the new moon, in the time appointed, on our solemn feast day."

Slane moved from around the screen as he answered, to face the ailing, irascible, brilliant Bishop of Rochester, dean of this church and considered the most able leader of the Tory party.

The younger man helped him to a chair and placed the crutches against a wall; Rochester suffered from gout in his legs and could not walk easily. "Well, Slane," he said, "is our broadsheet printed? I'm pleased with it, very pleased. It will prick old George in his tender places, like a thorn. He cannot control even his most illustrious fam-ilies. We must keep discontent stirred. And I think we do that. I've met this morning with some good men, good Tories, some of them our friends, some not—Walpole tries to make the Hanoverian believe that all Tories are Jacobites, but they're not. If they were, King James would already be wearing his crown. We held a meeting this morning to discuss Tory policy for the rest of the time Parliament meets. There was even a Whig or two among us, Slane. Walpole and the other ministers have made many enemies, and we all agree that we will do everything in our power to thwart every bill King George and his ministers desire this last session. We will move all our energies toward reminding people what this last seven years of Whig power has cost. Gussy read me bits and pieces of the broadsheet about Tamworth this morning as I dressed. Young Wharton is a clever rogue, isn't he? I understand he wrote most of it. My only regret is that Lady Devane's name had to be made so obvious."

One did not state the name, but printed the initial, Duke of T— for the Duke of Tamworth—or Lady D—for Lady Devane—giving enough description to make it clear who was intended.

Mine, too, thought Slane. He and Wharton had argued over this. Find a way not to indicate who the lady is, Slane had said.

Barbara would want us to, Wharton had replied.

Is she Jacobite? Slane had asked, startled, intrigued.

No, but if she were, she'd be among the best.

Then let us not describe the lady so vividly, Slane had said.

No, said Wharton. She moved in the highest circles; her husband was a South Sea director; the Prince of Wales desired her; her mother is Walpole's whore. She is what we need. She can be for us a symbol of this reign, of all that is wrong with it—its immorality and its greed.

Do you consider her immoral? Slane was curious, despite himself, as to Wharton's opinion. Wharton was a strange man, among the most brilliant Slane had ever met, and the most unstable. And he hated women, yet he did not love men in the way that Tommy Carlyle did.

I love Barbara, said Wharton, surprising Slane. She is like a sister to me.

Would you slander your sister?

For the cause, yes, as would you. Bab will forgive us, particularly if we win. If we win, we'll abolish the debt on her estate and marry her to a Tory duke and publish our apologies for taking her name in vain in every district. Will that satisfy you?

"The plan of invasion is here," Slane told the Bishop.

Rochester's face, a beefy square of wrinkles and set brows, changed color, became almost boyish.

"I must arrange a safe meeting between the messenger who brings it and those few you trust most completely," Slane continued.

"Tell me whatever about it you know. Quickly, man, for I have been in an agony of impatience and doubt."

As I know only too well, thought Slane. "The invasion is slated for spring, during the general election, as you advised."

"Yes, everything will be stirred up then, men divided and quarreling. What else? What else?"

"There must be money raised to be sent abroad to the Duke of Ormonde, who will head the invasion force." Ormonde, who had been Captain General of the English army under Queen Anne, was not of the stature of Marlborough or Tamworth, but he was beloved by Englishmen nonetheless.

"Ormonde! That is wonderful news," Rochester said. "Do you know the story—that when Ormonde fled the kingdom rather than be tried for treason, Hanoverian George said to his ministers, 'You go too far in your threats. You send to my cousin James the best of men!' " Rochester laughed, his square face alight, his eyes snapping and brilliant. "Ormonde. Excellent, excellent. He was loved by our troops, is loved by the people."

"He's to land at the spot you decide is best and lead troops from there to London."

"What troops? How many? Who is supplying them? The French? The Spanish? The Swedes?"

Slane took a deep breath. Here it was. If he could navigate Rochester past this moment, the way was clear. "The troops will be ones you and the others secretly rally."

"*What?*"

The word roared out of Rochester, hovered over their heads like a bad omen, then crashed and died upon the walls of the small chamber.

Slane walked to one of the arching windows and looked out to the courtyard below. It was the wrong move, but Rochester's reaction was so much his own, that, for the moment, he could not deceive. Slane's eyes, under his dark brows, were like stones. No foreign troops, he'd thought to himself last night. We had foreign troops to aid us, before. What a chance we take, to invade without foreign support. But it was not Slane's place to question, though he had sent off an immediate letter to Jamie doing so. Those in Paris and Rome had their tasks, and he had his. They must make a move, a bold move, and let the cards fall where they might. There would never be a time when everything was perfect. A man made his destiny, if he moved forward forcefully enough.

What had the Jesuits taught? To keep one's eyes upon the goal desired, not upon the delays and impediments. There was within him the growing feeling that if they were not triumphant this time, it was over. Eight-and-twenty was too young to feel such futility. He bucked against it. Listen to what moves within you, his mother always said.

"An invasion must be backed by foreign troops, Slane," Rochester said, his voice furious and impatient. He was the terror of the House of Lords, when aroused. "There isn't time to raise the force we need, by April."

Slane answered doggedly: "We have men in every court, from France to the Czar. Who knows what will have happened by April, what alliances will be formed, who will commit troops to us? We know for certain that the Irish in the French regiments will join Ormonde; the Catholic clans in Scotland will rise to help us too, as always they have before. We select the best men in each county to raise troops, men who know their neighbors, know who can be trusted. Men have only to keep their mouths closed, to collect weapons, and, when Ormonde lands, to march. Nothing more.

Then events will take over. Others will join. Their hearts will make them do so. It is possible even the English army will declare for King James. They still love the Duke of Ormonde, as you just said."

Rochester twisted and turned in his chair, as if there was no place of comfort. His face set stubbornly. "I cannot agree to this plan."

God in Heaven, thought Slane, you cannot desert us now. "We have a plan, which those in Paris have agreed to, which those in Italy have agreed to, which a man like the Duke of Ormonde risks his life to lead. Don't you see, having a plan and moving with it is half the battle. Moving forward with confidence and courage is what is necessary now."

Moving forward, not dithering like old women over their teacups, or old men. Old men lost their will. He and Wharton had talked of that the other night: The older Jacobites here were becoming too weary and too cautious, but would not allow the young ones their head.

"The Duke of Ormonde will make up the difference foreign troops might. I've heard it said you would follow Ormonde to perdition. Don't you think there are soldiers in the army right this moment who feel the same way?"

"Perdition is here, Slane, in this chamber. I carry it in my heart. I curse the day all of this began. There have been three failed invasions since 1714, Slane, three. During one of them I sat in the House of Lords as discovered traitorous letters were read, and listened to my own words."

"Your courage is well known. No one doubts it." Display it now.

"I have the courage of a dozen lions, Slane, with the right plan. I cannot consent to this. It is too weak."

"Another time like this may not come again soon. People still hold a grudge for the South Sea Bubble. Sir Alexander Pendarves and Lady Shrewsborough were talking of it only a day or so ago, and you know what a loyal Whig Pendarves is. Yet even he is troubled by the malaise that hangs over the kingdom. The time is ripe. The realm is unsettled, the dislike of the King as great as it was during the first year of his reign."

"Others must be consulted. I will not bear the burden of this decision alone."

Slane knelt before Rochester's chair, the bones of his face hard, as was his voice, absolute in its sincerity, the eyes blazing, compelling, drawing one in, so that Rochester closed his own eyes, as if he must do so or be singed.

"You are our leader. Leave perdition to me. I am here to serve only you—that is my command, from the mouth of King James himself. You served his father, James II, and his sister, Queen Anne, and you will serve him. Only you can bring him to the throne, and when he sits upon it, as is his God-given right, you will see that all wretchedness and all worry were worthwhile, and you will be rewarded, as no other man who serves him, for both your skill and your pain. I swear that to you. Where you lead, others will follow. Lead strongly now. I will be your right arm in all things. I am commanded to stay with you for as long as you need me. I will stay even past that."

"I feel as our Lord Christ did in the wilderness during his temptation. Are you angel or devil, Slane?"

"A little of both, sir, like every child of God."

"Nonetheless, I do not support this plan. I must talk with others."

"And if they agree to the plan?"

Rochester was silent.

Slane closed his eyes so that Rochester should not see the rebellion and anger in them, his mind on the arguments there would now be as some men, already frightened, backed away from Jamie's side, and thus frightened others off. We fiddle while Rome burns, Slane thought. And our leader does not wish to lead.

The Princess of Wales yawned behind her hand. Ah, tedium. She played another card, knowing she would win the hand. Her mood was not improved even by the fact that her windows at Hampton Court had the finest view of the gardens, with their avenues, their fountains, and Sir Christopher Wren's landscape canal, the Long

Water, which reflected now a magnificent sunset. The day had gone well enough, with the Prince playing at bowls and winning; later, there had been strolls in the gardens. The mistress, Mrs. Howard, and the old Earl of Peterborough became lost in the maze, to everyone's amusement and the Prince's open irritation.

A broad-shouldered yet feminine man, walking like a bear in heeled shoes, appeared in the doorway of her drawing room. He wore an outrageously large wig, rouge, lead paint to darken his brows, and—what he had become noted for, even more than for the paint upon his face—a diamond earring in one ear.

"Carlyle"—the Princess put down her cards and held out her hands for him to bow over—"you rescue me from death by boredom. Hervey, take my place at the card table so that I may speak awhile with this awful man." Tommy Carlyle had news, malicious bad news, about someone; it was in his face. It was one of the things she liked best about him. He could always be depended upon to know the worst, and to delight in telling it. He was a source of much information for her.

"Take me to the window," the Princess said, "and let us admire the sunset."

Once there, he handed her the broadsheet. The ink on it was so fresh it had been smudged by Carlyle's fingers. That was the way they did things here, with little news sheets printed on secret presses, spreading scandal and rumor, vilifying one's honor. People believed the written word, even if it was false. Her eyes ran quickly over the page: There had been a duel over the kingdom's most beautiful woman, a woman ruined by the South Sea, a woman who had had to flee to Virginia to escape a prince's lust. Lust, impiety, and immorality were the tokens of this reign, of this England ruined by parasites, bawds, and ugly whores who served His Majesty. There was another reference to the South Sea Bubble, a reminder of what all had suffered because of the greed that inspired it. "Ugly whores" was an insult to the Duchess of Kendall, the King's longtime mistress. The "beautiful woman" could only be Barbara, Lady Devane. In an uncharacteristic gesture, the Princess wadded the broadsheet up into a ball.

"The Duke of Tamworth and Tom Masham have dueled," said Carlyle. "I wonder if Tamworth's marriage is off, then. I was in the tavern when the quarrel began. So ugly. Tom Masham had been drinking, and he said—"

And here Carlyle abruptly halted, putting his hand to his mouth as if stopping himself from making the most enormous of mistakes. The Princess knew he amended what he was now about to tell her, just as she also knew that Carlyle did nothing accidentally.

"Masham brayed for all the world to hear that though Lord Russel's bed may be cold this winter, some Virginian's will be warm. You are shocked by my news, I see it. It is distressing. Awful. These lines about the South Sea—" Carlyle took the wadded broadsheet from her hand, unfolded it, and began to read: " 'Ministers protected those who were the cause of the distress of millions, the sinking of credit, the discouragement of trade, the lowering of stocks.' To my mind, Walpole didn't protect Lord Devane as he should have."

An expression of impatience crossed the Princess's face.

"I bore you. Everyone wants to be ended with the South Sea. With your permission, Highness."

As still as death, the Princess watched Carlyle go flitting like a giant moth from one person to the next, spreading the news. He had carried an extra broadsheet in his pocket. Of course. People were knotting into twos and threes, whispering what Carlyle told them now, what he had not said before: that Tom Masham had said that though the Prince of Wales's bed would be cold this winter, some Virginian's would be warm.

In a single moment, the Princess was transported back to two summers ago, when Barbara had walked through court and taken all hearts. And she, the Princess, who prided herself upon her calm, had been like a wounded lioness at her love-stricken prince.

The Princess hated court at this moment more than seemed humanly possible. Her image, if she had wished to walk close enough to see, was reflected back to her by dozens of pairs of eyes watching.

Does she know what was said? they wondered. Poor Princess, will she cry when she is alone? they asked. The Prince is not over his passion for Barbara; only look how he hangs upon her mother, Lady Alderley. Remember his grief at the news of Barbara's leaving; remember his rage. Barbara would have become mistress, if she'd stayed.

All of the Princess's life was played out before others: No quarrel was secret, no grief; even her suffering in childbirth had to be public so that others might see that the children born had in fact emerged from her royal womb, and no one else's.

The Princess could feel cold fury inside herself. Bad Barbara, wicked Barbara, how dare you walk among us again? If ever I am Queen of England, thought the Princess, I will banish you to a dungeon, the coldest, the darkest hole I can find, I swear it. And I will chain your mother there beside you.

Fury was good. It gave her the strength she needed to rise calmly, her gaze steady, and leave the drawing room with her expression serene. How can I hurt you, Barbara? she thought. Let me think of a way, I pray.

❧

"His Highness asks permission to enter," Mrs. Clayton, the Princess's attendant, whispered a little later.

The Princess felt a terrible futility for a moment. Why must her husband come now, when Barbara's name was still like a brand on her flesh? Except, of course, that he had no one else with whom to share the truth of his own feelings. And she had long ago accustomed him to the freedom of telling her everything, even when what he told could only hurt her.

It was one of her holds over him—a hold that cost her, but she had long practice at mastering emotion, at allowing good sense to rule. Now she glanced at herself in her mirror. Her hair was brushed to shining; there was an attractive bedcap upon it; her bedgown was thin, white, sheer. Much would be aroused in him. She loosened her nightrobe. Mrs. Clayton opened the door, and the Prince of Wales raged in, waving the broadsheet. He was squarely made, pale-skinned and pale-eyed, the eyes bulging slightly. He was brave in battle, stupid in policy.

"Listen to this!" He began to read aloud without so much as greeting her. " 'The duel is yet another example of the immorality and impiety which flourish like foul weeds under this set of His Majesty's ministers, men who would give succor to dissenters and atheists—' "

On and on he went, reading aloud the points the broadsheet so cleverly made, with its reference to various acts passed during these last years that had been unpopular. In this quarrelsome country, there was no act that did not displease someone.

You comprehend, the King had once said, that we rule here by a thread of English law, the law that he who rules must be Protestant. This law, which makes us the rightful King, can be unmade as well. Cousin James has as much claim to this throne as we, save that he is Catholic. They tried to remake the law the last year of Queen Anne's reign. If she had lived months longer, they would have. The English.

" 'A man who cannot command his gentlemen cannot command a kingdom,' he will say!" The Prince was still ranting. It was one of his faults: He could not control his temper. " 'Your gentlemen drink too much,' my father will say! 'They gamble! They whore! They plot and intrigue! You are not fit to follow in my footsteps. I ought to send you back to Hanover instead of allowing you to intrigue against me here!' Intrigue against him! I do nothing! My gentlemen do nothing! To duel over a woman is commonplace!"

He was making his way around to Barbara. The Princess sensed it. He wished to say her name. He wished the Princess to hear him say it, and to allow him to weep and bewail her absence.

The Prince laid his head in the Princess's lap, and she stroked his high, square forehead, knowing the workings of his mind far better than he did himself. He longed for those delicious, lazy, golden days of the summer before last, for the blossoming time of lust for Barbara, which had fooled him into thinking that with a young and lovely enough mistress—after all, Mrs. Howard was now in her third decade; the Princess and the Prince in their fourth—time would stand still for him. He saw that the King might live for years, and he, as Prince, be obliged to play the role of court second for an endless time. And he and his father did not agree; they quarreled often enough to have the English laughing over it. Mooning after Barbara gave him new worlds to conquer; it disguised the truth.

But they could none of them go back to that time, and Barbara was, after all, in Virginia.

"I regret the absence of the Mollies," he said.

The Mollies had been her two loveliest maids of honor, Molly Lepell and Molly Belenden. They had married and gone away from court. Like Harriet Holles, leaving quietly tonight with the Princess's permission, so that she didn't have to face the whispers and gossip about her fiancé and the duel.

And the huntress's whelp Barbara, thought the Princess. You regret her absence also. But you may not say so; your pride will not allow it. Her manner of leaving has hurt that pride.

I had thought the whelp might become mistress in spite of her disinclination, for who ever knows all of what is in the heart of another? Dear God, I thought, not such a young, beautiful woman with what under all that flirting may well be wit. The combination did truly frighten me, allied as it was to the huntress her mother, who has no heart.

I thought your loving pity for Barbara after her husband's death and the dismantling of his handsome house, would finally play out the game. I saw how beautiful, how drooping she was at her husband's memorial service, saw how affected you were by it. Defeat and humiliation looked to be my supper. I could not sleep at night. Walpole, I said, confiding in him, as never I have before, because he caught me in a moment of despair, what am I to do?

Patience, he counseled. See what Fate provides. And then word came that Barbara had gone to Virginia. The whelp just slipped away, like a thief in the night. Too amusing, too delicious. And so very, very foolish. It was good to know Barbara could be foolish. The Princess never was.

"And Lady Devane," said the Princess now, lingering over the name deliberately. "She was an ornament to our court, like the Mollies. But she was far more dangerous. First, the Landsdowne duel. And now this one of Tamworth's. Our young men will do better without her provocative presence. I must tell you I have always felt it thoughtless of her, hurtful, discourteous, to leave us the way she did, with no farewell. It showed a lack of regard for our position. For you. My dear little Harriet Holles has already left the court. It may be the marriage to Tamworth will not go through—a pity, for it was a handsome alliance. The Tamworths have not always been steady in their loyalty, my love. This marriage would have assured it."

"Well, then, Lady Devane is bad."

Very bad to still be so much in your thoughts, thought the Princess. The huntress knew, didn't she, that once her whelp became a habit to you, you would never stray. What luck I've had, for the whelp ran away, but I am here. I will be, always, the first and oldest and wisest of your habits. And one day, I will be Queen. And then, Barbara, beware. Beware, in fact, even now.

The Prince put his hand on the Princess's breast, visible through the sheer gown and the opened nightrobe; she put her hand over his.

He was lord and master, wasn't he? Prince of this kingdom, wasn't he? Without him, she would not be all she must be, all she was, wiser, more politic, more cunning than any man braying and striding on two legs through the court. He who hath patience may compass anything. Walpole knew that, which made him a far more clever man than people suspected.

There was no one but her whom this prince could completely trust. That condition came with being a prince. In his very deepest of hearts, in spite of his tantrums, his rudeness, his sulks, his anger with his father, he knew that whatever his foolishness, she would aid him past it; that she was, in truth, though neither of them ever admitted it, the more clever of the two. By far the more clever, almost as clever as her father-in-law, the foreigner, the "bumptious Hanoverian," as the English styled him, who had kept this querulous little island for himself a full seven years, more than had been prophesied. The Prince knew he had not his father's cleverness, but he knew that his wife had. A little knowledge was a dangerous thing, wasn't it?

"She is bad," the Princess agreed, leaning back, letting her white, plump legs go slack. "She needs punishment. We must think of a way to punish her."

He pulled at the front of her gown, like a demanding child. "Yes."

"Show me how you would punish her. . . . Ah . . ."

Yes, thought the Princess, as the Prince pushed himself against her. And so we will punish her, beginning now. I will remind you of her fickleness and faithlessness, her rudeness and snubs, so that into your love will grow such a fear that a saint—and Barbara is no saint—could not move past it. . . . Perhaps she will remain in Virginia. Yes, thought the Princess, the King feels guilt for all that Roger suffered unfairly. He has already granted her relief from taxes in Virginia. Perhaps, if more relief is granted, she will stay there forever and ever, amen. Now, there is a prayer. Keep her debt high here, her life good in Virginia. Can I accomplish it? He who hath patience may compass anything. And so may she.

CHAPTER 14

Diana sat at her dressing table trimming her nails with a pair of tiny ivory-and-gold scissors, a task of which Clemmie, her servant, did not approve, for there was a right day and a wrong day to do such tasks, the old country sayings were passed down for just such things, and her mistress had chosen the wrong day.

" 'Cut them on Monday, cut them for health,' " Clemmie muttered as she set out the gown her mistress would wear this day. The sounds coming from her—she resembled nothing so much as a barrel, round and large—were a rumble, but clear enough so that the words "Monday" and "health" emerged.

"You sound like my mother's familiar, that great crone Annie. Be quiet or I'll send you to Tamworth to do penance for me."

" 'Cut them on Friday, cut them for sorrow. Cut them on Saturday, your true love tomorrow—' " came from Clemmie's direction.

There was a knock on the door, imperious and impatient. Diana and Clemmie looked at one another; there was only one person who would have pursued Diana to Hampton Court.

Robert Walpole, one of the King's ministers, First Lord of the Treasury, and Chancellor of the Exchequer, and surely one of the most hated men in England at this moment, opened the door and walked inside, just as if he and Diana had not been quarreling since June.

"By God's blood! You might have at least let me know you were going to leave London," he said, pulling off his dark periwig, tossing it upon the bed, running one pudgy hand through cropped hair, taking in the spectacle of Diana at her dressing table, one stocking on, one off. The garter tied round the leg with the stocking on it featured an embroidered motto in bright thread.

" 'My heart is fix'd, I cannot range.' "

He quoted the motto on the garter. He knew it because he had given her the garter, and the stockings, too.

She was in her chemise and stays. The chemise was white lawn, as sheer as nothing, and through it Walpole could see her bare legs, her thighs, the dark hair between. The stays had been embroidered with silver thread, and over her shoulders she wore a Spanish shawl, its garish colors suiting her dark beauty. Her breasts rose out of the stays, almost completely uncovered, lush, full. Walpole was not a man easily discouraged, but the continued quarrel with Diana was telling on him. She had been his mistress for a long time, but since Barbara's leaving in June, they had been quarreling, and it hurt his heart.

"How dare you leave without telling me where you were going?"

She blamed him for the fact that Roger's fine was not more reduced, blamed him for Barbara's leaving. "Diana, I will not abide this treatment. No woman is going to deal with me so. I could wring your neck like a chicken's and not regret it once—"

Tiny scissors went sailing past his face. Just to the left of him they bounced from the painted paneling and fell like an ivory-and-gold butterfly to the floor. If they'd hit an eye, they would have blinded him. The action seemed to calm him.

"Everyone is talking of the duel," he said. "I'm told Tom Masham is quite ill."

The throwing of the scissors had not surprised him, but the immediate weeping that followed these words did. Diana was capable of the most beautiful weeping he had ever seen a woman do, with no reddened eyes, no dripping, red nose, just tears running down that once-matchless face from still-matchless violet eyes. It meant nothing when she did so, except that she had decided tears would obtain whatever it was she wished to have. But he knew her well enough to know that she wept genuinely now.

Some emotion within her was touched, some truth, some need. He was so used to her tricks and lies that it threw him off stride. Walpole felt his own throat tighten with emotion. Diana had had her share of sorrow. Children dead, her daughter widowed, gone away. Damn it, she was the most immoral, selfish, ruthless bitch he had ever had the misfortune to know, the fortune to bed, and the stupidity to care about. He went to her and knelt down at her side and took her in his arms, crushing her against his great belly. She felt as supple as any man's dream of an odalisque. He desired her, as he always desired her, and he loved her, the more fool he. Her weeping broke his heart.

He held her to him, and she was soon ruining his fine shirt with her powder and rouge and lead eyepaint, spoiling his expensive waistcoat and the lace cravat around his neck. Now, he thought. He half dragged, half carried her to the bed, and lay down there beside her. They had been quarreling for two months. He held her close and stroked her bare back under the Spanish shawl, his hands roaming to the front of her stays, untying the laces, as he murmured to her, determined, concentrated.

Clemmie, seeing which way the wind blew, put the gown away and closed the door to leave them alone.

"Diana . . ." Walpole's fingers kneaded the bare flesh of her back, then drifted again to her front; he had finally opened the stays. God, her breasts. He wanted to put his face between them. He wanted to touch them, lick them. It had been too long since they'd lain together.

"Barbara ought to be here. She ought to take advantage of this duel—" she was saying.

He kissed her mouth, kissed her face, and unbuttoned the buttons of his breeches at the same time; he was nothing if not single-minded. Diana had been out of his bed for too long over this quarrel, and while women were easy to find, a woman like Diana was not.

He could feel the desire in him like flame, licking at him the way a woman might, tongue hot and pointed. Her tears only made him desire her even more. He found her weeping extraordinarily erotic.

He groaned and bit her neck, even though she tried to move away. Her breasts were bare now, and he moved over onto her, stopping the litany of her daughter's name with his mouth. And then he could not help himself—the sight of her, her near nakedness, her smell, her lushness, their quarrel, her anger with him, his with her, made him a wild man.

He pulled off the chemise and held her legs apart with his and was pushing into her. And then he was home, he was in his glorious, wanton, maddening Diana, and only he knew he loved her and how dangerous that made their relationship. For she had no compassion, no kindness in her. She was brutal and primitive, the most selfish person he had ever known in his life; God help him for loving her. If his wife had been dead—and thank God she was not—he would have married her, knowing that he could count on neither loyalty nor passion to hold her. She was a wild beast; for this moment he tamed her, made her bend to his will, but for this moment only.

God, those thoughts made him frenzied. He wanted to crush her with his desire, his need. He wanted to scream it into the morning. He moved against her steadily, purposefully, quickly for a heavy man. He spent himself in her, and his tongue was down her throat, all inside her mouth, here, there, everywhere, he wanted her so, he needed her so. And she lay like a rag doll under him and did not caress him or kiss him back once. And then there it was, that peak all men climbed for, making him shiver, making him groan, making him sink against her and whisper her name. He had enough sense—but only just enough—not to tell her he loved her.

She wiggled out from under him; he half expected her to get up, to order him out, but she lay quiet beside him, and he thought to himself: Yes, she has missed my presence in her bed. We will mend this yet.

Sleep was coming over him with the safety of that thought, with the satisfaction of desire. God, he needed sleep. He had not had a peaceful night's rest since they had begun to quarrel, and now the mob in the streets was howling for his head—they called him Skreen Master, old Skreen, screening the guilty, called him many another vile thing. He felt like a bear baited by hounds, those pitiful moth-eaten bears pulling against their chain while dogs lunged at them, dogs whose jaws locked until death once they had you in their vise. The things said of him, written of him. He had feelings, like any other man.

God's wounds, it was good to be here in bed with Diana, his terrible, selfish love, who would forgive him. He'd make her forgive him. Sunderland. Wily, corrupt viper of a fellow minister he had no choice but to clasp to his bosom. There was a rumor that there were to be changes in the ministry, that the firm of Townshend and Walpole, as he and his brother-in-law liked to call themselves, was out—never mind that the Walpole of it had saved the King's favorite minister, the viper himself, from being forced to resign in disgrace. Trust; there was no one to trust at these levels. . . . He was asleep, like a baby, large and sated, for the moment.

Diana leaned up on one elbow and stared at him, beached beside her. She pushed him, and he rolled over with a snore. His shirt had opened to show the thick, dark, curling hair on his chest. His breeches were open, too, and he was exposed there, satisfied, limp. He had not even taken off his shoes.

"Rutting hog," she said. She pulled his wig from the table and wiped between her legs with it.

Later, when he woke, she was at her dressing table again, and Clemmie was kneeling to tie a garter upon her leg. Walpole sat up in the bed and began to pull off his crumpled clothes, throwing them to the floor. Dark, thick hair covered his shoulders, arms, hands. In his middle years, he was stout, solid, with legs like the trunks of trees.

" 'My heart is fix'd, I cannot range.' I cannot range, sweetling, for you have my heart. First decent rest I have had since you told me you never wanted to see me again."

He chuckled, plumped up the pillows, and settled himself back into them, for all the world as if he were in his own bedchamber, among his own family, the picture of good humor and sincerity. He was good-humored and sincere in it most of the time, two of his most valuable traits.

"Clemmie, my dumpling, my fine, fat cow, a cup of wine, if you please. Where are you going, pet?"

"I am supposed to walk with the Prince in the garden. This duel has upset him. He will complain about Barbara to me. A year," she was saying to her frowning self in the mirror, "it will likely take a year before she can be home again. If she were here, we could act—"

And do what? thought Walpole.

"It is a colony, for God's sake—what will she find to do there? I go half mad when I think too much upon it, all she gave up," she was saying.

Tommy Carlyle, one of the more outrageous courtiers, had appeared at court with a black band around his arm just after the news was everywhere that Barbara had gone to Virginia. For whom do you grieve? he had been asked. I grieve for Lady Alderley's failed ambitions, he answered. London and court had laughed over the answer for weeks.

"—She could never be satisfied watching hemp—"

"Tobacco," corrected Walpole, absently.

"—grow on the wrong side of the ocean. She is too headstrong, impulsive. She always was. I blame my mother for all this."

And me, and anyone else you can, he thought. Except yourself.

"I am writing to her, this very day, to come home now," Diana said. "And by the by, I am leaving for London this afternoon."

What's she up to? wondered Walpole. No good. "Come here and let me comfort you, my sweetheart. Let me hold you in my arms. Last time, I had thought only of myself, but this time, I will see you pleasured, too—"

"She would not have left, if the debt were not so large. The debt would not be so large if Roger's fine had been reduced."

"Diana, I could do no more than I did. How many times must I tell you that in time, the fine will be reduced. Although this broadsheet has done little to help. People are muttering about the South Sea again, as if it were autumn a year ago and the stock was just starting to fall. When memories are not so vivid, I will see that the fine is reduced."

If I am still a minister, he thought. Besides, Barbara's young. A journey to a colony was a moment in the longer span of her life. In a year or so, he'd have a fair portion of the fines returned; the King had promised from the beginning to support it. Will they use the Bubble against me for the remainder of my reign? the King had asked.

Yes.

"I said, come here."

To his great surprise she obeyed; but afterward, when she had finished her dressing and left him alone, he felt desolate. He lay back against the pillows on her bed, staring up at the design woven in the canopy above him, thinking about the broadsheet, so vicious, striking sharply and accurately, like a snake, to wake memories of loss and anger at that loss. The viper Sunderland, the King's favorite minister, argued that Tories ought to be allowed in the cabinet. They would not intrigue with the Jacobites here, he said, if they saw that they might be ministers. The policy of excluding them is wrong-headed. Is it? Walpole asked himself. Am I wrong-headed?

Only time would tell. A man had to trust time and himself and very little else.

❧

"You are eating too much toast," said Annie. "She has eaten too much all day," she said to their visitor at Tamworth Hall. It was Jane Cromwell, who was Sir John Ashford's daughter.

Scarlet leaves, scarlet berries, scarlet ribbons in her hair, thought the Duchess. October is a scarlet month. From where she sat, she could see a certain Tamworth hillock with its ancient oaks, dropping acorns now, their leaves a wonderful autumn mix of yellow gold and crimson. Jane and Barbara had used to sit under the oaks when they were girls and play at supper with the acorns as cups. Fairy cups, they had called the acorn shells, for the shells were small enough that wood fairies and sprites might drink from them.

On the ground now, under the oaks, were the ripe acorns, hundreds of them. The birds would leave the shells behind, but there were no more bright-eyed girls to gather them up and play. One was off to the colony of Virginia; the other was in the Duchess's parlor, with four children of her own, who had come one after another, like the steps of a stair. I don't like the way Jane is looking, Sir John had told the Duchess before leaving for London, determined to bedevil the Whigs this last session of Parliament. There is some trouble between her and Gussy. Now, Grandmama, I must ask you to look after Jane for me, Barbara had said, cajoling and charming as only Barbara could be. Bah, as if she needed asking. Harry and Jane had courted in the apple orchard. Jane was hers, as all things of Tamworth's were hers.

"Mother's cabbages have not blanched," Jane was saying to Annie.

"Did she put them on a stone floor?"

They might have been discussing a treaty, so serious were they, but fall was a time of purpose and activity for a country housewife: making preserves, harvesting and storing vegetables and herbs, making rushlights and tallow candles sweetened with beeswax, salting and smoking meat, preserving eggs in salt, protecting potatoes from frost; fall was a time of harvest and storage, a time to hoard against the cold, snowbound days of winter, when frost rimmed windows and kitchen pails.

Barbara would be seeing to something like it in Virginia, she or her servants. The Duchess imagined a vast platoon of servants against the large bulk of a handsome stone house; some of the servants would be dark, like Hyacinthe. The Duchess saw a smaller Tamworth when she thought of Virginia.

"Such a silly thing," Jane said. "On the way over, I thought I saw a witch."

Jane, always the possessor of a sweet and tremulous smile, had it still. She'd lost a child last year, a boy four years old. No hoyden like Barbara, no rogue like Harry, Jane had always reminded the

Duchess of the violets in her woods, their timid petal faces hidden, drooping away from the bold gaze of the world, which hurried by, thinking, because it did not have the patience to see, that there was nothing there. Blessed are the meek: for they shall inherit the earth.

The Duchess had never liked that verse. No one with any sense would want this earth, what with its greed and malice and ill-doing. Blessed are they that mourn: for they shall be comforted. That was more like it. Look after Jane, Grandmama. So ordered Barbara, keeper of the Duchess's heart. Even wood violets ought to have their day.

"No such thing as witches. Superstitious nonsense. This is 1721, not 1621," she said.

"Gypsies," said Annie. "I have heard there are Gypsies about."

"Have Perryman warn the stable boys to keep an eye out, Annie. I will not have Gypsies camping in my woods. They'll rob us blind."

"Yes," said Jane. "I must have seen a Gypsy woman in the woods."

"I have a mind," said the Duchess, "to send Barbara geese, sheep, a cheese press, and bees." Though her beemaster was being difficult about it.

"I do so miss Barbara," Jane said.

"And I have a mind to plan another herb garden for spring. Of course, I am old. Not as strong as I once was. My mind wanders and will not stay on its task, Jane. . . . Angelica and anise for the herb garden . . . perhaps broomwort and balm."

"I could help you, while I am here."

"Caraway and chamomile."

"Comfrey and coriander and cowslip," said Jane.

Jane humors me, thought the Duchess, in my dotage. Good, I need humoring, and taking care of. We'll have the roses back in those cheeks, Janie, yes, we will. You'll bloom again in the sun of a Tamworth autumn, planning my herb garden. Your mind will be busy with something other than grief.

"I have a cowslip pudding recipe in my mother's old receipt book; sweetest thing you ever put a tongue to. Pennyroyal and peony and pansy. Rosemary and rue," the Duchess said.

"Rue water kills fleas," said Annie.

"Thorn apple and thyme and violet. Such a pretty song I've made, Jane," said the Duchess. "You must harvest the herbs on a fine dry day, only the best of them. Dry them in the shade. Put them in bags to dry, and when they crumble, pour them into wide-necked bottles—"

"—securely stopped," finished Annie.

Jane looked down at her hands. "I cannot stop thinking of Jeremy."

Jeremy was the child who had died. Of course Jane could not stop thinking of him.

"He was always afraid of the dark. At night, I sometimes dream he calls to me. 'Mama,' he says, and I wake thinking the coffin is too tight, the sides press in on him. He was afraid of the dark."

"I'll want a good herb garden. There will be no shirking if you're to help with it. What about a kitten for those children of yours, heh? Dulcinea, shall we give Jane one of our kittens?" Dulcinea was the Duchess's cat. The Duchess named all her cats Dulcinea.

"Father would—"

"Mind? All the way from London? Unless the kitten is Whig, he won't be thinking of us. You leave your father to me."

You call upon Tony, she'd told Sir John, and you give him this letter. The letter told Tony that it was her wish that Sir John continue to represent Tamworth in the House of Commons. She also gave her opinions of the men on the various other properties Tony owned, but added, graciously, that since Tony was now duke he might do as he pleased, except for Sir John. She wrote to guide him, she told him, for he had been a boy at the last election of members to the House of Commons seven years ago. "You'll want men you can trust," she wrote him. "You'll want men who will vote as you ask them to, when there is some act you want passed. You'll need to make certain they understand, for they hold their places for seven years, and in seven years, a man can become independent of his patron, if he isn't reminded that that will not do." She'd written the names of men she thought he ought to talk to, men who were used to wielding influence through the members they controlled in the House of Commons. "Whether you are Whig or Tory," she had written, "I do not care, as long as you act in the interests of this family, as long as you select men who will do so, from their end, also."

"Letters."

Tim, her footman, who had been to the village for letters, walked into the chamber. Grinning a broken-toothed grin—his two front teeth were chipped off at the middle—he made a bow and put a letter in her lap.

It was from Tony. The Duchess's heart fluttered like a girl's. June, July, August, September, October. Finally, Tony forgave her for Barbara. On October the tenth, the Duchess thought to herself, feeling joy, my grandson and I were reconciled. She ripped past the seal.

"I told you he would write. My bones. I felt it in my bones," Annie said to Jane.

A duel. He was fighting a duel and asked her prayers if he died. Died? Tony could not die. There was to be his wedding, and an election. She saw suddenly Tony sitting next to her bed last spring, calmly discussing Barbara's troubles. She remembered the strength in that face, and the quiet passion. Enormous fear combined now with shock; she could not breathe; she clawed at the air before her, and the cat in her lap leaped away. The world was whirling. Everyone's face loomed large at her, Jane's, Tim's, Annie's, mouths all open at once saying things she could not hear. Why did they mumble so that she could not hear, when they knew she was old?

Richard, she thought, they've made me fall with their foolishness. Catch me.

"What is it?" The Duchess pulled her bed linens up stubbornly to hide her mouth.

"It is a syrup of violets for fever," Annie said.

"I do not have a fever."

"You are too warm! I felt your forehead myself. And your cheek. You are too warm!"

It was not like Annie to be so emotional. The Duchess opened her mouth to the syrup. Heartache was a tight band around her heart. Syrup of violets did not cure heartache. But try telling Annie that.

"Is Jane still about?"

"Of course she is still about! You must sleep. You must—"

"Send her to me; then I will sleep."

In the antechamber, Tim and Perryman, the steward, went to Annie and hovered over her like a pair of birds whose bad-tempered chick has fallen from the nest.

"What did—"

"Is the Duke—"

Annie swept past them to Jane. Of course the Duke was not dead. If he had been, they'd have known already. A special messenger would have been sent. The letter had been written before the duel, it appeared to Annie, in case the worst happened, and an idiot servant must have sent it by mistake.

"It's you she desires to see," Annie said to Jane, and to the men, darkly, "I will deal with you presently."

Annie ushered Jane into the bedchamber. The draperies were drawn now, the chamber quiet. "Do not tire her."

With a whirl of skirts Annie was gone again. Jane sat down carefully on the big bed.

"I've sent Barbara to a paradise," the Duchess said. "In Virginia there are grapes and poplars, pines and cedars. Wood grows at every man's door so fast that after it has been cut down, it will grow up again in seven years' time to firewood. There are cherries and plums and persimmons. I miss Barbara, Jane. She was the light of this house—our candle, Annie called her. 'There goes our candle.' The Duke of Tamworth loves her. Did you know that? He has not forgiven me for sending her away. But I did what I did for the best. Why can people not see that? That I act for the best, always. Do you remember the time you and Barbara and Harry fed my pigs brandy? I thought the grooms would die from laughing. And it was my best brandy, too."

"The duel?"

"If Tony were dead, they would have sent word by now." You thought I was not good enough for her, Grandmama, Tony said in her mind, but I am. The memory of those words hurt.

"I used to tell Jeremy about my adventures with Barbara and Harry. At the last, I told them over and over because they seemed to comfort him. He died in my arms," said Jane.

"No better place to die."

A woman was not a set of stone wheels and wooden ratchets, was she? the Duchess thought. Needing only grease to forever turn. Each child she bore took time to grow inside her, took strength from her. I will greatly multiply thy sorrow and thy conception, the Lord said. In sorrow thou shalt bring forth children. Easy enough for Him to command. He did not have to birth them, and He did not have to bury them. See to Jane, Grandmama, Barbara had commanded. But it seemed that Jane saw to the Duchess instead.

"See that miniature there," the Duchess pointed, and Jane took a portrait from the bedside table. "My son, Giles, was the only one of the three to resemble me; the others were Richard Saylor's to the inch. But Giles was mine, small, dark, bright as three brass buttons. He died of smallpox, Jane. He was away at school, and we'd heard there was smallpox near, and I sent Perryman to fetch him, and he brought him home, all right, but in a coffin. I did not see him before he died. I saw none of my boys before death. So you see, Jane, you have the better of me, for at least your Jeremy died with loving arms tight around him."

Jane touched at her eyes.

Yes, weep, thought the Duchess, go ahead. Don't let them tell you not to weep. Don't let them tell you not to sorrow. They do, you know. Her mind went to Richard, of how his grief and guilt turned inward and into madness, and reduced him day by day until in the end she had lost her golden man and buried his mad shadow. She would never love anyone the way she had loved Richard Saylor. Wood violets and lionhearts, impossible not to adore. Hold my hand, Jane, and let my old age find comfort in your shining youth.

In the antechamber, Perryman said to Annie, "She is—"

"Warm! More than likely feverish!" Annie turned on Tim like a thin brown whirlwind. "Have you no sense? Dropping that letter on her like that!" She slapped at him, and he raised his arms to ward her off. Her blows would not have hurt him much anyway; he was twice her size. "Let me have all the letters from now on! *All* the letters!"

"It would not be proper," said Perryman. "I do not think I will allow that. I am steward of the household."

" 'Allow that'! You fat old capon! You are nothing! I am the Duchess's tirewoman! I know what is best!"

And then, to their surprise, Annie burst into tears and ran out of the door of the antechamber. Tim stared after her; he had never seen her cry before. He did not know the Lord had given her tear holes.

"You will continue to deliver the Duchess's letters as always," Perryman said, after a moment in which he and Tim were speechless. Naturally, Perryman recovered first. "However, if one should be from His Grace, the Duke, you will inform me of it so that I may prepare Her Grace properly."

Tim, a big, bold, merry-faced fellow, did not say anything. Give the letters to Annie. Give the letters to Perryman. Ha. The Duchess would hack his head off with a dull ax for doing so, and those two would stand on either side as his head rolled across the lawn, Perryman saying, None of my doing, none of my doing, and Annie, Hack him again.

Wonderful little broadsheet, thought Slane, pacing his small room like a lion while Rochester and others argued over the plan of invasion. London sizzled and buzzed with the news of the Duke of Tamworth and of the duel. The details, so obvious from the broadsheet, were simply too delicious. Everyone was talking about the South Sea Bubble, who had lost what. They were glad to remember perfidy and lies.

Tony waited in a small antechamber at St. James's Palace for the King to receive him, as commanded in the summons he had received. The ceiling was adorned with intricate plastering, created to surround allegorical paintings, which consisted of the usual nymphs in trailing, diaphanous robes, the inevitable warriors in their chariots. Tony was staring up at one of the nymphs, his mind not on what he looked at, not at all. There had been his life before the duel, and there was his life now. It seemed to him that he could move nowhere without looking up to see someone watching him. Whispers died away when he walked into a chamber, then began anew. Masham was quite ill—a fever in the blood, the doctor said.

Forgive me, Tony told Masham, for he had gone to see him each day since the duel. There is nothing to forgive, Masham said. I was a drunken fool. The duel had cleared Masham's mind wonderfully, as it had Tony's. I am sorry that your cousin's name should be so bandied about, said Masham.

Masham refused to talk to anyone, refused to admit there had been a duel. Tony did the same. But sometimes, when he caught a glimpse of himself in a mirror—and there was no great house in London without its wall of mirrors—he didn't know who it was staring back at him. He hated the gossip about him, but hated even more the gossip over Barbara. It was vicious. Never had there been so wanton a woman as Barbara, it seemed.

And so it seemed to him that he had failed her. Even though he knew that she would forgive him, he didn't know if he could forgive himself. Was it only a few days since the duel? It seemed lifetimes. And his fool of a valet had sent off the letters, so that his mother and sister had done nothing but weep for days. You might have died, they told him, weeping. How could you? Barbara is bad for everyone, they said.

Behind him, someone remarked, "Yes, there is a resemblance to the divine Barbara in the nymph farthest to the left, I quite agree."

Tony looked to see who spoke so. Tommy Carlyle. Hulking,

rouged like a woman, standing on shoes with heels enameled a deep red, the clear signature of a gentleman of fashion and of a certain age. No younger men wore them anymore. Carlyle sat down on one of the silk-covered benches, crossed his legs, admired the bows upon his shoes.

"One hears that you were seen coming out of Holles House yesterday. How are Lord Holles and his countess—and your sweet young bride-to-be?"

Carlyle probed for news, like the bird of prey he was. Tony kept his face stoic. It seemed to him these last days that his face had frozen into place. "Very well, thank you."

"You may as well tell me all, as I shall find out one way or another. Is the marriage on or off? I am more a friend to you than you know, Tamworth."

I've lost what little reason I have left, Tony thought to himself, for I feel like telling him. Carlyle could not have kept a secret if his tongue were taken out.

"I have the honor to take Harriet as my bride in a year."

So much he did not tell Carlyle: the humiliation of having to wait for Lord Holles in the drawing room like a disobedient boy; telling Harriet's father the truth, the apology tight in his throat. Asking if he might see Harriet to apologize to her, but not being allowed to.

The Duke of Wharton was her cousin. He'd get Wart to take a private letter to her. In it he would beg her pardon for his behavior, tell her that though her father had merely put the marriage off for a year, she might step back from it completely if she wished. He would honor her wishes over her father's. It seemed only fair.

"Do I offer congratulations or condolences? You are too choice a plum, my dear Duke. If you were half-witted and crippled, they would marry their daughter to you."

"I have no wish to call off the marriage."

Carlyle was silent a moment, digesting this. Then, he said, "One hears that a certain banker has been to Devane Square: Sir Gideon Andreas, who I need not remind you is otherwise known as Midas Andreas. Sir Gideon is among trustees who are to sell the assets collected from the South Sea directors to pay their fines. Those board members will put more than one estate in their pockets, I would imagine. Has he a fancy to obtain Devane Square for himself, do you think? And I swear I noticed an infinitesimal slackening of vigor in Walpole, our plump Norfolk squire, at certain key points in the debates over the directors' fines, over Roger's fine."

"Roger and Walpole were friends."

"And friends never betray friends—is that it? Interest in self never wins out?"

"Are you saying Walpole did not defend Roger? That's one manner of interpreting it. But I saw a man who saved whomever he could, a man who now pays the price of great odium for having done so. I thought you and Walpole were friends."

"Ah, here comes the King's servant. You have an interview with His Majesty, do you not? Yes, I know that, too. Annoying, isn't it, how I know everything. People talk, and I listen. You have much to learn, my dear Duke, about policy and intrigue. Shall I be your teacher? First lesson, Tamworth: Some rise by sin, and some by virtue fall."

A servant stood silently in a doorway. Tony stood. "Do you include yourself in that?"

"Of course." And then, surprising Tony, Carlyle said, "Call upon me whenever you wish. I better than anyone understand betrayal, and friendship."

In the private apartments of the palace, a Turkish soldier who was one of the King's personal attendants—the King was known, and not belovedly, as the gentleman who kept two Turks—bowed to Tony and opened a door inset into a paneled wall. For a moment, Tony heard the sound of a woman singing—she had a pleasing voice—and the high, sharp notes of a harpsichord. Through the door he was able to obtain a quick glimpse of royal domesticity. A young woman, one of the Duchess of Kendall's nieces, sang like a human songbird to the composer Handel, who stood with her at the harpsichord. Kendall herself, jewels blazing around her thin arms and neck, stood by an enormous bird cage, its shape a duplicate of the Tudor gatehouse of this palace. The birds inside it were singing also.

Tony just caught the shape of the Duchess's mouth saying, "Listen." The man to whom she spoke was Robert Walpole. The King walked forward through the door; with him was his dwarf, a court jester, brought from Hanover. That was another thing everyone mocked, that the Hanoverians were so barbaric they still had court jesters. The door closed again behind them. Tony could still hear the muted music rise and fall, the voice and harpsichord point and counterpoint.

"Lovely music, Your Majesty," he said, bowing.

His heart was beating like a drum to summon soldiers to battle. There was every possibility that the King would ask him to give up his place as one of the gentlemen who served the Prince of Wales. That would be the closest thing to punishment Tony could expect, since Masham did not admit to a duel, and neither did he, and therefore, there had not been one. There was only a broadsheet about one.

"Lovely music from a lovely young woman."

The King spoke in French. The gentleman from Hanover, as the King was called when someone wanted to insult him, had a long nose and jowly cheeks, both objects of much derision in the news sheets. But his eyes, quite pale, were shrewd and not unkind.

"Your conduct . . ." The King had soldiered with Tony's grandfather, with Marlborough and Prince Eugene and William of Orange, against the mighty ambitions of France's Louis XIV. "Your conduct distresses us. I think it would distress your grandfather. He was an honorable man, more than that, he was a grand seigneur."

That phrase signified something more than "gentleman." It meant someone who was noble in the largest sense, in every aspect of his conduct, upholding strictly the rules of his class and birth, acting at all times as he should, with honor and decorum. Tony felt blood rushing to his face. He kept his eyes upon the King's shoes, with their blunt, square toes, their diamond-and-silver buckles, their red heels—the sign of old men, now, those red heels.

"He is young."

The King spoke to the dwarf, as if Tony were not there. "Such is youth. Impulsive. Fiery. My dear Lord Devane's family has suffered enough. Tell him so. Tell him I require prudence from him. Tell him that he does the lady in question no good by misbehaving. Ask him if she has arrived in the colony. Ask him if there is any word from her. Tell him I sent her a message of goodwill. Tell him that."

"There is no word," Tony said.

"I will see the fine against her estate reduced one day, Tamworth. But not now, when there is a certain broadsheet on the streets that howls of my greed, that calls those whom I love bawd and parasite. You English are cruel. We have been dealing with the South Sea Bubble for over a year, and now we must press on to other things. Yet this rumor of a duel has been used by unscrupulous men to raise old matters again, to bring divisions among us. People are reminded once more of what they believe they have suffered. We have all suffered."

The King had finished. The dwarf was opening the door for him, and the music swelled out. The door closed, and all was muffled again. Tony was left alone.

The interview had not gone as he'd expected. What did I expect, thought Tony, some kind of punishment? The King shouting at him, telling him he was a fool and a hothead, the way the Prince of Wales would have done? Lord Holles did not say, "You are no man for my daughter," but instead, "Let us wait awhile, let rumors die."

Some rise by sin, and some by virtue fall.

He walked under the gatehouse of St. James's Palace, his mind on his next errand. His aunt Diana had come to London yesterday from Hampton Court, and been exceedingly busy ever since.

"Darling," said Diana, leaning over the stair rail above Tony; he had a vivid, startling look at her breasts. The rouge on her lips was crimson. She wore diamonds and sapphires, and she was beautiful—remarkable, really—in the candlelight.

"I called to see you," she said, walking down the stairs and holding out her hands affectionately to him. She had been affectionate since she'd known he wanted to marry Barbara. "But your mother said you were away from home."

"I must speak with you, Aunt."

"Of course. But come upstairs with me first; let me introduce my guests—"

"No, if you please—at once."

She put her arm through his, led him to a parlor. "You look awful, darling, tired and ill. You remind me, at this moment, of your father. I haven't thought of him in years. He was my favorite brother."

"Today I went to Tom Masham to see how he fared."

She did not turn her eyes away or busy herself with something; he had to give her that. She knew what was coming, and she faced him.

"He said you had called on him," he continued, "offered him coins not to admit to the duel. You also called upon Lord Holles. He would tell me nothing of your conversation, but he did ask me if there were prior commitments to which I was obligated, or which might prove embarrassing later. I cannot imagine what you had to say to him. You are not to interfere in my affairs."

"Do you or do you not want Barbara?"

The question took his breath away.

"Because if you do not, tell me so now, and I will allow you to do exactly as you please. You may drink yourself into oblivion, whore yourself into the pox and an early grave, and stand at the altar and marry the insipid Holles chit, who will bore you to death within the space of a year. I will not lift a finger to stop you. But if you want my daughter, you'd best listen. At this moment, in my drawing room, are several men from the Board of Trade and Plantations, as well as a Virginian or two in the bargain. Now, why do you think I endure their company? It is not for their wit or charm, I do assure you. It is because I think they may aid Barbara, and anything I may do to help her from this end of the world, I will do. If that means I must commit mayhem and murder, so be it. She is the only child left to me, and I want the world for her, Tony. I want everything this life has to offer a woman. I want her debt cleared. Security in a marriage such as she deserves. Children, houses, gowns, jewels, whatever she desires. She is not going to spend her days dependent and—"

"She is also not going to spend her days as the Duchess of Tamworth."

"You— You asked for her hand in marriage—" Diana actually stammered.

"She made the decision for both of us at the time. It was the proper decision, I see now." His head felt as if a thousand fireworks had lit themselves inside it and split him away to nothing. "Tell me, did you think I would share her, whether she was my mistress or my wife, with the Prince? Was that part of your plan?"

"Of course not. I would never—"

"You married her off to the highest bidder when she was fifteen. You encouraged her love affairs; you held her up to the Prince as if she were a choice bone, and he just the dog to enjoy her. From whom do you think Barbara fled, Aunt Diana? It was not from me. I am not the first man to act the fool over her, and I won't be the last. My ardor did not frighten her. I did not frighten her. I think she fled from you and your limitless, loveless ambitions, ambitions which have now led you to act in a manner I will not countenance. I have obligations that go beyond desire. You are not to include me into any of your ambitions, unless I give you express permission. And I do not give it. And you are not to meddle in my affairs, ever again."

The footman in the hall had to run to open the front door for him in time. Outside, he stood a moment before summoning a carriage to take him to the edge of town, to Devane Square.

Carlyle's words were in his mind. What was it that interested Midas Andreas, who turned everything he touched into gold? Once there, Tony walked on one of the bricked streets of the unfinished square, a square filled now with weeds, with gaping holes where once trees had been planted. Everyone in London had walked in the garden that had once been here; Roger had brought in plants from around the world. Only one end of the square had been built up into townhouses. These remained, though shorn of their beautiful fittings inside. There was also a small church designed by Sir Christopher Wren. The church and townhouses faced each other in lonely splendor among the fields between the road and Hyde Park. Their windows were boarded over, the front door locked with a chain. The decoration of the interior of the church had never been finished.

Tony walked behind the church to a fountain, where the entrance gates to the house had been. Moss scaled the fountain's sides, scaled the stone figure of a nymph. The house had been here, but there was nothing now, only bits of broken brick from the wall that had surrounded it. One could see the church spire of the hamlet of Marylebone in the distance. Every plant, every iron ornament, every windowsill—all, all had been sold to pay the fine, or stored away in a warehouse.

The sun glanced off the water of a landscape canal. Gone were the hundred orange trees in wooden tubs, the small, perfect stone Temple of the Arts Roger had built at one side, like a summerhouse, to hold his collection of paintings and statues.

The bell in the spire of the church at Marylebone began to ring. Andreas must think the city will move this way, thought Tony. Prices for land were low now; nothing much was selling. There was no building. What building there had been, was stopped.

"See how a crafty, vile projector picks Britannia's purse by South Sea shams and tricks." So went the saying that accompanied a popular woodcut; the face of the South Sea Company director in the print was Roger's. He was among the chief scapegoats of the crisis. I did what I could, Walpole had said, tiredly. The howls against Roger were too loud. Give me a year, Tamworth, perhaps two, and I will see the fine reduced. She has only to endure a year or two.

The figure of a woman rose out of a shell in the center of the fountain, like the famed Botticelli painting of Venus rising from the sea, except the woman's face and form were Barbara's. Tony reached out to touch the moss that covered one slim leg.

What was Carlyle's game?

Carlyle and Walpole had long been friends. What a high price Walpole paid for his place in the ministry; but everything had its pricc. Tony himself paid a price for being a duke. The price was that he must put duty and legacy over love.

And, then, again, the price brought its privileges. No one, it seemed, would do more than shake a finger at him. Even Masham forgave him. In fact, there was a likelihood he and Masham might become friends. They had laughed over that today. I feel like a rag doll from which the sawdust has been expelled, Masham had said, his face flushed with fever. I am a changed man, I swear it, Tamworth. Are you?

The character of heroes, the stuff of legend. And speculators, on my grandmother's side, thought Tony. Gamblers. My father was little more than a gambler in land and buildings, his grandmother had once said. Interesting, to try to envision the future, to speculate which way a city might sprawl.

I'm going to ride through London over the next few days, he thought, and look at what is happening, so that I can make certain Barbara profits from this land I stand on; she must not lose anything more. And then I am leaving town; I am going on a tour of my estates, to meet the men who want seats in the House of Commons come spring. But first, he was going home to write two letters: one to Harriet, and one to his grandmother, from whom he was no longer estranged. That, at least, had been accomplished by all this mess.

As a church bell nearby struck ten, Tony walked through the dark streets to his Aunt Shrew's. He felt almost happy. The letter to his grandmother was written. He whistled a little as he climbed the stairs up to Aunt Shrew's drawing room. As he had imagined, she was playing cards with her lover. They were both richly dressed, she in a ridiculous youthful dark auburn wig that curled down to her bony shoulders, as many jewels as she could find a place for everywhere, her face splashed with its usual helping of white powder, red rouge, and dark patches.

Pendarves was equally splendid in dark coat and grand periwig.

Knowing them as he did, Tony knew they had done little more than go for a drive in her carriage and eat their dinner. Anything else took away too much from cards. When she saw Tony, Aunt Shrew smiled, waving an arm that displayed a ring on every finger and bracelets to her elbow. She loved to rattle and jingle with jewelry. She prided herself on her jewelry. I know how to pick my lovers, she bragged to her great-nieces, who laughed at her behind their fans but would never have dared to do so to her face, and my lovers know how to pick my jewelry.

"Have a look at Lumpy," she said. "He's had a bath and is fit to bed the Queen. You look exhausted, young man. How was your interview with His Majesty? Am I to visit you in the Tower?" She cackled and played a card with a grand jangle of bracelets.

"I was asked not to duel again."

"A reasonable request, I must say. You owe me twenty pounds."

Tony went to stand behind her so that he could see her cards. He leaned down and kissed the top of her wig, smiling a little at her hand. She was going to win.

"You owe me twenty pounds, nephew, not a penny more, not a penny less. Leave this Harriet Holles now that you have scandal on your coattails, marry a Tory, and I will forgive you the debt, leave you all my funds in my will, and dance with blue satin shoes on at your wedding."

"I thought the goldsmith fled with all your funds, Aunt Shrew. Sir Alexander"—Tony turned to Pendarves—"who other than the late Earl Devane owns land off Tyburn Road?"

"The Grosvenors; Lord Scarborough. I have no idea who else."

The door opened, and Laurence Slane came into the chamber; his expression was somber, the dark brows elegant slashes above the dark eyes.

"You look full of news, Slane," said Aunt Shrew.

Slane looked over at Tony, who knew suddenly that his title of duke, his legacy of fame from his grandfather, did not matter. He was not, after all, to be let off lightly.

"It's Masham, isn't it?" Tony said.

"Not dead?" said Aunt Shrew, putting down her cards with a crash of bracelets.

"Yes," said Slane. "Tom Masham is dead."

⁂

Tony walked down Russell Street toward the central piazza of Covent Garden. The sellers of fruits and vegetables at Covent Garden were gone now. The three shacks were just beginning their revels. A little flower girl stood at the commemorative column in the center of the square; at her begging, he bought some bunches of flowers from her, and at the coin he gave her, she ran away whooping into the dark. Across, under an arcade, he saw a young woman sitting at the windows. She played a game of solitaire, looking out into the square every once in a while. She was attractive—there to be purchased, if a man wished. All cats are alike in the dark, said Charles, and no woman is worth devotion. You are wrong, Charles, Tony thought.

A carriage rolled by, the horses' hooves clip-clopping on the cobblestones. Words said today echoed in his mind, like the last round of a church bell:

Friends never betray, do they?

Your grandfather was an honorable man, a grand seigneur.

Tom Masham is dead.

Barbara could have married him. He had been so far gone in love he would have rushed off to be wedded to her by special license. She could have been the Duchess of Tamworth, and the estate left to him would have been plundered to nothing as the Devane debt ate it up for anyone who married Barbara, married the debt. It was the law. You're a good boy, Tony, my boy. I have killed a man, thought Tony, and over nothing. Heartbreak pales compared to this anguish.

He separated one bunch of flowers from among the others and put it at the base of a column that was in the center of the plaza. In honor of his grandfather, the grand seigneur, who created the legacy he now carried.

Then he laid a second bunch down by the first, for his father, whom he had known only a little, but who had died as bravely as a man may die.

Then he put down a third, for Barbara, as a final farewell to the woman who had not taken advantage of a callow, lovesick fool, who taught, as his father and grandfather had, that honor knows no sex, no age, no limit; honor knows only, and finally, behavior.

CHAPTER 15

Philippe, the French Prince de Soissons, stood at one of the long windows in the great parlor of Saylor House, staring at handsome gardens in which leaves floated down langorously, as if they had all the time in the world, to rest upon straight gravel walks and beds of flowers. Gardeners were about, raking them into piles, burning them. It was a scene of order, decorum, nature brought to man's bidding, the design of the gardens emulating on a miniature scale those across the Channel at the palace of Versailles. Versailles had been the wonder of civilized Europe in its building, and every royal house had copied its design; even these Hanovers, who had fought France during the wars and who now ruled England, had a small duplicate in their continental province.

Philippe had just come from the English court, which like all royal courts made every effort to duplicate the intricacies of French court etiquette and yet could not compare in any manner to the original. He was looking down at these gardens, so very French in their design: the avenues, the landscape pool, the fountain. This parlor, too, was filled with objects and furniture created by the finest of French craftsmen, even though the man who built it had defeated the French in battle. His companion, Tony's mother, Abigail, was dressed in a sack gown, the height of current fashion, a style from the French court.

It was clear to Philippe that the humiliating peace treaties of 1713 and 1714 meant nothing; France was merely resting, allowing her precious boy King, the great-grandson of Louis XIV, time to grow into a man. The regent, who guided the young King, knew a masterly retreat was sometimes part of the battle.

Sniffling came from Abigail's direction. Philippe had brought her the news of Tom Masham's death. It was all London was talking of this morning, her son's duel and Masham's death.

" 'The moon has set, and the Pleiades; it is midnight, and time passes, and I sleep alone.' I quote from Sappho, the tenth Muse, my dear Abigail."

And when his dear Abigail, no Muse, did not answer, because of course she did not know who Sappho was, Philippe smiled thinly at the gardens, having succeeded in amusing himself at her expense. Roger, he thought, you would have known the verse. I miss you still. Will I ever recover from your death?

"Sappho was a Greek poetess," he said.

"Was? Is she dead?"

"As she lived six centuries before Christ, one can only assume so."

"Not Christian, then?"

Abigail dabbed at her face with a handkerchief, and spoke without irony. Very little in life was amusing to Abigail, who was daughter of an earl and had become mother of a duke, two distinctions she never forgot.

"No." The irony in Philippe's voice was deadly, stinging, and completely unobserved by her, one of the reasons they remained good friends. "How much longer must I endure these tears, Abigail? I must tell you I find you quite bourgeoise."

"I don't care how you find me. This duel; that vile broadsheet; now this death—it is all too dreadful. I have never been so upset. I have wanted nothing but my son's happiness, always."

"Nonsense. You want nothing so simple as happiness for your son."

The Hanovers did not rest securely in England since the South Sea Bubble, and though France was required by treaty not to succor one James Stuart, also called the Pretender, she was also required by survival to do that which was best for herself. He and the French ambassador had talked long into the night of that.

"Would you rather that Tony had allowed the insult," he asked, "and that the gossip flying through town this day was of how the Duke of Tamworth is a craven weakling who will allow anything to be said of the women of his family? He acted honorably. He acted the man. I would have done the same." He had done the same—too many times, now, to remember.

"He might have died."

"But he has not died. It is Masham who has done so."

Philippe sighed at the further sounds of Abigail's tears. Turning around, he faced her, and after watching her for a time, limped over to her. The limp was from an old battle wound. He bore another wound, a dueling scar from a sword across his face—a proud, arrogant face, reflecting the man inside. Philippe was a prince of the blood, related to the royal houses of Valois and Capet. Pride was something he had suckled in with his wet nurse's milk.

He sat down upon a footstool near her. "What if I can make your son's marriage take place in sooner than a year?"

"You? Can you do that?"

"I can do many things, my dear Abigail. Do you desire it? You have only to command me."

She stared at him a moment, her face puffed and proud. He knew what she would say. She hated and feared Barbara, if only because Barbara was Diana's daughter. She wanted her son safely married, to anyone but Barbara.

"Yes."

"It is done, then."

"How? What will you do? You leave for France today." She put her face into her handkerchief and began to weep again. "I will miss you so." And then, looking up at him, her fleshy determination showing through the tears: "Sooner than a year?"

He could read her mind. She was calculating: When might Barbara return, at the soonest? He nodded.

"You are very kind, Philippe, more than kind."

I'm not kind at all, thought Philippe. It was love, he'd told Barbara when she'd asked if Roger had loved him. She might have answered the same, if he had been foolish enough to ask her, but he was not as foolish, as impulsive as Barbara. Roger had loved her, more than Philippe had seen him love anyone, except her grandfather Richard Saylor. He did not forgive her for that. He would never forgive her.

"Barbara," scribbled Tommy Carlyle. With wig and rouge off he was just a large, almost ordinary-looking man wearing a diamond earring in one ear. In a bedchamber, sitting at a desk, he wrote, "Barbara, you must come home." He looked around at what he had assembled to send to her: pamphlets and broadsheets from over the summer. From one to the next, the image of Roger's face became larger and larger, while others' faces became smaller. Walpole had sacrificed Roger, made him scapegoat for everyone else, so others would survive. It was so clear. And no one would listen. Perhaps Barbara would not listen, either, but he had to make the attempt. He wrote out, carefully, slowly, what he thought. "Roger became scapegoat," he wrote, "don't you see it? Walpole could have made the fine on his estate less, but he chose to safeguard others. Come home, Barbara, and fight him. I have known him for twenty years, and I begin to think him the most ruthless man I know. I would never have said so a year ago. Come home." It was the least he could do for Roger, who had been his friend. There were very few people to whom he accorded that word.

Jane glanced outside the window of her mother's kitchen at Ladybeth Farm. The window had many small leaded panes of clear, thick glass, beveled at the edges and slightly uneven in the middle, at the spot where the glass had been broken off its blowpipe after it was whirled and flattened, so her view of the outside was distorted. But not so distorted that she could not see the afternoon was dark, over-cast. The wind was picking up; it reminded her a little of her daughter Amelia, in the random, heedless, almost happy way it scattered the leaves about.

"No," her mother said irritably. She and her kitchen servant stood at opposite ends of the great oak table used for baking. The tabletop was a scene of plenty, a cornucopia of wooden bowls of brown eggs and yellow-white butter Jane had helped form; burlap bags spilling out walnuts and currants; hard cones of sugar, now broken; piles of fine white flour and grated breadcrumbs.

"It is three pounds of fine flour to a pound of caraway comfits to a pound of butter, a quart of cream, a pint of ale yeast, eleven eggs, and a little rosewater with musk," said her mother.

They were making caraway cakes to send to her father in London. On a large wooden frame suspended from the ceiling oatcakes hung limply on lines strung from wooden end to wooden end. Bread for him was already cooling on shelves in the pantry. Never mind that her father could buy fresh bread in London. Her mother had made puddings also, covering the tops of the bowls carefully in brown paper. And into the servant's saddlebags, along with the cakes and bread and puddings, would go further jars of her mother's jellies and jams: cherries in jelly, green apricot, white quince. Never mind that her father had taken much with him.

Jane leaned over to poke at the fire with the long-handled toasting fork. Sparks spun upwards and a piece of coal jumped out.

"Is it a coffin or a purse?" asked the servant.

Death or wealth. She would just take a happy heart, which she'd had, once upon a time, before Jeremy's death, before Harry's. Every time she walked to Tamworth, she expected to see Harry step out from behind a tree. Harry and Gussy had used to sit out in the night under the oak tree, watching the fireflies, discussing the last days of Queen Anne, when the rivalry between Whigs and Tories had turned to hatred and vindictiveness. Gussy had liked Harry. Their last child, born after Harry's death, after Jeremy's, was named Harry Augustus. That had been Gussy's idea.

The coal was coffin-shaped. Somewhere a child began to cry. Jane untied her apron and reached for the thick woolen shawl that hung on a peg by the door. She pulled on the leather handle of the heavy arched door that led outside.

"Where are you going?" Her mother's question was sharp. "That is Harry Augustus I hear crying—Jane!"

A sudden gust of wind pulled her across the yard. She knew that if she looked back she would see her mother's face at the window, so she did not look back, but stepped quickly across the stones dotting the muddy yard, then to the little white wooden gate in the stone wall, and then past the stables and barn into the shelter of the woods, the Duchess of Tamworth's woods. She thought, I should have put on pattens—wooden soles raised on iron rings—for her own shoes, with their thin soles, were already damp from the leaves and cold of the ground. But she did not turn back.

The wind shook her skirts and whipped them around her; leaves, gold, crimson, orange—all shades—spun through the air around her. For once in her life, she was not with child. It was a heady sensation. The oaks and beech and horse chestnuts and elms of the Duchess's woods were dropping their leaves. All Hallow's Eve was around the corner, and Guy Fawkes Day lay ahead, and then Christmas. She stumbled a little over a root, or perhaps it was because the thought of Christmas made her think of her child, who had died at Christmas. He lay now in a little grave at the chapel of ease in Petersham, the hamlet where she and Gussy lived, near the village of Richmond. She had planted pansy seed and wood violets over his grave. Barbara had helped her.

Gussy was curate at Petersham's chapel of ease and also clerked at Fulham, in the Bishop of London's palace there. And now also for the Bishop of Rochester, at Westminster Abbey, which meant he was gone a good deal of the time. Jane stopped a moment to catch her breath. She was at the stream. It gurgled its way to wherever it went. She sat down among the damp leaves near the edge of the stream, held out her hand, and a leaf fell in it. Catching a leaf was good luck. She and Barbara and Harry used to fish in this stream—

not that they ever caught a thing, but what fun they had, for Barbara always managed to make her gown wet, and then she would splash Jane. Fly, ladybird, north, south, or east or west. Fly where the man is found that I love best. So she and Barbara used to chant.

How far away seemed those days of girlhood. She was not with child because she and Gussy were not together. Why must you be gone so much? she said to him. They quarreled; her temper was shorter since the death of Jeremy. Her heart had cracked open, and she could not quite mend it yet. She and Gussy quarreled, and she left him to visit her mother and father, and stayed longer than she wanted, wishing him to come and bring her home again. But he did not come.

Primrose, ribwort, rocambole, rodweed, rosa solis, rosemary, said her mother's receipt book, a treasury of recipes handed down from mother to daughter, into which she had looked last night. Angelica and anise, the Duchess wanted. Broomwort and balm. Annie had sent over an herb pillow to take away bad thoughts. Caraway and chamomile. Pennyroyal and peony.

Last night, she'd said the words to her children. "Peony and pansy," Amelia mimicked, making Thomas and Winifred double over with laughter. She slept with her children, a sow surrounded by sleeping piglets. An older child to their child, scolded her mother. Your place is with your husband. Thorn apple and thyme. Violet and willow. Again, again! her children had begged, until she could not say the words without laughing herself. Wintergreen and witch-grass. Wormwood and woundwort. Take me back to girlhood, when I had no sorrows and frets, only days in the sun with Barbara and Harry. What if my husband no longer cares?

She heard something. Was it a carriage? Was it Gussy come to take her and the children home again? The carriage was closer now. She saw it pitching from side to side down the road that led to Tamworth village, too fine a carriage for Gussy. The carriage crossed the narrow bridge under which the stream gurgled. No one ever came to the village. Excitement! The people would be beside themselves.

Smiling suddenly, Jane picked up her long skirts and ran like a girl, the girl she used to be, through the oaks and beeches and horse chestnuts as autumn leaves swirled and twisted through the air, toward the village. She would hide herself, just as she and Barbara used to do, and watch. She laughed a little as she ran, seeing herself hiding like a fool behind trees and cottages. Her mother would think her mad. But Barbara would have understood. Barbara would have run right beside her. Barbara would have said, "What, Gussy does not appreciate you any longer? Well, come here and let me dress you in this gown of mine, and put a patch upon this cheek—some rouge here, some powder there—and you just go to Gussy and make him see why he should love you again." The thought of seducing Gussy so made Jane laugh aloud. If Barbara had been here, she would have had the courage to do it. Barbara would have made her. But Barbara wasn't here, and all her own courage lay buried in the grave with Jeremy.

A cumbersome carriage swayed and jolted into the main lane of the village of Tamworth. Children playing in the dirt of the road ran inside to tell their mothers. Women spinning, their front doors crooked open for a bit of air, took their feet off the trestle that turned the wheel, and stared. Old men, dozing in chairs propped against cottage walls, enjoying autumn sun, opened one eye and looked.

The carriage was lacquered brown and rode on large wheels with metal rims. A coachman drove it, and two footmen hung on the back. The coachman pulled on the reins and with a jingle of harness and much pawing and stamping the six horses in front of the carriage were halted at one end of the village green. Someone inside rolled up a leather shade and leaned out the window. It was a man, and he wore a long periwig. A tricorn hat, its high brims trimmed with braid, indicated the passenger's position in society: He was a nobleman. The man rapped the carriage's side with a long malacca cane. The coachman leaned down.

"The church," the man said.

It was not difficult to find Tamworth Church; it was on the opposite side of the green, and it was also the village's most imposing building, being the only large one. The coachman clucked his tongue to the horses and set them trotting down one of the small lanes that ran along each side of the green.

The coach lumbered under the spreading arms of a row of oaks growing on the east and west sides of the green, oaks so huge they must have been planted a hundred years ago. They shaded the cottages on each side of the green, which was empty this morning of any village loiterers or sheep or cattle. Everyone still in the village was watching from window and door and fence, but not in a way an outsider would notice. The carriage stopped before the low, gabled front porch of the church.

⁂

"Tim says there are boys from the village here who need to speak with you," Annie said to the Duchess.

The boys were talking even as they entered the Duchess's bedchamber, interrupting one another, each anxious to be the one to tell her the news.

"A stranger is in the village—"

"In a grand carriage—"

"Foreign, French, Vicar Latchrod's housekeeper said." Which was enough to condemn the stranger, the war with France being still in recent memory. Anything within fifty years was in recent memory. The housekeeper might as well have said, a highwayman.

"A scar across one side of his face—"

"His cane has a gold head, like yours, Your Grace—"

"He is in your chapel. Toby here looked through the window and saw."

"Tim, go to the stable and have my carriage readied," the Duchess said. "Annie, I need my black gown, the one with green ribbons. Perryman—never mind ignoring me, I know you are at the door listening—be certain I have hot bricks for my feet and the carriage shawl." The Dutchess dangled herself on the edge of the bed, as

Tim, still questioning the boys, walked them from the bedchamber.

"You cannot walk four steps without falling," said Annie. "Who is this stranger that you must see him?"

"Never mind. Do as you are told." It was the only secret she had from Annie, the only one, and it was not hers to share. Roger's lover had come to see Richard Saylor's chapel.

"Well!" said Annie, the word one long, outraged breath.

"A deep subject," snapped the Duchess. "Are you going to dress me or must I ring for a kitchen maid?"

In the silence of the chapel, Philippe could hear his breathing. The vicar's housekeeper had been rude, all but slamming the door in his face when he asked if the chapel was locked. The Duchess don't lock the chapel, the woman had said, every bit as abrupt as any provincial in his own country. Among the gravestones had been a sundial with a carved stone pedestal. "Watch and pray," were the words carved upon it. "Time passeth away like a shadow."

The church had been designed by a countryman of his, one of those invading Normans who had come over with William the Conqueror in 1066. The influence of another countryman, Le Vau or Mansart, was here, too, in this chapel, built almost seven hundred years later to honor the memory of Richard Saylor, famed warrior. Atop a table tomb lay a marble figure, worthy of Bernini, the great Italian sculptor King Louis XIV of France had patronized. It was a figure of Richard.

But Philippe limped forward to a marble column, atop of which was a bust of Roger Montgeoffry, the Earl Devane, ordered by his countess, Barbara, no expense spared. The likeness to Roger was striking. Whoever sculpted it had been singularly gifted. Yes, Barbara had chosen well, but then Philippe had known she would. Her uniqueness had been there in the bud of a girl Roger had married but did not yet know he loved, uniqueness combined with beauty.

How labored his breathing was. He was the only living thing here. On the wall was a huge bronze plaque, giving the Earl's birth and death dates, naming his wife, and then listing the battles in which he had distinguished himself. Philippe put his gloved hand to the plaque to trace the last words: "How like an angel came I down."

"Magnificent, Barbara," he said aloud and in French. There was a code among gentlemen, among warriors, that an enemy deserved honor for a deed well done.

He closed his eyes, saw bayonets flashing in the sun, fifes playing, pennants waving, clouds in a blue sky floating. A king, large hat shadowing his face, on a restless stallion whose bridle was studded with silver and diamonds and glinted in the sun; young officers on horseback, all dressed elaborately, uniforms blazing with satin bows and lace ruffles and jewels and medals, wigged and hatted as if for a ball.

But it was not a ball, but rather a military review for their monarch, King Louis XIV, the greatest monarch the world had ever seen. Before that monarch stretched thousands of foot soldiers, France's finest, stepping smartly into position, performing their drills before their king. It was a memory of youth and valor, of honor and war.

Clumsily—the limp left him without grace—he knelt on one knee and pulled a rosary of pearl and amethyst from a pocket. He began to finger each bead slowly, saying prayers for Roger, whom he had loved, and who had loved him. It was love, he had told Barbara, and that was true.

The Duchess's carriage rattled down the avenue of limes. The Duchess had done honor to the importance of the occasion, wearing jewels and starched green ribbons on a formal black gown; a velvet-and-fur cape; black damask shoes with gold lace appliqué on their sides and great silver buckles in their middle; black silk stockings; a hoop, petticoat, undergown. A diamond or two glittered discreetly amid the folds of her cap. She wore diamonds in her ears; she had even insisted on a spot of rouge on each cheek, as well as a moon-shaped patch at the corner of one eye.

Within moments the carriage was in the village, and her coachman stopped it on one side of the green. The Duchess leaned out the window; there was the Prince's carriage, its coachman leaning against the side waiting, postilions playing dice on the stone steps of the church entrance. She took a deep breath. He would have to pass her carriage on his way to wherever he was going. Observing her, missing not a movement or expression, Annie sat in the corner. The Duchess looked down at her hands. She had had the vanity to wear gloves, leather gloves with pearls sewn on the crisscross design stitched across their tops.

"He is coming out of the chapel, Your Grace."

The coachman went back to stand by the lead horses and to steady them when the other carriage should pass. The Duchess clutched the edge of the window with both hands. She saw him. He was walking across the graveyard. He limped. Yes, Barbara had said he had a limp. Two servants ran to open the carriage door for him. He was climbing into the carriage. His periwig was thick, curling, his clothes rich, his cloak lined with scarlet. The carriage was starting up. His coachman whistled to the horses and cracked a whip over their heads. The carriage jolted forward.

She felt as if she were going to faint, but she could not faint and miss this. The carriage was passing by. There he was, an aging, proud face in profile, the scar Barbara had described not visible. Now he was turning to look at her, and the scar was there, as Barbara had said. The Duchess looked on him without smiling. He touched two fingers to his forehead, in salute, and then she saw that he was signaling his carriage to stop.

Sweet Jesus, he was going to speak to her.

When his carriage halted several yards from her own, the postilion who rode behind leaped off the back and ran forward to his window, then to her carriage.

"Letters for the Duchess of Tamworth," said the postilion.

"Ask your master if he will stop awhile. Tell him the Duchess of Tamworth invites him."

The Duchess held to her window's edge, listening to the beat of her heart, thinking a thousand things at once, none of them coherent. Vengeance is mine, saith the Lord. Sodom and Gomorrah. The fate of Lot's wife. Judge not, that ye be not judged. Here was another letter from Tony. No telling what was in this one. Had she the courage to open it? She saw the postilion had done as she asked, saw the carriage door open, saw the Prince descend and walk haltingly toward her.

"Who is he?" hissed Annie.

"Hush. Is my cap straight? My gown—straighten that fold there. One of my earrings has fallen—"

"No, it's there. You never looked better."

"Your Grace, I feel as though we've been introduced," said Philippe, standing at the Duchess's window.

His voice was purring, rich, touched with his foreign accent. Eyes narrowed, the Duchess faced him arrogantly, this man who had hurt Barbara. He has a proud face, proud eyes, and he was cold, thought the Duchess, cruel. Barbara had said he was the cruelest man she ever knew. Yes.

"How kind you are to honor me with your invitation, Your Grace, but alas, I've a long journey ahead of me, for I return to my home in France. I cannot tarry. I never saw where Lord Devane, who was my friend, as perhaps you know—"

Does he mock me? thought the Duchess.

"—was buried. And I thought, before I left England, to do so. Forgive me if I disturb the quiet of your village. I hope I have given no offense by entering the chapel. If I have, again, I ask forgiveness, for the manners of an uncouth foreigner. One letter is from your grandson, the other from his mother. I warn you they carry news which may be disturbing."

"I know of the duel. How does my grandson do?"

"The man, Masham, died. London, as you must imagine, talks of nothing else."

"Ah." Tony would take it hard. He had a kind heart.

"I believe the young Duke's mother asks you to visit, but that would be a hardship, would it not, for one of your years. Your influence would do much good now, but . . ." Philippe shrugged.

Did she imagine it, or did his eyes challenge her? French toad. Of course, it would be a hardship. She seldom traveled, being old, being infirm, as anyone with eyes in their head could see. But if need be, she could travel to London . . . if the family needed her. Well, of course they needed her. Where was her mind? Lost in its fog and old memories. She ought to have started out for London the day after she received Tony's missent letter. That way, she'd already be there. Her presence, her name, would restore decorum after all these despicable antics. She could call upon Lord Holles in London, settle everything between their two families once and for all. And she would call upon King George, talk to him about the large amount of Roger's fine, its ruin of Barbara. Yes.

"The marriage between your grandson and Lord Holles's daughter has been put back a year. A pity. Have you word from your granddaughter yet?"

"No." A year? What was this? Why on earth had Abigail not written immediately, by special messenger? Because she thought she could manage everything herself, that was why. Bah. Abigail was a proud fool. The Duchess had never liked her.

"Such a long way, Virginia. I make you my respects, Your Grace. The bust of Lord Devane is very fine, as is the inscription."

There was in his face a momentary glimpse of sadness, deep and frigid. Then he was wishing her well, wishing her good-bye. Good riddance, Frenchman, she thought. Richard ought to have slaughtered you all. Marriage put off a year? That would never do. A bird in hand was worth two in a bush.

It took all her determination not to hang out the window to watch him walk back to his carriage. As it was, she made Annie do that work for her, describing every movement he made until she heard the sound of his carriage wheels on the road. Then the Duchess moved to the window and watched with her own eyes, staring until even the dust from the wheels settled back to earth. She hadn't turned to a pillar of salt, had she? And neither had he.

"Shall we go home now?" Annie asked.

"Yes. Home."

The Duchess sat back against the leather carriage seat, the letters in her hand. Soon they would be off to London. Annie would not be expecting that, would fuss and flutter at the break in her routine like the stubborn stick she was. It would do Annie good, do them all good. One needed to do the unexpected, sometimes. Speaking of the unexpected, how surprised Abigail would be. She and the Duchess had never gotten along.

Ha.

CHAPTER 16

The wail of bagpipes, harsh, jarring, filled Slane's ears and made the flesh on his arms crawl. All around him, men's mouths had opened to scream the call of their clans, wild cries that set every man's legs into motion. The enemy was massed ahead, formation solid, un-yielding. Slane kept step with the man on each side of him, scream-ing out his family name, Duncannon, as a battle cry, though he'd never seen the home of his father in Ireland, and a clansman who had second sight said he never would. The soldiers toward whom he ran raised muskets as horses in the calvary behind them reared and screamed their fright at the sound of the bagpipes.

Slane woke with a start, heart pounding, fear a knot in his insides.

It took him more than a moment to know where he was, the small chamber in the outer buildings of Westminster Abbey. It took less than another moment to know he was not alone. Someone else was in the chamber with him, waiting, on the other side of the screen.

The dream fading, he stood, quietly, coolly, not a gesture wasted or awkward, and put his hand to the window, which opened sound-lessly. The courtyard below yawned open like the mouth of a dark well.

"Make a joyful noise unto the God of Jacob. I hadn't the heart to wake you."

In Rochester's voice Slane heard the verdict. Still standing on the cot, he put the heels of his hands to his eyes in relief.

Thank God, oh, thank God. Such nightmares he'd had these last nights. Now or never, the voices in him said. Come home, his mother urged in dreams. Leave Jamie. It can never be.

"Come out and show your ugly face," said Rochester. "Send couriers off, immediately, to France and Italy."

"And tell them what?"

"That I accept the plan. That I lead it."

You're certain? Slane wanted to say, but did not. Impossible, irascible, cruel, Rochester had been in his floundering, though one would not know it, now. There was no sense in telling Rochester he had done real harm, been among the most divisive, pointing out the flaws of the plot with brilliant clarity. Several key men had removed themselves, saying they would give their time and trust to God and the coming election, thank you, rather than to King James. They might have stayed if Rochester hadn't openly argued his fears.

"No New Year's gifts this year, Slane," Rochester said. "All our coin will go instead to King James. Come drink a cup of wine with me, to the year in which King James assumes his rightful throne. Long live the King, hurrah the King, but who that King, is quite another thing—"

"To revolution," Slane said, quietly, wanting to calm Rochester. He swung too high after being so low.

That evening, as planned, Slane met the Duke of Wharton late, in a tavern. To his surprise, Charles, Lord Russel, sat with Wharton. Slane bowed stiffly, thinking, Why are you here? Wharton and I were supposed to speak privately. Then, his brows drawing together as he looked Charles up and down: I still think I'd have been better for Barbara than you.

"Charles, I have the honor to introduce the Viscount Duncannon," said Wharton, "King James's most trusted adviser."

Slane was caught completely by surprise. No one was to know his name. That was imperative. His anonymity was the only thing that protected him.

Quickly, smoothly, a muscle in his face working, he recovered enough to say, "The Duke flatters me. I am simply Laurence Slane."

Struggling not to show anger or dismay, he thought: How dare Wharton be so foolish, so cavalier with information that he was privileged to know? Not an auspicious beginning to rebellion. I depend on a fool.

Wharton laughed wildly, his narrow, ugly face flushed. He's drunk, thought Slane.

"His Grace isn't himself," Slane said to Charles. "And neither am I. He confuses me with someone else."

"Don't fret about Charles," said Wharton, leaning toward Slane to whisper loudly. "He is one of us. I will swear to his loyalty. He is my most faithful lieutenant, directly under me as to the counties which are mine to maneuver. Look over there, Slane, in that corner. See that stalwart old man? That is Sir John Ashford, as staunch a Tory as the day is long. No Jacobite he. He stands for Church and home and God save the King. If you could convert him, Slane— What? What is it?" For Slane had leaned his hands onto the table and brought his face close to Wharton's.

"Come outside with me, now. Come outside, or I will drag you out. You, too," he said to Charles.

Once outside the tavern, Slane shoved Wharton into a wall, hard, and the younger man slid down it, his dark, brilliant eyes bewildered. Charles made a movement, but Slane said, "I'll fight you, too, not with pistols at dawn, but right here and now, with fists, if you try to interfere. This is not a game."

Slane looked down at Wharton. "This is life and death. If you cannot hold your drink, then do not drink. And if you ever introduce me to anyone else to whom I do not ask to be introduced, I will kill you."

"I meant nothing, Slane. You can trust Charles—"

"I trust no one, and neither should you."

Slane looked over to Charles, who was not drunk like Wharton, and who was standing with one shoulder against the wall, listening, his expression serious. You are handsome, thought Slane. Was that what she liked? "You and I have never met, except as Laurence Slane and Lord Russel. Do I make myself clear?"

"Quite clear," said Charles.

Wharton moved to stand, and Slane pushed him down again, hearing the breath go out of Wharton's body, hearing the raggedness with which he now took in air. He knelt, took the man's long chin in his hand. "Beware. Beware of yourself. And beware of me."

He stood. He must leave. He was so angry that he would do something he would regret if he didn't leave this moment.

When he was gone, the sound of his steps clear and harsh on the cobbles, Charles reached down to help Wharton up. "That was very foolish, Wart."

"Yes." Wharton brushed himself off, some of the drunkenness gone now. "It was. He is right, and I was wrong."

"We'll win," said Charles. "With men like him, we'll win."

"If men like me don't ruin it."

CHAPTER 17

The sloop seemed as if it, and it alone, existed in all the world as it cut its way through the waves, its sails billowing out with wind. There was nothing else as far as the eye could see, save water and sky. The line of the sloop's prow, the shape of its hull, were sleek, moving through the waves with the grace of a filly as she runs. The vessel known to Virginians as a Bermuda sloop, after the Caribbean island of that name, was known for speed—necessary in these waters, where pirates lurked. Spaniards, Frenchmen, Englishmen, they had been commissioned to pillage by their respective governments when war was on, but many remained to menace shipping whether there was war or not. The Caribbean was a haven for such predators. No government of Europe sent the number of ships that would have been necessary to patrol it. It was nothing to them, a sea dotted with islands on a map, a piece of territory to concede or war over, a place to send flotsam: restless younger brothers, and military men with no war to fight or money to buy promotion.

"He says he hears a ghost. Some of the others believe him. I thought you ought to know. He wants to offer sacrifice tonight," a mate was saying to Klaus, who stood at the big wheel that kept the course of the sloop.

The sight of the sails unfurled above them was magnificent, and the sound they made was music to men who sailed the seas, something Klaus missed on shore. On shore, sailors woke from dreams in which sails forever unfurled, white and grand, and the creak of rigging and rope was like a choir's chorus.

"Sacrifice of what?" Klaus said.

"A chicken."

"Give him his chicken. We'll be putting in at Spanish Florida soon, and we'll buy more fowl then. You'll be there tonight when he does it? Tell him to ask the ghost for good winds while he's at it."

The deckhand grinned and clicked his bare heels together in imitation of Klaus, who was liked by his crew. Once his stint at the wheel was done, Klaus went belowdecks, made his way past the narrow passageway to his cabin and stopped there for water, which he carried carefully, walking easily with the sway of the sloop to where the cargo was. The rows of barrels held some actual flour and pork, as well as tobacco. Bolling was nothing if not careful.

"Boy," he said. "Hyacinthe. Answer me."

He waited, but there was only silence. Having satisfied himself, as he had to do over and over again, that there was no way the boy's presence could be perceived other than through an African's percipience—one of the crew was a slave—he lit the lantern he carried and made his way among the barrels. The boy was hidden behind them, and the gag was still around his mouth. He stared up at Klaus with a slack, vacant expression. Klaus untied the gag, rinsed the boy's face, then carefully poured water into his mouth.

"Swallow," he had to say, before the boy would do it; it was as if the child had forgotten how to survive. Klaus tore some bread to pieces, soaked them in water, put one in the boy's mouth.

"Eat," he commanded, and the boy chewed a little before turning his head away and refusing. It was possible he would starve before they reached a port. One side of the child's face was still swollen, bruised to the texture of pulpy fruit so that it must hurt him to chew, but the bleeding from his ear had stopped.

"Do you know who I am?" Klaus kept his tone friendly, patient. "Tell me your name. What is your name, boy? You heard me call it, do you remember?"

The boy didn't answer. He never had, not since that moment Odell knocked him to the ground.

"I have to put this around your mouth now." Klaus redid the gag. He untied the boy's hands and feet to move the arms and legs a little. It was like moving a large cloth doll.

"Can you stand? Do you want to walk awhile?"

There was no response, but he asked anyway. He bound the boy again, even though he was certain the boy could not escape, had no thought to. In fact, Klaus wondered if the child had any thought at all. But if he didn't that was best—a blessing, really.

"I'll be back again. There's no need to be afraid of the dark—" Even as he spoke, the boy's eyes were closing. Klaus stood and stared down a moment, anger and a kind of sorrow fighting with common sense and self-preservation. Damn Odell. It would have been better for the both of them if the child had died as Odell stood there looking down at what he'd done, aghast, one dog snarling at them, one moaning. Then it would have been upon Odell's head; now, somehow, it was upon Klaus's. There was nothing for it. If the child didn't die, he would pay one of the slave merchants in Spanish Florida to come aboard and take the boy away in secret. Then Odell's sin would be his sin; but wasn't it, already?

"I have no choice," Klaus said aloud, angrily, to the boy.

The boy shouldn't have spied and sneaked. Odell shouldn't have panicked. The boy should never have charged Odell, like some little maddened beast of a child. Klaus thought of Lady Devane, of Barbara, of her face and the way she had looked upon the rooftop. The kiss between them would remain forever unfinished, the passion between them never acted upon. The boy stood between.

WINTER

FOR NOW WE SEE THROUGH A GLASS,
DARKLY; BUT THEN FACE TO FACE . . .

CHAPTER 18

In the earliest hours of morning, they hunted for game. Barbara's breath expelled itself unevenly; she tried to move more silently, easily, the way Colonel Perry's slave did, but to her own ears she was loud and clumsy. How could she not be, with frost on the ground, but Cuffy, Colonel Perry's slave, to her right, moved silently. Captain Randolph, Mrs. Cox's grandsons, the others hunting—none of them were to be seen. They'd gone on ahead of her, and she'd lost sight of them. She rested a moment, then walked on, to the sound of her boots in the frost-edged grass. After a time, she saw a clearing— and then, suddenly, she saw the stag, grazing in grass that glittered with frost.

"Look," she whispered to Cuffy, a white puff of air coming out of her mouth with the word.

Not a gesture wasted, Cuffy knelt, poured powder into the musket he carried, tamped it down. The stag lifted his head and looked from one side to another, suddenly wary, scenting the air. His head and antlers were etched in clear lines against the winter-bare trees behind him. The sight was magnificent. Barbara raised the musket and took aim, but the gun was heavy and she could not hold it steady.

"Help me," she said to Cuffy.

With a quick movement, Cuffy walked behind her, his hands going up under her arms.

"Yes," she said. The moment was perfect. She had only to press back the trigger.

"Now, Lady," Cuffy breathed into her ear.

The musket kicked hard against her shoulder, hurting her, and her ears rang at the loudness the gunpowder made as it propelled the musket ball out of the long barrel. Through the smoke rising from the barrel, she saw the stag rear, run wildly a few feet into the clearing, then drop.

I've killed him, she thought.

Within a few moments, Colonel Perry, his head protected from the cold by a battered hat tied down with one of Beth's scarves, ran out from the woods and joined Barbara and Cuffy at the fallen animal. The sun had risen, unmarked by clouds. Its light streamed down strongly through the bare branches of trees. The scent of pine was strong in the air, and Barbara took it inside her lungs like some kind of perfume; it mingled with the strong sunlight and the stag upon the frosted, glittering ground, as if he had fallen among dropped diamonds. I will remember this forever, she thought.

"A most fortunate shot," said Perry, and then, after Cuffy had said something to him in a mixture of his own language and English and Spanish, "Cuffy says he gave you his eyes with which to shoot, but the heart that pulled the trigger was yours. And it is a warrior's heart."

Barbara met the slave's eyes. Respect was in his face, and she smiled.

Beth was walking out of the woods. Perry called his daughter. "Come and see the stag Lady Devane has killed."

Cuffy had pulled out a knife from his belt, held it, his eyes on Barbara, up before his face, the blade flat. With an easy, violent elegance, he bent and cut the stag's throat. Out of the woods had come some of the men who were hunting, and their slaves. Shouts, like war cries, rose up from other slaves as the fresh, dark blood streamed in the cold. Looking at Barbara, Cuffy dipped his fingers in the blood, then held his hand out to her.

This was a slave custom. Barbara had seen the overseer, John

Blackstone, do it when he hunted with the slaves on First Curle. As the one who had killed the stag, she was to mark herself with his blood. It made the stag's might and cunning hers.

"You don't have to do it—" began Colonel Perry, but Barbara was already taking off her glove. Blood warm on her fingers, she marked her forehead, then—obeying some impulse—her cheeks.

One by one, the slaves followed suit, dipping their fingers in blood, marking themselves; Colonel Perry and Cuffy did the same. Barbara could see that Beth was shocked at the blood drying on her face, as were Captain Randolph and Mrs. Cox's grandsons; but they were too polite to say anything. They were careful of her; the story of her taking Bowler Cox's horse from him was known everywhere.

When the morning's hunting was done, she knelt by the fire to watch slaves hang her stag from a tree and begin to gut and skin it.

She and her neighbors were hunting. The men were provisioning for winter, now that the weather was cold enough to keep the meat, but also, she saw as she joined them, taking time away from plantation and duties, from wives and family, to perform a ritual of hunting—and something more, which she could not quite articulate: a kind of gathering, around hunting, that somehow strengthened their friendships.

They were kind about her joining them. Margaret Cox used to hunt with us, said Colonel Perry. And I loved it, said Mrs. Cox. I loved the quiet of an early morning in the woods. I loved the hunt. The challenge of aiming true.

It was interesting to listen to the talk, when hunting was done, as everyone stood around the fire to warm himself and drink a potent, hot rum punch made in an iron pot right over the fire. They knew who beat his wife and slaves, who put trash tobacco into hogsheads, who was on the verge of losing his plantation.

She had learned that they thought Klaus Von Rothbach had made an excellent choice in his widow because of the land and family connections she would bring to him if they married. She had learned that the Governor was greatly disliked, that the quarrels between him and his Council and members of the House of Burgesses had been so strident that letters had come from England, from the Secretary of State, reprimanding everyone. They wanted a different governor. Even now there were men in England—Virginians—doing what they could to see that another man was appointed in Spotswood's place.

Since the men talked of everyone else, they must also talk of her, she realized. She thought about that at night, when she was home from the hunting. They had plenty to say. She smiled a little at the thought of what they must say. Much. She had not been still since Hyacinthe's disappearance.

There was no word of Hyacinthe, despite the reward, despite the descriptions posted at every ferry on the river, despite the word spread at all county courts, at all churches, by special order of the Governor, who sent her letter after letter. "Come to Williamsburg," he wrote, "until your servant is found." She declined. He had traveled to First Curle to see her, but she, with John Blackstone as escort, had been on her way past the falls, a dangerous journey of several days, to talk with people settled there, to spread the word that there was a reward for Hyacinthe if he could be found. For weeks, she had ridden from one end of the county to another, the weather finally stopping her. Nothing else could have. I will not wait patiently at home, she'd said to Colonel Perry. You would not.

Many times at night, she did not sleep, but paced the floor, thinking of Hyacinthe, wondering if he was held captive by some savage tribe somewhere, their slave. There was an agreement between the Iroquois and the colonists that runaway slaves would be hunted down and returned, dead or alive. Be strong, be brave, she whispered to Hyacinthe in her thoughts. There was an ache in her throat that was his absence; unshed tears, her grandmother would have said. She missed her grandmother. It would have been good to have the Duchess's strength and presence in this time. But since she did not, she imagined what her grandmother would have done, and acted accordingly. No wonder they talked of her. What was it Bolling had called her in their last quarrel? Shopkeeper and fool.

So you're a shopkeeper now, are you? he'd said, hands on his hips, head cocked, glaring at her. Did he ever do anything but glare at her? You'll ruin the only landing for goods this far upriver, as well as a fine plantation.

Only if the razor was dull: She remembered. They might have been partners in the storehouse, in the rolling house; instead, she'd told him to take his share of the goods and be gone.

Now which of us is the fool? she'd asked him, glaring back, mimicking him, hands on her hips, her head cocked to one side. Me with my place on the river, or you, with none? He had so swelled with anger that she'd thought he would burst right there on the spot where they quarreled.

Colonel Perry joined her at the fire and spread his hands to it; her thought of Bolling went away. Barbara smiled at his battered hat and scarf.

"There's a juggler downriver," he said, "I've bought his services for my Christmas supper. You'll spend tonight with us. Beth is determined, and when my daughter becomes determined, nothing may change her mind."

Sweet liar. He was the one determined. He knew that tomorrow, on Christmas Day, Roger would be dead one year. Every day, no matter the weather, he rode over to visit or had Cuffy row him upriver, so that the sight of him walking into her hall had become as much a part of her life as seeing the slaves assemble at the kitchen house for their food, as Blackstone's walking to the house to greet her every morning and talk over the chores of the day, as the sound of the bagpipe jarring through the woods in the evening, a Jacobite military tune, their good night.

Klaus Von Rothbach was back. His sloop had been seen downriver, Margaret Cox told her. Barbara had walked in cold and rain to the second creek, but the sloop was not there. But then, it would not be. She had made Bolling take his goods from the storehouse. It was now hers alone.

There was in her heart a great yearning, a wildness like a fever. Hyacinthe's loss, atop Roger's and others: Too much. Too much loss. She kept going back to the kiss on the rooftop, to the passion there. When you come back from your voyage, Captain, she'd said to him, and his eyes had gleamed. And then, after Hyacinthe's disappearance, the kiss, the desire seemed large to her, the reasons not to lie with him small. She might just take him—never mind his widow—take him with a smile and a kiss and a coupling and show no mercy, let out all the wildness and grief in passion and flesh.

"I'm going to go home now," she said to Colonel Perry.

"What? No more hunting?"

"I've killed a stag."

"But there are others in the woods."

"I don't need others. I have this one."

"So you killed him to see if you could?"

"Yes, I think I did."

"Will you hunt again?"

"I don't know."

"You still have blood on your face."

She wanted to leave it on. She didn't know why. He led her to a stump, so that she could mount her horse.

"Would you like an escort?" he said to her.

"I know the way."

"Be careful, then."

"I am always careful."

"No, my dear, you are not."

You are brave, heedless, extraordinary, he thought, watching her as she rode away. Watch over her, said the archangel, take care of her; show her the way. What way? Why did he dream this, the same dream coming to him once or twice a week, waking him, leaving him frightened? Even prayer did not quiet the fear. What was taking place inside him was too strange. Everything within him struggled and flailed at the thoughts that came.

"I think you, like Lady Devane, should go home," he heard a voice say.

Perry turned; it was Beth, his daughter—his joy, as he always called her, except that she was not very joyful these days. She watched him with grave eyes, saying nothing as he went day after day to Lady Devane's. She did not understand. She was bewildered by his devotion to Barbara, bewildered and jealous. My regard for Lady Devane does not lessen my love for you, he tried to tell her, but her heart was young. It did not understand.

"Do you think so, my joy?"

"Yes, I do. I think you ought not to hunt any more this year. Cuffy can kill whatever else we might need. I think you ought to rest. You look so tired, Father. It frightens me. Do not go to Lady Devane's tonight. Send Cuffy to escort her to our house. You had another dream, didn't you?"

"I did. Yes, my dear."

"Well, that frightens me, too."

Perry put his arm around Beth, felt her solid flesh. Her robustness, her youth made him aware of how frail he was; she was only a year younger than Barbara.

A man kept appearing in Perry's dreams, the handsomest man he had ever seen, like some archangel with blue stones for eyes, an angel who had fallen to earth. Take care of her. Show her, the angel commanded. He'd told Beth a little of the dream, for she knew him too well not to know that something disturbed him.

There was a roll and surge inside him. Everything was changing. He could feel it. Barbara had told him much of her grandmother, making him smile, making him almost see the Duchess, with her white cat Dulcinea, her cane, her footman; making him see Annie and Tamworth Hall and the large portrait of Barbara's grandfather in the Duchess's bedchamber. She always says, said Barbara, pursing her mouth and frowning in imitation, Everything changes, and nothing does. Some great test was coming to him, greater than any he'd known.

"I think you're right, my joy. I will go home and rest, and I will not hunt, as you say, any more this year."

"Good."

The dream included Beth, the joy of his life. She turned her back on him in the dream. Things were shifting between them. He saw that, and could not stop it because he did not understand. Why? He asked when he woke at night with the feeling, when foreboding moved through him, fear, a wishing to pull away, to hide himself. Why? I have been Your faithful servant. Why?

Because everything changes, and nothing does.

❧

"She will return soon," said Thérèse. "I must go. We spend the night at Colonel Perry's tonight."

But she didn't move from Blackstone's narrow bed, in the overseer's cabin that had once been Odell Smith's. She put her hand up and gently grabbed his beard, thinking to herself, I like your face, John Blackstone—those eyes of yours, so bright, so alive with life. She traced the line of his nose, wide, flaring, sensual, the lips inside the halo of beard. Lover and friend, *cher*, she thought, how glad I am to have found you.

He sighed, a great, heaving sound, coming up out of his body like a groan and leaned his heavy head into her neck; she rubbed her bare foot against his back and thighs. He was so tall that he could not put all of his weight upon her. When he stood, his head came to the ceiling, so that he had to stoop. He towered above the slaves and most other men like some kind of merry giant come to them.

He was kissing her neck now, his mouth moving down to her breasts, to each tip.

"Why do you smile?"

"Because I am a man, and you are a beautiful Frenchwoman, and you are in my bed, and what we are about to do again, before you must go, makes me happy. Doesn't it make you happy? Move here, Thérèse, and let me look at you."

It was his laugh—booming, zestful—that she had first noticed. That, and his kindness to the slaves. The same as you and me, Thérèse, he'd said to her of the slaves, as much my friends as anyone I know. I am a slave, too, for the years George of Hanover's judges have decreed I must serve, but unlike the slaves, I'll be free someday.

He did everything hugely—laughed, ate, drank. Both she and Madame were amazed at the amount of rum he could consume without falling over. At the slaves' ring shouts, which were dances slaves danced upon certain nights when the moon was a certain size, a dance in a circle around a fire, the music from their throats and from drums and rattles they'd made, from flutes of wood, he would sit and watch and drink, and finally, near the end, stand like a tree rooted to the spot and sway to the music, calling out words he knew in their language—moon, fire, feet, rum—calling out the slaves' names— Jack Christmas, Moody, Mama Zou—while the slaves laughed and moved to dance around him, to celebrate him and his largeness. Friend, they called him, clapping and stomping and singing, Black- stone, they sang, brother.

I like that man, Madame had said, after her journey to the falls with him. He can be trusted. And after Odell Smith left them she'd said: Thérèse, I am going to make him overseer at First Curle.

Blackstone pulled Thérèse on top of him.

"Touch me," he said, and the mouth inside the halo of beard was no longer smiling.

She was ready, like some woman of the streets, like some bitch in heat, because she knew the pleasure that was coming, his mouth on hers, his hands, gentle hands, moving her easily to his pleasure, to hers, as if she weighed nothing, the essence of them, the masculine, the feminine, equal, wanting the same thing. The ring suspended from a chain around her neck cut into her.

"Move it," he said, his eyes slitted almost closed.

She had not taken off the chain since the day Madame Barbara had given her the ring. Thérèse held it in her hand tightly a moment before leaning forward to put it upon the sill of the window behind them. Blackstone grabbed her hips and sat her back down against him hard, and the movement brought such pleasure that she forgot the ring.

He kept the movement between them going, ground his teeth, arched back his head and said several words she did not understand. Were they some of his barbaric Scotch? Were they African? Fin- ished, he opened eyes that were bright and clear, and moved her off him; he made a place for her against his belly, put his hand to the sill, took the chain, held it up, looked at the ring. It was a mourning ring, of the kind given at funerals to those who loved the dead one best.

"Tell me."

Tell him? Lover, friend, companion, man, boy: Madame Barbara's brother, Harry, Lord Alderley; her dear lover, gambling in the South Sea, gambling too hard, too far, dying.

Thérèse said nothing, took the chain and ring from Blackstone. How to describe that mad, wonderful time when everyone must dabble in stocks, when everyone knew a footman or actress who would never work again, because they had bought South Sea stock and sold it, for huge amounts. How to describe its fall: no one believing at first; then a doom spreading, like a crimson stain, everywhere. Harry had owed much money. The boy in him could not face the loss.

Blackstone pulled a blanket over them both, rolled a leg over her, a heavy leg, imprisoning her. A tear was rolling down her cheek. He reached out a finger and touched the tear and brought it to his mouth and tasted it. Ah, she liked that about him, his appetite, that he must taste all of life. And he made himself happy with what was. Look at that tree, Thérèse, look at that moon, look at the slaves dance. What beauty, he said. Large Brother, the slaves called him, Large Heart.

If not for this, she thought, moving from the bed, finding her gown to put it on again, stopping a moment to savor her exhaustion, I would go mad. Spring. They were going home to England in the spring, home to London, to narrow streets and lanes, too many buildings, people everywhere, the street vendors with their cries, walnuts to buy, old clothes, fish and oysters, to life, teeming, crowded, cruel, vital, alive. But that was three full months away. Winter, said Madame, we have only to get through the winter, Thérèse. Madame might return to Virginia—indeed, she said she would—but not Thérèse. She would never return to this colony of river and wood and slave, never, not even for the warm hands, long legs, and very loud laugh of John Blackstone, overseer, Jacobite traitor, taster of women's tears, buried treasure, found by her here in the midst of a Virginia forest. Blackstone was not enough. Nothing was enough to make up for the life here, a life that caused the loss of Hyacinthe.

❧

At First Curle, Harry was in the picket-fenced yard. He barked and jumped up to smell Barbara's skirt and hands.

"Mighty hunter," Barbara said to him, kneeling down to scratch his head and back, "I now share your title. I killed a stag today. Did Thérèse banish you to the yard?"

Walking into the parlor, she saw that John Blackstone sat in a French chair. Thérèse stood behind him, cutting his hair with a pair of scissors. His beard had been trimmed, and for a moment Barbara almost did not recognize him. He might have been a Tudor nobleman, with his neat beard, except that in the portraits in the gallery at Tamworth, those noblemen wore pearls in their ears, like dashing pirates, and their beards were dyed blond or a brighter red than even Blackstone's. They were peacocks, her grandmother had said, for the peahen who ruled them—Queen Elizabeth.

"I am made civilized for Christmas, Lady Devane," Blackstone said, standing up. He took a long look at Barbara, at the blood of the kill still on her face, and then laughed. The sound filled the room, the way his size did, and warmed it, the way he did with his vigor and talk and interest in everything. He knew more about slaves than men who'd been here the whole of their lives. He knew about tobacco. He knew about secret paths through the forest and the best night for stars.

Be damned if you'll give that criminal the job I ought to have, the second overseer across the river had told Barbara when she rode to tell him she was putting John Blackstone in charge of First Curle. And so, like Odell Smith, he had left her service. She could have hired another, but the words "Tobacco will sell low; pull in your horns and live small" had echoed in her mind.

I came as close to dying as a man can on the prison ship over, Blackstone had told her during their journey together. It took me a year to feel like a whole man again. I vowed from that moment on to live each day as if it were my last. This is my home, until my indenture is ended. I will know it, and I will love it. I do know it, and I do love it. She had liked that, repeating the words as she sat out at night on the steps to see the stars or watch the slaves do a ring dance: I will know it, and I will love it.

"Blood becomes you, Lady Devane."

The dried blood of her morning's kill was dramatic, vivid, startling, upon her face.

"I killed a stag today. The musket hurt my shoulder when it fired."

"They'll say when you go home to England that Virginia has made you a savage. They'll blame me and add another year to my indenture once they know."

Blackstone flirted, making her want to laugh. Disrespectful, impudent, her grandmother would say of him, though he was not; she would like him, just as Barbara did, for the impudence and joy with which he faced life.

The afternoon outside was darkening. Winter here can be fierce, Colonel Perry had warned her. Have all tasks done—firewood cut, grain stored, meat salted, candles made—for there will be days when the horse paths are impassable, and you are alone with yourself and God and all your deeds, good and bad, to remember.

Thérèse was lighting the lantern they set in a window each night for Hyacinthe, so that he could see his way home to them.

"I think we should plant both Digges seed and the old seed," she said, picking up a map from the table, as well as the quarrel in which she and Blackstone were engaged. He was excited about her idea of growing a special sort, and willing to go further even than she, willing to plant nothing but Digges seed. That was why she had chosen him as overseer when Odell Smith left: After the journey with him, she had a feeling he was a gambler, like her—maybe even more of one than she was, unafraid to risk.

"What if the Digges seed does not take? What if the seedlings don't survive the spring? We know how the other tobacco grows, for you've grown it here spring after spring. What if we have little or no tobacco for next fall's casking? My grandmother would not be pleased. And you will not be the one facing her, Blackstone. I will."

You must plant more seed than you now think, said Colonel Perry. A seed for the blackbird, a seed for the worm, a seed to grow, is what we say as we plant.

Blackstone stayed where he was, towering over her, his words falling with force like stinging rain. She liked that about him, too, that he fought for what he believed.

"I will nurture those seedlings as if they were my own babies," he said. "I will sleep out in the fields with them. I will have Mama Zou say special prayers for them."

"I've decided. A mix," said Barbara. "A mix of our old seed and the new. We have to learn this new tobacco, Blackstone, see how it does. You can't know that, yet."

"You're a stubborn woman, Lady Devane."

She made him a bow, the way one man would to another. "Thank you."

He had found a marsh he thought they might drain. He was excited about that, too, making her tell over and over again Major Custis's story about the tobacco grown in one.

Major Custis has a theory, said Colonel Perry, that a man, like the plants of the earth, endures death and rebirth inside himself over and over again, and unless he is willing to endure that, he will die inside. Major Custis would say—here Colonel Perry had pointed to the lilies in the garden—Look, look at those. Their long, pointed, green leaves are listless now, brown, dying back to nothing. They rest, they go within, back to the earth from which they come; they ask not why, but know that in the spring there will be green furl and buds: hope become visible, faith become visible. And then glorious bloom.

Are you saying there will be glorious bloom for me?

My dear, there can be nothing else. Endure your servant Hyacinthe's absence with faith, I beg you; trust in the Lord—and Barbara had had one of those mad moments in which she imagined she saw Roger in his eyes. Except that Roger would not have told her to trust in the Lord, for he had not believed in God. He had been fashionable and disdainful in his disbelief. Yet she did not sleep well that night. She tossed and turned and dreamed confused dreams of Devane House, of running down long corridors at St. James's Palace holding lilies in her arms.

"We are not finished, you and I. Sit," Thérèse said, picking up the scissors. Obediently, Blackstone sat down again in the chair.

Barbara sat, too, and Harry leaped into her lap. She picked up a comb to comb the dog's hair. The firelight played over her and the dog in her lap, and all was shadow and fire, light and the darkness of the dried blood against her pale skin.

"I've walked all around the marsh I would drain," said Blackstone, "We would need to make a dam at one end and a canal at another."

"How long do you think it would take?"

"Well, now, that depends upon how many men work upon it. With five men, I think we could be done within a year."

"So that a year from spring, I might have it as a field?"

"You might."

The beds were being made for tobacco seeds. The ash of burned cornstalks, as advised by Colonel Perry, was being tilled into the beds, and soon the precious seeds would be sown.

As soon as the last frost was gone in the spring, when she would be leaving for London, the slaves would begin to till the fields, breaking up the winter earth. All day they hoe, Blackstone said. It is hard work. Precious seedlings would be moved onto the small mounds of earth called tobacco hills.

There came into the parlor the far-off sound of a wolf's howl. It was part of the winter here. Barbara touched the dried blood on her face, thinking that when she returned to London she would send Colonel Perry Roger's book of drawings by the sixteenth-century Italian Palladio. Colonel Perry wished to build a large house for Beth, as part of her dowry; he would enjoy the delicate, intricate craftsmanship Palladio displayed. She could just see his fingers tracing the drawings. It would give her pleasure to send them. She could see his surprise, see him gently turning the pages, absorbed. He had an eye for beauty, as Roger had had.

"Grandmama," she had written in a letter, "I know you would like him very much." And to Colonel Perry she had said: Come to England. I want you to meet my family. There was an idea in her, to introduce the two of them, the Duchess and Colonel Perry. She had the oddest feeling, like a tickle, that they would like each other, and more. It made her want to laugh, the thought of her grandmother and Colonel Perry.

Her mind went to Devane House, roamed the vanished chambers and parlors Roger had created. Her mind was much on Devane Square these days, on salvage, repair, beginning again. The fire spat and flickered in the fireplace. Barbara smiled at the idea of bringing her grandmother a beau, and slowly combed Harry's coat, amicably talking tobacco with Blackstone. She thought, now and again, about Klaus Von Rothbach and what she would say to him when she saw him again. Thérèse finished cutting Blackstone's hair.

Barbara excused herself and went up the stairs, the dog following. She opened the wooden box and sorted through the land deeds there. "Buy more land," she always wrote to Randolph in Williamsburg, "as much as you can." The new-bought land lay beyond the falls of the four rivers, because all the land along the rivers themselves was sold, even if not settled. They own it, Mrs. Cox told her. Colonel Perry, and Captain Randolph and Robert Carter. They hold it in keeping for sons and grandsons.

And now, I, too, hold something in keeping, thought Barbara, something not Grandmama's, but my very own.

Downstairs, Thérèse said, "You flirt with her."

Blackstone laughed and pulled her into his lap, but she slapped at him and stood up. "Do you desire her?"

"I desire all women, Thérèse, old and young. She is beautiful, but far above the likes of me. You have my heart. I merely admire her."

"Have you a heart? Does any man?"

"Don't be angry, Frenchwoman, because I think a woman beautiful. Come and sit on my lap and give me a kiss."

"No."

He stood, walked out into the hall. She couldn't help but admire the length of him, the way he walked and moved, the way his head sat upon his shoulders.

"There is always and only now, Thérèse. Do not spoil that."

"Don't you spoil it," she snapped.

Fiercely, Thérèse swept up his locks of hair and beard, carried them to the fire, threw them in. She knelt, thinking of Harry, of his unfaithfulness, which she had ignored because it was easier to do so and also because one did not expect men of his station to be faithful, particularly not to women like her, servants. She had seen the admiration in Blackstone's eyes, like snapping sparks of a fire. It had made her angry. What are we to them? she wondered. Nothing? Everything, Harry had said, but still he had loved others. It isn't love, he'd said.

What was it, then?

Spring: In the spring she would be far and away. And in the meantime, she might give John Blackstone her body, but she would be quite careful about her heart.

The afternoon was darkening, and the housekeeper began to move from table to table, lighting candles. "I see her at church in the Perrys' pew. Old Colonel Perry has taken a great fondness to her. He is always visiting."

The housekeeper of the plantation that belonged to William Byrd, absent in London, gossiped the gossip of the county to Klaus, who was doing what he always did once in from a voyage, riding from plantation to plantation, catching up on news and seeing friends, orienting himself again to home. He had not gone to First Curle, though his mind circled around and around it, around her who lived on it.

"There is no word of her missing boy, Captain Von Rothbach.

She rode all the way to World's End looking for him, talked with those foreigners settled there—in their own tongue, I'll have you know."

The falls of the river were called World's End. The foreigners she spoke of were Huguenots, Protestants the Catholic kingdom of France had exiled. William Byrd settled them above the falls, upon uncultivated land his father had laid claim to years earlier. Byrd had given ten thousand acres to the Huguenots, though they farmed only a hundred; ten thousand acres was nothing to men like Byrd and Perry, who held deeds to hundreds of thousands. I will have much land, thought Klaus, if I marry my widow. The thought was comforting, as if the land would erase the memory of Hyacinthe.

"She brought an Iroquois up from Williamsburg to see if he could find any trail the boy might have left, but the Iroquois found nothing. They say that's when Odell Smith decided to quit her, at the sight of the Iroquois. She asked the Governor to send out the rangers to hunt for her boy, but the Governor said they must wait until spring, when the mountain passages were open and clear. He wanted none of his rangers caught on the other side by early snows."

"Yes, I saw the boy's description posted at the ferry crossing."

The boy was not a slave. Klaus's uncle told him she had granted Hyacinthe his freedom while she was in Williamsburg. How was your voyage, Klaus? Bolling asked. You don't look yourself. She's thrown me out of the storehouse, you know. Dumped my half of the goods as close to the river as she could and told me begone.

Why?

She said, Because the razor wasn't dull. It killed my brother dead as dead can be.

"They are posted at every ferry on this river, Governor's order. She has closed down the other two quarters of First Curle. When Odell Smith left, she offered his post to that wild man, that Scotsman, and since Ephraim Crawley had been second overseer all these years, and not a criminal either, as he put it, he left her service also. The word is she is not going to plant those quarters across the river; she is going to plant only at First Curle."

"Only at First Curle," Klaus echoed. Odell was working for his uncle now, at a quarter beyond the falls. It had been good to know he would not have to see Odell. Now I can forget it, he'd thought to himself. I wish I could forget her as easily.

The door to the library opened and Beth Perry entered, stopping at the sight of Klaus.

"Captain Von Rothbach. I had heard you were back. How good to see you." She held out a book to the housekeeper, who took it from her.

"Finished it, did you? Well, take another. You know Colonel Byrd will not mind."

"How was your voyage?" Beth asked Klaus.

He did not answer.

"Where did you go?" Beth persevered.

"Jamaica, Curaçao, Tobago, Martinique. Islands. Blue waters so clear you see the fish swimming near the bottom. Lagoons hidden like precious pearls. Mountains rising up like a backbone in the distance. An adventurer's world, a pirate's world."

Beth went to the shelves that held Colonel Byrd's many books, which he shared with neighbors. It was the custom here, those having more, to share. She touched the spine of one. "Lady Devane recommended a book called *The Life and Strange Surprizing Adventures of Robinson Crusoe*, but I do not see it here. You know, of course, that her boy is missing."

"Yes, I've been told." Klaus felt an impulse to bolt, to leave Beth Perry talking in the middle of a sentence.

"She told me he was like a child to her. I can't imagine a slave as— Captain Von Rothbach, what is it?"

"It grows dark, and I have a long ride back home."

"Don't ride home. Come and stay the night with us. Lady Devane will be there."

"No, it is impossible for me to spend the night."

The thought of seeing her before he was ready made him abrupt.

"You're coming tomorrow?" Her fine eyes—she had her father's eyes—lingered on him.

"Tomorrow?"

"Christmas Day. Everyone is invited. Your uncle will be there. Father has hired a juggler."

"Yes, I'll be there."

"Good."

☙

Perry's house was filled with people. In every room, tables were piled high with food: maid-of-honor cakes dripping with icing; turkeys; hams; bits of dried fruit made sticky with rum and sugar. The tables were lit by large silver candelabra, molded in a heavy pattern of leaves and flowers. They had belonged to Beth's mother. Barbara had brought her silver trays and candlesticks from First Curle. Brown bottles of wine and rum were everywhere, the wine a clear Madeira Colonel Bolling brought. There was Colonel Perry's peach brandy, made from the peaches in his orchard. There were platters of trout and roasted chicken, pewter bowls of pecans and walnuts.

Barbara had spent days walking through her woods to find vines with some green left on them, to pick pine branches and cones. Last night she and Beth and Thérèse had made vine-and-ivy wreaths, which hung now on the walls. This morning, early, she had scattered the pine sprigs and cones among the trays, and the smell of pine woods mingled with that of the food. She wore a pine sprig in her hair, the green needles vivid against the red-gold, against the heavy black velvet gown she wore, the lace on it as white as new snow. There was not enough room for everyone who had come, so she sat on a window ledge watching the juggler.

"I've something to tell you." It was Valentine Bolling. All day she had managed to ignore him.

Barbara unfurled her fan with a snap, began to fan herself rapidly. "I am watching the juggler."

"I'll be bringing barrels of pork and hogsheads of tobacco into the rolling house."

She turned her head abruptly, the pine needles a slight green caress against her cheek, to look him in the eyes.

"It is custom to greet each person this day with compliments of the season, or with 'Christ be with you.' Compliments of the season, Colonel Bolling. You most certainly will not."

"It's the law. You cannot stop me. You have to accept hogsheads if I pay the fee. He who has a rolling house at the river has to store any hogsheads brought him."

"You cannot tell me there is no other rolling house to which you can take them."

"There is no other rolling house close."

Barbara snapped shut her fan. "Tell me the law again."

"He who has a rolling house at the river must store the hogsheads of his neighbors in it."

"Hogsheads. Of tobacco. Not barrels of pork. Bring your hogsheads, but nothing else. And you'd best put the fee into my hand that day, or something may happen."

He glared at her, unrepentant and challenging. "What might happen?"

"They might fall in the river. I would be so sorry, of course, but there they would be."

Once a day, she or Thérèse walked to the rolling house to count the hogsheads accumulating inside the long shed. Sometimes planters stopped by to tell her they'd left hogsheads. Sometimes they simply left them. Everyone was preparing for spring, for the first tobacco ship. Bolling had kept an indentured servant to live in the storehouse throughout the winter and early spring to keep an account of the hogsheads brought by neighbors, as well as to sell items from the storehouse.

Bolling had provided prizing, the packing of tobacco leaves into a hogshead. He bought raw tobacco from his neighbors, as did Colonel Perry. It was in Barbara's mind that she must bring someone to live in the storehouse, to sell its goods, to keep accounts, and—why not?—to prize, as Bolling had done. All the things necessary—the ropes, the pulleys, the heavy stones used to weigh down and press the tobacco leaves tightly into the hogsheads—were there. Why should she not, like her neighbors, buy tobacco?

"Where is Captain Von Rothbach?" she asked him.

"He'll be there." Bolling looked Barbara up and down. "He will escort his lady."

Barbara held the fan up so that only her eyes showed. "I promise not to flirt too dreadfully."

She promised nothing. She was wild to see Klaus, and angry. She'd learned today that he'd been to see the Randolphs, the Farrars, the Eppeses. But not to see her. He ought to have called, if only to condole with her on the loss of Hyacinthe, which he would know about. Someone would have told him. Pride stirred up that part of her that knew how to be both ruthless and cold, the tease, the flirt, deadly, said Harry. Beware what you do.

Those of us given the gifts of charm and beauty, Bab, said her grandmother in her mind, shaking a finger at a fourteen-year-old girl who didn't yet know she possessed them, nor what they meant, those of us given them use them kindly, discreetly, with honesty, for otherwise the hurt to others is too great. And one day the hurt will turn around and bite.

"Strumpet," said Bolling.

Barbara cocked her head to one side, moved the fan, smiled dazzlingly. "Yes."

He snorted and walked away.

Late in the afternoon, Klaus walked into the parlor, the dark-haired woman of Williamsburg with him. Barbara felt pride and anger flare out like a peacock's tail. I could take you easily, she thought. Look into their eyes, Richelieu had said. He was her first lover other than Roger, and he had coached her in the art of seduction. Once they trust you, hurt them. They struggle then to escape, but can't. The hurt paralyzes them, makes you the puppetmaster, them the puppet.

Among her admirers had been an earl, the son of a duke, and a duke, as well as handsome young men in King James's Jacobite court. Two men had fought a duel over her.

Why bother over a sloop captain? she thought. I'll leave it be.

She watched as he went around the chamber greeting people. Finally he came over to her.

Well, she thought, what do you have to say for yourself?

"You're as beautiful as ever."

"Why have you not called on me? I expected you to do so." She was direct, no flirting, no seductiveness.

He did not answer. She watched a blush come to his face, recede. There was that saying of her grandmother's: Nothing changes and everything changes. Something had changed: He no longer desired her. Well.

He might at least have had the courtesy to come and tell her so; but the thought of Charles came into her mind, and how she had used him so as not to love Roger—and had loved Roger anyway. Playing Richelieu's game, without the coldness, but playing, anyway. Leave it alone, she thought, her pride smarting. There was never love between us, only desire.

"I heard about your servant," he was saying. "I offer my condolences."

"I accept them."

"I can bring you another slave. You have only to ask it. The slave markets of Cartagena are filled with young boys—"

"Compliments of the season, Captain."

She went into another parlor, saw Margaret Cox's grandsons. Anger was rolling through her, that Klaus thought Hyacinthe could be replaced like a lost dog. To these people, he was a dog. I am dangerous, she thought. I'd best watch myself awhile.

"Someone has hurt my feelings," she said to the Coxes. James and Brazure and Bowler Cox were half in love with her. They came to call upon her only as a trio, as if it took all three of them to have the courage to visit her. "Let me sit with you awhile."

As they stood, one of them tipped over his plate of food upon himself; another stammered out something incoherent; the third was unable to speak at all. She settled between them, at her ease, amused by their clumsiness—and touched, too. The girl in her said, This is real, this is genuine, this is good. Enjoy their innocence. Find yours, again.

After a time, Colonel Perry came into the room. Barbara saw him look from one to another, until finally he found her, and onto his face came a smile. She felt her angry heart grow more peaceful. Here, now, was true love, kind, steadfast, safe. There was Roger's grace, Roger's courtesy, matured to something so fine she did not know how to put words to it. Really, her grandmother must meet him.

"Brazure, Bowler, James, do you take care of her?" he said, walking over to them.

The three young men stood again, one of them knocking into another as they did so, making Barbara laugh.

"I have to show Lady Devane my seedbeds," he said to the Cox lads. "Does your grandmother have her seedbeds covered? If not, go and tell her I think we'll have snow today. Well," he said to Barbara, as he walked her away, she leaning on his arm, "I have been a good host, talking with each and every one of my guests; I have been a good burgess, listening to complaints and frets; and now I intend to please myself by talking only with you. Have you enjoyed your day? Did you like the juggler? You're still in black. For New Year's, will you wear a gown of color, for my sake?"

Today Roger had been dead a year. Her period of mourning was over. Where is my wild grief for you, Roger, the grief I brought over with me? Has it simmered down to this wistfulness for what might have been but was not to be? Was not to be. The words no longer break my heart. Does the hurt for Hyacinthe overlie my feeling for you? Or do I hurt so much for him, as not to notice how I still hurt for you? Do I love you less, or is this what Grandmama means by time healing all? Am I healing? There is greater purpose to all than we know, Colonel Perry said. Believe that and life becomes, even in despair, a thing of adventure.

They were walking through the parlor. Klaus was still there, a crowd of women around him as he told fortunes, looking into palms. It's a slave trick I learned in Jamaica, he had told Barbara. People find it amusing. He had opened her palm last fall before he sailed away. I see a man who finds you very beautiful, he'd said.

"Did you have Blackstone order the slaves to sprinkle cornstalk ash among the dirt in which you planted the seedlings? Did he cover the beds with hay and cornhusks?" Colonel Perry was asking.

They were outside, he stopping to tie her cloak under her chin as if she were a child, pulling the hood over her hair carefully, his face concentrated. Near the riverbank, a large tree had fallen over; he had planted ivy and vines that Major Custis gave him to grow up and around it, making it green, making it handsome, even in its death. He had had a seat carved into it, so that he might sit and watch the river. My mind becomes one with my God, he said, as I watch the flow of the river. I find peace.

"Someone hurt me today," she heard herself saying. "Or perhaps, I hurt myself. Pride, you know; I am very prideful."

He listened, saying nothing, brought her hands up, kissed her knuckles. Where, her grandmother would demand, where are you hurt? Come here, my Bab, and we will kiss it and make it well. There was nothing disrespectful in Colonel Perry's kiss, only tenderness, which she felt like something warm all about her. I like you so, she thought. Did I like Klaus? I don't know.

A Christmas tune from home went through her head: "Well-a-day, well-a-day, Christmas too soon goes away." So had the hurt, somehow.

"Look"—she raised her face, and the purity of her profile was beautiful to see—"it's begun to snow."

"I must go and tell the others, so that they can make their way home."

"May we sit just a moment? The snow feels like kisses on my face."

In the house, Beth turned away from the window, from the sight of her father and Barbara sitting on the bench like lovers.

"You haven't told my fortune," she said to Klaus.

He looked down into her outstretched hand and said something about her marrying into King Carter's family. His mind was on Barbara, on what he'd felt at seeing her, again: mingled desire and guilt and regard. The mixed feelings were a tumult in him.

"I don't like my fortune, Captain Von Rothbach. Give me another one."

Surprised, Klaus met Beth's eyes.

"Change it," she said. "Only you can."

He said nothing, uncertain of what was in her voice—or certain, but not quite able to believe, yet.

"Change it."

"You will marry—"

"A foreigner, I think, and live happily ever after."

She took her hand from his coolly, walked from one guest to the next, telling them that snow had begun. It was what her father should have done. Many of them would need to go home, so that they would not be stranded.

"Shall we go?"

Klaus looked down into the eyes of his Williamsburg widow, blinking, almost as if he did not understand what she said. In a way, he didn't. His mind was still reeling from the stroke of fortune that had just opened up Beth Perry's arms to him. His future had become, suddenly and without warning, a widow's third against an heiress's whole.

The tumult subsided. Ambition—opportunity—covered it over.

CHAPTER 19

Blackstone was in the yard, playing his bagpipes. Ranged out behind him were all the slaves on First Curle, some holding candles, some pounding drums, some waving rattles. The sound of seeds in the rattles was like rain hissing. The drums, the rattles were exquisite things, carefully made from wood and stretched skin, or hollowed-out gourds or branches. Carving, feathers, beads, and shells decorated them.

They believe the drumbeat summons forth your heart, Blackstone had told her. The sound of the rattle summons forth spirit.

The sight was beautiful. Barbara opened the door wider. Blackstone broke off his playing and, as she stood in the opening of the doorway, he said, half laughing, "Wassail"—an old word, as old as England, meaning "wholeness to you," "health to you." It was a New Year's blessing.

Up the steps, moving past her, he said to Thérèse, on the stairway in her nightgown, "I am firstfoot in this house this night. I bring you your luck in the coming year. See the color of my hair, Mademoiselle Fuseau? It means good luck for you. Now, if my hair were dark, you should not allow me in, for I'd bring bad fortune, but since it isn't, here I am. Come along, ladies, I have the wassail prepared. You must drink a cup of it with the slaves and me."

"It is the middle of the night," said Barbara.

"Of course it is. When else can a new year begin?"

He began to play his bagpipes again, marching into one of the parlors and around the table and out into the hall again. Barbara and Thérèse pulled on boots and followed him outside, snow caking on the bottoms of their cloaks as they walked. The Christmas Day storm had shaken snow like white sugar over everything, knocking down trees and blocking the horse paths between plantations. Yesterday, the slaves had worked to clear paths to First Curle so that Barbara might receive any New Year's company visiting once the sun rose. She had seen no one in several days; the weather had made travel impossible.

Crowded into Blackstone's cabin, they drank wassail. The spiced ale, into which Blackstone had mixed rum, was strong; with three cups in her, Barbara began to sing, softly, the words of a melody Blackstone played every once in a while, a haunting melody. A melody of my home, he said to them, written before you English ever ruled us. It's a tune of the mountains in which I was reared. My mother sang it.

" 'Morning has broken, like the first morning,' " Barbara sang, her voice husky and sweet. " 'Blackbird has spoken, like the first bird. Praise for the singing. Praise for the morning. Praise for them springing fresh from the Word.' "

Blackstone closed his eyes to the sound of her voice, moved by the fact of Thérèse sitting close enough to touch, moved by the presence of all these people in his small cabin, moved by the good fortune that had come his way in the last months. You flirt, accused Thérèse, and her Frenchwoman's heart was cold. Yes—how could a man help it?—but with no motive save to pay tribute. Lady Devane was beautiful in her heart. He was a felon; his time had been given away as punishment for his loyalty to King James. She was not obliged to pay him a penny for the time he served. Jordan Bolling had paid him nothing. But she had said, I'll give you the same as Smith received for his duties of overseer. Then, when your time is over, you'll have something upon which to build. Hope had come into his life, like the first bird, like the first morning. The wassail and song brought tears to his eyes; so did the hope.

"New Year's gifts," said Barbara. "I have to give out New Year's gifts. Come, stand up. Pipe us outside and over to the house, Black-stone." She laughed. "I don't think I can walk in a straight line."

No one could, and it was wonderful: following her zigzag, the laughter in the night at themselves, the candles glowing, bobbing up and down with the movements of those who held them, the sound of drum and rattle and bagpipe. Once in the house, Barbara led everyone into her parlor and gave gifts: a cone of sugar to each slave, blankets for all, coats, gowns, shoes, clothing she'd taken from the storehouse. For Thérèse, there was a shawl woven by the French Huguenots who lived beyond the falls, the wool of it a rich red color, warm and vivid. Thérèse began to weep as Barbara draped it across her shoulders.

"What is it, Thérèse?"

"It is so beautiful. I miss Hyacinthe. He should be here."

Yes, thought Barbara. John Custis had sent a small tree, a silver maple, up with the Governor. The note attached read, "Green on one side, silver upon the other. I am sorry about your boy. Plant this so he may see it as he moves toward you to return. The sun will catch the silver in the leaves and make them glint, and the glint will guide him home."

Still weeping, Thérèse crawled into Blackstone's lap.

"It's the wassail," Blackstone said looking at Barbara, who smiled to see such a large man look so sheepish.

"Hyacinthe was like my child," Thérèse was saying into Black-stone's chest. "I cannot bear it. I made him something for the New Year. I was so certain he would be back with us."

Thérèse's weeping changed the mood. The slaves were standing, going to Barbara, thanking her, grave in their courtesy and drunk-enness. After they were gone, Barbara sat on the floor, her arms around her knees, staring at the fire for a long time, until she real-ized that Thérèse was no longer weeping. She had fallen asleep in Blackstone's lap, and he, eyes closed, gently rocked her back and forth. So, she thought, they're lovers.

Then Blackstone was standing, going up the stairs to put Thérèse in bed, coming down them again, nodding good night to Barbara.

Alone, she walked around the parlor, touching this and that, the ornate carving upon the frame of one of the paintings she'd brought with her from England, a pewter dish in the cupboard, the threaded thickness of the embroidery upon the French chairs.

Upstairs, she pulled a gown over her nightgown and found wool stockings. Harry followed her back down the stairs.

"We'll welcome the dawn, mighty hunter," she whispered to him. "Wassail, my Harry dog."

She walked to the river, then turned to follow a path along its bank to the second creek. In the distance, in a sky still more shadow than light, was smoke spiraling up from a chimney, the one in the slaves' house. This was a day of rest for the slaves. They were cooking the game they were not supposed to hunt—a law they and Barbara ignored—as well as two small pigs she'd given them. The meat was roasting outside in a pit they'd dug yesterday. She could smell snow and pine tree and roasting pig, delicious, wonderful, the river a dull, snow-iced murmur to her other side.

The sky was the color of a shell streaked with rose. The sun fell in patches before her as she walked back toward the house. Smoke was spiraling from the kitchen-house chimney. Curious, she went to see who was there. Blackstone smiled at her as she stepped up into the kitchen.

"Your cheeks are as scarlet as plums," he said. "Have you slept at all? Neither have I. I've been making an oatcake of Scotland. There is more wassail made, for your guests this day."

Pots hung from an iron bar in the fireplace—a cavern of a fireplace, the width of the kitchen house. Barbara leaned over and smelled the wassail. Any guest who drank much of this today would have to spend the night. Along small ledges at the back of the fireplace, built to put food upon so that it would stay warm, she saw thin cakes piled like so many Shrove Tuesday pancakes.

"I hear a bridle jangling. First guest of the New Year for you, Lady Devane."

This early it could only be Colonel Perry. He wouldn't mind her cloak and boots and hair hanging down about her shoulders. She stepped outside and was startled to see Colonel Bolling atop his horse at her picket fence, and with him Klaus Von Rothbach. She could not imagine why they were here but instinctively she didn't like it.

"We have news," Bolling called when she was close enough to hear.

She had heard that a solitary tobacco ship or two was beginning to show in the rivers. Were there letters from home? she wondered—the best of New Year's gifts—and she lifted her skirt to run, sudden, vivid joy in her heart, joy which must have showed upon her face because Bolling said, quickly, stopping her mid-step, "It's about your servant boy."

"Lady Devane, this way, please . . ."

Barbara could not move, unable to believe that this was how the day ended. A musty smell tickled her nose—hay for the cattle and horses; it was an undertone to another smell, one of death, something rotting, decayed. In spite of a lantern lighted, the barn was almost as dark as the January night outside the door. Her breath came out in little white clouds of puff. Cold, it was so cold. Beside her, cloaked, gloved, booted as she was, Thérèse made a sound, like a sob pushed back.

Under the wavering light of the lantern held by the owner of this plantation lay a blanket-covered mound. Hyacinthe, they said. The body of a boy had been found down the river, caught in a tangle of brush, preserved a little by the cold. A miracle that the body had been seen at all. Or so Colonel Bolling, in his official position as one of the justices of the county, had come to tell her.

Someone took hold of her elbow. Colonel Perry. Yes, she must do what she must do. Grandmama, she said in a quick prayer, send me your strength. I do not think I can stand this.

It took tremendous effort to lift her foot, to make the first step of the fifteen or so paces to where the body lay under the blanket, but she did it, Thérèse beside her, maidservant, friend, Hyacinthe's other mother.

As the planter pulled back the blanket, Barbara's heart gave a mighty lurch. It will jump out of my chest, she thought, as a hundred images, a hundred memories of Hyacinthe jostled one into another in her mind. She looked down, thinking, as she'd done the dawn she killed the stag, I will never forget this. It will mark me all my days.

The boy was naked. He had the long, gangling legs of a growing boy; the bones of the knee, the thigh showed. Something had eaten away flesh from fingers, from genitals and toes. His features were soft, almost formless, most of the face gone to bone. Who was this? How could she know?

"I am not certain it is he," she said. The words came out a whisper. Her throat was closed tight. She was frozen in horror at this death, for all death, for life. Colonel Perry still had hold of her elbow, thank God. The shock of what lay at her feet held her breathless, numb.

"Is this the boy, Mademoiselle Fuseau?" Colonel Bolling said; he leaned against one of the horse stalls, arms folded, face impassive.

Thérèse was weeping too hard to answer. Words were echoing through Barbara's mind. It was last spring, and she sat in one of London's most beautiful churches and listened to Robert Walpole give the eulogy for Roger. "No man is an island . . ." Walpole had read, intoning the words of Roger's favorite poet, Walpole's voice echoing and stern from the pulpit of the exquisite church. "Every man is a piece of the continent, a part of the main. . . ."

"The boy must have wandered from the plantation, become lost in the woods. Who knows how long he lived there before he fell into the river and drowned?" It was the sheriff, who had met them at this plantation, who spoke.

"Her boy was not raised to the woods. How would he survive?" Bolling said.

"What of the dog?" said Perry. "Someone shot the dog in the head. It was a deliberate act."

"The dog's back was broken, wasn't it?" said Klaus, who had accompanied them on this journey. "Perhaps someone came across her, dying, and killed her. Out of mercy."

"Why hasn't that person stepped forward then, to tell us?" said Bolling. "Everyone in the county and two more besides knows about the boy."

Barbara walked across the barn and pulled one of the heavy doors open, stepping out into freezing night. The darkness of it was complete, making her blind for a moment. If a clod be washed away by the sea, Europe is the less, as well as if a promontory were, as well as if a manor of thy friend's or of thine own were. Then she saw a pinpoint of light, feeble, a candle in the window of what must be the plantation house in which they would stay this night. She began to walk toward that light. It is the great mix of feeling, that is why I feel so ill, so faint and weak, so out of time and place, she thought to herself as she walked. Hyacinthe. Dear one, brother, child, sweet servant, Roger's gift.

Roger, where are you? Where is anyone? Grandmama, Tony, someone, help me. Any man's death diminishes me, because I am involved in mankind; and therefore never send to know for whom the bell tolls; it tolls for thee. Snow had begun to fall, the droplets of it lightly stinging, like the tiny, cold kisses at Christmas.

"Lady Devane—Barbara, my dear, sweet . . ."

She turned. Colonel Perry had followed her. The lantern he was holding made odd shadows dance between them, like the winged tips of angels or fairies, the fairies she and Jane had left food and ale for as girls. Upon her hands were soft leather gloves he had given her for the New Year. Appearing not long after Bolling had arrived with his dreadful news, Perry had insisted that he would accompany her to view the body—this man, her aged angel, sage, Virginia guardian. Tears coursed down her face. She was crying now, openly, hard.

"Let me accompany you back to the house. My dear, you must not be alone. What we have just seen is terrible. We are all affected by it."

"Where is God? I've lost Him."

Colonel Perry was holding out his hand. She put hers into it, like a bewildered child.

"Here, between you and me. There, in the barn. Everywhere, Barbara. He does not leave us, ever. It is we who leave Him."

Let that be true, oh, let that be true, she thought, as she allowed him to lead her to the house.

⁊

At the sound of a knock on the door, Barbara looked over, but Thérèse was at last sleeping. Hours had passed. She and Thérèse had cried, together and separately. It is not he, Thérèse said. I know it, I feel it. But they had cried anyway. What they had seen was so dreadful, touching something so deep. Barbara opened the door to see Klaus standing in the dim of the hall.

"You have been upon my mind all the night. I cannot sleep. Please tell me you are all right."

"I hear drums," she said.

"The slaves tell one another about your boy. By the morning, every slave for miles will know the news of it." There were tears in Klaus's eyes. "I am so very sorry. Let me bring you another boy. I will select him myself. The slave markets of the Caribbean are full of boys—"

She turned away and closed the door, gently, and went back to her chair. Everything changes, and nothing does. Who *was* he, this man with his Gypsy cheekbones? Had she ever really desired him? When? That seemed like another time, another world. There had been a Barbara who had arrived on these shores, and there was a Barbara now, who had seen the body in the barn. The shock of it still vibrated through her, like a fingertap against a violin's tautest string. She remembered this feeling, of glass breaking. She'd felt it that morning she saw Roger kissing his lover. The Barbara in her broke, and another stepped out of the broken shards.

Downstairs, Colonel Perry sat in a chair, his eyes upon the fire. Around him, upon the floor, rolled up in blankets, slept the sheriff and Bolling. Something nagged and pulled at Perry, but he could not put his finger upon what it was. Von Rothbach, who had gone upstairs to see about Barbara, came back into the parlor. He put his hands on the mantel and leaned toward the fire.

Like us all, thought Perry, he is touched by that body in the barn.

A dream, thought Klaus. I will pretend it is a dream I dreamed on the second creek.

It was here, wasn't it, that which I've dreaded, thought Perry. The roll and surge within him was so strong that he shook with it. They had covered his shoulders with two blankets. If you fall ill, Valentine had said, your daughter will have my head on a platter.

He had known the moment he had walked into the barn.

"The Lord is my shepherd," he kept repeating, trying to find comfort against the fear, the roll and surge within him.

In the morning, Barbara stood outside with Colonel Perry, waiting for the saddled horses to be brought to them.

"When you get to First Curle"—he watched her carefully, as if he could read her mind by doing so—"what are you going to do?"

"Bury this boy."

And more. He knew what, as well as if she had spoken the words. He shivered. On the way, as they all rode silently, each of them aware of the body across the saddle, words echoed through his mind, words that seared his soul: Inasmuch as ye have done it unto one of the least of these my brethren, ye have done it unto me.

Blackstone and all the slaves were waiting at the boundary of Barbara's land. Glancing at Thérèse, Blackstone put his hand against the neck of Barbara's horse, who was restive, hooves pawing at the snow.

"Was it your boy?"

"We don't know."

"No," said Thérèse.

"Where is the body, ma'am?"

"On that horse, there."

"Well, it's right that you bury him, anyway. . . . Letters have come for you, from your home, and some New Year's gifts from Williamsburg. Captain Randolph brought them."

Letters, thought Barbara, closing her eyes. Somewhere in all the frozen brokenness was joy at that, but it was muted. Let her do the difficult things, first, and then she would take the pleasure of her letters.

Home, she thought, looking past Blackstone to the fields, the trees all around them. Yet, this place, too, even with the horror strapped there across the saddle of a horse, was home. Everything changes and nothing does. She said good-bye to Colonel Bolling and Klaus, to Colonel Perry.

"Where do we bury him?" said Thérèse.

There was a small slave graveyard, set far back in the woods, where the sun came through the thick trees fitfully. Slaves had left their own monuments there—not stone monuments and wide table tombs such as those in the graveyard of the church in Williamsburg, but a log set upright with a series of figures carved upon it, or bits of broken rum bottles and broken gourds sprinkled upon the sunken earth of the graves—a custom, said Blackstone, meant to protect the living from the buried dead: Their lives revolve around their ancestors, said Blackstone, those who have gone on from life, but must be remembered and appeased. It frightens them, the way we ignore the dead. The dead are not dead, they say.

Barbara rode to it on horseback. "It is too lonely."

She and Blackstone and Thérèse walked along the river.

"Where you buried the little dog," said Blackstone, "it might be good to put Hy—the boy—there." They walked to the spot, overlooking the river, under tall trees, their trunks wide, old, their limbs spreading out to make a canopy of shade and coolness in the summer. "Yes," said Barbara.

They went to the barn. The body must be somehow washed and dressed. What will I do? thought Barbara. I can't see it again.

"I'll tend the body," said Blackstone. "You and Mademoiselle Fuseau go on to the house and leave it be."

In the house, Thérèse came downstairs with one of Hyacinthe's suits of clothes, one of his hats with a feather. He had been very vain about his clothes, his hats.

"Hyacinthe would want this boy to have these," Thérèse said.

"I'm going to ride to the vicar," said Barbara, but when she got to his plantation, which bordered hers, his wife told her that he was across the river and that she did not expect him until the morrow. Barbara scribbled a note and left it. By the time she returned to First Curle, the sun was setting. In her parlor, she found Margaret Cox, Captain and Mrs. Randolph, Beth and Colonel Perry.

"You have letters from England," Perry told her.

He looks ill, thought Barbara. He ought not to have come here tonight. "The vicar wasn't there," she said to Thérèse.

"It isn't Hyacinthe," said Thérèse, her pretty face as white, as still, as pinched in and grieving, as Barbara had ever seen it. "It doesn't matter."

Barbara saw Beth and Mrs. Randolph look at one another. They think Thérèse and I are mad, candidates for Bedlam, thought Barbara. Perhaps we are. You have no idea how mad we are. But you will.

"We've brought supper," said Margaret Cox. "Sit yourself down and let us wait upon you. Here, read your letters from home." She put them in Barbara's hands, and Barbara, noticing for the first time the packages upon her table, remembered Blackstone telling her that gifts had come for her. She sifted through the letters—from her grandmother, from her mother and Jane, and one from someone whose handwriting she did not recognize. She put her grandmother's letter against her forehead, as if it would make her well again.

"One of my slaves is making a coffin," Perry said. "It will be ready tomorrow."

"Why do we have it?" Barbara said.

The roll and surge within Perry crested.

"What, my dear?"

He knew. He had known on the slave ship last fall that this moment would come, hadn't he? This was what the dreams portended.

"Slavery."

He tried to speak calmly, over the sound of his heartbeat, so loud, so insistent, like the drums the other night.

"We have learned a lesson from the sugar islands to the south of us. It is more gainful to raise tobacco using slaves. One does not have to give one's slave a portion of harvest for labor. A slave has no claim upon the land upon which he toils. As master, I have only to feed and clothe him. Whatever children he has are mine.

"I never thought to own the slaves I do. In the prosperity since the French war ended, more and more of us have bought slaves. The Dutch, the Spanish, the French, the English in the colonies to the north, they bring them in from the Ivory Coast, where, I am told, they are sold by their own brothers for guns and copper. If I do not buy them, my neighbor will. My neighbor does. I cannot be behind my neighbor."

Perry felt events, dates, scenes tumble in his mind so that he felt dizzy: the trial of Frances Wilson, who had killed her slave woman, the trial splitting the colony up and down, reverberating among them, one side arguing that no subject had the power of life and death, while the other said that she should not be tried because the slave was property. She had been acquitted.

Law after law, he and his fellow slave-owners had passed, each one more restrictive, more binding, more convenient to themselves, a law that slaves did not have the right of headright, which was fifty acres of land, given to anyone who came over as servant. A law that if a runaway slave was killed in capture, no harm came to the killers, and the owner was compensated. A law that children born were slave or free, according to the mother who bore them. Year after year, this or that law passed, each one making those who were masters less than Christian.

We are not Christian enough to set ourselves up over others, he thought now. We fool ourselves to think so; we corrupt ourselves and blame those whom we hold in bondage.

"The house I live in now was the best my father could build," he said to Barbara. "I will build a better house on the backs of my slaves.

We have patented much land in the last twenty years. It is our law that land must be improved within a certain time, must be planted or pastured, or we lose it. We need slaves to take that land from pasture to tobacco. We need slaves to grow and harvest all the tobacco we will plant."

He saw how Barbara held her hands together in her lap in fists. She is furious, he thought, with our arguments. They pale against that which lies in her barn. So she should be furious.

"Please go home, go to bed," she said.

She didn't like the color of his face. They had done hard traveling these last days, through cold and frost, snow, full days on horseback. She herself was exhausted. He was far older. He must take better care of himself. Looking up, she caught a glance from Beth. She doesn't like it that I have brought him out again, thought Barbara.

"You don't look well, Edward," said Margaret Cox, fixing a dark, round eye on him.

"I'm going to ride back to my plantation and have the carriage brought," said Captain Randolph. "You're going home in my carriage, Edward, with blankets over you and hot bricks to put your feet upon."

"The carriage won't make it through the snow." It was Margaret Cox, always practical.

"My sleigh, then."

"You make too much bother," said Perry, but Captain Randolph was already pulling on his cloak.

"Open your gifts," Mrs. Cox said to Barbara.

She tore past the brown paper of the smaller one. Set among dozens of dried rose petals were bulbs: lilies, she saw from the note, for her garden, from Major Custis.

In the other, larger package was an Iroquois cloak, much like the one she'd had sent to the King's mistress, the Duchess of Kendall. Softest leather and hundreds of beads were on one side, and upon the other was dark, beautiful, lustrous fur. There were feathers all along the bottom. It was from the Governor, who wished her compliments of the New Year. Everyone touched the leather, traced the design of the beads with their fingers.

"That is the fur of beavers." Perry could not suppress a shiver. "This cloak cost the Governor more than a few pence."

Barbara swirled her hand through the fur. She wished she could feel something other than anger. This was lovely. She could see that, but she couldn't feel the beauty. She had seen a beaver's dam on a creek at Captain Randolph's, seen the wonderful, odd, flat-tailed creature who had made it. She'd sketched a picture of him for her grandmother.

She picked up the letter from her grandmother, loosed its wax seal, and spread it open, and scanned it quickly, but at the end she came to news so surprising that she could read no further. She looked up blankly, not seeing her guests here, the small chamber, the elaborate Iroquois cloak, but instead England, Tamworth, Saylor House. She'd thought of all of them at home remaining precisely as they were. The world had tipped to one side. When will it right itself again? I am not the same, she thought. Why would they be?

Colonel Perry reached across and took her hand in his. "Shall I stay the night?"

"No, you are not well. I saw you shivering."

But she did not read another letter, or let loose of his hand, until they heard the bells on Captain Randolph's sleigh.

"Tomorrow," Perry said to her, as they tucked blankets around him; and across the light of a lantern, Barbara met Beth's eyes.

"I think not," said Barbara. "Tomorrow, I will come and see you."

"You will need someone with you at the funeral."

"I'll be there," said Captain Randolph. "You are not the only justice of this county, Edward, though you try to act it."

Upstairs, Barbara spread the letters out before the fire and began to read. Her grandmother missed her, was sending her geese, a cheese press, other things. She wanted to send bees—there was a whole page on bees, on how her beemaster was quarrelsome and thick-headed, had no imagination. The Duchess quoted him: " 'How would one keep them gentle? How would one keep them from leaving the hive? How would they forage on the long journey over?' How do I know?" wrote her grandmother. "He is the beemaster, not I."

Barbara smiled and would have kissed the signature another time, if there hadn't been a body in her barn. She was to keep careful account of the plantation. She was to think about making wine. Her grandmother was having old clothing sent from London for the slaves. She was to take care of herself and come back home to visit as soon as she could, sooner, for Tamworth was too quiet without her. And by the way, Tony was to marry Harriet Holles, a maid of honor in the Princess of Wales's court.

Tony's to marry, thought Barbara. It was proper. He must do so, as duke, just as she had done as the granddaughter of a duke, rectifying her mother's mistakes by her marriage to Roger.

"Tony is to marry." She gave the letter to Thérèse.

She opened another, from Jane, reading news about the children, about Ladybeth Farm, where Jane was staying. "I am in despair," Jane wrote. "Gussy does not love me anymore." Nonsense, thought Barbara. Silly Jane. When Barbara got home, she'd see it settled. It was all the strain of the last year, Jane's losing Harry, losing Jeremy, birthing Harry Augustus.

There were two letters left, one from her mother, one from a writer unknown. From her mother, anything was possible, from kind words to cruel. She chose the other letter, reading it slowly once, then once again. Robert Walpole sacrificed Roger, the letter told her, allowed him to be scapegoat, so that other ministers of the King might survive.

She spread out the broadsheets enclosed, feeling ill as she looked at the pictures there—particularly an obscene drawing of Roger, buttocks exaggerated and plump as he raped a figure that represented Britannia. She read the letter once again, looked at the broadsheets. Was it true? Could it be so? She pushed the letter away. I am too upset for this tonight, she thought.

She opened her mother's letter, which was short, to the point. Tony had fought a duel but was unhurt; however, his opponent had died. Tony was to be married—would be married by the time Barbara received this letter—thanks to the interference of the Duchess. Barbara was a fool and a coward to have run away to Virginia. She might have been Duchess of Tamworth, rather than letting Harriet Holles have that title. Quietly, Barbara folded the letter up. And greetings to you, too, Mother, she thought.

I cannot believe Robin would betray Roger, she thought. They were friends. I cannot believe that Tony, my sweet, grave Tony, has fought a duel and the man died. How Tony must be suffering over that.

The obscene picture of Roger was in her mind. What vileness. What cruelty. But cruelty was everywhere. Look at what lay in the barn. God is everywhere, said Colonel Perry. Let it be so. It must be so.

"You're certain it isn't Hyacinthe."

"Yes," said Thérèse.

In the corner was an altar Thérèse had made. There was a pillow for her to kneel upon, a homemade carved wooden cross of Blackstone's. Like Thérèse, he was Catholic; he'd carved it the first year of his indenture. Thérèse prayed for Hyacinthe there. Sometimes for hours, she prayed. The times, she told Barbara, in which my mind goes around and around over him, I must pray or go mad.

She was there now, kneeling in her nightgown and the New Year's crimson shawl, fingering the beads of her rosary. Barbara took a pillow from the bed and knelt beside her. Her girlhood had been one of prayers; every evening her grandmother read prayers, and there was church on Sunday, she and Harry laughing at Vicar Latchrod's droning sermons, in a way they would have never dared to laugh at their grandmother. She'd let the habits drop once she married Roger. It was not fashionable to believe in God, and so, to please him, she had not. But now, like Thérèse, she must, or go mad. Bless me, God, in what I am about to do.

Did Robin betray Roger? Why?

She rode early to see the vicar the next day, but at first, he would not perform the service.

"Unless it is your boy, I cannot," he said. "The service is for baptized Christians only."

"My servant was a baptized Christian," Barbara said, the line of her jaw standing out.

The vicar looked her up and down. He's heard already that we don't believe it Hyacinthe, thought Barbara.

"He must be buried today. He was my dear servant. I swear it." The lie didn't trouble her at all.

Captain Randolph and Margaret Cox were waiting at First Curle when she returned with the vicar.

"Colonel Perry has a fever," Captain Randolph said. "There is another letter for you. The ships are arriving, one after another, to gather up tobacco, so more may come for you over the next months."

Barbara took it from him, recognizing Wart's scrawl. "You didn't have to come," she said to them, "but I am so very glad you have."

The afternoon was cold and dreary, threatening more snow. If she'd been in England, there would have been so much to do—funeral invitations to write and send; gloves, mourning rings, and black hatbands to give out; a white-velvet child's pall to buy for the coffin, which should have lain in state in the house for a while. But she was not in England.

Blackstone and all the slaves were at the grave, dug this morning. The vicar, clearly disapproving, made the service short. Onto the coffin Barbara and Thérèse threw clods of dirt and some rosemary Thérèse had found frozen in the garden.

"Earth to earth, ashes to ashes, dust to dust; in sure and certain hope of the Resurrection to eternal life," said the vicar, and it was ended.

"There is going to be a fine freeze this night," Blackstone said.

"How do you know?" Margaret Cox's question was sharp. Tobacco seedlings had to survive this and other shifts of weather until April, when, as leggy plants, they were moved into hoed fields during the rains that came that month.

Blackstone pointed toward one of the slaves, the one from whose foot several toes had been severed. "He is never wrong."

"I must be off," said the vicar, looking toward the sky.

"I'll have to be going, too," Mrs. Cox said. "You'll understand if I don't stay with you this afternoon. William, are you coming with me?"

Captain Randolph nodded his head. Barbara understood. They would be seeing that their seedbeds were covered with an extra layer of hay, just as Barbara would do today.

"With your permission," Blackstone said to Barbara, once Randolph and Mrs. Cox were gone, "the slaves would like to send him on his way properly before we cover the grave and then attend to your seedlings."

"Yes. Let them do what they wish."

It was wild and strange, and in Barbara's eyes, wonderful, far better than the vicar's thin, reedy voice reading the funeral service. One of the slaves put a homemade bow and three arrows into the grave. Another came forward and poured something over the coffin. Another broke bread and threw it into the grave. The yard slave put a knife beside the bow.

"Rum," said Blackstone, explaining each gesture. " 'I give libation to the Earth because she receives the dead in her pocket,' that is what he is saying. 'Receive this food,' the other is saying. 'Forgive them that they did not offer it first to you, O Mother Earth, as should be. They are ignorant in their hearts, like children untaught.' The slaves give him the bow and arrows, the knife, the food and rum, to sustain and protect his spirit on his long journey home."

"Home?"

"They believe their souls return at death to the place from which they came."

Now the slaves were throwing dirt upon the coffin. One after another they came and scooped up the cold, damp earth and threw it down. As some of them shoveled dirt onto the coffin, others began to sing; the sound of the words rose up lone and fierce to the low, gray clouds, alien, odd, somehow right. Someone began to beat a drum slowly. The three women Barbara owned—Mama Zou, the yard slave, the girl Belle—tore at their faces with their fingernails and added their cries—higher, piercing—to the men's.

"They mourn. 'It is your grandchild who has died,' they are telling the Earth," said Blackstone. " 'Bless him,' they are saying, 'upon his journey.' "

An impulse rose in Barbara. She felt suddenly as if pieces of herself were crying out for relief. She moved into the circle of slaves who were dancing in place, and pulled out the pins in her hair and shook it free, pulling at her face the way the women were doing. She stomped and shouted the way the men did.

"I weep," she cried. "I mourn, I do not approve! Bless this child! Bless me! Bless all of us! Take this grief from me. *Take it.*"

Blackstone put his arms around Thérèse and rubbed his chin in her hair as he watched. She is not the least ashamed, he thought, his eyes following Barbara as she danced and cried and sang. She acts like no duke's granddaughter now, no countess with her lace and patches, but some kind of wild woman. Free. Desperate, fierce, grieving, as much a part of the circle of slaves as if she were one of them.

He could see the slaves were startled, but they moved aside for her after a moment, accepting her and her feelings. Did she know she honored them by honoring their customs? She was saying, Yes, your gods are my gods. She would be blessed for that. They would bless her.

Her grandfather had been a famous general. Everyone had known of Richard Saylor, had heard some story of his bravery in battle, his kindness and steadfastness in life. The slaves would say her grandfather's spirit walked in her. If she were a man—my commander—I believe I would follow her to hell, Blackstone thought. Just like this, with her hair down, her face wild, and her spirit free.

CHAPTER 20

That night, Blackstone stood before Barbara in the parlor. He had been summoned there.

"I am freeing the slaves," she said to him, as cool as if she announced the choice of a different field to hoe for spring. "There will be a prison ship in the river in the spring, and you are to go and choose men from it, buy up their time—"

"The tobacco seedlings, the fields, the marsh—" Blackstone stammered. He was so surprised.

"That work will all be done. You are in charge, to decide when each slave is to be freed. It can't all be done at once, I understand that. As we add a man, we will free a slave. I have much land patented. We'll send the slaves there, have them build the dwelling that I must build to keep the deed to what I've surveyed and patented. We'll give them the wages we would give anyone else. Also some acres of land among the various tracts I've bought, so that they have something."

"Your grandmother—"

"My grandmother placed me in charge of this plantation. She has every confidence in me—has always had confidence in me. And you're free, too." She held up a paper; it was the paper marking Blackstone as criminal, sealed by the keeper of the Tower of London, stating the amount of time he was to serve. She walked to the fire and threw the paper in. "You do not owe me any more time."

"You cannot do this, Lady Devane. Your neighbors will hate it, will hate you. It will stir up—"

"I can do anything I please. And I intend to."

"You're mad."

"Very likely I am. What I saw in that planter's barn would make anyone go mad. You may leave my service if you wish, but there will never be another slave upon First Curle as long as I have anything to do with it."

He knelt, startling her because he was so big that the movements he made were always big, too. The eyes that looked at her were still a lively and a merry blue, but tears were coming out of them, at the corners, falling into his beard.

"Wild woman, I am yours, forever, your indenture for life. You know that what you do will bring you great odium? That those you count as friends will oppose it? And you?"

She nodded.

When she'd stood in the barn looking down at the body, she'd known it, known all that it would entail. But she'd also known that she was to do it. Who was there to fear? Her grandmother? The Governor? Captain Randolph or Colonel Bolling? King George? The Prince of Wales? There was no one and nothing she was afraid of any more. Absolutely nothing.

"Well, then, I'll have to stay as overseer because no one else will."

"Good."

"Sleep well tonight, Lady Devane. Know that the angels watch over you. They bless you."

As Thérèse brushed Barbara's hair, Harry sat on top of Barbara's feet, sleeping, and every now and again, he moaned.

"He runs with Charlotte in his dreams," Thérèse said.

"I forgot to read Wart's letter." Barbara took it from a pocket in her gown, opened it. "Come home," Wart wrote in a short scrawl. "There is an adventure happening, and you are needed."

"Oh, no . . ."

"What is it? Have I scratched my face, Thérèse?"

Thérèse brought the silver-and-ivory hand mirror up to Barbara. There in the mirror were reflected a few, first strands of gray, like shining silver purl among the red-gold of her hair. Like the silver maple leaf John Custis had once pressed into Barbara's hand.

Hyacinthe's, thought Barbara, and the boy we buried today. And the broken Barbara, her rebirth; she was a babe, crawling now, on her knees now, but soon, unfurling like the lily's leaves. She could feel it, far down, under the broken glass, a tough, green, strong, slender, grief-tempered unfurling. A new birth. A new Barbara.

She wasn't afraid, not even of the strands of gray. "Never mind," she said to Thérèse. "It's all right." And she meant it.

CHAPTER 21

"I don't believe you! You cannot do this! You are mad, insane! It is the fever speaking," said Beth.

Tears were running down Beth's face, and she wiped at them, staring at her father as if he were a stranger, as if he were an enemy. She was as angry as ever he had seen her, but the anger was not a child's. It was certain of itself, calm, determined. It was a formidable thing to see in one so young. She's like you, Margaret Cox had said to him. Yes, in his younger days, he had been formidable, too.

"In another month I will be one-and-twenty. I won't let you do it. I will take you to court if I must."

She turned away from him, her skirts whipping out, hissing in the movement. She walked out of the parlor, up the stairs. He heard the door of her bedchamber close, heard the key click as she turned the lock.

Edward Perry felt as if he had fallen, he felt the way he had the day he saw his son be thrown from his horse and lie still once his body hit the ground. He sat down and found that he was trembling. He touched his face and found that he was weeping. He tried to pray, but no words came. It was dark outside, but in a moment, he would call Cuffy and, fever or not, he would go to First Curle. Lady De-vane—Barbara—Barbara would succor him. That he knew.

All his life he had lived here. A part of his life, this last part, he had tried to live in peace and with honor, not that he had not been honorable before, but gain, land, acquiring, had been foremost in his mind. If he bested a man, cheated a little, well, that was part of the game. Now he would have no peace and no honor, not among his neighbors, whom he loved, whom he had served as burgess and justice for all these many years, not from his daughter, whom he adored, whom he had trained, as he would have trained a son, to inherit his earth.

He called for Cuffy, ordered the sleigh harnessed, wrapped a cloak around himself. He was ill. He'd caught a fever, but he was going to Barbara. She had buried that boy today.

Outside, Cuffy helped him into the sleigh, tucked a bearskin around him, told him he should stay home.

"Do as I say."

Bells on the sleigh jangled out. The night was dark, and it was snowing lightly, but Cuffy knew these woods, these paths, as well as Perry did. In two hours, he would be at First Curle. From there, he had to begin life anew. Grief for Beth's anger twisted in him. He wept, and he was old to weep, he had not the resilience of the young, who wept as if their tears had no bottom. Tears had a bottom at his age, called death.

Barbara was silent. Perry waited, exhausted. Cuffy had had to carry him into the house, and now he lay, swaddled like a baby in bearskins, upon the bed in her other parlor.

"Must you free them?" she asked.

He didn't answer.

She twisted a strand of hair. "Must you free them all at once, then? Is there some way to see that Beth does not suffer too much, does not lose too much for your action?"

He could give everything to Beth, save one plantation. They might work out a plan by which slaves were gradually freed, as others were bought. He would have nothing to do with their buying, but Beth was her own mistress. There was a place farther away, small, upon which he might live. He looked around himself.

He might live here, in these rooms that would be full of Barbara's presence after she left them. He might run her storehouse for her, live on the wages she paid, let it all go, let all of it, the land, the seeing to so many people.

"What of your place as burgess, as justice?" she asked.

"I imagine those will go, with my actions."

"You do much good."

"I can do good whether I am a burgess or not."

What if I do not give Beth all, he thought, but two-thirds now, with the promise that I will pay her for every slave freed, that they will be freed over some five years. What if I take my third—must it be a third? I have so much. A fourth, an eighth would be enough—and live from that.

Barbara pulled blankets up around his shoulders. He had a fever, and she was truly worried for him. "Are you going to free them? It is a large thing that you do."

"I am."

She smiled. It was her grandfather's smile. "I've thought to do the same. We'll be despised together, I suppose. The two of us."

He held out his hands, and she took them in hers. Pieces of a soul, he thought, closing his eyes, the fever in him hot, deep; fear hot and deep, too, for what he was about to do. For all he lost in the doing of it, for all he gained, pieces of a soul split in two and joined again.

"Show her," the angel said. She shows me.

CHAPTER 22

"It has come."

Tim, the Duchess of Tamworth's footman, held up the book just delivered to the back door of Saylor House in London. "What is it called?"

Annie took the book from him—it was a New Year's gift from Tony to the Duchess—and opened to the front page.

"The Fortunes and Misfortunes Of the Famous Moll Flanders, &c.—"

She stopped abruptly, frowned at Tim, and went upstairs to find the Duchess, who was resting. She heard the Duchess humming as she walked into the bedchamber, which had become completely the Duchess's own from the moment of her arrival; she'd brought her own bed from Tamworth, and it was now set up in splendor in the chamber along with various small tables, their tops a litter of papers, books, vases of flowers from the King, from Tony, from his bride-to-be, Harriet, from the Duchess's many friends in London. Well may she hum, thought Annie, and in her disapproval was pride. The Duchess had been fussed over like a queen since she had arrived.

Annie read her the remainder of the title page: ". . . Who was Born in Newgate, and during a life of continu'd Variety for Three-score Years, besides her Childhood, was Twelve Year a Whore, Five Times a Wife (whereof once to her own Brother), Twelve Year a Thief, Eight Year a Transported Felon in Virginia, at last grew

Rich, liv'd Honest, and died a Penitent. Written from her own Memorandums."

The Duchess pursed her lips, waved her hand vaguely.

"Leave it there on a table, and I will look it over later and decide if it is fitting—"

"I can answer that question now." Nevertheless, Annie laid down the book, saying warningly, "You must rest. You have the performance to see tonight, and tomorrow is New Year's."

New Year's. Tony married Harriet Holles tomorrow night. Finally, a wedding in the family again, a glorious wedding, the wedding of Tamworth's heir. My visit to London has been fruitful, thought the Duchess. She had been able to pour oil on troubled waters, move things forward by her devising. She was quite pleased with herself.

Closing her eyes obediently, but not so tight that she did not see the door close behind Annie, the Duchess snatched the book up. Daniel Defoe's latest. Defoe birthed books the way some women birthed babies, one after another.

She looked over to her window. The cold outside had misted the panes. Winter seemed to last a long time this year. It was Barbara who had introduced her to the writings of Defoe. She'd brought *Robinson Crusoe* to Tamworth last year and kept them all enthralled with it. The Duchess was fretting: no letter yet. Barbara's absence was an ache. Does she make her place in Virginia? she wondered each night before she slept. Is she well? Bees, she wanted to send Barbara bees. It was really only the queen that needed to be transported, her friend, Sir Christopher Wren, had decided. Would Virginia house and field bees tend a foreign queen or even accept her in a hive? asked her other friend, Sir Isaac Newton. What if the queen had not been mated? The three of them had many long discussions over the project.

The Duchess tapped her finger against the book, Tony's gift to her. Tony had forgiven her completely, fussed over and cosseted her the way he'd done before. And though there was no letter from Barbara, Robert Walpole said a ship from Virginia was docking this very day. Perhaps there would be a letter upon it. The absence of a letter—of Barbara—was the sole imperfection in this, her winter of triumph. But then, if Barbara were here, there might not be a wedding taking place.

She leafed through the pages of the book, pausing now and again to read when a sentence caught her eye:

". . . if my story comes to be read by any innocent young body, they may learn from it to guard themselves against the mischiefs which attend an early knowledge of beauty."

Trying to attach a moral to ease his own conscience for writing common vulgarity, she thought. Writer's trick. Defoe was full of them. She opened to another place:

"Then he walked about the room, and taking me by the hand, I walked with him; and by and by, taking his advantage, he threw me down on the bed, and kissed me there most violently."

The Duchess read as fast as she could to see what else happened to this Moll Flanders. Only the kiss, but the girl was clearly on the road to perdition.

Shocking, low, common, and wicked.

She ought to close the book now and read a book of sermons, prepare herself for the seriousness of the morrow, when she saw her only grandson carry the legacy of the family forward. She would. In a moment. She smoothed back the first page.

" 'The Preface. The world is so taken up of late with novels and romances, that it will be hard for a private history to be taken for genuine. . . . When a woman debauched from her youth, nay even being the offspring of debauchery and vice, comes to give an account of all her vicious practices, and even to descend to the particular occasions and circumstances by which she first became wicked, and of all the progression of crime which she ran through in threescore years, an author must be hard put to it to wrap it up so clean as not to give room, especially for vicious readers, to turn it to his disadvantage. . . .' "

Now I will read too long and have to hurry Annie to dress me. Defoe, you rogue, the Duchess thought, you've done it again.

CHAPTER 23

Not far away, alone with Slane in a private chamber at the Deanery of Westminster Abbey, the Bishop of Rochester fumed.

"I tell you, he is in a tavern somewhere, drunk as three lords."

"He has sworn temperance until the invasion," Slane said quickly. They were quarreling about the Duke of Wharton.

"There is not a temperate bone in his body. I don't trust Wharton, Slane, and I don't like him. I never have!"

"I remind you that no one," said Slane, "has done more for us in the last months than the Duke of Wharton. I remind you that ten thousand pounds of his own fortune was in the packet we just sent to Paris. I remind you that all of London expects Robert Walpole's resignation from the ministry at any hour. That is due as much to Wharton as to anyone."

"Robert Walpole has survived far more than this. The day he resigns as a minister is a day I dance naked in the streets. Wharton fools you. He is impious, immoderate, and unstable! I tell you—"

"And I tell you I will listen to no more. You let your bad temper and impatience cloud your judgment."

"Slane . . ."

The word was either a plea or a threat, but Slane was out the door, refusing to quarrel further, walking swiftly down hallways and corridors. I'll argue no more this day, he thought. He begins to make me doubt myself.

"Rochester is too old a man, too ill with gout, to bear this burden," Slane had written in a letter to Jamie, a letter he did not send
but threw into the fire to watch burn. The Bishop of Rochester isn't
a true Jacobite, said Louisa, Lady Shrewsborough. He came to us
because he saw that King George and his Whig ministers would do
more to destroy the Church of England than revolution. Remember
that, my pretty Slane. It makes a difference in Rochester's commit-
ment.

Too old, thought Slane, the leaders here are all too old. He envisioned them—Rochester, others, who with Rochester formed the
English head of this invasion. He moved lithely, silently, quickly,
with a grace that was sudden and sure, that made him, on stage, a
magnet for all eyes.

Once at Gussy's chamber, having walked to it without a con-
scious thought to do so, he knocked upon the door and walked inside. The fire blazed and crackled red-gold in the fireplace of the
small room. Every surface was covered with papers, as was a narrow
bed. Gussy, squatting at the fire, was stirring something in an iron
pot. He glanced up as Slane came in, but said nothing, simply
smiled. Quiet was Gussy's way. It was an immense relief after
Rochester's temper.

Rochester is excitable and too ambitious, Slane had been
warned. You are to keep him pacified, keep him to me, Slane, said
Jamie, for I fear no man can lead my way into England save
Rochester, who is also courageous and subtle. Jamie was correct.
Rochester was the strongest of those here. He was brilliant, determined, clear-thinking—but also violent of tongue when in doubt,
indecision, or fear. The closer the invasion loomed, the more in-
decisive he became.

"I've made some spiced ale," said Gussy. "Sit down and share a
cup with me. I almost did not recognize you. You look like a great
lord in those fine clothes."

"I perform tonight."

Slane filled his lungs with the smell of the spices, his heart with
the peace that was part and parcel of this small chamber. Outside, af-

ternoon dusk was falling over London, and old snow lay in white-gray piles against buildings. Almighty God, give us grace that we may cast away the works of darkness, and put upon us the armor of light, so each prelate of each church in London—St. Clement Danes, St. James Garlickhythe, St. Magnus the Martyr—each prelate in all of England had intoned to begin Advent, the season of vigil and prayer before Christmas and New Year.

Slane looked out Gussy's window—frost-rimmed, like windows everywhere. Where was Wharton? Late. Was that a good sign or a bad one? Rochester had so irritated him that he could not tell. He picked up an invitation from among the papers on Gussy's table, the card thick, the ink dark, the writing swirling and ornate.

"You've been invited to the wedding of weddings, I see."

"My wife and Lady Devane are great friends. For Lady Devane's sake, His Grace has always been kind to me. I am honored to be invited to his wedding."

Lady Devane. Barbara stood looking at Slane the way she had in his dream. They were in a garden in Italy, just as they had been once upon a time, and her lovely heart-shaped face was raised to his, her eyes amused, questioning, and something more, and he leaned forward, knowing suddenly that he must kiss her. But in his mind Slane turned away. He had no time for her now.

"Was I sharp? I meant nothing. My mind is on Wharton and how late he is."

My mind is on Rochester, and how impossible he is. Blackbird, you gave me too hard a task. Rochester is too old. He is not completely ours. He dislikes the invasion plan. His enthusiasm of the autumn has faded. His fears overwhelm him, overwhelm me.

And yet we persevere in spite of them. We make such progress, Jamie. I lie awake, unable to sleep. I am that elated. I make you copious notes—about what I observe here, about your followers and what you will find after you are King; I burn these, but they stay in my mind because I've committed them to paper. You are going to be King, Jamie. I can see it.

Gussy handed Slane a goblet and gently clinked his to it.

"Christ be with you, Slane. Do the children of Rome go a-gooding? No? Well, here, on St. Thomas's Day, children gather in groups and go from house to house, singing, and in return they're given coins, the coins to give them good things, thus it's called a-gooding. There's a sweet song they sing: 'Well-a-day, well-a-day, Christmas too soon goes away, then your gooding we do pray, for the good times will not stay.' "

And here will be one of your most faithful servants, Jamie. Christ be with you, Gussy. Christmas gone, thought Slane, the New Year tomorrow. This is the longest stretch of time that I've stayed in one place in years.

"Has the Duke of Wharton spoken to you of Christopher Layer?" asked Gussy.

"No. Who is he? What does he want?"

"I will leave Wharton to tell you. I know this only: Layer has been to Rome, has spoken to King James himself."

Gussy was excited for some reason. The Blackbird received many people, too many. Beggars cannot be choosers, Lucius, he'd say. One of them may be my salvation. How am I to know unless I speak with all? But that wasn't the sole reason Jamie did it. He must hear and see the love brought him, feel close to the country that was his by birth, or break from bitterness.

"What was it about the gooding song that made you sad?"

Sadness had been there on Gussy's face. Slane had seen it.

"My son died last Christmas, Slane. He loved that song. In his last days, his mother sang it over and over to him, and he, like a small bird, repeated it until he could not. He was a beautiful boy. Already he knew his catechism. My wife, Jane—"

Slane watched Gussy stop himself, as if he'd said too much. Gussy's words moved him, touched on wounds within himself. He, too, had lost a son. Because he liked Gussy so much, he was curious. This tall, silent, diligent man always kept himself in the background, took Rochester's rages and upsets without a word, was up at all hours deciphering the letters that came in code, writing letters in reply, so that Rochester's replies were as immediate as possible. Not a scrap left this chamber in Rochester's handwriting. It was a precaution Rochester absolutely insisted upon. Suspicious letters were opened at the Post Office. King George and his minister did not forget that there was another claimant for the throne. Codes, ciphers, were always used, but still the risk was great.

To correspond with King James, or with anyone known to be connected with James, was high treason. Day after day, simply by dipping his pen into the inkpot and setting another's words to paper, Gussy committed the crime of high treason, yet he never complained. There was a wife and many children somewhere—not here. Some trouble there, Rochester had told Slane, gossiping about his favorite clerk, the way anyone would, even a bishop of the church, even the irascible leader of an invasion.

Slane probed. "Do you take your wife to the Duke of Tamworth's wedding, Gussy?"

"No."

"A shame. She would like to see it. It is all everyone is talking of."

"She is some distance away, at her father's farm."

Ah, her father's. So there was some trouble between them. Gussy had a house in the hamlet of Petersham, not too far from here, an easy journey for a wife to make to attend London's most talked-of wedding.

"Your wife's father is Sir John Ashford, am I right in that?"

"Yes."

A staunch Tory, no Jacobite, yet friend to many a man that was. A keeper of secrets, loyal, steadfast, Rochester said. The kind of man who is the salt of the English earth.

"My poor father-in-law. He has taken the defection of the Duke of Wharton hard."

In a very public gesture last month, Wharton had abandoned the Tories and gone over to the Whigs. He had become the fair-haired follower of Lord Sunderland, King George's favorite minister. It was the kind of posture and maneuver that London loved. People fed on it like flies on carrion, talking of nothing else, wondering what it meant in the long struggle between Robert Walpole and Lord Sunderland for the King's favor.

"My father-in-law disapproved of Wharton, of course," said Gussy, "but relished it that the Duke's speeches in the House of Lords so infuriated the King's ministers, so inflamed opinion. It takes all my wits not to tell my father-in-law the truth, that Wharton is a spy in the heart of the King's cabinet. He says Wharton's leaving the Tories shows he thinks the party is finished."

"Make your father-in-law join us. Then he will know all our schemes and not have to fret."

"One Jacobite in the family is enough, thank you."

"Not if we win, Gussy, only if we hang." Slane stretched, tension, tightness leaving him, though not the sadness Gussy's words about his son had produced. Coming to this room and talking with Gussy had calmed him. He must be calm and alert for tonight, when he performed before the Princess of Wales and her ladies, in honor of the bride-to-be in London's famous wedding tomorrow.

The Blackbird shall make you an earl, Gussy, Slane thought, for your quiet strength, and your silent travail, and your wife, whom you clearly love, will be a countess. Perhaps she will love you again if you are an earl.

There was a knock at the door. Slane felt his heart leap. Wharton. Another man he had grown to like, as different from Gussy as night was from day. Wharton at last. As promised. Damn Rochester, thought Slane, that he should make me doubt my instincts.

"It has begun to snow, gentlemen," said Wharton. "Good God, Slane, you look like an earl in those clothes. I almost did not know you."

Brushing off his cloak, Wharton's dark eyes were shining, and it was not wine that had given them that gleam. I drink no more until the invasion, he swore.

What's he done now? thought Slane. Clever boy-man, not quite fully a man, nor fully a boy, but brilliant, as brilliant in his way as Rochester, and like Rochester unstable. In Rochester, the weakness expressed itself in rage. With Wharton, it was wine.

"Sunderland and I have been plotting against Walpole. There is a favorite minion of his whom I will accuse of bribery and high crimes when Parliament meets again after the New Year. It will cause a great fuss, and a committee will have to be formed to investigate, and Walpole will be furious, trying to find a minion of Sunderland's to accuse and disgrace in retaliation. Thus, while we plot, the King's best ministers tear one another to shreds. I am surprised either one can still stand."

It was true: There were a hundred petty daily quarrels over a hundred details of governing, which Wharton, as Lord Sunderland's newest friend and protégé, encouraged.

"You've heard what Walpole said to Will Shippen?" said Gussy, and Slane smiled to see him excited, drawn into their gossiping. Will Shippen was one of theirs, a Jacobite who was a longtime and respected member of the House of Commons.

"What?" said Slane, though he had, indeed, heard.

"He told Will Shippen he was quite tired of it all and hoped to leave soon."

Slane felt a shiver through his body. It had become a personal quest of his to see Walpole removed from power as a minister. *I stand or fall with the Whigs, and with King George,* Walpole proclaimed, like a cock on a dungheap. He would have no dealings whatsoever with Jacobites. Other ministers of King George were not so tidy in their loyalty.

Lord Sunderland was not so tidy. To remove Walpole before Ormonde invaded would leave King George to the mercy of ministers who would deal with whomever they had to, to survive.

But there was more than policy behind Slane's feeling toward Walpole. He felt a personal animosity toward him. Walpole—vulgar, forthright—was a man of the land, a squire like Gussy's father-in-law, Sir John, yet so different from Sir John. Walpole was a man of this age, rough, ready to buy any man's loyalty. It was as if he represented that ruthlessness within the English character that had betrayed James and his father before him. There was no honor in him, and Slane felt a need to crush him, to see him disgraced, abandoned, out of the public life that was so clearly life's blood to him.

"Beware of Lord Sunderland," Slane said to Wharton now. "He has not survived as a King's minister for all these years by being sincere. Rochester says that Sunderland promises much but delivers as little as possible— Why do you laugh?"

"Barbara said just that of Charles, more than once. Don't worry over me, Slane. No one is more duplicitous than I. Therefore, I recognize duplicity in others."

Here you are again, Barbara, thought Slane.

"I have a New Year's gift for the Bishop," Wharton continued. "Charles has found a man who says he can recruit many soldiers within the army for us."

Christopher Layer, thought Slane, and a feeling suddenly went through him, the tingling in his middle that always presaged success.

"His name is Christopher Layer. He has an impeccable background, comes from a good family in Norfolk, has been to Rome and sworn loyalty to King James."

"How will a man from a good family in Norfolk recruit soldiers within the English army?" asked Slane.

"A servant of his was once a soldier. The servant knows a man, an ex-sergeant, who knows many soldiers, many sergeants still on active duty. Layer says with the help of that man—who will not come to us cheaply—they can put together groups of soldiers out of nearly half the King's regiments who will fight for Ormonde. Those who don't do it for love will do it for the proper coin. Look"—Wharton held out a piece of paper—"what Christopher Layer gives us to show his loyalty, his sincerity, to show he knows of what he speaks."

The paper was a listing of regiments on duty, with the name of the town or village within which troops were barracked.

"We must verify this," said Slane. He was tingling all over. This was priceless information. If it was correct, Christopher Layer was a gift beyond measure to them.

"Of course." And then, in a way unlike himself, so that Slane was reminded how young Wharton was, in some ways younger than his two-and-twenty, a boy with no war, no stretch of hardship, no sorrow to make him grow: "Slane, persuade the Bishop not to doubt me. King James has my heart. I swear it on the soul of my little son."

Frowning at the thought that Rochester had been openly rude to Wharton, Slane said, "I didn't know you had a child."

There was a wife somewhere. Slane knew that, but she never came to London. It was said that Wharton would not allow it.

"I no longer have him. He's dead. Smallpox."

Gussy looked down into his cup of ale. So, I was wrong about no sorrow, thought Slane. Rochester is too open, if Wharton has known his distrust; too open, too angry all the time. . . . So the two men I have grown to care for have both lost sons. We share that, don't we, gentlemen, a grief for which there are no words, and at times, no healing.

He stood, the sadness vibrating in him so that he knew he'd have to walk it off, walk the feelings into numbness before he could be what he had to be, clear and alert, open to his instinct, at the performance tonight.

"This is not the day to deliver your gift," he said, softly, kindly, as an older brother or uncle might speak, "but it is a fine gift, precisely the gift we need. If you two will excuse me, I leave you to your plotting. I must earn my keep. I go to perform like a trained bear before the Princess of Wales this evening."

"Give her my regards," said Wharton, evilly. "I host a final party for the luckless groom tonight. We'll be at Pontack's tavern while you're declaiming lines. Join us."

"I shall."

Slane warmed his hands a moment at one of the street fires lighted to keep beggars from freezing.

The Duke of Ormonde was in Spain, buying arms for the invasion. Agents in France and Hamburg were purchasing more arms and ammunition, sending them to Spain. The Jacobites in England had just sent a packet of money for that. There was a chance that France would breach her treaty with England and provide regiments to invade with Ormonde. If France would be the ally to Jacobites that she had been under Louis XIV, if enough troops here would rebel, declare for James, then Jamie would ride down these streets as King.

Someone brushed against him, and Slane put his hand to his sword. This part of London, a good brisk walk from Westminster, was a wretched warren of narrow, labyrinthine lanes and alleys and dark courtyards. Here lived and worked the sellers of dog's and cat's meat, of watercress, old iron, coal, tripe, and used clothing. Here lived chairmen and sailors, watermen and porters, brickmakers. It was a brawling, ruthless world; the strongest, the largest, ruled.

In every lane down which he walked, there was a fire burning in the street, around which stood shapeless, cloaked women and ragged children, a few men. The water in the gutters that ran down the middle of the streets was frozen. The sky was gone, lost to lines of frozen wash strung from one side of the street to the other, blocking out dreary winter sunlight. I miss Italy, Slane thought. The sunshine. The people.

He went into a building with boarded-over windows, like closed eyes. There was no door, only the opening where a door had once been. This was one of his lairs, his burrows. Like a fox, he had several hiding places. Two flights up, at the second door, he knocked, and a boy opened a door.

Slane stepped into the room. Its windows, like the rest, were boarded up so that the landlord did not have to pay the tax on windows. A single candle guttered on the floor, highlighting the bed, upon which a woman and several children sat. There was a malodorous chamber pot and a dark hole of a fireplace. It was freezing in here. Why was there no fire? The woman stood up, and the smell of fermented geneva floated across to Slane. Geneva, gin, was the lifeblood of these rookeries, these slums, this England that King George and his ministers had had to themselves for eight years.

"Geneva" was a corruption of the word *genever*, meaning juniper; the liquor was distilled from malt or barley or other grains and then flavored with oil of juniper. The butcher, the baker, the greengrocer, the weaver sold it. A favorite trick was to give children, buying for parents, a free glass, until the drink became a necessity to them also.

The first time Slane had walked down London's back streets and seen men and women lying where they'd fallen in their drunkenness, seen their children around them, unheeded, abandoned, he had been disgusted. "You must forbid the sale of gin when you are crowned king," he'd written to Jamie, "for the sake of the people here." The coins he'd given for coal for the fireplace had gone toward gin.

The woman smiled drunkenly, brazenly at Slane. Most of her teeth were gone. She was probably in her early thirties. Her son had been outside to the water bucket; he brought the dipper for Slane, who saw, as he took it from the boy, how red the child's hands were. He motioned for the boy to follow him outside to the dark stairs.

"Any letters?"

The boy and his friends served as couriers, going into the various coffeehouses used as receiving points for letters from Italy and France, so that Gussy did not always have to do it. Slane knelt and handed the boy several coins. He felt as if the woman saw him through the door as he gave the coins. He could feel her hunger for the gin. It was a live thing with a will of its own.

"This is enough for food and coal for days if you are careful with it."

"Mam will take it from me."

"You buy geneva for her, enough so she goes to sleep. You wait until she sleeps, and then you and the children eat. Hide the coins, and you drink none of the geneva. Promise me?"

"Yes, sir. Thank you, sir."

If the children were lucky, she would go to a gin cellar, places where men and women sat on straw in a stupor, waiting for the drink to wear off until they could drink again. If she died, the children were better off than they were now.

Slane tried not to feel the whole of his disgust for her, his pity for the children, all the children of these streets, Jamie's children, all of them. Despair was all around him, on every street, in every house, here. If he began feeling it, there would be no ending to it.

The news is good, he reminded himself to pull his spirits up from the children, from the squalor and ruin sitting on the bed, living all among these streets.

Everything was falling into place as if meant to be. Why could Rochester not appreciate that? Wharton, clever boy-man that he was, had simply said one day, I'll go to Sunderland and tell him I'm bored with Tories. And he had.

Everyone was happy—Sunderland, who now had the notorious, influential Duke of Wharton among his followers; King George, who had grown to dread Wharton's barbed speeches—honed to absolute ruthlessness during the South Sea Bubble—against royal policy; Whigs, who saw Wharton's defection as a clear symbol that the Tory party was finished, who saw the coming election as theirs.

The quarrel between Whigs and Tories was deep, ruthless, something Jamie would need to deal with when he was king. It was too divisive, the determination to see the other side ruined costing time and effort that might have gone to better things.

Slane sat down on a chair. So Gussy and Wharton had lost sons. My son, he thought, no longer able to hold at bay sadness for his son and wife gone, the pair of them dying in childbirth, a woman's battleground. He'd loved her with his boy's heart—he'd been younger than Wharton when she died—and she'd loved back, clean, pure, open. The boy in him remembered her, remembered the sweetness between them. Barbara had looked at him with clear, girl's eyes, but she had been married, and he had been busy, and there was only time for a kiss under the cypresses in an Italian garden. He must go now and find a church, light three white candles for three small hopes stillborn.

On his way, later, to Leicester House, the London home of the Prince and Princess of Wales, Slane passed Saylor House. If Richard Saylor had stayed loyal to me, I would never have left England, old King James, Jamie's father, used to say.

Slane stood a moment before the ornate iron gates that opened on the courtyard. Huge lanterns beside the massive front door spilled out soft winter light. The house sat solid and splendid in its bare gardens.

Our house in Ireland was beautiful, Slane's mother had told him. Three-storied, it was shaped like an E, for the old Queen Elizabeth in whose reign it was built. Ireland is green, my Lucius, green like the most tender of spring grass. He'd never seen the house, nor Ireland. Among his memories were no paintings of ancestors and relatives such as were in other houses. His mother and father had left with what coins and jewels they could sew in his mother's skirts, after that last battle in Ireland that finished James II's hopes.

Slane had walked the huge, echoing, ornate chambers of Versailles and the Palais-Royal, had been a guest in the palaces of Venice, Rome, Vienna. As he stared at Saylor House—no palace, but a great and beautiful house, a monument to Richard Saylor and the glory of the French wars—he thought: When Jamie is king, I will ask for this house as my reward.

A woman crossed the courtyard, her hair red and gold, her face shaped like a heart. Barbara. Slane's heart beat fast. The image was as quickly gone as it had come. Would she forgive him for taking her family's house? To the victor belong the spoils. Did she still have girl's eyes? He would take her, too, if she did.

Slane played from one woman to the next in the front row of chairs.

" 'This wimpled, whining, purblind, wayward boy, / This senior-junior, giant-dwarf, Dan Cupid: / Regent of love-rimes, lord of folded arms, / The anointed sovereign of sighs and groans,' " he said, but he was thinking that at a signal, the clans would rise in Scotland, and there would be a rising in the west, under Lord Arran. They needed a rising in the south, too, so George's army might split itself in three directions—west, north, south—as Ormonde came in at the Thames River. There was no one yet designated to head a rebellion in the south, closest to London. The rising closest to London would be the most dangerous. King George's troops would reach there first.

The chamber in Leicester House was beautiful, an elaborate

painting across the ceiling, intricate cascades of molding along walls lined with velvet, portraits in heavy frames hanging from ribbons. Small armchairs, their legs and arms crusted with gilt, had been pulled into rows, a dozen or so women sitting on them: the Princess of Wales; her maids of honor; the bride-to-be, Harriet Holles; her mother; and her groom-to-be's relatives—his mother, Lady Saylor; the Duchess of Tamworth; Lady Shrewsborough.

Slane stood before the Princess of Wales. A man who knows many sergeants, said Wharton. Sergeants and corporals were the heart of an army. Take them and you had the men under them.

" 'See!' " said Slane, giving the Princess a passionate, languid look, " 'how she leans her cheek upon her hand: / O! that I were a glove upon that hand, / That I might touch that cheek.' "

King George and his family would have to be taken into custody. It was the Jacobites' plan to capture the Tower of London, which would become the prison of King George and his ministers.

Slane stood at last before the slight, dark-haired bride-to-be. She had a chipped tooth, which showed when she smiled. Her family had much land, several houses. She'd have to go to one of them when he took Saylor House.

" 'I would have thee gone;' " he said to her. " 'And yet no further than a wanton's bird, / Who lets it hop a little from her hand, / Like a poor prisoner in his twisted gyves, / And with a silk thread plucks it back again, / So loving-jealous of his liberty.' "

The young maids of honor sat staring at him with rapt faces, their eyes adoring. But the older women—the two mothers and the Duchess of Tamworth—were something else again. Thank God I don't have to seduce them, he thought. Let's end this.

He pulled Harriet up from her chair, walked her around, reciting love poetry, then went to one knee and stared up at her, as passionate as a bridegroom. " 'Good night, good night! parting is such sweet sorrow, / That I shall say good night till it be morrow.' "

He bowed his head, closed his eyes, listened to the applause. Charles was leaving in another month to make certain of their support to the north. Slane would do the same thing to the south.

"Thank you so much," said the young woman he knelt before. "It was beautiful, quite beautiful, a lovely New Year's gift. Come and meet the Princess. Your Highness, I have the honor to present Laurence Slane."

"My maids of honor have been slain by you, Slane," said the Princess, and Slane bowed very low, thinking, Plump arms, hair frizzed by keeping it falsely blond, diamonds everywhere, eyes that do not smile.

"You were very good. You're from Ireland, yes?"

"Ireland and other places, Your Highness. I left Ireland long ago. A man can starve there, and too many of us do."

"What other places?"

"Any small town that has honest labor to offer."

"You haven't the look of a man who does much labor, honest or otherwise. It's said of you that you've never acted before, yet you made all my young ladies fall in love tonight, Slane. What a light you've hidden under the bushel of honest labor."

She had not fallen in love. Again, he took a moment to deliberately meet her eyes. You could read a man's soul in his eyes. It was like going before an opponent in a duel to look into hers. A keen intelligence, he saw, made formidable by years at court. She trusts no one, thought Slane. And she is absolutely right. She'll remember that I played before her, remember this night, when she is in the Tower. She'll plot escape during every moment of every day that she is in the Tower. I must remember to tell Jamie that.

He smiled.

"Go and say a few words to my maids of honor," said the Princess. "I promised them they might have you to themselves for a few moments. I am so kind."

You are ruthless, thought Slane.

"Not too long, Slane," the Princess said. "I want none of them seduced by your dark eyes."

Slane stood among the young women who served the Princess as companions and surrogate daughters. They were the cream of society, the blossoms of the realm, offering large dowries and immense family connections, offering access to the court because of their service to the Princess. Tamworth does well to ally himself here, thought Slane. Of them all—he felt he was surrounded with delicious young flowers—he liked Harriet best. She seemed pleasant and bright.

The circle around him was broken up by a raucous cackle. Aunt Shrew—Louisa was how Slane thought of her—stood before him, rouge and patches vying with her wrinkles, jewels sparkling everywhere, as if she would make up in jewelry what she might have lost in youth.

"Enough, now," she said, moving young women aside. "He's mine for a time. Come along, Slane, meet my sister-in-law, the Duchess of Tamworth, and Lady Saylor and Lady Holles. Shoo," she said, "go on," waving her hand to the maids of honor as if they were dogs.

Slane stood before the Duchess of Tamworth, the great hero's wife, once a player among those who decided the fate of this kingdom. Richard Saylor had adored her, it was said. Coming up to London several months ago, in a carriage so ancient that it was the talk of London, she'd made certain the marriage moved forward as if there'd been no duel.

She sat regally, arrogantly, in a black gown and many emeralds. There had been a time when the only way to find favor with Queen Mary, and with Queen Anne after Mary, had been to find favor first with this woman. She might have been a dowager queen, now, staring back at Slane with dark eyes. She has no higher authority than herself, thought Slane. If I take her grandson's house, she will not forgive me. Like the Princess, she will plot against me. Where is Barbara in this tiny, arrogant woman?

"Irish, are you?" the Duchess said. "Where is your accent?"

"I lost it long ago. A man with an Irish accent finds little acceptance in England."

"Yes, we haven't been kind to your land, have we? My husband always said that we erred in Ireland from the beginning, and were too foolish or too proud to make amends. Are you Catholic, Slane?"

The question so surprised him that he answered honestly. "Yes."

"What do you know of bees?"

"Bees?"

"I wish to send some to my granddaughter in Virginia, but my beemaster says they will die on the way over. He has a small mind, not able to see the forest for the trees. He's good at what he does, mind you. My Tamworth honey is the best in the county, but he has no imagination. Tending the bee skeps, preventing swarms is enough for him. I've talked to Sir Christopher Wren—he built St. Paul's Cathedral," she said, as if Slane was a barbarian and did not know. "I've even spoken with Sir Isaac Newton—not that I believe white light is made up of colors, but, in spite of that Sir Isaac is a clever man. They're all clever men, and one of them, you would think, could design a bee skep that would keep the creatures alive across the ocean. Do the Irish keep bees, Slane?"

He was saved from answering by the Princess of Wales, who was up from her chair, walking about the chamber, surrounded by her maids of honor like a cow surrounded by nymphs.

"Do you still play cards with Lady Shrewsborough?" the Princess asked him.

"Whenever I may."

"He bests me, too, Your Highness," said Aunt Shrew, "more times than I care to acknowledge."

"Bring him to a card game of mine some afternoon."

"I would be honored," said Slane, but the Princess was turning away. He was dismissed. She and the Duchess were talking about smallpox. Someone tapped Slane on the shoulder—a lady-in-waiting with his bag of coins for payment. Forgotten except for a few lingering looks from the more bold of the maids of honor, he walked from the chamber. The Princess was telling the Duchess that she was going to give her children the new treatment for smallpox.

That was the topic in London this winter, other than the feud between Walpole and Sunderland. A cure for smallpox had been brought back from her travels by Lady Mary Wortley Montagu, a vivacious woman who was the daughter of a duke and Slane's favorite Jacobite agent.

"I am going to have it done to ten men at Newgate Prison. If they survive and are only lightly poxed, then I will have it done to my children," Slane heard the Princess say as he stepped out into the hall.

One scratched the arm lightly with a needle dipped in the active pox, then became sick, perhaps even broke into spots and fever. But the spots and the fever were not deadly, did not disfigure or kill as smallpox did. Some physicians opposed the practice, saying it was ungodly because it came from Turkey. Lady Mary's husband had been ambassador there, and she'd seen the custom.

If Wharton's child had had the treatment, he might not have died, thought Slane. Louis XIV had died of smallpox, and two of the Duchess of Tamworth's sons. It was the grimmest of reapers.

❧

"Have you heard from Lady Devane in Virginia?" the Princess asked.

"No."

"Will she settle there, do you think?"

"After tomorrow," said the Duchess, "it does not matter."

It matters to me, thought the Princess.

❧

Outside, the moon was full. It flung light randomly over building and shadow, snow and ice. Slane stood staring up a moment at it, his mind filled with impressions of the women he'd just left, their soft arms, flowing gowns, light laughter, flirting eyes—all colors—above elaborate fans. There was a shivering, delicate lightness to it all that made him feel off balance and exhilarated. He'd go home, change out of these clothes that revealed too much of who he was, put on his plainer, simpler clothing, and go to Pontack's tavern.

Thus the women celebrate the wedding tomorrow, he thought. And the men?

❧

Hours later, in the confusion and noise of Pontack's, Slane pulled his chair up where the Duke of Wharton was sitting. Whores sat on various laps, trading kisses for coins, pulling down their gowns to show their breasts, if the coins were plenty enough. Two of them were already quarreling. No one would notice him.

"You're drinking," he said to Wharton.

"Only a little ale for me, *duenna.*" *Duenna* was the Spanish word for chaperone. "I made a promise. I have the others drink what I cannot. Look at Tamworth. He hasn't had a drop since Masham's death, but tonight he might be me."

"What's he talking about?"

"His grandfather; it's all he's been talking for an hour. Go and listen. It's worth hearing. He tells the same story over and over."

"People were talking of Lady Mary Wortley Montagu tonight."

Wharton's eyes, the lids hooded like a bird's, blinked once. "What did they say?"

"They were talking about her remedy for smallpox, of how some physicians call it ungodly."

"I'll tell her. She will be angry. She says it is because she is a woman, that her remedy is not accepted more easily."

"I must meet her."

Again, there was that slow blink. "Why, Slane?" Lady Mary and Wharton were lovers. Such difficult duty you give me, Slane, Lady Mary had said. She lied. She was more than half in love with Wharton.

Slane laughed. "So that I know as much as possible about you."

He moved to sit near Tony, who was talking to no one in particular, but talking just the same.

"They said my grandfather was found wandering through his camp like a vagabond, which was likely the first sign, but everyone tried to shield him from the talk. Then it was said he wept before a meeting of the Queen's ministers. After that, there was no holding gossip back. All the stories came out, swirled through London like the snow outside. Wart, are you listening?"

Wharton grinned evilly at Slane, made a motion of drinking.

"He's listening," Slane said quietly, behind Tony. He could see that Tony was so drunk he would remember little in the morning. None of these men would, with the exception, and it was an exception, of Wharton, who, as he said, was keeping his promise.

"I was just a boy when the rumors started. They said my grandfather had broken down once too often during campaign, had to be replaced, though his command was not taken from him. He was so well known, and the war was still enduring—two wars, one upon a battlefield against Louis XIV, one in the cabinet room of Queen Anne. The rumors just kept growing. I didn't understand them, but I understood the insinuations behind them, of madness, insanity, possession. A sign of the devil, they said, a curse. Have you seen the Hospital of St. Mary of Bethlehem? They call it Bedlam. The men and women are caged, naked, tied to the walls of their cells like animals. They howl in their own filth."

Slane had seen it. It was one of the sights of London, one of the places young noblemen liked to go, just as they liked to visit Bridewell after a debauch and see the imprisoned women whipped, because the women were stripped to the waist beforehand.

"Some rise by sin, some by virtue fall. Tommy Carlyle said that. My grandmother brought my grandfather to Tamworth. I came to visit whenever I could. I was heir by then, and so in that, at least, I got my way. To me, my grandfather just seemed quieter, more gentle than ever, having need of more rest. We worked in the rose garden together. We walked. He let me rummage in his cabinets of precious medals and cameos, something Barbara and Harry were not allowed to do."

"Barbara and Harry?" prompted Slane. Tony turned to look at him, seemed to focus a little.

"My cousins. You haven't met them. It would be hard now to meet Harry. He's dead. And Barbara, she's gone far away. Too boisterous, my grandfather thought them. He collected lead soldiers, Slane, he had hundreds of them. We used to arrange them into his battle plans, small men of lead, their regimental colors bright with paint. Retreat, march, feint, fall back, charge. 'You are good for him,

Tony; he is happy with you,' my grandmother said. Have you met my grandmother, Slane? A word of praise from her is rare. She never liked it that I was heir. There were others, you see—my oldest uncle; his son; my father. They all died, and so it came to me. She never thought much of me."

"I met her this evening. I don't think she thought much of me, either."

Tony smiled, a shy smile, grave. "Barbara and Harry, they didn't think much of me, either. I was the interloper. I used to stand at a window and watch them. 'Anticipate your enemy,' my grandfather said. 'Hit him hard and strong with your foot troops.' Obviously, Barbara and Harry were the stuff of generals."

The scene around Slane and Tony was becoming wilder, the women half undressed, Charles with his face pressed between the breasts of a young whore. There was spilled wine everywhere, and the women's voices were too shrill; some of the men were already so drunk they couldn't stand, while Wharton sat at his part of the table, eyes gleaming, as if he were the conjurer who had summoned it all into being.

" 'I will thrash you, heir,' said Harry. He did it, too, knocking out a tooth."

"And Barbara?"

"She taunted me as I bled. I had no idea how to deal with them, except to avoid them."

"A wise choice."

"I never minded my grandfather's silences, the vagueness. I loved him, Slane. My grandfather was very kind, and I knew he was a great hero, so that his kindness seemed even more special. There was no criticism, no anger, no expectation which I did not meet, ever. We were in among the roses. 'You cut the stem this way,' my grandfather said. I've had too much wine, Slane. Somewhere, in the distance—I remember the hum of bees, the fragrance of roses—I remember the sound of Barbara and Harry quarreling. They were near. They liked to spy on us, to tease me, later. My grandfather scratched his forearm on a thorn, and he bled. I didn't notice at first.

I was tending the roses the way he'd shown me. I had no idea there was anything wrong until my grandfather cried out, this shocking cry, this groan from the heart."

Slane sat very still. In his mind's eye, he was in the garden he'd never seen, with Tony and his grandfather, the great hero, made man-sized now.

" 'Where are my boys?' he said. He was so loud. My grandfather was never loud, never shouted. 'My boys, my boys,' he said. He wouldn't stop asking where they were, and he kept pointing to the blood on his arm. Well, finally, I took him by the hand and led him down the path to Tamworth Church, to the chapel there. That's where the coffins of my father and uncles are. It was the wrong thing to do, but it was all I could think of. My grandfather sat on the marble bench in the silent chapel and began to weep. 'Dead,' he said. 'They are all dead.' How he wept, Slane. I cannot describe it—"

A whore sat down in Tony's lap, kissed his cheek, and slipped her hand into his pocket, looking for something to steal.

"Leave him be," said Slane. He gave her a coin. "Go on, there are plenty of others. Tell me the rest of the story, Tamworth."

"He was weeping like a woman. All the rumors I had overheard about his madness, the whispers, flew into my head, and I ran all the way back to Tamworth Hall to tell my grandmother. She was angry. 'Never take him there again,' she told me. Madman, madman, boo hoo hoo, that was Barbara and Harry later on the terrace—there is this big terrace at Tamworth, sloping in gentle steps down into the gardens. They were playing out the scene as they'd seen it, our grandfather being led weeping from the chapel. My grandmother had them spanked and sent them to bed without supper, but not me."

"Which finished you in their regard."

"Yes. She allowed me supper—in spite of my stupidity, she said— but I could not eat. I stared down at the silver plate. It had a dim sheen, I remember it still, and I was aware of a loss greater even than that of my father. I never knew my father, not really. Something precious, rare and fine, not easily replaced, not easily found to begin with, was gone. It sat in the chapel, sobbing like a woman, until servants brought it home again and put it to bed. Whom did he mourn? His sons or all those soldiers who had died in charges and counter-charges? Perhaps the two became mixed in his mind. 'O, noble warrior. O, valiant man. We will not see your like again.' "

"What's that?"

"Caesar White, a poet, wrote a requiem poem to my grandfather. I am going to be sick."

"Here, let me help you outside. Follow me."

Outside, Slane walked a little away, breathing in the cold air, glad to be out of the tavern with its noise and smoke and mayhem.

Tony stood, head leaned against a wall, retching.

O, noble warrior. O, valiant man. We will not see your like again. Slane thought of the Blackbird, when still a boy, hiding out in this and that castle because France had lost the wars and Louis XIV was not allowed to succor him any longer. He thought of friends who had died beside him in Scotland in the awful winter of 1715, when they knew they'd lost but fought on anyway, thought of his own father, drowned during the storm that had tossed Jamie's French invasion ships about like so many sulfur matches thrown upon water. He had been thirteen when his father died. He'd seen him drown. He would never forget it, watching water lap over the place where his father had been, then somehow making it back to France, where his courageous, vibrant mother waited. He'd had to tell her. She'd held out her arms to him, and for the last time, he had stepped into boyhood and wept in them. Your Jamie is cursed, said his mother, but that was in 1718, as yet another invasion, this time helped by Sweden and Spain, got all the way launched, and was yet again destroyed by a storm. Leave him, Lucius, she'd said. Slane shivered.

Tony did not move his head from the wall.

" 'Give me a kiss, and to that kiss a score; / Then to that twenty, add a hundred more: / A thousand to that hundred: so kiss on / To make that thousand up a million,' " recited Tony.

What's this? thought Slane. I should have recited it tonight. It's beautiful.

" 'Treble that million, and when that is done, / Let's kiss afresh, as when we first begun. . . .' I never once kissed her in passion."

"Whom, Your Grace?"

"Barbara."

Barbara, thought Slane, you'll be at the wedding tomorrow, in this man's mind. He put his hand on Tony's shoulder. I married my true love, he thought. I lost her, but for a time I had her. Ah, Tamworth, you do your duty and it has its price.

"Beloved," said Tony, and Slane closed his eyes. This was what came of staying in one place too long. A man began to care for people, even those who were his enemies.

"Tell me what you know of the death of Wharton's child," Slane said.

"Smallpox," Tony answered, still without moving his forehead from the wall. "There was smallpox in London, and although he asked her not to, his wife brought the boy to the city."

"Why?"

"She did not wish to be separated from Wharton. They married when they were both fifteen. Wharton was wild for her, for a time. But his father died, and Wharton blamed himself. His father had not wanted the marriage, had been angry that Wharton had acted as he did. After his father died, Wart went away to Europe, leaving his wife behind; when he came home, she was interesting to him again, and they had a child. He never sees her now."

"Tell me about Lady Mary."

"She is some ten years older than Wart. She lives alone, without her husband. Writes poetry."

Slane smiled at what was in Tony's voice, as if Lady Mary's writing poetry made him afraid of her. "I think you need a companion to walk you home, Your Grace."

They walked silently through the streets, Slane going after Tony and grabbing him by the coattails when he wandered off course. The moon lit their way like a lantern, and in some of the streets were the fires to keep the beggars from freezing. They walked into the courtyard of Saylor House.

"Good-bye, Your Grace."

"Come to my wedding. I want you to come to my wedding."

"I think you'll regret the invitation tomorrow, Your Grace."

Slane's shoes made a crunching sound in the melting snow as he walked back toward his lodging under the moon's full light. He stood at the window in his room and looked out. The moon spilled down like soft silver. O, noble warrior. O, valiant man. We will not see your like again. The words kept echoing through his mind. He remembered when word of Richard Saylor's madness had come; there was celebration at the French court. He kept seeing Richard Saylor standing in his garden weeping for his boys. And in Slane's heart was not hatred, or jubilation, but compassion, for Tony, for the Duchess—and, oddly enough, for himself, for he, too, knew what it was to lose someone you loved.

I'm losing my edge, thought Slane, and he sighed.

CHAPTER 24

Cursing himself for having called on the day of the wedding, Sir John Ashford walked into a parlor at Saylor House. Bunches of Christmas holly and ivy were cascading out of the Chinese vases, and there was ivy gathered at the corners of the famous and enormous tapestries on the walls of this chamber, the ivy twining greenly into the battle scenes of rearing horses and grimacing struggles. Roses and lilies were intertwined through it all, for the wedding. The young Duke of Tamworth married Harriet Holles at nine tonight. Sir John had sent his regrets. His gift for them had been given to Gussy to bring.

He cleared his throat. He did not see the Duchess among the people standing before the fireplace. But he did see the Duke of Wharton, and his face went red. Traitor, he thought.

He glared at Wharton, before seeing what was even worse—the hulking courtier Tommy Carlyle, rouge bright on each cheek and that infamous earring in one ear.

That does it, thought Sir John. I'll make some quick excuse and call upon the Duke of Tamworth when I return in January. But just then, a footman touched his arm.

"Her Grace, the Duchess of Tamworth, asks me to bring you to her."

The Duchess sat in a corner, talking to Sir Christopher Wren.

What is that contraption upon her head? wondered Sir John. There were feathers and whatever, springing out of it. She looked a sight, and it was clear she did not care. Sir John smiled and bowed very formally to the Duchess, the bow old-fashioned and stiff.

"Since when do I not deserve a New Year's kiss?"

The Duchess embarrassed him, as always she tried to do, but she also amused him, and so he smacked at her cheek, while she touched at something dangling down from the cluster of feathers on her head, something making a clatter.

"Bear claws." She spoke with what could only be described as tremendous satisfaction. "And look here, this is a necklace of them around my neck. Look at their size. The bears must have been monsters, not like those brown bears the dogs bait across the river. I am wearing a chieftain's bonnet, or so Barbara says. I've had a letter from her, John, this very day, along with these trifles I wear. She sent me a swamp laurel and cuttings for vines, which you'll need to take on to Tamworth Hall for me. I cannot tell you the weight that has been lifted from my heart. You know what I've suffered fretting about whether Barbara made it safely or not, old friend, yes, you do. But where are my manners? You know Sir Christopher?"

"The Duchess and I were speaking of bees," said Sir Christopher. He was quite old, as tiny now as the Duchess.

"So," said Sir John, who knew all about the Duchess and her bees. Who in London did not? "You've still got bees in your bonnet, have you? I congratulate you on receiving a letter from your granddaughter. She's well?"

"Quite well, thank you!" The Duchess jangled her bear claws.

"I've had letters too, from my wife. She says there are Gypsies in Tamworth's woods. They've found one of the Gypsy women. She's with child."

The Duchess lifted up her skirts, pointed to her feet. She wore some sort of soft slipper.

"Never mind Gypsies. Barbara sent these, also, along with a pair for Jane. I forget what these are called."

I haven't seen her this elated in months, thought Sir John. I'm glad she's heard from Barbara.

"Moccasins," said Sir Christopher, "and made quite well. Look at the beading, the design it makes."

The Duke of Wharton had stepped forward to join them.

Sir John stiffened. Arrogant young hound, he thought. We're too old, we're the party of the past, he'd said to Lady Shrewsborough, as long a Tory as he was. No wonder the young men leave us. Wharton was impious, irreverent, and unstable, but they had needed him. Don't whine, John, she had replied. I can't abide it. She and the Duchess were a pair. Of what, was the question.

The Duchess ignored Wharton.

"Barbara said the women who make these chew the leather to softness with their teeth. She's sent a parcel for Jane and the children, too, and something for the King and all the royal family. Go fetch me something to drink, Wharton. That's a good boy. —I can't abide him," she said to Sir John, as Wharton walked away, "and as cousin to Harriet, with the marriage, he becomes family."

"Who is here?" said Sir John, looking around.

"Everyone. Sir Gideon Andreas, Lord Sunderland, Lord Holles, Sir Alexander Pendarves."

"A Whig parley."

"A marriage party. It won't hurt you to mix with us. Perhaps you'll hear something Tories can use. It's being said the Whigs will sweep the election, John."

"I know it. My heart is breaking for it. We haven't the funds to buy votes, Alice. The King himself is giving money to buy Whig votes."

"Here's Wharton with my wine. Sir John has come to say goodbye to me before he goes to his home, Wharton. Sir John Ashford is a rarity these days, a man who follows his conscience."

"Is that for me?" Wharton asked.

The Duchess looked at him, pursed her lips. "Is it?"

Other people in the chamber were moving their way, they'd attracted attention. The Duchess began to introduce them one after another, just as if Sir John did not see them during the week in the corridors of St. Stephen's, where the House of Commons met.

"You know Sir Gideon Andreas, of course, and Lady Andreas. Lady Andreas is godmother to Harriet."

A goblet of wine had been put in Sir John's hand; he smiled in the direction of the woman he assumed was Lady Andreas and gulped down the wine, only to have the goblet immediately refilled by a footman. The guests were in satin coats and full wigs; there were jewels upon the women, at their throats and in their ears; while he was dressed simply, for travel, for he was beginning his journey home this very afternoon. He was stopping by to see Gussy before he left; then he was off, leaving London behind. A note had come from the Duke of Tamworth: "I would very much appreciate it if you might find the time to call upon me before you leave for Ladybeth." But where was the Duke?

"His Grace will see you now," a servant said, quietly, into Sir John's ear.

"What's this?" cried the Duchess. "Are you leaving us? Promise you'll look in before you go to Ladybeth. Even if I've gone up to my bedchamber, have a footman inform me. You must not forget that parcel Barbara sent for Jane. She sent Tony a—now, what was it called?"

"—hawk," Sir John thought he heard Sir Christopher say as he moved to follow the servant.

"Tomahawk," the Duchess called out loudly after him. "It's a war ax, John. They bash in one another's brains with it."

"More direct in their violence than we," said Wharton.

The wine made Sir John feel dizzy and happy as he climbed upstairs. The Duke of Tamworth was in his grandfather's library on the top floor of the house. It had been years since Sir John had been in this particular chamber, not since Richard Saylor himself was alive and they'd plotted strategy together in the last dangerous days of James II's precarious reign.

Sir John could remember it as clearly as if it was yesterday: Richard, no duke yet, saying, John, we are going to declare for

William of Orange. I am among those who have signed a secret declaration asking him to come over with an armed force. There may
be war, and I want you to be free to follow your conscience in it.

Then, unlike now, the party of the King had been Tory, and the
opposition Whig, but both Tory and Whig lords had signed the
declaration.

Richard had remained faithful to Tory principles under King
William and his heir, Queen Anne, but Richard's grandson Tony
might turn Whig; it looked as if he would. He was allying himself by
marriage with a Whig family. They had not discussed the coming
election. The Duke had been a boy seven years ago, when the last
election was held.

The wine made Sir John wish that he and the young Duke might
talk of Richard, of old days. He would tell a story Richard had loved,
a story from Sir John's grandfather, who had seen Charles I led to
the scaffold to be beheaded, not far from this very house. There was
a groan from the crowd when his head was severed with the ax, a
great collective groan, his grandfather had said, like one immense
sound of fear, as if the beheading had transgressed against God.

The divine right of kings. It was James's right to rule by virtue of
his birth, God having determined that birth. That was what they had
struggled with in those days of tumult. Was kingship divine, hered-
itary and inalienable, or did a king hold power on trust from Parliament? A revolutionary idea, republican, dangerous, but more and
more talked of. If James II had not convinced certain great lords of
Parliament into thinking he would rule without them, without the
sanctions of Parliament, he would have remained on the throne,
Catholic or not. And that was the truth of it, so Richard had said,
Richard, who was even then becoming a great lord.

I've had to wrestle long and hard with my conscience, John,
Richard had said to him that night. The struggle of it was there in
lines upon Richard's face, the darkness under his eyes. I give you full
leave to follow your conscience in this.

Have you followed yours? he had asked Richard. That was the
only time he had ever seen Richard at a loss for words.

One word of understanding from this young man, this grandson of Richard, and while Sir John could never turn Whig, as Wharton had done, he would bend. After all, he was old, and times were changing.

Downstairs, the Duchess looked up from admiring her moccasins to see her daughter, Diana, marching into the parlor. There was no other word for it than "march."

Diana spoke to no one, but came directly over to the Duchess. The crimson gown she wore was cut so low that the tops of her nipples showed. There were large jewels on her neck and at her ears. Every man was stopped, staring at her.

"I understand there are letters from Barbara, Mother."

They weren't reconciled, she and Diana. Tony had forgiven her for sending Barbara to Virginia. Diana had not. They were cool and distant to each other still. Walpole would have told Diana there was a ship in from Virginia. If I thought she had a heart, I would be grieved for her, the Duchess thought.

"Yes. Letters and parcels."

"Where is mine?"

"There was none."

Diana was turning away. She was always turning away. The Duchess felt her heart squeeze for this daughter she had never liked, yet whom Richard had so loved.

"You may read mine, Diana."

But Diana was walking away, over to the fireplace, dividing the men who talked there like Moses parting a sea. She took a goblet of wine from a servant. "Bring me another," she said, "and another after that."

"Letters from Lady Devane," Tommy Carlyle purred. He smiled down at Diana. "How happy you must be."

"Does Walpole come as your guest to the wedding?" Lord Sunderland asked her, viciously, knowing Walpole would be with his wife.

She shook her head a moment; she looked like a giantess surrounded by pygmies. "Walpole's not well, as you know," she snapped. "Why don't you just stab him in the heart and have done with it? More wine. Now."

Charles put a goblet to her hand.

"Congratulate Lord Russel," said Lord Sunderland. "We've been told this day that his wife is with child."

Diana drank. The wine left a stain against her upper lip. Her tongue came out to flick at it.

"How domestic, Charles," she said. "Barbara would love it. I congratulate you on her behalf."

"Someone hit her over the head with the fireplace poker," said Aunt Shrew, standing near enough to hear. She wore a bright red wig and a gown cut as low as Diana's, but without the same effect. "You seem unable to tear your eyes from Diana's gown, Lumpy. The top of it will hold, I assure you."

"It wouldn't kill her," said Tommy Carlyle. "She seems to be taking it hard."

"Which? Having no letter from Barbara, or what looks like Walpole's fall from grace? It is the only thing I can stomach about this betrayal of Wharton's."

"Both. Divine, isn't it? How I do adore to see others suffer."

"I hear someone is buying the land all around Devane House," Pendarves said to Carlyle.

"Midas Andreas."

"Why? Building has all but stopped out in that direction. Buying too much land is what helped ruin Lord Devane."

Carlyle shrugged, went to where Charles stood, looking out a long window at the afternoon. "I hear there is a letter, but only one, from Virginia."

"Have you also heard that I never pine over former mistresses?"

"Never? What fortitude."

Bend, rather than break: There was wisdom in that, Sir John was thinking. Those among his old friends who were Jacobites, who wooed with such compelling arguments, saying that only revolution would bring Tories into power again, could whistle in the dark for the sake of the memories the sight of this library room aroused, for the sake of that dear termagant downstairs clacking bear claws at the company, for the sake of Richard Saylor, whose grandson this was.

"Compliments of the season, Sir John," Tony said. The young Duke looked stern, a bit worn.

"Thank you, Your Grace. I return the same to you." There were account books spread across the table behind which the Duke sat, and a large map of London, the various streets and great squares of houses drawn on it. Hardly a task for one's wedding day, thought Sir John.

"You've been bailiff of my grandmother's estate for how long?" the Duke asked.

"Since before your grandfather died, Your Grace. Since his mind became dark, and he no longer made sound judgments."

"A long time."

Tears came to Sir John's eyes. Too much wine. I am ready to laugh or cry, he thought. I am a sentimental fool. What had the Duchess said tonight? Something about not knowing who was who anymore, when it came to party principle. It was true. Whigs had taken on Tory ideals and vice versa in the long years of treacherous fighting for favor. What did it matter if he sided once in a while with Whigs, particularly when they espoused an old Tory principle wrapped now in their linen, as long as he could vote his conscience on church matters, which were dear to him?

He plunged in, knowing he was clumsy and chose his moment poorly, but wanting the matter clear, that he was a Tamworth man, always had been, only there had been no Tamworth to follow for years, and so he had gone his own way, because the Duchess hadn't cared. Once Richard was buried, all that was political within her had been buried with him. Now there was a Tamworth again. There will never be Tories in the ministry as long as George is king, the Jacobites said. Those men downstairs did nothing to change that, but perhaps an old Tory and a young Whig could learn from one another.

"Not nearly as long as I've been the member in the House of Commons from Tamworth, Your Grace. We've not talked of that, and there is the election staring us in the face in the spring. I have had a thought to talk to you tonight, to tell you—"

"There are two thousand pounds of rents missing from my grandmother's account."

Time stopped, then started again for John Ashford, and in the moment in which he stared at the young man sitting behind the table, a young man whose glance fell over him contemptuously, he knew that Richard was dead, and the Duchess old, and he aging in a world he no longer understood.

"I— You must give me leave to gather my wits," he finally managed to say. "The South Sea—I bought shares in the South Sea, like all the other fools in town and countryside. I bought another farm, Your Grace, ordered a new carriage, dowered a daughter too high, did many another foolish thing with what I thought were my riches. When the stock began to fall, I was short of funds, so short that I had to—"

"Steal two thousand pounds and some odd shillings from my grandmother? She counts you as her closest friend, but I would call your action a failure of friendship."

"No!" Sir John tried to calm himself. "I never meant to hurt your grandmother, for whom I have all the admiration in the world. I had obligations that were insistent, and in the heat of the moment— surely you remember how mad that time was—only last year it was, Your Grace, and men were jumping from windows, slashing their throats. I had immediate obligations that threatened. Everyone was desperate for coin, calling in loans. I could not—"

"Jump from a window? So you stole from my grandmother and from me. The estate is hers only until her death, Sir John. Then, under the terms of my grandfather's will, it becomes mine."

We are foes, Sir John thought, in a state of shock. He regards me as foe and fool and thief.

"I cannot put my hands upon such a sum at the moment, but I will write out a mortgage to the Duchess upon Ladybeth Farm even as we speak. Ladybeth is worth far more than what I borrowed—or it will be, when land prices become stable again."

His hands were shaking, he could not stop them, and the ink blotted and ran, but he was writing out words crookedly upon a sheet of paper he grabbed at random from the table between them. He scarcely knew what he was writing, so upset was he. "If you would allow me a few months, I will have every penny of the money—"

"I do not require another farm, Sir John. And I find I do not require your services as the member in the House of Commons from Tamworth. I won't have Tamworth served by a—" The Duke did not finish the sentence, but he did not have to.

"Your Grace, you have the account books before you. Look them over, and you will see that in all the time—"

"I waited for you to come to me, Sir John. Once I found the loss, I thought, There must be an explanation, and Sir John will come to me and give it to both our satisfactions. He is my grandmother's closest friend. But you did not come, not yesterday, or the day before, or the day before that. I do not think you were going to speak of it today. If my grandmother cannot trust you, I, who do not know you, and have never counted upon your friendship in the manner she does, certainly cannot."

Words seemed to stick in Sir John's throat. He could feel tears again in his eyes—how different these tears were from those he'd felt coming before—and he said a quick, fierce prayer that he would not weep before this remote, cold young man. "I will return the funds, with interest, within the month. I always had the intention to do so, but— You have my word of honor."

"Then no more need be said. Good evening, Sir John."

"Your Grace, your grandmother—"

"I have not spoken of this matter to my grandmother, nor will I. But I remain silent out of regard for her and not for you."

The young man's contempt could not be borne.

"You're scarcely wet behind the ears," Sir John heard himself say. "My father owned Ladybeth and his father owned it before him, and they were able to live decent lives. They and men like them, honest men of the land, made this country what it is today. In my time, I've seen taxes upon land rise, and income from that same land fall. I've seen the great lords take more and more for themselves. I've seen good men reduced to little or nothing because they wouldn't go to court and lick some flatterer's boots and so be given a place or office. Yet any clerk with a head for figures and too heartless to forgive loans may call himself a banker, like that hard-eyed son of an old Dutch merchant, that Gideon Andreas downstairs, whose father was wise enough to ride in on William's coattails and be—"

"Good evening, Sir John."

In the hall, Sir John found he was breathing far too hard, his heart pounding, aching, a literal ache that made him think he would not be able to walk down the stairs and outside the house without fainting. He could feel grief and shame blocking his chest.

Out of his loyalty to the Tamworth family, he had abstained from voting when Lord Devane's part in the scandals came up from committee. He had had every intention of returning the funds to Alice. Only desperation had made him take them in the first place. She never looked at the accounts, left the money untouched sometimes for years because she had no need of it. He had not quite been able to catch up his affairs since the Bubble; nagging debts remained, and he had let more time than he realized slip by. All his life he had served—

Stop this, he told himself.

The world had changed. It belonged to the London moneymen and their clerks, who schemed bubbles and took honest men's coin and found themselves favored for it, like Andreas downstairs. It belonged to vain young dukes who squandered their fathers' patrimonies and know no love of the land and no decency, like Wharton. It belonged to churchmen who dealt in policy rather than God, not to old squires like him. It belonged to Whigs, the more venial the better. As Robert Walpole bragged, every man has his price.

Go on home, Sir John said to himself, as quietly as you can. He managed to walk down the stairs, even though the shame at what had occurred was like hot stones in his chest. The doors to the great parlor were mercifully closed; he would not have to see that company again.

One of the footmen standing in the large hall followed him to the front entrance doors. "Her Grace, the Duchess, asked that you join her upstairs."

"No, I am unable—tell Her Grace how sorry—"

He had just enough sense about him to give the footman a coin for Christmas, as the fellow put a parcel in his arms. That parcel for Jane, from Barbara. Barbara and Jane had grown to womanhood together in the orchards of Tamworth and Ladybeth. Why, Harry might have married Jane, had Diana not needed a better match to cover the funds she had squandered in her misspent life. The Lord above knew Diana was on her knees at that time, and a squire's daughter would not have been too low a match. How proud he had been of his years serving Tamworth. He'd seen a road put through, gotten funds for refurbishing the church, helped this or that family find places for extra sons in the army or navy. In one hand was the crumpled-up paper on which he'd written out the note pledging Ladybeth, his home, his life, to repay the money.

"Give this to His Grace," he managed to say.

Outside Saylor House, it was raining, but Sir John walked unseeing toward the lodging he kept in London and where his horse awaited him. He found he was weeping as he walked, weeping as if his heart was broken; and, truth be told, it was.

At a knock on the door, Tony started and put down the tomahawk, whose handle he had been so absently caressing.

"Come in."

In came Tim, carrying the Duchess, who still wore the headdress that had arrived this afternoon from Barbara. Does she intend to wear that to the wedding? thought Tony.

"Wait outside," the Duchess said to Tim, and to Tony: "What's this?"

In her hand was a piece of paper, which had been crumpled.

Smoothing it out, Tony read the words, "I, John Ashford, do pledge to the Duke of Tamworth . . ."

"How did you come by this?" He rubbed at the pulse in his temple.

"Why do you rub your forehead? Your debauch last night?"

Tony had a vague memory of inviting the actor Laurence Slane to his wedding. Had he done so?

"It says that he pledges his farm to you. What has happened? I can see in your face that something has occurred. He didn't come upstairs to say good-bye to me before he left. That is not like him. Have you quarreled? I've been meaning to talk with you about him, but there hasn't seemed to be the time. He has been the member from Tamworth since before you were born, and—"

"Sir John, and I say this with all respect to him, won't do. He agrees with me—"

"Won't do? What on earth are you talking about?"

"This is not something for you to involve yourself in, Grandmama. Trust me in my—"

"To whom do you think you are speaking? I know more about policy and intrigue than half the men downstairs. I wish Sir John to continue as Tamworth's member of the House of Commons."

Tony turned away. "I am sorry, Grandmama. That is not possible."

The Duchess pursed her lips. "Tell Tim to come and fetch me."

She saw Tony glance at her out of the corner of his eye. Yes, I am taking it well, she thought, because I have no intention of allowing it.

In her bedchamber, she was full of orders. "Go out on the street and hire a carriage," she told Tim. "Find my warmest cloak," she told Annie.

"There's a wedding at nine. Where are you going?"

"Never mind that. Give this to Tony."

And when Annie didn't move, only stared at the letter: "Go on."

"He's the best of those before him."

Were those tears in Annie's eyes? The Duchess set her mouth stubbornly.

"The servants adore him, cannot say enough good things about him. When all is said and done, he's the best."

"Do as I say. What's that?"

"Another New Year's gift for you."

"Open it."

It was a scratchback, wonderfully made, of chased silver, resembling a cane in its length, but with a slender ivory hand at one end, and, if she wasn't mistaken, a ring upon a finger of that hand. It was a wonderful gift, extravagant, and handy for reaching those itching places one could not reach when wearing a tight gown and stays.

"Who gives it to me?"

"Tommy Carlyle."

That rouged spider. Why? Never mind. Here was Tim.

Tony stared down at the map in front of him. It was Sir Gideon Andreas who had told him to look to his estates, who warned that bailiffs and stewards left unchecked while young heirs grew to manhood soon developed fingers to which many coins stuck. I have seen it time after time, Andreas said. It was Andreas who knew Sir John Ashford had been bitten deeply by the South Sea, and who had told Tony of it.

And it was Andreas who was buying land all around Devane Square, as quickly and as quietly as he could.

At the sound of another knock on the door, Tony expected Tim and his grandmother, but Annie whirled in like a dervish, handed him a letter, and tried to whirl out again before he could speak.

"Wait," he said. "What is this?"

Annie didn't answer for a moment.

"Lady Devane's letter," she finally said, and her mouth was grim.

Blood pulsed strong from head to heart, heart to head. Barbara's letter had come today. The moment he'd seen it, he had felt as if it were June, and she was freshly gone.

"Why does she give this to me? It is my wedding day."

Annie compressed her lips.

"To be kind, or to hurt me? You know, Annie."

"I know nothing, Your Grace."

Diana moaned. The carriage lurched, and she moaned louder and shifted backward. She pushed aside her cloak impatiently, pulled down the front of her gown, that crimson gown whose top was so low that no man could keep from staring.

She brought Charles's head to her breasts and closed her eyes. The inside of the carriage was dark, and cold in spite of fur cloaks and carriage blankets. Charles made an impatient movement, as if he would throw her down to the seat opposite, but she stopped him. She was sitting in his lap, facing him. Legs braced against the seat opposite, he had his hands on her bare hips under bunched folds of gown and petticoat.

"I can't cannot think," Charles said.

She leaned into him. Her breasts were at his mouth. He tasted the nipple of one, a diamond in her necklace sharp against his cheek. He kneaded the soft flesh of her hips as she pushed against him. . . . Ah, the pressure . . . ah, the feeling . . . the sway of the carriage, the cold, the ways they were dressed but undressed—

"Soon." Her tongue flicked a moment in his ear. "Oh, Charles . . ." She put her arms around his neck and the carriage lurched and swayed. They were on their way to who knew where, the coachman had simply been ordered to drive. The insanity of what they were doing made him insatiable. The pleasure was hurtful, it was so exquisite it was unbearable, and then—sharply, suddenly—over.

He sat there, watching her. He felt unable to move, but she was pushing herself back into her gown, straightening her jewels, touching her hair, pinning it back with its diamond pins. She pulled up her skirts to retie a garter. He wished he could see her face more clearly, but the shadows were too great. God, he felt so cold suddenly. As cold as ice. She pulled the edges of his cloak together and covered him with a carriage robe.

"You called out Barbara's name," she said. "Never mind. I am getting out now. Don't be late for the wedding. Are you listening, Charles? Charles!"

"Yes."

The carriage stopped, and she opened the door and was gone.

He lay back against the leather seat, shivering inside his cloak. He would have the carriage go back to his room in the city, near St. Paul's Cathedral, where he could wash off her rouge and change into another shirt and think about what had just occurred.

⁂

The room was cold. Freezing. Charles's hands shook as he lit a candle. He took the time to light a fire, knelt before the fireplace, holding out his hands to the small flames, willing the fire to grow before he died of cold. Parts of the fire were yellow-red, and he was reminded, sharply, of Barbara's hair in certain lights. He found another shirt and changed into it, shivering and cursing. Standing before the mirror, he stared at himself, rubbing at his face with the first shirt long after any trace of rouge was gone. You have a deceiving face, sir, Barbara had said in one of their quarrels.

He knelt before the fire again, holding his hands out for a last bit of warmth before he braved the street to find another carriage. What a jest it would be if he died from the cold, after a bout in a carriage with the most surprising whore he had ever had.

Diana, he thought, lingering over her name. Diana. What am I going to do?

But he knew what he would do. See her again, and again, until every lustful thought she conjured up was burned away in the ashes of coupling. Why not? She'd begun it. It was she who had touched him not an hour after arriving at Saylor House today, she who'd suggested they rendezvous in the carriage. A treat before the wedding. Are you hungry for a treat, Charles? Was this her heartbreak over there being no letter to her from Barbara? God.

This was the lodging where he brought women—whores, ladies of court, merchants' wives, the dancer or singer from the opera, whoever took his eye. Most men he knew had something like it. She said he had called Barbara's name.

The first time Barbara had walked through that door, she had been flippant and irritable and nervous, almost as if she were a virgin, rather than what her reputation said. She had been stiff in his arms; it had taken him a while to warm her, but the warming was a pleasure. What a strange affair they'd had; he never felt he knew her, except in a carnal sense, but he had loved her.

It was her habit to sit up in bed afterward, chin on her knees, talking to him of anything and everything, shops and hats and Harry's debts, what her dogs or Hyacinthe had done. He had sometimes felt an odd pang in the region of his chest, listening to her, feeling closer to her then, after the act of coupling, than when in its middle. He had liked Barbara in the way he liked his friends, and he had trusted her. Oddly enough, he still did, in spite of all that had happened between them. Someone, Tommy Carlyle perhaps, had said that the Prince's mistress, Mrs. Howard, in a drunken mood had confessed to having known both passion and love, but tenderness, Mrs. Howard was reputed to have said, tenderness is best.

Charles stood. He had taken Tony's friendship for granted; only its absence made him aware how deeply he cared that all was changed between them now, since the duel. If you don't fight him, I will, Charles had said, and so Tony had killed a man; that death had changed him, and remained in those grave eyes. If you looked closely enough, you could see it. You're a dangerous friend, Charles, Wart had said. It took one to know one.

The New Year was here. "Wassail!" they would say tonight, holding up goblets. To health and happiness. To triumph. To invasion. How he and Wart had laughed, that a great and noble Whig like Lord Sunderland, with such direct access to the King, should be embracing one of the highest Jacobites in the land. Wart.

Is Slane pleased? Charles had asked. I don't speak of Slane, Wart had said. Charles was impressed. Slane had certainly made his point. Charles did not even know who was the true head of this invasion, though he had his suspicions. He knew Wart, and through Wart's misspeaking, Slane, but not who was above them. Wart said, mad grin intersecting the long ugliness of his face—and Charles could see Slane speaking through him—It is now that the men separate from the boys. There must be no faltering, Charles, and if we are somehow found out, you must deny it forever, no matter who of us goes down.

Cursed be the wretch who seized the throne and marred our constitution. Cursed be the Parliament, that day who gave their confirmation. And cursed be every whining Whig and damned be the whole nation, so said a street verse.

Charles smiled, his even face made handsome and bold. What would Wart say to his seduction of the sometimes mistress of one Robert Walpole? Even the arrogant Laurence Slane would have to be impressed. The edges of the memory of what had happened with Diana in the carriage were suddenly sharper than the event itself had been. He wanted Diana again, as soon as he could have her. He would have her again. She liked the danger as much as he. What a useful way to pass the time until spring, until the invasion. He raked apart the coals and blew out the candle and shut and locked the door behind himself.

"What happened then?" Gussy asked Slane. They were talking of Tony.

"He said his grandfather was among the roses, when he somehow cut his arm. A thorn or something— Is that your father-in-law come to say good-bye? I'll wait on the other side of the door."

There was another exit from the chamber, and Slane stepped out into a hall, put his ear to the door, heard the sound of someone weeping.

Sir John was here to pick up letters and parcels to take to Ladybeth. Slane had helped Gussy select the gown that was his wife's New Year's gift. She will look beautiful in this, Gussy, Slane said. Why not take it to her yourself? Lace her in it, tight, then lace her right back out, and show her that you love her. Too many children, Gussy answered. Childbirth is difficult for her. She is afraid of having another child.

I'll buy you French letters, said Slane. Do you know what those are? Put on before a man enters a woman, it keeps him from catching the pox. But it also keeps him from giving away his seed. He'd shocked Gussy as he explained it all to him.

Carefully, Slane cracked the door. Sir John was sitting like a large child in a chair before the fire, hands to his face, crying, while Gussy moved around him in what could only be described as a fluttering way. There was some kind of disjointed confession going on—stolen funds, the Duchess of Tamworth's friendship, the Duke's contempt; Sir John wasn't to represent Tamworth in the Commons. Something about age, duty, the Tories.

Slane's mind went leaping.

Someone knocked upon the door Sir John had used. Gussy went to open it, and in came the Bishop of Rochester in his nightgown, nightcap on his head, upon his crutches, and behind him the Duchess of Tamworth, carried by her footman. What is that upon her head? thought Slane. Feathers and some kind of claws. Is that a wedding headdress?

"I have to speak with you," the Duchess said to Sir John, who jumped up at the sight of her.

The footman put her in a chair, and then Gussy and Rochester and the footman were going out the door. Slane stepped back down the hall, lightly, lithely, went around a corner.

Rochester stood with his ear pressed to the door. Gussy was peeping in through the keyhole. Only the footman had the dignity to stand away.

Slane went back to his own secret place, put his eye to the crack.

"I don't believe you!" The Duchess's hand, fastened to the head of her cane, clenched and unclenched. "You are not a thief. It is a mistake. We will call it a loan. I will give you—"

"You will give me nothing, because I accept nothing. I have broken the trust between us, stolen from you, and that is that. I am willing to go to trial, if the Duke wishes it."

Everything about Sir John was set and stiff, from the angle of his head to the way he stood to the jut of his jaw. Only his eyes, the rapid blinking of the lids over them, betrayed what this conversation was costing him.

"To trial? Are you mad? That would be a pretty sight, your fellow justices sitting in judgment upon you—or have you forgotten that you are also a justice of the peace? There will be no airing of dirty linen—"

"Dirty linen? It is a matter of the failure of trust! Do you not hear me, Alice? I took two thousand pounds from your rents over a year ago and have yet to pay back a penny of it."

"We have been friends for thirty years—"

"Which makes this all the more reprehensible upon my part. I understand that all friendship must be severed between you and me, that you can scarcely bear to look me in the eye. I will trouble you no more, except to say you have my pledge that I will repay every penny I owe, with interest, by the end of spring. Good evening to you, Your Grace."

"All finished? A thirty-year friendship does not finish in the expanse of a quarter-hour's quarrel, no matter the deed done. This is absolute nonsense, and I won't have it! You have let your dreadful temper and worse pride—"

"Pride? Pride! Yes, I have pride, enough pride not to allow you to treat me like a child. I am a man, madam, and I take my punishment with the best of them! Tim!"

Sir John had opened the door. To Slane's amusement, neither Gussy nor Rochester had time to move from their positions of obvious eavesdropping.

"Tim, come and take the Duchess away."

The big footman was leaning down to lift up the Duchess, still in her cloak and headdress.

"You may not tell me what to do, John Ashford!" Her headdress was quivering as much as her voice.

"I want to see no more of you, no more! Good evening, madam!"

Sir John had made her cry. The footman was carrying her away, she crying. Sir John was cursing, a long string of curses—good ones, thought Slane, who knew how to curse in Spanish, French, and Italian. He opened the door, but the others didn't see him.

"Impossible! She was always impossible. To act as if I am not a thief—"

"You are not a thief!" said Gussy.

"Of course, I am." Sir John turned to Rochester. "I am humiliated that you had to see my shame, but you may as well know the worst about me."

And just then, Rochester looked beyond Sir John and saw Slane.

Yes, thought Slane, you think the same as I. I wish I had known you when you were younger. Lion, they called you, you were the lion's roar, just as Richard Saylor was the lion's heart. Shall we, O Bishop of Rochester, gather the rosebuds while we may? Gather this old warhorse into our arms? We need a strong leader for our rising in the south.

"There is someone I want you to meet," Rochester was saying. "Turn around, Sir John, and meet Laurence Slane, a friend and, you may as well know, a fellow conspirator."

At the wedding, Diana stared at Charles, through him; he might never have existed.

It seemed to Charles that he could not keep his eyes from her, but when her glance locked with his, hers was indifferent. You are good, very, very good, thought Charles, but so am I. His wife, Mary—Tony's sister—looked almost pretty tonight. Light lashes and brows were combed with lead to darken them, a trick her cousin Barbara had taught her. Everything Barbara had done in dress and style had been copied by the young women at court.

Suddenly, Charles was bored.

"Wilt thou love her, comfort her, honor and keep her, in sickness and in health; and forsaking all others, keep thee only unto her, so long as ye both shall live?" the vicar was asking Tony.

In the candlelight, Charles saw a sheen of perspiration on Tony's upper lip.

"I will," said Tony.

Will you? Do any of us? wondered Charles.

Later, when they were back from the church, they gathered in Saylor House's great parlor and hall. Musicians had been hired, and guests who had not been invited to the wedding ceremony were invited to this celebration afterward. The King was coming, as well as the Prince and Princess of Wales.

"The Duchess says she wants to go back to Tamworth tomorrow," Harriet, the bride, was telling Mary. They were close friends. "She says she will go in spite of the weather and muddy roads. She says she wants to see the first robins in her gorse bushes."

"What was the Princess speaking to you about for so long yesterday evening?"

Harriet looked around to see if anyone was close enough to hear.

"Marriage," she whispered. "About men and women and the relations between them. The world is theirs, she says, and while you are young, they may, for a while, desire you. But always, another woman will come into their eyes, and like children who must have everything, they will have her, too, she says, because they can. She told me: 'Be a good wife to Tamworth, enjoy the sport which can come between you in bed—' "

"She said that?"

"Yes. 'But never, never take it to heart,' she said, 'for then your heart will be broken. Love other things—policy and intrigue if that is your bent, or your home, your children, your horses, your dogs—not only him. In fact, if you are wise, my little Harriet, you will not love him at all. I tell you this as my favorite maid of honor—' I'm such a fool. I've made you cry."

"No, no." Mary wiped at her eyes and looked around, as Harriet had done, to see who might be watching. No one. They put their heads together again.

"Lady Mary Wortley Montagu said something nearly the same. 'How I agonized,' she said, 'how I fretted, before eloping with the man I married. How I read and reread his letters to me and finally took on disgrace to have him' "—it was a great disgrace for a young woman of good birth and family to elope with a man—" 'only to discover my love was a pompous bore.' "

Mary laughed, and Harriet said, "That's better. You need to laugh more, Mary. You used to laugh—"

"A dance, madam," Charles interrupted their conversation abruptly.

"You have had too much wine, Charles." Mary's eyes were clear and gray, like her brother Tony's.

Charles pulled her up and kissed her, letting his tongue just brush her mouth.

"How very wifely of you to say so."

He felt her tremble, saw out of the corner of his eye that Tony's bride was taking it all in, and he looked up to see Diana, too, watching. He smiled, lazily, and then kissed his wife yet again, long and lingeringly.

"A dance, nephew-in-law." Diana walked forward, drawling out the words. "Mary, allow an aging woman a dance with a young man, if you please."

"This dance is promised," said Charles, and he led his wife toward the dancers. But when he looked at Diana, she was smiling, a cat's smile, and he felt his heart beating faster, and memories were in his mind that made him stumble.

He and Diana made love standing up in a corner down a dark hall. It was dark and bitter and too fast and better than any in his life. And this time, Charles did not call Barbara's name.

Later, when he told Wart, not all of it, but the essence, Wart laughed so hard he nearly choked.

CHAPTER 25

Francis Montrose and Caesar White, both of whom had once served the Earl Devane, shivered in a drafty warehouse in London, which held the contents of the Devane estate—those contents Parliament had allowed the estate to keep after assessing penalties for Lord Devane's part in the South Sea scandal. There were paintings, mirrors, gilded chairs, tables, marble statues, books piled atop one another, dishes from China to serve fifty, even a hundred, silver forks and goblets, silver bowls—the remnants of a man who might have achieved the reputation of a great collector, had he lived.

"It could be anywhere," Montrose said. "The Duchess desires the impossible."

"She always does," said White, who was by now inured to the Duchess's requests. "And we always oblige her. Here, I think I have found it." He lifted a thick cover. "Yes."

"Dear God," said Montrose.

"This harpsichord isn't going to bother that tobacco ship's captain," said White. "But I would give a shilling to see his face when he views the bees."

CHAPTER 26

Odell Smith pulled on the reins of his horse and stopped a moment to watch the river, easily seen through the winter trees. It was not yet the placid, lazy curl of downriver. Here there were small islands in it, which the water flashed around, showing white, rough edges before joining it again. The astonishing roar of the river's cascade could be heard. There were bluffs behind him, where the land rose up abruptly, punctuated by God's design of falls, rapid, swirling through rocks and more islands. This was World's End, except the world did not end. It did not precisely begin either, though there was more settlement than ten years ago. Colonel Byrd had a trading post and small plantation here. Past the falls, the Huguenots farmed in placid little quarters. A Randolph brother had the beginnings of a prime plantation.

The sky above was as hard a blue as he remembered Lady Devane's eyes being. It might have been a summer day, but for the cold, the drifts of snow, the bitter brown of the trees. The woods were silent against the dull roar of the river's cascade as he and his horse picked his way through them. Every now and again, he would see the tracks of a hare in the snow, or the slow circling of a hawk above. The winter was long for him. On the Bolling quarter where he lived there was a cabin, as required by law, but not much else.

I will send slaves to you first thing in the spring, Colonel Bolling had said, fresh off the ship, fresh from the Ivory Coast. We can make a late tobacco crop and corn and wheat. Life was at its simplest, a round of chores, morning to dusk, a little hunting now and then in early morning or late evening to keep fresh meat, an evening pipe. Solitude had become hard to bear because of the news, heard from Tom Randolph, that the body of a slave boy had been found, a body thought to be that of Lady Devane's boy.

Lately, Odell had had the same dream over and over: the sight of the boy running toward him; the way he had taken the boy by the shoulders and shaken him, pushing him again and again into the trunk of a tree; Klaus behind him, pulling at him, telling him to stop, only he couldn't stop. I will handle it now, Klaus had said, snarling the words, as he, Odell, had stared down at the body. Go away. Now. And he had, glad to leave the scene, still stunned from the swift rush of violence that had risen up inside himself. That night he had slept deeply, with no dreams, waking the next morning to a queasy feeling inside. He'd gone to the second creek, but there was no sign of the sloop, or of the boy—save one, which he had taken care of. Then, not knowing had been good. Now, he had to know what had happened. Klaus had to tell him, so that the dream would stop.

His horse snorted and shook its head, cold. He slapped his reins smartly on his horse's haunch, and the creature fought him, rearing suddenly—stubborn, purposefully stupid, the way a horse can be. The action caught him by surprise. Before he knew what was happening he was falling backward. He held the reins in one hand only; there was no time to harden his thighs to control and calm the horse. It was not the first time he had fallen from a horse. It was not the first time he had been thrown. Everything would have been fine, except that as he fell backward, a leg bent under him.

His body met ground, the leg between. He heard the snap of bone even as a pain dark and red throbbed enough to make him cry out, make him almost faint. His other foot hadn't come quite clear of the stirrup. His horse shied and danced, upset, to drag him a few unbearable inches, grinding the leg into agony before somehow, he was loosed.

He lay on the ground like a fish pulled out of water, gasping for air. In the distance, he could hear his horse. The ground he lay on was as cold as the grave must be. Into his gasping came a shivering that shook him ruthlessly. He fought it, fought the pain, fought the weakness, willed himself to think clearly. Carefully, he lifted himself up to his elbows. Pain made him light-headed. He was bruised all over, but it was the leg, the leg . . .

He saw his horse, watching. Odell breathed in and out for a while, until finally he had summoned the stamina to push past pain and make the small, clucking sounds that would lure his mount to him. Sure enough, the animal came, nosing at him a little.

"Bastard," he said, but whispering, careful not to frighten. He lunged and caught a stirrup. The movement shifted the leg bent under him. For a moment, he thought he was going to faint dead away, going to lose the stirrup and fall back. But he didn't. He waited until the pain lessened enough for him to think through it. He knew what he had to do. Grunting, he pulled himself up along the length of the girth. It was a slow thing; the pain in his leg radiated whitely, hot enough to make his body shiver. His horse sensed it and moved restlessly, bringing fresh bouts of agony.

"Bastard, bastard, bastard," he sang softly to his horse.

His strong fingers dug into the leather; his hands, powerful, seasoned with years of work, locked themselves around the soft hump of the pommel.

"Be good," he told his horse, hoarsely, breathlessly. "Let old Odell rest awhile. Be still, boy."

He had pulled himself up enough so that he was standing on his good leg. The other leg was useless. Leaning on his horse, he thought out the next moves carefully. He would put his weight onto the muscles of his arms and shoulders and lift the good leg in the stirrup, letting his thigh push him up and into the saddle. Somehow, he had to get the other leg over. It was going to be hell. He might faint and fall right off the horse. All right, he could face that. He must do it quickly, not ruminate upon it.

He counted off to himself, one, two, three. His muscles bunched.

His leg was in the stirrup, but that effort frightened his foolish horse. The beast whinnied and trotted off. He couldn't hold himself on. He tried, grimacing, panting, praying, cursing. But, in spite of his efforts, his hands were coming loose from the pommel. No . . . not again . . .

He fell back, into a soft drift of snow and the baleful branches of some shrub.

For a while there was just the pain. He did not fight it. He had not the strength. Then he became aware of cold upon his face. He opened his eyes, looking through branches to sky. Snow was melting on his face, snow that had dropped from the branches of the shrub he fell into. Snow was all around him, like a soft pad, like the beginnings of a white shroud, the drift into which he was sunk. The cold burned. He heard his horse in the distance, restless, impatient, fretful without him. Sometimes he thought that day at the second creek was a dream he had dreamed. Maybe, this, too, was a dream. He saw, far above, a hawk circling in the sky, that sky the color of Lady Devane's eyes.

In his mind were words the slaves sang, a song he'd never understood, only now he did. The dead are not dead, they sang. They are not under the earth. They are in the rustling trees. They are in the groaning wood. They are in the moaning rocks. The dead are not dead.

The boy had his revenge.

SPRING

. . . NOW I KNOW IN PART

CHAPTER 27

Slane sat up, his whole body alert. He lit a candle and stared at the flame. He was on the last leg of his journey, near Tamworth, plotting the rising with Sir John. He'd been all over the south of London this last month, talking with Jacobites, ascertaining support, priming them for Jamie. He was exhausted. But he was glad he'd left the intrigue of London and gone to the country, where love for Jamie was still clear and clean in people's hearts, where without a second thought, women sold family jewelry to give to the cause, and saw their men ready to march to London.

Something was wrong. What was the time? Not dawn for several hours. He tried to slow his breathing, so that his mind would be clear. Was Rochester ill? Dead? Was it Jamie? What made the flesh on his arms tingle this way?

He pulled the blanket from the bed, sat down at the chair by the window, and stared out, closing his eyes, willing his mind to quiet.

It was a false quiet. Before light had done more than etch the horizon, he was in the stable, saddling his horse, coins left in his chamber for the innkeeper. The day was misty and cold, and the March sleet yesterday had turned to ice in places. There was a saying here: "March damp and warm doth the farmer much harm." What about March damp and cold? His horse picked its way through the muddy, churned paths, pulling its hooves out at every step, and Slane pulled his collar up, flattened his hat down. Italy was in his mind—the thought of the sun shining down on a bay dotted with fishing vessels, himself swimming in water that was warm and tasted of salt.

His horse stumbled. Slane patted a haunch. With the paths this muddy, it would be two days before he was in London. He heard a bird singing and looked up, his hands slack on the reins. The horse stumbled again, falling almost to its knees, and he was thrown out of the saddle, falling headfirst over the horse's neck. Shock kept him still a moment, then he got to his hands and knees. I didn't break my neck, he thought, but I'm bleeding like a slaughtered pig.

There was a fallen log. He lay back against it, face skyward, and picked up a handful of snow and held it to his brow to stop the bleeding. The snow burned, and he felt sick. When I stop bleeding, he thought, I'll remount. But the bleeding didn't stop.

Trying to decipher the spidery handwriting of some Tamworth housewife from long ago, Jane bent over the old leather-bound books in the Duchess of Tamworth's stillroom. She loved this room, its jars of preserves and dried flowers, its wooden and marble bowls. It was a refuge, a place of memory, of solace, of girlhood. In the autumn there were apples on shelves, and the last of the roses for the Duchess's potpourris, just as there had been for as long as Jane could remember. In the spring, flower after flower lay upon shelves, drying. Barbara had used to sneak away the jars of jellies for them to eat in the apple orchard. She and Barbara had used to hide in here and play for hours in the cool and shadows.

Last night she had dreamed of green gloves and the pale green eyes of the Gypsy woman who'd been made to sit before the church three Sundays in a row, her distended abdomen the evidence of her crime. The woman's eyes had been downcast, her face pale, while above her, from the wooden pulpit, which was built so that it seemed suspended in air, Vicar Latchrod had thundered about wicked women and sins of the flesh. I could not do it, thought Jane, watching the woman. I would weep or go mad at the shame. Perhaps Gypsies don't feel shame. Later, parish officials had walked the woman to the boundary of the parish, told her to be gone.

Every time Jane walked the woods, she thought of the woman. Where could she go? How would she survive? It's the law, said her father, irritable the way he was when he didn't quite agree with the law. We in the parish don't need a strange mouth to feed. We have enough of our own. If the baby was born in the parish, her father and others would have to be responsible for it. She'll find other Gypsies and be fine, said her father. You think too much on it, Jane.

I think Gussy loves you very much, said Laurence Slane.

Last night her mother had locked Amelia in the cellar for badness. You are too easy on that child, her mother said. You have been since Jeremy died. She is out of hand. Amelia was in a little sobbing heap at the top of the cellar stairs when Jane opened the door. She had wrapped her arms and legs about Jane like a burr. Dark, Amelia had said through her sobs. Be good, Jane whispered, be good tonight and I will take you with me to the Duchess's tomorrow. Spare the rod and spoil the child, said her mother. You think too much upon it. Jeremy's death, her mother meant. It is time to let it go. You have other children. Grief has its own progress, said the Duchess. It cannot be hurried. I saw Gussy weep for Jeremy, or perhaps it was for you, Slane said.

There was some new tension between her mother and father. Her father had brought it back with him from London at the New Year. There was the sound of raised voices from behind the heavy thickness of their bedchamber door. Her mother's eyes were red-rimmed at times, as if she had been crying. Her father's answer to any question was short, and the children bothered him, when never they used to. Strangers came to call, late at night, when the house was asleep. Jane woke from her bed and peeped out the window, saw her father leading their horses to the stable. What was the secret? When she asked her mother, her mother told her to be quiet, not to speak of it again if she had any care for her family.

And then Laurence Slane just showing up one afternoon. An acquaintance from London, said her father, an actor. She saw him and her father walking in Tamworth's woods. What did her father talk of with an actor? Why did Slane ride five and six miles away to an inn in another village? He is hiding from those to whom he owes money, her father said. The theater in London always closed for the winter, so an actor might owe funds.

Why did she feel that wasn't true?

Come to London and see Gussy, said Slane. He must come to me, she answered. Do you want to be right, asked Slane, or do you want to be happy?

The stillroom was suddenly too silent.

"Amelia, come and give Mama a kiss."

No answer. She looked under the table, where her daughter Amelia had been playing with Dulcinea. No one was there.

"It's more than I can bear, Annie," said the Duchess. "Thirty years we've known each other, and now we might be strangers. He returns my notes to him unopened. Unopened."

Annie, brushing the Duchess's hair, didn't reply. The Duchess continued to attempt reconciliation with Sir John, and he would not allow it. She would not give up, and he would not give in. Annie didn't know how it would end.

"And this letter from Barbara," said the Duchess. "I cannot believe Hyacinthe is kidnapped."

"You're shivering." At once, Annie put a shawl around the Duchess's shoulders, then went to the fire and stoked it higher.

"You'd think it February instead of the beginning of March." Out of the corner of her eye, she saw someone in the doorway, someone small. The cat, Dulcinea, sauntered into the bedchamber.

"Look whom Dulcinea brings," Annie said to the Duchess.

Jane's daughter Amelia walked forward to the chair where the Duchess sat, glancing at the Duchess with a wise, sideways look. She pointed to the magnificent portrait by Watteau.

"That is Bab. I love Bab." Amelia's face was plump; her neck was plump; her arms were plump.

I wager the little legs under that gown are plump, thought the Duchess, staring down at the child, who gave her back stare for stare. She'll know something. Children always know something.

The Duchess patted her lap to Jane's child. "Come and sit here."

"Yes, Your—what am I to call you? I forget."

"Your Grace."

"Your Grace."

Two peas in a pod, thought Annie, going behind the Duchess's chair and beginning to pin up her hair.

"Who visits your grandfather these days, Amelia?"

"A man with black brows. You are very old. I am four. How old are you?"

"A hundred and four. A man with black brows, heh?"

"Amelia." Jane stood in the doorway.

Amelia rolled her eyes at the Duchess, as if to say, We are in trouble now.

"Ha! This child is the image of her grandfather, Annie, may she lead him a merry chase. In another few weeks, all over England, men will be voting for who will sit in the Commons for the next seven years, and for the next seven years, Tamworth's man will wear an earring. An earring."

The Duchess referred to Tommy Carlyle, who was Tony's choice to represent Tamworth.

Jane heard what you said, thought Annie. It is no good trying to pretend you were talking of something else.

"Jane, you and this child stay and have crumbling cake with me."

It will do you no good, thought Annie. Jane never tells much.

"Annie, ring for cake and tea. Amelia, we will have crumbling cake and honey rings. Bah. This might be February. The only thing which tells me it is March is all the robins."

"Their red breasts are crimson surprises."

"A pretty image, Jane. Crimson surprises amid the dreariness."

"Dreary, dreary, dreary," said Amelia. "Grandpapa is dreary."

"Crumbling cake gives her wind. I will be up half the night."

Annie, on her way to obey the Duchess, whispered to Jane: "Watch her. She can't be trusted."

"Well, now, Jane, who is this man with the dark brows I hear about?"

Jane stammered, caught off guard by the Duchess's directness. She was certain her father would wish her to say nothing.

"A—A friend from London."

"What friend?"

Jane was saved from answering by the Duchess's steward, Perryman, who as always resembled a pigeon with his puffed-out chest. "Forgive me for interrupting, Your Grace, but Tim has found a person in the woods over near the next village," said Perryman.

"And what is Tim doing in the next village?"

"A sweetheart, I believe. Thrown from his horse—"

"Tim's been thrown from a horse?"

"The person."

"Well, send a carriage to fetch this person. I'm surprised that you had to ask. Things have come to a pretty pass when we don't help our fellowman here at Tamworth. Now, then, Jane, who is it you said visits from London?"

I didn't say, thought Jane, as you well know. "I don't think you know him."

"I know many people, Jane."

"Have you heard anything further from Barbara?" Jane crossed her fingers for luck. It might work. Sometimes, the Duchess's mind floated away like a cloud in a summer sky.

"Not a word, other than that dreadful letter to say Hyacinthe was gone. I've written her to come home. Louisa, my sister-in-law, wrote to tell me London was in a ferment about it, that there was a broadsheet bringing up the South Sea Bubble again. Barbara's had her share of sorrow, Jane, more than her share. She loved Hyacinthe as if he were her own child. Spoiled him. The tricks he pulled when he was here with me, letting my geese out, fighting with stable boys. 'You ought to cane him,' I told her. She didn't listen. Tony promised he would call upon the King on Barbara's behalf, but what can any of us do from here? Tony ought to go to Virginia. I've written to Abigail to tell her I think he should go. I should never have sent her there in the first place. I regret it now. Pirates. I had a thought of pirates. Annie will tell you. I dreamed of them, last fall, long before this happened. Pirates took Hyacinthe. I know it. I feel it. Pirates are said to roam up and down the colonial coast, even though the worst of them were hanged several years ago. . . ."

Safe, thought Jane, I'm safe.

An hour later, as Jane left Tamworth, the carriage was rumbling down the drive. She and Amelia stood near a tree to watch, both of them equally curious.

"It's Grandfather's friend," said Amelia, as footmen carried Laurence Slane into the house.

From Tim's arms, the Duchess stared down frowningly at the actor, Laurence Slane, whom she'd seen in London. Was this the man with dark brows who visited Sir John? It would have to be. Now, why would Laurence Slane visit Sir John Ashford? The Duchess pursed her lips.

Slane was muttering, and his movements were restless, dangerous, his arms flailing out, so that Annie, who was trying to tend the deep gash on his brow, said to Tim, "Come and help me. Hold his arms."

"It's not French he's speaking," said the Duchess, listening intently. "I know French."

"What then? Spanish? I'm going to have to sew this." Annie shook her head. "We'll need someone else to help hold him. It is going to hurt."

Come out, come out, wherever you are! Lucius laughed to himself and hid behind the altar. The King, his friend James, was visiting, and though James was six years older, making him fourteen to Lucius's eight, they played hide-and-seek. It was an honor to his family for the young King to visit.

You make him smile, Lucius, his mother said. He has great need of that.

The King moved slowly down the aisle, one hand on the hilt of the sword tied to his belt. Lucius put his head out, then pulled it back in quickly, laughing to himself. The King was close now. He was walking up the altar steps. Lucius backed into a corner of the marble altar, holding his breath. He could see the King's legs. Suddenly, he lunged, grabbing an ankle, and Jamie shouted, and Lucius began to laugh, and Jamie, dark eyes shining, suddenly did, too, high laughter, clear laughter, the laughter of a boy. His courtiers forget, his mother said, that he is still a boy. Jamie's father had died in the last year. All hope now rested on Jamie.

You frightened me, Duncannon, the King said, but he was smiling. He pulled off a ring, giving it to Lucius. You'll be the best of my servants, someday, the one I trust most.

"Italian, I think," said the Duchess.

The next afternoon, Jane walked through the woods that separated Ladybeth from Tamworth Hall. Her father was waiting for her near the stream.

"He is not awake yet, Father. He is feverish, making no sense, Annie said. I saw him. Annie let me go in and put the plaster Mother made upon his forehead, but I couldn't give him the letter. The Duchess asked if he was the man who'd been visiting you."

"Bloody hands of Christ Jesus our Lord! How does she know that? Has she spies behind every tree? She is impossible, she has always been impossible, and she will never change. What did you say?"

"I said, no, that I did not know him, that he had not been to Ladybeth."

"Good, good."

Her father was almost feverish himself. "Go again tomorrow and see how he does. They'll think nothing of your visiting. I'll have your mother make something else to take him. And if he is awake, you must give him the letter."

"What if he doesn't wake?"

"He must. He will." Sir John put his arm around Jane, and they walked toward Ladybeth.

"Tell me what is happening? Tell me why the letter is so important. Tell me what you hide, Father. I know you hide something. You have since New Year's. You can trust me."

Without breaking his stride, he hugged her to him, carrying her against his side a full step or two, so that she was lifted off the ground. "I know I can trust you, Janie, but this I cannot share."

"Gussy? Does it involve Gussy?"

"No." He said it so quickly that she knew it did.

The woman in Tamworth's woods stopped. Her pupils, if anyone had cared to look, were distended, so that the odd green shade of her eyes could hardly be seen. She gave a cry, bent over, panting like a dog in summer when there is no water near. Her belly heaved, rippled, as if it had a life of its own. It did: a life trying to be born.

The woman walked a few steps farther, stopping when the pain was too enormous, holding on to trees, panting. Another step. Another. The pressure was so great. The child would be born in the mud and cold.

There was the back of a great house. The woman walked a few steps, fell. She began to crawl, stopping when the ripple of her belly, the pressure, seemed as if it would burst her apart. Making little cries, she managed to crawl to the kitchen garden, where green sprouts showed through the hay covering. The woman lay on her side, her body making spasms that arched her into the shape of a bow. "Help," she tried to say, but no words came out of her mouth.

Annie sat by the fire in the kitchen, waiting for water to boil. Pulling a book out of her pocket, she put it in her lap, glanced around. There was only Tim, sitting at the great oak table cracking open walnuts. She began to read.

" 'One morning he pulls off his diamond ring, and writes upon the glass of my sash in my chamber this line—"You I love, and you alone," ' " Annie read, her heart palpitating with the boldness of it.

It was Defoe's book, which the Duchess had given her to burn, and which she had been reading since.

"What are you reading?"

Annie started, slipped the book into the pocket of her apron. "Nothing."

"Something. The Defoe book," said Tim, standing.

Annie stood, too, moved so that there was some distance between her and Tim. Their time together with the Duchess in London had made him much less afraid of her. In fact, sometimes he dared to tease her. He would not be above chasing her down. He was bold and impudent, a bad servant. No wonder the Duchess adored him.

"It is not the Defoe book. It is a book of sermons— What's that?"

"Your left eye squints when you lie."

"Hush. Listen."

"It's the wind. It is cold enough for January outside."

Annie went to the kitchen door, opened it, and stepped outside. "Tim!" she cried. "Hurry!"

Slane opened his eyes, but with effort. It hurt to lift his eyelids, hurt more than he could have imagined such a thing hurting. Carefully, he felt the bandage at his brow, but just the touch of his hands made him wince. He sat up carefully, the throb in his head intensifying, like a drummer tapping harder and harder. He felt sick.

Where am I? he thought through the drumming. Then: How long have I been here?

He tried to stand, but could not. He sat on the bed, willing himself upright. The effort made him grit his teeth and break into a sweat. Standing, he felt sick, as if he would faint. The throb in his head was becoming all there was. It was hard to keep his eyes open against it. He managed to pull on his breeches under his nightshirt. He kept his head completely level. Even the slightest jar to it made him groan.

Out in the hall, he had to stop, one hand to the wall, to keep from falling. His head was large, enormous, a giant iron ball someone was hitting with a mallet. At any moment the iron would split open and he would be nothing. He groped from one piece of furniture in the hall to another, trying to get his bearings, to keep concentrated upon what he was doing. There were stairs. Careful, one foot down slowly, hand on the railing, careful, then the other foot, pull yourself with your hands, keep your head level. God, the pain.

He had managed to get upon a lower floor. He was in a wider hall, far wider. Likely this hall held the bedchambers of the owners of the house. He put his hand to the nearest door, opened it, gritted his teeth at the nausea in his middle. I'm going to faint, he thought. He saw that he was in a withdrawing chamber, with draperies the color of pale butter. There would be a bedchamber beyond, windows he could look out of.

So there was.

He leaned a moment on the knob of the door, wondering if he could walk to the windows. There was a great four-poster bed with its curtains drawn nearly closed. Portraits in heavy gilt frames hung from faded velvet ribbons. A cat leaped from nowhere and wound itself around his legs. He moved toward the light of the windows, but one of the portraits caught his eye.

He stood a moment before it, swaying. Beautiful girl, captured in that moment of time in which she was moving into womanhood, with diamonds in her hair and around her neck, diamonds upon the edge of the glorious fan she held open.

"Barbara," he said, aloud.

"How do you know my granddaughter's name, Laurence Slane?"

Startled, he turned, and the sudden movement was his undoing. His head seemed to burst open and, as the cat wove between his legs, he fell.

"The afterbirth. Did she push it out? If I don't get all the afterbirth, she'll die." Everything about Annie was sharp, efficient. The Gypsy woman lay on the floor before the kitchen fire, and the cries of a newly born baby were louder and louder, rising up to the high, dark, vaulted kitchen rafters. A bell among a series of bells, an indication that someone upstairs wanted a servant, began to ring.

"The Duchess's bell! Now of all times!" Annie looked over at Jane, who had walked in in the midst of the birth and now held the woman's shoulders. "Go upstairs for me, Jane. See what it is she needs. Tim! Give the child to Cook and go with Jane."

Upstairs, in the bedchamber, Jane half walked, half ran toward the bed, speaking so fast that half her words were swallowed, "Your Grace, Annie could not come to you. The Gypsy woman—you remember, she sat in church three Sundays in a row—well, she is in your kitchen at this moment and just gave birth to a baby. It is a boy, and she is in a very bad way. Almost starved."

The Duchess was staring at Tim's hands. They were covered in blood. Tim looked down at them. "The baby," he said. "I was holding the baby."

Without a word, the Duchess pointed toward the other side of her bed, and Tim walked around to see.

Dulcinea sat upon Slane's chest, purring loudly. Tim looked over to the Duchess, staring at him from among her nest of bed pillows, the cap she wore dwarfing her thin face.

"Are you all right, ma'am?"

"Apart from having strangers barge into my bedchamber at their will, I'm fine. Take him to his bed, Tim. Jane, is this Gypsy woman going to die?"

The groan Slane made at being moved made Jane clutch her hands.

"I'm not certain, Your Grace. Please, Your Grace, may I go now? I am worried for the woman."

"Yes, yes, go on."

"Well, Dulcinea"—the Duchess stroked the cat, who had leaped up onto the bed—"Gypsies in my kitchen, actors in my bedchamber." She pursed her lips. How did Slane know Barbara? How?

Her mind slipped into fret for Barbara, for the depth of Barbara's heartache. Roger, and now Hyacinthe, gone. Please, God, Barbara has been through enough. Lead her to green pastures, to still waters.

Anoint her head with oil, fill her cup with joy. Come home, Barbara. Come home. Let us comfort you.

"Tim, tell Annie what has happened." Jane pulled the covers back over Slane. "She'll know what he needs. And bring back with you the poultice my mother made. I think I dropped it on the table."

Slane was groaning, knotting his hands into fists.

"I have a letter for you. It came three days ago." Jane spoke quietly. "Can you hear me? Do you understand? Do you know who I am?"

Without opening his eyes, Slane gritted his teeth, a groan coming through them. "Yes. Read it."

Jane had to bend over him to hear him. She took the letter from her pocket, but for a moment was unable to open it. My whole life is in this letter, she thought; then: Jane, stop this. You are being fanciful. You are a woman with four children, whom few know and fewer see. What do you know? Nothing. You are nothing in this life.

" 'Rochester has bolted,' " she read. " 'Come immediately. We've come apart at the seams.' "

Slane groaned. "Any signature?"

"No."

Gussy. It was Gussy's handwriting. Her hands trembled.

Slane reached up, startling her, and took her wrist; he opened his eyes. There was a trickle of blood seeping down from the bandage.

"I . . . have . . . to leave," he breathed, slowly, a breath between each word. Speaking was costing him great agony. "Help . . ."

"Help you?"

How? Was she to sneak into this house and bring him out a back stairway, this when he could not stand? She'd be seen. She'd be caught. She could never do it. Gussy's handwriting. Something in her hardened.

Did she not know this house as if it were her own? Had she and Barbara not hidden in every passage, in every chamber at one time or another just for the sake of doing it, the pair of them swallowing their laughter until they had to laugh or choke? Jane is cunning, Harry. She could just hear Barbara saying it. Yes, there had been many a time when her thinking of a story to tell had saved the three of them from caning. She couldn't *say* it—Barbara and Harry had had to do that—but she could think of it. Just stand there and cry, the way you always do, Barbara would say. Leave the talking to Harry and me. Your weeping softens them, Jane, so that Harry and I have an easier time of it.

She would bring her father in a back way. She knew a door seldom opened; she would go right now and see if it was locked, and if it was, she knew where the key was. She knew a back stair. They would spirit Slane away. It would just have to be done. The handwriting was Gussy's.

"Rest now. Drink what Tim brings. It will be better for you if you do."

"I . . . must . . . be . . . awake."

"You must be well. Father and I will take care of you. I promise you that."

He opened his eyes again, with great effort, and stared up at her.

Measuring me, thought Jane. She let him see all her fear and all her courage. He closed his eyes again. She took that as a sign that he agreed. When Tim returned, she had the bandage off and was dabbing at the blood as gently as she could. She made Slane drink several spoonfuls of the thick syrup Annie sent, put her mother's poultice upon his forehead, which was so horribly bruised and swollen about the brow and into and around the eye. She tied on another bandage.

"Tim, I'll sit with him. I'll stop in the kitchen before I leave home. Thank you, Tim."

When she was certain Tim was gone from this floor, she opened the door and began her explorations. The door leading outside was unlocked. It squeaked when she opened it. She'd have her father bring oil for its hinges.

Evening settled around Tamworth, dark going into its far corners, behind chairs, under tables with a familiarity that brought quiet to everyone. All through the house, people did the things that brought them comfort, made the event of the afternoon settle into something smaller, something they could understand. Downstairs, Perryman lit a few candles to take away evening gloom. In the kitchen, Cook fussed over pots and kettles that held the Duchess's supper. The parlor and bedchamber maids gossiped about the Gypsy woman, now up in the attic chambers with her child. "Bad luck," they told one another. "It is bad luck to have a Gypsy in the house." Tim sat by the fire, whittling a stick, thinking about the birth he had witnessed, the woman's great pain and her courage, thinking about the child slipping out like some small miracle, thinking about God and Mistress Barbara across the sea and the book she'd read them last year, about old Robinson Crusoe and his adventures. Larger worlds, thought Tim, content by the fire, content with his life, with his position, with his world. There are larger worlds out there than we, sitting by the fire, can ever know.

"I found her by the garden. Tim carried her in. She was in the last stages of childbirth and nearly starved to death. She must have been in the woods since the parish officials cast her off."

Annie, as tired as she had ever been, sat in a chair by the Duchess's bed, drinking a glass of wine the Duchess had told her to pour for herself. The Duchess, too, was drinking wine, a little before her supper to help her digest better.

"Will she live?"

Annie shrugged.

"She may stay here until she is well or dies. Where is Tim?"

Annie smiled grimly. "Resting. All the men are exhausted."

"He said Barbara's name."

"Who?"

"That man, Laurence Slane."

Annie frowned, stared down into her wine. "Perhaps he's seen her portrait in London. There is one at Saylor House. He might have seen it there."

"I hadn't thought of that."

"I'll go see to him."

"No, not yet. You're exhausted. Sit here by the bed awhile longer. Tim told me Jane gave Slane the syrup of poppies. Slane is going nowhere this night. We'll ask him tomorrow how he knows Barbara."

Annie sipped her wine. "I'll look in on him before I go to bed."

In the middle of the night, Annie opened her eyes and listened a moment, before turning over on her side. This was an old house, always shifting, always groaning, creaking, settling. This would teach her to sit up late by the fire and read novels that were better off burned. Would Moll be faithful to the man she'd married but did not love? I'll wake earlier than usual and read awhile before beginning my duties tomorrow, she thought.

The Duchess stared down at the bed in which Slane had last been seen.

"We've searched the house," said Annie. "I do not understand. If Jane gave him syrup of poppies—"

"I saw her do so," said Tim, defensively. Somehow, without a word, Annie had managed to imply Slane's disappearance was Tim's fault.

"So you keep saying."

The Duchess pursed her lips. "You've looked in every chamber?"

"Every chamber."

"It is a mystery," said Tim.

"Walk to Ladybeth and see what Jane says."

The Duchess was sitting before the large window in her bedchamber when Tim returned. She was thinking of Barbara and of Tony, of his insistence that Tommy Carlyle was to be their representative to the House of Commons now; of Tony's dismissal of John Ashford, of Tony's marriage. "It's going quietly," Abigail wrote. "No quarrels."

"Mrs. Cromwell was resting, and so I could not speak with her, Your Grace, but her mother, Lady Ashford, said that Mrs. Cromwell had said earlier the actor was sleeping when she left him last night."

"Go outside, Tim, look around, see if you see footprints, anything out of the ordinary."

Hyacinthe kidnapped. How Barbara must be grieving. Too far, she'd sent her too far away. Walpole was to be dismissed at any moment, so the Duchess's letters said. How did Walpole and Diana do? Tony's earringed minion said that Walpole had not done all he ought for Roger, for Barbara, about the debt. Was it true? Walpole's friendship with Roger, his relationship with Diana, made the betrayal doubly deep, made Walpole a man not to be trifled with. If he'd betrayed them all, as Carlyle said, he was stronger, more ruthless than anyone imagined.

She tapped a finger against a cheek. A sweeter day today than yesterday. Spring. Richard had loved Tamworth's spring. How did Slane know Barbara? The Duchess was dozing before the large window in her bedchamber when Tim returned.

"Wagon tracks cross part of the drive."

The Duchess pursed her lips.

"Annie says to tell you the syrup of poppies is gone from the still-room."

CHAPTER 28

Slane lay on his bed in his lodging room in London. Around him sat the key leaders of the plot: Lord North, Lord Arran, Dr. Freind, Lord Cowper, Will Shippen, Lady Shrewsborough, the Duchess of Ormonde, Harry Goring, the Duke of Wharton, the Duke of Norfolk, and he who was clerk, messenger, keeper of papers, and friend: Gussy, the Reverend Augustus Cromwell.

The Bishop of Rochester was not present. Sir John Ashford was on the street, keeping watch. "Salt of the English earth," Rochester had called him. It is true, thought Slane, and of his daughter, too.

Freind, a physician, had taken off the bandage and was examining Slane's head. Slane tried not to groan. He had thought he would die during the journey. He'd lain in the back of the wagon as it lurched through the muddy roads, and thought: Let my head separate from my body, let me have a second, a single second, in which it does not pound.

Freind opened the jar of syrup of poppies and smelled it, as the others attempted to explain what had occurred.

"To give him credit, Rochester's wife is quite ill. The physicians attending her are saying her illness is fatal." Lady Shrewsborough was speaking. Aunt Shrew, Slane heard Tony call her in his mind, but to Slane, she was Louisa, his dear Louisa. Is the Duke of Tamworth here? he wondered. Of course not. I'm ill, he thought, very ill.

"Rochester's wife has consumption," said Freind, quietly, as he leaned over, putting his head to Slane's chest.

"He had called a meeting," Aunt Shrew was saying. "After all, the invasion is all but here. It took days for the Duke of Norfolk to arrive, and that made Rochester even more impatient. 'Will it take days when the invasion comes?' he snapped. 'It's winter,' I told him, 'you know how impossible the roads are.' He wanted details of everything, how North and Arran had divided up the country into military districts, how many men could be counted upon as troops, how the Scots clans were doing, what were their numbers, who led them. 'Lord Russel is reconnoitering the north, Slane the south,' we told him. 'We haven't full details yet. You know that.' "

"*I* told him," said Wharton, "that Sunderland will side with us, if he sees that there may be a military victory. And that if Sunderland came to us, there are four others among the ministers who would do the same."

"He wanted a counting of the monies collected, and that is where, as the saying goes, the fat hit the fire." Aunt Shrew slapped her hands together, her many bracelets jangling.

"Only a tenth of the money is in our hands," said Wharton, "but we have pledges for much of the rest."

"How much?"

Unbearable to speak, unbearable. Tears came to Slane's eyes, and seeing them, Freind took his hand, felt his pulse. Aunt Shrew sat down on the bed, and Slane groaned. She took Slane's hand from Freind.

"We have promises for ten thousand pounds," said Wharton, "and the rest of us will make up an additional thirty thousand the day an invasion ship is sighted—the day, I swear it."

I brought back pledges, thought Slane. Charles will, too, when he arrives. Why didn't Rochester wait?

"Once Ormonde lands," said Aunt Shrew, "I know ten merchants here in London who will open their coin chests to us, a certainty of at least ten thousand pounds more. We have ten men poised to ride all over England alerting men to rise, collecting coin, another ten thousand pounds, perhaps twenty thousand. It can be done. It was done for Charles I, and his son Charles II. I tried to tell Rochester, but he would not listen."

"He became furious, said we played at invasion, we had not done our parts well enough. He insisted we write to Ormonde and tell him to cancel the entire expedition," said someone.

The faces Slane looked at, when he could bear to open his eyes, were blurred. Listen to the voices, he said to himself. They will tell you everything.

"We have a ship ready," said Aunt Shrew, "to send to Ormonde. Rochester refused to countenance our sending it, if you can believe that. He struck Goring, who told him we would send it anyway; he would have choked Wharton, if Gussy had not stopped him. As it was, he was foaming at the mouth in his anger, calling us dolts and idiots. The insults he gave were unendurable. If I were a man I would have challenged him to a duel. He told us we must call off the invasion. Great bloody coward, to leave us at the last moment. It is always confused at the last moment. I ought to know; he ought to, too, as much as he and I have seen in our lifetime. The younger Rochester would have done it."

"Rochester was always one to twist with the wind," said Lord North.

"Perhaps Rochester is right."

Slane opened an eye. It was the Duke of Norfolk who spoke, and Will Shippen, standing just behind him, nodded, or so it seemed to Slane. Damn Rochester, thought Slane, to divide us further now.

"And I say, nonsense," said Aunt Shrew. "We have this young Christopher Layer and his rebellion within the army. We may never have that again."

"King James has faith in me. You'd think Rochester might," wheezed Lord North.

Is there anyone other than Wharton and Gussy who is not a hundred years old? thought Slane.

"I've thought hard on this, Slane," said Aunt Shrew, "Ormonde invading with the Irish on leave from the French army, the arms he'll bring. There are the arms we've already collected, waiting in cellars and barns for us. We have three risings we can count upon. We have Layer's rebellion. We can do it, Slane."

"Hear, hear."

Their backbone is showing at last, thought Slane. As for his dear Louisa, she was all backbone.

"There's more."

It was Gussy. Good Gussy, thought Slane, I've brought your wife. Do you know? Was Jane in the chamber? No. Of course, she was not. He had a vague memory of waking to find her dressing. She had been pulling the gown Gussy, or rather he, had bought her over her chemise, so that he saw, as much as he could see with his head the way it was, her bare shoulders and neck. Fetching, he thought he remembered saying to her. He'd embarrassed her.

"Rochester sent a letter to Paris," said Gussy.

This was worse than Rochester leaving them at the last moment. Slane lay still on his pillows.

"How?"

"He used someone other than me to write it. George Kelly, you know him."

"Yes."

A good man, a steadfast Jacobite, a courier and messenger, completely trustworthy.

Slane could hear self-reproach in Gussy's voice. Yes, Gussy would take much of the blame on himself, unlike North and Arran, who had great and onerous responsibilities, yet did not discharge them well enough. "They are weak links in our chain," Slane had written to Paris. He had no doubt why Rochester had become angry at them. Their planning had been too vague and trusted too much to chance. I know they're old fools, Louisa had said, but one of them is brother to the Duke of Ormonde. He must be consulted. And they're all we have, Slane. Beggars can't be choosers. That was why he and Charles had made these journeys, to cover for North and Arran.

"What did it say?"

"Tell him." Aunt Shrew was sharp. "Go on. Let him hear the worst. He's already been half killed by falling off his horse."

"There is no union, no spirit. Tories are worried for the election and little else. Too many decline to join. Any schemes are wild and impractical, and cannot succeed."

There was a silence in the chamber.

Rochester should have toured the country with me, thought Slane. Then he'd have felt differently.

"They'll understand in Paris that it is Rochester's opinion of things here. We are a month from invasion. They won't know their heads from their tails," said Aunt Shrew.

"I'm going to Paris," Slane said. He could almost hear the sigh of relief. "Write it all down for me—everything: the quarrel; what you think you can pull together; what you have done already. God, Freind, give me the syrup."

Slane held tight to Aunt Shrew's hand. He had to sleep. Only the syrup of poppies allowed him some rest, when the pain stopped. "You'll see I'm put on a ship," he said to her, "see I get to Paris."

"He ought not to go," said Freind.

"He must."

She brought Slane's hand to her withered, powdered, rouged cheek, the bracelets making their music. "I will see to it. You drink your syrup and whatever else this bag of bones who calls himself a physician prescribes, and when you wake, you'll be in Paris. You tell them to never mind what Rochester has said to them. You tell them he no longer leads us, but that we may lead ourselves. You've ruined your eyebrow, Laurence Slane. It breaks my heart to see your handsome face marred. If I could kiss it and make it well, I would. —Oh, your letter. I'm forgetting your letter."

She reached into the bosom of her gown and pulled out a small, folded square.

"It is from your mother."

Dear God in heaven, thought Slane. How does she know where I am? Who in Paris has been talking to her? No one is to know where I am. Are the weak links not only here, but stretched all the way to Paris, too?

Jane, after rummaging through the papers on Gussy's desk, sat down and held out her feet to the fire. She ran her gloved hands over the beautiful gown she wore. She'd made her father stop in Petersham, where she and Gussy lived. There she'd knelt and pried up the loose floorboard in the parlor with her fingers, taking out the box there, opening it, looking at a pair of green leather gloves that smelled of cinnabar. They were the only gift she had ever accepted from Harry after she had married Gussy. She had always hidden the gloves, even though Harry was dead, even though Gussy, with his kind and remote wit, likely would not have minded, would rather have said, Oh yes, Janie, they are lovely. That Harry was a fine fellow.

Would you rather be right or be happy?

When Gussy opened the door, Jane was sitting in a chair, the green gloves upon her hands.

"Jane!" he said, not unfastening his cloak but crossing this small chamber to kiss her, not chastely, but fiercely. "Jane, my Jane." Then, "The children—"

"Are at Ladybeth, still. I know, Gussy—every single thing. There is to be an invasion, and my father heads Tamworth and neighboring counties, and you, you are in it, too."

He put his hand to her mouth, roughly for Gussy. "I don't know what you've heard, but this is no game, Janie, to prattle about—"

"No, it is true, and dangerous, and you, Gussy, are not going to do it without me." She had always preferred King James over King George. After all, her first love had been a Jacobite, and he'd talked politics between kisses under the apple trees at Tamworth. She'd follow her heart, be Jacobite, too. Who would stop her? Her father? Her husband?

Harry gone, Jeremy gone; life was so short, so uncertain. She caressed Gussy's face with soft green leather gloves. Whither thou goest, I will go. And where thou lodgest, I will lodge. These last months, she had been right, but not happy.

Diana sat down at a table, tapping her foot impatiently to the sound of March rain against her windows, paper, inkpot, pens, seal, wax, sand all laid neatly before her. She seldom bothered to write letters; in her girlhood, she hadn't needed spelling and penmanship to get what she wanted. Swearing at her mistakes, she crossed through words and spilled ink here and there, but after a quarter of an hour's struggle, she had down on paper what she wished to say:

"Daughter, Sir Hugh Drysdale will take Sir Alexander Spotswood's place as deputy governor of the colony of Virginia. He will come to the colony aware of your family and your welfare, and you may put yourself under obligation to him. I desire nothing but your return to the home of your birth and the bosom of your family. Your second letter arrived in January. Everyone talks of your missing page boy. The Prince of Wales was filled with sympathy, asks of you and sends his regard. Written by your loving mother this the tenth day of March in the year of Our Lord, 1722."

She sprinkled sand over the paper and then blew it off, folded the paper into a square, melted wax, dribbled some of it onto the letter, and pressed her seal into the wax at the meeting of the folds. A footman came to tell her there was a visitor.

"I don't want to see anyone."

She frowned at a valentine, forgotten, left over from the month before. Today might have been a day in February. Rain beat against the windowpanes like the fingers of beggars' children asking to be let inside. But there were far more robins in the trees in her garden than a month ago. Robin . . . the frown deepened.

Charles stood in the doorway of the parlor, Clemmie behind him. Clemmie gave Diana a long, blank glance before closing the door.

"Nephew, finally back from your journey, are you? I was writing to Barbara."

Charles put his hat and cane upon a table, as if he had every intention of paying a long visit. "Were you?"

"Indeed, I was."

"How are you?"

"Very well, thank you."

"And Walpole?"

"We've quarreled. I wish the King would simply dismiss him outright and put us all out of our misery. It is all Robin talks of—when he will be dismissed, what he will do. The new rumor is that the King will make him an earl, to compensate, but Robin says he would rather remain a minister than become an earl. I'm quite tired of it. 'You've been in disgrace before and survived it,' I told him. 'You can survive this.' He can. He can survive anything, Charles. And of course, he is making himself ill over the election. He and Sunderland fight for every seat in every town and borough they see an ally in. There have been betrayals Robin didn't expect. I will be so glad when the votes are taken and things are more clear."

"Sunderland and Wharton remain friends, I gather."

"Friends? I never see one without the other. Have you heard about Hyacinthe?"

"One of the first pieces of news told me when I arrived in London. And I saw the broadsheet. I gather the woman weeping in the forest is Barbara, and the fat minister with his back turned to her distress, Walpole. What did it say, something about woe—"

" 'Woe is me, the South Sea hath taken all from me.' The King and the Prince of Wales are both upset. Robin says the Prince told him that it was his fault Barbara traveled to Virginia. You know Tommy Carlyle says Robin didn't do all he ought in the matter of Roger's debts. He says it to anyone who will listen. Sometimes I listen, and I think, No, Robin would not lie to me. Then other times, I think he might. When it comes to survival . . ." Diana looked down at the small knife she used to sharpen the point of her quill. "If it is so, I swear I will cut out his heart and eat it before his eyes."

"And what does Robin say?"

"That Carlyle is a vicious half-man who can't be trusted, that Roger was his friend and he did everything possible, that the King's personal letter about Hyacinthe is going to the Governor." She touched the sealed letter on the table before her, mockingly. "You don't seem distressed for Barbara."

"I am. I want you to add a postscript to your letter."

He walked toward her, and Diana closed her eyes a moment, almost as if she felt weak, or afraid.

"It is foolish of you to call here, Charles."

But Charles was kissing her neck and shoulders and then her breasts through the material of her gown.

"Charles, we cannot be long. I play cards with the Princess at three—"

He kissed her mouth. She dug her fingers into the column of his neck. He pulled off his wig.

"Here is my postscript for Barbara. And see if the Princess smells me on you." After that, there was no talk, there was only the desperate heat of the joining, and a kind of despair for them both.

CHAPTER 29

Linnets, redstarts, and hatters settled in the trees of Tamworth to nest. Annie had Tim fetch periwinkle from the woods and wove it into a wreath to place on the Duchess's legs for cramp. She had nothing for heartache. Now the Duchess fretted not only over Sir John and Barbara, but over Laurence Slane.

The Duchess wrote to Tony about Slane. "How does he know Barbara?" she asked. "He left Tamworth like a thief in the night. I don't like it. Find him in London and demand an answer."

The Gypsy woman rose from childbed, pumped water from the kitchen garden pump into a bucket, found a brush, went into the stillroom. Perryman, informed by Cook, sent for Annie. Annie stared for a long moment before speaking.

"Why do you scrub the floor, girl?"

No answer. Annie looked her over. Dark hair pulled back into a tight knot. Eyes kept downcast; occasionally one glimpsed their fern green. Hands red from the scrubbing water and years of work. Gypsies were said to be fugitives from Egypt. They spoke their own language, possessed secret, sinful signs, read fortunes, sowed ill will, stole livestock, picked pockets.

"I see you are up from your bed at last. The Duchess will give you a coin. We'll find you a bit of food to tide you over, some clothing for the child. You'd best be on your way now. Spring is coming."

Spring was easier to survive than winter. Perhaps the child would live through it.

The woman did not raise her head. Something about the way she knelt on all fours, continued scrubbing as if Annie had not spoken, not with pride in the action, but with a kind of stubbornness that was enduring in its insistence, made Annie remember the scene of birth in the kitchen. An abandoned, disgraced woman was among the most despised of all God's creatures.

"Are you a Christian?"

No answer. Scrub went the brush. Water circled and crested near the toe of Annie's shoe.

"It is cold out still. The baby might perish. For that, I will allow you to stay a month or two more. Only that, mind. Then you must go."

There was the tiniest of quivers in the woman's body, a movement that touched Annie to her soul.

"Mind, if one item is found missing, it will be on your head. I will have you dunked in the village pond and tried for a witch. Your name?"

"Bathsheba."

Annie pursed her lips. She ought to have known.

"You've picked a Gypsy to mother, have you?" said Tim, later in the kitchen. "Might as well have picked a wild animal."

Annie glared at him.

Tim held up a book. Annie made a grab for it, but he held it out of her reach easily.

"This book of sermons you're reading," said Tim, who could not read, but was still too clever for his own good, "I'd like to hear them, too."

CHAPTER 30

Barbara stood staring down at the seedlings, slender, rich green, that had moved up out of the earth, the hay around each plant haloing it like a necklace. Kneeling, her skirts belling out around her, she touched the closest seedling, her fingertip gentle upon the stalk, searching for the small bumps that would be leaves. But it was too soon. First Curle's pride and joy, she thought, Grandmama's sort. Thrive while I'm gone.

"And what are you doing?"

It was Blackstone, tall, his heavy head cocked to one side, watching her from across the seedling bed. He knew these were their children; she and Blackstone had been going to see these plants each day, discussing the individual plants at night: Had they grown? Which were taller? Which looked stronger? When would be the best time to move them?

"I'm saying good-bye."

"Not good-bye; never good-bye. Only 'fare thee well for a time.' They will fare well. They're the handsomest seedlings I've seen in many a year."

Yes, her grandmother's sort stood an inch above the others.

"We should have planted only Digges seed," he said.

She stood up, dusted off her hands. "See how these do over the summer—they still have to endure the summer, you know—"

Blackstone smiled at her tone, as if she'd been raising tobacco all her life.

"—and perhaps next year we will."

She would not see them moved into the fields Blackstone was so carefully preparing. The business of spring in Virginia was to have the field dirt hoed as loose, as easy as river sand; once the rains of April and May began, the seedlings were moved to fields to finish their growth, growing under blue skies toward the sun—but not too tall. I'll pinch them back, Kano and I will, said Blackstone, Kano has a feel for tobacco, like I have. Thus strength would move into their leaves, those precious leaves that when dry made tobacco.

"Walk with me back to the house," said Barbara.

"Sinsin says the rain will come early this year. He says already the places where his toes were feel it. It's hard when the rains come too early. The first spring I was here there was a storm of hail not two days after we got the last seedling planted. I don't think half Jordan's crop survived."

Once the rains began, every man and his slave was out in them, moving seedlings to fields, each field dotted with row after row of small dirt hills, made by the slaves pulling soft dirt up around one leg, pulling out the leg, and tamping down the top of the hill made. Tobacco hills. Each would be crowned with a seedling planted in the rain, the better for it to thrive—unless, as Blackstone said, a storm of hail came, or a flood, or there might be a terrible, unimaginable storm, the kind called a hurricane. There had been one of those in 1713, said Colonel Perry, ruining the tobacco for that year and a year to come.

"In two springs, I predict we'll have the marsh drained. Will you come and see the field we make for your grandmother's sort?"

"Yes."

Her mind was moving over the plantation, seeing the fields, the two creeks, the path through the woods to the slave house, seeing her plans for it all. She had worked hard this winter to plan First Curle's destiny, talking with other planters, with the Governor, who was unhappy with her. You do me no service with this matter of the slaves, he'd said to her, as if she were a child who had been disobedient without him there to watch over her. That work was now ready to lay before her grandmother in rough maps, inked drawings, page after page of her thoughts and others' conversations in an account book.

"Have you enough coins, do you think?" she asked Blackstone.

A prison ship roamed the York River, she'd heard. Blackstone and Colonel Perry were going to find it and begin the purchase of indentured men to take the place of slaves.

"There is credit if you need it in Williamsburg." She said this though she knew he knew it. It had all been said before, planned out carefully. She couldn't help herself. Time was so short now. "John Randolph holds notes I've signed, which will give you more funds if need be. Then, once I'm in England, I'll arrange a proper line of credit for you."

They walked by the kitchen to the house. In the yard sat her trunks and boxes. This afternoon, the slaves would bring them to the second creek.

"With your permission, Lady Devane, there are things I must do before tonight."

"Yes, go on."

She knew she'd done nothing these last days but quiz him on what he would do in her absence, as if he were a boy who could not follow instructions. First Curle would thrive under him. She knew it.

Two geese came rushing at Barbara from around the corner of the picket fence.

"Shoo!"

She stamped her feet, waved her skirts. The geese stopped, but stood as close to her as they dared, honking at her, their long necks thrusting out like snakes ready to strike. They were bad-tempered, awful, Tamworth's fattest, gifts from her grandmother.

"Harry! Rescue me!"

From the house, the dog came bounding out. The hatred between him and the geese had been immediate. It had reminded Barbara of the rivalry between Annie and Perryman at Tamworth.

He began to chase them, and the geese, furious, hissing, wings flapping, disappeared around the corner of the fence again.

"My hero," Barbara said to him. "Come, say good-bye with me."

They walked through the field and woods toward the slave house, stepping up into it. Barbara moved from one narrow bed to another, her skirts shushing against the wood floors, in her mind the man who slept in each. Jack Christmas, Moody, Sinsin, Kano—in her account book were drawings of them. Some of the slaves would leave First Curle and go and settle the land she had patented. Cuffy's gone, Colonel Perry had said. His personal servant, Cuffy, had been the first slave he'd freed. I offered him wages to continue to serve me, but he left without a good-bye. All these years he has served me, and I never knew what was in his heart, Barbara.

In the hall of the house, Blackstone stood watching Thérèse, who was kneeling before a trunk, frowning, as she packed. She looked up and saw him. They stared at one another, a long look, much in it.

"When?" he said, a muscle working in his jaw, which his beard hid. His heart was beating like a boy's.

"In another hour."

Barbara walked through the woods. Upon the trees and shrubs, leaf and flower buds were fat, fecund, deliciously close to opening—or else open, daringly there, petals soft as velvet, leaves rich, lushly yellow-green, as if half the sun were in them. Birds sang and fluttered from tree to tree above. At night, the frogs were a chorus drowning out sleep. The river, to her right now, was fat and rolling with melted snow from the mountains far to the west. When you come back, Blackstone said, we'll journey to the mountains. I hear they rise to the sky in shades of purple.

A fish jumped out of the river. The sun glimmered on its scales. Another fish leaped from the water, and another. It was their spring journey. All about her was birth, promise, striving.

She couldn't sleep nights, instead slipped out and sailed her dinghy at all hours. Come home, Wart had written. There is an adventure happening. Avenge Roger, Carlyle had written. Tony is married, wrote her mother. I miss you, said her grandmother. This work she had done for First Curle seemed a preliminary for Devane Square. Devane Square was on her mind always now: what she might do with it.

There was the grave. Barbara stood under the trees that sheltered it, the oak limbs as thick as her waist. He is not dead, said Thérèse. She had such faith. Faith is all there is, said Colonel Perry. Clear faith belonged to Thérèse and Colonel Perry. Barbara couldn't have it, wavered, faltered, felt anger, questioned.

If you come back, Hyacinthe, she said silently, every justice in every county knows of you. There are coins in Williamsburg to pay for your journey to England. Thérèse had refused to pack Hyacinthe's clothes. She was leaving them here. He will need them, she said, when he returns.

Harry, farther on down the path at the river's edge, barked. Yes, Barbara thought, walking away from the grave, time to move on, to leave this. But it was hard, like burying Roger, something she did not want to do; and when she did not want to do something, all the King's men and all the King's horses could not convince her otherwise. She was no wiser in that than when she'd left England.

God is with Hyacinthe, Colonel Perry said. Believe that, know that. When the sun sets, and darkness comes, the light has not died; it only waits a time in the darkness for its new day to be born.

I don't understand, she'd said.

In the hurt is good, he had answered. Keep your mind upon the good, upon the fact that there is a greater purpose, and we are but servants to it. Is there greater good in your quarrel with Beth? she'd flashed. She could not help it. He might be a saint, but she was not.

Yes, he'd answered. I know there is.

There was her saint now, talking with planters here at the second creek, planters seeing to their hogsheads, talking with the tobacco ship's captain about charges for freight, deciding whether or not they would send their hogsheads on this ship, or another, which might charge less.

In the river was the ship, its sails folded, masts rising pointed to the sky. Tomorrow her hogsheads and those of neighbors would be loaded upon it. And she and Thérèse would board it to return to England. Home. She was going home. She saw Colonel Bolling and frowned.

Stepping carefully across the small, floating bridge at the narrow, marshy head of the creek—Colonel Perry's design, one of the ways in which he kept his mind from his daughter these months—Barbara joined the men. They took off their hats at the sight of her.

"And to what do I owe this honor?" she said to Bolling.

The men around her shifted from one foot to the other. No one knows what to think of you, said Margaret Cox. No one knows what you will do.

"I haven't come to see you. I've come to see about sending my hogsheads. You'll allow me that, I believe."

"I must by law, mustn't I?"

"Did you get your other barrels loaded, Colonel Bolling?" The mischief in her preened. "Did your nephew Klaus hoist his anchor and sail?"

"I did; he did; no thanks to you. I am surprised you allow me here at all. I am surprised that you didn't insist that I settle with the tobacco captain by letter, or by rowing out from my land to his ship."

"I considered it, but I thought you'd take me to county court."

"And indeed I would. I've as much right here as any man who has hogsheads in the rolling house."

"Well, then."

"Well, then."

They stared at one another, he glaring, unrepentant, she not glaring, but certainly unrepentant.

"You bewitched Edward Perry into running your storehouse for you. Bewitched him into freeing his slaves. Little wonder his daughter has filed suit against him in county court. I'd do the same. The colony is well rid of you, madam."

"Be certain you don't linger here too long."

"I have as much right as the next man. I may want to buy something from the storehouse."

"Coins only, Colonel Bolling. No credit will be extended to you."

He swore, but Barbara walked away, going back to the planters, shaking hands with each of them, asking about their families, telling them that she'd put some of the clothing her grandmother had sent into the storehouse, and that they might find something for their wives or themselves there. One of them gave her a letter. She took it, promising it would get to its destination in England.

One of the slaves was standing knee-deep in the river, pulling out a basket in which Barbara could see fish gleaming, like silver caught. A paradise of shad and sturgeon and trout and pike and eels and perch and crab was in these rivers and creeks, the colonials had bragged when first she'd come. Dip your hand in and see, they had said. The slave let the basket slide back into the water. When first she'd come here, that late August when she'd been ill with fever in Williamsburg, the colonials had come to visit her, had chattered to her of their colony, bragging of its beauties. In her fever, she had imagined they were mettlesome horses prancing before her. She wished she might present this basket of shining fish to the King to show him the abundance of his colonial paradise.

She was going home tomorrow.

In his bed, Blackstone put his head against the flesh of Thérèse's bare shoulder. "I was going to make you weep for me in this time we have, Frenchwoman"—his face was against her shoulder—"make you beg for mercy and know that you cannot do without me. . . ."

Thérèse cupped her hand against the side of his face, feeling the softness of his beard. He would let it grow long and ragged again when she was gone; she knew he would. She wrapped a bare leg over him, tracing with her toe the length from buttock to knee, a length she liked, reveled in. I adore your legs, she said to him often in French, refusing to translate. She put her hand to the thick hair curling at his neck. His neck was strong, solidly made to hold the heavy head. Often, she'd kissed the back of his neck. This piece of your flesh, she thought, now it's mine, forever, I brand it now with my lips, that and the long length of your thighs. When you die, send me your thigh bone, Blackstone, and I will put it in a place of honor in my house.

She moved onto his back, lying down upon him as if he were a bed, snuggling sensually against him, her breasts flat on his shoulder blades, her belly and abdomen in the curve of his back. She closed her eyes, thinking of the pleasure they had given each other these last months.

Blackstone sighed, a deep sigh that she could feel, and stretched out his arms; she put her arms atop his, laid her face in the back of his neck. I have desired you greatly, Scotsman, she thought. After a time in which they both lay quietly, she moved off him and sat up, her hand caressing his back, as she chose the places to kiss good-bye: that sweet, broad space of neck; the ribbon of spine; the small but-tocks; that long thigh; the back of his knee.

She moved down and held his heavy calf a moment against her, as if it were a child. She put her hands in his thick, unruly hair, feeling the shape of his head under her hands, thinking of the mind inside that head, so keen, so watching, intent on enjoying all around it, in-tent on missing nothing of life. There was a kind ruthlessness to him. He would do what he would do, and she who loved him would have to bear it.

He lay with his eyes closed. She put her finger to his lips, traced the quarter-moon of them thinking how smooth they were, how greedy. Whom would he take to his bed once she was gone? There would be someone. He was too sensual a man for there not to be someone. And he would enjoy that someone to the fullest, as was his way.

Stay, he said. Here? Thérèse had almost laughed, though she was tempted a moment. Who would not be tempted by such a long-legged man with such a big laugh? There was a dream she had, an old one, of a small shop with a cat in it, and women working for her, sewing the gowns she made for noblewomen to wear. Threads were bright in the shop, crimson and garnet and butter yellow. Fabrics were rich, lustrous: velvet, satin, lutestring. Women sat in dainty chairs, the cushions thick with embroidery she had done herself.

The fur of their cloaks framed their haughty faces, and they stroked their pet dogs and were impatient and rude, as they looked at fabrics and said, No, that won't do, I like it not. But always, there would be a yes, for Thérèse knew what she knew, and there was no one better. Already it was in her mind to weave Iroquois feathers and beads into Madame's hair when she went out, to take the soft buckskins and feathers and beads of the Iroquois and weave them into Madame's clothing, to mark her as different, as having gone to this rough colony, as having survived it. Thérèse knew London, knew the tastes and boredoms of those she served. Everyone would be wild for it, would try to copy it.

Hyacinthe was to have been part of her shop—to sell the fabric, to serve wine to the ladies, to run her errands. She closed her eyes. He was not dead, though doubt of that came to her in darkest night and shook her the way a cat does a mouse. She and Madame's dear Colonel Perry had talked long about it. Keep your faith to you like a treasure, he said. Do not speak of it to others, do not allow them to soil it. What you know and feel in your heart is true. He was, as Madame so often said, an angel.

Stay? No, her destiny was not here, in these woods, where a man or woman could live for months without seeing another soul. It was Blackstone's paradise, but not hers. She stared down at him—at his small waist, his long legs—thinking about the way he talked about stars and drank too much rum and shouted out slave words. In France, they would say he was an original, and all the noblewomen would want him. He would be like—what was it the savages took?— a scalp upon their belts.

He turned over, aroused now, as she was. He was watching her face. She laughed. It must be so clear what was upon her mind. I will miss you, big fool, she thought. I will cry, but not now, not in these last hours we have. They are for other things. You know. He stroked her breast to its point, eyes half closed, in the way he had, a way that always made her catch her breath. He looked in her eyes a moment, daring her: "Are you ready?" his look said; then he put his mouth to her breast, but just flicked it with his tongue. He showed his teeth to her and then lay back, like a large, lazy cat, waiting, the dare greater than ever.

"What shall we do now, Frenchwoman?"

He knew. She knew. They would be here a long time, a very long time.

"You said you would make me beg for mercy." She bit her lip, ran her hands through her hair, stretched, playing at indifference. "I don't think so. But you might try."

She touched him, and he groaned.

"Just a moment, now." Barbara held the candle as steady as she could to the dried twigs, which began to smoke.

"Keep the flame to them longer," said Colonel Perry.

"I'll burn my fingers."

"A while longer, or the twigs will do nothing but smoke."

"I know that."

Perry smiled to himself and folded his arms. He'd taught her to build a fire, and she'd made the act her own. There was not a clear night that she was not here on the bank, carefully redigging the shallow pit in which the last night's fire had burned, carefully piling the small twigs into the old ash to make yet another fire. When she did not appear for supper, he and Thérèse would look at one another, their look saying, Yes, she's at the river. He'd walk to the bank to be certain she was all right, and there she'd be, sitting before the fire she'd made.

"What did Kano give you?"

"A branch of dogwood, the flowers not open yet."

The slaves had been bringing her gifts for days: a bird's nest, a smooth stone, a small mat woven from reeds, a single feather—treasures for them, honor for her.

"There."

Barbara sat back, satisfied, looked up at the sky—it was streaked now with evening—the line of her jaw smooth, perfect.

"There will be stars tonight," she said.

"And a full moon. Everything is packed?"

"Everything. Bay myrtle candles, baskets, everything but that which I will pick up in Williamsburg."

"Have you bought all of John Custis's garden?"

"Nearly all."

He was going with her as far as Williamsburg, sailing down the river. From there, he could find out precisely where on the York River the convict ship was and send a message to Blackstone to join him there. Come to England, she had said. And the voice had told him yes. His Beth would not see him, his sweet girl, his joy, strong in her anger, straightforward in her purpose. Beth had filed suit against him. Even though he gave her nearly all, she fought him in court for that which he kept, fought to keep him from freeing a single slave—the child of his loins, allowing Klaus Von Rothbach to court her. He would not have chosen Klaus.

"Your second creek will make a good small port. A mile away to the west is the church at which your neighbors worship. A tavern, a larger storehouse, perhaps a small yard to repair boats and ships. After all, yours is the last place a large ship may anchor."

"It is all written in my account book."

"And more and more people are settling beyond the falls."

"So the Governor says, too."

Spotswood had come to see what in the world she was doing. "Such rumors," he told her. "You've set the colony on its ear." He spoke of how much land was being patented beyond the falls of all the four rivers of the colony. Planters would need a place below the falls of the rivers to bring their tobacco to.

Make such a place, Barbara, suggested Perry.

"Have your grandmother send a bell for the church, some altar silver, money to build a tower in which to ring the bell. Every time people hear it, they will be reminded of your grandmother's landing, of what she offers there," he was saying now.

To make a proper dock would require funds, people willing to invest. There were ten pages in her account book, written by Colonel Perry, as to why the idea was a good one. He pledged to invest in it himself. So, thought Barbara, more entries to the account book before she left tomorrow, about church bells and altar silver.

Someone called from the top of the riverbank.

It was Blackstone, and with him Captain Randolph and Major Custis. They slid down the bank.

"There's to be an assembly of the burgesses in May," Captain Randolph said. "I just received word that the Governor has called it to meet. I rode over to tell you, Edward."

Randolph bowed to Barbara.

"And I came to see the captive of the madwoman of First Curle," growled Major Custis. He shook Perry's hand, bowed to Barbara. "How do you do, Lady Devane?"

"They think me mad?" said Barbara, her hands in Harry's fur. He lay in her lap.

"A portion do, but they allow it because you are a duke's granddaughter, and so you may have your whims. Edward here—now, for him to free his slaves, there is just no excuse. Except that tobacco prices from our last year's crop are low, lower than anyone imagined, and so there's talk of what we may do to salvage ourselves, talk of an import duty on slaves, such as once we had. Edward may be ahead of his day, freeing his slaves. That is, if his daughter allows it."

"An assembly," said Perry. "It's been two years since the Governor called the last one."

"The Iroquois have agreed to make a treaty with us. He calls it for that. And to tell us His Majesty wants us to send more tar and pitch."

"Pinelands," said Colonel Perry, and to Barbara's questioning look, "Pine trees make the best tar and pitch. That portion of your land with many pine trees can now be turned to gain."

"Tell Her Grace your grandmother I thank her for the bees, Lady Devane," said Custis. "The ship they were on is still in Williamsburg. She sent them over in a box that had to be seen to be imagined, and they weathered the journey, but a sailor dropped the box while the Governor was aboard ship, and the bees have swarmed to my garden. There is a harpsichord aboard that ship, also. You'll need to leave word to the Captain about whether you wish it unloaded or not. Peach brandy." Custis slapped at a leather bottle tied to his belt. "My best peaches. I brought it to celebrate. I've news that I rode all the way in from Williamsburg to tell you, cousin."

"And what is that?" said Perry.

"The Governor is to be replaced. I've had a letter from Will Byrd that says it," said Custis, excitedly taking a letter from his pocket and giving it to Perry, who read it, then gave it to Barbara.

"We'll have to make a real push in the assembly for what we want," said Randolph to Perry, and Barbara saw that this was the real reason he and Custis had called. "The Governor is wounded. Whom else do we gather to us?"

"Does the Governor know?" asked Perry.

"As to that, all I can say is that his hand has to ache from all the land patents he is suddenly granting to his friends. Yes, I think he knows. So, do you plot with us, Edward? We ought to be able to get around him on certain laws we've been wanting."

Perry smiled, didn't answer.

Custis handed him the brandy bottle. "You've become boring since you've become a saint, Edward. Lady Devane, I hold you responsible. I see you're not a saint about peach brandy, Edward, and a good thing, too. What's this?"

"Supper," said Barbara.

Thérèse was sliding down the bank, in her hands a basket. Blackstone was going to meet her, to help her.

They began to eat, the fish, hot, steaming, delicious. They ate with their hands, wiping them in sand or going to the river to wash. They passed the brandy bottle from one to another, the men talking about laws they wanted to push through the assembly: laws loosening the rules on patenting land and limiting the amount of tobacco that might be grown. They talked of hiring more sheriffs to see the limits enforced. By the time the brandy bottle had made its way around the circle several times, they were talking about who on the Governor's Council would ally with them, and for what favor.

Barbara stood. I will remember this, how one forms allies over fires, during hunting, during dinner. My aunt Shrew does this. She is always feeding Tories dinner, playing cards with one and all. She knows everything that happens in London. They say my grandmother did, too, once upon a time, that while my grandfather battled the French, she battled his enemies at court.

Carlyle's words were in her mind, his claim that Roger had been made scapegoat. Passing Thérèse and Blackstone, who were murmuring, feeding each other in the shadows of the riverbank, Barbara began to climb the bank.

"The Governor wants that treaty with the Iroquois so that the land he has patented will be safe. All of it borders on Iroquois lands," she could hear Major Custis saying. "He has feathered his nest in his time here, that I can guarantee. Word is, that plantation of his in the mountains is now thousands of acres. I'll wager my best wig that by fall it will number thousands more."

"The treaty is a good thing for us all," said Perry. "Remember that."

From the top of the bank, she looked down. Major Custis was now in the river to his knees. When he walked back out, he brought a small barrel with him.

"That's Bolling's brand on that barrel," said Captain Randolph.

"Captain Von Rothbach sailed for the West Indies the other day," said Colonel Perry. "This must have fallen off when they were loading."

"She still won't let him use the creek?" said Custis. "Where is Lady Devane?"

From the fire, Colonel Perry pointed her out to Custis.

"Is it true you are the only one those geese like, Edward?" asked Captain Randolph. "Do you know they chased me all the way back to my home the other day when I walked over to call."

"Geese like saints," said Custis.

I smell jasmine, thought Barbara, and dogwood, night and river. Harry ran ahead of her as she walked away from them. The full moon lit their way. At the first creek, she stepped out of her shoes, ran lithely along a plank, and stepped into the dinghy, Harry following. The moon above was like a coin. In the river, its reflection smiled upward. She began to row, taking pleasure in her skill, her strength, much increased with time.

Keep thy heart with all diligence, for out of it are the issues of life.

In the river, she undid the sail, tied the ropes fast, pulled in the oar, put her hand on the tiller. The wind on the river was just right. It was like sitting upon the back of a bird.

She sailed by the party upon the bank. They waved and whistled to her, and daringly, she stood and bowed to them, the dinghy skimming along.

Around a bend, when she felt safe and secluded, she dropped the anchor, lay back to stare up at the moon, bits of conversation echoing in her mind. Land: The Governor had talked of land in two new counties when he'd come to call, telling her she ought to patent it, that he would personally see her deeds approved. So now she'd patented land in those counties.

She undid the lacings of her gown and the pins of her undergown, pulled her chemise from her body, and dropped, like a stone, into the water. It was cold, too cold. In her mind was the image of Blackstone, the expression upon his face as he kissed crumbs from Thérèse's fingers. She began to swim.

Harry barked. He would bark until she was aboard, but she swam until she was tired and numb with cold. Shivering, she pulled herself into the dinghy and dried herself with the chemise, looking down at her pale body, chaste now. She breathed in the moon and the river.

Charles would never believe there had been no lovers for her, but then, the truth be told, she'd never been as wild as people thought. The wildness had been for Roger. See me, it said. Love me, it said. Others do. Why not you? Roger. She breathed in the moon and river.

What will I do with all this passion inside me, she wondered, all the fire and grief and tenderness mixed within me? I could be like Aunt Shrew and collect men like jewelry. Do I want to do that? No.

Make the bones which thou hast broken rejoice. Hyacinthe's loss has broken me, and I am not the same. Will there ever be rejoicing again? What have I learned in Virginia? What do I take back with me? The ability to build a fire, to sail a dinghy. She looked up at the moon. The ability to survive, to run a plantation for months, to make decision after decision about it. I am not frightened now to go back to England and look at the debris of my estate.

The girl in me is clear-eyed, absolutely determined—worse, in some ways, than ever. She laughed softly, and the laughter was like a spring gurgling, beguiling and charming. If Roger knew me now, she thought, he would be mine. But if I knew him now, would I be his?

It saddened her, that into her love for Roger had come questions and disillusionment, as if in her maturing, she looked at him and saw his flaws. What a burden he had left her—the debt, the fine. She had no illusions about what she faced. Yet she loved him. He was the love of her girlhood, and that she would always honor.

If you hurt Roger, Robin, I will avenge him, she thought, and the bones of her face set in a look those at home knew only too well. She was going to make an entry when she returned. Her arrival was not going to go unnoticed. She was going to bring the finest, the most remarkable gifts she could find to His Majesty, to the Prince and Princess. They were not going to be able to ignore her or dismiss her.

Lacing herself back into her clothes as well as she could, she thought: The flirtatious, talking, jangling Barbara of my failed marriage is gone. Loss has burned her up, chastened her, tempered her, so that, like wood hollowed out to make a music pipe, I am something else now. What? Who? What is it now that I want to do with my life? What is it I desire? What is it I need? Truth: I want to live a life of truth and not lies. That, at least, has come out of this winter of grief.

She wiggled her toes in the water, staring down at them. She was going to begin the fight, the campaign, the dance, to return Devane Square to that which was thriving and vital again. She was excited by that, proud of her labors here.

She was going to seek a position at court. It would give her a place of safety—those she owed would be hesitant to force anything—

from which to maneuver. There was other land Roger had bought. If land was important here, was it not important at home? Roger had had a gift for knowing what would be desired later, what would or could develop into something special. There was a warehouseful of furnishings, treasures Roger had accumulated, not touched by the South Sea fine. They might be sold, carefully, piece by piece. They'd sell even higher if she seemed reluctant to let them go.

Tommy Carlyle. He knew all. He was an arbiter of taste. She was going to befriend him, use him to guide her. People followed his lead. He'd help make her tobacco fashionable.

Adventure, said Wart.

No, no more adventure for a time. She would proceed in an orderly fashion, a quiet fashion—Tony would be so pleased—to salvage herself and her estate. She would be placid and quiet in all her affairs, obedient, good, kind, meek. She smiled. She had never been able to be any of those for long—and likely her time here in Virginia had just made her worse. Never mind it, her grandmother would say, at least you are not dull. You're fine as you are, my Bab.

Grandmama.

Barbara closed her eyes. You are so dear to me. I love you so. It will be so good to see you again, and Tony, and Jane.

I will make friends with Tony's wife so that she allows me a little of his company. Oh, Tony, you were so kind when Roger died, and I was too distraught to see it. But I see it clearly now. How can I repay you? What if I don't like your wife? What if she is mean-spirited or cruel to you? What shall I do? I won't behave, I know it. Oh, well.

Rowing back around the bend, she saw her fire smoldering. Everyone was gone. She rowed as close as she could, stepped into the water, pulled the dinghy up, and poked at the coals with a stick; the fire burned brighter. She dragged some large limbs across it, and it flickered up at them. There was a blanket; Thérèse must have brought it. She wrapped it around herself and lay down in the sand, her cheek against it, moving her fingers in the soft sand.

When I was a child, I spake as a child, I understood as a child, I thought as a child. Within you is all you need, said Colonel Perry. That is what you bring back with you from Virginia.

Harry moved to lie against her stomach. The Governor would likely wish her to take letters, begging letters, pleading for his position.

Robert Walpole lies with my mother. She'd not told the Governor that, but she smiled at the expression she could imagine upon his face if he knew. Walpole is your enemy, said Carlyle.

She turned on her side and slept for a time, waking with the feeblest light of dawn. There was Colonel Perry, against the bank, wrapped in a blanket, asleep himself; upon her, another blanket. She stood, shivering, stretching, saw the barrel Major Custis had fished out of the river. "Pork," read the stamp on its side. Someone had broken it open. Walking over to it, she stared down.

Colonel Perry opened his eyes to see her squatting, rifling through wet tobacco leaves.

"Many smuggle, Barbara," he said. "I've done so myself. By law, all the tobacco must go to England, and we must take the price we can, besides pay import duties, so that in hard times, we make less than nothing for our tobacco, pile up a loss to send it over. Tobacco is selling low, lower than anyone imagined last year at this time. I'm not the only one who knows it now. It may be years before we look at profits. You cannot blame a man if he finds a better market elsewhere, particularly when his plantation is mortgaged. Men make laws, Barbara, men like myself, like you, men with faults, with greed in them, with malice. There are bad laws, as well as good ones."

"I could take Bolling to court."

"For what?"

"On a charge of smuggling. With this as evidence."

"You could. But half the men who tried him would have done the same, and would be reluctant to convict him for a crime they all commit and see little harm in."

"I could tell the Governor."

"You could do that. Remember, however, he is governor only for a time. He will have other things upon his mind, such as salvaging what he can; adding more enemies to his list of those already there will not be wise."

"Why not, if he is no longer governor?"

"I don't think he intends to return to England. I think he intends to live on his plantation in the mountains. He won't want more enemies."

"I feel as if something significant, something large, has just brushed its wings against me, and for the life of me I do not understand. It has to do with this barrel."

"The sun is rising. Here's the new day. Come and sit by me. How I will miss you. Do you know the psalm of David that begins, 'He that dwelleth in the secret place of the most High shall abide under the shadow of the Almighty'? You must, if your grandmother reads prayers every night. I thought so. Say it now with me, as we watch the sun rise."

She lay back against him. He took her hand in his and brought it to his mouth and kissed the fingers one by one.

" 'I will say of the Lord, He is my refuge and my fortress: my God; in him will I trust. Surely he shall deliver thee from the snare of the fowler, and from the noisome pestilence. He shall cover thee with his feathers, and under his wings shalt thou trust: his truth shall be thy shield and buckler.' "

"I know no more," said Barbara.

He continued alone: " 'Thou shalt not be afraid for the terror by night; nor for the arrow that flieth by day; Nor for the pestilence that walketh in darkness; nor for the destruction that wasteth at noonday.' "

He hugged Barbara, skipping several verses.

" 'For he shall give his angels charge over thee, to keep thee in all thy ways.' Remember that, Barbara."

The sun was up. A new day had begun.

CHAPTER 31

"Just don't stand there. Put them all about the altar," said Annie.

They'd heard the first cuckoo. It was April. Bluebells and lady's-smocks were blooming.

In Tamworth Church, Annie watched Bathsheba begin to arrange boughs from the plum and apple trees, the cherry and almonds, blossoms shut tight yet, but lovely, like lacy, airy fairies landed, wings held in. "Laurence Slane is not in London," wrote the Duke of Tamworth. Annie gathered a handful of willow branches to begin hanging them about the church walls, but then walked instead to the window and looked out. Her view was the graveyard, in which leaned gravestones and cracked table tombs, a scene defined by the lead crisscrossings in the window out of which she looked.

The election was just over. The men who were allowed to vote in Tamworth had elected Tommy Carlyle, as the Duke of Tamworth had requested them to do.

Clouds were gathering above yew trees, whose tops had begun to sway a bit as the wind grew rougher. There would be rain tonight, thought Annie, trying to still the sensation of foreboding within her. They'd have to walk to church in the rain on the morrow. It was Palm Sunday.

The coming celebrations of April spread themselves out in Annie's mind. On Maundy Thursday, the Duchess and all the servants would wash the feet of vagabonds and beggars, giving them food and coins. On Good Friday, Cook would make his hot cross buns, the cross of sugar sticky and sweet atop the bun, and then would come Easter.

Festivals and rituals, marking their year.

Christ our passover is sacrificed for us, Vicar Latchrod would say, therefore let us keep the feast; Not with the old leaven, nor with the leaven of malice and wickedness: but with the unleavened bread of sincerity and truth.

"Tell me the rest of the last lines of your duty toward your neighbor." She was teaching the Gypsy the catechism. She didn't know why.

" 'To keep my hands from picking and stealing, and my tongue from evil speaking, and . . .' " The Gypsy spoke so softly. "I forget the rest."

"You'd best remember."

Bathsheba the silent, outcast, accepted by none of the other servants, eating alone, working alone, always alone. The Gypsy had braided apple blossom into the willow of the basket in which her baby slept. There was something not right with the child. Annie saw it in the set of his eyes, the shape of his mouth and nose. The Gypsy would have him on her hands forever.

The foreboding did not go away. A dark cloud merged into another one outside the window, and there was a rumble of thunder. The church felt damp and cold to Annie.

"Storm coming."

Bathsheba's voice was soft.

Yes, thought Annie, Bathsheba feels it, too.

CHAPTER 32

April. In London, Slane shook his head. "No, nothing else, Louisa. You've fed me as if I was a prince."

There were candles burning everywhere, a long tablecloth of Belgian lace on the table at which he sat, before him the remains of a feast: roasted chicken, quail, fish. He was only just back from France. Aunt Shrew had all but fed him herself, so glad was she to see him. She poured more wine into his goblet.

"The physician in Paris said I must not drink too much wine."

"And what else did he say about your hurt?"

Ride nowhere on horseback. Rest every day in a darkened chamber. Slane crumbled a piece of bread to nothing. "To take care."

"And you've been on horseback since you arrived. We have some time before Lord North and the Duke of Wharton arrive. Tell me how you found Rochester."

Arrogant, melancholy, somehow pitiful.

"Distraught about his wife, who is near to dying."

His wife's illness had pushed Rochester to the edge. He had not the courage for both the invasion and her death. Time, thought Slane, lessens courage. I see that. If we live long enough, we become cowards. He rubbed his brow. The choice of Rochester to lead had always been fraught with risk. Everyone had known it, only no one wished to pay the forfeit.

"He wished to know if I despised him."

"He wanted absolution for abandoning us."

"He does not abandon us."

"I hope you didn't give absolution to him. You did, I see it."

Slane sidestepped her. "He voices what are true concerns for our success, supports us in any way possible—"

"Except to lead us? You may forgive him, but I never will. I don't like the new plan, Slane, this waiting until King George goes upon his summer pilgrimage to Hanover. It takes the edge off, to wait too long. Disgusting is the only word for what King George's ministers have made of the election. There were riots in Westminster and Coventry over how voting went. Never has there been such open purchase of votes. Besmirched, I feel besmirched by it all, as if everything, every one of us might be bought at the market. I am not the only one who feels that the tone of our court is ugly and venal. The time is ripe. Why can they not invade as planned?"

He did not answer.

Rochester's letter had shocked those in Paris and Rome and Madrid who were feverishly pulling together the last threads. The letter made them cautious. It was his duty to persuade those here to the new plan, but like Louisa, Slane did not like it that the invasion was put off.

Ormonde had ships, soldiers, arms ready in Spain. King James was poised to join him. They were confident France was going to supply thirty thousand troops. Slane had argued as forcefully as he could that Rochester's letter should be ignored, that they should proceed as planned, that those in England would not fail, never mind what Rochester thought.

"So, the invasion is put off until May, you come to pull us all into obedience again, and who, in their great wisdom, have those in Paris decided will now lead the rebellion here?"

Slane told her the name. It did not matter. What was necessary now was simply a figurehead, a symbol. The man who had agreed to lead, to take over for Rochester, was an old Tory lord whom time had mastered. Once he had been the wiliest of Queen Anne's ministers, but he'd been sent to the Tower of London after King George came to the throne. The man had listened carefully to Slane, who explained how the plot was in its last stages. I'm not what I once was, he had told Slane.

No one has to know that, Slane had replied. Simply tell the others what I ask you to. It is your name I need, not your vigor. Aunt Shrew was pleased. If she accepted, so would the others. Slane felt relieved.

"It's a good choice," she was saying. "He is the only man every one of us respects. It is, in fact, a brilliant choice. I feel more hopeful myself, knowing he has agreed. Well, what a busy man you've been, Laurence Slane. Did you call upon King George himself and request that he leave early for his journey to Hanover? Was that among your instructions for salvaging us? What is it, Pinchwit? I told you I was not to be disturbed."

"Tommy Carlyle asks to see you, madam," the servant said, and to Slane, "The little dog is crying. We've given it milk."

"We have time before the others come," said Aunt Shrew. "Carlyle will have some gossip no one else yet knows. I'll go hear it, and then I'll send him on his way. You know, Tony has taken Carlyle as his creature. Still waters may run deeper than we know. What dog?"

"A little spotted dog. A gift."

"For whom?"

"For Rochester."

She bristled. "For Rochester! From whom?"

"King James."

"Since when does King James give gifts to cowards?"

"Its leg has been hurt on the journey. I've brought it to London with me to heal. It is sent to Rochester's wife. Such is called, I believe, respect for another's grief; called, also, not biting off one's nose to spite one's face."

He spoke evenly. Jamie played all sides against the middle. He would need the Bishop of Rochester to solidify loyalty within the Church of England when he was on the throne. And so he would not punish him. Yet.

"I'm going to show you my Easter gown, Slane, once I see what Carlyle wants. I looked very handsome in it."

She left in a rattle of jewelry and hiss of skirts. It was the custom to wear new clothes at Easter, which had just been celebrated. Walpole had not resigned as a minister. He hung on, despite their plots. There had been a scandal over one of his men's actions in the Treasury in February, and he'd survived it. There had been an uproar over the news about Barbara's kidnaped servant. The Duke of Wharton had done a wonderful broadsheet, making everything Walpole's fault. Walpole had survived that. If Walpole was tired of it all, he was not so tired that he walked away. That was the good thing about Lord Sunderland, though. He never gave up, either. He would continue to invent scandal, to harass, to maneuver until Walpole was gone. Even Wharton was impressed with Lord Sunderland's single-mindedness.

Slane closed his eyes, wanting to rest a moment from machination and plotting. When he opened them, she was standing before him, and her face was grim.

"Sunderland is dead. That's what Carlyle came to say."

Slane felt cold move up his back.

"This morning," she was saying. "It is a great surprise to everyone. The King is in great distress."

As are we. The Jacobites' key to the inner workings of George of Hanover's English ministry was gone, like the blinking of an eye. Sunderland would have betrayed the King, had betrayed him, in a dozen small ways.

Slane stood, walked to the window, looked out to the night, the river; a few boats rode on it, lanterns to light their way.

Every instinct in him said, Go back to Paris, now. Tell them they must invade now. If he could have willed Ormonde to appear on the next river tide, he would have done so. He touched his brow, tender, a dull ache always there, sometimes terrible pain.

What was the saying from his childhood? Bad news came in threes. Here was the second. He was going to Paris. What was the saying about April? Some country saying of it being the cruelest month.

CHAPTER 33

April. Several days later, the Princess of Wales sat in a parlor at Leicester House, where she lived when in London; pretending to read, but her mind was very much upon her husband, and upon a summons he had received to attend his father at St. James's Palace.

Nothing unusual in that. The King was going to Hanover in another two weeks, was pleased about the journey, for he'd not been there in two years. The South Sea Bubble had not allowed it. The Prince would be regent in his place. There were doubtless many details to discuss. She herself was looking forward to the summer, to the power that would be theirs. It was like stretching her wings in anticipation of that time when she would be Queen. Hard to fold the wings back in when the King returned, but she who has patience may compass anything, may she not?

So.

Little tendrils, lightest of tendrils, most delicate of tendrils, out to Robert Walpole: Was it in the best interest of the kingdom that the Devane fine even be discussed in the next Parliament?

Might it not be better to let sleeping dogs lie just a while longer—a year, six months? Nothing more, of course; we are too fond of Lady Devane for it to be longer.

What can we do, she asked the King, to make our dear Lady Devane's stay in Virginia more pleasant? The Princess would retreat now that Sunderland was dead, allow the dust to settle, see who pushed closest to the King, base her further conduct on that.

She walked out to her terrace, raised her face to the sun. What did the death of Sunderland mean? Carlyle swore that Walpole and his brother-in-law, Lord Townshend, would be the chief ministers within two years, now that there was no Sunderland as competition. She thought of some of the other ministers, shuffling them in her mind, considering what she knew of them. Possibly Carlyle was right. Sunderland had possessed a truly remarkable deviousness and longevity.

Ah, there was her husband.

The Princess smiled, genuinely pleased to see him, though he would soon spoil that with some rough word or some slight, which she would have to pretend to ignore but which would be added to the burden of those already borne.

"I'll talk a moment with the Princess."

He spoke rudely to the attendants who followed him, gentlemen of the bedchamber, constant companions. Foolish to offend when offense was not necessary. But he could not learn that.

She scanned his face. Something had happened. He was breathing too heavily. His face was too red. The fingers of her hand, resting upon the balustrade of the terrace, gripped it a moment. Had he quarreled with his father? This was not the moment, when in another month they would for all purposes be upon their own. But when had the moment of something ever mattered to him? She had to guide him in everything.

"There is to be an invasion," he said.

The Prince was looking out over the terrace to their gardens as he spoke to her. Fear clutched the Princess's heart.

"The Regent of France sent a messenger to tell us. Ormonde is in Spain, with ships at his command. We do not know how many soldiers or ships. The Pretender has asked for three thousand men from the Regent, as if there were no treaty between France and England."

France had helped Cousin James before, treaty or no. That was the truth of treaties. "When?"

"We're not certain. Soissons—"

"Who?"

"Philippe, the Prince de Soissons. It was he who was sent by the Regent to inform us of the invasion plan, and he says they have a date of May tenth. But no one is perfectly certain of that. The French have word from their army that the Irish in certain regiments are gone, on leaves of absences. I cannot believe it. We are on the brink of war."

The Princess rubbed at the suddenly cold, cold flesh on her arms. "Will there really be war?"

"Ormonde is a fine soldier."

Yes. Ormonde had been Captain General of the army when Queen Anne died. He was singled out by Whigs as one who plotted to make James the Queen's heir. Oh God, who could forget that treacherous year of 1715?

You go into a web of terrible quarreling, the Prince's father had been warned by his closest advisers. The two English parties, Whig and Tory, hate each other, and each will try to have you rule without the other. It was true; the hatred between the two factions had been something one could feel. There had been a time in 1715 when their throne was so uncertain, when civil war seemed so imminent, that the King made plans for them to leave England and seek refuge in Holland should the Duke of Ormonde come out in open rebellion. It had been clear the soldiers in the army would support Ormonde, their general, over the foreigner, their King. But Ormonde had fled the country. That's what had saved them: the flight of fearful Tories.

What had they sung in the streets, as Tory after Tory was accused of treason, of plotting to bring Cousin James to the throne? "Farewell Old Year, for thou with Broomstick Hard had drove poor Tory from St. James's Yard. Farewell Old Year, Old Monarch, old Tory. Farewell Old England, thou hast lost thy Glory." Awful song. Someone had had the audacity to sing it under her windows at St. James's Palace.

I am given no choice, the King had said then. Neither side will work with the other. I must choose one and attempt to contain the other. Seven years, and the enmity, the deceit, were not ended yet. The other would not be contained, it kept bursting out. This was the fourth invasion attempt. Perhaps they would not be safe until Cousin James died, but he had a child now, hadn't he? So the mantle would be passed on to the child. It might never end, it might go into time endlessly, forever and forever, amen.

"There is to be no word, no sign, no whisper on our part yet. We are gathering what information we may; letters are being opened at the Post Office and ships stopped in the Channel," said the Prince. "Walpole said there had been odd rumors about Cadiz from certain agents. Our ambassadors at the courts of France and Spain and Rome are instructed to find out what they may as soon as they may. All agents here and abroad have been alerted. I'll go again to St. James's tonight."

"Is it Cadiz that Ormonde will leave from?" Cadiz was on the coast of Spain.

"It seems so."

She shivered. In an uncharacteristic gesture, the Prince put his hand over hers upon the balustrade.

Is it war? she thought. And can we endure?

CHAPTER 34

They appeared again, the angel women. For a moment, the boy stopped his work to listen to their voices, knowing, yet not knowing, the words they spoke to him. The slave driver raised his cat-o'-nine-tails, a stem of rope some eighteen inches long, at one end of which were fastened nine tails of leather with three or more knots upon each line; the whip whistled its particular sound as it whirled through the air. But the boy was stronger now, nimble again, a quick pupil of survival. He leaped out of the whip's way and ducked in and between other slaves who were bent over planting the green strips of hollow cane in a patchwork of water and dammed-up soil. Once out of the driver's reach, he bent down, as the others were doing, to work. The driver shook his head, leaving well enough alone. The boy did not have all his wits; everyone knew it.

The sky over the boy was blue, as blue as his memory of the color of someone's eyes. He could make no complete sense of words yet, just as he made no complete sense of the pictures in his mind, crowded images of dogs and gilded chairs and two women, their faces pale. The other slaves around him sheltered him. They put him to work between them. They motioned for him to do as they did. When he fainted, as sometimes happened, they carried him into the shade to rest, one of them fanning him with a palm leaf. They nudged him when he stopped too long, lost in his dreams. Over and over he bent, all the day. His hands bled because the pieces of cane cut. His head ached, a perpetual ache from the sun and bending, so that by evening he could not think nor speak, could only shake with weakness. The other slaves were gentle with him, respectful of his pain, respectful of his confused visions, of the dreams he woke them with at night.

Clear memory began with awakening in a small, bare room. He lay upon a floor, a threadbare blanket over him. There were others in the room with him. They sat crouched against the walls. Some of them were weeping. Their hands and feet were chained.

"Madame?" he said, as from the window sounds came to his ears: a carriage passing, a cry like a street vendor's, though the words were in another language unknown to him. He made an attempt to crawl to the window, but there was no strength in him. Some time later, a man came into the room; he was pale, plump, in the rich, sober clothing of a merchant. Exclaiming, the man spoke to him in questioning tones, but he didn't understand. Thus was born the first truth of this new life, that he was in a world in which nothing was comprehensible. Day by day, the others in the room with him disappeared. The plump, pale man would come for them, and only he ever returned.

That was the second understanding, that his own time to leave this room was coming. The boy ate the strong broth with chunks of meat mixed in it; he drank the wine mixed with egg the man brought; and he saw in the man's eyes that he measured the boy's growing strength. The boy prayed, the prayers welling up from a source he couldn't remember; he knew in his boy's heart that what lay ahead was nothing good. The angel women came often. They told him how much they loved him, that they would guide him and protect him, that he must be brave and ever vigilant. He wrapped their warnings, their promises, their love around his heart like a cloak.

The day the man took him outside the room, he stood in a courtyard and blinked at the sun, at the sight of masts rising behind houses, gulls circling, their cries shrill. The man gave him a shirt to wear, nothing more, so that he felt shamed. It had been in his mind to run at the first opportunity, but the man seemed to know—Others have tried before me, the boy thought—and fastened an iron collar around the boy's neck, connected by a small chain to the man's wrist. The shame of near nakedness was nothing compared to the shame of that.

"I'm not a dog," he said in French. The man ignored him.

When he was aboard a sloop, one of many in a harbor, the chain was undone. A sailor motioned for him to descend down a ladder into the bowels of the sloop. Something in him broke. He ran to the side of the sloop; he kicked and clawed at the sailors who wrestled him; he kicked, clawed, screamed "Madame!" over and over. When they had him pinned, the man was there, raising his hand. In that hand was a club—and the boy thought, His soul is dead, have mercy on mine, before he could think no more.

He woke in pain and dark, unable to see, a ringing in his ears, the press and presence of another being on each side of him frightening. In that dark was a stench that could not be described, made up as it was of filth and fear, of desperate degradation. The dark was horror. Weeping, screaming, sobbing, fierce foreign chants made up a babel of sound. Something scrambled over his leg, a creature, a ship's rat. He screamed, himself, after that, for a time, until the angel women hushed him. Pray, they told him, and he did, aloud, into the din, prayer after prayer: The Lord is my shepherd; I shall not want. He maketh me to lie down in green pastures. God is our refuge and strength, a very present help in trouble. The Lord is my light and my salvation; whom shall I fear. Sometimes he sang the prayers, sometimes he cried them, sometimes he whispered. Madness was tangible, a pressing, hovering presence in the bowels of this place. It waited in the dark and took those not strong enough to withstand it.

One after another in the darkness was ill with the bounce of the sloop on the water. The mess of it was everywhere, touching the boy's feet, his hands, making him gag and weep amidst his prayers. After a time—time had pressed back upon itself; he had no idea of its passing, of whether he had been here one hour or one day or one month—sailors appeared, their faces shadowed by a lantern, and with shouts and kicks pointed the way to a ladder, which led to light, to outside, to sun, which led to sanity, the sight of clouds, sky, sea. Ears ringing, head aching, stomach reeling, the boy clung to a mast as if it were life. He would do whatever he had to to stay in the light, but there was nothing to do. He and the others were allowed to stay atop from that point on; in the sun, laughter came, smiles, talk, as if there were no dark below; though at night, what the sailors came and did to the women was dark, and evil, and made the boy weep.

Once land was sighted, rising green out of the sea like an emerald, he thought again about escape, but it was clear the sailors had seen many attempts at escape. Chains were made tighter. Every movement was watched. Once the sloop was anchored, he and the others were immediately herded down a gangplank and into wagons; then, for two days, they jolted along twisting roads.

Three of the brave ones, a woman and two men, who fought back, growled and spat, tried to jump out of the wagon, were tied to a tree at the first stopping point and whipped. They were not allowed back into the wagons after that, but made to walk behind them, tied to them, until one of the men fell, and then he was dragged, mile after mile, until they stopped for the night. The sight of the deliberate, ruthless, implacable punishment was something the boy never forgot. Physical strength was not the answer. The man who lay in the dust behind the wagon, bleeding, silent, possibly dead, had been strong. Cunning and patience must be woven into this existence. You can be cunning, said the angel women. They do this to break your spirit, your power to resist them. They must cow you to nothingness. Do not resist them, or they will break you. A way will come, a time when you will see your way clear to us. Make me to hear joy and gladness; that the bones which thou hast broken may rejoice.

Memory of before was just there, beyond reach, ripe fruit upon a limb, tempting but too high to yet reach. He survived. He lived for his dreams, in which the angel faces hovered low, murmuring confused blessings in his ear. "Flower," they called him, "dear flower." Except that he now knew his name was Hyacinthe.

Who knew what began it? Beginnings are often vague and without meaning. Slaving was an old thing, as old as war, as old as man, as old as time. The children of Israel were slaves to Egypt, the Hebrews and Egyptians, Greeks and Germans, Gauls to Rome. The Renaissance city-states of Italy grew fat on their Christian slave trade with the Sultanate of Egypt; even papal decrees did not stop it. The Ottoman Empire was based on slaves. The first Portuguese sailors, greatly daring in their small ships, meandering down the coast of what would be called Africa, saw little significance in their capture of those they called Moors. It is written that one of the captives himself owned slaves, and redeemed himself from captivity with them. Beyond, farther down the African coast, was the state of Benin, with a thriving, ancient trade in slaves and ivory and pepper with the Berbers and Arabs of the desert. The Portuguese discovered soon enough there was a Christian market for slaves.

In 1492, in the name of the kingdom of Spain, an adventurer, explorer, and seeker of gold named Columbus searched for a quicker route to the riches of Asia, sailing blindly to the west from Spain. He found to his astonishment the West Indies, as islands of the Caribbean Sea would be called, their name reflecting the explorer's yearning to find Asia. To the north and west and south of them were huge continents, virgin, immense, populated by native tribes who hastened their own destruction in welcoming the strangers who brought guns, horses, and disease, smallpox and measles. Guns combined with death from disease soon conquered; the southern continent of the New World belonged in a short span of years to Spain.

There was gold and silver on that continent, gold and silver that gave Spain preeminence in Europe; but gold and silver had to be mined, and the native labor was dying too quickly to meet the demands of the market across the sea. A trickle of slaves brought to the West Indies by the Portuguese, by the Dutch, both clever traders, began to take their place. They died also. But their source was far more inexhaustible, as inexhaustible as the continent of Africa herself.

Other kingdoms—the French, the English, the Austrian Empire—looked at Spain, saw immense, amazing wealth, and wanted a share. They sent their adventurers to explore the continents for more sources of gold and silver, to found colonies so that they might stake their own claims. They sent their buccaneers to plunder and steal from the Spanish. These kingdoms followed the lead of Portugal and began trade along the African coast with the kingdoms of the Ashante and Oyo, Fon and Yoruba, Dahomey and Mandingo, and Hausa; all sold slaves.

Another event merged into the search, often futile, for gold; the growth of a crop in the New World that sold well in the old. Sugar grown in the West Indies went to Spain, which found Europe's appetite for that sweet, whitish substance inexhaustible. Growing sugar required the labor of many in the fields. A base grew into being for a triangular trade, with gain in three places: goods to Africa for slaves, slaves to the West Indies for raw sugar, raw sugar to Europe for refining and sale. With the crop of sugar, the trade of slaves to the Americas became so lucrative that the Spanish government institutionalized it into a licence, called an assiento. The slave assiento was a gold mine without the gold.

In time, through war, which was continual somewhere in Europe throughout the century, Spain sank back into the shadows as other kingdoms—the French, the Dutch, the English—moved forward. In 1701 the French obtained the slave assiento; in 1713, the English took it from the French as spoils of war. Men and women from Africa were being poured into the New World by the early 1700s, as another crop, tobacco, required much field labor, as would rice when it came to be grown in the new colonies of the Carolinas, and later, cotton.

Exploration to find fabled riches, but, instead, vast new lands found . . . planting when new lands did not possess enough silver and gold to meet the cost of exploration . . . a market for the crop of that planting, a gain when the crop was sold, more of a gain if there were slaves to plant and harvest . . . a market, therefore, for slaves, sold by native kingdoms of Africa for goods and gain themselves . . . such was the beginning, vague and without clear meaning, as beginnings so often are . . . though evil has, ultimately and always, both its meaning and its price, if not paid today, then come due tomorrow.

SUMMER

. . . BUT THEN SHALL I KNOW EVEN AS ALSO I AM KNOWN

CHAPTER 35

May . . . The milkmaids in London decked themselves with all the silver plate they could borrow to make a pyramid of plate, flowers, and ribbons upon their heads. With a fiddler to fiddle the way, they danced from door to door to celebrate the first of May. Young women crept out at dawn to gather the dew from the hawthorn, called the May, budding but not yet open to full blossom, to wash their face in it, for it was said the maid who washed her face in dew from the hawthorn tree would ever after handsome be.

In London, King George and his ministers read the copies of certain letters intercepted at the Post Office, read special dispatches from ambassadors, spies, and agents, and knew themselves as gravely threatened as ever they'd been. Ten thousand English troops marched through London and into Hyde Park at the city's western edge on the seventh day of May.

❧

Tony, his mother, and Philippe watched atop the flat portion of one of the roofs of Saylor House the startling spectacle of thousands of soldiers marching in formation and pomp. Drums thumped like a pulse heard aloud. Fifes sang out their shrill, merry tattoo. Feet stamped in rhythm. Bayonets were fixed to flintlocks, as flags and regimental banners waved atop poles, as rough voices called out commands and horses of the cavalry neighed and pranced. Officers rode by, proud in splendid uniforms of gold and braid and crimson and blue, the hooves of their horses clattering on cobblestones.

"Extraordinary," said Philippe.

"I cannot believe it." Abigail moved closer to her son, put her arm through his.

"It was madness once we got to the edge of London today," Tony said. "Our coach could scarcely make its way upon the road toward London Bridge, jammed as it was with other coaches, with wagons, with carts, with people walking, their children upon their shoulders, leaving the city. You must be the only Catholic allowed in London tonight, sir."

"Myself and the French ambassador," Philippe said. The announcement of a plot to put the Pretender upon the throne had been read by the King's herald at all city gates, and Catholics had been ordered to leave the city by the morrow.

"Is it true the King was to be killed?" asked Abigail. "Such things I've heard—London to be set to fire, burned to nothing, the Prince and Princess kidnapped, arms for Jacobites at secret places all over London."

"I'm told the hall of the Bank of England was mobbed this morning," said Philippe, "people rushing to take out their coins and go and hide them. Catholics were not allowed to claim theirs."

"I've heard Lord Sunderland's papers were searched," said Tony. "Walpole and Lord Townshend were looking for evidence of knowledge of the invasion."

Abigail sat down on one of the elaborate chairs brought up to make their view of the troops more comfortable. London stretched out verdant, peaceful, green before them, church spires lovely marks to the May sky, the sound of drums reverberating up to them again and again.

"I do not believe you. Lord Sunderland was not a Jacobite. I am afraid. Ought we to stay? What if they come, Tony, what if they take this house? What if there should be a war?"

War, thought Tony. Yesterday I was walking in the gardens at

Lindenmas with Harriet, with no thought of this, only the thought of how good my world was, and today that world has tipped to one side, is changing even as I stand here. Now, the time at the lovely country house belonging to Harriet's parents seemed a dream.

"You will come, of course, to France if there is war, my dear," Philippe kissed Abigail's hand. "Stay with me in Paris for as long as need be, while your son raises a regiment here and repeats the exploits of his famous grandfather."

"What a mercy Diana's husband, Kit, is dead." Abigail dabbed at her eyes. She had been crying on and off since she and Tony had crossed London Bridge. "He would be in this, part and parcel, and not upon our side. Oh, I feel as if I have stepped into a nightmare. Look there!" she said, and Tony and Philippe saw, in the distance, over the rooftops of the houses on St. James's Street, the first lights from campfires as the soldiers made camp in Hyde Park.

Dusk, thought Tony, the end to an extraordinary day.

As more and more fires appeared, hundreds of them, it was as if portions of the stars had fallen to ground and burned.

"A stirring sight," said Philippe.

"There you are," said Charles. He had not come with the rest of the family to Lindenmas, but had stayed in London. There are things I must do, he had said. "All of London is a place fit only for madmen, today."

Charles kissed Abigail's cheek.

"Or soldiers," said Philippe.

"Oh, it is too dreadful. How glad I am Mary is not here. What if she had the child in the midst of this," said Abigail.

"Yes." Charles spoke slowly, almost as if he were drunk; Tony, watching, thought, He is not drunk, but something is wrong. "It is best that she be gone."

"You look ill."

Charles shrugged off his mother-in-law's words and went to stand near Tony. "Will there be an invasion, as they claim?"

"If there is, it looks as though we are prepared."

"So it does. I am restless, I cannot be still. I feel as if the drums the soldiers beat are inside in my head. Tony, walk with me to Hyde Park."

Abigail started to protest, but Philippe put his hand upon her shoulder, and she was silent. After they were gone, he said, "You must leave them be. They are young, and this is a night when the blood in young men's veins rampages with the thought of war and valor, honor and country. I will amuse you with my version of the Duchess of Kendall weeping about her precious king, worried for which jewels she should take with her if your Pretender comes."

Charles and Tony walked through streets that were strangely quiet. In windows of houses, draperies were already drawn, as if people wished to shut out the world. They walked past fields and farms, and Tony thought of Sir Gideon Andreas, buying land or building leases all over this part of London, easy enough to do now, since the South Sea Bubble. Tommy Carlyle said Andreas now held two of the largest notes of debt Barbara owed. Why? Tony had asked, and then: Will he sell them, do you think? Carlyle had shrugged his shoulders. Tony was thinking of that as he walked past lanes that would one day be streets, if building should ever start again, the way it had before the Bubble. When building did begin again, this part of London would belong to Andreas and, interestingly enough, to Barbara. Roger had bought much here, too.

They were at Hyde Park. It seemed as if a thousand, two thousand tents were there. It was a stirring sight, a clear symbol of England's might and King George's will. Challenged by guards, Tony gave his name, and they were allowed to walk in.

"The Duke of Marlborough or your grandfather would be more than welcome, now," Charles said.

The Duke of Marlborough was dying. Tony had thought of visiting the old general, to hear some last word, some tale of his grandfather, but somehow the days at Lindenmas with Harriet fell one into the other, and he did nothing but enjoy his wife. Marlborough and his grandfather had soldiered together, had won the wars of King William and Queen Anne, had been uncrowned kings of Europe, admired and fêted everywhere, for a time. Before the intrigues began. They always begin, said Carlyle. Envy, like a snake, must rear its head and bite that which it at first admires.

"The servant who answered your door had a pistol in his belt," said Charles.

"My mother is afraid."

"Any wise man is afraid this night. Will the King call in extra troops from the Dutch, as he did in 1715?"

"I have no idea, Charles."

"I may come back to Lindenmas with you."

"My sister would be glad."

"I'd like to stay the night at Saylor House. Have you any objection?"

"Of course not."

They walked along silently for a while, the ease that once had been theirs gone, and they were both awkward, too aware of what was no more.

In Tony's mind was a picture of the old days, when he had admired Charles, accepting without question that Barbara should love Charles rather than himself, because in his eyes Charles was better in all things. Like a boy, he had not envied Charles for being better, but loved him the more for it.

Stopping where he was, Charles spoke abruptly.

"Men make errors in their lives, Tony. It is my understanding that only God may judge. Let us go back. I think I can sleep now." He did not look at Tony as he spoke, but at some point in the darkness, his words, his expression, fierce.

Do I judge? thought Tony. Then: Yes, I judge you to be a poor friend, when all is said and done. You could have stopped the duel. You know you could have. And I know it, too. "I'm going to walk awhile longer."

"Please yourself."

Tony walked for a long time among the tents, stopping to watch the soldiers as they squatted before their campfires, listening to their talk, their laughter and complaints. An officer came up to him, and when Tony said his name, a grizzled soldier nearby called out, "The

Lionheart's grandson, are you? I'll drink a dram of rum to your grandfather tonight, Your Grace, for he was one of us. We could use him in this fight we're facing."

When he was finally tired, he left the park, crossed the road to the smaller Green Park, which lay at one side of St. James's Palace. Tony stood a moment, looking at the palace, thinking of the Hanovers.

In 1715, for months after King George had landed, a rising had been expected, a civil war. We accept a foreigner before the English-born son of our late king had been one of the sayings. Rise in the name of James, he who is our own. There were riots in Bristol and Oxford and Bath. He had been sixteen, then, and his uncle, Barbara's father, Kit, Lord Alderley, was one of the Tories around whom rumors of treason wove themselves. Alderley, Bolingbroke, Marr, Oxford, Ormonde—great Tory lords, mighty in the last years of Queen Anne.

If there was war, Tony's loyalty was with this house, this king, this family. The crown was theirs by law, a Protestant must sit upon the throne, and King George had been generous, granting favors and honors to him and to his sister. If there was a war, he would raise a regiment and fight.

Halfway across the park, he thought about Aunt Shrew and turned his steps toward her townhouse. She was playing cards with Pendarves and Laurence Slane. Diana was with them, sitting in a chair, not playing, but watching. Diana did not look her best. The elemental vitality that even powder did not dim was missing tonight.

"Give me a kiss, boy," Aunt Shrew said, her bracelets jangling as Tony hugged her.

"I will sleep safer in my bed this night knowing you are in town. Did your sister birth her brat yet? No? Last time I noticed, that rogue of a husband of hers was in Twickenham, staying with the Duke of Wharton, and the pair of them were drinking the village dry. What do you say to a wager, Tony, that when I wake in the noon tomorrow, I will feed breakfast to a handsome soldier who walked out of Hyde Park to turn Jacobite in the night?"

"This is no time for jests, Aunt," Diana said.

"Jest? If Ormonde sets foot on English soil, King George can kiss his troops upon their buttocks, because that is all he will see of them, their backs as they march to join Jamie's general. You sulk, Diana, because you have made your bed with the Whigs, in more ways than one." She slapped a card viciously upon the table. "My point, Lumpy."

"You're speaking treason," Tony said.

There was a moment's silence. Aunt Shrew threw back her be-wigged head, narrowed her eyes at her nephew.

"Since when has truth become treason? Do you arrest me?"

"I would not dare. I simply ask you to think before you speak. We're on the verge of war, and what people say may be taken in the wrong manner. I've been wanting to see you," Tony said to Slane.

There was a deep, not quite healed scar breaking the fine, thick line of one of Slane's dark brows, and he looked tired, the darkness under his eyes as dark as the eyes themselves.

"Have you, Your Grace? Here I am. How may I serve you?"

"You were at Tamworth, I understand."

"I fell from my horse." Slane touched his brow. "And I have this to show for it. Your grandmother nursed me most kindly."

"You left Tamworth Hall without a word."

Slane smiled. "There was a woman I had to see. The situation is complicated, Your Grace. Unfortunately, there is a husband in it."

"How do you know my cousin, Lady Devane?"

"I do not know your cousin."

"My grandmother said you said her name."

"I could not. I do not know her name."

"Do you deny saying the name Barbara?"

"The name of my amour is Barbara, Your Grace. I must have said it aloud, not knowing your grandmother was about. To tell you the truth, I remember very little more than fainting, though I do have a memory of a cat sitting upon me."

"Why did you leave without a word to my grandmother?"

"I went to see my friend, thinking I would return, but there was a complication with her husband, and it seemed best to leave the area. What can I add, Your Grace, except that later, it was easier to continue on to London than to stay and explain my lack of manners. I hope I caused no distress."

"You did cause distress. She was greatly upset."

"Then I offer a thousand apologies. Will you convey them to her on my behalf?"

"What does it matter?" said Diana.

Tony took Diana's hands in his, knelt, looking into Diana's face. "Are you well?"

She looked quite pale, the circles under her eyes dark, like Slane's.

"Never better. Only frightened, like everyone else."

"She wanted to be with family on a night like this, or so she says," said Aunt Shrew. "Play me a hand, nephew. Lumpy has lost this game, and I know all his moves anyway. I tell you, this story of invasion is folderol."

"What has gotten into you?" said Pendarves, shaking his head. Then, commenting on what was as important to his heart, "Stocks will go down over this. And we were only beginning to recover from the Bubble."

"We'll have to send for our regiments in Ireland if war does break out," Tony said. "I walked among the troops in Hyde Park this evening. They're saying the word is Ormonde has six to eight battalions of foot soldiers with him. The spirit of our men is good, though. They are ready for a battle. I don't think they will desert."

"It is the Saylor coming out in you. Blood will tell every time, won't it?" Aunt Shrew's bracelets jangled harshly. "Did your grandfather ever tell you about Malplaquet, Tony?"

"Malplaquet?" said Diana.

"A battle, which you ought to know," snapped Aunt Shrew, "as it was one of your father's finest. James, of course—may I call him James, Lumpy, or must I say the Pretender?—fought upon the side of the French against us, but he fought so well, charging the Dutch and English lines twelve times in one day, even after he was wounded in the arm, that the English soldiers drank to his health around their campfires that night. Your grandfather did, also, Tony. The armies faced each other across a river nearly all of that summer, and James would ride beyond the French outposts and sit atop his horse watching the English soldiers drill. Not a man of them would have thought of shooting at him, Brother said. He said he would have hanged the first who lifted his musket. What honor there was then, Tony. It makes my heart quicken to think of it, the way men fought each other face to face in the morning and drank to the other's valor at night, a kind of honor of which there is no evidence any more. Brother told me that sight haunted him all the summer, James atop his horse watching his countrymen, men who might have been his to command. The love for them was plain, said Brother, even from across the river."

I will not weep, Slane thought.

"Look out the window, Diana, and tell me if you see any ships yet," said Aunt Shrew.

"Stop it," said Diana.

"I must go." Slane bowed to Aunt Shrew, and for a moment the two of them looked at each other. Under the jangles, the rouge, the harsh flippancy, she was as stunned as he. They had no idea what was happening, whether Ormonde had sailed or not. Slane had only just returned from an exhausting trip to Paris. He'd offered to go to Spain, to give Ormonde an order to invade immediately. The invasion is set for May tenth, they said. King James approves. Even a day may make a difference, he had argued. And so it did. This day was May seventh. Was Ormonde stopped in his tracks, or had he sailed? There was no way to know. They could only wait.

"You have a care," she said to him.

And you also, my sweet friend, Slane thought.

"Please give your grandmother my apologies and tell her I thank her for her nursing of me. Tell her I am a ragamuffin Irishman with no gratitude nor manners in me," Slane said to Tony.

"Why are you still in the city?"

"I beg your pardon."

"All Catholics were ordered to leave. You have only until morning."

"Am I Catholic?"

"I believe you told my grandmother so."

Slane took a breath. Tony's forcefulness was a surprise. But why? He was of Richard Saylor's blood. And the Duchess's. "I haven't prayed in so long a time I've forgotten what I am. I think the truth is, I believe in nothing."

"It might be well if you left the city for a time. If you stay, as my aunt says, have a care to yourself," said Tony.

Out on the street, Slane walked toward Hyde Park, to see with his own eyes the troops in camp. There had not been one whisper, one rumor of this. He felt the same sense of stunned stillness as when he'd been thrown from his horse, and lay on the ground. It was masterly upon the part of King George, and frightening. Was Ormonde stopped? What was known? How long had the ministry been intercepting Jacobite letters?

Slane leaned a moment against the brick wall that enclosed one side of Hyde Park. Feeling sick, he touched his head, the bad pain of it with him again. He had waked early in the morning, waked to the sound of drums, the throb in his head matching the beat of the drums.

Five days ago, six, if the Duke of Ormonde had landed then, these soldiers would have still been scattered across half of England, in their various postings. The first plan would have accomplished that. The Paris advisers clung to their second plan, their precious date of May tenth, saying King George would be gone. There was a possibility Ormonde would still be able to leave Spain. If so, all was not lost. Let him land, let there be one battle, just one battle, here, at England's heart. For that I would give my life, thought Slane, to be able to look once into the faces of my enemies and battle them for the throne.

"Here, now," said one of the guards posted along the fence. "What do you think you're doing?"

"Looking at the King's fine army."

"Never mind looking. You move on, unless you want to talk to my lieutenant and tell him why you linger."

He must find Wharton, must go to Arran, to North, to Lord Oxford, to Rochester, convince them to hold strong, even in the face of this, to await Ormonde. Bad things come in threes. The saying stumbled over itself in his head. There had not been a whisper of this. God, he wanted to weep. The sight of James watching his English troops from across the river at Malplaquet was in his head so clearly. Not a whisper of this. That's what came of losing Sunderland. They'd have been forewarned, if Sunderland had been alive.

A few hours later, Tony walked with Diana to her townhouse. On the way, they passed the house in St. James's Square where Barbara had lived when she was in London.

Fortunate that Harry is dead, thought Tony. In his heart was the ache that was Barbara, only changed now, lessened by his wife. Thank God for that, thought Tony, staring at the tall, narrow front of the house, leased now, to someone else, so that Barbara might collect the rents. Barbara.

"Do you think there will be war, Tony?"

"Yes, I do."

He took Diana's hand. "Come back with my mother to Lindenmas. It is far enough away from London that you will be safe, at least for a time."

She allowed him to hold her hand a moment. They were standing before her townhouse. "You're kind, Tony. Does your wife please you? You act as if she did."

"She does."

"Barbara would have pleased you more, you know. In every way."

Diana ran up the steps, leaving Tony to stand in the dark, staring after her.

Inside the house, a man stepped out of the dark of the hall, pinned Diana against a wall, began to kiss her neck, her shoulders, pushed her gown down, roughly.

"Eat, drink, and be merry," whispered Charles, "for tomorrow, we die. Sit on that table. Pull up your gown. Yes, like that. What if we die on the morrow, Diana?"

He bit the tip of her breast, uncovered now. "I leave for Lindenmas tomorrow. I must have something to remember. Your leg, here, where your stocking stops, is smooth, Diana. I have only to think of you to feel desire, and no whore but you satisfies me any longer. Does that please you, whore?"

In the dark, Diana lay back on the table; there was the sound of candlesticks falling. "Which of us," she said, digging her nails into his sides, as he entered her and began to move, and the table swayed with the movement, "is the more faithless and lying? Which of us is the true whore?"

At Saylor House, even though it was dark, Tony found his mother in the garden, overseeing the footmen. At her orders, they were burying all Saylor House's silver plate and china, and there was much of it.

"What are you doing?"

"There will be looting. And don't think for a moment they will overlook Saylor House."

He shook his head at his mother, but found himself only moments later thinking, What would I miss if the house should be looted or burned? The idea of Saylor House being burned touched off something fierce in him. They'd do it, if only to take revenge on my grandfather, he thought, who might have saved James II and therefore the throne for the House of Stuart. But Grandfather chose otherwise, and so do I. He looked around at the walls of Saylor House, festooned with the finest carving, with heavy portraits and velvet damask. My home, he thought. No one will have it, if I must die defending it. There would be children with Harriet. This is theirs.

By morning, he had all his grandfather's journals and plans of maneuver in a neat pile to send back to Lindenmas with his mother. And he walked to St. James's to call on the King, to offer his services in whatever manner might be useful.

CHAPTER 36

In Virginia, the rains of April had led to the warmth of May, and at First Curle, the seedlings sat in their tobacco hills. Shirt off, sun warm on his back, Blackstone hoed in his garden, the fresh smell of the soil good in his nostrils, the sound of the hoe breaking up clods satisfying, his mind moving over what he'd plant in this soil, moving over Thérèse, missing her; missing Lady Devane, too. She'd be proud of the seedlings. They did well in their hills. They'd do even better in the drained swamp. The finest tobacco on the river, some-day. His hoe hit something, and he leaned down to pick up an arc with a grimed ribbon hanging from one end.

Turning it over a time or two in his hand, he put it into his pocket and continued to hoe, placid in the sun, in his work and thoughts, when suddenly there came a picture of the boy, Hyacinthe, sitting behind Lady Devane on her horse, a bit of shining silver at his neck. It shows I belong to her, Blackstone saw the boy saying, showing the metal arc held with ribbon at his neck. I am proud to belong to her.

At once he put down the hoe, went into his house, and rubbed soot onto the metal, watching the darkness turn to that dull shine that was silver. He found a cloth and worked at the metal until the arc was as it had once been, shining and beautiful, the Devane crest raised slightly at its center.

What did it mean?

Colonel Perry was in Williamsburg. All the burgesses were in Williamsburg, at their assembly, where they made laws and listened to that which England desired of them. Could this wait until Colonel Perry's return?

No, thought Blackstone. I'll ride into Williamsburg and show the Colonel myself.

CHAPTER 37

The buds of the hawthorn, England's clear sign of May, began to open, to fill the air with their sweet fragrance. In every village and every town, word of the plot was sent by special messengers as soon as possible from London.

"It's a detestable and terrible thing," Tim said to Annie. "We must be prepared."

Annie handed Cook the ancient muskets and swords the Duchess had ordered pulled down from the walls of the great hall. All the servants at Tamworth would be given them. Anything left over would go to the militia.

An hour later, an odd procession set off across Tamworth's lawn, Tim carrying the Duchess, the coachman pushing a wheelbarrow that held a rigid wooden chair, Cook carrying weapons, and the beemaster and Perryman bringing up the end.

Tim sat the Duchess in the chair at the edge of the meadow. Cook wrapped a blanket around her legs. The beemaster handed her Dulcinea.

"Go on," the Duchess said to them, "duty calls."

The news of a plot had been read aloud in Tamworth village yesterday after a soldier beating a tattoo on a drum had summoned a crowd to listen. In loyalty to King George, Tamworth village prepared itself for invasion by forming a militia, with Sir John Ashford as its commander, a commander of farmers' sons; of the village smith, Vicar Latchrod, and Squire Dinwitty; of a few of the village weavers; and of servants from various households, including her own.

The Duchess shivered, and it was not from cold; she was thinking of an old verse: Thunder in May frightens summer away. I am old, she thought, too old for all of this. In her grandfather's time, when Cromwell and King Charles I had battled, estates from both sides had been burned to the ground, as brother turned against brother, and father against son. If she had to watch Tamworth burn, she would die from the sight of it.

She looked out to the field, to the men marching there.

You make a fine commander, she thought, watching John, who did not deign to notice her. The Duchess stroked Dulcinea. Cook ruined the marching drill by bowing to the Duchess every time he passed her chair. Squire Dinwitty quarreled about what should be done. If the Duchess knew Squire Dinwitty—and she did—he was indignant that he was not commander. One of the farmers' sons kept tripping over the long pike he carried.

Not a pretty sight, thought the Duchess.

The beemaster stood where he was and hummed. He'll be gone within the hour, summoned by his bees, thought the Duchess.

"We may as well surrender," she called out to Sir John, but he ignored her.

Not even in this crisis did he relent and speak to her. He paid her the debt, as he'd promised, but by mortgaging his farm to a moneylender in London. Fool. Appalled at what he had done, she refused to touch the bag of coins. Moneylenders charged a rate of interest that was often impossible to pay. She who loved Tamworth as if it were a piece of her soul knew what it must have done to him to have mortgaged Ladybeth so desperately. She would have allowed him as long as he needed to pay the sum back, but no. Pride goeth before destruction. Someday she would take the coins and have them melted down and cast in the form of a donkey and send it to him, with her compliments. View yourself, she'd say. Ass.

Dread, thought the Duchess, I am filled with dread, truly afraid. Any day—such was the word—Ormonde was landing with a force of men. And the Duchess of Marlborough had written to tell her that her husband, a soldier who, like Richard, had defined the times of King William and Queen Anne, was dead, after a long time of suffering. Was it an omen?

They had belonged to her other life, that life of policy and intrigue, a life she had been born for, had played until her last card was taken from her, that card being Richard.

Oh, Richard, she thought, the last of the warriors is gone. His funeral will rival the pomp of yours. But King George was ordering it put back, fearing what mobs in London may do. Richard, I wish you were here with me. Another war looms; more bloodshed, more anger and revenge. It should be finished, Richard, but it is not.

"Picture an anthill," wrote Louisa, her sister-in-law, from London, "which has just been stepped upon. So it is in London, among the offices of the ministers. Men come and go at all hours, and no one in London sleeps, expecting Ormonde and his fleet daily. The wildest of rumors fly about. No man or woman speaks freely nor leaves home for more than an hour at a time. The naming of those who are supposed to have headed this plot range from the ridiculous to the foolish."

Where was Tony? There was no word from him. He should come and see to her. The Jacobites would murder her in her bed because she was Richard Saylor's widow. Richard would have been Jacobite, but for her. Who knew that? She and God and Annie. The times made her think of it. It was not something she wished to think upon. It was a regret.

She was old for regrets, but she had them. Barbara, Harry would have been in this, and you and I would have been fretted to death. He'd have involved us in his plotting; we would not have been able to say no to him. War. I am afraid.

May moved to its middle part in the calendar. Robert Walpole sat alone in a garden, pudgy, strong fingers moving, slowly, methodically, along the back of the bench, his face, with its plump jowls and perennial jolly-squire smile, showing little, only the steady, almost unblinking stare indicating the forward movement of a mind that was practical, tough-fibered, amazingly shrewd, and born to the task at hand.

The view from the bench upon which he sat was of the Thames River, its boats, wherries, small yachts, even a barge or two. He was surrounded by the buildings that had formed the texture of his life: St. Stephen's Chapel, in which the House of Commons met; the Treasury Building, made from what had been a royal cockpit, an arena for a favorite and bloody sport in which roosters were pitted against one another to fight until death. The cockpit was among those buildings left of Charles II's Whitehall Palace, which had once covered these grounds in its sprawl.

This was a place of odd little courtyards, a magnificent church, a prison, private gardens and houses, lanes, alleys, narrow streets, the law courts, buildings spared when Whitehall burned, half their stone fronts barnacled with small taverns and shops, hundreds of years of history, of intrigue and machinations, plottings and secrets, all squeezed between the river and the royal parks. This was his life. He knew every nook, every odd corner, every silent garden here. And it was to one of these gardens, small and half forgotten, that he came in times of turmoil to think.

Another invasion attempt.

The troops were still encamped in Hyde Park. The King's mistress, the Duchess of Kendall, drove with the King's granddaughters to look at them daily. The royal family was outraged, and under that outrage, fearful, the Prince of Wales blustering, full of bravado.

His Majesty, upon the other hand, was another story: quiet, mostly silent, listening to the daily reports of his ministers as information was slowly gathered in, as the best of their agents broke Jacobite codes. Who, he asked Walpole, are the chief plotters?

There was no one with them, and the King spoke English—fairly well, better than Walpole would have imagined. Walpole had a sudden, startling moment in which he remembered all the times he or another minister had tossed off quick, slighting remarks, trusting that the King's English left him unable to grasp them.

Sunderland knew, thought Walpole, knowing the way Sunderland always did certain things, how good the King's English was. How he must have laughed at me at times. How he must be relishing this moment, and my discomfort, in the hell in which he burns.

Walpole told His Majesty the names, names he and Lord Townshend had carefully pieced together from references in the letters. No one was named directly; all had a code name or cipher given them.

The King had been silent a long time.

There were no great surprises, still it was hard to know that a man who had bowed before you only the other evening in a drawing room had also actively and carefully plotted treason against you for a year or more.

Proof? he had asked after a moment.

Here was the hard part.

Nothing yet which will stand in court, though we have someone in Paris who is supplying information, Townshend and Walpole said. There's the matter of reference to the gift of a dog which might aid us. It's mentioned in letters we know are Jacobite.

His Majesty was not impressed.

How pleased I would be, said His Majesty, to see the back of this insidious plotting broken once and for all. Something like a trial, said His Majesty, someone significant losing his head would give people pause. How grateful I would be for pause.

Tap, went Walpole's fingers upon the bench.

Rochester.

Would it be possible to capture the best-known, the wiliest, the most outspoken of Tory bishops? Rochester led this; all the signs in the letters pointed to him; a dying wife, his gout, his calling as a priest.

To convict him of treason.

Off with his head.

And so break the bad habit Tories had formed of consorting with Jacobites when things did not go their way? It would break the Church, too, make it more amenable to policy.

Tap went Walpole's fingers upon the bench, once more.

There was knowledge, there was instinct; and then there was proof.

Could he prove Rochester guilty in a state trial that would linger in the public's mind for years afterward? That ought to earn the King's eternal gratitude.

What, precisely, did "eternally grateful" mean?

I think, said the King, that the man who crushes Jacobites once and for all must be my chief minister. For he will have the audacity and the coldness I most assuredly need.

CHAPTER 38

May moved to its end. Diana sat at the window in the bedchamber of her townhouse. The window before her was open to catch the breeze. Clemmie, taking away a slop jar, glanced over at her mistress and then away, knowing better than to be caught doing so.

A seller of gingerbread wandered onto the street. Dressed like a nobleman with ruffled shirt, white stockings, a cocked hat, he saw Diana and began his song: "Here's your nice gingerbread, your spiced gingerbread, will melt in your mouth like a red-hot brickbat and be rumbling in your inside like Punch in his wheelbarrow."

The sweet, spicy smell came before his words, and Diana put her hand to her mouth. Clemmie brought the slop jar over at once, soaked a cloth with water and gave it, silently, small eyes blank, to Diana, who held it to her mouth.

"I would kill for a bit of winter ice, just to allow it to melt in my mouth," Diana said. She caught sight of herself in her dressing table mirror, staring a moment at herself.

She threw the cloth at the mirror, then a jar of rouge out the window, missing the seller of gingerbread but making a satisfying clatter of breaking glass outside, and silencing his song.

"What is the date?" she asked Clemmie.

"Eight-and-twenty days into May."

"The King's birthday fête tonight. I wish I did not have to go. If

Ormonde weren't coming, I wouldn't, but we all have to be on our best behavior these days, Clemmie, or we'll be thought Jacobite. Have I a gown I can wear?"

"If anything, you are more thin."

"I won't be for long."

Clemmie scuttled downstairs to her lair in the kitchen. Her mistress had insisted upon hot baths for a week and had gone horseback riding early in the morning and again at dusk. Three days ago, she had tried a purge. The only recourses left were a visit by Clemmie to certain shops for selected pills and powders, and, if those failed, a fall down the stairs.

Let Robin Walpole try to save the nation; they had other things to deal with, here.

CHAPTER 39

In the last days of June, a ship sat at anchor in the Thames River, not yet at its destination, London. Gulls, hundreds of them, had settled themselves into the rigging, but as sailors moved among the tall masts, the gulls swooped away in a gray-white, winged cloud. It was a beautiful sight.

"We're moving, I believe, Thérèse. The tide must be in."

"Tide and a strong wind," said a sailor. "You bring us good fortune, Lady Devane."

Barbara looked upward. Sails were descending, creaking and moaning in their journey. Gulls hovered above the masts, screeching and crying out and whirling away on strong wings as one by one sails opened to whipping majesty, the sailors' calls mingling with the gulls' cries, the sailors laughing, happy in their perilous perches in the rigging of the ship. The ship's anchor was being pulled up.

Her heart was beating strong enough to shake the inside of her throat. A shudder shook the ship. Slowly, like a great and clumsy swan, the ship was moving. Now the tide had it. Wind was filling the sails and they billowed out, full and splendid. The ship settled into the tide's current more securely. Around them were other ships, and ahead of them, and behind, all using the incoming tide to reach London Bridge—merchants' ships, yachts, dinghies, skiffs, and wherries, sails unfurled to the wind, a procession on water toward London.

After a time, as the marsh and fens of the shore began to change to a line of houses and cottages, Barbara could see in the distance masts, the pennants and flags on them waving in the strong wind. They belonged to the ships docked at London Bridge.

She looked up at the pennants flying on this ship, brave and whipping in the wind. Home. I'm home. She felt as if her heart would burst.

"The Tower of London." Thérèse, on deck beside her, pointed.

Oh, yes, there it was, one of London's most famous landmarks, England's most famous prison. Massive, impenetrable, looking of another age with its turrets and bulwarks and moat, Queen Elizabeth's prison and other kings' and queens', and even, once upon a time—for the briefest of times—her grandfather's. The Tower of London was a symbol of Fate's whims, for the being who entered through Tower Gate might emerge to become queen—or England's finest general.

I thought I'd lost him, said her grandmother, spinning out a tale that had left her and Harry fascinated, one they played over and over again, imprisoning one another in an imaginary tower, but there is no prison made that could hold your grandfather's spirit.

Barbara smiled, the smile dazzling. The sun caught and tangled itself in the red-gold strands of her thick hair, pulled up and caught by pins with heads of pearl. Her face had never been more heart-shaped, more true, and her heart itself, in spite of Hyacinthe, happy. That was a gift from Virginia, to know so clearly what those here meant to her.

She squeezed Harry so that he barked. "We are home."

"They're not expecting us so soon," said Thérèse.

Grandmama. Tony. Jane. "No."

Leaning against the railing, she looked down at the water cutting away in white-green spray from the ship's hull. Droplets touched her face, like tiny blessings. Purge me with hyssop, and I shall be clean: wash me, and I shall be whiter than snow, she thought, the familiar verse comforting. She'd call upon His Majesty, the Prince and Princess, then go home, to Tamworth, to her grandmother.

The ship took its place amidst a crowd of ships. Lightermen rowed the small cargo boats called lighters among the anchored ships, like dozens of small insects upon the water. Barbara paced the deck, waiting for the order from the captain that would allow her to leave. There it was. Skirts bunched under one arm, she climbed down the rope ladder and into a small boat. A lighterman rowed them toward the dock, and men reached down to pull her upward. Harry, in his wicker cage, snarled and whimpered. Barbara put her foot down upon solid ground.

"Hush, silly dog," said Thérèse. "We are home."

There was the strong smell of river water and fish. There was the sight of fishwives with baskets of herring, Spanish onions, oyster, and cod to sell, calling out to one and all to buy, men unloading barrels and boxes, merchants bargaining for corn and coal and tobacco. They moved through bearers and customs men, beggars and street vendors, toward a street. There was a carriage for hire.

At once, Thérèse walked over, haughty, imperious, in her element, ready to bargain for a good price on this carriage ride, every inch of her a great lady's personal servant, cynical, world-weary, imperious.

Barbara noticed soldiers standing guard on the quays. Others marched by in formation.

"Has there been a riot?" she asked the carriage driver.

Certain troops were always barracked in the Tower of London, while the rest were scattered about in different cities and villages. There was a continual quarrel between the King and his ministers and the Parliament concerning how much of a standing army to maintain. "Not much," was always the vote.

"Oh, no, ma'am. There's to be an invasion. The Duke of Ormonde is coming with twenty thousand Spanish and Irish at his back."

What? An invasion? "When is he coming?"

"We thought before now, my lady. You should have seen us a month ago. There wasn't ten people on this quay. Old Robin the Skreen is holed up at the Cockpit, like a hunting dog, following every scent. Jacobites meant to kill the King, it's said. I have no love for the Hanoverian, but, as I said to the wife, at least with the Hanovers, we know what we have, don't we?"

"Did you hear?" Barbara said to Thérèse, inside the carriage. "I cannot believe it."

"Come home," Wart had written. "There is adventure happening." Lying, duplicitous Wart. Telling the truth for once.

The carriage began to rattle down Fish Street Hill. The sounds of the street mingled with the clatter of the iron carriage wheels. Street vendors, as numerous as beggars, were working their trades, imminent invasion or not.

"Cabbages O! turnips!"

"Knives to grind!"

"A tormentor for your fleas!"

The carriage moved closer and closer to Saylor House; soldiers were everywhere on the streets. There was no one at Saylor House. The housekeeper who came to greet them was like a pot boiling over with words instead of water.

"Lady Devane, is it truly you come home? I could hardly believe my ears when the footman told me. The family are from town, madam. I'll send a footman to the dock for the remainder of your trunks and boxes. I have scarcely closed my eyes at night these last two months, expecting any moment to see foreign soldiers marching down the Strand. The Duke has done nothing but travel back and forth from Lindenmas—"

"What is Lindenmas?"

"The new Duchess of Tamworth's house, ma'am, belonging to her parents. He said we was to leave the house if they invaded and he was not here, said we was to go to Tamworth Hall or Lindenmas. But will there be time to leave the house? is what I ask. Do you desire to rest? Shall I have the bed made down for you? Is there a time you desire supper? Have you need of anything? Only tell me, and it shall be yours, the Pretender on his way to us or not. You'll want to know that Lady Russel was delivered of a boy. We're all so proud."

A child? Charles and Mary had had a child?

"When?"

"Three weeks ago, now."

"My grandmother?"

"Fit, as far as I know. The Duke went to fetch her to take her to Lindenmas so that she would be safe."

"Tell me about the invasion."

But the housekeeper could tell her little more than that the Duke of Ormonde was to come. That the great Bishop of Rochester himself was said to be the head of it all—caught, so the rumor in broadsheets was, by word of a little spotted dog sent him by the Pretender himself.

Rochester had been a friend of Roger's.

"Has the Bishop of Rochester been arrested?"

"No, ma'am."

Barbara went to a long window and looked out at the gardens. Trees hid the streets beyond, cushioned the house from the busy sprawl all around. One might have been a mile from town, in the country, and yet just beyond the entrance gates was Pall Mall with St. James's Palace, where the King lived, and Green Park at its end. I must call upon the King, the Prince and Princess of Wales, she was thinking, as she took Harry to walk in the gardens. I must get at the lay of the land here again. But does it matter, if there is to be war?

War.

Dread filled her.

Watching Harry run about, roll himself in the flower beds, bark at the weederwomen bent over, weeding, she thought, My brother always said, One day there will be an invasion and we will be in the thick of it, Bab. But by then, she no longer took what was said by Harry and the others in Italy seriously. The afternoon wine the men drank as they sat in Rome's sunny plazas gave them bold words and bolder dreams, but on the morrow, there seemed to be only more wine and more words. She had soon grown bored with it.

The arbor under which she sat was heavy with roses, fat, pink-white, as petaled as cabbages, all the warmth of June in them. In another day or so, it would be July. The petals of a spent rose fell gently in her lap. Barbara stared at them, tore one to bits, thinking,

Charles is a father. Tony is married; will, perhaps, soon be a father himself. Ormonde is coming. What else has happened in my absence?

❧

"I must go and call on Mother and on my aunt Shrew," she told Thérèse later. Both of them would know almost all there was to know.

She splashed in a wonderful bath that washed the weeks aboard ship from her. She stood still for a lovely gown to be put upon herself, for powder, rouge, a patch placed roguishly by her right eye. She stood still for feathers and Indian beading woven into her hair. She looked at herself in a long mirror. Feathers and fuss, wonderful, pleasing, fun, yet strange after the simplicity of First Curle.

She touched a patch on her face and thought of the slaves' ritual scars, flicked at a feather and saw the Iroquois again in the Governor's hall. We, with our patches and powder, are no different, she thought. We, too, must have our masks, our disguises, our ways to summon spirit and courage.

"Shall I come with you?" asked Thérèse.

"Not this time. The evening is yours, Thérèse. We are home. Never mind unpacking trunks yet, please yourself this evening."

She had lied to Thérèse about where she was going.

"The Duke of Wharton's house," she told Tony's coachman.

But no one was at home. Wharton had leased the house to someone else and was living in the village of Twickenham, she was told.

"Well, my lady?" said the coachman.

She hesitated, then said, "Devane Square."

❧

The church was one Thérèse had gone to, often, when she was in London. It was small, wedged between narrow houses, and there was no one in it, except for one man. The man was an agent for Walpole, and he was writing down descriptions of anyone who came to worship in this church.

But Thérèse couldn't know that. She went at once to light a candle for Hyacinthe and another for Harry, Lord Alderley and another for the baby that she had had taken from herself; long ago, now, it seemed. What comfort, she thought as the flames glowed in the soft dark; how I have missed this. There had been no church for her in Virginia. At once, a great peace came over her.

She went to a pew and knelt to pray.

Slane was looking out the slit of the curtain in the confessional. To the priest on the other side of the intricate wooden grille that separated them he said: "There is someone here, a woman. Walpole's spy is watching her, scribbling away. Why doesn't she know we are suspected, one and all? Do you know her, Father?" Something about her was familiar.

The priest left the confessional; when he came back, he said to Slane, "She used to come here some years ago. I do not know her name."

Who is she? thought Slane. Where have I seen her?

"Warn her," he said to the priest. "Tell her when she comes to give confession that she is being watched."

Barbara stood still, taking in the sight before her. She'd never seen the final destruction of Devane House; she'd left before it was done. I was wise to do so, not to see this, she thought. Standing in the lane before the place where the house had been, she thought, I couldn't have borne it.

Nothing was left but the fountain and the landscape pool, in which sunlight glimmered. In her mind was the magnificent house, its adjoining Temple of Arts, the acres of gardens, all of it the talk of London. Now, where the house had been, there was only this clear desolation, bits of broken brick, ground not yet healed; then, beyond, the gentle hills, shepherds herding in the sheep, and the spire of the church in Marylebone. The house might never have been.

To the west, someone was building, someone was dredging out streets. She tried to remember. The Oxford family, yes—she remembered Roger writing in his letters of their plans for a six-acre square called Cavendish Square, near his; of the two squares rising side by side, now that the Oxfords had married into the wealth of the Cavendish family. The Duke of Chandos, challenged by Devane House, had been planning a house as part of Cavendish Square, a house to rival Roger's.

There was no house from Chandos yet, only what looked to be its outbuildings, kitchens or bakeries or stables. London had whispered, Look at Devane, he builds his house in the wilderness. He's mad. Yet they flocked to see what he did. London will come to me, Roger had written. London does come to me.

A coach lumbered down Tyburn Road, and she turned to watch it. There was Hyde Park. She could see the tents of the King's soldiers, so many tents. Roger had been King George's man, knowing and serving the family before they came to the throne. It had been part of his triumph, to anticipate that it would be George who came to the throne, and to leave England and go to Hanover to serve him personally. Was this his reward? Was this how King George treated his friends? Or was it, as her grandmother would have said, that time and chance happen to all?

She stepped back into the carriage, thoughtful, the exultant shipboard mood completely gone now. The sight of the desolate square was unnerving. Can I do it? she thought. Am I mad to dream of rebuilding? She gave the coachman Aunt Shrew's name.

The area around Whitehall, where her aunt lived, was more crowded than she remembered it being on summer's eves in the past. There were soldiers everywhere.

Stepping out of the carriage, she had to stop a moment, because feeling was pushing up at her. Grief, real and deep grief at the destruction of Devane Square. Not now, she thought, not yet.

The servant said her aunt was home. Barbara ran up the stairs. There was Aunt Shrew rouged and powdered, five patches on her face, jewels at her ears and neck, an elaborate wig with ribbons in it, dressed as if for a court fête, and doing nothing more than playing cards in her own drawing room. In a flash that made her laugh, Barbara had a vision of Aunt Shrew, visiting Virginia. How would Bolling react to her? Or Perry?

Aunt Shrew stood up from her card table at the sight of Barbara, who ran forward to kiss her.

"Barbara, my dear. I cannot believe my eyes. You could knock me over with a feather. As if there isn't enough excitement in London today. Oh, but I am delighted you are back. Give me a hug and a kiss as well. I cannot believe it. I forgot how gorgeous you are. Where is my mind? You've confounded me, Barbara, I don't know up from down. This is Sir Alexander Pendarves. He is a particular friend of mine."

Barbara smiled at Pendarves, snuff-stained, grimy; he had been one of her mother's choices for her after Roger died. How could her mother have ever thought she would look at him, never mind marry him? Coins, Barbara, she could remember her mother saying, and plenty of them; he has land, plenty of that, too. But he's dirty, Mother, she had said. A little dirt, what's that? Diana had retorted. He'll die years before you do, and you can enjoy a pleasant widowhood. You won't mind his dirt then.

"We've met."

"Of course you have, of course. I am so amazed to see you that I have lost my wits. Tell me everything. Sit down. London has gone mad. We might all be better off in Virginia. Did you bring tobacco with you?"

"Yes, barrels of it. They are sitting on a London quay."

"This is a summer for surprises, is all I can say. I had no idea you were coming home. London will go mad all over again, over you. Of course, your grandmother wrote not a word of this to me."

"She doesn't know I'm here yet."

"Tell me, did you ever find that little page of yours? We grieved about it, for you."

"No." She spoke softly. The hurt was still alive, deep.

"His disappearance was all the gossip here for a while, you know. Well, how could you know, leaving us to go halfway across the world the way you did? There was a costume fête given not long after word about him came. I must say that Lumpy and I—"

Lumpy? Who was Lumpy? It took Barbara a moment to realize that her aunt referred to Pendarves.

A bubble of laughter was suddenly in her, delicious, like summer wine. They're lovers, she thought. How amusing, how funny! Charles is a father, Tony is married, and Aunt Shrew has chosen as a lover the man my mother once thought of as a husband for me.

Oh, Colonel Perry, I have so much to tell you already.

"We were the hit of the fête. I came as you, Bab. I wore a wig the color of that glorious hair of yours, and Lumpy came as Hyacinthe. We were all everyone talked of all evening. Lumpy, see if that broadsheet is somewhere about. There've been a number of them about you, Barbara, you might as well know, but this is the one that came out after we heard about Hyacinthe. Look on my dressing table, Lumpy. 'Let her stay here to face her demons,' I said to your grandmother, who was never one to listen to anyone, your grandfather included. And I think you are little different from her, Barbara, when all is said and done. Coming home, like this, without a word of warning to anyone. Well, you took us all by surprise in your leaving, and I suppose we should expect you would do the same with your return. Did you find it, Lumpy? Good. Look here, Barbara."

The broadsheet was a rough drawing of a woman who looked like Barbara herself. She was in a forest weeping, while a plump minister looked the other way, a rope labeled "South Sea" around his neck and pulling him away. "Woe is me, the South Sea hath taken all from me."

So it did, thought Barbara. Did you do all you could for Roger, Robin? For his memory? For me? If you did not, I will make you pay. How odd it felt to see herself used so.

"Is that supposed to be Walpole?"

"Yes. Have you seen the King's legions in Hyde Park yet? Walpole and his brother-in-law, Lord Townshend, are screeching 'Jacobite plot, Jacobite plot!' over and over, like two parrots."

"The plot is real," said Pendarves. "I am privileged to be helping with the discovery of it. I may not say anything, but I will tell you, it is real."

"It was quite a day," said Aunt Shrew, "the day the soldiers marched in and set up camp. Quite a spectacle. Lord Townshend sending a proclamation that was read at the city gates. Soldiers have been stealing from my kitchen garden, I'm sure of it. Not a fresh lettuce leaf or green pear is to be had. I told Robert Walpole that it was a pity we citizens had no protection from our own troops. I told him the Pretender's troops might be a welcome change from the thieves and beggars he calls soldiers."

"That tongue of hers is going to see her arrested," said Pendarves. "It is only a matter of time."

Aunt Shrew leaned over and patted Pendarves's hand. "It is why I keep on with you. So that you will warn me in time for escape. You will, won't you?"

"Her slave," Pendarves said to Barbara. "I am. I can't help myself."

Slave. Barbara had a momentary vision of Sinsin and his toes, of the eyes of the slave for sale on the ship. He does not know what he talks of, to speak so of being someone's slave.

"I brought you something from Virginia, Aunt. A blackbird with red feathers in his tail. Is the King at St. James's Palace?"

"He has just gone up the river to Hampton Court. The Prince and Princess are at Richmond House. You'll need to go and make your obediences right away. This is not time to be careless about one's obeisances to the King. I'm glad your father is dead. He would have been up to his elbows in this, no doubt, and we'd all be imprisoned in the Tower or sitting before Walpole and his henchman for our connection to him."

Barbara went to the window. The sun had not set. She looked out on London's mellow, sweet, long summer's dusk, thinking of dusk at First Curle, the shadows the thick woods threw, the slaves gathering at the kitchen house.

"Walpole has spread it about that the Bishop of Rochester is the head of this plot. What nonsense. He might as well be saying I am the head. Isn't it convenient that treason should settle upon the ministers' most vehement opponent, upon a man who says the Church has become a tool of the Whigs and the King? As it has, as everything has. What is that in your hair, Barbara? I like it."

Barbara turned from the window. "Beads, and these are eagle's feathers. Only a brave Iroquois warrior may wear them. He has to have counted coup to wear them."

"Counted coup? What is that?"

"Faced down a formidable enemy. Your war cry is so fierce, your bravery so profound that your enemy is somehow tricked for a moment, and you touch him, unharmed, and take his spirit, his courage, from him. You make it yours. It's a mad game of chance the warriors play with their lives. When did the Duke of Wharton go to live in the village of Twickenham?"

"This spring. Lord Sunderland died in the spring, and with him Wharton's chances for a place among the Whig ministers."

Wart a minister? thought Barbara. A Whig? No.

"Lord Sunderland had taken Wharton under his wing, but no one else trusts him. I don't think he's drawn a sober breath since May."

That was unchanged. "And my mother. Is she at home in London?"

"The last I heard."

"There are still some hours of light; I think I'll send Tony's carriage back and walk over to see my mother."

"You do that. And go tomorrow to see the King without fail. Give me a kiss, my dear."

Outside, Barbara sent Tony's coachman home and walked, her mind on the scene around her, on the invasion, on treason, on King George and King James. On Harry's whispers eight years ago under the apple trees. Unrest back then too, in 1714 and 1715. Father's gone, Harry had said, slipped away to escape being imprisoned. She had cried impetuous, deep tears at that. The last time she'd seen her father was in 1714, and she, like the century, was four-and-ten. Her father had come to Tamworth to visit from London, a rare thing for him to do. She'd been excited to see him, but he had quarreled with her grandmother, from whom he had tried to borrow funds. The Queen is dying, he told her grandmother, and her wish is for the throne to go to her half-brother. Barbara knew because she had been eavesdropping, standing in the hall, as close to the door as possible, to hear what was said. It was how she found out so many things about her mother and father and Tamworth, by eavesdropping.

Then you'd best pass a law, and quickly, her grandmother had flashed, to say that the king of England may be Catholic. The law now says Protestant. You're a fool, Kit. George of Hanover is a soldier, a king over his own territories. Do you think he will let the crown of England go from his hands without a fight?

We'll win the fight, her father said, angry himself.

Later, Barbara had slipped in to see him. He was drinking, her handsome, feckless father. She knelt before his chair. My lovely pet, he'd said, how you're growing. I must marry you well, Bab. Ormonde has sons, and Oxford. Can you say, Long live the King, Bab? Say, Long live King James. She had repeated the words and then given him her coins, saved over time, and he'd stared down at her hands holding out the coins to him, and then looked at her, his eyes glistening. Tears came easily to her father.

My Bab, he'd said, you are a treasure. But he was gone the next morning, and she did not see him again until Italy. Until he was dead.

Italy. Barbara shook her head.

The next thing she knew, she was sprawled on the ground; she had walked into someone, stepped out of her shoe, stumbled back, falling. Her hands were scraped; she'd scraped the palms of them cushioning her fall, and they hurt. That will teach me to woolgather about Italy, she thought.

"Here, madam, I'm sorry, give me your hand—"

The man whom she'd walked into was apologizing, asking her if she was hurt. She looked up at him, and for a moment she couldn't think. She was looking into the dark eyes of Lucius, Lord Duncannon. A still-healing scar marred one of his thick brows.

She saw in his face the surprise and shock that must be mirrored on hers. If ever she had doubted that the plot was real and King George's throne was in danger, she knew it now. Viscount Duncannon was James's most devoted friend.

Before she could speak, he was gone, leaving her as she was, sprawled on the ground, in shock. He disappeared down the alley out of which he must have stepped when they collided.

Sweet Jesus, she thought. What have I come back to? Then: I must follow him. Where is my shoe? But she couldn't find it.

Holding up her skirts, she ran down the alley, one shoe on, one gone; she ran to its end and out into a garden.

The Thames River was like a sweet, broad ribbon before her, and there was a man sitting with his back to her, on a bench; but it was not Duncannon.

In a flash, she realized he was the reason Duncannon had been in the alley. She knew it as certainly as if he had told her. The black-browed Duncannon had been spying on Robert Walpole, Lord Treasurer for King George.

She stepped back into the alley between the two houses that shared this garden, took off the shoe left her, and ran quickly, lithely on stockinged feet back to its end. She wasn't ready to face Robin, not yet. She walked toward the sedan chairs she could hire to take her home. There was a sudden need in her to get away. She wanted to see her mother, who was heartless, yes, cruel, yes, but her mother nonetheless. There was an invasion. She needed her family.

She told the chairman the name of her mother's street, but when she got there, her mother, like Wart, was not home. She'd left today, the servant said. No, she hadn't said where she was going.

A brandy was placed before Slane, and he drank it down as quickly as he'd done the first, letting the burning fill his head with fumes. "Another."

He touched the shoe set out on the table before him, a gray damask with beautiful beadwork all over its front.

Barbara was in London. He did not even try to question how or why. In the last two months, life had become a series of leaps from one surprise or disaster to another. There was no question that she had recognized him. He would go to his dear Louisa. She'd know something.

She met him on the back servants' stair.

"You certain she recognized you?" Aunt Shrew asked.

"I'm certain."

"If Harry were alive, I'd say you were still safe, because Barbara would do anything for him. But now, I don't know. Barbara has never spoken of politics. The talk before she left was that she was going to become the Prince of Wales's mistress—not a good sign for us, I'd say."

In the dark, they reached toward one another and held hands, for strength. It was all they could do these days, and it was not enough.

"I could weep," she said. "But once I begin I won't stop. How is Rochester?"

"How do you expect? This rumor about the dog has driven him half mad. He startles if a door opens too quickly."

"Walpole would have moved if he had something other than guesses. Tell Rochester to hold fast, to remember 1715, when the Whigs tried this same trick of rumor-mongering and innuendo."

The King's agents had arrested no one important. Once questioned, every man was let go. The questions asked were about Rochester, over and over again.

Walpole's guesses were too good. What game did he play? What did he know? All up and down the Jacobite network, talk was of whether to stay and brazen it out, trusting the matter would blow over—or to flee. "Stay," James wrote directly to Slane. "The invasion is not canceled but only put off."

You haven't mentioned the irony, Slane, said Rochester.

What irony?

That I should have abandoned you all the way I did, and yet my name is foremost among the plotters.

"Do you think they will arrest Rochester, Slane?" Aunt Shrew asked. "He is old, he has gout, and he is not over the death of his wife. A year or two in the Tower, if it comes to that, could very well kill him."

Doubtless that was in Walpole's mind, too. That was another reason Slane did not leave England. He must see if he could thwart Robert Walpole. It had become imperative, to thwart Walpole.

"I thought you wished Rochester dead," Slane said.

"I've changed my mind. Where do you go now?"

"To see Barbara."

"Be careful. She's my niece, and I love her."

He didn't answer; he was already halfway down the stairs.

"And have a care about yourself," she said to the dark stairwell. "I love you, too."

Barbara sat in bed at Saylor House, Harry snuggled near her thigh. The long windows of her bedchamber were opened full to the night, and she was thinking of Duncannon and of Devane Square and of Thérèse.

The priest told me they make note of all who come to the church, Thérèse had said tonight, nearly crying. All Catholics. His words frightened me. I shall not go back, I shall pray at home. We leave Virginia at last to come home, and find madness here as well.

Barbara felt angry, knowing what her church, her prayers there, meant to Thérèse, who had not complained once all those months in Virginia when there was no marble saint, no darkened altar rail at which she might kneel. It is not against the law for you to worship as you please. Act as if the priest had not spoken. You've done nothing wrong, Thérèse. And neither have I. We will not act as if we have, she'd said.

Duncannon.

He was Harry's hero. He had rescued King James's bride-to-be. On her way to Italy to marry James, King George had seen to it that she was taken and imprisoned—she brought James a large dowry, money which could be used toward invasion—and it had been Duncannon who had rescued her from a castle high in the Alps and brought her to Italy to marry James. It was a romantic story. He had been the hero of the hour, all the contessas sighing when he walked into a salon. Other exploits were whispered of: journeys to the court of the Czar, trips to France. He was a man of romance and action. Duncannon never spoke of these adventures, but others did, includ-

ing Harry, who had admired him so. It was said he was King James's
most trusted servant. He was certainly the most famous of the
goslings.

Her dog leaped from the bed and went running to the opened
windows, out to the small balconies before them. Barbara wiped at
tears on her face. Devane Square. She'd known the house had been
dismantled, but to see the bare land was hard, as hard as seeing the
dead body of a loved one. What grief she felt at this moment. How
could she ever think to remake it? The task was impossible, too large
for her, with the debt and the fine, also. Her plans in Virginia
seemed child's dreamings here.

She touched her palms, which were sore and stinging, put them to
the wet of her face. If it did not have to happen, if Devane Square
had been torn down needlessly, she would never forgive Robin,
never, for no matter what she achieved, she would not achieve the
beauty Roger had. That had been one of his gifts, the making of rare
and splendid beauty. To have torn his work down was sacrilege. She
could not believe she had allowed it. I had to, she thought, but that
knowledge did not lessen the pain. It was as if she experienced
Roger's death afresh, seeing Devane Square today.

She looked up just as Slane stepped into the bedchamber, and her
breath caught in her throat.

"This dog is easily bribed." Slane walked forward toward the bed,
holding Harry. "Why do you cry? I hope I did not hurt you today."

He reached in his pocket, took out a handkerchief and her damask
shoe, set both upon the bed, frowned at her when she didn't answer.

"Virginia became you."

Beautiful, he was thinking, you are more beautiful than any portrait could capture. And in your eyes is what so drew me in Italy, so
that I followed you across a crowded drawing room, asking everyone
your name, only to find that you were my friend's sister. Essence of
girl is in your eyes, strong, sweet, tender. Fierce, too. You stare at
me fiercely. Has Virginia made you fierce? Or your husband's
death? She loved him, Harry said, adored him. This was a woman
who loved hard when she loved, like his mother, like his dead wife.

When you loved hard, you lost hard. Losses are there, like the sweetest of shadows, in the shape of your mouth.

London does not become you, Viscount Duncannon, Barbara thought. There were terrible dark circles under his dark eyes, and that scar. London, it seemed, took its toll on heroes. Harry had admired this man tremendously.

"I came to ask for your silence," he said. "It must not be known who I am."

"Robert Walpole was in the garden. You were spying on him, weren't you?"

Her voice. He'd forgotten how husky, how sensuous it was. Or had he? Wasn't it always there, in his memory, like the promise of the girl in her eyes.

"Where is your other dog? I remember there being two."

"Charlotte died in Virginia."

"Listen to me carefully, now. I am no threat to you or anyone. The invasion will not come. I stay only because I must for a time. Grant me the favor of your silence."

The ship sent from London for Ormonde had come back without him. Ormonde had never even been able to set foot on board. Agents and ambassadors of King George had moved too quickly in that little space of time at the end of April. Twelve thousand arms, said the captain of the ship, lay in barns in Spain, and we could not get to them. Ormonde himself was on shore, in disguise, and we could not touch him. Officials from the court of Spain came aboard, every day for over two weeks, looked in every corner of the ship, took down names of passengers, made a listing of our cargo. We finally sailed without Ormonde. We did not know what else to do. Saints' finger bones, thought Slane, rubbing his brow.

He saw Barbara shrinking from him and found himself saddened, then angered by that. He reached out and took one of her wrists, and though she tried to pull it away, turned it over and looked at the scrapes on the palm. She'd hurt herself today when she'd fallen hard.

"What did you say to Walpole?" he asked.

"That you were Viscount Duncannon, a gosling. The most famous of the goslings. And that he'd best find you. He thanked me profusely and promised he'd see me made a duchess."

Without a word, Slane dropped her hand and walked toward the windows. In another moment he was gone.

Barbara leaped out of the bed, ran to the window, leaned out over the balcony's edge. He had jumped to the gardens below, and he was nowhere to be seen. Then, thinking a moment, she stepped back, moved herself into the soft draperies of the window, and waited.

It seemed a long time. It was a long time. But finally she heard a movement, faint but definite. Tiptoeing, her heart beating so loudly she could barely hear past it, she edged onto the balcony. There he was, walking toward the darker shadows of the trees of the gardens. He'd been hiding in shrubs below, waiting until he thought it safe to move on.

I was more clever than you, she thought, but then he turned and walked back toward the house. She stepped behind the drapery. He stood, in the open, as if waiting.

Does he wait upon me? she thought. After a time, curious, she showed herself.

Slane stared at the figure on the balcony, the woman as slim as a candle in her pale nightgown, but he really didn't see her.

Jacobites were drawing back, waiting to see what Walpole did, though a few still planned and plotted, tried to salvage what was in place. Slane plotted with them, unable to give up, yet. He could taste how much he wanted to see Walpole and the others frightened, on edge, humbled, the way the Jacobites were. After the soldiers at Hyde Park are sent back to their garrisons, they said, then Ormonde can invade, in autumn. Slane had a feeling it was a fool's dream, but he couldn't stop himself, dreaming it.

There had been a chapel in the house in France in which Slane had grown up to boyhood. He could still remember how the sun came in to the chapel, colored and cooled by the stained-glass windows. There had been wax tapers as tall as he at each end of the altar, and when they were lighted, the altar silver gleamed dully. There were statues of the saints, a carved memorial to various ancestors of the owner of the house. Upon a stone table was a small carved chest holding a relic, the finger bone of a saint, brought, it was said, from the Holy Land during the Crusades. As a boy, he often opened the small chest and viewed the slender ivory bone, wondering at it, daring sometimes to touch it, then later to lift it from its cushion and hold it in his hand.

He had secreted in the chest the small gifts from King James, his senior by only six years. He could remember a knife, a bird's feather, a letter, a gold ring with a ruby stone. He'd gone into service to James early, when he was thirteen, following him from place to place— Jamie the Rover, the King was called, as he was forced to move from place to place as the English won their battles and demanded that France would not succor the Stuarts. He'd gone from the court of the Czar to Florence for James, looking always for money or promises of soldiers with whom to invade England, looking always for ways to exploit grievances with the Hanover George and his policies.

He'd forgotten about the chest for a long time, and then, this last time he was in Paris, he'd gone back to the estate upon which he had lived as a boy, gone to the chapel to see the finger bone once more, to see if he could recapture his boy's feeling of mystery and certain vision. The small carved chest sat where it always had, upon the stone table, under the memorials, and he had opened it, heart beating strongly, to find all was gone, finger bone and gifts. The priest who looked after the chapel had no idea what had happened; neither did the owners of the estate.

My heart hurts, Louisa had said when she learned the ship was back without Ormonde. It has all been for nothing. Not for nothing, he answered her. We have a network in place. We will plan for another time. King James says we'll invade when the element of surprise is ours again. Louisa had not replied. Despair and fatigue were etched in deep lines upon her aged face, like solemn good-byes to boyhood and dreams of saints' finger bones.

Slane bowed to the figure on the balcony and was gone, stepping like a ghost into dark shadow and disappearing.

Barbara shivered, stepped back, pulled down the window as

quickly as she could, then another, then another, locking them all. She ran to her bedchamber door and locked it. She ran to the bed, pulled the linens up to her chin.

He'd known she was waiting because she hadn't closed the windows at once. That would have been the natural thing for her to do, close and lock all the windows. He had been listening for sounds of that.

He showed himself to her to tell her so, to show her she was not as clever as she imagined. We were counting coup, she thought, and he wins.

Why did I tell him I told Robin? I'm not going to betray him. And that had something to do with her brother, Harry, but it had something to do with Duncannon himself. Hero, he'd been called. He was revered in Italy for his daring exploits for King James. He lived what he believed, had risked his life more than once, was here now, doing it again, in a way that Harry, for all his words, never had.

Her reasons for not informing Walpole had to do with her father and with Harry, with growing up loving them, listening to them. They had wished to be what Duncannon was.

He'd kissed her in a garden. She had waited for him to call the next morning, after that kiss in the twilight; she was certain of herself, of her effect upon any man she chose to charm and many a one she chose not to. He did not call. Later, they learned he'd left Rome unexpectedly, left the night he kissed her. Adventure more compelling than you, Harry had teased. Perhaps he was warned how fickle and cruel you are, Bab, how no man ever pleases you.

Keep thy heart with all diligence. Something in her had responded the moment she saw him walking forward with her dog; it was not the response she had to a Charles or a Klaus, but something deeper. The way I felt toward Roger, she thought, and she closed her eyes tight, just as she used to when she was a girl and believed wishes came true.

Tomorrow, she'd begin the journey to Tamworth. Richmond House and Hampton Court were upon the way, and she'd make her obediences. And, as soon as possible, she must talk to Tommy Carlyle and to Wart. Tommy she must question to his face; and Wart—well, Wart she simply must talk to. He was a friend. He wouldn't lie.

In the morning, she left instructions for Tony's coachman that they were leaving in the afternoon; then she rode back to Devane Square. Leading her horse, she walked into the heart of it. She would look at it more carefully this time; move past the confusion and grief, to think, to come up with a plan. You have all you need inside yourself, Perry had said.

Only one end of the square had been finished into townhouses, they and Sir Christopher Wren's tiny, perfect church were all that remained. Another section of houses had been framed in wood, but the wood was gone now, so the church and townhouses faced each other in lonely splendor among fields. The windows of the townhouses were boarded over, as were the windows of the church; its front door was padlocked and chained. The interior had never been finished, she remembered.

There had been a beautiful garden in the center of the square, and a lawn, gravel walks, flowers, trees. The garden at the square's center had, in its moment of abundance, rivaled the curiosities in the royal gardens at Kew House. Even Major Custis had heard of her husband's garden at Devane Square—he'd sent twenty swamp laurels to it, all gone now, grass growing up unevenly over the wounds where once a wealth of rare trees and shrubs had been, where people had strolled on neatly raked gravel walks and sat upon heavy stone benches to admire the view.

She mounted the horse again, urged it along the lane beside Wren's unfinished church. The house had been behind the church, toward Marylebone, upon its own road, Barbara Lane. Great gates had opened to a magnificent setting, the house in its midst. There was nothing now, only silence broken by the morning twittering of birds, as her horse moved to the fountain, searching for water, of which there was none. The nymph's shell was dry. Barbara stared at the nymph, who had been modeled after herself, it was said, to the scandal and delight of London.

She was at the place where the entrance gates had been. Before her was the outline of the drive. The house was gone, as were the hundred orange trees in silver tubs and the small, perfect Temple of Arts built at one side of the house, near the landscape canal. Roger had called it a summer temple, and in it had been his growing collection of paintings and statues. All was gone, nothing to show any of it had ever existed, except what was stored in a warehouse, the items Parliament had allowed her to keep, anything which could be proved to have been purchased before 1719. The horse shied and danced, and she turned her head.

Another rider was approaching. She remembered the man vaguely—she'd seen him at court more than once—but she didn't remember his name. He was older, stocky, his face marked with the myriad tiny, puckered stars that a light case of smallpox made. He circled his horse around her twice. The second time she became angry.

"This is private property," she flashed.

"Well, I know it, and you are its owner." He pulled his horse short. "How do you do?"

She didn't answer.

"I am Sir Gideon Andreas. We were introduced once, but I doubt you remember it. I knew your husband. I ride this way every morning that I am in London and the weather allows. I give my horse a drink from your landscape pool there, before going on to Marylebone. I hope you don't mind."

His eyes, gray eyes, light eyes, moved from her to the stone nymph and back again. Barbara raised her chin.

The nymph was naked, holding out a shell. When there had been water, water had dripped from the shell into the larger pool in which the nymph stood. I ought to duel with Roger over this, Harry had said, on first seeing the nymph's face.

"When did you return from Virginia, Lady Devane? I had not heard you were back, so it must have been just recently."

"Yesterday."

"And already you come to look over your property. Quite right. A woman of sense as well as of great beauty, I see. I've been buying land all through here, and you and I must talk someday soon. We shall. Now, I'll say good day and disturb you no more."

She trotted the horse to the tangle of wild grass that was the churchyard, dismounted, and leaned her elbows upon the yard's stone wall. Andreas was at the landscape pool, allowing his horse water. Then, with a bow to her, he was galloping away toward the quaint village of Marylebone.

Andreas, Andreas, thought Barbara, as she rode back toward Saylor House. That was it—if she was not mistaken, that was one of the names among those to whom Roger had owed funds. And so, now must she. He reminds me, faintly, of Bolling. I'd best remember that.

CHAPTER 40

At Tamworth, Tim lifted the Duchess out of her carriage, an ancient, unfashionable vehicle that she refused to replace. She was just returned from Lindenmas, half a day's journey away. She had been there all of June, waiting for Ormonde to invade. She was tired of waiting now, and missed Tamworth, so she'd come home. I may as well die in my own bed, she told Tony. I'll come to see about you, he said.

"Chapel, Your Grace?"

"I must rest first. Then, yes, chapel."

"One of the hives isn't thriving." Tim glanced back through the opened door, but Annie was still outside, Dulcinea in her arms. He said, "It's the Gypsy, I think."

As he carried the Duchess up the stairs, he told a tale of sitting up all night on the summer solstice in the porch of the church because custom had it one might see the spirits of those who were going to die in the next year. Bathsheba, out gathering herbs for Annie—St.-John's-wort, fern frond, vervain, and rue, which must be gathered at night, and what better night than solstice?—had unpinned her long, lank hair, crept up to the porch church, and peered suddenly around its opening at him.

"I ran for a mile before I stopped. I thought her a witch. Now one of the hives isn't thriving and there is quarreling among the kitchen maids," said Tim.

Later, when Annie was fussing about the bedchamber, making certain everything was as it ought to be after their absence, the Duchess said, "I won't have a Gypsy upsetting my household. She may well have cursed my bees. One of the hives isn't thriving. How long has that Gypsy been here? She was only to stay until spring."

"There is a letter. It came while we were gone."

Some timbre in Annie's voice distracted the Duchess momentarily. "Who is it from? And never mind preparing me. You will send me to my grave one day preparing me."

"It is from Lady Alderley."

Diana.

Annie held up the letter. The pair of them stared at it as if it would explode.

"Open it."

Annie slit open the letter—it might have been Diana's throat—and handed it over.

"She writes to tell me that she comes to Tamworth. From the date of this, she should be here today or tomorrow. Like Job, I have not enough suffering at the moment. Invasion, a Gypsy cursing my hive and my household, and now this. I doubt I will sleep a moment, and I am old, and I need my rest."

"Then rest."

"I won't sleep. I won't close my eyes."

The Duchess closed her eyes and fell asleep at once.

Later, in the evening, England's wonderful summer evening in which light stayed for a long time, Tim took the Duchess to chapel, going by way of the hives so that she could see them for herself. They were kept at the garden wall, each straw skep shaped like a bishop's hat, sitting in its own enclosure, built into the wall. He showed her the poor hive.

All kinds of flowers were planted here to entice the bees. Beyond the wall was her orchard—apple, pear, plum trees—and beyond that a field of clover, the fat heads of the blossoms growing up thickly together, moving gently, like waves on a sea, in this summer's breeze.

At the wall grew an ancient, vining wisteria and brambleberries, mint and violets and Queen Anne's lace, rosemary and daisies and an old, varicolored damask rose planted so many years ago that no one knew how old it was. The bees loved it.

The Duchess breathed in the smell of the flowers, the sight of roses and clover. Bees were everywhere, their hum a wonderful chant to her, better than a choir at evensong. Now that war loomed, all was doubly precious. Each moment must be treasured. She must fill her eye with this view of Tamworth, her favorite. Barbara, she thought, I wish you were here, but if we're to have war, I'm glad you're not.

Chapel was as always, a cool dip of water for a hot, troubled mind. It was so peaceful. Tim helped her to sit in her favorite spot. Richard's marble tomb, with its reclining figure of him, dominated all.

"Ormonde isn't here yet," she said to Richard. "Barbara is still in Virginia. You would approve of Harriet. The marriage is a success." Weary not in well doing, for in due season we shall reap, if we faint not. She'd done well, led the family into further wealth. The Tamworth legacy was secure, buffered and enlarged by all that Harriet brought. Nothing could hurt it now. The remaining problem was Barbara, what to do about the debt, the shambles her dearest's life had become. She closed her eyes and drifted into memories of her sons and Richard, of Barbara and Harry and Jane in other, younger days. Her head nodded.

Tim touched her shoulder.

"Tell those children I'll cane them if they feed the pigs brandy again," she said.

Tim bent down to pick her up in his strong arms. She looked at him. He was a bold-faced fellow. It was difficult to resist the smile in his merry eyes.

"Bah."

He grinned, showing his broken front teeth.

"Shall I take you by the beemaster? Now that you have seen the Duke, you ought to be up to quarreling."

"I do not quarrel. I never quarrel. What goes on at Ladybeth?"
How did Sir John get on? Was he still ridiculously angry?

But Tim didn't know.

They took a way back that brought them through Tamworth
woods, verdant green and wonderfully shadowy. And there was the
house, built in the time of King Henry VIII and his daughters, Mary
and Elizabeth, rising ivy-greened and many-gabled before them.
Octagonal bays in its front corners, woods and park, garden maze
and iron gates opening to a curving avenue of lime trees, the house
was a part of the life of everyone for miles around. The Duchess
made Tim stop a moment, so that she could enjoy the view. Ormonde may not have this, not one acre, not one brick of it. I will die
for it, she thought.

"Richard's roses are at their best. Just look there."

Together, they admired the crimson heads of the roses in the garden. It was the first day of July. July was a good month for roses.

"Scarlet ribbons in her hair . . ." Tim began to hum the old folk
tune as they walked toward the house.

Her servants would sing another tune if Ormonde and James
came and scattered them all to the four winds, burned this house to
nothing or gave it away to loyal followers. To the victor belong the
spoils, and well she knew it. She had seen it three times in her life
alone, the victors dividing up the spoils. She'd been among the victors.

In her bedchamber, a bouquet of blue forget-me-nots, crimson
pimpernels, and yellow agrimony lay upon her pillow.

The Gypsy, thought the Duchess. Bah.

When she woke the next morning, a handful of tiny strawberries,
like little red babies, lay atop her book of sermons. But there was
more: a chain of wild roses festooning Richard's portrait and Barbara's and strewn across the bed in which she slept.

Dulcinea pounced and killed a sweet rose.

"Things have come to a pretty pass," she told Annie and Tim and
Perryman, assembled like punished children, "when anyone may
march about in my bedchamber as she pleases. I could have been

murdered in my sleep. There is an invasion, in case you have forgotten—marauding Spaniards and Scotsmen, Jacobites who knows where."

And to Annie, "It is bribery, pure and simple. You told her of my weakness."

"I never said—"

"Bah. You, Perryman, tell me the truth of the Gypsy."

"She does whatever is asked. There is no rude talk from her."

"No talk at all from her," put in Tim.

"No one in the household will eat with her or sit beside her," continued Perryman. "No one will share the chamber in which she sleeps. Anytime a thing goes wrong, anytime a plate is broken or a finger cut, the others blame her, saying she put a curse on them. She is always alone, save for her babe, whom no one will touch. He has the look of an idiot to him."

A Gypsy and an idiot in my household, thought the Duchess. Fitting. She had Annie summon Bathsheba from the kitchen.

"Is this your doing?" She gestured toward the twined roses across the portraits, across her bed, toward the strawberries lying on her book of sermons. She could see Annie drifting back and forth in the withdrawing chamber just beyond. Like a hen brooding over a cracked egg, thought the Duchess.

The Gypsy's thin chest rose and fell, too rapidly. A sign of guilt if ever I've seen one, thought the Duchess. Guilty of wantonness with wildflowers, of bewitching bees. Off with her head.

"Yes, Your Grace."

A soft voice. Soft voice, hard heart. Come unto me, all ye that labour and are heavy laden, and I will give you rest. Now, why had she thought of that verse? But she knew. A sudden thought entered the Duchess's head.

"What goes on at Ladybeth Farm?" she asked.

"Strange men come calling, late at night. Him that fell, the man—"

"Laurence Slane?" The Duchess was suddenly excited and intrigued.

"Yes. He came to see Sir John."

Slane? Here again? Tony said he had a sweetheart nearby, but why would he call at Ladybeth?

"I see something in the tea leaves, something small, with a tail, spotted. It will bring trouble. I see muskets and swords and Lady Ashford crying."

Second sight. The Gypsy had second sight. That and her knowledge of the goings-on at Ladybeth were enough for the Duchess.

"Do you know our Lord's catechism?"

Bathsheba nodded her head, then shook it. "Hard to remember," she said.

"If you can remember the catechism and be baptized like a decent woman, you may stay here. Cat got your tongue? Dulcinea, give the Gypsy her tongue. Answer 'Yes, Your Grace,' or 'No, Your Grace'—and, mind, either answer suits me."

"Yes, Your Grace. Thank you, Your Grace."

Those eyes were the shade of fern fronds. They'd have their work cut out for them taming this one. Typical of Annie to pick a Gypsy to mother.

"I never said a word," Annie said in defense of herself later, fluffing up pillows and pounding at imaginary dust upon the cushions, to have an excuse to find out what she could. "She's a Gypsy. She read your mind."

"Has she a way with plants?"

"Such as I've never seen."

"Take her out of Cook's hands and put her in the stillroom."

Where she was half the time, anyway; but the Duchess did not need to know that, Annie thought.

"By the by, it was the Duke, you know, who was fond of strawberries, not I." Roses had always been her undoing. The Duchess picked up one of the roses. Gather ye rosebuds while ye may.

Tim put his head in the doorway.

"A boy has come from the village to say a carriage is passing through."

Diana.

The Duchess had Tim carry her to the terrace. Purge me with hyssop and I shall be clean. Wash me and I shall be whiter than snow. Make me to hear joy and gladness; that the bones which thou hast broken may rejoice. Richard, Diana has ignored me for over a year, and now here she is. She wants something. She only visits when she wants something. The continual game between us.

"Mother," Diana said.

The voice, unmistakable, low and husky, came from behind her. The Duchess did not turn or move or indicate that she had heard. Lips as cool as grass touched her cheek.

"Dearest Mother."

The Duchess saw out of the corner of her eye Diana kneel in a rustle of skirt, an air of musky, heavy scent.

"You weren't so sweet last summer, Diana, nor at Christmas. What has changed your mind? Come around here where I may look at you."

Diana moved to stand before her. Unlike another, who might fidget and fuss under scrutiny, might blush or look away, Diana cocked her head to one side as she waited, as lazy, as uncaring, as a cat sunning on a fence. Her face was too thin, the lines from her nose to her mouth deeper. There were dark circles under violet eyes, eyes men had once dueled over, quarreling over the exact shade. It was still a face of matchless beauty, but now it was haggard, time-edged, hard. She leaned upon a cane, and one of her wrists was bandaged.

"What's this? Has Walpole taken to beating you?"

"I fell. Never mind it."

She lied. Nothing changes, and everything changes. Of her children, this child had done as she so pleased, always. Of her children, this child had said, Leave me be. She had cared for this child's children, had paid this child's debts, had dampened what she could of this child's scandals, but she had not liked her. Yet there was something between them that went beyond regard, some fine-grained, steely quality each possessed and recognized in the other; and in the end, perhaps that was stronger than any affection. Amazing to think that out of Diana came Barbara.

"Settle yourself, and tell me the gossip in London. When I was at Lindenmas, they were gossiping about the Bishop of Rochester. Do they still say he is implicated in treasonous correspondence by a letter about a little spotted dog?"

"Oh, yes."

CHAPTER 41

The small village of Twickenham was just across the river from Richmond House, where the Prince and Princess of Wales lived in the summer. Barbara had the coachman find out where the Duke of Wharton lived. Wharton's servant told her he was in the back garden. Walking back to it, she saw him in a chair by the river, saw, too, that he had been drinking. She called his name.

Wharton stood, steadying himself on the back of the chair, held out his hands. "My very dear Barbara, am I drunk or just dreaming?"

She hugged him.

"Drunk, I think. Oh, Wart, it is so good to see you." He was her substitute for Harry. When you lost people you loved, you were less unforgiving of those left.

She looked around. There was no one but them and the river weaving its way greenly among reeds. She pushed him down in his chair, pulled another one close.

"Tell me about the invasion. Everything. No lies, but the truth."

"There are plans for an autumn invasion going forward, and my part is, as you may imagine, to be in the thick of it."

So Duncannon lied? Barbara frowned down at a fold in her gown, disappointed—no, more than disappointed. No one now, except her family, and not even all of them, would be telling the truth, but she'd expected more of Duncannon.

"Tell me something, Wart. Tommy Carlyle wrote me that the fine Parliament put upon Roger need not have been so high, that the ministry, that Robin, did not defend Roger as they might have. That Roger was a scapegoat."

"It is possible, Bab. Anything is possible."

"What do you remember?"

"Only the vile baseness of the Hanoverians and everything their greedy hands touched. They were like highwaymen, piling up South Sea stock and selling it again. No one was worse than the Duchess of Kendall. And Walpole is beneath contempt. He always has been."

"Why?"

"Because he has no honor, Bab."

A woman was wading through the shallow part of the river, through the reeds, her skirts pulled up. Barbara recognized her, Lady Mary Wortley Montagu. She was older than Barbara and Wharton, by perhaps a decade; her face was lightly marked with smallpox scars. There were no lashes around her large, dark eyes. The same smallpox that had marked her face had taken her eyelashes. The lack gave her an odd, staring, almost rude look. She walked forward into the grass, her feet bare and wet, the ends of her skirts dripping, at her ease.

"It is easier to come by river than by garden path, and I have to confess I enjoy wading in the river like a child. You're Lady Devane, aren't you? Yes, I remember, quite the loveliest young woman at court. I thought you were in a colony somewhere. Wharton, you're drinking wine already, and I have walked over most particularly to invite you to one of my gatherings tonight. Try to be sensible when you arrive. Senesino, from the opera, is going to sing. His voice is divine, Lady Devane. You must come, too, though you haven't to splash by river, as I have. Wharton, I depend on you to join me tonight and to behave. Good-bye, Lady Devane."

She walked back into the shallows of the river, her gown dragging. Barbara watched her, remembering that Lady Mary's sister was married to a Jacobite, one who'd fled England in 1715. Lady Mary is in the plot, thought Barbara. I'll bet coins on it.

"I've been told there will be no invasion," she said.

"Ormonde will come in the autumn, when the soldiers in Hyde Park go back to their garrisons. Do you think it will be possible to remain neutral, as you did in Italy? You had not a serious thought in your head then, Bab."

"As if you and Harry were serious—"

"We were."

"You were drunk."

"But deadly serious, nonetheless. What are all these feathers and beads about your person? You look magnificent."

"I go to see the King at Hampton Court. I must make an impression."

"Playing both ends? Coward."

She stood, irritated.

"I think you tilt at windmills, my friend. Did you see the number of soldiers in Hyde Park? And I was told that more were available, upon notice, from the Dutch. The war is lost before it is begun."

"Never."

"Dear Wart, please be careful, please. I would not want to see you beheaded. That is still the penalty for treason, you know."

"Would you cry?"

"Indeed, I would."

"Then you would be the only one. Did you hear of my hour of triumph, Bab? Lord Sunderland and I were like father and son. He was maneuvering to see me brought into service as one of the King's ministers. Is that not amusing? We were maneuvering to see Walpole gone. How I want to see Walpole gone. Everything was right there, in our hands, Bab. And then Sunderland died."

She was silent. She knew better than anyone the twists of Fate, when life seemed to spiral downward.

"It's good you're back, Bab. I am going to make you Jacobite. See if I don't."

"If Harry couldn't do it, what makes you think you can?"

"I am more clever than Harry. . . . I miss him, Bab." He looked at her, a tear in his eyes. The wine he drank brought emotion up.

"I do, too," she said, softly.

At the gate, she turned to have a final look at him, Harry's friend, and, when she'd gotten to know him, hers, too. He made gestures—see no evil; hear no evil; speak no evil—and then pulled his hand across his throat in a slashing movement.

What was it Harry had said to her so long ago, the night, in fact, she'd learned she was to marry Roger? Politics, it is all politics, my innocent little sister. Hanover or James III. King or Pretender. One is supported by a majority of the powerful men in the country. One is not. Not the divine right of kings, Bab, but the divine right of power.

Slane, who'd been watching from the window in Wharton's house, walked outside once Barbara had gone. Wharton was slumped in his chair, hands under his chin, frowning at the green reeds in the river. Swans were among them, the swans of the river, which belonged to the King of England.

"What did she say?"

"She wanted to know about the invasion. She won't betray you, Slane. I know her."

"She said she'd told Walpole."

"If she had, she would have told me, first thing. Trust me in this. She didn't even mention you. She's protecting you for some reason."

"How can you be so certain what she will and won't do?"

"Barbara is one of the only people in this world whom I trust. Where do you go?"

"Off to follow your trustworthy friend. I have no desire to end my days in a dungeon in the Tower of London."

She wasn't far. She was at the river, stepping into a boat in which three other people sat. Slane recognized the dark-haired woman at once as the woman in the church. Was she a friend? wondered Slane. Or perhaps a servant? Yes, she must be Barbara's maidservant. That was why he felt he knew her. He'd likely seen her with Barbara in Italy. The two men in the boat he didn't know, but they were laughing and talking with Barbara as if they knew her quite well. One of them had a crippled arm. There were various boxes and baskets in the boat with them.

What are they doing? thought Slane, walking closer as the men rowed the boat out into the river. They were heading to the opposite shore, where the crumbling archway of an old riverside palace defined the village of Richmond. Slane watched as the boat was landed, as the men helped Barbara step ashore without wetting her gown's hem. She looked wonderful, with some kind of topknot of feathers in her hair, and beads braided into it. Pieces of softened doeskin, each decorated with hundreds of beads, were sewn to her gown in harlequin's patches. She wore a waistcoat that was nothing but layer after layer of intricate beading, with a tail of white feathers cascading down its back. And her maidservant had a single feather in her hair.

New World finery, thought Slane, used well. The men were gathering up some of the baskets. Slane watched as Barbara beckoned a boy, gave him a coin, and the boy stepped into the boat with the remainder of the boxes. The four walked toward the crumbling archway.

She goes to Richmond House, thought Slane, to call on the Prince and Princess.

Slane was correct. Barbara did know the two men with her well. They were Caesar White and Francis Montrose, and they had been servants in her husband's household when she'd married him. They'd seen her grown from girl to wife in a space of months.

As she walked with them down the long avenue that led to Richmond House, she thought, Does my father's ghost ever walk along this avenue, searching for old friends and allegiances? Richmond House had belonged to the Duke of Ormonde. They're gone, Father, scattered to the four winds. New conquerors, Father.

Standing under one of the trees that bordered the avenue, Tommy Carlyle saw Barbara before she saw him. He stepped in front of her, huge in his shoes with their high red heels, blocking the way.

"You have abandoned Virginia. How delicious. What a shaking you shall give our weary little court today, afraid of invasion, yet bored at the time it begins to take Jacobites to make good their invasion threats. 'There *is* an invasion,' I shall tell them. 'An invasion of one, come to ravish us all with her beauty.' My dear, you are a dream come true. We're dreary, Barbara, dreary and frightened and bored, and here you are, landing like an omen in our midst. What do you portend, divine one?"

Barbara looked up at him, meeting his eyes directly. "I received your letter and the broadsheet."

"Send these minions on their way," he said, waving his hand disdainfully at Caesar and Thérèse and Montrose. "I make myself your humble servant from this moment forth. Command, and I obey."

"I'll keep my servants, thank you, but join us, Tommy, for we must talk. Take me to see Their Highnesses, first."

"I know precisely where everyone is. I make it my duty to know. The Prince is fishing. It is the first time he has allowed himself the pleasure since the invasion was found out. He was ready to lead a regiment, himself, and now chafes at how long it takes Ormonde to make an appearance. Let us surprise him."

The Prince, in a satin coat and embroidered waistcoat, stood among the reeds, shallow water to his knees, soldiers upon the bank to guard him. Seated in a French chair some distance away was a woman dressed in a satin gown: his mistress, Mrs. Howard.

An attendant, seeing Barbara and Carlyle and the others, splashed out to the Prince, in the midst of casting his line. Impatiently, he turned to look, and the expression upon his face as he recognized Barbara would once have upset her. He threw down his pole, stamped out of the water.

"His eyes bulge more than usual, at the sight of you," said Carlyle. "Who was it among our small court who named him Frog?"

It had been Barbara.

"Ah, trouble to the east of us. Mrs. Howard has seen you. She's no longer sitting placidly in her chair. She is standing up and the expression upon her face is worth the price of a ruby necklace. Here he is. . . . "Your Highness, I found this vision of loveliness wandering in your avenue and brought her at once to greet you."

"What's this? What's this?"

The Prince was breathless, angry, repeating himself in his distress. His eyes swept over Barbara furiously.

"I've returned from Virginia, Your Highness."

Barbara sank into a deep curtsy.

"You left us without a farewell."

She came up out of the curtsy with the grace of a lily unfurling. "So I did, and I ask your pardon for it. I was so greatly grieved over the loss of Lord Devane, over the loss of Devane House, that I was not quite myself. Will you accept my humble apology and forgive me for my rudeness? I hope so. I want your forgiveness."

"Do you think you may put yourself among us again, just as you left us, with no warning? Do you stay among us this time? Or will some whim take you off again?"

"I have something for you."

Barbara knelt and Thérèse stepped forward and unfastened the wonderful knot of feathers in Barbara's hair.

"Only a great warrior is allowed to wear this." Barbara held out the knot of feathers to the Prince. "He has to have proved his bravery in battle again and again. These are the feathers of an eagle, the most fierce of birds in the New World. Will you accept this with my compliments? This is an Iroquois warrior's knot. The Iroquois are the finest warriors in all the colonies. Governor Spotswood told me that if we did not ally ourselves with them, they could push us all out into the sea. The French woo them, want them to ally against us. Governor Spotswood says that no one here understands the importance of treaties with the Iroquois. It is an honor that I have this. I did not have to purchase it. I told them who it was for, and it was given to me, to honor you as a king's son, and to honor your exploits in battle. For I told them you were a warrior also."

The Prince ran a finger down the long feathers, along the beading where the feathers joined. Her gift was clever. He was happiest when soldiering, most in his element among men and animals and the smell and feel of war. Then, his roughness was only part of a larger brutality.

"And this"—Caesar stepped forward at her signal and held out a package—"is a cover made from a bear. Large, brown bears live in the mountains at one end of the colony of Virginia. They've left the paws and claws. The paws are as large as my head, the claws are as long as my hand, and the cover itself is huge. He was a magnificent beast. It is very warm. I hope it will give you pleasure and keep you warm and that some of the bear's spirit will come to you as you lie under it. I wish only to move freely among you all again, as once I did. I would like that, and to have your regard."

The Prince was glaring at Caesar, at Thérèse, at Montrose, at Carlyle, at everyone but Barbara. It was as if he couldn't bring himself to meet her eyes.

"I'm going to Hampton Court this afternoon to see His Majesty the King. Do you wish me to carry any message for you?"

The Prince shook his head.

"Have I your permission to retire now, to go and call upon the Princess?"

At his abrupt nod, Barbara backed away, the others doing the same.

When they were some distance away, on a path leading up in the gardens, Carlyle said, "Look."

The Prince had walked over to Mrs. Howard and was holding up the huge cover. He was waving to them, stiffly, no smile, but waving nonetheless—this from a man who had no social graces.

"Let me accompany you to Hampton Court."

"No, Tommy."

The Princess sat in a summerhouse, called a folly, her back to them. Positioned upon a slight hill, the folly was of white stone, shaped like a temple, its sides open to breezes. She sat with her favorite companions and the maids of honor. They were eating pears, slicing them with small, sharp ivory-handled knives they wore fastened to their gowns with belts of silver links. They laughed as the pear juice dribbled down their chins. As one after another of them saw her, Barbara felt she was moving across a vaster space than the ocean she had just crossed, into a well of silence and hate. The maids of honor were staring at her with grave faces, as if she were a moon fallen from the sky before them. They were young, fifteen and sixteen years of age, serving the Princess until they should marry. She could remember herself at that age; it seemed a lifetime ago.

Barbara stopped at the bottom step of the folly, her servants fanned out behind her. There was a long silence, into which Barbara curtsied.

"Lady Devane, you are unexpected."

The Princess's voice was cold, as cold, as unwelcoming as the expression on her face, an expression mirrored to some extent by everyone around her. Barbara took a breath. This woman she must make a friend, and if not a friend, at least not an enemy.

"But I hope not unwelcome, Highness. I've brought you something from Virginia: fifty-two candles made from the bay myrtle that grows there, in a basket fashioned by the oldest slave on my grandmother's plantation. The design upon the basket is quite intricate, and the candles have an enchanting smell once they begin to burn."

One of the maids of honor walked down the steps to take the basket. Barbara explained her other gifts, a child's moccasins, a comb made from the bone of a whale, a board and cradle such as Iroquois mothers carried their children in. The Princess scarcely glanced at any of them.

"I wanted only to make my obediences before going to Hampton Court."

"Obedience from you, Lady Devane? How you must have changed in Virginia."

I won't respond, thought Barbara. I'll act as if all is well. "I wanted you to know I had returned. You have my humble service."

"Humble?"

The Princess laughed, and there was no mirth in the sound. Barbara waited where she was, until the Princess was no longer laughing.

The women's eyes met, both blue, one pair fierce, cool, disdainful, the other pair quiet.

"Yes," Barbara repeated, clearly, "humble."

Once they were away from the folly, she told her servants to wait for her at the boat. To Carlyle she said, "Let's go and sit where we have a view of the river."

When they had found a bench, she had to gaze at the river for a time. What he was about to say was going to affect her whole life. She could feel it. "Explain yourself. Tell me to my face what you tried to tell me in the letter."

At last, thought Carlyle. He began to speak.

"Two springs ago, when everything was chaos, His Majesty's most trusted servants were charged with high crimes. The royal family had partaken liberally of South Sea stock and bribes. And your husband was a South Sea director. It was he whom the South Sea Company depended upon to obtain royal approval and patronage in their doings, and he was wonderful in his task. When the price of the stock fell, and fell again, and when it was clear it would not rise, the howls of rage toward him, toward all the directors, were deafening. Roger's carriage was stoned in the streets. He was accosted outside the House of Lords by angry holders of stock. He tried at first to pay friends who had lost, out of his own funds, but that was useless. It was like trying to empty the ocean with a pail. And then he died. A tragedy, that. But perhaps also a stroke of luck—"

"Luck." She could feel something—was it anger? Was anger this mighty?—like a flame in her from head to toes. He spoke truth. She was reacting to hearing truth.

"—for those who were trying to salvage the ministry and royal family. Public rage was turned not only toward the directors. As you must remember, the King and all his family and all his ministers and favorites felt it, too. You have seen the boys throw stones at the Shrove Tuesday cock, throwing harder and harder, even after the bird is dead, caught up as they are in their frenzy of bloodlust? Barbarous custom, but satisfying, too, a venting for rage and violence. The cries of rage against your husband, even dead, continued to build. It is my belief that they were inflamed a bit, once it was realized that a scapegoat had appeared, and such a convenient scapegoat, a dead one, unable to defend himself. After all, heap as much abuse, as much hatred as possible upon his head, and the others can somehow creep past the howling crowd that wants something for its woe, someone to rend and tear. Above all things, Barbara, Robert Walpole is a practical man. He bows to the inevitable. I was there; I saw the maneuvering and pretexts used to protect others. But when the subject of Roger's fine came up, there was not the same intricate dance of defense; some zest, some purpose or determination, was missing. True, the hounds were howling loudly, but they had howled before. I saw Robert sit silent time and again, as Roger, a man who had helped both him and Townshend back into favor only two years before, was defiled beyond words. There watching with me were certain ministers, men as guilty as your husband ever was. Or guiltier. But they were alive, weren't they? In the rush to plunder Roger's estate, Robert neatly plucked out certain allowances, certain rights for other directors, all of them living. And all the while, Devane House was being pulled down, brick by brick, as London flocked to see it, and said, 'See, we have our revenge. We are eating his soul.' "

She felt sick, dizzy, with fury.

"Do not take my word alone, Barbara. Ask the Bishop of Rochester, he whom they now claim has plotted against the King. 'I kept my office because Lord Devane died,' Sunderland told Rochester, and Rochester told me."

She stood up, shook out the folds of her gown, but Carlyle was not fooled by her action, the calmness in it. Her face was very white, the dark patches placed on it standing out in contrast.

"Perhaps you speak from envy, Tommy, for what Robin has, and you do not."

"Do you really believe that?"

"No."

"A little advice from a seasoned courtier. Never, never reveal to another what you think, as you just did to me. It is fatal to do so, absolutely fatal. You are no longer in the wilds of Virginia, my dear. You are at court." That reproof made, he put his hand over his heart. "I had the honor to be called friend by your husband, whom I loved. I remain his friend, even in death. For his sake, I am yours."

She walked away from him at that, not looking back once, and Carlyle watched until she was just a tiny figure in the distance. He fluttered open his fan. Walpole, he thought, I may have you, after all.

She had left a rambunctious, scattered beauty and returned something else again. She was more grave, more aloof. The irrepressible mischief of her, chief among her charms, was transformed to a more mature willfulness, quite alluring in its way, and also a little frightening. In this court of whining complacency, she was unmistakable, gold among the dross. Has she the depth and strength necessary to challenge Walpole? he wondered. Will she? Was that do-or-die recklessness gone, erased by Virginia and by Roger's death? Or did it simply lie dormant?

Someone sat down beside him. Carlyle turned and narrowed his eyes at Laurence Slane.

"I am to play cards with the Princess at three," said Slane. "Do you know where she is?"

"Of course."

"Who is the lady I saw you sitting with?"

Slane lazily sprawled himself out upon the bench.

"The widow of the Earl Devane, one Barbara Montgeoffry. She has just returned to us from Virginia, has just made her obediences to the Prince and Princess of Wales."

"They were glad to see her?"

"His Highness had all the grace of an ox, freshly pole-axed. The Princess would have gladly stabbed her through the heart with one of the knives with which she was slicing pears."

"A varied reaction."

"Yes; extreme, from love to hate in a matter of moments."

"And where does the lady go now?"

"To Hampton Court to see the King."

"Will she arouse the same emotion?"

"I think she will arouse respect."

"You smile like a cat who has seen a nice, fat bird."

"Do I? Odd that you make no comment upon Lady Devane's beauty. Beauty such as hers is quite rare, placing her at once into an aristocracy all her own. She may be stupid, ill mannered, vicious. It does not matter. With that face, any virtue seems twice magnified, and vices are ignored. Passions are set for and against her before she even speaks. Most men speak of her beauty right away."

"Is she stupid, ill mannered, vicious?"

"No. Her late husband had an eye for that which was above the ordinary. He collected many beautiful objects, and he married her when she was just a child, not even sixteen years of age. He saw it, then, I believe, that she would be above the ordinary in all ways. Of course, he was mostly interested in the property she brought with her as part of the marriage. When she returned to us at the end of 1719, after an absence of four years, she was all everyone talked of. All the women must have their gowns cut the way hers were, must wear their hair, place their patches the way she did. She'll do the same again, this time, with all those feathers and beads on her person. Ah, Roger. His eye was wonderful."

"Do you go to Lady Mary's gathering tonight?"

"Of course. Most of the Prince's court will be there, perhaps Their Highnesses themselves. I would not miss it. Will you be there, Slane?"

"Of course."

"And where do you go now?"

"To walk along the river awhile. I must have my wits about me to play cards. You're wrong, you know. I did notice how beautiful she was."

Trailing her hand in water, Barbara leaned over the rim of the boat that was taking her to Hampton Court. Her head was aching, and her heart was on rampage. Thérèse was pinning another set of feathers in her hair, and it was all Barbara could do to allow it. She had trusted Robin to take care of the disgrace, of Roger's part in it. Carlyle's words stirred up the grief and pain, the horror of two springs ago, when Roger had died despite her care.

Thérèse was telling Montrose and Caesar about the slaves at First Curle, how they would not cross the river until they had obtained permission of its spirit.

"If this river has a spirit, it is a mild one," said Caesar.

"We must give it an offering, as we did in Virginia," Thérèse teased. He and she were good friends. "Your wig," she suggested.

Barbara pulled a patch from her face and threw it into the water, thinking, All Robin's letters, all his assurances—Roger is my friend, I will see to him—were they lies? She had left it to Robin. She'd not even thought to go to London and sit through the hearings.

Swans floated by, majestic, stately, undisturbed at sharing their river. Gardens and lawns ran right to the river's edge, where willows and reeds grew.

"Look," said Montrose, pointing. "He's made himself one of them."

There was a goose in among the swans, his long neck dark, his bill bumped and ugly, not beautifully shaped like the swans'. As if he heard Montrose, the goose honked at them.

Duncannon, thought Barbara, Jamie's gosling among the swans. Goslings were the sons of the Irish nobles who'd fled Ireland in 1689, after King William and his generals Marlborough and Tamworth had defeated them in one disastrous battle after another. James II had made a last stand for his throne from Ireland, and it had been futile. Hundreds of Irish fled with him. They went with James to make a home in France, under Louis XIV. The exodus had been called the flight of the wild geese.

Irishmen—and Scots, who also fought—filled European courts serving as everything from ministers to mercenaries. The goslings, grown to manhood in foreign courts, served as spies for James, elite and secret, their loyalty renowned.

King George would want to know there was a gosling, would clip his wings and imprison him in the Tower, show him off to crowds, the way the lions at the Tower were shown, or the elephant. Barbara shut her eyes tight against the sight that rose in her mind of Duncannon, a rope around his neck, being paraded before a crowd, which pelted him with rotten fruit and vegetables. Do you lie, too, Duncannon? she thought.

They were at the river stairs that led into the gardens of Hampton Court. It had been the favorite palace of Henry VIII and his daughter Queen Elizabeth, she who, it was said, died a virgin. Hampton Court was a favorite of this king, too. There were soldiers along the stairs, stationed at intervals along the great façade of the house. I should have stayed in London, thought Barbara. I should have seen the hearings for myself. O, Robin, I will never forgive you. And I will make you pay.

❧

"There you are."

The voice made Bathsheba shiver.

"It's no good hiding. Come out and show yourself. I know all about you."

Bathsheba moved from the corner of the stillroom in which she was standing.

"So," said Diana, "you're the witch, are you? A witch and a Gypsy, with an idiot for a child. Is this your idiot?"

Diana bent down to a basket.

Bathsheba tensed, but after one glance Diana had moved, hobbling, to the shelves of the stillroom, touching the jars and crocks, the drying roses and fern fronds. Bathsheba edged the basket under the table with her foot.

"How fortunate for me that you've come to stay at Tamworth. I had no idea, you know; I came upon a whim. But then, someone must be watching over me, I do vow." Diana laughed, small teeth white against crimson lips. "I want a favor, witch. I'll pay you for it, more than you'll ever see in a year here. I want to be rid of something, you see."

Diana rummaged among the drying potpourri, picking up the lavender and cardamom seeds to smell, then dropping them as something else caught her eye.

"You're the one to help me, I know."

Inside Hampton Court, Barbara gave her name and a small bag of coins to a servant, then waited in a chamber filled with others who, like her, came to see the King. She stood at the windows and stared out at the gardens, not joining Thérèse and Montrose and Caesar in their talk and laughter. Several men were walking through the chamber, and there was a stir of whispers and movement among the waiting crowd as they recognized various ministers to the King. Barbara walked from the window and put her hand on the arm of one of the men.

"Robin."

He turned, eyes widening under those preposterous, thick brows. "I cannot believe my eyes."

The next moment she was being pulled forward into a ruthless hug, Robert Walpole both laughing and wiping at the sentimental tears rolling down his cheeks as he held her out from him, looked her up and down.

"You're safely returned. When? How? God's blood, Barbara, it has been a continual prayer of mine to know you are safe. You are acquainted with my brother-in-law, Lord Townshend, and this is Lord Carteret. Gentlemen, I give you Lady Devane."

"I've only just returned, Robin. I've come to present myself to His Majesty." She felt cold as ice. Surely he could sense it. She made herself smile. Never tell another all you know.

"Give me your arm, my girl. I will take you in to see His Majesty myself. He will be as pleased as I am. Not a week goes by but that he asks after you."

They walked down a long corridor, he smiling, expansive, talking all the while. People approached him with rolled-up petitions, but he waved them off.

"Why are the Virginia planters sending letters of complaint because our tobacco merchants have added a charge to honor bills of exchange?"

"They were never charged before, and they are afraid tobacco will sell low. Therefore they watch their pennies and want no new charges."

"They'll have to accept it. God's blood, it is good to know you are back. How I have fretted about you, blamed myself for your going to Virginia. Now, I'll tell you once and for all that your fine is going to be reduced. I swear it. I have to deal with this plot"—he laughed and corrected himself to include the other men with him—"we all do, but I can command the votes in the Commons to see the fine reduced, and I intend to do it. Ah, what a friend Roger was to me, Bab. How I have missed him, missed his counsel. He was a wise man, could always twist the Duchess of Kendall around his little finger. She doesn't like me. If I suggest south to the King, she whispers north into his other ear."

His sincerity, his forcefulness were immense. It was like being carried upon a wave. You're good, thought Barbara, very, very good at this. Well, so will I be.

"You," Walpole said to the dwarf, who was sitting in a chair. "Go and tell His Majesty that his Lord Treasurer desires an immediate interview because he has brought him a treasure from one of his colonies. At once, little man."

And as the dwarf ran to open one of the heavy, double doors, "Did you grow tobacco while you were in Virginia, Barbara?"

"I did, and one day I intend to have the best snuff in all of England."

Walpole threw back his head and laughed, as pleased as if she'd told him she was growing gold. "I told your mother you weren't going to pine away over there. I told her you'd find something to keep yourself occupied, that likely the whole adventure would do you good, and so it has."

"My servant was lost over there. Is that good?"

"The boy—what was his name?"

"Hyacinthe."

"Hyacinthe. Yes, too bad."

The heavy doors swung open, and there was the King of England, standing before huge windows.

"Your Majesty," Walpole said, "look what I've brought you." With a flourish he pulled Barbara forward.

The King had been solemn, but at the sight of Barbara, a smile of real pleasure broke across his face. He walked to her and pulled her up out of her curtsy and kissed her cheeks, a rare spontaneous gesture of favor not lost upon Walpole nor the other men.

"Gentlemen," he said, "I will allow myself the pleasure of an hour or two of this lady's company, that is, unless you have some news for me that cannot wait."

"No, of course not," everyone was saying, bowing a good-bye, smiling at Barbara, who signaled for her servants to leave the gifts and go themselves. When the door was closed, and she was alone with the King, he said, in rapid and flawless French, "Your husband was one of my most faithful servants. I have grieved over your leaving England in a way you cannot imagine, grieved over your sufferings. But now you are back, and things will be different, that I promise you. I am so delighted to see you here"—he looked around this chamber, with its high, ornately decorated ceilings, its walls of priceless paintings, its heavy gilded furniture, its huge fireplace— "where you belong."

"Thank you."

"Tell me about my colony of Virginia."

She heard herself describe the rivers, the trees, the largeness and abundance, as if she were not enraged and in shock. She described the huge bay, the dolphins that accompanied ships as they neared shore; she told him of growing tobacco, of the care and time it took, going through each step of it as if he were a tobacco planter and as interested as she.

He was interested.

She told him of the Iroquois, of their splendor and fierceness, and of Governor Spotswood's feeling that the English must ally with them.

"I have a letter from Governor Spotswood," she said. "May I present it?"

Spotswood was begging for his old position of governor back. You see me made governor again, he'd said, and I'll see Bolling fined for the smuggling somehow.

The King took the letter from her, listened to her describe the mountains, the large creatures with wooly heads that were said to roam vast plains that had no end.

"I would like to see Virginia," he said. "When I came here as king, my English ministers tried to tell me I could not visit Hanover once a year. It was quite a quarrel between us. I won, but can you imagine what they would say if I now told them I also wished to see my colonies? And yet I do. Your dress today is magnificent. Tell me about the feathers in your hair, about the waistcoat you wear."

Barbara told him about counting coup and taking scalps, about warriors said to run lithely through woods, never breaking a twig. As she talked she brought the King a war club, a knife whose handle was a long bear claw, and a scalp, all of which pleased him, particularly the scalp, which seemed to fascinate him.

She brought out a bear's head, the teeth long and grimacing. It had been made into a headdress, magnificent and fearsome; the fur came down over one's shoulders, like a cloak.

"Their wise men wear this before they go to hunt for bear. They dance a certain dance and sing to the bear's spirit."

At once, he tried it on.

She brought out a long rattle that wise men used to cure illness, and a peace pipe; he examined the pipe's carving and beads and feathers.

"They smoke tobacco only to show reverence for a treaty made or a friend come," she said. "They sprinkle tobacco in the river to make safe crossings. They aren't prodigal with it the way we are."

She spread open a large square of beaver skins sewn together, describing the creature to His Majesty. He stroked the dark, soft fur, as she began to talk about the slaves.

There was a knock upon the door, which opened to show three girls, accompanied by the King's mistress, the Duchess of Kendall. The girls glanced curiously at Barbara and went at once to the bear's head, touching the long teeth, making faces to one another.

"Come and greet Lady Devane," the King said to them.

Nine, eleven, and thirteen, they were his granddaughters. By his express command, they lived with him, rather than with their parents, the Prince and Princess of Wales. He knows it breaks the heart of the Princess, the Prince had once said to Barbara. He does it to crush my pride.

This royal family was not a peaceful one. Before Barbara had returned to England in 1719, all the talk in Rome and Venice had been of a public quarrel between the King and the Prince. There had been a rumor that King George would make James the heir, rather than his own son. Roger had been part of reconciling them. But the King did not allow the Prince's daughters to return to their father.

"The cloak you sent me was beautiful. It is quite my favorite thing," the Duchess of Kendall told Barbara. Queen in all but name, she was very thin, with dyed dark hair, and dark drawn around her eyes. Talkative, full of her own opinions, she had been the King's mistress for years.

"How handsome you look, Lady Devane," she said now, and, bowing her head to the compliment, wordlessly, Barbara took off the waistcoat she wore. Kendall put it on at once and went to a mirror to admire herself, the girls clustering around her, touching the beading, the tail of feathers and fur.

Barbara turned back to the gifts, uncovering three small reed cages in which redbirds sat.

"These are for you. These cages were made by the slaves on First Curle. Have you ever seen birds this color?"

The girls ran to Barbara.

"An old woman among the slaves on the plantation on which I lived was said to understand the language of birds and beasts, and that of the trees and wind. She said these redbirds will bring you good fortune. There are many wonderful animals in Virginia. One of my slaves captured a raccoon, a beast with dark about its eyes, like a masked highwayman. How I wish I might have brought you the tiny, tiny birds, no bigger than my thumb"—Barbara held up a thumb to show their size—"that come in summer to feed on certain flowers in the colony. They dart about so quickly that it is almost impossible to see them. They never rest, it is said; they fly continuously."

"I wish that we could see the tiny birds," one of the Princesses said.

Barbara moved among the gifts and uncovered a cage in which sat a raccoon.

"Will this do instead?"

"The highwayman," said Princess Anne, the oldest, laughing. "Oh, do look at his eyes. It is as if he wore a mask."

"Did you bring tobacco with you?" the King asked Barbara.

"Yes."

"I will come down to the quays myself and see the hogsheads opened in the customs house," he said.

"And here finally are swamp laurel trees—twelve, which I thought was a good number, like the Apostles. They have a flower which makes the most beautiful perfume in the world. The blossom is the size of a woman's face."

Barbara walked to the windows, pointed. "You could plant the laurels in a row, there, Your Majesty, and from this window you'd see their blossoms in the spring, and be able to smell them."

"I shall name them after the Apostles: Matthew, Mark, Luke, John," said the King, pointing to each tree, making his granddaughters laugh. "What shall I do with the one called Judas?"

"Plant it to remind yourself there are always traitors," said Barbara.

"May Lady Devane walk with us in the garden awhile?" asked the youngest girl, Princess Caroline. "Make her, Grandfather."

"She will not wish to walk in the garden," said the Duchess of Kendall, sharply.

"I would be honored to do so. His Majesty's granddaughters remind me of my sisters."

"Please, sir," begged Caroline, holding on to the King's hand. Barbara saw that he had a special softness for this child.

"If you would be so kind, Lady Devane," the King said. "As you can see, I spoil them."

The girls left the chamber with Barbara, prattling about the tiny birds no bigger than her thumb and the old slave who understood the talk of animals.

⁂

The Duchess of Kendall, still at the mirror, turned this way and that to see herself in the waistcoat.

"Exquisite," she said, "absolutely exquisite. Though it looks far better upon Lady Devane than it does upon me, I have no intention of giving it back."

The King, looking down at the gardens, smiled, while the woman with him rummaged through the other gifts with the thoroughness of a street vendor, stroking the fur, touching the bear's headdress with a frown, lifting up the knife. She picked up the scalp, and as the King explained what it was, made a face and put it down again.

"That scalp is my favorite thing. That and the Apostle trees." Then the King said, "Roger was a good friend to me."

"There was no one more charming. I shall have this fur made into a stole for my shoulders. I did not know Lady Devane had sisters."

"They are dead, now. Smallpox, I believe."

In the garden, Barbara sat upon a bench, a princess upon either side of her, while the youngest danced and fidgeted in place as she talked. It was clear Barbara was telling some long story. The King, watching them, said, "It is time the Princesses had an attendant."

The Duchess of Kendall poked a skinny, ringed finger at the redbirds. "Aren't they cunning? Look at the little crests on their heads. Look at the black among the crimson of their feathers."

"They need an attendant all their own. Not these old witches of court, but someone young. Someone delightful," the King continued.

CHAPTER 42

That evening, the music from Lady Mary Wortley Montagu's house rose into the night, mingling with the soft rush of the river, with the fragrance of summer roses. Her garden was filled to overflowing with people. All the world came, strolling under lanterns she'd had set in trees, walking to the rivers, where musicians sat in boats, playing violins and flutes. Later, in the evening, the singers, from the opera company that had been formed in the last year, and about which everyone was excited—all London flocked to see performances—would add their voices to the music.

Lady Mary wore a turban upon her dark hair, gauze scarves and pearls around her neck, an embroidered vest over her gown: Turkish clothing from her travels, from when her husband had been an ambassador. Her dark eyes were shining as she went from one person to the next.

"She owns a pair of scandalous Turkish breeches," Montrose said. He was standing near the garden hedge, with Caesar White. They had been invited because they lived in the village, and also because Caesar was a poet.

"What do you know of Turkish breeches?"

"I've seen pictures of them. The harem women in Turkey wear them. They're . . ." Montrose made a gesture with his hand.

"Yes?"

"The material," whispered Montrose. "One can see through it."

"And what does one see through it, Francis?"

"Never mind."

Tommy Carlyle sauntered up, extravagant in a blond wig, demanding to know where Lady Devane was.

"She is at Hampton Court," said Caesar.

"She stayed there, did she?" Carlyle waited for them to tell him more.

"The King *asked* her to stay," Montrose said.

"Ah," said Carlyle, as if everything was explained. "I am not surprised." He strolled away.

Slane sat under a tree near the river. Gauze grazed his cheek.

"All the world is here." Lady Mary was leaning over his shoulder, her mouth close to his ear. "You have only to listen to learn more than you will learn standing in a council chamber. Walpole is coming soon. Remember, there's a boat just down the river should you need to leave us quickly."

She moved away, lively and full of herself, all gauze and pearls and dark eyes, pleased that she had lured Walpole to her gathering, excited that Slane might have to make a quick escape.

Slane, on edge, alert, aware he might have to leave on a moment's notice, ahead of soldiers or King's messengers sent to arrest him, looked around. There was the frail, hunchbacked poet, Alexander Pope. There was the Earl of Peterborough, and Captain Churchill, Molly and John Hervey, Lord Lumley, Philip Stanhope, Lady Cowper, Mrs. Clayton, Mrs. Howard. All of them were attendants or frequent guests of the Prince and Princess. There were Lord Townshend and Lord Carteret, ministers to the King himself. Lady Mary was wonderful. He, and the other agents here, would learn much.

He saw the Duke and Duchess of Tamworth strolling arm in arm, on their faces the expression of two people happy in each other. Does Tamworth know yet that Barbara is back? thought Slane. He felt in himself curiosity to see the Duke's response once he learned the news. And there was Charles with his wife. Slane liked Charles no better than he ever had. Of the two, he thought, watching Tony and Charles, I prefer the Duke, who is my enemy, over you, Charles, my ally.

Two men strolled to the riverbank near where Slane was sitting. One of them, a dueling scar across his face, crumbled bread and threw it into the river; swans suddenly appeared, arching their long necks greedily.

"So," Philippe said to his companion. "You saw her."

"Yesterday morning," said Sir Gideon Andreas. "I had forgotten what a beautiful woman Lady Devane is. Will she be here tonight?"

"So others are asking. Divine Barbara, I thought her in Virginia forever."

There was an edge in Philippe's voice that made Slane sit up straighter.

"You know her, then?" asked Andreas.

Philippe smiled. "A little."

"Slane, how do you do?" said Andreas. "I did not see you sitting there. Sir, are you acquainted with Laurence Slane? Slane, this is the Prince de Soissons."

Slane rose and bowed to the Prince, whose eyes flicked over him and then away. He didn't answer, or acknowledge the bow, and Slane, knowing he had been dismissed as a nobody in the French prince's mind, sat down again in the chair.

His head was aching. In a moment, he must stand, he must walk among the crowd and hear what there was to hear. Somewhere in the distance, he heard Wharton laughing. Three parts drunk already, thought Slane. Wharton had started drinking again in May.

There was Gussy, talking with Alexander Pope. More stoop-shouldered, even quieter, Gussy had labored to keep all together; his fingers must be permanently cramped from writing letter after letter. He was, like them all, tired now, discouraged, but not quite ready to give in. He saw Slane and smiled his quiet smile.

Dear friend, thought Slane, I wanted to see you given a fine estate, a high office in the Church. You deserve that. Anger filled Slane at

the people walking around him, rich in their honors from the
Hanovers, when someone like Gussy had nothing. I will do anything
to hurt this reign, Slane thought. A sudden, driving pain in his head
made him know he must calm himself. He touched the scar on his
brow, closed his eyes, sat in the chair as if sleeping.

After a time, hearing someone say that Walpole had arrived, he
stood and walked among the crowd.

Was Barbara here?

He didn't see her. Did that mean he would be arrested, that she
absented herself so as not to see it? His watchfulness, his wariness
were at their highest level. He wouldn't be taken. No one was clever
enough to do it.

"Is Lady Devane coming?" he heard someone ask.

Tony was standing near the speaker, and Slane saw the jerk of his
body at the question.

Yes, thought Slane, she's back. Fit that into your life now, O
young duke who has been given all things. He walked by the maids
of honor describing Barbara's dress today, talking about the feathers
and beads. Someone asked them where the Prince and Princess
were, and they answered that the Princess had the headache.

"Yes," said someone. "It is called Lady Devane."

Slane saw Tony go up to Tommy Carlyle, Tony's face somber,
questioning.

Carlyle began to talk, his arms sweeping out extravagantly. Describing this day, Barbara's meetings with the Prince and Princess,
Slane surmised. He looked for Charles but did not see him; instead
he found Walpole telling a story, surrounded by avid listeners, a certain sign of Walpole's current favor and increasing power.

"Lady Devane gave the King's granddaughters a raccoon, a little
beast from the colonies with dark about its eyes, like a highwayman's
mask," Walpole was saying. "The thing somehow got loose from its
cage and attempted to climb up the skirts of Lady Doleraine."

Lady Doleraine was the Princesses' governess.

"I am told Lady Doleraine screamed as if she were being stabbed,
then ran about the chamber like a crazed woman, then fainted at the

King's feet. Apparently, the Princesses were laughing too hard to be of any help. Lady Devane sent everyone from the room, including the King and the guards who had run in at the commotion. She managed to coax the raccoon out from under an enormous japanned cabinet by giving it biscuit dipped in French brandy. She got the thing drunk—I swear it is the truth. His Majesty told me he never laughed so hard in his life as he did when he entered the room again and saw the raccoon staggering about in ever-widening circles."

The crowd around Walpole laughed.

"She is like one of my daughters," said Walpole.

"And where is Lady Devane?" asked the Earl of Peterborough.

Walpole arched one of his heavy brows. "She is a guest of His Majesty this evening."

There was a murmur at that, and as Slane moved from one group to the next in the garden, all people were talking of was Barbara, of the infatuation the Prince of Wales had felt for her before she left for Virginia.

What does Walpole know? thought Slane. He showed nothing, did not seem to even notice Slane. But that would be the way, to act as if all were well, and then to spring the trap. Certain of Lady Mary's servants were posted in the village to watch for any sign of soldiers or King's messengers. Slane sent his concentration through the crowd, searching for danger, but nothing came back to him. It was like slapping water and hearing the slap, then nothing more. Was there danger? He did not know.

Later, in the evening, a barge appeared on the river. It was the royal barge; the King, the Duchess of Kendall, the three Princesses, and Barbara were visible in the light of torches held by footmen. At once, word spread through Lady Mary's fête, and people crowded to the river's edge of the garden, pointing. Lady Mary went to the river's edge and called to the King to come and visit.

"Shall I swim out to him and give your invitation firsthand?" Wharton asked.

Before there was an answer, he was stripping off his clothes, the maids of honor squealing and covering their eyes as Wharton walked naked into the river. Charles glanced at Slane, as if to say, "Ought I to stop him?" But Slane ignored the look.

"Madman," Slane heard someone say, "he's drunk enough to drown."

Not only drunk, thought Slane, but bitter, spent, needing to shock and outrage. It is the only revenge left us upon the rest of you, until autumn. Yes, Charles, she's here. You wish you were the one swimming to the barge. That is clear from your face. And Tamworth, standing just beyond, what an interesting mix of emotion upon his face, also.

Wharton was talking with Barbara, who knelt at the edge of the barge. She was laughing, shaking her head at him. He probably threatened to climb onto the barge, naked as he was. The King, smiling, came forward to talk to Wharton, too. You make Wharton palatable, Barbara, Slane thought. What a courtier you would make.

Wharton swam back. As he walked out of the river, careless of his nakedness, Harriet, the Duchess of Tamworth, handed him a long coat, which Wharton shrugged on.

"The King sends you greetings, says that for this evening he will remain where he is, but he thanks you for your invitation," Wharton said to Lady Mary. "He asks if Senesino and Mrs. Robinson have yet sung."

"No, but they certainly will now."

The singers from the opera were brought forward, excited to be singing for the King, and they began a duet there at the river's edge. Their voices were beautiful, strong and rich, rising and intertwining up into the night. The sight was beautiful, the shadows and lanterns, the singers, the richly dressed crowd around them, the barge, looking fantastic and fiery in the midst of the river.

Slane took it all in, Tony at the river's edge, gazing out at the barge, his face strained, grave. His wife was talking to Wharton, who had pulled on breeches, but whose bare chest showed between the lapels of the coat he wore. She and Wharton are cousins, thought Slane. I'd forgotten that. What does she ask him, I wonder? Does he reassure her or make her suffer? There was no way to know with

Wharton. The Duke and Duchess of Tamworth would leave this gathering in a different way from which they'd entered it.

Slane found himself suddenly saddened at that. Do I wish him well, after all? He stared at Tony, the man who was his enemy. Or is it that I wish anyone well, anyone who finds a moment of happiness in this life? Ah, I am, as Louisa says, becoming a cynic.

He looked around himself at the willows, the reeds, the swans, the men and women favored of this reign, in their rich dress; he looked at Lady Mary's large stone house, whose windows and doors were open to the night. In his mind was James's court, where courtiers soon became pinched and vicious, feeding upon themselves and others, such was the futility of a court in exile, always having to beg for coins, for favors from other kingdoms. I want to crush them all here.

Walpole and the Prince de Soissons were talking. They did not see Slane, who was almost one with the bulk of a willow tree at the river's edge.

"I knew Lady Devane and her brother in Paris," Philippe said. "Her brother and the Duke of Wharton were friends. He and Wharton journeyed from Avignon to Paris in the summer of 1716. They made their obediences to the Pretender when he was in Avignon."

"Boys will be boys, won't they?" Walpole was jovial, as if it did not matter at all that they had called on James and promised loyalty to him.

Wharton had been given honors by King George when he returned to England. He'd laughed when he told Slane of George's attempt to purchase him, he said. They believe everything, even honor, has a price. I took what they gave. Why not?

"I don't trust a man who hasn't sown a few wild oats. Half the families in England have a Jacobite in them," Walpole said.

Philippe reached into a tiny pocket sewn upon his waistcoat and pulled out what looked like a coin. He gave it to Walpole. It was a medal; upon one side was a profile of James Stuart, upon the other a white horse, symbol of the House of Hanover, trampling the English lion and unicorn. In the background was the figure of Britannia weeping, the city of London, London Bridge. Walpole read the words, translating the Latin: " 'James as the only salvation.' "

"This was sent me from Paris," said Philippe. "James's rewards to the English faithful."

"I should like any information upon Harry, Lord Alderley within your archives, no matter how old," said Walpole.

Philippe touched the dueling scar upon his face. "Only Harry? Barbara was with him in Italy in 1717 and 1718. She made quite an impression in Venice and Rome."

Walpole didn't answer.

"I have information that King George will want to know," said Philippe.

How smooth his voice is, thought Slane, listening intently, though he felt sick at what he heard. Ormonde would not come, not even in autumn. It was there in his middle, the way disaster always was.

"The information is so important that he who delivers it must rise in the King's regard," Philippe went on.

"Why not deliver it yourself?"

"I have no need for your king's regard. But there is something I want."

"What might that be?"

"I want the Devane fine left as it is. I want no reduction of it."

Walpole was silent. Then he said, "Roger was my friend."

"And mine. This has nothing to do with Roger, who is dead."

"The information would have to be extraordinary."

"It is. You have a gosling among you. Word has come to me from someone who can be trusted in Paris."

There was an intake of breath from Walpole. "Who is he?"

"That, alas, I do not know. Ah—" Slane had bumped into Philippe.

"I beg your pardon," said Slane.

"Clumsy, likely drunk," Philippe said, dismissively.

Slane walked toward the house, in his middle a vibration so strong he almost could not walk. This was much worse than could be imagined. The Prince de Soissons was supplying information from Paris, from the Regent of France himself. So the Regent, once their ally, was betraying to the English whatever Jacobites asked of him.

Who among the Jacobites in Paris betrayed information to the Regent? There was no way the French should have known there was a gosling. Only three or four men in Paris knew, and only one of those knew the gosling was Slane.

It would be a great coup for King George's men to capture a gosling, renowned for his loyalty. Men so chosen could not be bribed; it was part of their oath of loyalty, part of becoming a gosling—unswerving loyalty to Jamie, sworn the way a priest made a vow of poverty—and that could not be said of many another Jacobite. Waiting, as time lengthened into years and invasions failed, had proved, again and again, too difficult a test for many men. As they succumbed to poverty, they succumbed to bribes—always there—from King George's court.

He was a personal friend of Jamie's, one of the devoted inner circle, a man whose father had sailed away and left his estate and property behind in Ireland rather than support William of Orange. They would parade him in the streets like a wild animal captured. They would imprison him forever, gleeful, gloating to have him in their power.

I must go to Paris, tell the two I trust completely that there is a break somewhere, up high, and that they must no longer, under any circumstances, talk with the French. He must tell Wharton and the others plotting the autumn invasion. Charles must call off Christopher Layer. There is more danger than we realize. My God, what extent does Walpole know?

He ground his teeth in frustration, seeing in his mind's eye Gussy, Louisa, Wharton, others, his friends here. I'll be back, he thought. I won't abandon friends, not until I know they are safe. Let it be as Louisa says, that Walpole may suspect but cannot prove. Heaviness settled on him. It's over.

The singers had finished. There was a burst of loud applause. On the barge, the King could be seen to be applauding. Barbara's face was a pale and beautiful oval in the light of the torches. Slane stood in an upper window watching; then his vision blurred, and he knew he must lie down. He did so, thinking: She holds the key to my discovery. Huge honors and awards would go to her if she told, but she won't tell. He knew that—had known it, really, in her bedchamber; only the caution he must always practice required him to verify it.

He allowed himself to feel the full and certain extent of his attraction to her. It didn't blunt the ache in his heart, but it helped. She was another reason he would return. And to see Walpole thwarted in any and all ways.

Later, Lady Mary came into the house to wake Slane, to tell him of a furious quarrel between Walpole and Tommy Carlyle, something about the South Sea, she said, something about Lord Devane and friendship. Carlyle had thrown a glass of wine on Walpole, and it had taken two men to restrain the usually jovial Walpole from striking Carlyle.

"Is there to be a duel?" Slane was amused at the idea of Walpole and Carlyle facing each other with pistols or swords at dawn.

Lady Mary shook her head. "No, but the expression upon Walpole's face frightened me."

This was a perceptive, intelligent woman. Slane respected her opinions. "Why?" he asked.

"He's always said he is a humble man." She spoke slowly, as if she, too, were trying to understand. "A Norfolk squire with mud on his boots. But I think he is very aware of being a King's minister, of rising, and Carlyle offended against that."

"And will pay for that offense?"

"Somehow. Yes."

Yes, he'd be back. He couldn't leave friends to Walpole.

CHAPTER 43

Diana appeared at the edge of the lawn, a sheaf of wild bluebells in her arms. She walked up the broad steps of the terrace to where her mother, the Duchess, sat, taking her time because of the limp, the cane she must use. She'd had a fall, so she said. Diana was a mossy step or two away. The Duchess tried to calm herself, but she couldn't. The invasion has taken my strength, she thought, I have nothing left for Diana. I need Barbara now.

"I've been to see Father's tomb," Diana said.

"You're with child," the Duchess replied.

There was a moment's silence. Diana looked down at the bluebells.

"I might have known your toady would tell you."

"You did know she'd tell."

The eyes that now stared back at the Duchess were the color of the bluebells.

"Tell me everything, Diana."

"I cannot have the child."

Why not? Walpole would support it. Diana would have to disappear, of course, lie, but she was good at that.

"Leave it be, Mother. Let me to do what I will. It's for the best. The child isn't Robin's."

The Duchess's heart was fluttering, birdlike, in her chest, making her dizzy. Diana laid the sheaf of bluebells in the Duchess's lap, and the Duchess stared down at the color, which seemed to swim at the edges of her vision like deep blue water. She lost herself a moment to time and space, became suspended in the blue. A young Diana looked back at her, chin lifted, the way Barbara lifted her chin. I will do as I please. And so she had, always.

"Leave it be." Diana balanced on the cane. "Tell the Gypsy to do as I ask. She knows the herbs that will do the deed. Order her, Mother, I beg you. When, in all our life together, have I ever begged you? I beg now."

Swirling, swirling blue. The third child was a girl child. At last, said Richard, holding the naked, squalling baby aloft to the nymphs painted upon the ceiling, none of whom were as beautiful as this child would grow to be. My pet, my sweetling, my lovely little girl, crooned Richard. Diana.

"Not only have the French betrayed us, but so has someone else, someone among ourselves, at the highest levels. I don't know whether from France or from Italy."

The Bishop of Rochester sat without moving. Lord Oxford closed his eyes, placed his hands, which Slane noticed were trembling, in his lap. Oxford, you were considered the most treacherous, the wiliest man in Queen Anne's court, thought Slane. We need that guile now. Where is it? Did you leave it in the Tower of London? Old man, old man, go home and close your door.

Wharton went to a sideboard, poured himself more wine. Aunt Shrew, playing a game of solitaire, had stopped somewhere in the midst of Slane's speaking to gaze out a nearby window. Dr. Freind was silent. Will Shippen swore softly. Gussy pinched at the bridge of his nose, a quiet gesture that for some reason angered Slane.

Is that where your heartbreak is? thought Slane, watching him, watching them all. Others—Lord North, the Duke of Norfolk, Lord Arran, Lord Cowper—were not here. Divisions deepened as summer progressed.

"North, Norfolk, Arran, Cowper must be told," Slane said, looking to Rochester, upon whom most of the King's suspicion rested. The gossip at Lady Mary's gathering had been that Rochester would be arrested within the week. Lady Mary and Alexander Pope had both reported hearing it.

"I can have you escorted from the country within two days. King James will receive you with all love and appreciation," Slane said to him.

"Leave the grave of my wife, the country of my birth, my parishioners, my church, my daughter and grandchildren, my friends, never to see them again? Upon Robert Walpole's vindictive use of rumor and fear? No. I will see it out. Walpole toys with me." Rochester spat the words out. "He tries to break my nerve."

Slane met Aunt Shrew's eyes. If Rochester is arrested, she had asked him, forthrightly, the way she would, will he betray the rest of us, or not?

He will not, Slane had replied.

Word had come to him from Paris this morning. The Duke of Ormonde was in Spain, fighting off his debtors, for he had mortgaged and borrowed upon everything he had to buy arms for the invasion. The French had ordered all Irish soldiers back to their regiments, on pain of hanging. Officials all along the Spanish coast had been ordered to put embargoes upon any suspicious ships. Two—Jacobite, sent to help Ormonde—were already embargoed. King James wrote letters to keep up the spirits of those here, sent them medals in appreciation. "Plans are simply put back," he wrote. He could not yet accept truth. Slane would tell him truth.

People here were exhausted. This was the fourth time in ten years that they'd hoarded coins, mortgaged lands, sent money abroad to support an invasion. I'm bankrupt, Wharton had said today, with his odd, cruel smile, as if it were nothing. He'd given nearly everything he owned toward this invasion, and told his bailiffs, who questioned him about the emptiness of his coin boxes, that he had gambled and lost. His patrimony was in ruins. Oh, don't look so upset, Slane. I can hold off those I owe. Wharton didn't complain, and Slane loved him for it. He'd drink himself to death instead.

There was a knock at the door. Gussy went out to talk with the servant who knocked.

"Lady Devane, on her way to Tamworth, is below, wishing to speak with you," Gussy told Rochester.

Slane saw Rochester's face soften.

"You will forgive me, I hope, if I take a moment to visit with her. Her husband was a great friend to me, as was her father. I am touched that she takes time to see me."

Rochester stood unsteadily, as Gussy helped him with his crutches. Everyone was silent as he limped from the chamber.

I am a leper among my own, he'd said today. Those who are not afraid to be seen speaking with me do not trust me and won't speak to me. I've made my own hell, Slane. I won't betray, no matter what befalls. Slane believed him. Everyone's courage was showing. There was in his throat a growing knot at seeing it—the loyalty they gave Jamie, the sacrifices made, which they must live with ever after. He must salvage as many of them, as much of their time and trouble, as he could before leaving. He must, or die trying.

"He'll betray us," said Will Shippen.

"I think not," said Slane.

"I must remember to tell Jane Lady Devane is home."

Gussy spoke to no one in particular. He had the stunned look of someone who has been given a great shock. Like Wharton, like Slane, he had harbored hopes of an autumn invasion.

Jane had become a favorite of Slane's. She came to London often now to visit, the children with her, and they piled into Gussy's small chamber like pumpkins. Slane liked those days Jane came to stay, the chamber lit by candles in the evening, Gussy stirring some thick soup in a pot, Jane putting children to sleep in the bed, she and Gussy fretting and fussing over them. There was something warm and comfortable and good in Gussy's chamber on those days. A time or two, he had watched over the children for them. He had given Gussy a key to his own lodging, and he always liked to see their faces when they returned, Jane beginning to blush, as Gussy explained, in too long and detailed a manner, how they'd seen the lions at the Tower or gone to view the waxworks, as if a man could not rejoice that he took time to make love to a beloved wife.

"No one is arrested yet. As far as I am concerned, we have come out of this beautifully," said Aunt Shrew. "In another two years, who knows what will have happened. Walpole may be dismissed. The King may die. That would be a mercy, for the Prince of Wales is openly despised by those who serve him. It will come together again, if we do not lose hope. In 1715, two of my dearest friends lost their heads on Tower Hill. I saw Bolingbroke, Marr, Ormonde, Alderley flee, and the Hanovers take their estates. Lord Oxford here was sent to the Tower to rot. He is free now. We still have our heads, and what's more, we still have our freedom. Rumor may nip at our heels, but rumor is not proof."

❧

Barbara walked down a gravel path in Rochester's garden. She slapped her gloves in her palm absently, her head, her thoughts, her heart awhirl. Rochester had confirmed Carlyle's words. Walpole had sacrificed Roger, the debt, and therefore her, to his own purposes. A false friend—no friend.

She opened the garden gate; across the road was the flash of sun on water. The river. She walked to it, leaned against a willow. In her mind was a memory from Virginia: the morning she'd killed the stag.

She remembered her surprise at herself, the surging triumph she had felt as she saw the animal stagger, run a few feet, then drop. Later, riding back, the stag hung by its hooves upon a pole carried by the slaves, she had known a new thing: that—in spite of her laces and skirts, her birth, her manners, her sex—savagery was within her, just as deeply as she had imagined it within the slaves, with their braided hair, scarred faces, and angry eyes. She called on that savagery now.

Purge me with hyssop, and I shall be clean: wash me, and I shall be whiter than snow. The game Robin played was subtle and brutal. The better part of valor is discretion, Colonel Perry had quoted when she'd insisted she would tell the Governor about Bolling's smuggling. She would be discreet. She would have to be. Robin was the stag.

A stone went skimming across the water of the river, three leaps before it sank. She turned to see the boy who threw it, and there he was: Duncannon. He skimmed another stone before he joined her. Willow touched the cloth of his coat at his shoulders. How tired he looks, thought Barbara, how sad.

"Walpole makes inquiries about you," he said. "I overheard him. About you and your brother in Italy. Be careful, Lady Devane. Beware."

"You lied to me about the invasion."

"So I did. Forgive me. I do not lie now. There will be no invasion."

Great emotion, great sadness was in his voice. I feel as if I've known you forever, she thought. So much to tell him: that she had not betrayed him to Robin; that she was after Robin herself, now.

"Walpole won't reduce the fine," he said.

He'd promised, she had just heard him promise it. "Why not!"

"He was given information that is valuable, and not reducing the fine was the price."

How I hate Robin, thought Barbara. "Who asked him not to?"

"The Prince de Soissons."

Philippe. I hate you, too. But I always have.

"What name do you go by, here?" she asked.

"Laurence Slane. I am known as Laurence Slane."

She repeated it: "Laurence Slane."

He kissed her then, leaning forward easily, a light kiss, on the lips, surprising her. He said nothing, and neither did she.

In another moment, he was across the road, going wherever it was he went. She looked down at her hand. He had put something into it, a stone. She had no memory of his giving it to her.

Could she still skim a stone across water? When she was a girl, she could do it. Yes, three leaps, as good as his.

Later, in the carriage, she put her fingers to her lips; his kiss was still there. How odd she felt, as if some spell upon her were lifted. Roger's no more, she thought, and in that was sadness, but also joy. When she was a girl, she'd known exactly what she wanted. Her feelings had told her where to go and what to do. It had taken cruelty and betrayal to mix her to pieces. Loss to make her find herself. Like the girl of old, she knew what she wanted now, Robin's head, Devane Square's rise, and perhaps, Laurence Slane.

"To Tamworth," she told the coachman. She'd rest there for a time before beginning. It would be peaceful.

⁂

"She vomits again, but nothing more," reported Annie. "No sign of blood."

The Duchess had Tim carry her to the bedchamber in which Diana rested, wan, pale, white-faced against even whiter pillow coverings. The crimson hangings of this chamber were overpowering; for once, they even overpowered Diana. When these chambers had been built, Richard had been upon his rise. His beloved daughter must have whatever she wished; he'd lure her to Tamworth with a bedchamber hung with finest crimson cloth. Diana had been like a lovely, dark moth in them. She was the wickedest woman at court, which he would not see. Or did he see, and yet love anyway? Oh, Richard, it would have been the way you loved, accepting all that was in another, the good and the bad, loving simply and purely. You were always better at love than I, thought the Duchess.

She made Tim and Annie leave, though she allowed Diana's faithful fool, Clemmie, to remain. What that serving woman had seen in her years of service would most likely put another in the grave.

Diana was waking. Her hands atop the covers went at once to her abdomen. She looked to Clemmie, whose expression, as far as the Duchess could see, did not change. But Diana and Clemmie must have an unspoken language such as the Duchess and Annie did, for Diana turned her head away, brought her hand up to wipe at her face.

A true tear? thought the Duchess. If so, it would be worth the price of a diamond for its rarity. Diana's cast-off lovers would rise from early graves to see it.

"I've been thinking, Diana. Is there no fool among the men you know who will marry you?"

Diana made a face of disgust. "After Kit died, I vowed I would never put myself in another man's hands again."

"You put something there, however, didn't you? Now, listen a moment. I assume you still believe, as always you did, that coins are there for the spending, and nothing else. A marriage might be just the thing. It would give you a resting place for your old age. You are not becoming any younger, you know. Barbara received my land of Bentwoodes as dowry, but I have a farm or two all mine that I might give you, some bank funds invested I might be persuaded to part with as bribe to a reluctant bridegroom, if need be. Could you not make Walpole think it is his, have him arrange that one of his minions marry you? You'll soon see the darker side of your years, Diana, and this child, who seems determined to stay among us, will take its toll. Think upon it, it's all I ask. Clemmie, call my footman to come and fetch me. Your mistress has, as usual, exhausted me."

"Mother . . ."

The Duchess waited, fearful of what else Diana might ask. Nothing was ever simple between them. Always, always, they bartered.

"May I stay awhile, here? At Tamworth?"

A pain as piercing as unrequited love squeezed the Duchess's heart. She nodded.

CHAPTER 44

A carriage lumbered clumsily down a dirt road. Barbara bounced from one side of the carriage to the other. In the fields, grain was beginning to show its precious heads. Laborers in other fields scythed the long grass, their blades flashing in the sun. Wildflowers peeped out of ditches and fields: crimson pimpernel, crimson corn poppy, golden agrimony. Barbara closed her eyes, smelling the cut grass in which wild marjoram grew, smelling summer, smelling home. In Virginia, Blackstone would have the seedlings all moved. They would not be seedlings now, but plants. He and Kano would be pinching back some leaves, nurturing others. Had he bought any indentures from the prison ship, and how was dear Edward Perry? He should be with her, going to meet her grandmother. She heard the sound of bleating, opened her eyes to see a stone circle fence, and in it, men shearing sheep. Lambs, outside the circle, bleated and cried for their dams, who bleated and cried at being sheared.

"We turn into the avenue of limes," said Thérèse.

"Tell the coachman to stop."

The sound of the horses' hooves in the dirt was no louder than the beat of her heart. She opened the door, tossed Harry out, then jumped down.

"You go on ahead," she told Thérèse and the coachman, and she began to walk down the shaded avenue toward the house. Home of her childhood, haven of her girlhood, her wonderful, unfettered girlhood, when she'd run through the fields and pastures as free as any boy, free until the day she left to go to London to marry Roger. Oh, Grandmama, she thought, how good it will be to see you again.

There was the house now, visible at the end of the avenue of trees, quite perfect, exactly what should be at the end of such an avenue. The brick of it mellow, faded, covered in most places by ivy. The child she'd been, playing at fairy cups with Jane, looked at her with solemn eyes; the girl she had been, who had sat in those bays upon many a day, barefoot and dreamy, waved at her. The wild young woman who had inspired duels and desired what she couldn't have ran across the expanse of lawn, skirts swaying, arms creamy white in lacy sleeves. Hello, Barbara, she said to all her selves.

She called for Harry and walked around one of the long sides of the house. Her grandmother sat on the vast flagstone terrace, dozing, as always she did. Nothing changes, and everything does.

Barbara stood where she was, tenderness in her heart welling, it seemed, without end. Grandmama. Dearest Grandmama, she thought, how small you are, sitting there in your chair. Have you always been that small? Barbara smiled, all her love in that smile. There were no words for what this woman meant to her. Her heart felt like a summer wildflower, open and bold to the sun, full of love.

Harry barked; Tim, leaning against a huge stone vase, straightened and saw Barbara. She put her finger to her lips, lifted up her heavy skirts and began to walk up the grassy steps in that graceful movement so particularly her own, her face alight and smiling.

Dulcinea leaped from the Duchess's lap to run at Harry. The pair, old friends, met halfway and wrestled one another on the grassy steps. The Duchess lifted her head, opened her eyes, pursed her lips.

"Tim!"

At once, he knelt by her.

"I dreamt I saw Lady Devane, there, on the steps."

"It is not a dream, Your Grace."

Dulcinea and Harry dashed into the shrubbery in a merry, remembered game of chase.

"Grandmama," Barbara called from a middle step. "I decided to come home. I have come to report to you about Virginia."

Then, quickly, she was at the top step, she was kneeling, she was putting her head against the Duchess's breast.

"Precious, precious girl, darling child, I thought I'd dreamed you. Tim, I thought I'd dreamed her. Barbara, pet, sweetling, my dear child. You are back."

The Duchess was stroking Barbara's hair, rubbing her cheek back and forth into the red-gold of it as if she could not get enough.

Better than Defoe, thought Tim, wiping at a tear in his eye, and it's our life.

Then the Duchess sat up straight. "You've picked a fine time to come home."

"Do you mean because of the invasion?"

"Worse. Your mother is here."

In the great hall, Thérèse and Annie were supervising the servants bringing in boxes and trunks from the carriage.

"Have you pulled the crossbows from the halls and issued them to the parlormaids to protect us from the invasion?" Barbara teased Perryman. "I might have been a Papist Irishman, you know, coming in to cut Grandmama's throat for the Pretender. There!" Barbara made an evil slashing motion across her own throat. " 'Die, dread Duchess,' I might have said, and ordered you to give me all the Tamworth silver for my king. But first, I'd say, kiss this rosary, and swear upon the holiness of the Pope, over all."

"She has not changed," Perryman said to the Duchess. "Not a bit."

Yes she has, the Duchess thought. My girl has become a woman.

The Duchess motioned for Tim to take her over amid the boxes and trunks.

"Hyacinthe?" The Duchess said his name quietly to Thérèse, so that Barbara might not hear.

Thérèse struggled not to cry, and the Duchess asked no more.

"I've learned the ways of the colonial savages," Barbara was saying, "and if you do not obey me in every way, I will cut your hair from your head and wear it upon my belt; a scalp, it's called, with the flesh dried to leather upon it. I've brought you a scalp, Perryman. You must wear it instead of your butler's wig."

"Barbara . . ."

There was no mistaking Diana's voice. From the bend in the stairway, Diana stared down at Barbara, as if seeing a ghost, then ran down the steps to embrace her.

"I knew you'd come back. I told everyone you'd come back. No one believed me, but I knew."

Barbara stroked the tears from her mother's face with her thumbs and kissed her mother's cheeks, one then the other, and Diana crumpled down in a heap on the very last stair, sobbing as if her heart would break. Barbara sat down beside her and put her arms around her and rocked her back and forth, as Annie and Thérèse and a servant went up the stairs, Barbara's boxes in their arms.

It was as if Diana were the child, and Barbara the mother, thought the Duchess, watching. But isn't that how it always was? It was Barbara who was mother to her brothers and sisters, not Diana, ever. Such tenderness in Barbara's face, her touch. New tenderness, deep and true. How will anyone resist her? thought the Duchess.

"I've seen the King, and I've seen the Prince and Princess, and now I am home for a while, no more curtsies and false smiles. . . . Everyone still expects invasion," Barbara said to her grandmother.

"And the Bishop of Rochester?"

"It is said he will be arrested before this month of July ends."

Other servants were in the hall, now: Cook, the groom, the stable boys, various maidservants, all to see Barbara. The word that she was home was spreading through Tamworth. By nightfall, everyone in the village and nearby houses would know it.

"The Prince!" said Diana, reviving at once and interrupting Barbara's greetings to servants. "You've seen the Prince of Wales? Good. What did he say?"

"Nothing of importance. Ah, I must take off this gown, these shoes, all my feathers and froth. I've made a report for you about Virginia, Grandmama, a long report. I'm draining marshes and freeing slaves and making a special tobacco."

Barbara stood. I want to walk to chapel, she thought. I want to explore every room of this house. I want to lie at the foot of Grandmama's bed and tell her everything about Virginia. I want to see Jane, my dear and true friend.

"Is Jane at Ladybeth?"

The Duchess shook her head. Barbara kissed the top of Diana's head, kissed her fingertips at her grandmother, ran up the steps.

"She saw the Prince," Diana said to the Duchess. "I could not have arranged it more perfectly myself. 'Nothing of importance.' Bah. I would imagine he was astounded. She is more beautiful, is she not, Mother?"

"Leave her be. She has only just arrived. You have your own business to contend with, Diana."

"She is my business."

It begins, thought the Duchess. I haven't the strength for it, but it looks as if my Bab has. What happened to you in Virginia, my pet? More than we imagine.

In her grandmother's bedchamber, Barbara could hear Annie and Thérèse in the next-door chamber, her grandfather's. Annie was questioning Thérèse, gathering information to be duly reported later. Barbara smiled. She went to the footstool on which, as a girl, she'd sat listening to many a lecture. She touched all the items on her grandmother's bedside table: the miniatures; the books; the vase filled with roses, a mix of wild ones and ones from her grandfather's garden. She went to the large portrait of her grandfather that hung over the fireplace, put her hand against the dried paint, smiled up at him. She had no idea how much she favored him at that moment.

She left the bedchamber to roam in and out of rooms on the lower floors; everything about her—the dark Jacobean paneling, the ancient chests and cupboards, the creaking steps and floorboards—was familiar and welcoming, a comfort to her, a touchstone of her girlhood. In the attic rooms she touched the things that had belonged to her brothers and sisters, held a doll a moment to her breast. Never would she have believed that out of them all, only she would survive.

In Annie's straightforward, neat chamber, she noticed the corner of a book peeping out from under a pillow. At once a spark of old mischief was in her to see what Annie hid. The intrigues of Tamworth, precious beyond words.

"*The Fortunes and Misfortunes Of the Famous Moll Flanders,*" she read. Interesting. She put the book in the pocket of her undergown. She would change and walk to chapel. Later, in the quiet of the evening, she would give her gifts and begin to tell her grandmother of Virginia.

In the woods, Harry ran ahead of her, roaming but always circling back to keep her in view. In the stream that ran through her grandmother's woods stood the new servant someone had spoken of. Bathsheba. She was silent, Cook said. Perryman called her a Gypsy and sniffed dismissively: Annie's whim. Standing bare-legged in the water, her skirt pulled up and bundled into the band at her waist, the woman gathered something, pulling green bunches of it and tossing them near the stout basket that must contain her babe. An idiot, said Cook. Pitiful, said Perryman.

"What do you gather?" called Barbara as her dog ran forward and barked. "I am Lady Devane, come to see my grandmother."

The woman did not answer, in fact stood more still than Barbara would have believed a being could stand, her hands filled with mint and water flags, with their purple banner of a flower. But her eyes went to the babe, a pale green flicking, as Barbara bent down to the basket and pulled back the ragged linen with which the child was covered. He lay there smiling. Sweet little idiot, thought Barbara, precious child of God.

"Your child has eyes the color of the mint you gather. He's beautiful. I leave you to your harvest."

Bathsheba tucked the linen carefully around her child, put the mint and water flags into the basket with the child, and hoisted it up.

"Voice be the same," she said to the child, "but the heart be different."

Inside the chapel, dust motes leaped and danced in the afternoon sun. Barbara walked to the marble bust of Roger and stood a long moment, her hand against the cold cheek of the face.

She went to the bronze plates that commemorated her uncles, her brothers and sisters, touching the plaques tenderly, remembering them all; though she was surrounded by the dead, though their coffins were in the large vault under her feet, she felt no fear. There was nothing frightful here, only people she had loved. The dead are not dead, sang the slaves, they are in the tree that rustles, in the wood that groans, in the water that sleeps. The dead are not dead. Good words, thought Barbara. A tablet for Hyacinthe must be added.

Duncannon came into her mind, and Rochester. Yes, the Bishop of Rochester had told her, Roger's death was neatly used. Vengeance is mine, saith the Lord. No, thought Barbara, it is mine, too. The book chose that moment to fall from her pocket. She picked it up, went to a bench, and began to read absently pulling at a curl. " 'The world is so taken up of late with novels and romances, that it will be hard for a private history to be taken for genuine. . . .' "

Outside, the sun moved farther west. Trees threw longer, slanted shadows upon the stones and table tombs of the churchyard, some of which were so old that the marks, made to last forever, had weathered to nothing. Somewhere a bell sounded, as sheep came to the stream to drink. Blue dragonflies darted above bluer forget-me-nots. In the cornfields, the scarlet pimpernel, called poor man's weatherglass or shepherd's clock, closed its deep-dyed petals; that was a sign of rain. Stillness settled and became profound, as afternoon at Tamworth moved to long summer twilight and Barbara sat reading in Tamworth's chapel, at peace, at home.

She looked up from the book. It was near dark now; she'd read longer than she'd meant to. Noticing the basalt vases lacked flowers and thinking to pick some before it was too dark to see, she walked out of the chapel, and there, on the steps before her, were water flags, dozens of them in purple and green glory, inside a pail of water. She'd not heard the Gypsy's step, and neither had her dog.

At the house, there was a carriage in the drive. Who's here? thought Barbara. She meant to walk to Ladybeth, to visit Sir John and his wife, ask after Jane, but if her grandmother had visitors, there would not be time. She looked up. A full moon tonight. She would walk over to Ladybeth in its light, later.

She met Annie halfway up the stairs.

"Prepare yourself," said Annie.

"Who's here?"

"Everyone. The Duke, his Duchess, Lord Russel, Lady Russel, the baby, Lady Saylor. Come to see you."

"Tony? Tony's here? And Mary and the baby? Where?"

"They're in the library. Where are you going? Aren't you even going to change your gown?"

But Barbara was running back down the stairs. Rushing into the library—it was filled, as Annie had warned, with people—she saw that Perryman was just beginning to light candles, struggling with the breeze wafting in through the opened doors. There was Tony. She called his name, ran to him, and hugged him fiercely enough to make him stagger.

"A husband, are you? You look no different." She pinched his cheek hard, before going from one to another, almost dancing in her joy.

"You are Harriet," she said to a dark-eyed young woman. "I remember you from court. I am so glad you are part of the family." She leaned forward and kissed Harriet's cheek. "You've married the best one of us."

There was Mary, the baby in her arms. Barbara kissed her cousin, held out her arms for the baby.

"He is beautiful, Mary, quite, quite beautiful! I congratulate you. Hello, nephew," she crooned to the baby. "You have your Uncle Tony's eyes."

Charles walked up to her. "They're my eyes."

Barbara nodded gravely to Charles, then saw her aunt and went forward and kissed her. Abigail was as stiff as if she had swallowed a fireplace poker. Her mostly uncovered bosom was heaving, always a sign of emotion. Barbara wanted to laugh. She hates me still, she thought. Nothing changes and everything does. How delightful.

It's summer at Tamworth, with Grandfather's roses in full bloom, scenting the air. I can smell them this moment. My dear Tony is here with his new wife, and I'm holding Tamworth's first baby in many a year. Mother watches everything with sardonic violet-blue eyes. I had not noticed her limp, her cane. What has happened?

And there is Grandmama, in her favorite chair, queen of us all, unhappy with this unexpected visit, see how her hands clench and unclench the lion's-head top of her cane, how she looks from one to another, assessing. She is willing us all to behave, to have no untoward emotions. Awful family, dreadful family, dear family, passions and needs in us intertwining and falling over one another, how glad I am to be among you all once again. Which of you will help me take Robin?

They'd eaten a late supper served in the library, picking apart the roasted chicken and fish with their fingers, exclaiming over steaming pear tarts dusted with sugar and fresh mint. They'd talked of the invasion, of the gossip swirling around the Bishop of Rochester. Barbara had talked about Virginia and held the baby until he began to cry and Mary told a servant to take the child to his wet nurse to be fed.

Now, at last, dark had fallen on the house, the terrace, the lawn, the woods. It was late. Mary was gone to see about the baby. Diana and the Duchess, Tony and Harriet played cards while moths fluttered in at the candles. Charles sat apart from them, watching the terrace through the opened doors. The moon spilled ivory light onto it, and Barbara leaned her elbows on the stone balustrade in that moonlight.

Because she was not there, they talked of her, describing to Diana and the Duchess the sight of her upon the barge with the King and his mistress and his granddaughters, the gossip about her gifts to the royal family, her interviews with them.

"The Prince is still caught, if he's the catch you want for Barbara," Charles said to Diana, and Harriet pulled up her nose as if in disgust.

"I don't care to see Barbara as mistress to the Prince," said Tony.

"Everyone is talking of her, are they?" Diana was blooming. It was as if she had never been ill.

"It is said she will have a place at court, like that." Charles snapped his fingers. "In spite of the Princess's dislike. She isn't happy that Barbara is back, is she, Harriet? Go on, you're among family, tell us the truth. Tell us what the Princess says."

Harriet blushed, looked down at her cards.

"Jealous, is she?" said Diana. "Well she should be."

Charles stood, walked out to the terrace.

Watching him, Abigail changed color, and Diana said, "I doubt there will be a seduction on the terrace before us all. Rest easy, Abigail. She can do far better than Charles."

A place at court, thought the Duchess. Yes, it is fitting; it is, in fact, perfect. It will help to resolve the debt. It could be a form of protection. Barbara has the stamina, the guile, now, for court. She could always lie to me without blinking an eye. A position would give her the beginning she needs to become all that she may, again. I would not have to fret so. And, of course, she could help the family.

Across the table, Harriet rolled her eyes at Tony, but he was gazing out toward the terrace.

"I hate you," Abigail said to Diana. "I always have, and I always will."

Diana laughed, a sound like a hundred small silver bells. "I wondered when you'd break down and say it."

Abigail was enraged. "She is like you."

Diana tilted her head. "I'm gratified. Thank you."

"Enough," said the Duchess. "If you two must quarrel, go and do it in another chamber before you disgrace us before Harriet."

"Disgrace? Your daughter is the disgrace, and your granddaughter! Let it all tumble about our ears. I don't care!"

For a moment, the only sound was the hissing of Abigail's skirts, expressing her anger, as she left the library.

"Your play," Diana said to Harriet, who looked startled, then quickly laid down a card.

"Wherever is your mind?" purred Diana, picking up the card and taking it as her own.

❧

On the terrace, Barbara observed the play of moonlight over Charles's face, over the bones of his cheeks, over his mouth, a mouth she had kissed more than once in passion and with more than something of love. All this evening he had been light and taunting to Mary, who became quieter and quieter with each flicking, lightly stinging comment he made. It was clear he was indifferent to her. As he would have been to me, if we had married, thought Barbara, or been lovers long enough. He only loves that which he cannot have. I would have had to be unfaithful for him to continue wanting me.

She could see him in ten years, the smoothness of his even face bloated, the belly even bigger, the eyes red-rimmed and restless as they moved over every woman in every room. He had not even the kindness to hide his contempt for his wife; he displayed little if any interest in his son.

"You're getting fat, Charles. I noticed it at once. There in your stomach. Too much wine and too many late nights."

"I thought of you often," he said, in his old beguiling way, except that it did not beguile. "Had you a lover in Virginia?"

"Dozens."

"You said tonight you'd seen the Bishop of Rochester. I want to warn you away from him, Barbara."

"He was an old friend to Roger."

"It's not safe—"

"Safe? One does not fret about safety in seeing a friend."

"In times like these, wise men do."

"Will Robin put me upon a list for visiting the Bishop of Rochester? I really don't care, Charles."

"How like you. You're as heedless as ever. You've been gone for a year. You have no idea how dangerous these times are. There is evidence of an attempt to invade. This is not some child's game. There will be no mercy for those who are found out to be traitors. I try to warn you, Barbara, out of concern. And out of old memories between us."

"My memory of you in Virginia was of something larger. You've grown smaller in my absence, Charles."

In the library, Tony put down his cards, stood abruptly, and walked outside to the terrace.

Glancing at Harriet, who stared very hard at her cards, the Duchess suddenly sagged. "I'm tired." Her voice was trembling, and at once Tim was bending down to pick her up.

Diana swept up the cards, shuffled them, dealt them out.

"Just you and I, Your Grace," she said to Harriet.

Harriet stood. "No, just you."

Outside Tony said, "Do I interrupt?"

"Yes," said Charles.

"No," said Barbara.

Charles bowed stiffly and walked back into the library, where only Diana was now. She motioned toward an empty chair. "We must talk, you and I."

Tony struggled for what he wished to say. He felt as if he had taken no wedding vows, such was the rampage in his heart at this moment. He felt capable of anything. But in that was feeling for Harriet.

"I never kissed you in passion," he heard himself saying. It wasn't what he meant to say, at all.

In the library, Charles stood, as if he'd been touched with a heated iron, and looked down at Diana, a muscle in his cheek working. "I don't believe you."

"Believe me."

"How do I know it is mine?"

There was silence.

Charles tried to recover. "There is nothing I can do, Diana. It was part of the chance we took. You knew that."

"You could offer support; or, if not that, regard. Or perhaps, at the least, condolences—"

"I interrupt." Harriet stood in the doorway. "I was looking for Tony."

"He is where he was when you left, on the terrace enjoying his visit with his cousin. Charles and I quarrel," Diana spoke lazily, easily, flicking at imagined dust upon her gown, her violet-blue glance whipping in and about Harriet. "Come in here and make Charles behave. He is quite cruel to me."

"Cruelty seems to be Charles's forte, at least with women," said Harriet. Breathlessly, as if she were walking before tigers, she walked across the library to the opened doors.

"Shall I close these?" she asked.

"No," said Diana. "We won't quarrel anymore."

Harriet took a deep breath. "Good."

Diana smiled, a brilliant glittering smile that matched the light in her eyes.

"What a worthy Duchess of Tamworth you make. You know, for a time, I so hoped my Barbara would be duchess. Tony was wild for her, wasn't he, Charles? Everyone knew it. But he made the wiser choice, didn't he? Head over heart."

On the terrace, Harriet saw that Barbara and Tony were talking seriously to one another, Tony's head bowed gravely in a way he had. Moonlight played with shadow and expression.

Nothing ventured, nothing gained, thought Harriet, striding toward them. The heels on her shoes made defiant clicking sounds on the terrace stones. Barbara and Tony turned their heads toward her. Tony's expression was strained, Barbara's fierce.

"Tony and I were just talking of the wedding. I wish that I might have been there. I've brought you a wedding gift from Virginia, but

I wish I might have seen you married. I'm going to walk on the lawn for a while. Tony says he is too tired. Will you walk with me, Harriet?"

"Yes."

Tony watched his wife and Barbara make their way down the grassy steps, arm in arm. She had told him Walpole betrayed her. She wanted his help in somehow avenging that. Walpole had done what he could, Tony argued. The trouble was the circumstances, not Walpole. Tony felt as if nothing made sense, as if all were out of balance. The emotion in him was so strong. I ache inside, he thought. For what? For them both. I wish I could have them both.

"Temptation."

Tony turned. Charles had come out to the terrace again and stood beside Tony, watching the two women walk down the steps.

"Temptation separates the saints from the sinners, Tony. We are all of us saints until tempted. Then—well, then is another story. It was easier when she was in Virginia, wasn't it? Duty, I mean; honor; the keeping of vows. Welcome to the world, pilgrim."

I would like to strike him, thought Tony, there above the nose, not once, but twice. Blood would gush out everywhere. I would like that. But he said, in even tones, "Good night, Charles."

Inside the library, Tony saw that Diana was alone. There was a forlorn expression on her face. "Play me a hand of cards," she said to him; then, very quietly, "Please."

Not knowing why, he sat down.

"I adore this place," Barbara said to Harriet. She stopped every so often to take in a deep breath, as if she must breathe Tamworth, its moonlight, to her soul. "It is as if my heart resides here. Listen to me: My mother wanted me to marry Tony, wanted me to be duchess. She will do and say anything to hurt you because of that. You have three choices with her: Play her game—and I warn you, she is ruthless; hide when you see her; or ignore her. Jealousy is an awful thing, isn't it? I know. I was so jealous of Roger and his lover

I thought I would die from it. I did a hundred things to make him love me, and now I don't know if you can make someone love. They do, or they don't. Marriage seems to agree with Tony. I like what I saw tonight."

"And what was that?"

"Regard in his eyes when you spoke. Respect. He seems more a man, somehow. I won't take Tony from you."

"Perhaps you can't."

Barbara laughed. "Marvelous! I have no doubt he is yours. . . . Virginia was an interesting experience for me, Harriet. It was wonderful and awful at the same time. I made a dear, dear friend, one I will have with me always, and I learned what I wanted there among the river and trees—trees so huge, Harriet, that three men could not encircle their trunks."

"And what is it you want?"

"To live a life of honor, as I have not always done before. To hurt no one and to try to see that no one hurts me. You might let the Princess of Wales know that—that I do not wish to hurt anyone. I'm going on alone now. I may well walk for hours. Sleep well, cousin."

In the moonlight, the two women separated, no parting kiss between them. Barbara walked on toward Ladybeth Farm, and Harriet went back toward the house, a dark bulk in the night, with candles in some of the windows, in the window of the bedchamber she and Tony shared. He was still awake. Thinking about Barbara, no doubt, thought Harriet. On the late-night journey back from Lady Mary's fête, Tony and Charles had both sat like two lumps, not a word from them about the fact that the woman they both loved had just reappeared in their lives. The next morning, Lindenmas was a hive turned to one side, and Barbara was its buzz. Mary came into Harriet's bedchamber to cry and say that Charles would take Barbara as his mistress again, that she just knew it. Harriet's mother and her sisters came to her, separately, but in essence saying the same thing: Poor Harriet, they said, what will you do now? And in their pity, Harriet had seen a kind of perverse satisfaction. Why? Because she and Tony might be happy, or had been happy. What a sad, narrow little world, in which one begrudged any other person happiness, no matter how slight. She's back, Wart had said to Harriet. Let's you and I elope, leave England together and shock our friends. What had the Duchess said at the wedding? Something about the greatest love flying out the window without truth, duty, and honor to anchor it down.

She and Tony had not started with greatest love—or any love, for that matter. Theirs was a mating of families, of land and pride, as were most marriages between people of their station. But Tony was unexpectedly kind, and she liked that grave smile of his. There was passion between them when they lay together, a passion that surprised her. She found that she increasingly liked him; it was an unexpected gift, that liking, something to build more upon. She'd known when she married him that he loved someone else. She understood quite clearly that love between husband and wife was not a duty of this marriage. So it really wasn't fair to be angry at him now that the someone else he did love had reappeared. The time to be angry might come later, depending on his behavior. Would he humiliate her by openly courting Barbara? Would he grow cold and rude, the way Charles had, despising Mary's least gesture, so bored by marriage that he could not be still? Would he be quiet and hidden about his passion, leaving her to imagine anything and everything and then be told what was happening, as surely she would be, by others?

She'd wait to feel anger. She'd see what happened, how he behaved. If he remains a friend to me, then I will be a friend to him, she thought, and felt better immediately. It would be interesting, she thought, stepping up onto the terrace, to see if Barbara was a woman of her word. So many things were said of Barbara. Which of them was true?

Up above the porch at Tamworth's front entrance, a candle showed in the window.

"Walking across toward Ladybeth," Annie, at the window, reported to the Duchess.

"Alone?"

"Alone. Her Grace has returned to the house."

Leaning back into her pillows, the Duchess looked up at the canopy over her head. The big, four-poster bed she lay in had been her mother's. Her grandmother's mother had embroidered the curious, fanciful pattern of flowers and birds that decorated the bed-curtains, something done all those years ago that had lasted. There was a continuity to it, a rightness in this passage, from mother to daughter and on. The woman who had bent over her needle, to push the brightly colored silk threads, crimson, yellow, green, gold and silver gilt, to push the heavy purl made of twisted gold and silver wires, in and out, in and out, was long gone. What patience it had taken. What time. But the woman had persisted. She was dead now, but not her work, which lasted past lifetimes.

Barbara was likely to have a position at court. It was heady news. What influence she might wield. The Duchess thought of her own years at court, of her own rank and power, her deceits and machinations, the twists and turns. She had loved every moment of it, until Richard broke from it all. Richard, her fair Richard. You killed him, Louisa had said, you and your ambitions. She stared over at the portrait above the fireplace, not even knowing a tear was rolling down her face, until Dulcinea touched it with her paw. Had Walpole betrayed friendship, betrayed honor for expediency, as Barbara said?

She ought to know; she of all people should recognize betrayal. She had forced Richard to do what he had not believed in. He would have followed King James across the sea into exile, but she wouldn't allow it, told him he must choose between James and her. Richard had believed in his heart that James II was the true, the rightful king of England. That was what had destroyed his mind, in the end; he saw his sons' deaths as punishment, he told her, for his sin.

Richard, most honorable of men, she thought, what possible sin could God have punished you for, save the one of loving me too much? Regrets, regrets, life was filled with them. Of them all, this was the one she found impossible to bear, this was the one she must keep buried. She was too old to face it. She sniffed, and with all the will she was capable of, and it was much, pushed her mind to another place, so that Richard and James and herself in those old days might never have been.

Thank God Tony is married, she thought. The marriage likely wouldn't dissolve before there was an heir. She could only hope he and Barbara didn't break Harriet's heart, but if they did, well, it was not her trouble, was it? That was what she'd known downstairs, that she was too old to make it all right again, to send Tony one way and Barbara another, as she'd once done. Life could be cruel. She'd done her duty. No more could be asked. The family was preserved.

When Barbara returned from Ladybeth Farm and walked into her bedchamber, candles were burning, and flowers were everywhere— thistles, dandelions, dog daisies, rose-a-rubies, convolvuses, and bear-bine. Shades of white, silver, crimson, blush—shy, difficult flowers, half weed. Mixed in among them were water flags and mint.

She picked up a candlestick and went upstairs. Knocking softly, she walked into Bathsheba's tiny chamber. Bathsheba was awake. She knew I'd come, thought Barbara.

"Thank you for the flowers."

Bathsheba didn't answer.

"There is a dog at Ladybeth. Have you seen it?"

A look of intense relief came over the woman's face. "Yes. Danger." Barbara nodded and left.

She walked into her grandmother's bedchamber, set the candle on the bedside table, and shook the Duchess awake.

"Richard, we'll do as you say, we'll leave court and follow King James—"

"It's me, Grandmama."

"Who?"

Barbara tried not to be impatient. Sometimes her grandmother's mind drifted. It always came back. "Barbara, Grandmama. Roger is dead, and I went to Virginia and now I am returned."

"I was dreaming, a lovely dream of your grandfather. When did Roger die? Never mind. You know how my mind does, Bab, I can't quite remember, but I will. What's happened? Has Abigail killed your mother?"

"Grandmama, when was the last time you were at Ladybeth?"

The Duchess pursed her lips, a sign of stubbornness Barbara knew well. "Sir John and I have quarreled."

"He has the sweetest little dog with him, Grandmama. A tiny dog, with spots on it. Its leg has been hurt, however, and it limps. Yes," said Barbara, as comprehension came into her grandmother's face. She might not remember when Roger had died, but she well understood this. "The Bishop of Rochester is implicated in treason by reference in letters to the gift of a little spotted dog. Or so the rumors say."

John's a Jacobite, thought the Duchess. Certainty went flooding through her. I should have known. Sweet bloody hands of Jesus Christ our Savior. Like pieces of a wooden puzzle, certain things, certain events slid into place, made sense. Gussy was clerk to Rochester. It all fit.

"A new pet? I asked him. 'I keep it for a friend,' he said. I told him the rumor, Grandmama. He hadn't heard it. 'I've been staying close to Ladybeth,' he said, and though he tried to hide it, I could see he was upset. What do you suppose he's done?"

"There is no telling. Bathsheba mentioned strangers coming at night. He's been collecting coins, most likely, to finance the invasion—"

"And weapons. I would bet there are weapons hidden all over Ladybeth."

"He's in it up to his neck. He does nothing halfway. Oh, Barbara."

"I'm going to walk back over there tomorrow. I'm going to take the dog away, Grandmama. Where will we hide it?"

Oh, thank God Barbara was here. Treason was so slippery within the bowels of their own family that John's didn't shock her. Barbara had nerves of steel. She always had, even as a girl. It had been she who arranged the details of her father's burial in Italy; Harry had been too distraught to do it.

"In the chapel vault."

"Good, yes, that's good. Oh, Grandmama, the flesh on my arms is prickling. I feel afraid for Sir John, for us all." Gussy's in it, thought Barbara. I know it. Jane, what is your part?

She crawled up in the bed beside her grandmother, just as she'd used to do when she was a girl and needed comfort. At the foot of her bed was the book on Virginia, which now seemed far away and long ago, another world from this one.

CHAPTER 45

Barbara traveled to Petersham to see Jane. Her thoughts were a mix—Sir John; Jacobites; Duncannon, who was Slane; Gussy; the dog; Robin—so that even though she stared out the window, she did not notice the fields on each side of the road upon which the carriage moved. Thérèse sat quietly in the carriage with her. Is it only eight days since I've been home? Barbara thought. It feels like forever.

The dog was in the chapel vault. Tim would secretly feed and walk it. Her grandmother and Sir John had met in Tamworth's woods, like conspirators, Barbara standing guard while they whispered angrily to one another:

You're mad.

You'll say differently when James is upon the throne.

Bah. The dog is evidence; kill it, said her grandmother.

I can't, said Sir John. Neither could anyone else. That is why I have it.

I'll kill it, said Barbara's grandmother, but she couldn't either.

Amusing, thought Barbara, that we can plot treason and prepare for war, but we can't kill a dog.

They were quite close now to Petersham. In another quarter of an hour, or less, she would see Jane.

Fly, ladybird, fly, fly to the man I love best. So she and Jane used to chant as girls. If in October you do marry, love will come but riches tarry. Good St. Thomas, do me right and let my true love come tonight. All the sayings of girlhood. Girlhood was Jane, and now Jane was involved in treason.

Keep her safe, dear Lord. Barbara thought of Jane's children. The jest was Gussy had only to drop his breeches for Jane to find herself with child. In the Bible, Sarah was barren, she had no child; Abraham's Sarah and Roger's Barbara. Jane had the children for Barbara, one after another. Suffer the little children to come unto me. How shall I bear it, Barbara? Jane had said when her son Jeremy had died. She and Jane had planted pansies and wood violets around his small grave. Kit be nimble, Kit be quick, Kit jump over the candlestick— so she'd used to say to Jeremy and also to her brothers and sisters. What a sweet little boy Jeremy had been.

Something red caught her eye. Gooseberries were in season. They hung bright crimson and tempting on passing shrubs. July was a month of red—pimpernels, poppies, gooseberries. Red for blood. Would Rochester be arrested? Who else? Barbara sat up straighter in the carriage seat. The woman walking upon the road looked familiar.

"Stop the carriage."

Stepping down from it, Barbara recognized the woman as Cat, one of Jane's maidservants.

"Cat, I'm Lady Devane, do you remember?"

"Lady Devane. We're looking for Mistress Amelia. She's run away."

"Thérèse, go on to Jane's. Tell her I too am looking for Amelia and will join her soon."

"Your gown will be covered with dust—" Thérèse said.

"It doesn't matter, Thérèse."

The carriage rolling on without her, Barbara questioned Cat as to where she had looked, then stood a moment, thinking about Amelia, about where she might go.

Petersham was a hamlet, a stop on the road to Richmond; Richmond itself had once been a quiet village, not so quiet now that the Prince and Princess lived at Richmond House part of the year. There were only a few houses in Petersham, and the chapel of ease for those who lived too far from parish churches. Gussy conducted services in the chapel on certain Sundays. Nearby were the river and Richmond Park. The river, had Amelia fallen into the river? Into Barbara's heart came a sudden, jabbing pang. Hyacinthe. She could see the boy's body, lying in the barn. Jane must be frantic at Amelia's absence. Jane would have thought of the river, too.

Crossing a field, dirtying her gown, as Thérèse had said she would, Barbara came to the river and walked along its bank, her mind ranging as she looked for Amelia.

Her mother was gone. She'd left Tamworth yesterday, a day after the others, with all the suddenness of a summer storm. Her mother would not talk much about Robin. I'm not well, Bab, she said. I need time to think on what you say.

The King had set the date for the Duke of Marlborough's funeral. It was to be in London ten days into August. The Duchess had received a formal announcement from Marlborough's widow. We'll have to go, she said. It will be expected. The river flowed by, cool and green.

Hyacinthe, thought Barbara. She had to stop, stand there and breathe in and out for a moment. Amazing how deep, how clever pain could be, hiding away, then striking out. Amazing how swift and hard it did strike when it reared its head. Hyacinthe, I miss you so, Barbara thought. What happened to you, my dear boy and servant and companion and friend? Are you alive? Be alive.

Was that crying? Surely it was. She followed the sound.

And there was Amelia, crying, sitting before a gooseberry bush, her gown wet, dirty, as was her face. There was a red stain all about her mouth, as red as the ribbon on the letter from the King.

The King had sent a special messenger to Tamworth Hall with a letter asking Barbara to come to Hampton Court as his guest and his granddaughters'. It was a great honor to be asked. The letter had arrived as everyone was leaving for Lindenmas. They all had had to read it—Tony, Harriet, Charles, Mary, her aunt, her mother, her grandmother. She was on her way now to Hampton Court. But she had to see Jane first.

"Amelia."

"Bab!"

The child hurled herself into Barbara's arms, no question from her that Barbara should show herself again after so long a time, just gladness she was there. Barbara hushed her.

"What is it, my sweet? Why do you cry?"

My child, too, she was thinking. In her mind were Jane and Harry, all the times the three of them had run wild through Tamworth's fields and woods, never knowing they would grow up and away, never knowing one of them would die. There would be no children for Harry or for her. Jane's children were their children. Always, Jane had shared them because she was a friend. Friendship, the integrity of it, had never been more important.

"I've torn my gown and fallen in the dirt, and I can't find my way home."

"I will show you the way home. Plump Amelia," Barbara whispered into the child's neck, kissing its round sweetness, "round Amelia, sweet Amelia, gooseberry Amelia."

But best of all, Jane's Amelia.

CHAPTER 46

Home from his voyage, anchored in Williamsburg, Klaus Von Rothbach paid his crew just enough of their earnings to allow them an evening in the tavern, but he stayed on board awhile. It took him time to untangle the threads of himself from the sloop at the end of a voyage. It was always as if he must give the sloop an extra portion of time, as if she were a mistress he must assure of continued loyalty before he abandoned her for shore.

He walked the deck of the sloop, looking her over, making notes to himself of what small repairs she might need, then went below to his cabin and wrote them in his logbook, going over his account of the voyage there. A good voyage. He was a good captain, though these days were ending. When he wed Beth Perry, he'd sail no more. There would be too much land to see to. Had his uncle realized that yet? That when he married Beth, he became an equal in land? Those thoughts in his head, he took a nap in the small bed built along one side, waking to the hush of a hot July afternoon, birds calling to one another, water lapping placidly at the hull.

"I'll be going in now," he told the man left on board, who helped him lower the other rowboat and rowed him to the storehouse on the creek, a squat square of clapboard hastily built, the earlier building having been burned by some of the convicts those in England insisted upon settling here.

The keeper of the storehouse, knowing him, came out to greet him. They talked about the Assembly of Burgesses, which had just ended its meeting. They had appointed Spotswood to go up to the colony of New York to make a treaty with the Iroquois; they'd set bounties for the making of naval stores; they had passed an act to improve the staple of tobacco. Now none could be planted after the end of June, and any who received tobacco must obtain a certificate from a justice as to its quality.

Outside, Klaus walked through the pastures at the back of the college building, up the steps onto its back portico, then through the great arch and down the steps into the village, which spread out before him. It was always a shock to him when he returned from a voyage to see how small this village was compared with most of the port towns he visited in the West Indies. There was not even a cobbled street yet, only dusty lanes and alleys. The few taverns and shops and houses were clustered toward the other end, where the capitol building was. He walked out of the college yard and down the main lane of the village to the church, where he crossed to Custis's house.

Custis was settled at the edge of the village, with few neighbors to bother him, ravine and woods behind him.

Custis was in his garden, on the other side of the ravine, digging up a small tree, gesticulating wildly at the slave helping him. Klaus had brought some seeds from Cuba, but he had forgotten the name for them. No matter. Custis would be happy in the simple sight of what they grew to be.

He waited on a twig bench until Custis finally walked up out of the ravine; the slave with him carried a young tree whose roots had been wrapped in old sacking.

"Good to see you. How was your voyage?" Custis slapped Klaus on the back.

"Do you think to take the entire forest?"

"I steal from her like a thief and hope she forgives me. Here comes your uncle. He's been before the council. You know Lady Devane left a letter for the Governor? She found a barrel of tobacco and claims you smuggle. The Governor's trying to have your uncle dismissed from the burgesses, tries to have his office of justice taken away."

"When did this happen?"

"Right after you sailed, right before she left. It will come to little, be lost once the new Governor comes."

"New Governor?"

"Byrd and the rest in London have done the deed. Spotswood is Governor no more."

"You're certain."

"Everyone is certain. Spotswood himself announced it, though I heard he gave a letter to Lady Devane to take back with her."

Valentine Bolling was walking into the yard.

"I've lost your cargo and scuttled your sloop," Klaus said to him.

"Decided to come home, have you? It is good to see you. I'm to be hanged for smuggling. You'll have to hang beside me, Klaus."

"I've told him," said Custis.

"Your cargo sold well, more than well," Klaus said. The West Indies was always hungry for tobacco.

"That's good. Quitrent tobacco sold at low prices again." Quitrent tobacco was the tobacco given by planters in the place of coins for taxes due. It was auctioned by the colony several times a year.

"We grow too much tobacco," Custis said.

Bolling shook his head. "You sound like Edward Perry."

"I think he is right. I think we're looking at several years of low prices from our sales in England."

"I brought a pineapple," Klaus said. "It is in the house. Tell me about the Governor."

Inside, as Custis was cutting up the pineapple, Bolling sat down heavily in a chair, took off his wig and put it on his knee.

"We expect a new man any day now. But that is not the news you need to hear, Klaus. One of Carter's sons sniffs around Beth Perry like a hound. And that Scots overseer of Lady Devane's found the boy's silver collar in Odell's garden. Edward Perry has gone to England to take it to her."

Klaus stared stupidly at his uncle. The shock was so great that he could not think. With Odell's death, he had put it all away. "What collar?" he finally managed.

"The boy wore a silver collar with the Devane crest engraved upon it."

"The Scotsman says murder, and Colonel Perry supports him," said Custis. "That's why he has gone to England."

"Murder?"

The flesh along Klaus's forearms and at the back of his neck tingled.

"They think Odell Smith killed her slave. Why else would he bury the collar?"

A moth flirted with the flame of a freshly lighted candle. Klaus's eyes fastened upon the tiny drama, trying to make sense of it. He felt as if he were going to choke. He couldn't breathe properly. Odell had buried a collar? When? Why? How could he be so stupid?

"Damn me, Klaus, but this pineapple is the sweetest thing I have tasted all the year," said Bolling.

"Are you not going to eat yours?" Custis leaned over to spear the slice from Klaus's hand.

They moved on to talk about the bills passed this assembly: a bill to improve the breeding of horses, a bill to prevent swine from going at large within the village, a bill for the better government of convicts imported. Custis fanned at moths with his napkin to save them from the candle flame. Klaus told them the news he'd picked up on his voyage, that the Spanish claimed English buccaneers still attacked their ships, and all English ships in the Caribbean were warned to beware any Spanish; that the maroons in the island of Jamaica were said to be joined by fresh slaves every day. It was said a rebellion of all slaves was greatly feared by the planters there. All the while, the knot inside Klaus grew larger and larger, and his voice seemed to come from some dim, distant place, but the other two noticed nothing.

"The act to improve tobacco will be impossible to enforce. There are not enough sheriffs or justices to ride the plantations and see that people follow the law. I tell you, we'll have to limit the importation of slaves. That will slow down the growing of tobacco," said Custis.

"Those in London won't want it," said Bolling.

They began to argue. Klaus excused himself and walked outside. He gulped in air, unable to fill his lungs. The heavy fragrance of magnolias stung his nostrils, made his head hurt. He gulped air like a man drowning. Odell had never mentioned a collar. Why bury it? Why not throw it in the river?

That hour on the creek had become something he no longer thought of, with Odell dying, with the body of another boy being buried, with Lady Devane going. It had been easier than he would have thought to let the memory slip away. At this moment, he felt as if he had seen a ghost of the boy come into being before him—a duppy, as the slaves called such things.

Shall I regret my impulse of kindness? he thought. Was I, in my turn, a fool? Did the boy live or die? God help me, I must think. There is no manner in which I can be connected to any action of Odell's. Or can I?

And Carter's son pursues Beth?

"The night is not cold. Why do you shiver, Klaus?"

It was his uncle, whom Klaus had not heard come up behind him.

"These gardens are beautiful, are they not? Smell those magnolias. You were upset about the boy. I saw it at once. I cannot make it leave my thoughts, either. The wantonness of something like that. I've been thinking, Klaus; you were fond of Smith, knew him as well as any man. Was there any reason he might have for killing—not that I say he did kill—the boy."

"It is—" Klaus groped a moment in the enormous void of his uncle's question. "It is inconceivable to me."

"To all of us. . . . When do you intend to call upon Beth Perry?"

"As soon as I may."

"Good. This charge of smuggling, Klaus, it is no jest. We're both going to have to testify before General Court."

General Court was made up of the Council and the Governor. It was the highest court in the colony.

"She gave them the barrel, the tobacco, as evidence. I've had the brand destroyed, and another made with different lettering, so they will not be able to prove anything. We may have to pay a fine. If we do, I'm taking it all from your part. You ought to have noticed that a barrel was dropped. Spotswood vows he will talk personally with the new Governor, vows he will have us watched, but I think these empty threats. Still, she's made it damned uncomfortable for me."

They talked about the voyage, Klaus giving Bolling a precise accounting of what had been done.

"Good, good," said Bolling. "Go and see Beth Perry, as soon as you can."

A dog barked as Klaus crossed the college yard; otherwise the night was quiet around him. At the creek was the rowboat his crew had left out near the storehouse. He rowed toward his sloop. Pale, flickering light shone aboard. He called up to the man on watch, who caught the rope to secure the rowboat. Closing the door of his cabin, he lay upon his bed, pulling his blanket up over him in spite of the heat, shivering for a time, as if he had the ague. There was no manner in which he could be connected to Odell's deed. There was no proof of Odell's deed, only speculation. He must remember that. He would.

It was late the next afternoon when Klaus sailed a borrowed dinghy to the broad stretch of river before Perry's Grove. He waited for Beth in a chair in the parlor, at a window where he could see the horse chestnuts in the yard, and beyond them the river.

It was a long time before Beth came down the stairs, longer than she should have taken given word that a suitor waited whom she desired. Is it Carter's son? wondered Klaus. Or the collar? I must remember there is no way to connect me with the collar.

Finally there she was; did those cool eyes of hers look guarded, or was he imagining it? Something is wrong, he thought. There was warmth in that glance when I left.

He took her hand, kissed it, held it a moment to his cheek.

"I've missed you. You're all I've thought of," he said.

She took back her hand. "How was your voyage, Klaus?"

"Good. Everything went well, sold well."

"The tobacco?"

He didn't answer.

"It is said you smuggle tobacco. Lady Devane said so." She glanced at him and then away.

"No," he said. Why all the fuss? Many smuggled tobacco. At times, smuggling was the only way to make a gain. It was not looked upon as a crime, more as a fact of life those in England did not understand. "There is an old quarrel between my uncle and Lady Devane. She tries to injure him. What of you? What of your suit against your father in General Court?"

"It is to be settled this fall, I hope."

"He's gone to England, I heard."

A shadow passed over her face. "Yes."

He waited. There was no sign from her, of any kind. She might never have held out her hand to him, told him to change her fortune, might never have walked with him in the woods and allowed kisses.

"Tell me what you've been doing."

"So much. There is so much to do. I had not realized all that must be done on an estate as large as this. I stay busy from morning until night."

There was zest in her face. So she liked the running of her father's properties. Liked being the one in charge.

"The evening will be beautiful. Later, we'll walk in it, and I will show you some of the stars I steer my sloop by."

"No, thank you. I go to bed very early these days."

He was refused, and without an offer of refreshment. No offer that he stay. She was a stranger. He had not left a stranger.

"Is it the collar?"

She looked surprised. She didn't understand; he could see that at once. It was something else, then. He should not have spoken.

He bowed to her.

"I will call in the morning."

"I won't be here. I'm riding over early to another plantation."

"In the afternoon, then."

"Perhaps. I'm so very glad you came by to see me. Good evening."

Outside, he walked over to William Byrd's plantation. Byrd was in England. The house was large, pleasant. It was said Byrd wished to build a grander one, like houses in England. Why not? His father had acquired much land. Byrd was one of the young kings here. Klaus pushed open a gate and walked toward a garden house on the riverbank. The sky above was as blue as Beth's eyes, the grass and leaves a fresh green. Birds twittered and sang among the trees. Wisteria and honeysuckle bloomed all about the roof of the garden house, and hummingbirds fought by the dozen over each blossom.

Klaus walked among the gravestones by the church built close to the house, stopping at a stone column with the names of Beth's brother and mother upon it. There was a fine view of the river from here.

Something had happened. She no longer esteemed him as she had before he left. What was it? The collar, the smuggling, Carter's son? Was it the simple fact that she liked the running of her father's property, found power, satisfaction enough in that? What an irony that would be. He considered all the things he might do—fall to his knees, declare his love, ask for her hand in marriage, beg it. Continue to court her, waiting for some small change. Something in the coolness of those eyes warned him.

He had abandoned the widow for her.

If I am wise, thought Klaus, I will pay a visit to my widow tomorrow. She will be angry, more than angry, but I will endure it, see if I can win her over again.

And then there were always other widows. He looked back at the garden house, thought of the hummingbirds all fighting over the same blossom when there were others free. Beth Perry is no longer mine. Why? What happened?

A widow's third, versus an heiress's whole. For a moment, he had envisioned taking his place among the kings here. Now he would have to be content with less. The widow's third would have to do. His sons would be the kings, not he.

Barbara came into his mind—that kiss on the roof of the Governor's mansion, the passion of her, a passion he had forgone, choosing something else: the satisfaction of deflowering so great an heiress, of knowing that he became master of all that was hers. Barbara. The boy. Odell. The collar. Beth. Life was a strange thing. To have come so close to having all, and now to be so far away.

CHAPTER 47

July became August. . . . Grain was ready, ripe in the fields for harvest. . . . We have ploughed, we have sowed, we have reaped, we
have mowed, we have brought home every load. . . . The Lord's
bounty would be celebrated with harvest festivals—roasts and meat
pies to eat, mead and ale to drink, the songs of good harvest to sing.
. . . At Hampton Court, in the garden, the sight of Barbara and the
King's granddaughters was before the old Duchess's eyes. Bounty.
She was there as a guest, because Barbara requested it. Barbara could
have asked for the stars, it seemed. The rumor was that the King was
going to ask her to be a lady-in-waiting to his granddaughters. Triumph, thought the Duchess, watching Barbara charm all those
about her.

Walpole and Townshend had stepped up their investigation. The
technique was frightening: a knock on the door, and there was a
King's messenger demanding one's presence at the Cockpit, where
Walpole, like a hound, chased any scent. Everyone was suspect—
landladies, shopkeepers, physicians, anyone, everyone who might be
Jacobite, who might be a link. Yet there were no arrests, not one,
though the rumors about the Bishop of Rochester did not decrease.
And the troops did not leave Hyde Park.

August. Walpole sat in his favorite garden, near the river, tapping his fingers slowly upon the back of the bench upon which he sat. Rochester, he thought, I cannot take hold of you.

No one questioned admitted to anything, much less gave any hint concerning the head of the plot. No one released led them anywhere. They dealt with flotsam, with riffraff, no one solid, no one important. After two months of questioning, he was little further along than he'd been in May, and he'd lost the excitement of May, when the King had been eager to allow him anything. He had codes broken, by God, but nothing to link code names with their English counterparts, other than his instincts, and certain references—like those to the spotted dog—that left little doubt who the person was, but were not, unfortunately, proof.

We cannot convict the highest Tory bishop in the land because we think he *may* be guilty, said Townshend. They had not one scrap of independent evidence that their guesses were correct. All this time, all these questionings, all the letters with their codes broken— and no independent evidence to verify.

Why were there no arrests? asked the King. Walpole did not tell him that, as yet, he could furnish no proof that would stand up in an English court of law. The King expected results. He had led the King to expect results. He did not at this moment know if he could produce them. It drove him wild to see all he desired so close within reach, yet be unable to grasp it, legally.

He questioned again and again about a gosling. No one had anything to say. France, as a source of information, had completely dried up. I can give you nothing, said the Prince de Soissons. There is no more news.

Walpole kept the tension building with hasty little broadsheets announcing the names of those taken up for questions and promising, at any moment, arrests of high personages in the kingdom. All he could do was hope to frighten one of the chief conspirators into making a false move. It was a war of nerves, but his own were wearing thin. Other ministers want us to fail, said his brother-in-law. They want us to fall over our own feet. We must make arrests.

On what basis? How?

I'm to have a child, Diana had told him. Your child. Concentrated as he was on this plot, he was mildly interested, mildly excited, congratulating her, handing her a bag of coins.

Fool, she hissed, can you think of anything but Jacobites? I need a husband. I'll see to it, he said. He would, eventually. A child. After all this time. Amazing. Perhaps it was an omen, an omen he'd succeed in this.

Today, he met with a little man named Philip Neyoe, who swore he had important information and, for the price of a guinea, would give it over. Amusing, that this little man came to dicker and bargain, as if a King's minister were a merchant. Walpole was tired of seining through the small fish, but he had no other choice. So seine he would. But not kindly.

The Duke of Marlborough's funeral was in another few days. Perhaps by then he could present something to the King. He let it be inferred he would. He needed to present something soon; he could see it in the King's eyes.

Risk was part of the position he held, but a man got tired of risk, longed for certainty.

Tell His Majesty we cannot do it, said Townshend, as tired as Walpole was. That meant dismissal—not immediately, perhaps, but down the road.

He would not be dismissed. This was his life. He was destined for even greater things. Surely someone would break, run out into the open like a frightened hare, and he'd have him, then, the hare that led to the bishop who led to glory.

There was another name that had come up, whose trace he must follow. He sighed, tired of small fish.

Christopher Layer was the other name.

CHAPTER 48

A week later, Slane, just back from Paris, looked at the lines sent him for the part he would perform at the end of August in London's traditional Bartholomew Fair.

He could not concentrate, and he put the lines to one side to play with his finch, to lay his hand atop the table and crumble bread upon it. The finch was flying about the chamber, and he waited for her to settle, to land on the table and hop to his hand for the bread. This was a new chamber he'd moved to, and she was not happy in it yet. He'd left the door of her cage open for days, but only today had she ventured out to fly. It was almost as if she sensed the trouble brewing, and preferred the confinement of her cage to the uncertainty of freedom.

In the last week, some significant arrests had been made. Before, it had been the fringes Walpole mucked in, but in the last three days, he'd swept into his net three important agents—men who, if frightened badly enough, could give evidence against important nobles, secret Jacobites. The Bishop of Rochester was just a breath away from these noblemen, as their immediate superior.

What source had Walpole stumbled upon?

Slane had just seen one of the agents onto a boat for Ireland. The other two were under house arrest and he could not get to them.

Tomorrow the Duke of Marlborough would be interred in Westminster Abbey, a grand event in which most of the court and the highest officers of the army would participate. It was all but accepted that Rochester, who was to conduct the funeral service, would be arrested immediately afterward, that others, dukes and earls, would join him in the Tower of London. The city rattled with expectation.

Slane had met with Rochester for a long time yesterday, trying to persuade him to leave England clandestinely, not to perform the funeral service at all, but the old Bishop was adamant: Walpole will not run me from my duty, will not frighten me into unnecessary exile. And yet Rochester was frightened. His gout pained him so that even with crutches he could barely walk; his temper was so short that even Gussy showed the wear of bearing it.

Slane could feel it, could feel Walpole's mind moving over what was known, tenaciously searching. Walpole was calling him, this gosling—this prize an ambitious minister wished to present to his King—out into the open. He could feel that, too. A true gosling would be delivered to Walpole tomorrow; there would be no message, just the creature. It was Slane's way of taunting Walpole and, perhaps, distracting him from his hunt of the others.

They knew who had betrayed them in Paris. The betrayal was disheartening; the man was one Jamie had trusted totally. He had helped form the invasion plot itself. Save those you can in England, Jamie had written. Slane had gone to Rome to see him. I do not wish my subjects to suffer any more than they must. Help them, Slane, until you consider it too unsafe to do so. Succor Rochester. I know he failed us this time, but there are past loyalties to consider. And he is old, Slane, and alone. Jamie would think of that. It was one of the reasons Slane loved him.

The finch dove low at the table. Slane did not move his hand. Exercises in patience were good for him, strengthening resolve, the ability to wait, to allow events to unfold. Walpole was a master of patience. Look how he prodded and probed, not giving up. Would he act tomorrow?

Gussy, Slane had said yesterday, you must think about leaving England, my friend. He himself would travel soon, north and south, to encourage the leaders—they were hidden away in their country homes, like mice hoping the cat would pass them by—to leave England. He would offer them King James's support. He knew, and they knew, that the offer meant little, for Jamie had nothing to give—no land, no houses, no great court offices that meant anything other than plotting. To leave meant exile and a hand-to-mouth life. Nonetheless, that was what he was requested to do, offer them Jamie's profound gratitude and succor, such as it was.

Coins and muskets must be collected, hidden away in safe places, for another time, for the next time, so that they could say—when the next chance presented itself—"See, we have many arms, much coin awaiting us in England."

The finch hopped onto the table.

"Yes, sweetheart, that's it. Come and take the bread."

He coaxed her as sweetly as if she were a woman he loved. He was anxious to see the woman he loved. Such rumors about her. She'd not been still this last month. Slane smiled at the thought of that.

There was a knock at the door.

Startled, the finch flew at once to the highest perch in the chamber, a peg that held some of Slane's clothes. In another moment, Slane was at the window, and out of it, dropping down onto a porch roof. No one knew where he was, save Louisa and Gussy.

Instincts up, like a cornered animal's, he scanned the street below, but saw no soldiers, no King's messengers sent to arrest. There to his right was the bulk of the Tower of London, its high, massive wall a barrier no one penetrated, few escaped. Some Jacobites—those captured in 1715, those whose heads had not been severed from their bodies—languished there still, in dark, forgotten dungeons. Fitting, somehow, that Slane should be near.

He dropped to the street, tensed, a cat ready to spring. The drop started his head aching. He walked across the street and into another alley, and from the shadow of a doorway, watched.

A man walked out of the building in which Slane lodged: Louisa's servant, her most trusted one. Slane stepped out onto the street and called his name.

"You're to come at once," the man said.

"What's happened?"

"I don't know, sir, but something. She's been weeping all the morning."

Rochester must have been arrested. Finally Walpole had made a move. He could feel a tremendous tension inside himself. Who was next? And would Rochester hold firm?

In the carriage, he again questioned the servant, but the man could tell him nothing but that a note had arrived this morning, and that Lady Shrewsborough had fallen to her knees on reading it and begun to weep.

Slane climbed her stairs two at time, and there she was, sitting in a chair, her face so pinched-in that it made his heart hurt.

"You've come," she said.

"Close the door," he ordered the servant. He took her hands in his, rubbed them tenderly. Your brother was called the Lionheart, he thought, but so might you be a lion's heart, dear Louisa.

"Is it Rochester? Is he arrested? When?"

"It's Lumpy. He's married."

"I don't understand." He did not. His mind was somewhere else completely.

"Lumpy. He's married Diana."

Slane was silent, struggling to take in the news, not to follow a sudden impulse to laugh.

"They went down to Fleet Street like a common sailor and his whore, and were married this morning. They are now on a journey to his home in Newcastle. He did not even have the decency to tell me to my face, but wrote me a letter, which I spat on before burning, curse his ancient hide. I ought to have known she was up to no good. She'd been like a Christmas pie, all sweet inside, since she returned from Tamworth last month. Said she and Alice had reconciled. Said seeing Barbara filled her heart with joy. Called on me especially to tell me, she said. Her telling of it brought a tear to Lumpy's eyes. 'Oh, Sir Alexander, I've hurt my ankle and it is not well yet. May I lean upon your arm?' "

She mimicked Diana with precise bitterness, and Slane was glad to see the rage. It would hold the pain at bay.

"I was thrown off the scent by the worry about this invasion, by these terrible rumors about Rochester and other men who are my old friends. I was the only family she had in London, she said. Could she stay near? Which ought to have warned me at once, since nothing truly frightens Diana. But I was stupid. And all the time she was stalking Lumpy. 'Sir Alexander,' she called him. Stalking him like a cat, smiling at him in that way she has. 'Dear Aunt Shrew,' she said to me yesterday—yesterday, Slane—'how glad I am to be with you.' Curse her lying, tiny pebble of a heart. I loved that man. Unfair tactics, sashaying around all plump and smooth. Of course he succumbed."

"Louisa, I have no words—"

"I have, and plenty of them, if I ever lay eyes on either of them again, at which point I will end hanged at Tyburn Tree for murder. Promise me you'll be there to pull on my legs so that my neck breaks clean. And tomorrow I must go see my old friend Marlborough buried. And perhaps I'll see them arrest Rochester, too. And there will be talk of this marriage—people will know by then. Tommy Carlyle knows of it; he saw them on Fleet Street. He has already called to tell me he saw them coming out of a church, and so I told him the truth, pretended I did not care, said they had my blessings, but I know he did not believe me. Everyone will be laughing over it tomorrow, and I will have to pretend I do not care, and I do. I love that man, Slane!"

He raised her hands to his lips, kissed them.

"I know you do."

His action broke past the rage, and she began to cry, her wrinkled face puckering in like some grotesque child's, the weeping that way too, open and abandoned, the way a child might weep. Slane pulled her forward into his arms, thinking My dear, dear Louisa; and she wept in them, wept the way a woman of passion weeps, deeply, completely. It would have been frightening to see, if he had not had a mother who was a woman of passion also. There was nothing halfway in such a woman's love. To have her at your side was to have vigor and force and determination mingled with startling tenderness. How tender they could be. His wife had been so; and his mother had loved and lost and yet on she marched into life, fan furled, head tilted. Like a cat that must heal its wounds, she might go and leave life awhile, might retreat into a convent or some chamber of her house, but always, always, she emerged, faith in something—in herself and in her God—intact once more. I must experience tears as well as joy, my little one, she'd told Slane. That is life, and I want all of life. I will have it. And so love had come to his mother again, because she was not afraid of its coming.

He held Aunt Shrew close and patted her back, and thought, I will stay with you, dear friend, all this day and tonight, too. I'll see that you are rouged and dressed to within an inch of your life tomorrow. You'll go to the funeral, go on pride if nothing else. You must go anyway, so that we see what happens with Rochester. Ah, sweetheart, you are as brave and gallant as a man. Too bad of Pendarves to break your heart.

Barbara would be at the funeral tomorrow. Her cousin, the Duke of Tamworth, would march near the front of the procession in honor of his grandfather, Marlborough's colleague and fellow general. O noble warrior, O valiant man, we will not see your like again.

Barbara would be there as the King's guest. She had been at Hampton Court almost since arriving from Virginia.

Rumors were rampant: that Barbara would be made lady-in-waiting to the Princesses, that she was the King's new mistress, that she was the mistress of the Prince of Wales, that the pair shared her. People were talking about Devane Square, saying that it was going to be made what it once had been; people were saying Walpole had explicit instructions from the King to see her fine reduced, that the King was going to build a palace where Devane Square had been.

Early the next morning, Slane was up, and walking through St. James's Park from Louisa's house. There were fields between Piccadilly and Tyburn Road, and in those fields he'd find rose-a-ruby blooming, so Jane said. Jane had told him about the red flower, one of the last ones thriving as August turned to fall and chill: The country maids believe, said Jane, that if they don't have a sweetheart before it goes out of flower, they will have to wait another year, until it blossoms again. It would not do for Barbara to wait another year for a sweetheart.

A great bunch of rose-a-ruby picked, he walked to Devane Square, passing the few townhouses finished, the church. More rumors: that Sir Christopher Wren, quite old now, was wild to finish this church. It is my best, he said, a jewel of its kind. Sir Gideon Andreas held large notes against Barbara's estate and could take Devane Square, except that the King demanded otherwise, it was said. Barbara had clearly maneuvered herself into a good position since she'd returned.

Slane walked to the fountain. Moss scaled its sides, scaled the stone figure of a nymph. The house had been beyond, he'd been told. There was nothing now, except a landscape canal. One could see the church spire of the hamlet of Marylebone. The bell in the spire of the church at Marylebone began to ring as Slane walked around the fountain, gazing at the nymph from every angle. The sculptor had left nothing much to imagine. There was the slim grace of the naked body, the sweet roundness of the arms, the long back curving into hips and buttocks, the beautiful stone face half hidden by cascading hair. What kind of man were you, Devane, thought Slane, to show your wife so? Did you brag or did you love?

Only the outward was captured in this stone, none of the inward, and so to Slane's eyes it was not nearly beautiful enough. He dropped a blossom of the rose-a-ruby in the nymph's arms and blew her a kiss before walking back toward Aunt Shrew's, back toward this day on which Rochester and who knew who else might be arrested.

❧

"Pet, it is not that I do not love you. . . ."

Pendarves stepped back, as if Diana were a witch and he the newt that would be tossed into her brew. She was in his bedchamber, but not upon the bed, rather sitting in a chair, skirts raised, head thrown back, eyes closed, touching herself, giving herself pleasure, as boldly as any whore. More boldly. He couldn't take his eyes from her hand, moving in a sure, circular rhythm against herself. She made sighing noises in her throat and bit her lip and put her other hand to her breast. She could completely satisfy herself this way, and Pendarves found it more exciting, and more frightening, than anything he'd ever seen.

"You must stop. . . ." He couldn't catch his breath. He was too old for this on so frequent a basis, he'd tried to tell her that, but she didn't seem to understand, and he—well, he was weak, a man, flesh and bones, after all. Sometimes it crossed his mind that she was a witch and trying to kill him. Like metal near a magnet, he moved closer to her, cursing his weakness, yet unable to overcome it. Diana put her hand on him and growled. She is going to kill me, thought Pendarves. Then, as she began to unfasten the buttons upon his breeches: What a wonderful way to die. The next thing he knew he was fainting, and it wasn't the first time. His last thought was the hope he always hoped these days—that he'd wake alive.

The funeral was over. People milled about one of the courtyards of Westminster Abbey, the Bishop of Rochester among them, as well as Robert Walpole and the King of England. If there was to be an arrest, there was no sign of it, but there was a tension in the court-yard, a tension that had been inside the cathedral and that was al-most visible, so present was it. People vibrated with it, rustling and talking, something restless and odd in their rhythms, looking again and again to Walpole, to the King, to Rochester, waiting for the façades to fall, almost willing it.

Barbara, following an impulse to be alone, to escape the unnerv-ing tension, some of which was her own—everyone had stared and whispered when she had entered the cathedral as part of the King's household—had managed to find a quiet spot behind one of the sup-ports of an archway. She hid in its shade and took a moment to gather her wits. Gussy was here. She did not know what she would do if they took Gussy away. Or Wart. She did not know if she could be silent in the face of that, be discreet.

She heard the sound of someone's footsteps, a distinctive footstep, halting, short, as if someone possessed a limp. Finally, she thought, here we are, face to face. What would he say to her?

"You dropped this," Philippe said. In his open hand was a medal. She knew it at once. "James as our only salvation," the Latin upon it read. Prince of darkness, she thought, how you would adore to trap me. Well, you won't. What had Tommy advised? Never reveal your thoughts. It's court, pet, he told Barbara. The motto of a court is caress the favorites, avoid the unfortunates, and trust nobody.

"It isn't mine."

The dead are not dead, the slaves sang, and yet the Duke of Marlborough had just been given his death song, and Roger was gone, and she and Philippe seemed doomed to be left behind arguing over whom Roger had loved best. That was what this was ultimately about, wasn't it? Whom Roger had loved best?

"How proud Roger would be," he was saying, "to know you are giving yourself to so worthy a man as the Prince of Wales. I congratulate you upon your cleverness."

Cruel man, with your smooth and malicious voice, how dare you insult me so? Do you think me fifteen and a girl still? Do you think I have learned nothing, that I have no weapons, no claws of my own? She knew what to do. She'd thought it over carefully. Here was a man, if ever there was one, to use. She must not let her anger with him interfere in her use of him.

"Wouldn't he be proud of the pair of us? My curtsying to a frog and your aiding a false friend."

She had him, this man of ice, this man of disdain and deliberate cruelty.

"What do you mean by 'false friend,' my dear?"

"Walpole, the King's most gracious minister, our dear, fat Lord Treasurer, my mother's paramour, Roger's friend: Walpole allowed Roger to take the whole of the blame for the South Sea Bubble. Such is his idea of friendship."

"There was nothing else possible."

"No? Go and ask Tommy Carlyle, who was every day in the House of Commons during the investigations. Walpole allowed Roger's estate to be ruined more utterly than anyone else's. Why? Because there must be a scapegoat—and who better than a dead man? There must be a scapegoat who takes the attention of the mob, and thus others—those alive—creep by while everyone else is looking elsewhere. Lord Sunderland told the Bishop of Rochester that it was agreed among the King's ministers that they would fan the flames against Roger, see how large the hatred grew, how it might be useful. It was agreed to reluctantly, I'm told, but that isn't the point. The point is that they agreed at all. You're a man of subtlety. Don't you see? There was anger against Roger, yes. But so much anger that his fines were among the largest? That his face was drawn on broadsheet after broadsheet? That he was made the largest villain? No, I think not. That anger, that vileness, was helped along, not by his enemies, but by his friends, so that they might survive."

"I do not believe you." But his face was pale.

He does believe me, thought Barbara. "There will never be anything built as glorious as that which Roger built, and all of it was needlessly destroyed so that those still living might have smaller fines or keep their places in service to the King. Devane House would have been a monument to Roger, and the house is gone, because it satisfied the mob to see it gone, to see it dismantled. Roger's name is forever besmirched, and why? For the same reason you imply I would bed a frog. Ambition. Expediency. Roger was dead and others were alive. Ask the Bishop of Rochester. There he is, in the courtyard. Go and ask him before the King's soldiers drag him off to the Tower and he is forever silenced. Ask him what the Earl of Sunderland said about it all. Ask Tommy Carlyle. Go on, sir, see if this woman you so despise knows of what she speaks."

She watched in satisfaction as he approached Rochester. The two men moved, Rochester slow because of his crutches, to a quieter place to talk. She leaned her head back against the stone of the archway. It was set in motion. Her first powerful move against Robin. Easy enough, perhaps too easy.

She touched her face. Tears. Why? Because she began a dangerous and ruthless game? You might need years, said Tommy. Could
she give it years? Would she? Roger, to build it all back is hard.
More, sometimes, than I think I want to do. She moved to a door,
opened it. An empty chamber. Good. She closed her eyes and put
her arms around herself, as if to give herself comfort. Her stepfather
wished to loan her funds to finish the church in Devane Square.

"Why do you do that? Is there no one you trust to comfort you?"

It was Slane, actor, hero, spy, Jamie's favorite. When had he returned? She'd dreamed of his return. She'd not heard his approach.
He closed the door to the chamber.

"What is this?" she said to the bunch of dying wildflowers he held
out to her.

"Rose-a-ruby."

"What am I to do with it?"

"Put it under your pillow until your sweetheart comes."

She looked at him. These last weeks in the King's household had
brought forward the hypocrisy that was court. The rumor that she
was to have a place in the household meant that everywhere she
went people gathered to compliment her and be her friend. It was
good to feel, to see, after the disgrace of the South Sea, after all that
she'd lost, but something in her warned, over and over again, Beware, know the flattery is for a purpose, not your purpose but theirs.
Pick and choose friendships with care. Trust nobody.

"I want to come courting. Have I your permission?"

"Courting whom?"

She knew whom. I want this, she thought, never mind it might
end tomorrow.

"Thérèse, of course," he said.

She laughed. "She won't tell you anything of the King's household. Her lips will be sealed."

"I won't be asking her of the King's household, and I'll be kissing
those lips, instead."

"She has been betrayed before. It has made her wary and unforgiving."

"She will have nothing to be wary of, nothing to forgive."

His words made her heart stir. Actor, hero, spy, Jamie's favorite. Man of honor, they'd called him in Italy. Harry had honored him, been like a boy in his worship of him. There was that in her regard for him, respect.

"May I call on her? Allow me to call on her tonight."

She liked that, the way he pushed for what he wanted.

"I do not know how much time I have," he said.

"She'll be at St. James's Palace. Won't that be dangerous?"

"I like the danger."

"And if they arrest Rochester?"

He stopped smiling.

"I'll be late."

She took the rose-a-ruby, and before she could speak, he was gone. She was alone again in the chamber. Later, on her way to the carriage, she saw a bloom of it atop a gravestone, as if waiting for her. She went to it, stood a moment reading the words carved there in the stone: "Honor is like an island, rugged and without a beach; once we have left it, we can never return."

Harsh words, untrue. She'd left honor and returned. So must others.

The sweetest wooing she'd ever know was about to begin.

CHAPTER 49

Three weeks later, at the end of August, a pleasant twilight descended over the first day of Bartholomew Fair in London. The open square of Smithfield Market, at the northeastern edge of the city, was filled with tents and booths. A cattle and sheep market, Smithfield was surrounded by narrow streets and houses that crept up from St. Paul's Cathedral and Aldersgate Street, and it was the center for this fair, celebrated for as long as anyone could remember.

A bedlam of sights and sounds, everywhere were tents and crude wooden booths in which, for a coin, one could see puppet masters, the woman with the beard, the dancing dog, the fortune-teller—and plays. Outside the tents, acrobats walked daringly high in the air across ropes strung from one booth to another. Anyone and everyone came to Bartholomew Fair, from the boatmen who made their living rowing up and down the river to the Prince and Princess of Wales themselves.

Looking for the tent in which Slane would perform, Barbara stopped to watch a masked harlequin dance to the sound of a flute. The harlequin wore a wonderful costume, diamond-shaped patches of different colors, and Barbara felt happy, like a child. There was so much to see, to do, and in another hour she would be in a crowded tent, one of the many watching Slane. She loved to watch him.

The way he walked, held his head, smiled, pleased her. How much she liked him. Liking, respect, desire: what a powerful mix of feelings. Sometime this night, he would find her—he always found her—and take her somewhere quiet—he always knew somewhere quiet. He would hold her hands in his as he told her of his boyhood in France, of James and all he felt for him; and she, in turn, would talk of Tamworth and her marriage and Virginia. And they would end with kisses; it was as if they put everything they did not yet say into those kisses; she dreamed at night of those kisses. They had so little time together. He was gone for days on end. When he appeared, he looked exhausted. I call on the faithful, he said, and offer them aid. Then he would be off, again, for more days at a time.

Rochester was not arrested; no Jacobites were. There was the possibility that all would simply fade away. So Aunt Shrew said that Walpole couldn't make good his threats. That they'd won. By October, when Parliament began, this would simply be an embarrassment to the ministry, something they could not prove, a festering sore upon the body of this reign, she said.

That meant Jane was safe, and Gussy and Wart, and he whom she now waited to see, Slane. It meant Walpole would be dismissed. That was the rumor again. Was it so simple, that Robin would so soon be out of office? She wanted to crow at how easy it was, far easier than building Devane Square again.

The King had told her he wished her to become a lady-in-waiting to his granddaughters. It was official, everyone knew. It was a triumph. Her grandmother was proud, told her so, told her she continued a tradition her great-grandmothers began. Her mother was beside herself. Even Aunt Abigail gave stiff congratulations. I at last do as I am supposed to? Barbara had asked her. Yes, replied Abigail. Her mother's townhouse, where Barbara stayed when she was not at the palace, was filled with callers.

Wonderful, said Carlyle, who was her guide in this. Act docile and obedient; quietly remark against those you wish to harm, so that your words are like tiny drops of poison.

I do not know if I can be docile and obedient, she said. You must, he replied, if you want what you want. Look at the Princess of Wales, how clever she is, how strong. Yet she never appears too openly so, for she knows the men in her life would crush her, despise her, stop listening. You will not get what you desire from the King or his son another way.

Gideon Andreas circled like a hawk above Devane Square, but the circling did not frighten her much. Her position at court, her favor with the King, protected her.

Philippe was gone from London, disappeared.

And in the midst of all, was this romance with Slane.

Barbara laughed a little, now, thinking what her mother, her aunt, Tony would say to her treacherous liaison with a Jacobite when troops to fight Ormonde were yet in Hyde Park. You build with one hand and try to destroy with another, her grandmother would have said. Barbara knew it, did not understand it yet, simply followed her heart, which began to love this man in a way unlike what she'd felt for anyone before, even Roger. Roger she had loved with her girl's heart. Slane she was beginning to love with a woman's heart, in which the girl had a part, but was not the whole. This love was deeper, more complex: If she gave herself to him, everything would change. Somewhere deep inside herself she knew that: The place at court, the rebuilding of Devane Square, all would shift because of alliance to him. She could accept the shifts, but others in her life would not be pleased.

Someone touched her arm. Wart. Before she could speak, he was dragging her toward a tent. Upon a crude board scaffolding set up overhead outside the tent, Slane and an actress performed just enough of the play to entice anyone passing to buy a ticket. Near them, another actor blew upon a trumpet every few moments to attract attention.

Slane, gesturing with a sword in one hand, holding the actress with his other arm, declaiming his love for Helen, his determination to take the city of Troy, looked down and saw Barbara and Wharton.

His mind went to this night, to the later hours, when he would be with her. She filled his thoughts, as much as they could be filled past the endless waiting to see if there was to be anything to come out of Walpole's special, select committee to investigate the invasion. It was as if King George had great suspicions but very little proof. Already, some here were puffing up their feathers again, talking invasion, taking up the threads of the plot again.

"Bab," said Wharton, "the Bishop of Rochester has been arrested."

"When?" In a single moment her world tipped.

"This morning."

Fool, thought Barbara, furiously, I am a fool. I thought because nothing was happening that nothing would. "Are you safe?"

"I have no idea. He is already in the Tower. They took him this afternoon, in his own carriage rather than a state barge. Walpole was afraid a mob would form to defend him. People are gathering at the Tower even now, outside its walls. The Bishop was still in his dressing gown this morning when they came. An undersecretary of state, and messengers, burst into his study at Westminster. They rummaged through every drawer and cupboard. They even took the paper from his close stool. He was not allowed to dress, but went in his dressing gown to the Cockpit. Walpole and his committee accused him of high treason."

High treason. The penalty was beheading.

Death.

She felt the flesh on her arms prickle, the hair at the back of her neck rise. Not an echo of this from the King and the Duchess of Kendall, from Robin and Lord Townshend, whom she'd seen only yesterday. She, who should know, forgot what sharks swam beneath the quiet waters of court, forgot that when the waters were quietest, they were also most dangerous. To think that only a moment ago, she'd thought she had Robin where she wanted him.

"You must leave London, Wart. Take the first boat to France."

He smiled crookedly, and she saw how frightened he was. So he should be.

"That would be running away."

"If the Bishop of Rochester confesses, you will be arrested, too."

"Tell Slane for me, Bab. He must know as soon as possible."

He pointed up toward the scaffolding, and Barbara saw that Slane, the actress clinging to one arm, was declaiming his speech but watching them, too.

Wart kissed her cheek. "I mustn't be seen with him." And at Barbara's look, "Not for my sake, damn your bad thoughts of me, Bab, but for his."

He was walking away before she could answer. She looked up at Slane, anger filling her. Why did you not begin with me sooner? she thought. Why did you begin at all? Now I may never know you. I may lose you before I really have you. Damn you, Slane, damn all men everywhere with their machinations for power, their need to make war and punish and refuse to let bygones be bygones. —Wart, I may not see you again! Where are you? I didn't tell you good-bye.

Standing on tiptoe, turning round and round, she looked for him, but he was nowhere to be seen. She saw that her mother and new stepfather, Pendarves, were close—they would see her if they only turned around themselves—so she walked to the side of the tent, out of their sight. She must somehow get word to Slane. How? Then, there he was.

"I'm to tell you Rochester is arrested—"

He put his finger to his lips to hush her, took her hand, and led her wordlessly around tents until she wasn't certain where she was. Some caged pigs grunted at them. A man fumbled to light a lantern. It was not quite dark yet. The fair was transformed to something magical when lanterns were lit. The noise and din hovered somewhere behind them.

"When? When was Rochester arrested?"

"This morning, Wart said. They came for him at Westminster, took him in his dressing gown to the Cockpit, and he is now in the Tower."

She was shivering so, she could hardly speak. She saw her last words shocked Slane. What will happen to you? she thought.

"Already in the Tower?"

"So Wart says. He was taken by private carriage, so few people would know of it. Robin and Townshend do not want public outrage over this. The last time a king or queen of England tried to prosecute an official of the Church, there were riots everywhere, and the man finally had to be released. I was a girl then, but I heard about it even at Tamworth. Perhaps he will be released, Slane. Perhaps all will be well."

He wasn't listening. In his mind was a memory from boyhood, of sitting with his father, who read a tale of Rome. The book had an inked drawing of the Emperor standing in the Colosseum, an arm extended: "Let the games begin." Walpole had begun the games.

What was Barbara asking? Whether Wart would be arrested; whether he himself would. He had no idea. Rochester knew enough to bring down every Jacobite, high and low, in England.

"Can you make your way back alone?" he asked her. He must return to the tent, must continue the play—the one inside the tent, and the one outside, in life. He could feel all his senses move away from her, to protect her, to enable himself to pull away, to let her go.

Were His Majesty's soldiers even now surrounding the streets and alleys of Bartholomew Fair? What was she saying, this beautiful woman? Had he been selfish to begin a courtship? Gather ye rosebuds while ye may, / Old Time is still a-flying, / And this same flower that smiles today / Tomorrow will be dying.

"Slane, go to Devane Square. Hide there. You can pry boards off a window and stay in the church or a townhouse, if you have to."

She would risk her head for him. Was there time to kiss her the way she deserved to be kissed? Was there time to show her all that was in his heart?

He took her slim white neck in his hands, cupped her head, tilting it back slightly, as if her neck were a delicate stem and her face the full flower he must view. She allowed it, was yielding in his arms, with the same graceful yielding that Slane knew would be there in coupling. There were tears in her eyes—like stars dropped there, to his mind. One fell. He put his thumb to it, his purpose to have it mingled in his skin.

Tender woman, he thought, I have wished to know you for the rest of my life, but I do not know if I have more life. Is this good-bye? I do not know what lies ahead. Rochester can implicate me.

"I must go, Barbara. Can you make your way back?"

She nodded, and he was gone, walking off back into the fair, lost after a moment among the tents. Anger, loss, fearful uncertainty was in her. And then into her mind came a picture of Jane. She stood, then, the shock of her next thought sending her running into the fair like a thief.

Gussy would be arrested, if he had not been already.

Slane had missed his cue. It didn't matter; the actors had gone on without him, and half the audience had been drinking gin and did not care, anyway. He walked onto the stage and began his part, the entire time considering whom he must see—Louisa or Wharton, Shippen or Oxford; what he must do—get immediate messages to Paris and Jamie, alert everyone. A while later, to his surprise, the play was ending. It looked to be pretty much of a failure. The fragment of the audience that remained—most had left sometime during the performance—booed and threw the remains of their food at the actors. He could not remember saying a single line, so aware had he been the entire time of the tent's entrance, of who came in and out, so aware had he been of Rochester, alone in the Tower, faced at last with what he had most feared. Would he hold fast to his vows of silence, easy to make when a man was free, harder to keep inside a prison?

"Are you drunk or just bent on ruining me?" Colley Cibber was outraged. "Our performance was a shambles—"

Slane saw a child, one of his beggars' legion, waiting for him, and he pushed past Cibber. The child whispered that four candles burned in the windows of Westminster Abbey: the signal from Rochester that meant, "I am taken, save yourself."

Slane gave the child a coin, as into his mind slipped the realization that his good friend Gussy, Augustus Cromwell, prelate and clerk, scholar and father, best of Jacobite couriers and secretary to the Bishop of Rochester, must surely have been arrested, too.

❧

Gussy was late. He'd said he would be home by noon. Jane dipped a brush into the sand and whitener and scrubbed madly at her front step. Where was he? What had happened? Rest in the Lord, and wait patiently for him, Gussy had read to her the other evening, fret not thyself because of him who prospereth in his way, because of the man who bringeth wicked devices to pass.

Where were her servants? Did they not hear her son Thomas crying? Cat had overturned the salt cellar when cleaning the table this morning, and Betty threw her apron over her head, crying that salt fell on the master's chair. Oh, Jane would have liked to shake the pair of them to death. As it was, she put both Cat and Betty to scouring the pots with salt.

Could they not hear Thomas? Why were they not seeing to their duties? Jane put down her brush and went into the house, and sure enough, her two servants were at the hearth scrubbing pots with brushes for all the world as if a child were not crying. Amelia was pouring salt onto the floor and stepping in it.

Upstairs, Jane smoothed and kissed her child's forehead, sat with him in a chair, and began to hum, "Hush-a-bye, don't you cry, all the pretty little horses, when you wake we will take all the pretty little horses. . . ."

Where was Gussy? And now who else was crying? It was Amelia. No one cried as loudly as Amelia.

Downstairs again, Thomas in her arms, she saw Betty brushing at Amelia's face with a rag.

"Salt in her eyes," said Betty over Amelia's roars.

"I can't see, Mama!"

Jane dipped a rag in the bucket that held their drinking water, gave Thomas to Betty, put the rag to Amelia's eyes.

"Can't see, can't see—"

"There, now, yes, you can. All we need is more water."

"I hate you." Amelia turned on Betty. "She put salt in my eye."

"I never—"

"Hush! No one thinks you put salt in Amelia's eyes. Be quiet, Amelia. Give me Thomas, and finish the pots. Where is Winifred?"

But Jane saw, even as she spoke, placid Winifred under a chair, and Harry Augustus slept in his basket. At least two of her children were bearable. She took Thomas and Amelia, who were quiet now, but sullen in a way boding no good, outside, to the garden. The vines she and Slane had planted were bedraggled now, ready to be cut down. There was lettuce and cabbage, turnips and marigolds, parsley. She set Thomas down where she could keep an eye on him, gave Amelia a stick with which to dig, and then picked up the hoe and began to loosen the ground.

Fly, ladybird, fly, north, south, or east or west, fly where the man is found that I love best.

By dusk, she had cleaned all the steps, swept the hearth, sung ten lullabies, made seedcakes, churned butter, herded in her cow, and fed the chickens. By dusk, her heart was a sick thing in her breast.

Her children and her two servants sat around the hearth fire now, eating supper, bread and milk and jam. Jane stepped outside to walk by the river. As she walked, she made her plans. Tomorrow, she'd put on her best gown and hat and walk to the village of Richmond and catch a rowboat at the river steps. Once in London, she would go to Westminster Abbey, and if he was not there, then to Saylor House. He is disappeared, she would say to the Duke of Tamworth. He had been kind to them, for Barbara's sake; he would help her. And she'd go to Barbara. Barbara would know what to do.

Yes, she thought, standing at the river but not seeing it, that is a good plan. Things are happening, Gussy had whispered to her the last time she was in his chamber at Westminster. Some of the others—Goring, Sample—are going to make their escape. The plan has Slane's blessing.

Do we escape? She could not imagine leaving her life here.

Gussy did not answer.

Turning back to the house, she saw a horse tethered outside the chapel of ease, and she began to run, her heart rising up like a bird in her breast. Gussy was home. She forgot to curtsy to the altar inside the chapel, could only take him and hug him over and over.

"Where were you? I was so worried—"

"I was detained. They questioned me."

He was trembling.

"Who? When?"

"This morning. They've arrested the Bishop, Jane, and I thought they were going to arrest me, but they allowed me to leave. They looked in my chamber for letters, but I had had time to burn them."

She was trembling, an involuntary trembling that would not stop.

"Robert Walpole himself came to me and told me I would hang on the gibbet and then be broken on the rack, if I lied. He told me I would be buried in the deepest, darkest dungeon he could find for what was in the letters they'd found in the Bishop's chamber, in my writing, he said. Then he smiled like a different man, Janie, and said that if I aided him, he would see I rose to be Bishop myself one day. 'Tell me what you know,' he said. 'Save yourself, because the others are doomed.' I told him, 'I am innocent. My father-in-law is Sir John Ashford; my patron is the Duke of Tamworth.' I think that is why they allowed me to go—I mentioned the Duke's name."

"And the Bishop of Rochester?"

"In the Tower. I must leave London, leave England. Some of us got away safely yesterday. Slane has been urging it. I think that is why Walpole ordered the Bishop arrested—he was afraid Rochester would leave England."

How calm she felt, below the screaming disbelief of this. Leave England? This was not happening, except that it was, like Jeremy's dying.

"We will say a prayer, Gussy."

The only thing worse than Jeremy's dying would be his father's hanging. Gussy must leave. She must face that, that he must leave.

"The one you said to me when Jeremy died. Do you remember that, my love, how you held me in your arms and whispered these words. I hated you, at that moment, hated God, too, but I loved the words. 'The Lord is my shepherd; I shall not want.' He will guide us, Gussy. 'He maketh me to lie down in green pastures: he leadeth me beside the still waters.' Still waters, Gussy, green pastures, ours for the asking. 'He restoreth my soul: he leadeth me in the paths of righteousness for his name's sake.' You said that to follow King James was what God guided you to do. 'Yea, though I walk through the valley of the shadow of death, I will fear no evil: for thou art with me; thy rod and thy staff they comfort me. Thou preparest a table before me in the presence of mine enemies. Thou anointest my head with—' What's that?"

They heard the jingle of horses' harnesses, horses trotting by.

"Slane always comes alone—"

They held hands tightly a moment.

"Leave now," Jane said, "this moment—"

"Augustus Cromwell."

The voice echoed in the chapel, bouncing off the stone walls. Gussy stood, as did Jane. A soldier was framed in the chapel's doorway, a lantern in his hand.

"In the name of King George, I am commanded to search your house for treasonous papers and to take your person with me."

"They followed me," Gussy said. "That is why they allowed me to go, to follow me and see where I led them."

Calmly, Jane walked with her husband to their house.

It was bedlam, soldiers searching, pulling things out of cupboards and trunks, the children and her maidservants crying. Jane took a crying child and sat down in a chair near the hearth. Feathers drifted down the stairs. They were tearing up her mattress, her pillows. Burn the codebook and any letters if I am gone for more than two days, Gussy had once instructed her.

One day, said Slane.

She saw the agony in Gussy's face as he held a child in each arm and one of the guards walked back and forth across a certain section of the floor. No! thought Jane.

But a soldier lifted the loose floorboard, lifted out Jane's green leather gloves. And letters. And a book that held Jacobite codes. Jane and Gussy looked at each other. Slane had told her to wait one day, but Gussy had said two.

Fly, ladybird, fly where the man is found that I love best.

They took him away, she and the children and the servants all crying, following after, out into the night, to where the soldiers had their horses, in her garden.

"Oh, please," she and the children begged, weeping.

"Father!" the children cried.

"I beg you, have mercy, there is some mistake," she said, but they took him and rode away to London and left her there among trampled vines and weeping children. That was where Barbara found her, some time after ten of the night hour, sitting in her garden, silent and bereft, surrounded by crying children.

Slane leaped down from the horse and pounded on the Cromwells' front door with both fists. Barbara opened it, then shut it behind her, standing before him on the front step. He was startled, not expecting to see her.

"Gussy—"

"Taken."

"When?"

"This night. He was gone when I arrived. Jane has only now fallen to sleep."

"The children?"

"As well as can be expected considering soldiers tore their house apart and took their father away before their very eyes."

He heard the anger in her voice, and the deep sadness, as if she knew grief and loss well.

"Amelia screamed for an hour," she told him. "Winifred was silent, but like a clinging burr. Finally, she whispered, breathlessly, as if she were afraid to say it, 'Bad men took my father away.'"

There on the steps with Slane, Barbara put her hands to her face. I won't cry, she thought. Enough tears have been shed this night.

Slane pulled her down the stairs, pushed her against the house so that her back was against it, and, with a kind of sigh, leaned into her.

My beloved, my darling, my heart, Barbara thought, whither thou goest, I will go; and where thou lodgest, I will lodge. You are not taken, Slane, not yet.

"Why do you cry?"

"Jane is my"—her voice broke—"the children cried so—you are here."

"Barbara," he said, and then he was kissing her, greedily, selfishly, as if there were no time for all that must be done. And there was not. He kissed her neck, her ears, and then, wonderfully, how clever he was to know just what she wanted, her mouth again. More, she thought. You are alive, and well, and now there is no time. So let us make time. More. He raised his head, and in the dark, she could half see, half feel the smile on his face. She traced it with her fingers. She loved his mouth, the shape of it.

"I love you," he said. He said it in French, in Gaelic, in Italian.

She began to laugh. She'd never felt more alive in her life.

"Say no to me now, Barbara, for I have no manners left to stop if you should later want it."

"Yes."

"Say yes to me again, so I am certain you mean it."

"Yes."

He took her hand and led her. Thoughts whirled in her like small bats: You're mad, Barbara, you never do this lightly, you'll regret it, we may never see each other again, you don't want to be grieving over a man who has to flee England, grieving over a lover locked in the Tower, grieving over a beloved beheaded. For once in your life, Barbara, be sensible, she was thinking, but they were in some shed, and he was piling hay with one hand, the other holding her, as if she would run away. How little he knew her. And then with great clarity she thought the words she wished to live by: Keep thy heart with all diligence, yes, her heart, her mind, her soul must do what they must do. The bats settled their wings and were still.

Her fingers fumbled with buttons, with hooks, with the hundred and one intricacies of her jacket and dress, hose and garters, the traps and intricacies of a woman of fashion. He had pulled off his coat and flung it on the hay. He was saying her name, and the way he said it, the desire in his voice, was enough, it was right; her heart went upward to meet that desire the way a dove does its mate calling. And then he was pulling her into the hay beside him, and there wasn't time to think anymore, there was only time to feel, to touch, taste, be with this man, join him in that deepest of joinings, the one with the most promise, the one with the most heartbreak. It had begun to rain, and the smell of rain, damp leaves, musk, shadow, came into their lovemaking. They were both still half dressed.

Against ever-expanding bands of sensation, Slane was aware of different things: her arms cool and smooth, her thighs sleek and silky, the arch of her neck, her kisses on his face, dream kisses, rain kisses, raining down. Like the earth outside, he was parched for this, and he would have it, every bit of it, as much as he wanted and more. There was no stopping. He put his hands to her hips to move her against him, lost himself to the movement made. The rain cooled the place where they lay, and the sound of it was mixed, steady, and drumming, into his heartbeat, into the rhythm between them. There was nothing else—no failure, no fear, no arrests, no friends gone, perhaps lost forever like fathers and brothers before them— there was only this woman who held him, whom he held.

"What of a child?" he managed to ask, to see what she would have him do, before it was too late and he could do nothing.

"No children for me, Slane," she said, very softly.

Later, he would explore the vibration he heard in her voice. Now, he closed his eyes to the pleasure. She was whispering his name, biting a little of his ear, saying "Ah" in a soft voice as she moved, kissing his neck, his ear, his cheek, his mouth, running her tongue over his lips, across his teeth. He twisted his hands in her hair. Barbara, you are a wanton witch who has my heart, he thought, I knew you would be generous in love. And then he stopped thinking; there was only her, only him, only this between them, and it wasn't enough, there must be more, there would be more, he must have her again and again. He said her name as he moved toward that which his mother called the losing of souls, the intertwining of man and woman and desire and God into one.

When it was over,—the frenzy of the end left both of them laughing, then silent, chastened—he held her close. I cannot let her go, and I must, he thought. He stroked her hair, her bare back; the riding jacket had left her person, and somehow they'd pulled off her stays, in their need to touch each other's flesh. Into his mind came the knowledge that this act was not random, that her being here when he'd arrived was not random, that there was now an allegiance between them. He remembered the day Jamie had knighted him, one of the proudest days in his life. His mother had wept, and his heart had been so full that he'd thought it would burst. Scots pipers had piped a song of valor and war, and the sound of the pipes rising up in the vaulted church hall was as piercing, as deep as walking into war beside men you loved. He'd been fourteen. I pledge you my undying loyalty, he'd told Jamie, and meant it. He kissed the top of Barbara's head. She, too, had his loyalty.

That which was, intruded. Gussy, Rochester. Jane asleep in the house. Everything that must be done. She must have felt his thoughts, because she sat up and began to pull her stays about her. He wished he could see her face clearly, but he couldn't.

"Let me help you," he said, and together they tied the stays. At one point, he took her hands in his and kissed them, and she moved toward him and they held one another a long moment. How small you are, how slight, delicious woman, Slane thought. She put on her jacket, he his shirt, and, holding hands, they walked out of the barn.

In the house, she lit a candle, and now he could see her face. At the expression upon it, he said, "I love you."

She ran to him and put her head to his chest, a movement that touched him, made something in him move and settle deeply, at the unspoken covenant between them.

"Come and see Jane," she said and led him to the bedchamber where Jane slept, all the children in the bed with her, nestled as close as they could get. Back in Jane's parlor they talked in whispers.

"I want to ride on to Tamworth," Barbara said. "I must warn Sir John, tell him about Gussy."

"He may already be arrested."

"So he may, but I must make the effort. I was ready to leave when you arrived." She smiled, touched his face a moment. "I will leave now, if you will stay here for Jane. She and I have talked. She wants to go to London in the morning. She has an aunt there with whom she can stay. She'll do more for Gussy in London than anywhere else. She has to begin the rounds of calling on people, Slane, asking for favors, for support."

Yes, Barbara must do her duty, too. For all that was said of her, for all the duels, flirts, mistakes, she was a person of duty. "What did they take from here?"

"A codebook and letters."

Gussy will hang, Slane thought.

"Will they behead him?"

He didn't answer. Barbara stood up and walked to the door and opened it. He found her leaning against her horse, crying.

"Don't tell Jane what you believe," she said. She put her hand on her horse's pommel; Slane helped her swing up in the saddle, then kept one hand around the ankle of her boot.

"You can ride safely at night?"

"There's enough moon to see. I will be careful. I rode all over one end of Virginia for weeks looking for my servant. Take care of her, Slane. I've written a letter to my mother, telling her I had to go to Tamworth for a few days. See that she gets it, or she'll tear London apart searching for me. Remind Jane to call on Tony, on Aunt Shrew, to enlist their aid. She and I made a list of those in London who might help her."

"Go with God, Barbara."

"With God. I like that. A friend in Virginia told me that the Lord would give His angels charge over me. Good-bye, Slane. If you have to leave London before I return, please let me know—not where you go, of course, but that you are gone. Otherwise, I will fret and think you in the Tower."

Spoken as if they'd not just held one another in their arms, as if he were gone already. She held out her hand. He took it, held it tight.

"I would never leave you without a farewell."

His reward was a smile, dazzling, her heart in it.

"I'll take you down from that horse and make love to you again if you look at me in such a way."

She laughed, leaned down, nuzzled her head against his shoulder, kissed his ear. "Is that a threat or a promise?"

"A promise, Barbara."

"Good friends call me Bab."

"May I call you Bab?"

Lighthearted talk between them, except that it was not.

"You may call me anything you please."

"Then I'll call you Beloved."

The look she gave him was worth everything. When I die, my last memory will be this expression on your face, Barbara, of tenderness, fierceness, and devotion, all mine.

He did not want to let go of her hand, but he did.

CHAPTER 50

A few days later, Barbara unpinned her hat and set it wearily on the table in the hall of her mother's townhouse. Her legs and backside hurt. She had been in the saddle for too long. Take my carriage, her grandmother had begged, but being inside a carriage for two days, at the mercy of broken wheels, rutted lanes, or lame horses, would have driven her mad. Better, faster, to ride by horseback. So her grandmother had insisted that Tim go with her. Poor Tim was even now in the stable, groaning at the thought of having to ride back toward Tamworth tomorrow.

The house was quiet, almost as if no one was home. Good. Solitude would give her time to quiet herself; a bath and a rest would refresh her, soothe her, strengthen her to face whatever was happening. Sir John was not arrested—not yet, anyway. He was on his way to London, to see what he could do, as a man with many friends in both the House of Commons and the House of Lords. We must play it as Walpole's word against Gussy's, as a ploy of Walpole's overweening ambition, he said.

In the bedchamber, Thérèse was at a window, sewing beads onto one of Barbara's gowns. One glance at Thérèse's face, and Barbara said, "She did not tell you I sent a note to say all was well, did she? Don't cry, Thérèse. I am so sorry to have fretted you. It did not occur to me she would not tell you. Help me to undress. I am so tired. I have been on horseback for days. Tell me the news—what is happening? Who has been arrested?"

"The Reverend Mr. Cromwell—"

"Yes, I know. Who else, Thérèse?"

"Lord Russel."

Charles. Charles arrested as a Jacobite? There must be some mistake. To have committed himself to Jacobitism required a loyalty, a steadfastness Charles did not possess.

"No one else?"

"No."

Thank God. Barbara went to the pile of invitations and letters on a table, and sifted through them, opening at once the one whose handwriting she did not not know. I love you, it said in French; there was other writing in a language she did not understand. The letter was signed with an *L*. His given name was Lucius. My mother calls me Luc, he had told her. Someday you must, also. She traced the *L* with her finger. He had not been arrested. Rochester held fast, and Gussy, but there had been no question about Gussy. Perhaps not about Rochester, either.

"Tommy Carlyle has called for you several times, left notes," said Thérèse, "and there have been messages from the Prince and King."

Barbara was writing a quick note: "I am home, please call on me at your earliest convenience. Bab." She opened her mouth to tell Thérèse to take it to the theater, then quickly changed her mind. She must be as wary, as careful as ever she'd been in her life. My life of deceit deepens. I hope I don't lose myself in it.

She opened some of the other notes. "My divine," wrote Carlyle, "a position as serving woman to the Princess of Wales is open. I suggest you put forth your own servant. It has come to my ears that the Princess would like to have her among her serving women. The positioning of pawns is as important as one's own position. It would be a favor you did the Princess, to offer someone who is so dear to you."

No, thought Barbara. Not Thérèse.

She opened a note from Sir Gideon Andreas, who told her he had the honor of holding two large notes upon her estate and would like to speak with her, at her earliest convenience, about them. So the hawk took aim, did he? He chose his moment well. She was distracted by this plot, by her lovemaking with a hero.

"Has there been any protest over the Bishop's arrest, Thérèse?"

"All the first night he was in the Tower, people gathered outside—a great crowd, it is said, who were there all the night. It is an attack against the Church, people are saying."

Good, thought Barbara. That won't help Robin, to have people saying he tries to destroy the Church of England.

"Your mother wishes to see you, now." It was Clemmie, standing in the doorway, blocking the servants who brought water for Barbara's bath.

"Tell Mother I will come to see her in an hour."

"If it was me, I'd go now."

Thérèse brought forward a shawl and gave it to Barbara, whispering: "She's been in a rage for days. She fainted when she heard the news about Lord Russel."

Barbara nodded and went out the door.

Thérèse stood a moment in the empty room, then began to pick up the notes scattered haphazardly across a table. She could not help seeing her own name. She spread open Carlyle's note.

Barbara opened her mother's bedchamber door just in time to see Diana slap Clemmie.

"Won't come to me now?"

Diana's voice was shrill. Barbara knew the tone well.

"I'll beat you until you are bloody, you great, fat fool. You go right back and tell her I require her presence immediately. Tell her I demand it."

"I'm here—never mind beating your servant, Mother."

Diana swung around to take in the sight of Barbara, standing there in a chemise and shawl.

"Do messages from the King, from the Prince of Wales, mean nothing to you? Are you so dowried, so moneyed that you do not need anyone? Carlyle has called three times, ready to brim over with the news he has. Where did you go? Were you with a lover?"

Barbara didn't answer or move.

"I told everyone you were ill. It was all I could think of. This is no time to disappear from London, when everyone is frightened at what may happen next. Charles has been arrested, have you heard that? Have you no feelings for that? Where were you?"

Her mother had crossed the chamber as she spoke, raised her hand to slap her. Barbara caught it, held the wrist tight.

"If you strike me, I walk away from this chamber, from you, and never return."

"Walk away! Leave me! Do you think I care a fig what you do!" Diana spat out the words.

Halfway down the hall, Barbara heard Clemmie call after her.

"She's weeping, Mistress Barbara, go see to her."

"No."

"Please, Mistress Barbara. She is not herself." Then in a whisper, "She's with child."

"I don't believe you!"

"It's true, Mistress Barbara."

Back in the bedchamber, Barbara saw that her mother lay upon her bed, saw how white Diana's face was, how pinched in at the nostrils. There was something tired and strained about her mouth. Barbara sat down on the bed, took her mother's hand in hers. Diana allowed it.

The hand was swollen, so that the rings cut into the flesh. Barbara had a sudden memory of being a girl, of looking at the rings on her mother's fingers and wondering why the fingers were so fat. They were only fat at certain times. Her mother would descend on Tamworth, cursing and screaming, slapping them all, then disappear again; six months later she'd return for long enough to have a baby. After a while, Barbara hadn't minded the rages, or the slaps, because she knew they meant she'd have another brother or sister to love.

There was to be a child. She could feel the meaning of the words beginning to sink deep inside her, into a place of joy.

She began to pull off Diana's rings, to chafe the flesh of the hands and fingers.

"Why will you wear these when they must hurt your fingers? Are you with child?"

"Do I show it already? Of course I do. I look like a cow. I hate it, hate myself, hate this child. I don't want another, Barbara."

But I do, thought Barbara. Sweet Jesus, dear God in heaven, all the others were mine. This one will be, too. We're to have a child. Suddenly, words the Gypsy had said at Tamworth came into her mind: Babies be everywhere. Barbara had been sitting by herself, thinking about Hyacinthe, feeling sorrow at all that was not to be.

"Why on earth do you think I married, for the love of Penny's snuff stains?" said her mother. "Now I will grow huge and suffer to have a bawling, red-faced urchin. I tried everything to rid myself of it, everything. And you, the world in your hands, just up and leave London in the midst of a crisis when everyone—everyone—is under suspicion, and we must all be so careful. They know Gussy Cromwell is your friend, that Charles was your lover. It doesn't look good for you to disappear at the arrests. So you must change your gown and go to St. James's Palace at once. And you must call at Leicester House. The Prince has been most insistent to see you. I hope you weren't with a lover, Barbara. This is the time for discretion. Carlyle says he has an interesting proposition for you. Take care, Barbara. Position yourself while you still can, while you still have your youth and your beauty upon your side. If I die in childbed, I want him named Richard Alexander Pendarves."

"You are not going to die in childbirth, but you very well may give birth to a girl."

"I won't. It's male. It makes me quite tired, Barbara, quite feeble, in a way that none of the rest of you did."

Barbara put her hand to her mother's abdomen.

Miraculous, that life should be held inside this. She felt a sudden surge of love for her mother, ruthless, vain, treacherous as she was.

There was to be a child, out of Diana, for Barbara. Thank you, Mother. All things are possible, said Colonel Perry, especially joy.

"I have an amusing book for you to read. I found it at Tamworth, about one Moll Flanders of Newgate. I will have Thérèse bring you the book. She will read it to you. You'll like Moll, Mother. She has no honor of any kind."

"You must offer Thérèse to the Princess of Wales. It won't make her less your enemy, but it will placate her for a time, and it will give you a spy in their household. You need a spy. The Prince still desires you, Barbara. He and I talked of it only the other day. He is ready to offer you whatever you wish. To be mistress of the future King of England is no small thing."

So: Carlyle had told her mother about Thérèse in an attempt to force her to do what he thought best. She was not to be forced. Did people not understand that?

"Are you still brooding about Robin?" said Diana, sitting up, taking Barbara's chin in her hand, pinching it hard. "Listen to me. You mix in what can be very dangerous to you. Accept what you have already: a place in the King's household, the fine reduced. Robin swears he will see it done."

"I've heard otherwise."

"He swore it to me, on this"—Diana touched her abdomen—"our child."

This child is Robin's? thought Barbara. Well, whose did I think it would be?

"He is happy you are to be in the King's household. He counts you as an ally there. Be his ally. Rise with him, for I tell you, Barbara, he is on the rise. I can smell it. He will become one of the King's foremost ministers if he can prosecute Rochester. Smile and be beautiful. More will be yours, much more, if you bend a little and forget much."

Barbara lifted her chin up and away from her mother's hand. I will do what I will do what I will do, she thought but did not say.

It was evening, and she walked down Pall Mall. There was Saylor House. Had Jane called upon Tony there yet? Barbara bought an apple from the apple woman who stood under the statue at the center of Charing Cross and bit into it, watching children toss stones and mud at someone who had been sentenced to the pillory.

The man's head and hands were exposed through holes cut in the pillory's wooden frame. A common punishment, the pillory was a punishment whose severity was very much dependent upon the crowd's mood. A man or woman might stand in the pillory and not be bothered all day. Then again, anything from rotten fruit to pieces of jagged brick might be thrown. To judge by the blood upon this one, the crowd had no liking for him.

"Barbara . . ."

Was someone calling her name? The sound was so harsh, so hoarse, she was not certain. She looked around, to the Royal Mews on her left, to Northumberland House across from it, toward passing sedan chairs. The apple woman pointed a crooked finger.

Barbara walked carefully, gingerly, toward the pillory. The face of the poor creature in it was covered with blood. His wig had been stolen. He could barely hold himself upright. "Sodomite," read the crude sign hung around his neck. No wonder the crowd had been so brutal to him. Likely he'd been selling himself around the streets of Covent Garden, and the beadles had arrested him. But how did he know her name?

"Barbara," the creature said hoarsely, "help me. . . ."

She stepped closer.

It was Tommy Carlyle under that blood. Horror filled her.

She shouted at the children to stop throwing things, pulled the sign from his neck, tossing it away. She put her hands to his face and held it up. She would never have recognized him. One eye was swollen shut; his nose was broken.

"Help me, Barbara."

She stamped her feet at the children, who were like little birds of prey, waiting for her to go away.

"Here." She flung coins out of her underskirt pocket. "Throw nothing else at him, and there will be more for you."

Find the house of the magistrate who had signed the paper for this punishment, have the man unlock him from this thing—that was what she must do. She began to ask people passing by, but they shook their heads to her question. She went to the apple woman, but the woman shrugged. What do I do? she thought. She half ran, half walked toward Saylor House.

Tony was in the hall. He avoided her whenever he could, would not agree with her about Robin. But he was still her cousin, still family.

"Tony, Tommy Carlyle is in the pillory at Charing Cross. He is bloody and broken. We have to do something. His neck will break if he faints, and I am afraid for him."

"I'll find the magistrate. You stay here and wait."

Good Tony, dear Tony, like the Tony of old, there when she needed him. Already he was calling for his carriage to be readied. She slipped out in the confusion of servants coming into the hall and went back to the pillory.

Across one of Carlyle's eyebrows was a cut open nearly to the bone. What must have been thrown at him? thought Barbara. People went into a frenzy sometimes, throwing and throwing. Some had died from the actions of the crowd.

"Don't leave me again," Carlyle said.

"I won't."

She sat against the railing of the fountain, waiting. Every now and again, she stood and stopped people from throwing things. Tony was taking a long time. She walked a little down Pall Mall, then came back to walk a little down Whitehall Street, but there was no sign of Tony. Dusk was here. Carlyle was weaker. If he passed out completely, he might slowly strangle. Where was Tony? How long had she been here? Dark was here now.

"Barbara," Carlyle said, hoarsely, "I am going to die. I want you to know Robin did this to me. Avenge me, Barbara."

"You're not going to die. I'm going to fetch someone right this moment to break the locks. Wait for me half an hour. Keep your eyes open half an hour, that is all I ask. Will you do that, stay alert for half of an hour?"

Tim would do it, Tim could break the locks, and Tony would see that there was no trouble over it.

Within the promised half hour, Tim was hitting at the locks on the pillory with a iron mallet. It took only a few blows before they were mangled, half hanging from the wood. Carlyle sank to the ground, groaning, beginning to weep. It took Tim and Pendarves to put him in Pendarves's carriage, but once they were inside, Tim drove off with rattling speed. What they were doing could have them all fined, at the least, put into a gaol at the worst.

Some time later, with a servant holding up a lantern so that he could see in the dark, Tony walked slowly around the pillory. The top of the frame, which held the head and hands, hung from the bottom half by a single hinge. Where would she go? he thought. She'd go where she felt safest. Then, he knew.

Barbara bathed the cuts on Carlyle's face. They were in the kitchen of one of the townhouses at Devane Square. Dear Pendarves. He'd seen her talking to Tim, wanted to know what was wrong, and on impulse she'd told him. Now he was in the thick of this.

Carlyle's face was a mangle, the bruises on his throat dark.

"What happened?" Barbara asked.

"I was in a house, a certain kind of house . . ." He couldn't talk above a whisper.

He meant a Mollie house, where men went to buy pleasure with other men.

"And bailiffs came—not the first time, mind you. A few coins, and I go my way. But this time, they were uninterested in my coins and we were taken to the house of the justice of the peace, late as it was, and it must have been past midnight. Once there—you must remember I'd had much wine—I began to realize that I was the only one, other than the Mollies. Where are the others? I thought. Am I that befuddled? I was not the only customer when the evening began. I was fined, but there was no coin in my pocket to pay. Again, strange. I had had coin when the evening began."

"Don't speak anymore. I can see it hurts you to talk," said Barbara.

"No, I want to say this. I was sentenced to the pillory, led there in the night and locked in. In the morning, I watched more than one man recognize me and look away. By noon, I doubt my own mother could have known me. I might have died. All day, the crowd threw things. The sign telling my crime, someone read it to them, and once they began throwing, they did not stop. For a time, I quite lost my reason. 'Am I not one of God's creatures,' I screamed, 'the same as you?'"

Carlyle ground his teeth. "Robin has paid me back ten times over for my talk against him. I should have known he would. The justice is a particular henchman of his."

"Surely, Walpole did not do this," said Pendarves.

They heard the sound of another carriage. Tim had time only to walk in the kitchen door and say, "The Duke of Tamworth," before Tony strode in. He barely glanced at Carlyle.

"Did it not occur to you to wait for me?" He spoke only to Barbara. "The magistrate was not at home. I ended by going to Chelsea and seeing Walpole. I have in my pocket his paper freeing Carlyle."

"Who did you think ordered this in the first place?" she said to him.

"Nonsense."

"Your own man says so. Tell him, Carlyle."

Carlyle began to speak, but Tony cut him short.

"Walpole sends his express regards to Carlyle. He could not sign the paper to free him quickly enough; he even offered to come with me to see it done. Do not tell me he is the villain in this. Barbara, you must think about your position now. What if the watch had caught you?"

"Old men, easily outrun."

"Don't be flippant. Why didn't you wait for me?"

"I didn't think he would survive, Tony. He told me he was dying. You weren't there."

"You are too impetuous and headstrong."

"Why are you so angry at me?"

"My brother-in-law is in the Tower for treason, my candidate for Tamworth has been pilloried for sodomy, and my cousin, whose reputation is shaky at best, cannot even allow me to handle the matter but must make a rescue reminiscent of a highwayman. I thought you were ill. Your mother told everyone you were ill. And yet you act as if you had the strength of ten men."

"Tony, you have the paper from Robin. There can be no scandal now. He is freed. I simply freed him a little early. Is that it? Are you angry because you weren't a part of it? But you are. I knew you would see that there was no trouble. I knew you would make it right. And you have."

"I don't want to always be making things right for you—"

"Your Grace," said Pendarves, "Mr. Carlyle is bleeding very badly."

"I want to talk with you about Gussy," said Barbara.

"Not now."

"When? He is your man, too, just as Tommy is. You have a duty to them, Tony."

"Don't talk to me of duty, Barbara. I know my duty."

Outside, as they helped Carlyle into the carriage, Pendarves assured Tony he would see to Barbara.

"Try to keep her from making any scandals until she begins her duties as lady-in-waiting," Tony said to him.

"Yes, Your Grace. I'll do that, Your Grace."

In the carriage, Tony pulled off his jacket, wadded it into a ball, and put it against the cut in Carlyle's head. It was, as Pendarves had said, bleeding far too much.

I wish she were gone from here, he thought. I wish I did not love her. Your man, she lectured him, as if he did not know duty. Robin betrayed me, she said, this when he was now married into a family allied with Walpole's. Walpole had been patient when Tony had approached him about the fine yet again. I am like a lovesick fool, thought Tony in the carriage, shaking his head at the thought of that scene. I did what I could, Walpole said. I always do what I can.

Sodomy, Walpole had said tonight. Carlyle's been openly punished for it now. You might think about finding a new ally, Your Grace. This one will no longer be received in certain drawing rooms. I tell you this as a favor to you. Poor Tommy, he and I were great friends once. Even though we are no longer friends, I regret that this has happened to him. Here, take this paper and release him. Tell him I am thinking of him.

Barbara should have heard Walpole. He did do his duty. God, my heart hurts, he thought. She didn't care a flip for him. He was simply, as always, her cousin Tony. The turmoil in his heart was unbearable. He almost hated her.

In the carriage, Barbara said to Pendarves, "Thank you for helping me."

Sometimes, when she couldn't sleep at night, she roamed her mother's townhouse, her mind full of all she wished to do, and there he would be, too, roaming the house. Sometimes they played cards. It was almost as if her stepfather feared to go to his bed. It was how they had come to know one another, those nightly roamings.

"I've decided I'm going to live in a townhouse," she said. "In fact, the one we were just in. I had a note from Sir Gideon. He wishes to talk to me about Devane Square."

"He is making his move to try to get the land from you," said Pendarves. "Don't let him frighten you. I've an interest in this square myself. Others do, too. The Oxfords, to the west of you, are granting building leases, though there is no rush to buy. Caution is the word these days, what with the arrests and fret over the invasion. It is a good thing for your land that the Oxfords plan to build. In twenty or thirty years, this quiet spot will be as bustling as Covent Garden or Pall Mall. You remember that when Sir Gideon comes to call. Do not sell him the land in exchange for the notes he holds."

As the carriage stopped, and a footman came to open the door, Barbara said, "I don't think it would be a good idea to tell my mother of this."

"Good God, no," said Pendarves.

Barbara opened the window, walked to the bed, left a candle burning. Robin is dangerous, she thought. I underestimate his ruthlessness. Do I want to continue this? He will hurt me as surely as he hurt Carlyle if he thinks I threaten him, and now I am head over heels into treason. He would see my head chopped off, if he had to; he'd weep copiously but see it chopped off. But then Slane was there, walking in through one of the windows, pulling off his clothes as he walked into the room, and thoughts of treason went out of her mind as she admired his body.

"Where is your dog?"

Barbara pointed toward a cupboard. Slane opened the door, picked up Harry, scratched his head.

"Behave," he said, "and you may stay."

"Am I to behave, too?" Barbara said, a shiver moving up and down her as Slane lay down beside her, took her in his arms.

"No."

"A good thing."

He was kissing a breast. "Why is that?"

"I don't think I can."

"I am a most fortunate man."

Later, Slane felt tears on her face. At once, he untangled himself and set her on her back, sprawling atop her, putting his cheek against hers.

"What is it?" He felt fierce, protective, angry with himself. "Have I hurt you? I will never forgive myself if I have hurt you in my lovemaking."

She didn't answer for a moment, only rubbed a foot against his leg. Then she told him about Tommy Carlyle.

"My King is the better man, Barbara. You ought to convert to him."

"King George is a worthy man."

"Think back about what Walpole did to Carlyle. A man's disciples reflect the man."

"And if James were king, there would be no bloodshed, no betrayals, no treacheries?"

Rochester was under strictest guard, allowed to see no one, yet he had found a way to get a note out. "I do not betray," he wrote. "I think Charles, Lord Russel does."

How much time do I have? thought Slane. Am I selfish to continue to make love to this woman when I do not know what my next moment holds? I won't let them have Gussy, he thought. If there's any way to save Gussy, I intend to find it. He won't be scapegoat for Walpole's ambition.

"Touch me, Barbara—yes, just like that, just there. How clever you are," he mocked, until she kissed the mockery away, and all he felt was desire.

In the dawn, Barbara moved from his side, found his coat, put it on, and sat in the window. Palest quartz and rose, faint azure marked the dawn. Marks from his mouth were on her legs, and she touched them one by one, thinking of how they'd been made. This, or this? he'd asked her. Here, or here? Delicious questions. Clever man. I am yours, she thought. And what are we going to do about it? She saw that he was awake, watching.

"You slept well," she said.

"Did we sleep? When? That is not what I remember. Come here, Barbara."

She dropped the coat and walked naked, surefooted and graceful, to him.

The sun was rising. A boatman called up to those on the ship that he'd take passengers to the quays now. Colonel Perry looked around for his small valise, and finding it, took it in hand to walk toward the rope ladder. Dawn showed the Tower of London and London

Bridge and many church steeples. It was a thrilling sight after the weeks of sailing. Sailor after sailor called farewell to him. He had shared his treasured peach brandy with them on the crossing as well as listened to the tales of their lives. He knew the sorrows and joys of their hearts now, prayed sincerely for each and every one of them, as they also knew.

"You'll come to dinner and allow me to introduce my wife?" said the captain of the ship. "You'll send a note to let me know where you are settled?"

Colonel Perry agreed.

"You beware London," said the captain. "It can be a cruel place."

Colonel Perry filled his mind with prayers, with God, as the boatman rowed them toward the quays. Once there, with the bustle of London around him, he thought: I am as excited as a boy.

Barbara returned from Devane Square, where she'd walked to look at the Oxford land. Pendarves said he had word that the Earl of Scarborough was going to begin building again on Hanover Square, to the south of her. He said the Earl of Burlington was going to break up the farmland behind his house on Piccadilly and put in streets, a certain sign there would be building. She'd also walked in Soho Square, a fashionable older square in the area. The Duke of Monmouth, a bastard son of Charles II, had lived there. He had rebelled against his uncle, James II, and been beheaded. Slane had spoken of it this morning, telling her the story: The ax was dull, and after the first blow to his neck Monmouth had stood and rebuked the executioner before laying his head upon the block again. Extraordinary courage, Slane had said. What you and I must have. You must let no one, not even your maidservant, know of me. I can stand my own head falling to the ax, but not yours, Barbara. I will ask no treason from you—he stroked her face—except to have your love. You have my word on that. Be kinder to your cousin Tony, Barbara. He loves you. How long did they have, she and Slane?

An old man sat before the gate of her mother's townhouse, atop one of the bags and valises around him. Even before he stood and took off his hat, Barbara knew who it was. Colonel Perry. She smiled. He must have come to keep charge over her. He could not have chosen a better time. How delightful, how wonderful, how right.

❧

In the Tower of London, in the Lion's Tower, Charles spoke impatiently to the one-eyed servant who brought in his food. He'd been promised by Walpole that he should have the best of treatment. It was a fair trade, considering what he knew.

"Damn your eyes, if that broth is cold, I will send you back for more."

Slane took off the wig he wore, pulled away the eye patch, and knocked Charles to the floor. When Charles struggled to rise, Slane put his knee in his back, an arm around his throat. The other hand held a knife.

"Give me one good reason," he said, "why I should not slit your throat and leave you for dead where you lie."

CHAPTER 51

The priest came to bless the sugar pots, to celebrate that harvest was done. He smiled at Hyacinthe, nodded his head. They had a secret. Hyacinthe knew enough Latin to intrigue, to piece together his story. Madame will pay for my freedom twice over, he had told the priest at the end of it, painting a grand and wonderful picture of her beauty, her fame, her generosity. I am her favorite servant. Write a letter to Lady Devane, First Curle, Virginia.

The blessing done, slaves gathered in groups, and began their walk to the sea, half an hour from here. They were to spend the night, dance, drink rum, roast a pig, their reward for the sugar boiled and cooling in its clay pots. The first sight of the sea, its blue-green majesty, waves cresting white foam, was beautiful from the top of a hill. Like everyone else, Hyacinthe felt a shout come up from inside himself, and in another moment, he was running among the rest of them, determined to be the first to feel the delicious, salty freshness spreading out in frothy ripples. The day was heaven. They swam, caught fish, built a fire, opened the rum, began, once night came, to dance around the fire, singing the songs of their memories, of the life where their hearts still were, far across the water they'd enjoyed today.

Hyacinthe sat with the priest.

"I have written your letter," the priest spoke in Latin, tapping a pocket of his long gown.

Hyacinthe heard the paper rustle. Hope was suddenly so large inside him that he thought he would choke on it.

"You will be made a bishop," he said, with boy's enthusiasm, boy's certainty. "She will reward you greatly. May I see it?"

The priest, glancing around for the overseers, gave him the letter, but Hyacinthe did not know the words. They were not French nor English. They were Spanish.

How would she know them? He could survive this, if it was not to be forever; but if it was, he would do as some of the fresh slaves did, the ones brought new from across the water. He would lie down and simply die.

"Someone will tell her," the priest soothed him. "See your name written there?"

He saw it.

"Well, she will see it, too, and will she not do everything she can to learn what it is the letter says about you?"

Yes, yes, she would. She loved him.

"We will put it into God's hands, my son."

God's hands, yes.

He went to sleep to the sweet sound of the sea, dreamed of the sugar harvest, dreamed he was cutting cane, running beside the wagon that brought it to the mill, then standing in the boiling house. Everyone was moving, the pace set by the overseers. The boiling house was a hell, the heat unmerciful, the fires under the copper kettles terrible beasts to be fed constantly, the sugar constantly stirred and ladled, slaves moving at all times to the shouts and blows of overseers—feed the fires, turn the stone wheel that crushed the cane, ladle sugar from pot to pot. Everywhere he looked slaves were stirring, muscles in their arms bunched, perspiration pouring from them; they were witches, he dreamed, demons sentenced to die over caldrons. The treasure, thick, ropy, dark brown sugar, lapped in its great pots, hissed warningly at him. Scalded sugar stuck to skin, ate it away in a matter of moments; in his dream, slave after slave fell into the caldrons, became one with the sugar. You! shouted an overseer. Into the pot, too. And then he was in the chamber in which the sugar was cooling in hundreds of clay pots. Madame sat upon a stone mill wheel.

Come home, she said to him, eyebrows drawn together, impatient. I need you.

Hyacinthe woke to see several men standing in the surf, pointing. The clear of yesterday was heavier, as if a weight lay upon it. It was hot, still. Hyacinthe waded out to them, his dream heavy like the day.

"Trouble," one of them said, "a storm is coming. Go and wake the brothers and sisters."

The men went to the overseers, told them what they saw. Back in the village, everyone worked to move the sugar pots to better shelter. Only when that was done were they allowed to go to their houses, to look to their roofs, to bring in cattle, to tie up dogs.

"We must leave here. The sea is angry."

Hyacinthe stood near the men chosen to speak to the overseers after the first day of rain. Wind had begun, strong wind. The overseers, drinking rum, sated by their favorite slave women, shook their heads.

The rain did not stop. Hyacinthe watched as turtles, snakes, deer moved among the huts, unafraid of people, moving inland in the face of the driving rain, the hard wind. Village dogs had begun to howl. The overseers came, shouted. Everyone had to leave, but they must take the sugar.

They labored to load the wagons in wind fiercer than they were. The rain fell in such driving sheets it hurt. The donkeys snorted and kicked at harnesses and would not be buckled to wagons. Water lapped above their ankles. A huge gust of wind picked up a wagon and turned it over, spilling clay pots everywhere, crushing slaves nearby. The rain fell and the wind rose and water from the sea and sky came, inching higher and higher, after a time, rising so fast that everywhere one looked there was only it.

There was nowhere to run.

The water was too high, the wind too strong. Hyacinthe saw dear friends die, drown before his eyes. He saw everything around him, the mill house, the boiling house, the huts, the cabins of the overseers, destroyed. There was a lull, in which those remaining thought it was over, but then, like some dreadful jest, it began again, even fiercer. Monstrous circles of dark devoured whatever was in their path. Overseers died. And the priest.

He survived, how he did not know, for the storm, he would learn, was called a hurricane, and there was nothing more feared in all the Caribbean. Belonging to no one now, his own again, he determined to journey to the port, a wild port, he'd heard, a nest for pirates. A port meant ships, and ships meant passage, and passage meant a way to Madame and Thérèse, guardians of his heart.

He walked to the sea, calm now. In his mind was the memory of the celebration only a few days before. In his mind was the sight of the destruction he'd walked through, trees uprooted, buildings nothing but boards, bodies of men, women, and animals lying bloated in the sun, survivors sitting stunned and silent amid the dead. He looked to the left. He looked to the right. His stomach gave a growl of hunger.

Which way?

That was the question, wasn't it? Which way? For a moment, a terrible futility filled him, and he wanted to shake his fist at the sky, curse God, but then into his mind came the memory of sitting before the fire at Tamworth, listening breathlessly as Madame read the story of Robinson Crusoe. His boy's heart lifted a fraction. Then more. Well, yes. Of course.

What would Crusoe do?

FALL

AND NOW ABIDETH FAITH, HOPE . . .

CHAPTER 52

September . . .

Perryman ordered Tamworth fowls fattened on rice boiled in milk. They'd be sent to Saylor House for Michaelmas Day. The Duchess was there because Lord Russel had been arrested. Off she and Annie and Tim and Bathsheba went to London once the news was known. In the Duchess's woods, children hunted for double nuts, two on a stalk, said to ward off rheumatism, toothache, the spells of witches. Evenings were cool enough for a cloak, and the trees under which the children scampered wore the colors of autumn, gold, russet, red sunset, amber.

In London there were rumbles, whispers, seethings as others were arrested, high nobles: Lord Orrery, Lord North, the Duke of Norfolk. And a man no one had heard of, Christopher Layer. Broadsheets appeared: A reward was offered for any word of Lucius, Viscount Duncannon, a Jacobite spy. People locked their doors at night, afraid of spies, afraid of an uprising by all the secret Jacobites said to be in London, Jacobites who would storm the Tower, release the imprisoned, kill anyone who did not cross himself and swear allegiance to King James.

September, said the almanac, wife, into thy garden and set me a plot, with strawberry roots, of the best be got.

Slane looked at the body at his feet. It lay in the mud on Privy stairs, near to St. Stephen's, where the House of Commons met, where the ruined palace of Whitehall reigned, home of His Majesty's Treasury. Robert Walpole was Lord of the Treasury, lord of Whitehall.

A King's messenger stood guard against the curious crowd who'd gathered around the body. What were you doing in this part of London? wondered Slane. No good, his middle told him. The man, Philip Neyoe, was one of their agents, a courier and scribe under Gussy. Slane hadn't heard word of him since Gussy's arrest, had been searching London for him.

Someone ought to cut Lord Russel's throat for giving out your name, said Louisa.

He will give out no more. Slane had accomplished that, made Charles believe he had more to fear from him than he had from Walpole. No guard will keep me from you, he'd told Charles. All Walpole had was the name. It must be driving him mad not to have more.

Slane had sent Walpole another gosling, roasted this time, with a white rose in its mouth. Anything to distract him, to threaten him, to make him uncertain.

"He was living in that house there," a man near Slane said, pointing out a house that backed onto the river. "I saw him."

An official had arrived, told the King's messenger to keep the crowd back. The official touched Neyoe with the toe of his shoe, his face showing disgust at the white, doughy look of the body. At his signal a pushcart was wheeled forward and the body was heaved into it, like garden fodder or trash, carted away.

Slane followed the cart and official through archways and a garden to a back court of Whitehall. The official disappeared into a doorway. The carter walked away from the cart; Slane stepped forward, rifled through sodden pockets, and took a piece of paper just as the official and other men came through the doorway. Slane was walking out the courtyard entrance as the official began to shout. He tossed his hat over a fence and unfastened his cloak and folded it under his arm.

On the street, busy with people, Slane took his time to sift through the apples in an apple woman's basket.

"Picked only yesterday off trees in Chelsea, and sweet as your sweetheart's lips," she told him.

Slane bit into an apple.

"Not sweet enough," he said, and winked.

The apple woman laughed. "I like a man of passion."

The official and the carter appeared in the narrow arch of the courtyard, looked from one direction to another. The official barked something at the carter, and the carter, hesitantly, pointed toward Slane.

"These don't feel as if they were picked yesterday," said Slane. "They feel older. I want to buy at least a dozen, but I want good ones."

"You."

Slane looked up from his searching, his expression pleasant, un-ruffled.

The official, red-faced, angry, was glaring at him. Slane could sense his uncertainty. Slane smiled at the carter, offered him an apple.

"You look like a man of discretion," he said. "Are these as fresh as she claims?"

"Did you see a man come from that courtyard there? It could only have been a few moments ago." The official was impatient. Slane offered him an apple, but he shook his head.

"A man? In great haste? Why, yes, I did. That way?" Slane pointed toward a narrow opening leading to a side street.

"Or was it that way?" Asking the apple woman, who shrugged, Slane pointed in the other direction.

The official heading one way, the carter the other, Slane bought a dozen apples.

"It was you came out of that courtyard," said the apple woman.

"Was it?" asked Slane. "Why didn't you say so?"

"Didn't want to."

He pinched the apple woman's cheek, asked her if she wanted a cloak, gave her the one folded under his arm, and then began to eat apples as he walked down Whitehall Street. In the broad expanse of the park by St. James's Palace, tossing an apple core over his shoulder, he leaned into a tree and pulled the sodden paper from his pocket.

The ink was smeared, not legible in many places, but what was legible made him swear out loud. Code names for Rochester, for Gussy, for Lords Orrery and North. Details about Ormonde's expedition, questions as to number of troops, commanders, ships. Names of lesser agents. Did Walpole have this information yet?

Leaving the park, Slane headed west along the river, back to the stairs where the body had been found. He went to the house that had been spoken of as Neyoe's and knocked on the door to see what he could learn. A woman answered.

"I'm looking for a lodging," he said, smiling at her charmingly, "and was told you had chambers to let."

She frowned and called someone; Slane saw the King's messenger who'd been with the body.

At once, he put his hand to his face and backed away, so that the man might not see him clearly. At the bottom of the steps, he walked quickly away, even though the messenger called him to come back.

Later, disguised—it was easy to borrow wigs and clothes from the theater—he watched the house. It took a day to determine that the house belonged to the King's messenger, a man named Modest Welsh, that the woman who'd answered the door was Mrs. Welsh.

Several days later, he finally saw the man who said he'd seen Neyoe at the house.

"Oh, yes," the man answered, surprised at Slane's accosting him. "A carriage would come for him, and he'd go off for hours. I saw him in the going and in the coming."

"Did he often come and go?"

"Often enough," said the man. "Now, if I may be so bold, why is it you ask?"

But by then Slane was walking away. So. Neyoe had been in the custody of a King's messenger, been taken somewhere for questioning, brought back to stay under lock and key. Slane stood at the back garden wall of the house, examining it. The wall was higher than a man, and its side gate was locked.

Had Neyoe tried to escape? Any man who managed to climb that wall would look down into the Thames. Had he tried to escape and drowned? Or had he been killed?

Neyoe, thought Slane, Walpole found you first. You knew enough to convict Rochester. It was the Jacobites' hope that Walpole would be unable to go to trial. It meant dismissal if he could not take Rochester to trial; all Slane's sources of information told him that. Barbara told him that, offering the information with a dazzling smile.

Did Walpole have the information upon the note found in Neyoe's pocket? Or had Neyoe for some reason—let there be a reason—not yet given it to him? What did you tell Walpole, Neyoe? Slane thought. Everything? Nothing? Or something in between?

Set me a plot, of strawberry roots, the best be got.

CHAPTER 53

October . . .

Wrapped in shawls, the Duchess sat in Saylor House gardens with Harriet. Too old, I am too old for all this, she thought. I ought to have stayed at Tamworth.

Harriet was describing her morning at Walpole's house. He'd had a tragedy. His daughter had died two days ago and lay now in state in London.

"The parlors are so crowded there is no place to sit," Harriet was saying. "Everyone is there, but the Walpoles are allowing only a select few to come upstairs to see them. They say Mrs. Walpole is beside herself with grief. Everyone is talking of the King's speech to Parliament, of his threat that there will be more arrests. Who else, do you think, Your Grace? I myself would never have imagined Charles, not in a hundred years—"

"Arrest is not proof. We have laws that a man may not be found guilty on someone's hearsay. There must be direct proof of treason. Remember that," said the Duchess.

"We played the game of who Duncannon is while we waited. Molly Hervey made us all laugh by suggesting he was the King's dwarf."

"Who knows who he is?" the Duchess snapped. "It could be the dwarf. It could be the Duchess of Kendall's favorite groom. It could be the gardener there." She pointed with her cane to one of the garden servants raking smooth the gravel in the broad garden walks. "I've lived through too much not to know that nothing is as it seems. We can all wake up tomorrow and find our worlds tipped over."

John must be ruined, considering the coin he was spending now, and the coin he'd lost in the South Sea, and the coin he'd given to King James's invasion. Jane and Mary were heartbroken; Gussy was in the Tower; Charles, and other friends from long ago, like Norfolk and North, were locked in cells, allowed to see no one. Tears were in her, and she was too old for tears. Passion was in her, and she was too old for that, too; passionate regret, passionate guilt, rough gravel in her chest for the mistakes she'd made in this long life, mistakes whose fruit she was yet reaping, whose results were playing out before her eyes even now. Those she now loved were caught in them, just as those she loved had been caught in them years before.

Not settled, after all this time, all these years, all the men and all the women, among them herself, plotting, lying, pushing, pulling, quarreling over who was right and who was wrong so that their man might win.

"Poor Mary," said Harriet.

No visits of any kind, no letters were allowed anyone in the Tower. Men had died with their eyes closing on the oozing bricks of their cells.

"Here's Mary," said Harriet. "Look away so she won't think we've been talking of her."

"Why shouldn't she know we've been talking of her? A fine family we'd be if we didn't. Mary, come and sit by me. We've been talking of you. Harriet, take the baby and go amuse him. You'll be fine," the Duchess said, patting one of Mary's hands. "This will pass. There are others worse off than you."

Like Jane, thinner each day as she dragged her children hither and yon, from drawing room to official chamber, talking of Gussy's innocence, carrying letters of reference that spoke of his character and goodness, attempting to make someone listen, attempting to be allowed to see him.

Her father was beside her, doing what he could among Tories and uncertain Whigs, to twist the arrests into a sign of Walpole's ambition to break the back of the Tory party and the might of the Church of England. Odd that so much was true: Gussy was treasonous and innately good; Walpole was overweeningly ambitious and a clever tracker of treachery.

" 'If October you do marry,' " Harriet was chanting.

Love will come, but riches tarry—so Barbara had told Jane's little girl Amelia, playing with her, teaching her the rhymes she and Jane had grown to womanhood upon. Marry in green, ashamed to be seen. Marry in gray, you'll go far away, said Barbara the other day, trying, like the Duchess, to keep Jane's spirits up.

If Gussy died, what would Jane do? Harriet said she could find her a position as lady's companion, but what would happen to the children? No one wished to take on a companion who brought along four children. I will care for her, said John, his jaw setting full and stiff. She is my own dear girl. How the devil would he care for her if he himself was impoverished? It hurt the Duchess to the core of her being to see her old friend's trouble.

Tony walked out of the house and dropped his black gloves—he'd have received these mementoes today at the Walpoles'—onto the bench beside his sister. "You look pale," he told her. "Walk around the garden with me."

"Walk with your brother," said Harriet. "I'll see to little Charles."

What would you do if you knew the secrets I keep? thought the Duchess, her eyes on Tony, who looked pale himself. You keep secrets, Tony.

He kept his love for Barbara secret. She knew it. She suspected Harriet knew it, too, but Tony said nothing, only was more grave, more stiff, more demanding of everyone around him. He would be furious if he knew what she knew.

It is this Christopher Layer who implicates Charles, Tony had told her, and Layer's evidence is full of wild contradictions. There's nothing in it about the Bishop of Rochester.

That was whom the men in a chamber at Whitehall hunted: Rochester. Walpole was convinced the Bishop had headed the invasion plot. The King desired to see him beheaded, wanted Jacobitism crippled once and for all, frightened to death by Rochester's fate.

Did Rochester head the plot? the Duchess asked Sir John, who told her she already knew far too much and did not need to know that, too.

Barbara said the cruelty of the interrogations had broken this Layer person, and nothing he said could be depended upon. She'd overheard Walpole telling Diana this, debating whether to bring Layer to public trial and show what chaff he rested accusations of treason upon. He thinks he will ride into the King's clear favor if he convicts the Bishop of Rochester, Barbara had told her. But maybe Walpole won't be able to take a bishop's head. Maybe there won't be the evidence. There have to be direct witnesses. There have to be letters. Some say there are neither, just supposition and guess and unsworn testimony.

Barbara was up to something. The Duchess could feel it. If she'd had more heart, she'd have questioned her, found out, but she was too dispirited.

The King won't be happy if Walpole can't give him Rochester, la, la, la, Barbara sang.

They'd broken Layer. What did that mean?

What, in God's dear name, had been done to Gussy? It drove John to despair, she could see it in his eyes, and it drove Jane, what might be happening to the man they loved in a dark cell of the Tower of London.

Visitors were entering Saylor House gardens: Colonel Edward Perry and Sir Christopher Wren. Wren, small, alert, like the bird that shared his name, darted toward the Duchess.

"I've found a book in which there is an interesting fact, a reference to nomads of the desert sands carrying their bees with them when they travel," he said.

She was moved a little past regret and fear, but only a little. "How?"

"It does not say. Baskets, perhaps?"

Perry, Wren, and Pendarves had become fast friends. Like ancient boys, the three were always together. They liked to sit in the afternoons in Devane Square's church to watch Wren, as busy, as driven as any bee, up among the workmen on the scaffolding, among the woodcarvers and painters, as if not a one of them could paint a stroke or chip a splinter without his knowledge.

"I've had a thought about Hyacinthe," said Wren. "Could it be that he discovered the overseer in some crime, and was killed for that?"

That was another thing they did, discuss everything that had to do with Barbara, including what had happened to Barbara's servant and why. Perry's bringing of the collar had been a shock. Barbara had been ill for days over it, carried it now in a sadness in her eyes.

"What kind of crime?" asked the Duchess.

"Well, Colonel Perry informs me that it is not unknown for colonials to smuggle. Perhaps the boy saw something."

Edward Perry met the Duchess's gaze with the serenity of a marble angel. He had fine eyes, a clear stunning blue, angel's eyes, Barbara called them. I used to think I saw Roger in them, she said. The Duchess had another fancy. She thought it possible to see Perry's soul, a clear thing, full of joy. Unlike her, he had no regrets, no unconfessed sins that pressed him down, made it difficult to breathe, sleep. She envied him that.

"Smuggle, do you?" She frowned.

"We've been known to. Your duties upon us are unfair when tobacco sells low. We must put food upon our tables to feed our children, the same as you."

"If the boy caught him smuggling," said Wren, "he might have killed him."

Wren had an imagination, was building plots, rather than churches, in the air. She sniffed and didn't bother to answer.

"I must go," said Wren. "I've carvers working cn the altar rail at Devane Square church, and you cannot trust a carver not to whittle too much of his own ideas into what is already a perfect design.

"I've taken the liberty of drawing what I think might be a handsome building to put planters' tobacco in for your port," he told the Duchess. "I'll show you when you come by later."

"I need a simple port building, not a monument."

"Nothing fancy, good, strong brick. You could make it there. Perry here has brickmakers among his slaves—"

"Had," Colonel Perry interrupted gently. "I no longer own slaves."

"Well, your daughter, then. Simple lines, I thought, a column or two, three, making a porch, where the men might gather and talk. If you were to put in a tavern, a few beds for those who have far to travel and might like a night to rest, it would be sound commerce. You'd have the makings of a town."

"Are you going to design the tavern, too?" The Duchess's question was tart. They took it upon themselves to redo First Curle. Barbara was in the thick of it, urging them on.

"I might. I did the college building in Williamsburg, you know. Why not a port building and a tavern? Wren's, you could call it. Now, I really must leave. Think on those nomads. How on earth would they transport bees? I am intrigued by the question."

Wren was bowing to Harriet, walking down a gravel path to the gate the way he always walked, as if there was always much to do and little time to do it.

"Who is Duncannon?" Harriet said to Colonel Perry. Jests about Duncannon were fashionable among the young people.

"Who?"

"The King's dwarf. Isn't that wonderful? We laughed and laughed over it."

"I have another for you. Who is Duncannon?"

"Who?"

"Robert Walpole's horse."

Harriet gave a trill of laughter, and the baby in her arms laughed too, clapped his hands.

"Your port," Colonel Perry said to the Duchess, "I am not the only one who might be interested in putting some coin into it. Wren is interested, so are Sir Alexander, here, and Lady Shrewsborough, Sir John Ashford."

"Sir John hasn't an extra coin. The South Sea ruined him." She spoke harshly, too harshly, but she couldn't help it. John's plight upset her. And what the South Sea didn't take, contributing to Jamie's failed invasion did. Not to mention this arrest. John had left his farm, his fields, to deal with it. I was more selfish than you, Richard, always. I only knew how to love when it was too late. For what do I sit here and yearn? Peace? Quiet? Lost love? That the dead rise from the grave and walk with me again? Forgive me, I would say to the dead. I didn't know.

Tony was pushing Harriet away. The old Duchess sat here at Saylor House and saw it, a perfectly good marriage—the possibility of true tenderness in it—going sour. Because Harriet was not Barbara. Well, she would never be.

"Carlyle was at Walpole's today," said Colonel Perry.

"That surprises me," answered Harriet.

"Walpole would not receive him. Carlyle said he would return later, with Barbara."

Tony and Barbara had quarreled over Carlyle. You abandon him, she'd said. Tony told her not to interfere in matters that did not concern her. The running of my house and my estate and my men in Parliament are my affair, he'd said to her, as cold as ever the Duchess had heard him, no concern of yours.

Carlyle is of little use to me now, he'd said later to the Duchess, when Barbara had left. I'm sorry for it, but it is the truth.

He was turning cold. She could see it, did not know how to stop it. He was walling himself away from life. And in part it was her fault. There he was now, walking back with his sister. I've helped to do this, thought the Duchess, with my pushing and prodding, my interfering and plotting. I should have left all alone.

"Jane Cromwell was at Walpole's when I was there," said Colonel Perry. "The children were with her. They sat in a drawing room until Walpole's servants moved them on. I was not the only one affected by the sight of it. Is there any word of when treason trials may begin?"

If Gussy dies, I won't be able to bear it, thought the Duchess. Somehow, it would be like watching Richard die all over again. Her fault, that Richard had died. Here, in London, guilt and regret would not lie still, quivered and flailed and tormented her. I'll die if Gussy dies, she thought, I shall.

Last night Annie had brushed her hair. She'd stared at herself in the mirror, thinking, Where did I go? How could all her Alices—girl, woman, wife, mother, countess, duchess, widow—be contained in the tiny, withered woman staring back at her? But they were. All her Alices, and all Alice's deeds, good and bad.

Absolve me, angel, thought the Duchess, looking over at Perry, who held the baby and talked easily with Tony and Harriet. If only he could.

A few streets over, Barbara touched the funeral garland she and Bathsheba had made for the Walpoles, in her mind a country saying she'd told Amelia the other day: Marry in brown, never live in town; marry in red, wish yourself dead. She and Bathsheba had made the garland, and it was beautiful. Composed of two small hoops of wood, with bands crossing them, the garland resembled an open, arched crown. White roses, rosemary, rue, silver ribbons, combined with rosettes of white paper, covered the bands. Inside hung a pair of paper gloves. It was a country custom, a garland for the death of a maiden, the gloves an indication of her maidenhood. In Tamworth Church, such garlands hung from the rafters, some of them years old, rustling like dry leaves, for the young unmarried women who had died.

The best of the tobacco from First Curle was being made into snuff; the rest had been bought by French and Dutch merchants. She was excited, had visited the London merchant who would make the snuff, to question him, see how and what he did. There was no word yet from Blackstone. She dreamed of fields, of tobacco growing in them. How did her grandmother's sort do? Next year they would have tobacco from it. She could not wait. Had Blackstone bought indentures? Were any of the slaves freed?

She'd met the man who was to take Spotswood's place as deputy governor of Virginia, and dined with the Earl of Orkney, the colony's true governor, who sent men to govern as his deputies. What a long and wonderful talk they'd had. He said he might visit, but she didn't believe him. How odd to send someone else to do your task. He would never see the vast bay, the waves rolling in, the dolphins, the savages, the fields, the magnificent trees, the wide rivers, the streams and creeks and fish.

You must go and inspect in my place, Lady Devane, Orkney had told her. Go there again and tell me how this new man does.

"Ma'am."

It was her mother's footman, come to tell her that Tommy Carlyle was here. They were going together to the Walpoles'.

No more rouge, no more wigs for Tommy Carlyle, just a scrubbed face with a mangled nose and scarred forehead, as if he demanded that the world see what had been done to him.

But the world did not wish to see. No one spoke to him, no one returned his visits. No one sat beside him when he took his seat in the House of Commons. Only she remained his friend.

Before she was even settled in the carriage, Carlyle said, "You'll tell Robin?"

"You know I will."

She stared down at the funeral garland. Here was tangible evidence of what brutality accomplished. Tommy was changed, reduced, a ghost of himself. You mustn't judge, Slane had told her. We all have a breaking point, a point at which we snap, like dry wood, and are no more. Tommy, as she'd known him, was no more. And Wart. He was not arrested, and he did not flee, but fear and the crushing of Jacobite hope took their toll on him.

Carlyle was looking out the carriage window.

"Dear God, everywhere one looks these days are these broadsheets on Duncannon. Who is he? I wish I knew. I'd give him over for the reward they're offering."

Under the garland, Barbara gripped her hands together. There was no trusting anyone now. Danger was everywhere. At the first sight of the broadsheets posted on buildings, on fences, she'd run all the way to Slane's lodging.

Who told? she demanded.

Nothing more will be said, he assured her, not answering her question.

How do you know that? she said. How can you? Are you amused, challenged by the broadsheets?

He'd taken her hands in his. I am not. I take their position on walls and buildings of London quite seriously. He stayed in England for her and for Gussy. I don't want Walpole to have him, he said. If I accomplish that, I can live with myself.

Are you planning a rescue? she demanded. But he wouldn't answer.

At the Walpoles' there were too many people, and they overflowed into the parlors and chambers of the ground floor. Giving their names to a footman, she and Carlyle tried to find some place to sit. A footman came forward and held out a box, in which were dozens of black gloves.

Tommy took a pair, examined them. "The finest cloth. He spares no expense. I hear he'll give gold rings to those invited to the funeral tomorrow. I am not invited."

Two months ago he would not have cared.

Barbara had to turn her face away from what he'd become. People smiled at her, nodded their heads, came forward to speak to her. She was allowed her friendship with Carlyle. One false step, said he, any sense that you are falling in favor, and you will not be allowed it. The higher you climb, Barbara, the longer the fall.

She saw her mother, huge with child in a flowing gown, showing her bosom, and Pendarves jewels over that bosom. Pendarves was nowhere to be seen. Likely her mother had sent him on his way. People crowded around her mother as if she were second-best wife to a sultan, the sultan being Walpole.

"I finished the book last night," Diana said when Barbara stood before her. "Moll Flanders, whore, highwayman, thief, liar. A woman after my heart."

"How do you feel?"

"My back aches, my feet ache, my head aches. This child is a stone dragging me down."

This child is my brother, thought Barbara. Don't curse him, Mother.

"Remember your promise to me, Barbara."

"You are not going to die, Mother."

"But we die all the time in childbirth, Barbara. We just close our eyes and go, and they marry another who takes our place."

"I don't want to hear this, Mother."

It wasn't like her mother to think of death. She did little these days but lie in bed. Barbara would have been frightened, except that she could not imagine death having the courage to take on Diana. She made Annie read the tea leaves, and Bathsheba, too. Both agreed. Diana would survive.

Sir Gideon Andreas walked forward, bowed to Barbara and Diana. At once, Diana's mood changed. She sat up straighter and swept her eyes over the banker, assessing him, making no bones about the fact that she found him interesting.

You summon the strength to flirt with a man you find attractive, thought Barbara furiously. Now summon the strength to guard my little brother while he is inside you.

"I hear the tobacco merchants are asking that an act be passed to require planters to leave the stem on tobacco leaves when they're put into the hogsheads," Barbara said to Andreas.

She and Colonel Perry were all over London, she to learn all she could about this end of tobacco farming, he to reacquaint himself. Everything is changed from when I was here before, complained Colonel Perry. The South Sea Bubble has hurt many merchants. They gambled with our credit reserves.

Andreas's cool hawk eyes fell over Barbara, considered her, weighed her, assessed her; then, like a hawk, he let a hood fall over them. He smiled politely. "When the stem is taken from the leaves, and only leaves are packed, the planters send fewer hogsheads, Lady Devane."

"Since the planters pay for freight and shipping by the hogshead, why should they not send as few hogsheads as possible?"

"Customs duties are upon the hogshead. Fewer hogsheads mean smaller duties paid to His Majesty's Treasury. How does your church progress?"

As if he didn't know. He was there every morning, riding, as he said, to Marylebone, but stopping always at the church, to look at what Wren was doing, to quiz the workmen, or her grandmother or Colonel Perry if they were there. That man is no simple merchant, said her grandmother. He starts with a little and then takes all, Tommy warned.

"The body is in the grand parlor, Barbara. Go and see it. They'll be calling your name to go upstairs soon. —Dear Walpole is so fond of Barbara," Diana said to Andreas, her marvelous violet eyes flirting with him, once Barbara had moved away to obey.

"As we all are."

"You've been so kind, so generous in your handling of the notes. Barbara speaks of it to me all the time, how kind you've been." Diana gave Andreas a look that would have melted ice.

"But of course. I want to help her with Devane Square. Has she told you that?"

"We all want to help her," said Diana. She placed a hand on her bosom, on the huge swell of breast into neck. She watched Andreas's eyes run over that swell, and she smiled a cat's smile. There was a long jewel centered in her necklace. She stroked it.

"You must call upon me some afternoon so that we can talk of Barbara and all her troubles," she said.

Barbara stared.

In the grand parlor, Walpole's daughter lay in state, a huge velvet pall over the coffin, candles burning everywhere; six young women, there to publicly mourn her, sat nearby. Tonight Barbara would return, with Harriet, to sit for a time by the coffin. And tomorrow she would be among the young women who would walk before and behind the coffin, carrying candles and singing.

She'd never met Robin's daughter, who had been this past year in Bath, drinking and bathing in the waters there, which were said to restore health. She stared down at the mourning gloves in her hands, thinking of loss: Roger, Harry, Hyacinthe. Was Gussy to be added to the list? And Slane. She must eventually lose him. He must eventually leave England. They had not discussed it, but it was there, between them, all the time.

She started when her name was called. People, many of whom had waited far longer than she, parted for her as she went to be received upstairs. She could hear murmurs, hear her name. She was famous now, a favorite of the King. It was true; the King did like her, did seek out her company. Gossips said other things, too: that she was the King's mistress; that she was the Prince's; that the father and son shared her. That, too, was part of her fame, the envy for one rising above others.

Carlyle stood at the stairs.

"Tell him," he said.

"I will."

Upstairs, she walked down a quiet, dark hall in which there was no one but a servant opening a door for her. Robin was alone in this ornate chamber, black cloth over the mirrors, the custom for death, so that no one could look in them. Grief had puffed out his already plump features. Barbara put the garland in his hands, and he stared down at it.

"How very beautiful. Forgive the absence of my wife. She was overcome and could receive no more company this day. It is she who took the time for her, Barbara, not I. It was she who took our precious girl to the physicians, to the cures and treatments. She feels this deeply."

"My servant helped me to make it. I am so sorry for your loss."

"It's a country custom, isn't it?" He held the garland close to his face, smelled the fragrance of the roses, the herbs, lovely, hauntingly sweet.

"In Tamworth Church, such garlands hang from the rafters. Some of them are years old. They rustle like dry leaves when there is a breeze," said Barbara.

"Rosemary, rue, bittersweet, like her young life. I had such hopes for her."

"I thought you might put it in the church where she is buried."

"Yes, we'll do that. Your gesture is kind. How do you do, yourself?"

Devane Square rises; I rise; my love is a Jacobite and must leave London; my dearest friend is heartbroken; snuff is being made from First Curle tobacco; Wart drinks too much; Carlyle no longer exists; my treasured servant, Thérèse, leaves me; I begin to like Harriet very much, but I don't like Tony, not anymore. Restlessly, she touched Hyacinthe's collar, at her neck, tied tight with ribbon, worn today, worn nearly every day, in memory of the boy who was more than a servant, was part of the family she'd made for herself. Could Odell Smith have killed him? Was it possible for men to be so base? Thérèse, like Barbara, had wept at the sight of the collar. The sight of it shook her faith in his being alive. Thérèse . . . Barbara walked to a table piled high with papers, glanced at them. Were they about the plot? Was Gussy here, living in these papers?

"Well enough. Robin, I want to ask a favor of you."

"Doesn't everyone?"

"It's Tommy Carlyle. He's below, waiting. He came this morning and waited also. Please receive him. Allow him to express his condolences to you. He is sincere in them. A gesture from you would mean so much at this low point in his life. Think of all the years when you were friends, rather than of this last one, when you have not been. He asks that I tell you that he begs your pardon for all he has done, he swears he will do no more."

"Can do no more, you mean. I'll think on it. Your mother tells me you're giving Thérèse to the Princess of Wales's household in the next week."

You're not going to receive him, thought Barbara. Yes, I give Thérèse over, and not happily.

"Wise of you, Barbara, very wise. I'm pleased to see you can be so amenable. You try to mend old breaches of trust, I hear, try to encourage the King and the Prince to understand one another. The

Jacobites among us would not be pleased. They like it when the King and the Prince of Wales quarrel. You're happy at court? Happy with your duties? Good. Good. The King called on me this morning, along with the Duchess of Kendall. Their kindnesses to me, to my wife, during this time have been most flattering."

He spread out his favor like a peacock's tail, but it was far from certain he would keep it. He wouldn't keep it if he couldn't try Rochester. In the King's mind, Rochester was the head of the plot. In the King's mind, Rochester must be punished.

She was in the King's household now. She knew.

"You resemble the roses in this garland, Barbara, fresh and somehow pure. It eases me to know there is someone among those around me I may trust."

"Allow Augustus Cromwell to receive a visit from his wife, a single visit, nothing more."

He laughed, genuinely amused.

"Two requests within the space of moments. You've become a true creature of court, Barbara."

"It is so little, and would mean so much. She's my dearest friend—"

Walpole held up a hand, and Barbara was silent.

"As we all know. Not even for you will I do that, nor could I do that if I wished it. It is the King's will that there be no visitors."

Your will, thought Barbara. He's given the handling of this plot to you. Walpole's as tenacious as an old hunting dog, the King had told her. He will find Jacobites. He'd better.

"This is not a matter of friendship, but one of state, of treason, which you mustn't bother your pretty head with."

She wanted to strike him. They were speaking of life and death, as well as treason. They were speaking of policy, of survival—his and Gussy's. You'll sacrifice Gussy the way you did Roger, thought Barbara, and far more easily, for Gussy is nothing to you but fodder to feed the crowd's bloodlust for Jacobites that you foster, the King's bloodlust. I don't like this, thought Barbara. I don't like any of it the way I thought I would.

In the carriage, Carlyle said, "I will buy a jewel for the Duchess of

Kendall. You will give her the jewel, Bab; ask her to see that I'm given an interview with the King. Tell her there will be another jewel if I am. An interview with the King will restore me. I know it."

Walpole's cruelty has broken Tommy, thought Barbara, and I am reminded of Harry, and I don't know why, but I feel afraid, for Tommy and for myself.

❧

Walpole told his footman to bring up no callers for a time. He stared at the papers piled upon a table, papers that even the death of his daughter did not distract him from, papers he sifted through again and again, looking for the path that would lead him to what he wished. Even during the King's call of condolence today, Rochester's name had come up.

He has used the Church all these years as the platform from which to attack me, said the King. He has used his vestments to cover treason for who knows how long. It must be stopped. The enemies of my house must be crushed.

Despite Philip Neyoe, despite Christopher Layer, there was not the direct and definite evidence of treason necessary to prosecute in a court of common law. There was only hearsay. He had yet to tell the King.

The fickle, changing bitch that was opinion had begun to shift. The sight of Jane Cromwell, dragging most of her children with her from drawing room to drawing room—including his own, this morning—telling anyone who would listen of her husband's innocence and virtues, did no good. It made him look like a tyrant, an ogre. He tried to quell the power of the Church of England; he was godless and immoral, rumor said.

I cannot win if they pit me against God, said the King. You must prove that Rochester has acted in an ungodly manner, plotting against his King and country.

Had he taken himself too far out, promised what he could not deliver? He was going to try Christopher Layer and Augustus Cromwell. He could prove their guilt. But the King wanted more.

Just this one head, thought Walpole, staring down at the papers, on Traitor's Gate, and I am where I wish to be. But I cannot convict that head. The Bishop and his adherents are yet wilier than I.

It was all he thought of. When the news of his daughter's death had come, he'd thought: Good, a few days' respite from the King's questions about my progress. His wife had been disgusted with him.

There was a knock upon the door. A servant entered with a single white rose.

Walpole read the note attached, and said, cordially, "Who gave you this?"

"The downstairs footman, sir."

"Send him to me at once. At once, do you hear."

He knew, even as he gave the order, that the footman would be able to tell him nothing.

"My sincere condolences," the note said, and it was signed "Duncannon." The white rose was the flower of the House of Stuart. Duncannon trifled with him. What was it Barbara had told them stories of? The savages counting coup. Duncannon counted coup, against him, and won. What sums he'd spent trying to find him. What time questioning others. He wanted this Duncannon almost as much as he wanted Rochester. He would see the reward on Duncannon doubled tomorrow. I so enjoyed the chase of you, your élan, he would say, right before the axman beheaded him.

Spies and goslings.

Into his mind came the names of young noblemen suspected and discarded for lack of evidence: the Duke of Wharton, Philip Stanhope, others. If Barbara's brother Harry had been alive, his name would have led the list. A child of Diana's was capable of anything. He set the rose down beside the garland Barbara had brought, made with her own hands, she said, a garland with white roses in it, white for maidenhood.

Or for Stuart.

He remained where he was, staring at the garland. What if the gosling was not, as they supposed, a man, but a woman? A woman whose brother and father were Jacobites, a woman who had been received by King James in Rome, a woman who, according to his notes, had dined with every Jacobite in Italy. A woman who was now in the royal household and, on the strength of her charm and wits, rapidly rising. She reads aloud to the King in the evenings, the Duchess of Kendall had confided the other day, and the Duchess of Kendall did not even like Walpole. He says he likes the sound of her voice.

What does she read to him?

Robinson Crusoe.

Walpole's heart beat faster.

If he could give the King a gosling in the place of Rochester, that might do. Did you ruin my daughter for your ambition? Diana had asked him. If you did, I will cut your heart out and eat it. But their coming child distracted her. Robin, you are disgusting, his wife had said. Is nothing sacred to you but your ambition?

No, not really. Nothing. No one.

It was sad but true.

CHAPTER 54

Pendarves and Barbara walked through a townhouse in Devane Square. All of the wonderful interior molding upon the walls, around the doors, around the ceiling—the cascades of wooden flowers, shells, violins, musical notes, children playing—was gone. So were the chandeliers, which had been of silver. The wall sconces had been silver, Roger at his extravagant best. Above her remained the glorious scenes painted upon the ceiling, gods and goddesses floating upon clouds. There'd been no way to remove the paintings whole, or else Parliament would have done it when Roger was fined for his part in the South Sea. The chamber they were in was light-filled, windows all along its three outside walls.

"I thought to have everything finished simply," she said, "as they do it in Virginia. Plain panels of wood inset in the walls, rather than ornate carving. All the chambers painted the palest of greens and blues. That will save expense." She would live here soon. Pendarves was paying for the finishing of this.

Pendarves pointed, and she saw out a window that Andreas was dismounting, going into the church.

"What do you think he will do when he knows?" she asked.

"One of two things. Demand at once that you repay the notes you owe him—"

"Which I cannot."

"Or demand that he be allowed to build here, as I'm doing. You haven't answered about the ground lease for these townhouses."

"I won't give away the ground lease. It remains mine. By my figuring, you'll be paid back what you've spent, including interest, from rents before five years are passed, so I will give you all the rents for six." He wouldn't own these three townhouses, but he was building more, and those he would own. She had the land they sat upon, however, and he'd have to pay her rent for that.

He considered what she said, then slapped at the window ledge, chortling, clearly pleased. Papers were ready, papers that gave him the right to finish this row of townhouses, to lease them in his name, to build more.

"I'll have you in here by Christmas, Bab."

The townhouses would lease faster with her living in one. She was in fashion, and her stepfather, no fool, wished to use the fact. That was all right. She understood. It was to her advantage, too. Tomorrow, the King drove out in his carriage, with his nieces, his granddaughters, to view the church, to walk the square. Wren was excited.

A church bell tolled in Marylebone, announcing the hour. On the last ring, she and Pendarves went outside, and she saw Bathsheba walking down the lane. Loyal Bathsheba, come to fetch her, so that she would not be late.

Why take a half-wild Gypsy as your maidservant? her mother had asked.

Why not? Barbara answered.

Tim carried her grandmother out of the church, Colonel Perry beside her, Wren and Andreas following. The coachman brought forward the carriage that would take them to Diana's townhouse.

"We're going to make a Virginia garden in the square," Wren said to Andreas.

Barbara sighed. Wren was just no good at secrets. At once, Pendarves scuttled into the carriage, but her grandmother and Colonel Perry remained where they were.

"Are you?" Andreas was looking at her, trying to read her, she could see.

"Yes. I want lilacs, which are my colonial friend Major Custis's favorite, and wild pansies, which have markings like a slave's scars."

"A fountain in the middle, I thought," said Wren. "Trite, I know, but people do love water. And hyacinths, Lady Devane, tell him of the hyacinths. Dozens and dozens of hyacinths," he said, not able to contain his delight, "blooming everywhere, in honor of the servant boy. The trees all from Virginia; vines; perhaps the garden a little wild, I thought—daring, I know, not done, not formal, but it's time I stretched myself to something different."

"Quite an undertaking," said Andreas, "and an expense."

"A dream at this point. We're nothing but a quartet of old dreamers," said the Duchess. She was putting money into the square. "Excuse us, but we really must leave."

"You go to Leicester House?"

"Yes," said Barbara.

"And tomorrow His Majesty calls?"

"Yes."

"I hear you are collecting for vagabond children." Andreas smiled at Perry, the smile not reaching his eyes.

"He is," said Wren. "He will go walking in the worst of London, and so he sees our dregs. He says they live like wild dogs among the warehouses at London Bridge. He wants me to design a shelter for them."

"You may put me down for two hundred and fifty pounds," said Andreas.

"You're not to tell Wren a word of your plan of the townhouses," the Duchess said to Pendarves, very sternly, once the carriage was driving away. "He'll begin to talk of design and forget that we wish to keep this secret."

"What do you think Andreas will do when he knows about Pendarves's lease?" Colonel Perry asked her.

"He'll want me to pay the notes he holds, but I'll go to the King and cry, and since he also wants the King's favor, wants to be made an earl, he'll have to be gentle." Barbara's tone was more flippant than she felt.

"I hope it's as easy as that," snapped her grandmother.

Such an odd feeling I had, thought Barbara, standing there, talking with Andreas and Wren, that I won't see the Virginia garden made. The slaves' song for the dead was in her mind, but it was lost in the carriage stopping, and her rush to go upstairs to her bedchamber and change her gown. Thérèse was there to help, but Barbara, still angry, still unforgiving, stopped her. Today she was to present Thérèse to the Princess of Wales at Leicester House. The last of her family, save her dog, was gone.

"Bathsheba is my maidservant now."

Those fern-frond eyes of Bathsheba's flicked once at Barbara as Bathsheba handed her a gown. Sweet Jesus, thought Barbara, have I taken on an Annie?

"Wait for me downstairs," Barbara said to Thérèse.

"Yes, madame."

"I didn't want to weep before her," she said to Bathsheba the moment the door was closed behind Thérèse, "not that it is your place to have to know that. I don't wish her to leave. I regret being talked into this. I will miss her. You're not to lecture me with looks and glances. I won't have it. I receive enough lectures from my grandmother and Annie. All right. Now, did Caesar White find the cradle yet?"

Caesar and Montrose were searching in the warehouse for a lovely cradle Roger had had made for his hope of their child, not knowing there would be no children. She'd never told him she was barren. It was going in the kitchen, for Bathsheba's boy.

Bathsheba shook her head.

"Where's your child?"

Bathsheba didn't answer, kept her face empty, an emptiness that always touched Barbara's heart.

"My mother told you to keep him in the kitchen, out of my way, didn't she? Never mind her. You bring him with you when you come to dress me, when you do your work for me. No feathers today."

Everyone was wearing them now. Herbs, thought Barbara,

Bathsheba knows herbs and flowers, and when spring comes, I'll have her twine them all in my hair. Perhaps we'll twine them into a necklace for me to wear. Herbs in the tobacco—she turned slowly, so that Bathsheba could straighten frills and ribbons, pull out and fluff lace—there's an idea. The snuff from First Curle tobacco was going to be presented to His Majesty as her grandmother's New Year's gift.

Outside, in the hall, Harry barked at her, then ran down the stairs. He'd run to Thérèse, then back to her—a habit of his, to run himself to nothing between them. She had to stop a moment. She touched the collar at her neck. Her household, the family she'd made for herself, was undone now. Thérèse had read Tommy's letter, asked to go into service in the Princess's household. No, said Barbara. Yes, said Colonel Perry; her desire to move to the Princess's household has nothing to do with you nor her regard for you. She has her own dreams, which you must allow. She's my family, said Barbara, the family I made when Roger and I could not make one. Everyone is leaving—Harry is gone, and Hyacinthe and Charlotte, now Thérèse. It hurts me. I feel left alone. I feel afraid. Another family will come to you, said Colonel Perry, in time. Allow Thérèse her dreams. We must never interfere in another's hopes. It is hard for me to let go, Barbara told him, particularly of those I love. All the more reason to learn, he replied.

The dead are in the child who is wailing, in the firebrand that flames, in the fire that is dying. The dead are not dead, so the slaves sang.

A dozen memories swirled in Barbara's mind: Thérèse and Hyacinthe; the dogs and her brother in the garden in France, in a gondola in Venice, on a cypress-wooded terrace. Make me beautiful, she'd said to Thérèse, for Roger. Roger, she thought, Devane Square begins to rise again. But my heart isn't in it the way I thought it would be.

In the bedchamber, Bathsheba carefully smoothed the riding habit Barbara had stepped out of, opened a little bag at her waist, and sprinkled lavender and geranium in the folds. So much to learn. Thérèse at her, Annie at her, with all the things she must learn. The mistress of this house had violet eyes that looked coldly upon her. The other servants sneered. Gypsy, they said. Witch.

A cradle for the child, Lady Devane had said, a lovely cradle with cherubs carved upon it to watch him as he sleeps.

I can't bear to see your idiot, Violet Eyes said. Keep him out of my sight or I'll have him put in with the horses.

We'll live in the townhouse, Lady Devane said, and you will have the kitchen and the chamber beside it all for your own. You will be housekeeper and servant to me, Bathsheba. Can you do that? I think you can. When your child grows large, we can teach him to be a stable boy. I think he will like the horses. I think he will do well with them.

A whole chamber; a cradle for her son, who would be a stable boy. Bathsheba pressed in lavender, geranium with nimble fingers, long and clever fingers. It might have been love and good fortune she was pressing in. It probably was.

Downstairs, the Duchess was lecturing Thérèse.

"You remember who you began with. You remain hers even if you do go to them. She has been good to you, better than you deserve."

"As Mademoiselle Fuseau well knows," Colonel Perry deftly steered Thérèse to Barbara, who had just stepped into the chamber.

"Tommy Carlyle is not here yet," said the Duchess.

"We must wait, then."

"You cannot, and you know it. The Princess will be offended."

"Everything I do offends her," said Barbara. If the Princess felt gratitude, she was not showing it. The great are monsters who must be forever fed, cannot stay full, Carlyle had told her. One day, if you stay among them long enough, you'll be like them, too.

No, she'd said.

Yes, said Carlyle. No one escapes.

"Nonetheless, go on," said the Duchess. "We'll send him on if he arrives here. Likely he is already at Leicester House, proclaiming to one and all how clever he is, how he has arranged all this."

"He did arrange all this."

"You're too softhearted."

"He'll ask about the jewel," said Barbara. "I've given it to the Duchess of Kendall, but she has not said anything yet."

"Tell him that," said the Duchess. "He won't like it, but there it is."

"What is that?" Barbara pointed to a hat Thérèse had crushed in one hand.

It was one of Hyacinthe's.

"Never mind," Barbara said. "I know whose hat it is. Come, Thérèse, we must leave."

Thérèse went from one to another, very quiet, very pale. She feels this, too, thought Barbara. Oh, Thérèse, I never thought we'd part. Depend upon nothing but change, said Colonel Perry. It is the very nature of life. Barbara saw Pendarves press some coins into Thérèse's hands. She smiled to herself. She was always finding coins in the pocket of her gown or in some chamber to which Pendarves knew she'd go. Debt fairies leave them, he said. He was far too kind to survive living with her mother.

In the carriage, Barbara and Thérèse were silent. The quarrel between them was still too fresh. I cannot believe you wish to leave me, Barbara had said.

It is service to the future Queen, Thérèse had replied. Please understand.

"Listen to me," Barbara said now, as the carriage made a sharp turn. "Mrs. Clayton is the favorite servant of the Princess. I am told she is a good woman; her loyalty to the Princess is well known. She will be watching you to see how you serve, and it is she, besides the Princess, whom you must please. There will be jealousies among the women of the bedchamber; there always are. Mrs. Selwyn and Mrs. Pollexfen do not like Mrs. Clayton, Carlyle tells me. They may try to advise you wrongly, so that you make foolish mistakes; therefore, listen only to Mrs. Clayton. Take your orders from her and her alone. You will encounter many petty quarrels. I tell you this from my own experience now as lady-in-waiting. People are always looking to quarrel. Try to take no sides, to do your work and be discreet. Mrs. Clayton values discretion above all else, as does the Princess."

"You forgive me?"

"No."

They jolted down the streets that led to Leicester House. The carriage stopped. It ends, thought Barbara. A Leicester House footman was holding open the door.

"I have loved you more than a servant. I wish you well."

Barbara reached across the space that separated them and held out her hand. Thérèse took it.

In the house, a footman led the way to a long drawing room. There sat the Princess, surrounded by her maids of honor, her ladies-in-waiting. The Princess saw Barbara and nodded. Her eyes gleamed.

She is pleased, thought Barbara, grateful that I give Thérèse. Does she finally begin to see I wish her no harm? She looked for but did not see Carlyle. He should be here.

"I must speak with you," the Princess said, and Barbara followed her some distance from the others. She is going to thank me, thought Barbara.

"I have some sad news," said the Princess. ". . . hanged," Barbara heard. "They found him this morning."

"I don't understand," Barbara said. She didn't.

"Get Lady Devane some water," the Princess said to someone. "Of course it is a shock. We are all shocked."

"I am afraid. Your name is upon broadsheets pasted everywhere. I want you to leave England. It's a sign, I tell you. I've felt it since I saw the broadsheets: You must leave. I should have known how despairing he was. No one would receive him. People would not talk to him when he went to drawing rooms. I knew how proud he was. Tony and I quarreled over it today. He says I blame him for the death, which I never said. He said the fault is no one's. No one's! How can that be? Isn't it, really, when all is said and done, all our fault? I gave the Duchess of Kendall a sapphire so that she would cajole the King into giving him an interview. 'Hurry,' I told her. 'He is in a bad way. Five moments of time will satisfy,' I told her. 'The simple fact of the King's receiving him, of it being known, will mean so much, help him to feel he may establish himself again.' And do you know what she said today, about his death? 'Now I won't wear the sapphire. It will be bad luck,' she said. He used to spend hours entertaining her, entertaining her dreadful nieces, telling them all the gossip, the rumors, gathered like so many thorned flowers, to amuse them. Is that all it meant to her?"

Tommy Carlyle had hanged himself.

Tears were rolling down Barbara's face.

I love you, Barbara, Slane thought. The returning of Hyacinthe's collar had hurt her. The continuing vendetta against Walpole tired her, as did the maneuvering over Devane Square. I no longer draw an honest breath, she said to him. I must hide my thoughts from morning until night. How did this happen?

Slane was part of her dishonesty. He knew it, knew the tension his continuing presence created for her. She has too much heart for court, said Louisa. We ought to have known it.

"No man knows the heart of another," he said. "I could decide tonight to kill myself, and your caring for me wouldn't stop it, if that was what I had decided in my heart, if I felt that alone, that desperate.

"Who else will die before it is ended? 'No man is an island. . . . Every man is a piece of the continent, a part of the main—' "

He grabbed her hands.

"Did you do all you could? Were you kind, forebearing, patient?"

"Not always."

"Who is, *always*? Were you so for a good portion of the time? You are not God, Barbara; you cannot command another's living or dying. It was his choice. He had his own life, his own contract with his own God. I was taught that it is a sin before the eyes of God to take my own life, but, under certain circumstances, I would take my life and then, my chances with God. Now, who are these tears for? For Carlyle, who is dead, or for you, who, perhaps, were not all you meant to be to him? You're not a saint. You aren't, Barbara. And don't quote John Donne to me again. I know every man's death diminishes me. But what about every man's birth, every man's triumph? If I must partake of the loss of all, may I not also partake of the joy of all? Isn't one man's triumph also mine? It must be so. It has to be so."

He'd just received word that Walpole was going to try to convict Rochester on a bill of pains and penalties. It was a bold, brilliant maneuver. It meant Rochester would not go before a court of law. Walpole hadn't the direct proof he needed—a letter in Rochester's writing, or a reliable witness who would say, Yes, he is head of the invasion. So the minister would introduce a motion to make Parliament a court. Parliament need follow no rules of common law, might be presented with any and all evidence, no matter how flimsy. Walpole changed the rules, so that he might win.

It looked as if Charles, the others, would not be tried at all, would simply endure prison for a time. But Christopher Layer would be tried, and so would Gussy, because there was direct evidence, evidence admissible in a court of law, and because Walpole wanted them beheaded. He would behead them and exile Rochester.

Except that Slane was going to snatch Gussy from the Tower. How, he wasn't certain yet. He'd take Layer, too, if he could. "Do it," wrote Rochester, "do whatever you can to humiliate Walpole. I should have left England when you first warned me. Thank you for your message about the bill of pains and penalties. It is a shock to me, but I shall fight. It will be a duel of honor between us, and though he may come out the victor and exile me, he shall not come out the victor with the public."

Barbara touched the collar at her neck.

"I have lost so many people I love. I can't lose you, too. I won't be able to bear it. I really won't. I'll break, Slane."

Time shortened. He could hear his heart beating. There was so much they had to say, to plan.

"Do you love me?"

"You know I do."

"Tell me again."

"I love you."

He threw the two pieces of a broken coin on a table, and his finch in her cage fussed. Jane had told him the custom: Break a crooked ninepence and each take a piece. Then you were betrothed, she said. He wondered what was going through Barbara's head—thoughts of her position, surely, and Devane Square, and the birth of her mother's child. Men were around her, too, seeing her rise, knowing her fine was to be reduced, seeing her again as an asset in the marriage market, someone to bring fortune to family, and fame.

"Marry me," he said.

She looked from the pieces of coin to him, her expression grave.

"When?"

"Someday."

"I can't have children, Slane."

They had never discussed it. He had never pursued the tremor he'd heard in her voice the first time they lay together. Was this why? He could feel the shock of her words in himself, and he hated himself both for feeling it, for showing that he felt it.

"Put the coin away," she said.

I do plight thee my troth, he had been going to say to her. So much to do: go to Italy, report to Jamie, go to France, begin to make a life there. The letter was already off to his mother. "Find me a regiment," he'd written. He was going to become an officer in the French army. When I have a home, he was going to say, I will send for you. If you still care for me, come. If not . . . And then they were to have kissed the way men did when one has knighted the other, chastely, briefly, pledging fidelity to an ideal.

"Come and walk with me, Barbara."

"No, it's too dangerous."

"Pull the hood of your cloak up over your hair. No one will know you."

They walked the twilit narrow streets around the Tower, walked as a man and his sweetheart might, openly, for all the world to see.

He bought her something to eat, and they passed by windows in which families were gathered by candlelight. They sat on the river steps, the enormous wall surrounding the buildings that made up the Tower dark and massive behind them. He told her things in Gaelic: that she was his beloved, that he hated to abandon her—things he could not yet bring himself to say in English. "I wanted children with you," he said in Gaelic. "I wanted a son to replace the one lost to me. This breaks my heart."

In his chamber, they lay in his bed. She stroked his face, and he felt a little peace.

"Tell me more about your life in France."

"You know my mother is married to a French duke, my sister to another. I have an uncle who commands a regiment of Irish soldiers under the French flag."

"So that you could have them buy you a command. You would be a wonderful colonel."

He shivered. There was a misty vision in his mind, of Barbara singing in a beautiful room, the doors open to the outside, silk draperies with cascading tassels, wood floors polished and shining, someone playing a lute. A man in uniform stood near watching her, a man wearing an eyepatch, missing a arm. Was it himself? The more he tried to see, the quicker it disappeared. There were women who followed armies—whores, yes, but wives, too, who camped outside the army's camp and followed husbands over mountain and river, who nursed the wounded when the battles began. He could envision Barbara doing both, thriving on it. The vigor and passion in her would rise like cream.

He turned her on her back, kissed a shoulder blade. Tomorrow was Friday. Charles must receive his single white rose, wrapped in a crude drawing of a man hanged. It always amused him to send Charles that. I can touch you whenever I please, he'd told Charles. When he left, he must arrange for the roses to be delivered.

"I want you to leave," she said.

He moved his hands to her breasts, his mouth to her neck and her ear, moved himself into the shape of her naked body. She quieted, sighed, moved his hand to the slight swell of her belly, a movement that excited him.

"Not now," he said. "There is nothing you can say to make me go. I shall go soon, but I have a little something to do first. Night is passing, your friend has died, you are naked and sighing under my hands. You want me. I want you. This is not the time for talk, Barbara."

Yesterday a public herald had announced two November trials, Layer's and Gussy's. The city was seething again, a volcano that did not quite spew. The time was chosen well. Guy Fawkes Day was in November. Fawkes, a Catholic, had tried to blow up Parliament a hundred years ago. The trials would be after Guy Fawkes Day, after Queen Elizabeth's Day, when candles were lighted in windows in memory of her reign and the end of Popery. The King and his ministers played upon the old fear that Jamie would make England Catholic again. Slane would try to take Layer and Gussy before the trials, so that Walpole lost his public display.

He closed his eyes on fierce and bright pleasure, forgetting everything else. When it was finished, she nestled against his back, stroked his abdomen with light fingers, whispered to him that he must not tempt Fate. She pressed her cheek against his back.

"I adore you," Barbara said in French. "Friend, dear one. Darling. Month of blood, so November was called in the old days. Slane, I begin to feel afraid, and it is not a feeling I like. Do you know what Colonel Perry says? To know there is good in every event, to believe it. My grandmother says that he is a dreamer and a madman, or a true holy man. But wouldn't it be lovely if there was good in all things, a good maybe we were too small to see, but a good nonetheless? Could it be that simple? To look for the good?"

"Sleep, my sweet. I'll wake you before morning."

"I want you to leave. Now," she said in English.

Something rattled claws at him, a warning so urgent that he had to be silent a moment.

"I'll leave after Gussy's trial. I swear it."

The claws' rattling lessened but did not cease.

Barbara started to tell him of her feeling that she wouldn't see the

Virginia garden, but she didn't. She kept her cheek against his shoulder blade, thinking of the expression on his face when he'd learned she was barren.

This death, the coming trials, makes us all feel fragile, makes us all madmen, thought Slane. The feeling in his middle persisted. One of us is in danger, he thought.

He got up from the bed and stood at the window and looked up into the cold night's stars, looked at the Tower, lights shining in various towers within it. He thought of Gussy, of friendship, of love, thinking things he seldom allowed himself. His dreams of sons were ashes in his mouth. Who knew what twists life held? Where is your good in this, Colonel Perry? he thought. The broken pieces of ninepence sat abandoned on the table.

Marry in yellow, ashamed of your fellow, marry in black, wish yourself back.

It was only in the late night, when dawn was near, that he thought beyond himself, to her, to what her barrenness must mean to her. He woke her, and she sat up, bewildered and sleepy, like a child. She must have been a beautiful child, all wild hair and wilder heart. Weren't we all so, once upon a time? A demanding child, he imagined. She liked to win, said Jane. She liked to shout. She cried the hardest and the loudest when hurt.

"What sorrow it must give you," he said, "that there will be no children. Tell me."

The expression on her face touched him to his soul. If he'd had a thousand diamonds, he'd have poured them into her lap to ease her sorrow.

"I can't speak of it."

"Marry me."

"No. You go, do what you must do, think on me, on what I cannot give you as well as what I can. And if there comes a time when you want me as I am, when you see me not as something imperfect and flawed, but as a woman with whom you wish to share life, then ask again."

"What will you say?"

"Who knows, Slane? Do we have to know now?"

No. Because he already knew. She loved him.

One of them was in danger. He felt it again. Which one?

"We must be careful in how we see one another from now on. You mustn't come here again, Barbara."

"Why?"

"I have a feeling."

"Yes. So do I. Please leave, Slane."

"I will. Soon."

Tony poured himself another glass of wine. Barbara had called Carlyle's death a failure of friendship. And more than that, a failure of stewardship. He was your man, and so you were to take care of him, almost as if in marriage, Tony, in sickness or health. He was a valuable man to you, and you let Robin blind you. You are Robin's tool. Tomorrow someone or another will tell you that Carlyle was a sodomite and not worth your regard; someone will discuss his flaws, his faults, tell you you did what was right, but they will be lying, Tony. And if you believe them, you will be lying too. To yourself.

She was harsh. She was very harsh. And she was always right.

In Rome, Philippe stood before Michelangelo's statue called the *Pietà*, of the dead Christ in his mother's arms. Ensconced among the treasures of St. Peter's Basilica, it was one of the sights of Rome. He remained where he was for a time, contemplating the genius of a man who managed to instill both grief and grace into a block of marble, until he saw the same priest he'd seen for the last four days. Then he moved along the assigned path, from one statue or painting to another, before at last standing at the magnificent altar of dazzling green marble and gold. At a side altar, he lit the required seven candles, then walked out of the dimness of St. Peter's into the bright sunlight of the piazza that spread before the church and through which all Rome passed.

He had three more days in which to perform the ritual. He must wait, so he had been told in Paris, for contact from Jacobites. He had no doubt they would contact him. A convert such as he would not be ignored.

Walpole had hurt Roger beyond what was necessary for expediency, and how? By not doing all that could be done; by, with a subtlety that Philippe could respect, encouraging events to a fuller shape than might have happened had he let them alone. The thoughts drove Philippe mad, goaded him almost beyond endurance. He understood necessity, understood there came a time when one could do nothing further for a doomed friend, but to have used that doom, to have deepened it, for one's own purpose was unforgivable, particularly unforgivable because it was Roger. Devane House had not had to be destroyed. Philippe had accompanied Roger to commission paintings for it, had accompanied him when he sifted through antiquities from ancient Rome—with the eye of a master—to display in his Temple of the Arts. In his mind, he could see Roger, the grace of him, reflected in those choices. Devane House had been all that was best in Roger.

At night, Philippe woke from a restless sleep and paced the floor, going over in his mind every word of his conversations with Rochester, with Tommy Carlyle, going over the events of the South Sea Bubble. Barbara was right. Roger had been made scapegoat. It was a brilliant tactic upon Walpole's part. But Walpole was not the only one of brilliancy and cleverness in this secret drama.

High Jacobites in Paris were the ones Philippe insisted upon seeing, and they had at first not believed in his sincerity. Weeks he had waited for them to receive him, while events in England took their course. Philippe read the dispatches sent by the French ambassador. More arrests. A tax proposed against Roman Catholics of the kingdom. The suspending of an act which allowed those imprisoned to be brought before a judge and told what they were charged with. Clever of Walpole to suspend English justice to his need. The publication of a reward for any information concerning one Lucius, Viscount Duncannon, said to be a secret spy for the Pretender.

He did not waste the time they made him wait. He called upon Lord Bolingbroke, the ambitious courtier of Queen Anne who had fled England in 1715. He and Philippe strolled the gardens of the estate outside Paris upon which Bolingbroke now lived. I long for my home, said Bolingbroke. I long to serve my country again. I am a wiser man than once I was. I am humble.

Humble? Bolingbroke? No. But clearly anxious to be back in England.

Bolingbroke and Walpole were old enemies. Old hatred, nourished lest it die, was a useful thing. Walpole joins King George's most trusted ministers, said Philippe. I think if he is able to bring the Bishop of Rochester to trial, he will be foremost among them.

Satisfying, the look upon Bolingbroke's face.

Philippe moved impatiently among the crowds on the piazza. Here it was October, and he had yet to see King James. Looming against Jacobite slowness was the coronation at the end of the month of France's boy Prince, who would become Louis XV. Philippe, the Prince de Soissons, could not miss it. As a royal cousin, a prince of the blood, he had a part to play in the grandeur and pageantry that would mark the event. It had been far too many years since a king of France had been crowned. They'd saved this boy from the smallpox and the dread red rash that killed his great-grandfather, his grandfather, and his father. This boy was a miracle; his survival, his coronation, were a sign that France was destined for the greatness dimmed by England's generals Tamworth and Marlborough. Three more days. It was foolish to make him wait. He would lay waste the earth to avenge Roger. He had pledged a quarter of his fortune to the Jacobite cause.

Barbara, mentioned in the dispatches by France's ambassador to England, walked the corridors of his mind. "We must court her," the ambassador said. "It is clear she is a favorite of both King and Prince, yet apparently she graces the bed of neither. Interesting."

Dear Barbara. He could have seen her crushed beneath the debt like an insect crushed beneath one's foot. But Walpole betrayed friendship, betrayed Roger. So, Philippe would see that betrayal avenged. And Barbara, dear Barbara, must rise now, so that Walpole might fall.

⁂

Thérèse tried to stop crying, but she could not. It was All Hallow's Eve; the night ghosts and spirits roamed, and in the Leicester House kitchen, servants were roasting nuts in the fireplace and telling tales to frighten one another. Thérèse needed to hear no ghost tale to be frightened. They'd taken everything this time and turned it upside down. The straw mattress was pulled from her bed, the straw ripped from inside and tossed everywhere. The water in her pitcher was puddled upon the floor. Her clothing, her letters, her combs, her needles and thread, even the pins in her pincushion were thrown about. The laces she'd been sewing to the Princess's dress were torn from the sleeve, dangling like shredded ribbon. The word "Papist" was written across one wall with rouge, the "i" dotted with one of her patches.

Why did they do it? What did they want?

Four days ago, the pillow had been at the other end of the bed from where she'd left it. Three days ago, all her gowns had been dumped on the floor, but nothing else was touched. Two days ago, the linens had been pulled from the bed and folded in a neat pile outside her door. The first time and even the second, she'd thought: Someone teases because I am new, because I am French.

Yesterday, as she had walked through the series of grand front parlors, she saw written upon a mirror, the word "Treason," and with it a stick figure of a woman hanged. She left the house then, had herself rowed upriver to the village of Twickenham, to find her friends, Caesar and Montrose and tell them. They were upset.

This was a difficult household. The Prince had a temper, which he could not manage. It fell at will upon everyone from his wife to the random groom who handed him his horse. And Mrs. Howard, the Prince's mistress, lived in the household as bedchamber woman to the Princess. Swift, constant currents of malice flowed from such an arrangement.

The Princess did not forgive the King for keeping the three Princesses, did not forgive Madame Barbara for being made their lady-in-waiting. It was said the Prince's mother was locked away in a castle in the mountains of Hanover, her crime an old adultery, the reason the King had divorced her and banished her. He'd killed her lover, buried him under the floorboards of the house of their tryst, it was said. There was a curse upon the King: He was to die a year after his wife. Thérèse had heard the Princess believed she would die upon a Wednesday and was always restless and difficult upon that day.

This house had an air of unhappiness as tangible as the stone of the walls outside, unhappiness that spread to her. Now she must go to Mrs. Clayton and explain that the gown would not be ready for this evening, when the Princess had particularly asked for it.

Her whole inside vibrated with the harm wished her. She could feel it. Who did this to her? And why?

CHAPTER 55

The first of November.

"Visitors," Bathsheba said, in that soft whisper of hers. "They wait."

Barbara opened the kitchen door. Thérèse and Caesar and Montrose stood under the trees of the park behind her mother's house. She smiled, happy to see them. Montrose met her at the garden gate, which creaked with cold as Barbara opened it.

"Something's happened. Pretend all is well. We're likely watched."

"Watched? Why?"

"Please, Lady Devane."

Montrose waved cheerfully, falsely for Caesar and Thérèse to join them. One look at Thérèse's face, half hidden under the hood of her cloak, and Barbara felt her insides tighten.

"We'll go inside. After all, what harm is there in visiting Lady Devane, for whom we all used to labor?" Montrose said, too loudly. He was a poor actor.

In the kitchen, Barbara listened to Thérèse with what was at first bewilderment and then became anger.

"Last night," said Thérèse, "I was told you'd come to see me, and I went downstairs, and then out into the garden, looking for you, and two men were there. I'd never seen them before. They put me in a coach, threatened me with harm if I spoke out or tried to escape them. They covered my eyes, madame. They kept the cover upon my eyes even after the carriage stopped, until I was in some room, and there they questioned me. I must say nothing, they told me, or I would be sent to France, to prison there, lost to the world and all I love. 'You know your countrymen imprison without trial and throw away the key,' they said to me. 'We can make certain that is done to you.' "

"Questioned about what?" Barbara said.

"About— About Paris, Monsieur Harry, the Duke of Wharton. A-About you."

Wariness moved, snakelike, through Barbara.

"They asked about Rome, about your father, about Monsieur Harry and his actions there. About *your* actions. I did not know what to say. Had you called upon the Pretender while in Rome? they asked. 'Of course,' I said, 'everyone did.' They asked about Virginia, about the overseer, Blackstone. 'Were you and he lovers?' they asked. 'No,' I told them. How dare they ask such a thing? I said. Did I know he was a Jacobite? They threatened, madame. They said I would have to leave England if I did not tell the truth. 'I have told you the truth,' I told them, but they asked me over and over again, until I became tired and cried. They liked it that I cried. They told me if I said anything about being questioned, they would find me no matter where I was, and have my tongue cut out."

Robin. Barbara felt cold. Do not underestimate his determination or implacability. Words of Carlyle's, before the pillory. Sentiment had not served Tommy and would not serve her, for sentiment died before the push of Robin's ambition.

She made Thérèse repeat everything again.

"You're to stay here this night, behind a locked door," she said. "I think someone tries to implicate me in the Jacobite plot."

All everyone was talking of was the treason trials. Barbara could feel fear stalking the corridors at St. James's Palace. One could feel the tension gathering everywhere, like dark clouds.

"Who would do such a thing?" cried Montrose.

"Are you safe?" Caesar's face was grave.

"No, I am not. I want the three of you to remember this. If I disappear, look for me in the Tower."

"Who threatens you so?" asked Caesar.

"Robert Walpole. Remember that, too. Walpole."

They were silenced. Yes, thought Barbara, if I disappear, you will have to take on the mighty.

What to do? A note to Slane. They must not see one another again. He must leave London. I can see the danger coiled, tongue flickering, ready to strike, she thought. A visit to her grandmother and to Tony. Tony was angry with her, but he was family. He would help. Walpole pushed. She must push back. She must use her own strength or be trampled.

Children sang the songs and rhymes of the season:

> Remember, remember!
> The fifth of November,
> The gunpowder treason and plot;
> There is no reason why the
> Gunpowder treason should ever be forgot!

Revelers paraded a scarecrow figure of Guy Fawkes. London's Catholics, who had been allowed back into the city, kept their doors locked tight this night. Church bells rang. Scarecrow figures of Fawkes curled up and burned in the smoky evening bonfires throughout the city.

Barbara, watching with her grandmother, Lady Doleraine, and the young Princesses, shivered. She was in a carriage among a crowd of carriages at Lincoln's Inn Fields, where there was a giant bonfire burning, where Londoners danced around the flames and threw in straw figures of Fawkes. Her grandmother reached over and took her hand.

"Can you endure until tomorrow?" her grandmother said. Their interview with the King was then.

"Yes."

There was a knock upon their carriage door, and Lady Doleraine leaned out the window.

After talking a moment with someone, she said to Barbara, "It's Lady Shrewsborough. She asks if you'll walk around the fire with her."

"Oh, let us go too," said Princess Amelia.

Lady Doleraine, their governess, shook her head.

To the sound of the Princesses' begging, Barbara stepped out of the carriage.

Lord Carteret, a minister to the King, had told her that the King talked of building his granddaughters a house on Devane Square, on the spot where Roger's house had been. Princess House, thought Barbara, seeing it in her mind, nestled at the crest of a slight hill, behind it the quiet fields and lovely village of Marylebone, before it the vista of the Virginia garden and the roads that led to St. James's Palace.

Laurence Slane walked up behind Aunt Shrew. His expression was solemn, his eyes on Barbara's face. He had arranged this.

"I prefer to walk with my aunt alone," she said to him. If he couldn't read her coldness, couldn't see her fear, he was a fool. Why hadn't he left? Sweet Jesus, she was frightened. "Stay away from me and leave England," she'd written.

"Why did you send Slane away? He's harmless enough, and I like a handsome fellow holding my arm," Aunt Shrew said as she and Barbara began to walk around the fire. It rose some twenty feet above them, the flames hissing, crackling, roaring from deep within its kindling heart. The light from the fire made flickering shadows.

"I didn't want him to hear what I have to say to you. I've told no one, not even my mother. Walpole has been looking into my past."

"What on earth for?"

"To see if I am Jacobite."

"My God."

"Yes. Let us keep walking, keep talking the way an aunt and a niece would. There is no one close enough to hear us, but I want to take no chances. I have an interview tomorrow with the King and with Walpole. I intend to challenge him openly. Tony and Grandmama will be there."

They walked for a time in silence. Londoners around them were drinking gin from dark bottles, then throwing the bottles into the flames.

"It is wise to bring Tony and your grandmother. I couldn't have chosen more astutely myself. I'll be thinking of you, Bab. Know that."

"Thank you, Aunt Shrew. Let's go back to the carriage."

Many people were walking around the bonfire.

Mrs. Modest Welsh and her husband walked. Mrs. Welsh admired the height of the fire, the way the flames roared. They were at the cluster of carriages where the nobility had gathered to watch. Women leaned out of carriage windows, jewels at their necks and ears. Men, lace spilling out of the sleeves of their coats, buckles and sword hilts gleaming in the fire's light, stood in groups. Their wigs were long and thick and fine, their hats wide-brimmed and dashing.

One man, quite handsome, with dark brows, stood a little apart. He was listening to an elderly woman, one of the few women not in a carriage. She wore a huge, sloping hat like a man's, with dark, false curls spilling out of it, and many jewels, many bracelets.

"I will kill him," said Slane.

Aunt Shrew put her hand on his arm. "You will leave London, and at once. Barbara would say the same."

"She already has." He couldn't leave. He wouldn't leave. The details of the rescues weren't in place. He mustn't leave without Gussy. Two days ago, a guard's child had delivered a white rose from Gussy. Forever loyal, it meant. Even if he was convicted, his gesture said he would reveal nothing. Would Gussy like France? Too bad if he did not. And now Walpole threatened Barbara.

"Well, God curse you, why didn't you listen? Your part in this is over. You must face it, and leave us to our own devices. It would break my heart to see you beheaded."

"It's him," said Mrs. Welsh.

"Who?" said her husband.

"The man who asked about the lodging that day."

She pointed Slane out to her husband.

"You're certain?"

"His is not a face one forgets," Mrs. Welsh replied, tartly.

Taking her by the hand, her husband dragged her among the carriages, asking coachmen if the Lord Treasurer was here. They moved from carriage to carriage, until finally a coachman said, "He is, and just who might be wanting him?"

"Modest Welsh, King's messenger."

"The Lord Treasurer is otherwise occupied. You'll need to wait, King's messenger."

Instead, Welsh knocked loudly on the ornate, varnished carriage door. The curtains of the windows and door window were pulled shut.

Why does he come to the fire, if he doesn't view it? thought Mrs. Welsh.

"Here now," said the coachman, but Welsh rapped on the door again.

The coachman climbed down and stood before Welsh, ready to fight, but the carriage door opened slowly, and a plump man, richly dressed, with eyes that seemed lazy and sated, stepped down. Mrs. Welsh caught a glimpse of a woman inside the carriage, leaning back against the seat, her eyes closed, her gown pulled up untidily, a gown under which an abdomen swelled large with child.

"Modest Welsh," said Walpole. "How may I serve you this fine evening?"

"Forgive me disturbing you, sir, but it's important, sir."

"It had better be. What is it?"

"Stay here," Welsh ordered his wife, and he and Walpole walked away, lost to Mrs. Welsh's sight after a time among the carriages. When they returned, Walpole was smiling. He winked at Mrs. Welsh before stepping back up into the carriage.

"You're to have a new gown," said Welsh to her, "compliments of the Lord Treasurer."

"Two new gowns," came a voice from inside the carriage.

"Two new gowns," corrected Welsh.

Slane cooked himself a good breakfast and thought about the Tower guard he was going to bribe at this ungodly hour before dawn. His finch flew about the chamber and perched from time to time on the table so that he could feed her breakfast too. Time to leave. Dawn was an hour or so away, and the man went on duty at dawn. Slane held out his hand to the finch, but she went flying up into a corner of the chamber, perching where he could not reach her.

"If you don't go into your cage, I have to leave you," he said. The finch cocked her head.

"Come, sweet, into your cage."

She remained where she was. Stubborn little bird, he thought. Tonight she'd fuss at him for not putting her inside. He'd find her perched somewhere, exhausted from her day of freedom. You should take better care of me, she'd scold. He ran down his lodging stairs. The morning was still, dark, with that absolute quiet that comes at dead of morning, before dawn. Slane's guard said he knew others who could be bribed. At this point, Gussy was not allowed out of his cell. If Slane could somehow arrange that Gussy be allowed exercise, perhaps he could snatch him up. Otherwise, he was going to have to take him as they moved him back and forth for the trial, two weeks away. That meant staying in England longer than he really wished to, but—

They came up from behind and took him. His mind was on an escape plan. He was not even wary until their arms were linking into his.

Walpole. He knew it at once.

"Thief! Help me! I'm being robbed—" He struggled with them, the way any man would, but he was deposited briskly in a carriage. At once, he put his hand on the door opposite. It was locked.

"What is this?" he demanded, his mind flickering and turning, looking for any escape. "Who are you? I'll have you called before a bailiff. What do you want?"

"No need to get upset," said one of the men. "Someone high up is wishing to speak with you, privately-like. Someone high up has asked us to be gentle, but we can only be gentle if you are, too."

"Someone high up? Who? This is a trick. You try to rob me—"

He heaved himself toward the carriage door, but was stopped.

"Do we have to hurt you?" asked the first man.

"Anything but my face. I am an actor. Take what coins I have. They are in this pocket, here. Then let me free. I'll say nothing. I swear it."

"We're going to blindfold you now. Easy, easy, no tricks from you, no tricks from us. Hold his arms. I don't trust him."

He made a last attempt, but they hit him hard enough to let him know they'd hurt him if they had to.

"Careful of his face, now," one of them said.

When the carriage stopped, he was helped out, his arms held tight, one of the men on each side of him, and led into a building, up stairs, into a room. Once their hands left him, he pulled off the blindfold. They sat in chairs on either side of the door. Behind him was a cot.

"Lie down," one of the men said. "Him who wants to see you will be a while. He has other business to take care of today."

The King stood at his fireplace. Through a small door, set so beautifully into the wall that it did not show, came one of the King's personal servants, Mehemet. He nodded to Tony and the Duchess, smiled at Barbara.

Then Walpole and Lord Townshend were ushered in, and for the briefest of moments Walpole's face went blank at the sight of Barbara and her family. So. The King had given them no warning of this interview I've requested, thought Barbara. Good.

Walpole smiled, came forward to kiss her cheek as if nothing were wrong. Barbara turned away from him. He looked surprised.

Clever man, thought Barbara. And so dangerous.

Walpole glanced at the faces of the other members of her family, his expression questioning, perplexed, innocent.

"There has been an awkwardness, a misunderstanding. His Majesty feels his English is not enough for all that will be said, and the subject is too delicate to entrust with another minister," said Mehemet. He was very grave, very dignified. I am praying to Allah of this, he'd told Barbara when they'd met in a palace corridor, that all may go as it should. There were few secrets from a personal servant. That's why a good one who could keep secrets was so valuable.

"I have been asked to speak for him. There has been a certain handling of Lady Devane's former French maidservant which seems to involve Lady Devane herself. She has come to us—I speak, of course, for the King—with her cousin and their grandmother, to ask that whatever suspicions are held of her, she be allowed to address."

"Suspicions?" Walpole said.

"Her maidservant has been ruthlessly snatched up, ruthlessly questioned, and also threatened to keep silence," said Tony.

Tony was angry. Barbara had never seen him so angry. Hero, she thought, defending family honor. Bravo, cousin.

"There were questions, as I understand," Tony was saying, "to the maidservant about Viscount Alderley and Lady Devane, about their activities several years ago in both Paris and Rome. There was also, as I understand, a certain slanderous accusation—which I will not repeat because I find it too offensive—about her time in Virginia."

Softly, Mehemet repeated this in French, but, impatient, the King cut him short with a gesture. He understood.

"My grandson's Jacobitism, his father's, is no secret," said the Duchess. She was dressed in black, with diamonds everywhere, the medals of her husband's honors pinned among the diamonds like beacons. "If you begin to suspect those of us with relatives who are Jacobite, you suspect over half the families in England. One of our own—Lord Russel—is in prison even now, but that does not mean that we share his sentiments."

"Nor does it mean," said Tony, "that he is guilty. He has been accused by Layer, who, as we all know, is half mad. An accusation is not proof of guilt. At least, not by my understanding of English common law. If there is an accusation against Lady Devane, we wish to know of it at once. I want no more of my family imprisoned in the middle of the night, with no writ of charge, with no opportunity to go before a magistrate and show just cause. My sister still has not recovered from the manner in which Lord Russel was arrested. I will make no excuses for Viscount Alderley, who lies in his grave and therefore can harm no one, but I will say there has never been so much as a breath of rumor or a single fact to indicate that Lady Devane ever joined him in his sentiments. That she loved her brother, no one will deny, but to love someone is not to support them in treason."

"Lady Devane," Mehemet said, "will you please repeat what your maidservant has told you."

Barbara kept her eyes fixed on both ministers as she repeated Thérèse's story. Neither spoke, though Townshend showed irritation and embarrassment.

"Have you any firm reason to suspect Lady Devane?" said the King in English to Walpole, his accent heavy, the words clear.

"No."

"Is there any evidence, any letter to her, any description of her, any reference, anything apart from her relationship to her brother?" asked Mehemet for the King.

"No."

"Then how dare either of you imply—" began Tony, but the King turned sharply, his expression stern, so that Tony was silent.

"Will you withdraw a moment while I speak with my ministers?" the King asked Barbara and her family. And to Mehemet: "You also."

When he was left with Walpole and Townshend, the King said, in English, "You did not come to me?"

"We desired more evidence concerning Lady Devane, Majesty, before burdening you," said Townshend.

"Have you more?"

"No."

"The maidservant?"

"French, a Catholic, with them in Paris and Rome."

"And before service to Lady Devane?"

"In Paris, among the servants to the daughters of the Prince de Condé."

"The Prince de Condé is suspected?"

Walpole ignored the King's irony. "The overseer in Virginia—" he began, but the King stopped him with an abrupt gesture.

"Nothing else other than a colonial overseer who is Jacobite—"

"And a father and a brother," put in Walpole. "All the Jacobites courted her in Italy."

"—to make you suspect her?" finished the King, as if Walpole had not spoken. "I wish to be certain upon this."

"The matter of the gosling," began Townshend. "He—we thought perhaps it might be someone known to us, a woman, perhaps. . . ."

Townshend stopped speaking, as if he heard how feeble he sounded.

"The woman being Lady Devane? She was in Virginia all of the spring. How long has she been this dread Jacobite, this gosling said to have penetrated my kingdom? Before Lord Devane's death? After?"

The King picked up a bell and rang it, abruptly, impatiently. Mehemet appeared. The King began to speak to him in clipped French, and Mehemet translated, his voice soft, his expression wooden.

There was no need to translate anger, an anger large enough that the King had been unable to continue in English.

"Then why did she go to Virginia?" Mehemet said. "To plot uprisings in my colonies? Did she devise the taking of her servant boy so that she would have a reason to return? You've been clumsy. If I am not mistaken, you have made enemies of the Duke of Tamworth and his grandmother."

"I can win the Duke around again, if need be," said Walpole, quickly.

"If you wish us to halt our investigations—" began Townshend, stiffly, almost arrogantly.

The King cut him off. "Tell me now, once and forever, if there is any reason to suspect Lady Devane?"

Neither man answered.

"Then you will issue personal apologies to her in my presence and in the presence of her cousin and grandmother, and you will leave the maidservant in peace."

The King smiled. Anger vanished. "You persecute the enemies of my house. Your zeal is appreciated, although clumsy. I have a high regard for Lady Devane. I am glad she is guilty of nothing, but if she were . . ."

The silence after his words told all. Walpole and Townshend responded like dogs chastened but then patted upon the head by their master.

"It pained me beyond words to even contemplate that she might have Jacobite connections," said Walpole. "She is like a daughter to me. A gift to the maidservant might mitigate our clumsiness. Fifty pounds, perhaps."

"Twenty," said the King. At his nod, Mehemet fetched the others.

Lord Townshend's apology was formal, but Walpole shook his head and placed a hand over his heart.

"I am a fool, and I ask your forgiveness. I have allowed my loyalty to the throne to overbear my good judgment. I would not hurt Lady Devane, who is like a daughter to me, for the world. Please tell me I am forgiven."

The Duchess and Tony were silent.

Barbara said, "I was so frightened and confused by it all. I didn't know where to turn."

Walpole took her hands in his.

"Tell me how I can make it up to you. Tell me how I can repair our friendship."

"Reduce the fine in the House of Commons, now, before Christmas," answered Barbara.

Walpole smiled. He understood bargains. "Consider it done. With His Majesty's permission, of course."

"It has always had my permission."

The King dismissed the ministers, listened to Tony's stiff thanks. It was clear the Duke was unsatisfied and still angry.

"A moment alone with Lady Devane," the King said.

"I thank you for this, sir, for the opportunity to face my accusers," said Barbara when the others had left.

"Too harsh a word. You were accused of nothing."

She met the King's eyes directly. "It felt as if I were."

"I give you a gift."

"I don't require a gift, Your Majesty."

"Your Jane Cromwell may have one night, one night only, with her husband before his trial."

"Do you do this to please me, sir, or to annoy Walpole?"

"You are too clever. Both."

"Thank you from the bottom of my heart. This means a great deal to me. She is my dearest friend."

Just as she was opening the door to leave, he said, "There's more."

Barbara waited.

"The date of execution for Augustus Cromwell has been set. We decided it yesterday."

"Your Majesty, there's been no trial—"

"Ah, but he will be found guilty. I've gone over the evidence myself. We will take his head from him the last day in February. And on the next day, we begin against the Bishop of Rochester. . . . You're on duty this night?"

"Yes, sir." Her throat felt closed. She could barely speak.

"You'll come and read to me after the Princesses are in bed?"

"Of course, Your Majesty."

"No voice pleases me as much as yours."

"Thank you, Your Majesty."

"What will you do when you do not have the fine to worry over?"

"I will sing like a lark in the sun."

In the carriage, with her grandmother and Tony, Barbara would have liked to have wept. The King gave with one hand and took with the other.

"Was that one of the King's Turks?" asked the Duchess.

She meant Mehemet. "Yes. He is the King's personal servant, captured when he was a boy. He handles all of the King's private accounts, and the King is very fond of him."

"So it is a good thing that this Mehemet was there."

"I think so. It meant the King wished to keep everything discreet."

"I have no intention of being discreet," said the Duchess. "I intend to tell everyone who calls upon me of Walpole's conduct toward you. I will never forgive him, not until the day I die."

"Do you see of what Walpole is capable?" Barbara said to Tony. "Do you see that he will, in the end, betray anyone?"

Tony looked at her, his expression set. "I am his enemy now, Barbara. Be assured."

That's how they're alike, thought Barbara, looking from him to her grandmother. That implacability, that stubbornness. How glad I am to have them, their steadfastness. Oh, Gussy.

"Assured," said the Duchess. "There is no assurance at court, among ministers or favorites. Either can change in the blink of an eye. I was there when the Duchess of Marlborough led Queen Anne around by the nose, and the Duke of Marlborough and Richard won victory after victory, and I was there when Queen Anne refused to so much as nod in the direction of her friend, when Marlborough was relieved of his command, never mind the victories. Put not your trust in princes."

Except, thought Barbara, occasionally. I intend to weep very quietly when I tell the Prince of Wales about Robin and today.

At her mother's, Barbara rushed up the stairs, knocked upon the door of her mother's bedchamber and entered without permission to do so. Andreas, in the midst of buttoning his breeches, stared at her, appalled.

Barbara sat in a chair near the bed, as if this were the most natural thing in the world, and waited. After another moment, in which it was clear she was not going to leave the chamber, Andreas finished dressing, pulling on his coat, picking up his shoes.

Her mother lay on her side. Was she asleep? Andreas said goodbye in firm tones, so that it was very hard for Barbara not to laugh. Her eyes danced at him. The moment the door closed behind him, Barbara shook her mother's shoulder.

"What?" Diana didn't turn over.

"Robin tried to label me a Jacobite."

Diana turned over at that, her face slack, tired.

"He was gathering evidence against me. I confronted him before the King, and he backed down, admitted he had nothing but Harry's old adventures and his own hope."

She doesn't look well, thought Barbara. Where is her old vehemence, her fire, her cursing, her shouting?

"Have you nothing to say, Mother?"

"You won."

Is it my brother who takes away your strength? Barbara thought, and for the first time, she considered the possibility that, in spite of tea leaves, her mother really might die in childbirth, was perhaps dying now. Women did die so, it was true, all the time. And she thought about Andreas, this scene she'd just witnessed a portion of. Her mother was sapping him, taming him. Why? Then she knew. For her. In her own way, Diana loved.

It was late afternoon now. Robert Walpole sat before a table, some papers on it, a decanter and two glasses. At one end of the table was a clerk, pen poised.

"Sir," Slane said, "what is the meaning of this?"

"Allow me to introduce myself."

"Everyone knows of you."

Walpole smiled, cold, cordial. "Wine?"

"No, thank you." He'd had time to think. If Walpole knew he was Duncannon, he'd have been taken at once to the Tower. He felt calmer at that. What happened in your confrontation with my love today? I can't tell a thing from your face. Did my love best you, Walpole? She's a wiser man than either of us. She told me to leave, and I wouldn't listen.

"Just a few little questions answered, that's all I need," said Walpole.

"I'll answer anything you please, but did I have to wait all day?"

"Had you something better to do? Where were you off to at dawn? Dawn was what they said, wasn't it, Bone?" He spoke to the clerk.

"I was going fishing."

"I myself like to fish, but there is never time for it. Well, we'll be finished before we begin, and you can be on your way again, I'm sure. Where were you on September twenty-sixth?"

"I have no idea."

"You've been in London, what, two years? Are you comfortable with your lodging?"

Slane folded his arms, impatiently. "Very comfortable, thank you."

"Not wanting to move?"

"I move as I need to."

"That need being?"

"To hide from a jealous woman or someone I owe. My life has its ups and downs."

"You go to Leicester House to play cards with the Princess of Wales. You are a favorite of Lady Shrewsborough. I see more up than down."

"I am fortunate sometimes."

"I've a Mrs. Modest Welsh here who says you came to her at the end of September and asked about lodging. She remembers you quite well." Walpole peered at the paper. " 'A handsome man, dark eyes, dark brows, a scar.' Since she doesn't run a boardinghouse, it was strange to her to have a stranger ask."

"It wasn't I."

"Then you won't mind if I ask Mrs. Welsh, will you?"

"No."

"Excellent. Bone." Walpole motioned to the clerk, who rose and walked toward a door set in a side wall.

Mrs. Welsh came into the chamber.

"It's him," she said to Walpole. "That's the man."

Slane stood, bowed to her.

"I've never seen this woman before in my life. I've never seen you before, madam."

"I opened my door and there he was. He asked if I kept lodgers."

"You have mistaken me for someone else." Slane was patient, but only just.

"No. It was you."

"I think not."

"Thank you, Mrs. Welsh," said Walpole. Bone closed the door behind her.

"May I leave now?" Slane asked.

"Let us talk until I have this a little more clearly in my mind. You did not ask Mrs. Welsh about lodging?"

"I did not."

"Are you certain you remember nothing about September twenty-sixth?"

"Quite certain."

"I am going to bring Mrs. Welsh in again. Bone, one more time with Mrs. Welsh."

"It is her word against mine. You'll get nowhere with this, sir."

But Mrs. Welsh was not the person who walked through the door. It was the man Slane had asked about Neyoe.

Slane felt himself go slack.

"Bone, I asked for Mrs. Welsh. You've made a mistake. Ah, well, Slane, I believe you know Mr. Webster Adam. Mr. Adam, is this the man who asked you about Philip Neyoe?"

"One and the same. I saw him that day the body was found, and about four days later, he came up to me and asked about Neyoe— Had he lived in the Welsh house? Did he come and go? I told him, not knowing I might be doing wrong."

"Thank you so much, Mr. Adam. Your help has been immeasurable."

There was a silence after Adam left the chamber. Slane listened to the sound of the clerk scribbling. He summoned outrage to his voice, his face.

"I don't know that man. I have never seen him before. Someone is lying to you, sir—"

"So he is, and doing excellently, too. Bravo, Slane. Tell me how you knew Neyoe?"

Slane sighed, sagged down in the chair, sullen. "We grew up in the same village."

"In Ireland?"

"Yes."

"And what village would that be?"

He said the first name that came to mind.

"Did you come to London together?"

"No. I hadn't seen him in years. We ran across one another in London, and he asked me, every once in a while, to pick up letters for him at certain taverns and coffeehouses."

"Letters for him?"

"Him, other men sometimes."

"What names?"

"Burford, Rogers . . . I don't remember any more." These were Jacobite code names. Neither one was Gussy's; neither one was Rochester's. God forgive me, Slane thought.

"And it didn't trouble you that Mr. Neyoe received mail under names other than his. You had no questions about it."

"Not really. I was just glad for the dinner he bought me once in a while. It meant nothing to me. It wasn't my affair."

"To correspond with the Pretender or any of his adherents is high treason."

"The Pretender! I wrote no letters! Received none! I did a favor for a friend."

All I must do, thought Slane, is get out of this chamber.

"He was a Jacobite. You must have known of his Jacobite feelings."

"No."

"He never tried to recruit you, never asked for more than your picking up a letter for him?"

"He asked for money whenever he could, nothing else."

"He didn't wish to be presented to Lady Shrewsborough or the Princess of Wales?"

"Good God, no. I would never have presented him. He was a sniveling little wretch."

Walpole didn't even smile. "And when you saw him on the stairs, how did you feel?"

"Upset, frightened, I don't know. Philip owed me a debt, and I'd been looking for him. I never expected to find him dead."

"Frightened, you say. Why, frightened?"

"Doesn't death always frighten?"

"Indeed. And so you saw Philip Neyoe after his death, were told by Mr. Adam Webster that he lived in Modest Welsh's house, yet still say you didn't go to the door and ask Mrs. Welsh about lodgings."

"No, I didn't."

"Someone took something from Neyoe's pocket after he was dead. Did you follow the cart carrying Neyoe's body to Whitehall, take something from the pocket?"

"I did not!"

If Walpole brought the official in, the man would identify Slane. I asked him if he'd seen a man running, the official would say, and he told me to go that way. Offered me an apple, the cheeky rascal.

"And so you didn't discuss with Neyoe any of your high friendships—your card games with the Princess, with Lady Shrewsborough—"

Slane stood and pulled the table up into Walpole, who fell back in his chair, the table atop him. The face of the clerk was shocked. He was still sitting in his chair, pen poised. Slane was at a door, opening it. There stood the two men who'd captured him. They pushed him back in the chamber, took in the sight of Walpole rising from the debris, and pushed Slane into a wall, slammed fists into his face and abdomen. The shock of his head hitting the wall took the fight from him. A familiar sickness rampaged in his middle, a ringing in his head, bad enough to mute the pain of their fists.

"Enough."

Walpole spoke. Slane couldn't think against the rising, nauseous pounding in his head and middle. I've hurt my head again, he thought before he fainted.

When he opened his eyes, the clerk, Bone, was kneeling at his side. There was a wet cloth on his head. He sat up, leaned over and retched up some of his breakfast. Bone made a disgusted sound. Thank God I ate, Slane thought.

"Can you sit?" he heard Walpole say.

He ground his teeth. "No."

Walpole held a handkerchief to his nose. "The stench."

"Open a window," gasped Slane, before he gave up more of his breakfast.

"Do it," commanded Walpole, and Bone rushed to obey. The cold air was wonderful. Everyone breathed it in. Slane half crawled toward the window, followed by Walpole's henchmen.

He pulled himself up, saw that he was only two windows high, managed to cover their shoes with more breakfast, porridge, bacon, toasted bread. One of the men made a gagging sound. The other stepped back. In another second, Slane was out the window and dropping, catching one hand to a drain spout a moment to stop himself long enough to gather his wits, to soften his fall. He still landed too hard. He heard something snap in his ankle, felt it in ringing arcs up his leg and into his hip. His head, too, was ringing, and his abdomen, where they'd hit him. Some days, it didn't pay to rise from bed.

He glanced toward the window. No one there. Walpole's men were already on the stairs, coming down for him. He half ran, half limped—he'd crawl if he had to—stopping only to pull off his wig and coat, stuff them under hay in a cart. He knew this part of London the way he knew his own hand. He knew any part of London as if it were his own hand. To steal another wig, a cloak, would be nothing. To get to Seven Dials, London's infamous slum, festooned with gin cellars and rotting buildings, would be nothing. All he had to do was reach one of his army of beggar's children, one beggar's child to lead him, and as the game of his boyhood said, he was home, free. Good-bye, Gussy, I cannot save you. Walpole wins. How bitter that thought was. His finch. What will happen to her? Good-bye Barbara. Be well, my love. We aren't finished, you and I, but I'm leaving England. The Fates have spoken far too loudly and far too clearly.

" 'This was a dreadful Sight to me, especially when going down to the Shore, I could see the marks of Horror, which the dismal Work they had been about had left behind it, viz. The Blood, the Bones, and part of the Flesh of Humane Bodies, eaten and devour'd. . . .' "

Barbara read aloud to the King. He was like a boy, listening. She read until she stumbled over words.

"You are fatigued," the King said. "It has been a long day."

In the bedchamber at St. James's that belonged to Barbara as a lady-in-waiting, Bathsheba helped her to undress, brought her a cloth and water to wash herself with. There were no words from Bathsheba, and Barbara was glad. At the sound of a knock on the door, Bathsheba went to it, opened it, called Barbara, in that soft way she had. There on the floor lay a bouquet of roses. Barbara brought them in, knelt by the fire to look at them. They were deepest, darkest red, like blood, and in among them was one white one. Slane. He was gone. She didn't know how and she didn't know why, but he was gone. Thank God.

She put the white rose into the flames. The rest she held to herself, as if they were Slane. No, not Slane anymore. Duncannon. There was pain in her heart, and she began to cry, but there was also gladness. What was the verse, the beautiful, beautiful words? Make me to hear joy and gladness; that the bones which thou hast broken may rejoice. Much yet to do, Gussy's trial, the fine, Gussy's death to survive, but Slane was safe. She could sleep now, the way she hadn't in days.

Tomorrow, Jane went to see Gussy. There was that, at least.

CHAPTER 56

They were gathered at Aunt Shrew's, dressing Jane as if she were a bride. Jane's hair had been curled with heated tongs, and Barbara had brushed it, pinning in her most beautiful feathers. Jane wore an ornate gown of Aunt Shrew's and one of Barbara's necklaces, and Barbara brushed powder on her face, screwed earrings in her ears, put patches at her mouth.

Lady Ashford was pinning the gown where it hung too loosely.

"Too thin," she said to her daughter.

"Enough for Gussy," said Aunt Shrew.

"Done," said Barbara. She clapped her hands together. "Ladies and gentlemen, I give you Mrs. Augustus Cromwell."

She held Jane's hand, made her turn in a circle. The room erupted into applause.

"Now, you listen to me, Jane Cromwell." Aunt Shrew held up a small leather bag. "You are to flirt with every man in the guardroom of his tower, and if you can't do that, at the least give them coins and tell them to drink at a tavern later to your husband's health. Trust me in this, Jane. Make allies of them. Smile and be kind and flirt if you have it in you. You may need them for kindness later on."

Barbara looked at the rouged puff in her hand. She'd told no one yet of the execution date.

"I don't think she has it in her," Aunt Shrew said to the Duchess.

"She will be inspired from on high to do whatever she has to," said Colonel Perry. "I am going to be praying for you, Jane. Once you leave this chamber, I am leaving my vagabond, wayward friends and going off to pray."

"Pray for Gussy, who will need strength this night," said Aunt Shrew.

There was laughter, then kisses and a little crying and fretting from various children as Barbara tied her best fur-lined cloak securely about Jane.

"I want to go," said Amelia, when she saw her mother and her grandfather leave the chamber.

Barbara picked her up. "Wouldn't you rather wear a patch?"

Amelia wasn't to be had easily. "Three?"

"Five, if you want."

"I'm for a hand of cards," said Aunt Shrew. "Who will join me? Has anyone seen that rascal Laurence Slane? He was to play cards with me last night, and he never showed. A woman, I suppose." She dealt out cards to the Duchess and Lady Ashford. "I think I'll go to live in Twickenham when this is all ended. I'm tired of London. I haven't the heart for it all anymore."

" 'Mary, Mary, quite contrary, how does your garden grow? With cockle shells and silver bells, and pretty maids all in a row. If in October, you do marry, love will come but riches tarry. Marry in green, ashamed to be seen, marry in gray, you'll go far away,' " Barbara quoted to Jane's children, gathered around her. Her children, too; Jane had always shared them. She looked over to the trio playing cards, thinking of all the years among them, all the wisdom.

"What is true love?" she heard herself say. She was thinking of Slane and of Roger.

Colonel Perry, putting on his cloak, glanced at her sharply.

"Give me a man who plays cards well, pleases me in bed, and doesn't borrow all my funds, and I am happy," said Aunt Shrew. "Richard, I don't think looked at another woman once he won your grandmother, here."

He killed himself loving me, thought the Duchess, but that is another story.

"What is it the Bible verse says, thinks no evil, envies not, bears all things—what else, Alice?"

" 'Believeth all things, hopeth all things, endureth all things,' " said the Duchess.

"Is that love, or foolishness? Simplicity or error?" asked Aunt Shrew. "The essence of life or a lie? Who but a saint could live it?"

Jane, thought Barbara, enjoy this treasure of time with your beloved.

In the first great yard of the Tower, the one that extended across the moat, Jane stepped down from the carriage, shook out her skirts so she wouldn't fall walking in them. They went into the grim building at one end and Jane followed a woman to a small chamber, while her father waited.

When the woman was finished examining her, Jane brushed quickly, furtively, at the tears that had come at the woman's brisk manner, probing fingers. She and her father, shivering in the cold, followed the guard across the bridge that crossed the moat, walking alongside the high outer wall. There were walls to each side of her. She felt suffocated and looked up once to see if she could see stars, but there were none this night, only the light from the guard's lantern. They walked through an archway. Another few days, and Christopher Layer's trial began. Where has the time gone? thought Jane. It seems only yesterday that I came to London with the children.

"Bloody Tower over us," said the guard, and began reciting details, that the Tower was eighteen acres, that the high wall all around was ninety feet high, surrounded by a moat. It was an ancient fortress, he told them, added to by each king. There were many towers inside the walls, each with a particular name: White Tower, Bell Tower, Lion Tower. Jane stepped out of the archway. It was too dark to see much, but she saw lanterns here and there, the bulk of a building behind them.

"We're like a small village," said the guard. "The mint is here, where the King's coins are made and kept, the crown jewels are here, the royal menagerie is here, lions and leopards." He began to describe certain dungeons. "They've earned their names: Cold Harbour, Little Ease, Little Hell."

"Be quiet, man," said Sir John.

But all Jane was aware of was a distant wall, rising up the sky it seemed. The guard knocked on a door before some building, and opened it. They stepped into a hall.

"Up those stairs," he said, motioning. At the top was the guardroom. Jane presented the paper signed by the constable of the Tower. The guardroom was long, with a fireplace at one end. Women and children sat there.

"Family of the guards," her father said to her.

Jane began to put coins in the hands of the guards, who, though startled, immediately accepted them.

"I'm Mrs. Cromwell. I am so happy to see my dear husband. Drink to our joy this night. Drink to the King's mercy when all is said and done."

One of the doors set in the walls was open. Jane saw stairs leading upward.

"We opened it for you," said a guard.

So. That was the door to the stairs that led to Gussy's cell upward, nestled in a side tower of the building.

Jane took off her cloak, folded it carefully, stood before her father.

"I feel as I did the day I gave you away in marriage," Sir John said.

"Bless me the way you did that day, Father."

He put his hand on Jane's head. "Father of us all, bless this beloved child and her beloved husband. I put their care into Your hands."

Jane walked to the door. A guard was already there, on the stairs.

"The door above is open. I unlocked it for you. Don't pull it all the way shut or you will lock yourself inside."

She stopped somewhere about halfway. It was dark, but there was light ahead. The wooden door of the cell was ajar, and light spilled out softly like a welcome. She touched the cold stone of the wall around her. It felt massive, impenetrable. She stepped inside, a small chamber, a fireplace with the fire going, though it was still cold. She would imagine this stone never warmed.

She saw him, standing in shadow. Barbara had warned her that there might have been roughness, but to see his face, the hurt to it, was hard. At that moment she hated Walpole more than she had ever hated anyone in her life. I'll remember this, she thought. It will keep me strong.

He was walking toward her, and upon his face was the most beautiful of smiles. Under the bruises, the swelling, was still Gussy. I love you, she thought. You are my heart. How will I live without you if they convict you? She touched his face, the emotion in her so strong that it hurt to breathe.

"What have they done to you?"

"Many things. But it isn't me who's changed. You look like a queen. I almost didn't recognize you."

He touched her face where Barbara had placed a patch.

"I wanted to look beautiful for you."

"You've always been beautiful to me, Janie."

They held one another. She smelled his shirt, his chest, him. Gussy. Too thin. Swellings on his back. What had they done to him? There was only tonight to see.

They stood apart from one another, their presence, this closeness, a feast. Holding his hand, for she couldn't bear to let loose of him, she went to the narrow bed.

"Wait," he said.

He pulled back the cover. Everywhere were white rose petals.

"A gift from friends, I don't know who. I heard a knock on the door, a turning of the key, and I found a bag on the top stair, filled with these. Our bridal bed, Jane, better than the first time."

She sat down. He was kneeling before her, holding her face in his hands, kissing her lips and brows and forehead, kissing the places where Barbara had placed the patches. The tenderness of his kisses, the way they made her heart shake, was almost too much to bear.

"Foolish Janie, don't cry. My dove, my sweet, my angel, let me move these foolish feathers, unlace this gown and see where else your bad Barbara has placed patches. . . ."

❧

"Where is your mind, Alice?" said Aunt Shrew. "I've won again. You know, don't you?" she said, "that there's talk the King will build a house for the Princesses at Devane Square. Wren is beside himself, thinking of it, what should grace that hill where Devane House was. It would be difficult to build anything that beautiful again, he says. He thinks whatever is built ought to complement the Virginia garden. You've done well, Barbara. You've taken Roger's muck and made something grow from it."

Behold, thou are fair, my love, thou hast doves' eyes. The Duchess was thinking of Richard. Behold, thou art fair, my beloved, yea, pleasant: also our bed is green: so Richard had said, their wedding night. Richard, I am going to die. It was said, through Barbara, through Diana, through Andreas, that Sir John was going to lose his farm. Crops were poor, and he owed money from the South Sea. Send him to Virginia, said Barbara. Why not, Grandmama? He and Lady Ashford and Jane and the children. He can be your agent there. Do it.

" 'Marry in pink,' " Barbara sang to Amelia, the other children, nestled about her skirts, " 'of you he'll aye think. Marry in blue, love ever true.' "

CHAPTER 57

The first trial began.

"It is the judgment of the law that you, Christopher Layer, be led to the place whence you came, and from thence you are to be drawn to the place of execution, and there you are to be hanged by the neck, but not until you are dead, for you are to be cut down alive, and your bowels to be taken out and burned before your face. Your head is to be severed from your body, and your body to be divided into four quarters, your head and quarters to be disposed of where His Majesty shall think fit."

There was a long intake of breath from the crowd gathered in Westminster Hall. The entire long hall was a jostling, whispering mass of people, so many people pressing in to see and hear that witnesses could scarcely move to and from the witness box.

Layer was being led from the chamber, weeping, crying out that he had been betrayed.

"He is no one, of no rank, having no fortune, no family of consequence," said Aunt Shrew. She and Tony and Colonel Perry had come every day to the trial. "It is inconceivable that he could be important to a plot of the magnitude presented. Capturing the Captain General of our army, capturing Lord Cadogan, the Prince and Princess, Walpole and Lord Townshend. It is sheer nonsense that he had a key part, the ravings of a mad dreamer."

It was pieces of the actual plot, but she didn't say that.

"As to those who testified against him," she continued, "I wouldn't take their evidence to hang a dog. It ranks up there with this wild rumor that Laurence Slane has left London because he is a Jacobite agent. An Irish good-for-nothing, yes, but an agent, I think not."

"Layer did plot to overthrow the King. You cannot deny that, Aunt Shrew, cannot deny the evidence presented us," said Tony.

"And so he must die. I quite understand. The penalty for treason is death."

The crowd had cleared enough to allow them to begin to make their way outside. Just below the windows of this long hall, at the point where Gothic arches to hold the roof began, battle flags captured in war hung down in rows of ragged and frayed glory. Aunt Shrew pointed out the flags to Colonel Perry, talking about her brother, Richard, about his victory at Lille.

"This trial has been a show to whet the tastes of the mob," she said. "There was nothing presented to link Layer with the Bishop of Rochester, yet listen to how everyone around us is talking of Rochester, of how close we've come to war. Jacobite troops. Jacobite weapons. Jacobite evil. Walpole is a clever man. I thought you were angry with him, Tony, because of his encounter with Barbara."

"I am angry, but I can't deny truth when it is presented, and my anger with him has nothing to do with my loyalty to the King."

"Well, it took a jury only six days to convict Layer. They will proceed far faster with Gussy Cromwell. Is Jane prepared?" Aunt Shrew said.

"Are we ever prepared to see a loved one sentenced to die?" said Colonel Perry.

"Tell Barbara."

"To prepare her? How will Barbara do that? Why must Barbara do that?" asked Colonel Perry.

"It's her lot," said Aunt Shrew. "She's the heart of this family."

That evening, the King gave an evening drawing room to signal his pleasure at this first verdict. Everyone was there, pleased or not.

Barbara stood with Sir Gideon Andreas, who was not happy with her.

"Why do you allow Pendarves to finish the row of townhouses?"

"He asked."

"I also asked."

"Ah, but he asked first."

"What are the terms?"

She didn't answer.

"See here," he said, "I am not your enemy."

No, thought Barbara, my mother has seen to that.

"It would be in your best interest not to make me one, and yet you try. Do you want me to demand that you pay the notes I hold?"

"I can't pay the notes you hold. Demand all you like."

"As I well know. I try to allow both you and myself to gain from your husband's mishandlings, and you won't have it. Ride with me one morning to Marylebone, where we can look back on the vista of Devane Square. Let me tell you my schemes for it. Come, one ride with me won't hurt you. Is it true the King will build a house for the Princesses at Devane Square?"

"No one has spoken to me of it."

It was to be her New Year's gift, the King's dwarf had told her. The King would present her with a set of plans.

"Well, it is being spoken of. I want to buy ground leases at Devane Square."

"I don't sell the ground leases."

"Finally I know at least one of your terms. You give the rents over to him who builds?"

"For a time which he and I agree upon."

"The whole of the rents?"

"The whole. How else would it be fair?"

"Fair?"

"An important word to me, Sir Gideon. Someone once told me another man's gain is also my own."

"Who told you that?"

"Colonel Perry."

"He who leases the second townhouse."

"Yes. Lady Doleraine is signaling me, Sir Gideon. Excuse me, please."

"I want the other two sides of the square," said Sir Gideon. "I want them now. I am willing to be, as you say, fair."

He wanted them before the fine was debated in Parliament, as it soon would be. Walpole was true to his word. If the fine is reduced, Pendarves had said, every man in town with an eye to building will be after you.

"We'll talk soon," Barbara replied.

"We certainly will."

Barbara led the Princesses upstairs, to their private quarters. They were full of questions about the trial today as Barbara saw to their undressing, the putting on of their bedgowns.

"They'll quarter him and hang him," Caroline, the youngest, said.

"Would the Jacobites have taken us, too?" asked Anne.

"I don't know," said Barbara. "You mustn't ask me these questions. You must go to Lady Doleraine."

"She won't answer. She'll tell us to hush, not to think of such things. You know that. Were they going, truly going, to kill Papa and Mama and Grandpapa?" asked Caroline.

"Kings and princes don't kill one another," said Barbara. "That wouldn't be honorable."

"They imprison one another instead. We'd all have been in prison," said Amelia.

Barbara left the Princesses to the bedchamber women and to Lady Doleraine, who oversaw prayers and thoughts and actions. She walked back through the corridors that would bring her to where everyone was gathered, her mind on the verdict today, on Slane, on Gussy's coming trial. She sat down a moment in a window seat in one of the halls, leaned her head back, closed her eyes. Everyone needed her, and she was tired. What it was taking to sustain her present life was much, more perhaps, than she wished to give.

"There you are. Not trying to sneak out on me, are you, Bab?" said Pendarves some moments later.

"As a matter of fact, I am. I don't think this is the night to approach her."

"Now, Bab, you promised me."

"Do I always have to keep promises? Why do I always have to keep promises? I am a creature of court and tell lies with the best of them."

He didn't answer.

"Go into the alcove at the end of the gallery," she told him, and went to search the various chambers. She finally found her great-aunt playing cards. Aunt Shrew wore a black wig as dark as coal dust and a black gown with red ribbons; upon her shoulder was the Virginia blackbird with red topfeathers that Barbara had given her, the bird as silent and docile as if it were stuffed. It moved only to nibble at the diamonds hanging from her aunt's ear.

"If Laurence Slane is a Jacobite agent," Aunt Shrew was saying, "then so am I. Robert Walpole is just jealous of his handsome actor's face."

Barbara whispered to her.

"I've changed my mind, Bab. This verdict has put me off my feed."

Barbara pulled the bird's tail feathers. With a screech, he flew at the person across the table. Once the crow was caught, the coins and cards picked from the floor, apologies made, Aunt Shrew followed Barbara toward an alcove at the end of a long gallery.

"I'm a fool to do this," she said, "Fool, fool, fool."

"You promised. Look, he's already there, waiting. Just hear him out. You haven't to do another thing than that. It's all he expects. He thinks he is dying. A physician has been to see him twice."

"It is the only reason I agreed to see him, you may count upon that."

Her aunt handed her the crow; Barbara walked a pace or so away. The gallery, long, filled with statues and paintings and heavy tables piled high with books, was empty of people.

"Lou," Barbara heard Pendarves say, "forgive me. I've no words for what I've done, but she bewitched me, I swear it. If it were not for the fact she carries my child, there are times now when I think I could see her burned at the stake. The things she does, Lou, I could not withstand them; flesh is weak—"

"Good God, man, you're not going to describe it for me, are you?"

"I think it is upon her mind to kill me with lust and then have my fortune. I'm afraid of her, I tell you. I no longer sleep there, not trusting her not to lure me to my death. Bab will tell you I've taken to sleeping in one of the townhouses. I know what a fool I've been, that it is you whom I love in my heart, have always loved. Forgive me, forgive an old man his foolish passions. I am so lonely without you. I am like a ghost. It is as if I do not exist anymore, I but wander about from place to place—"

"How I let myself be talked into agreeing to this, I will never know, except that Barbara could convince a saint when she is in the mood. You are a liar and a cheat and a coward—"

"Yes, Lou, you're right, Lou, how I've missed talking to you, Lou, your honesty and forthrightness . . ."

After a time, the silence was just too intriguing. Barbara couldn't help herself. She had to look. She tiptoed toward the alcove.

Her great-aunt sat in a chair. Pendarves was upon his knees before it; his face was in the lap of her gown, his arms were around her waist, and his shoulders were shaking. He was weeping. There was upon Aunt Shrew's face the most curious expression: anger, pity, exasperation, consternation, self-mockery, all mingled together. Her hand, gloved in black, ten priceless bracelets above it if there was one, stroked the back of his neck gently, as if to comfort him. Or perhaps it was herself she comforted.

"What fools we all are," her expression seemed to say. She saw Barbara and shrugged. Barbara opened her hands, and the crow flew from them to Aunt Shrew, took its place at her shoulder, then stared down with beady eyes at Pendarves, who hadn't moved.

Barbara walked toward the stairs that led to the chambers below, where most of the guests would be. Coming up the stairs toward her was Wharton. His face was flushed. He'd been drinking.

"Have you gotten them together?"

"They are in an alcove at the end of the gallery."

"She did not strike him on sight?"

Barbara shook her head.

Outside, alone, the night too cold to bear without a fur-lined cloak, she looked up at the stars, then went to the chamber given her and put on her cloak. Outside, again, she called for a carriage.

In the gallery, Wharton waited until Aunt Shrew saw him. She left Pendarves, who was wiping his face with a great white handkerchief and blowing his nose loudly.

"Word is he's safe at his mother's, outside Paris," said Wharton. "He's asked us to steal a royal swan for him and to rescue Gussy."

"Thank God, oh, thank God. I haven't slept in days," said Aunt Shrew. "The bouquet of roses is off to Layer?" White roses would tell him he'd be taken care of on his execution day, given something to deaden pain.

"Done this afternoon."

Pendarves joined them. "Always tell a woman you love her when you do," he said, still wiping at his eyes. "It's important. Nothing else in this life may be as important."

"There'd be too many," said Wharton. "I wouldn't know where to begin." Another drink, he was thinking, until I feel nothing. Sometimes he wondered if it might not have been better to have been arrested, though the fear he'd felt in those weeks when all was suspense as to who would be next was not something he wished to endure again. You'd endure arrest no better, said Slane. Was it true? He could see himself in a cell—now that he was certain he would not be put in one—nobly remaining silent, the way the Bishop of Rochester and Augustus Cromwell and Charles—bless him—did.

We wait, said Lady Shrewsborough, and see what happens. And

when we know, we plan again. He who hath patience may compass anything. Another drink, and then patience was just possible.

❧

A servant led Barbara up the stairs to a small chamber in which sat Sir John and Lady Ashford. The room was dark except for the fire in the fireplace. Children lay sleeping in beds. Barbara went to them and kissed their foreheads.

"Where's Jane?"

"In the chamber just beyond. She wished to be alone."

"Where is King James?" said Jane's mother. "He was to come, with his great general Ormonde, with his soldiers; he was to have triumphed, not left us all here, stranded, like fish who have swum too far toward shore, and the wave that brought us in is pulled back, and we struggle here in the sand, some of us to die. Our dear Gussy is going to die."

Barbara took Lady Ashford's hand.

"I know."

Lady Ashford began to weep.

"You'll wake a child," Sir John said to his wife. "When the trial is over, Barbara, I will want an interview with the King."

"He does not see Tories these days. I won't be able to get it for you." She made a helpless gesture, and Sir John nodded.

Barbara knocked on the door and opened it. Jane sat in a rocking chair, her oldest and her youngest child with her. Harry Augustus was asleep in her lap; Amelia was awake.

Barbara took Amelia, kissed her plump face, brought a candle near to look at her. Little one, she thought, you're not so small that you don't understand what lies ahead, are you?

"She won't sleep," said Jane.

No, thought Barbara, I don't imagine she would. She sat down in a chair, kissed Amelia, began to stroke her face, her arms, to tell her she loved her. On and on she went, her voice quiet, reciting the rhymes and messages of girlhood.

"Fly, ladybird, fly, north, south, or east or west, fly where is found the man I love best."

Lids on Amelia's stubborn eyes were staying down. She was dozing. Barbara looked over to Jane. It was better the way Roger died, for I didn't believe he would, and so I could bear it, she thought. "There is nothing I can think to say, Jane."

"I'm glad you've come. It's funny how everyone is talking of Laurence Slane. Last Easter, he persuaded Gussy to take me to Greenwich Hill. We tumbled down it as the sweethearts do, all tangled together. I've never laughed so hard in my life. I keep thinking of that, of Greenwich Hill and that tumble. I've been amusing myself this night with last wishes. One more year than I had with Jeremy. One more tumble down Greenwich Hill. One more child, and every time I have a child I think I will die."

Mother, thought Barbara.

"One more girl's spring at Tamworth. Do you remember the way we used to wassail the apple trees so that there would be a good crop for the coming year? We'd all go to the orchards, everyone, your grandmother, Mother, Father, the laborers, and we'd sing to the trees, what did we sing, Barbara, what was it? 'Old apple tree, we wassail thee and hoping thou wilt bear—' "

" 'For the Lord doth know where we shall be, till apples come another year,' " sang Barbara with her. Their voices were sweet together.

In the adjoining chamber Sir John, hearing them, stood and walked to a window, in his mind three wild children, two girls and a boy, running the woods of Tamworth.

"We'd sing to the trees and drink their health and pour buckets of cider on the roots. We'd shout and stomp to frighten away anything that might keep them from growing. And we'd leave bread soaked with cider in the trees for the birds. That was my favorite time of year, the spring, because of your grandmother's apple trees. If I close my eyes, I can see them, smell them this moment. That's where Harry and I fell in love, in the apple orchard. He was chasing me, and I fell and cried and somehow in comforting me, he kissed me, and we knew we loved one another."

"How old were you?"

"Thirteen. No, fourteen."

"Where was I?"

"Running ahead. You were always ahead of me, Bab. The only thing I've bettered you in is children, and anyone may do that."

"Do you know how much I admire you?"

"Me?"

"To go from house to house as you have all these months. To write letter after letter. To sit in halls and parlors for hours, to be turned away and yet return. To persevere, as you have. All our lives, you will have my admiration for the courage you've shown in the last months."

"Thank you, Barbara. I have a favor to ask. If Gussy is convicted, I want you to help me write a petition to present to the King. I am going to ask for his mercy toward Gussy. Will you help me write it?"

"Yes."

Later, Sir John walked Barbara out to the street, insisting on waiting until he saw her into a carriage. Barbara gave the driver Aunt Shrew's street. Her great-aunt was up, in her bedchamber, playing solitaire.

"Your mother is as big as three houses," she said. "If I weren't told otherwise, I would say she is further along than anyone guesses. Lumpy is worried for her. He says she believes she is going to die in childbed. How's Jane?"

"How do you know I've seen her?"

"Everyone knows you left the gathering tonight, and most people made a shrewd guess as to why."

"Did the King seem angry?"

"It is not yet a crime to be a friend in this town, though before he is finished, Robert Walpole may make it one. I have something interesting to tell you, Barbara. I've heard that Lord Bolingbroke is asking to return to England, asking to be pardoned by King George, asking for his estates and titles back."

"Surely the King won't pardon him! He was King James's secretary of state!"

"It is said that ten thousand pounds is going to the Duchess of Kendall to help ease Bolingbroke's way."

"They will hang Gussy but forgive Bolingbroke?"

"Bolingbroke can give them information upon King James, upon agents. And he has tasted exile, tasted poverty. He will be more amenable this time around."

"It isn't fair."

"No. Wharton left a note for you, Barbara."

Barbara opened the note. "He's safe in France," it said. "Ask for nothing more. Burn this."

"Why do you smile?" said Aunt Shrew. "Don't tell me you have a yearning for Wharton. He is trouble, Bab, through and through."

". . . hanged by the neck, but not until you are dead, for you are to be cut down alive, and your bowels to be taken out and . . ."

Jane stood up. Even though Barbara had been expecting a reaction, she was not prepared for Jane's swiftness. Jane was running, people were parting for her, making a cleared path down which she ran, before Barbara could even gather her wits together. The judge was calling order to his court, but people were murmuring and twisting and trying to see. Tony had already leaped up from his seat and was after her. Harriet reached over and squeezed Barbara's hand. Beside her, Wharton shook his head. The Duchess was crying, tears solemn, clear rivers down her face, as was Lady Ashford.

Pushing through the crowd to the outside, Barbara looked around.

"There," said Harriet. They saw Tony and Sir John just at the edge of the courtyard, where the openness closed to narrow streets and alleys. Tony held Jane, was talking to her.

Sir John took Jane from Tony.

"Oh, God," Jane said, her face white and sick, "Oh, God, help me, help him, our children. I knew it but I cannot believe it now that it has happened. I cannot believe it."

A carriage had come around. Sir John helped his daughter and his wife into it. Tony, Harriet, and Wharton stood across the courtyard; Tim held the Duchess. Others were there: Aunt Shrew, Pendarves,

Colonel Perry. Barbara went to her grandmother, whose face resembled Jane's.

"What is it, Grandmama?" Barbara said. "You are not going to die because Gussy is. Stop it."

Tony's carriage was here. Barbara told them to go on without her.

She found the small garden near the river, the one where she'd first seen Walpole upon her return from London.

Slane would weep to know Gussy died. She wanted to weep herself. Bad luck, the Duchess of Kendall had said of Tommy's death. Now I won't wear the sapphire. Ten thousand pounds and Lord Bolingbroke, an infamous traitor, is forgiven. Treasonous letters and Gussy Cromwell is hanged, drawn, and quartered.

Aunt Shrew's words were in her mind: Love beareth all things, believeth all things, hopeth all things, endureth all things.

Love or foolishness?

Simplicity or error?

Who but a saint could live it?

CHAPTER 58

Three days, three nights, and the petition asking mercy for Gussy was written. Barbara sneaked Jane into St. James's Palace. "He always passes through here on his way to walk along the gallery. He is in a meeting with his council. You may have to wait a long time."

Windows jutted in a buttress shape, and inside this gallery, wood-carvers had carved seats into the shape. Jane sat down in one. Fly, ladybird, fly, north, south, or east or west, fly where is found the man I love best, she thought. Gussy wrote lists of things she was to do after his death. He was being allowed visitors in these last days; two people at a time might visit him in his cell. She didn't tell him what she was doing. He would not wish her to do it.

The hardest thing I have ever had to do, thought Jane, pressing her hands together to give herself courage, was put flannel over my child's face. It was the custom to cover the deceased's face with a square of flannel. That was harder than this, facing a king. Would she wash Gussy's body the way she'd washed Jeremy's? How did one wash a headless, disemboweled body?

How did she keep her mind from breaking? Go to Virginia, Barbara had said. You and the children and your father and mother. Go to Virginia and make a place for yourself. Barbara had described the French Huguenots living above the waterfalls, their neat farms and tiny houses. Marry a Frenchman when your heart is well again, said

Barbara. Have more babies, for my sake if no one else's. Have more babies. Jane was good at that, her only triumph in this life, having babies. . . . She started.

Men were moving toward her down the gallery, and she'd been somewhere else in her mind, she was always somewhere else these days, not even hearing people until they were almost upon her. Jane stood up abruptly, recognizing some of them—Lord Townshend, Lord Carteret, Lord Cadogan—men in whose hallways she had sat many an hour.

She took a step and nearly fell to her knees. Her foot had gone to sleep. They were going to pass right by her. These window seats were cut so deeply into the wall that a person could disappear in them. She mustn't disappear. They must see her. She lurched toward them like a drunken woman, her foot worthless, betraying her, not even there. What they must think, she could not imagine.

She fell against one of them, and several men moved back, their faces serious, startled. She half fell, half sank down onto her knees in what was supposed to have been a curtsy and held out the petition to the man in the middle of them, a man who looked at her with remote, light-colored eyes.

She said rapidly, "Your Majesty, I am the wife of the unfortunate Augustus Cromwell, and I humbly beg that you receive my petition—"

But the King, looking at her no more, was moving on. He did not touch the paper she held.

No, Jane thought. He must at least hear me. I will make him hear me. He must take my petition.

She reached up and caught hold of the skirt of his coat, twisting it fiercely in her hand, not even knowing what she was doing anymore, knowing only that she must be, she would be heard. But he kept on walking, and she was being dragged upon her knees across the gallery, but she didn't care. She would not let go.

"Your Majesty, please, I beg you, only take my petition. Let me know that I have done that— Ah!"

Hands were on her, on her shoulders, her arms.

One of the King's men pried her hand from the King's coat skirt;

another took her hard by the shoulders so that she fell back onto her elbows. The shock of it, the shame, was unimaginable. She felt seared all the way through her body.

The King was moving away, surrounded again by his gentlemen. Half sprawled in the middle of the floor, she sat where she was. The King had dragged her halfway across the gallery before his ministers could make her loose him.

God have mercy on him, she thought, for I never will. Humiliation was like a candle's light in her, but now there was a smaller flame, too: anger.

And now here was Barbara, dear Barbara, straightening her skirts, helping her up, chafing her hands, saying her name over and over, walking her to the window seat, into which Jane sank like a rag doll, for her body felt as if it belonged to someone else.

"I cannot believe they treated you so," Barbara was saying, and in her voice was the anger Jane could feel, far down inside herself, under the shame.

"Lady Devane."

In another chamber, a guard called out Barbara's name.

Barbara froze. Jane saw fear move into her expression. Barbara squeezed Jane's hands tightly.

"I have to leave you for a while. Can you get home?"

"Yes. Are you all right?"

"No. I am in dreadful trouble."

I did not think of that, thought Jane, what it meant for Barbara to do this for me. The King will know she placed me where I would see him.

Barbara followed the guard. In her mind was the picture of Jane being dragged across the floor as if she were nothing, was the picture of three men, all of them twice Jane's size, pulling her away from King George and leaving her as if she were nothing, in their wake.

The King was in his closet, most private of places, the little chamber attached to the bedchamber. He was standing before the fire, arms raised to the mantel, leaning into it.

The guard announced Barbara and closed the door. She was alone with the King, who raised his eyes from the fire to move them over her.

Furious, thought Barbara, he is furious.

"Never again do I want to endure such a thing. Never again will I."

Livid, thought Barbara. I am to be dismissed.

"I dragged her across the floor upon her knees. She was weeping piteously, begging me to hear her. Do you think I have no ears, no heart?"

And now he stepped from the fireplace to face Barbara, and she wished he had stayed as he was, for he was, quite literally, trembling with rage. His eyes raked over her, furious, scathing, unforgiving.

People do not give him enough esteem, thought Barbara, a rapid, darting thought, like a summer's bat, and she sank to the ground in a curtsy instinctively, her head and neck bowed.

"Do you think I have not seen Cromwell's children? Do you think I do not understand that with his death they will have no father? Do you think I have not heard over and over what a good man he is, what a careful priest he was in the tending of his flock? He plotted treason against me, do you understand the meaning of that? And I cannot allow it, not the smallest part of it. I must crush it wherever I find it, and crush it I will."

She stayed as she was as his words beat down on her. She clasped her hands together tightly.

"My granddaughters adore you, but I will not have you foment discontent and malice against me in my own household. I have family which do that."

"May she—will you still allow the visits, her visits and the visits of friends and family?" Barbara spoke breathlessly, raggedly, each word chopped and short. "It is all they have. Please don't deny the visits because of this. Augustus Cromwell is her husband, the father of her children. She could do nothing other than plead for his life. If your life were threatened, don't you see that the Duchess of Kendall, that your granddaughters, would do the same, would plead for you?

That is all my friend did, Your Majesty, attempt to make a plea for a beloved husband. There is no crime in that. There is only love."

The King was silent, his expression grim, and Barbara closed her eyes. It would almost be easier if he struck me, she thought. This moment is endless. Have I lost all?

"I will not deny the visits," he said. He held up his forefinger, warningly. "But I wish never to see her again."

"I understand, Your Majesty."

"You may go."

She could feel his eyes on her, cutting through her, feel the anger still flickering out from him. As she walked back to her chamber, she thought about what an older lady-in-waiting had said about court, how heartbreaking it was, how difficult. I am to hide inconvenient friendship and heartbreak, never mention them, pretend they do not exist, she thought. That is what they expect.

I don't know if I can do it, thought Barbara. How can I behave as if Gussy's death doesn't matter? What do I become if I can? What am I becoming?

"Diana thought you ought to know," Pendarves said. "It is all everyone is talking of. A dozen people saw Jane Cromwell dragged across the gallery this afternoon."

"Is Barbara dismissed?" The question was Tony's.

"Word is, His Majesty spoke to her, and harshly, but she won't speak of it, and no one dares to ask him."

"Give Diana my thanks." The Duchess held her hands out to Pendarves, who bowed over them and left the bedchamber.

"I'll ride out to see about Barbara," said Tony.

"See if she will come here awhile, stay with me. Tell her I need her, Tony."

Tony knelt. "What is it? Tell me."

"All this. Sir John."

The Duchess could barely get his name out. Go to Virginia? he had said. He said the word "Virginia" as if she had suggested traveling to Sodom and Gomorrah. Leave me be, Alice, please. As soon as Gussy was executed, the Duchess was leaving for Tamworth. The trial of Rochester would be the event of the spring, a final clash between the old ways and the new, but she would miss it, letting Tamworth's woods and ways, its seasons and bees be what her eyes finally closed upon.

Tony was reaching out to her, moving her, sitting himself in her chair and putting her in his lap, as if she were a child, and he the parent. He was holding her close. They are made of playing cards, thought the Duchess, our ambitions in life. Don't follow James, I told Richard, so that we would not live in exile or lose our fortunes in a war. If, years ago, I had allowed Richard to do as he truly wished, would things now be different? Would he be alive? Would my sons? Had she treated Barbara, treated Tony, like pieces on a chessboard, moving them to her will? What of their will? Futility and sorrow were bitter in her heart.

CHAPTER 59

Jane pressed her hands together, now that all was said. The next few moments determined the course of her life, and Gussy's.

"It will never work," her father said.

"If we're caught—" her mother said.

"We all end in the Tower," her father finished.

Jane stood. She'd do it upon her own, then. She gathered up her cloak, thinking of all that would have to be done: women found, clothing packed, the children arranged for—so much, so much, between now and then.

"The Duchess must be safe," said her father. "No harm must come to her because of this."

Yes, the same with Barbara. "Quarrel with her, publicly."

"Tell me the plan again," said her father, "more slowly."

Jane did it, the words tumbling out. They are going to help me, she thought. Light was spreading inside her. She felt faint with it.

"Why not?" Sir John said, when Jane was finished.

"And if we're caught?" her mother said.

"Is that worse than this?"

"Janie— John, catch her!"

When Jane opened her eyes again, her mother was looking at her in a way mothers have when no secrets are safe, for they know you too well.

"Are you with child? If you are with child—"

"No." Yes. The jest about Gussy having only to drop his breeches lived true. The one thing she knew was having babies, even now, in the midst of this. "I haven't been eating."

"Clear to anyone with eyes."

It was her father, fierce, angry, scowling, a caged bear. "Well, you'd best begin. We can't have you fainting in the Tower the day we rescue Gussy."

When Jane was gone, Sir John said to his wife, "Our Jane—who would have thought she had it in her?"

"We die if we're caught."

"I'm already dead inside."

Jane waited in Devane Square Church for Barbara. Sir Christopher Wren was there; he brought a lap robe over and tucked it about her legs, his gesture kind, quick, before he walked back to the carvers at the altar. He'd heard of her disgrace yesterday. He'd tell about the scene in his church today, the quarrel between Jane Cromwell and Lady Devane; he wouldn't be able not to.

Here now was Barbara, bold Barbara, brave Barbara. She must give me some of both qualities, thought Jane. They sat together, held hands under the lap robe the way they used to do years ago in Tamworth Church.

"I'm going to quarrel with you, Barbara," Jane said. "In another few moments, after I tell you what I'm doing. I'm going to try and take Gussy from the Tower—"

"A rescue! You have a plan!"

"And I don't want you hurt by it, whether I succeed or fail."

"It's madness. I can't believe you do it. What do you need? What can I do to help?"

"I need a woman to help me. I need coins."

"Bathsheba—"

"No. She is your servant, and I do not want this in any way connected to you. I'm with child, I think, Barbara."

"Oh, Jane, you have one of your wishes. Where will you go afterward?"

"Virginia."

"Yes, I'll write a letter for your father to give to Blackstone. He'll help you. Are there any ships in? It's nearly December. I'll find out about a ship and have word sent to you."

"Hold my hand for a long moment, because I am going to begin to shout at you, to accuse you of not doing all you could for me, and I won't see you again. We mustn't see each other again after this. Don't tell your grandmother. Father thinks it better that she have no idea, until afterward."

"I love you, Jane."

"I love you, Barbara. Give me something of yours. Anything."

Barbara untied a silver ribbon from her sleeve. They held hands tightly a long moment, all their lives together in the moment, all their friendship. Harry and the apple trees. Tamworth and the lane to church, all their golden girlhood.

❧

"It cannot possibly succeed."

"I'm with child."

Gussy took Jane's hands in his. There was nothing more to be said. She'd told him her plan; even now, as she said it yet again, she thought, How silly this is, too simple, it will never work. If Gussy says no. . . .

"It is in God's hands, then, Jane. We'll pray."

"You will do it?"

"Yes."

Outside, later, as Jane walked away from the Tower, to the rented chamber where her father was, she thought, Ten more days, ten more days, and then my life changes forever.

Her mother was even now secretly selling everything—plate, pots, jewelry, clothing—so that they would have funds to pay the captain of the ship on which they sailed. She was on her way to see the Duke of Tamworth and borrow a hundred pounds from him.

He'd give it without asking a question as to what she wished it for. Barbara had already sent fifty pounds, would send more. Jane needed two women to help her, for her mother was going to have the children on her hands.

Who could help her?

Who would be safe in risking it?

Annie, in the kitchen at Saylor House, read once again the note Barbara had sent.

"What are you up to, Annie my love?" said Tim.

Annie looked away from Tim's impudent face. She'd just done tea leaves. It was in the tea leaves, all of it. Even Tim.

"I will not have it," Sir John Ashford said, silencing even guests at the other end of the chamber. "You are to keep your meddling hands out of my affairs once and for all."

Lord Cowper moved quickly away from the guest he was talking to, toward John Ashford and the Duchess of Tamworth. Ashford was making a scene, accosting the Duchess as if she were a yard woman.

"I know all about it," Sir John was saying as people around them murmured to one another and watched. "You've asked to buy Ladybeth from Andreas, don't bother to deny it. You always wanted it, didn't you? Greedy woman."

"No," said the Duchess. "You know that is not true."

Lord Cowper was just able to keep Tony from putting his hands on Sir John. As it was, Tony followed Cowper and Sir John down the stairs, Cowper whispering to this man, an old friend, but a friend who had gone too far, "You forget yourself, John. You must leave my house at once."

Tony pushed past Cowper and took Sir John by the arm. "You are never to speak to my grandmother in such a manner again."

Sir John pulled away. "Will you duel with me? Or call me thief? Young Whig rogue. I spit on you and every Saylor I know."

Lord Cowper stepped in front of Tony. "I beg you, simply allow him to depart. Remember all that has befallen him—"

Upstairs, Barbara stood by her grandmother. Annie had gone for their cloaks. Her grandmother was silent, but her face was too pale and her hands were clenching and unclenching her cane.

"He didn't mean it," Barbara said softly. "It is the strain of everything. Did you offer to buy the farm from Andreas?"

"Yes, but to give it back to John, not right away, but in time. When you're grieving you need the familiar, that which you know, to comfort you. He won't survive all this without his farm."

A tear seeped down the Duchess's cheek. Death, she thought, I am ready.

※

"It broke my mother's heart," said Diana to Walpole, who visited her. "She has given Sir John nothing but faithful friendship in this time. I never liked him."

"Shall I put him in the Tower for you?"

"No, let it be. You're going to lower the fine, yes?"

"Yes. It will be our last piece of business in Parliament before we all leave for Christmas. If anything, Diana, Barbara may be more in favor with the King than ever. 'She is a true friend,' he says, 'That is rare.' I don't understand."

"Neither do I," said Diana.

※

"Don't grieve," said Barbara, patting the Duchess's hand. "Please don't grieve. Sir John will send an apology. I know it. Let time pass."

Whig and Tory matter no more to me, thought the Duchess. George or James—it matters not. Oil of violets: If she were at Tamworth, Annie would be making oil of violets, violets' leaves boiled, steeped, strained, put into a glass with fresh leaves and left alone for a time, good against melancholy, dullness, and heaviness of spirit.

John, you have broken my heart.

※

Colonel Perry found Barbara walking around the centermost portion of Devane Square, where her Virginia garden was to be. He got down from his horse.

"I've found out about a ship to Virginia, as you asked."

"Thank you."

He cocked his head and watched her as she moved along the long lines of string Wren had stretched from wooden stakes to show the shape of the garden. He was dreaming of her. The angel was there again, telling him to watch over her, carefully.

"How can I help you?" he said. He knew nothing else to say.

"Be my friend," said Barbara. "Walk with me as I see this garden in my mind. Assure me that Walpole really will reduce my fine. And pray for Jane."

"I do nothing else. I pray that that which is best for all, that which is good and loving, happen."

"Yes."

∽

Five days. Annie walked down the street where Mrs. Cromwell rented a chamber in a building. She knocked upon a door at the top of the stairs. Jane opened it.

"I want to help you," Annie heard herself say.

Jane's face became closed, guarded. "Help me?"

"Take him from the Tower."

"How can you know that! How?" And when Annie didn't answer: "I need two women. Can you find women who will go to the Tower with me? All they have to do is to bring in clothing for him to wear out. I'll give them each twenty pounds."

"Your mother?"

"She will have to be with the children. The children would behave for no one else, except Barbara."

"I've brought green tea and two eggs. We'll let the tea steep, then beat in the yolks with white sugar. For strength. Tell me your plan."

∽

Four days. Annie folded gowns. Where to find another woman? She herself would be the first. She saw the Duchess watching her and coughed.

The Duchess pursed her lips. "I don't like that cough. Are you becoming ill?"

"I am never ill." Annie coughed again, put the gown down, and left the chamber. Tim caught her in the servants' hall and backed her into a corner.

"Tell me."

She looked him up and down, her face expressionless. "Mrs. Cromwell is going to take Mr. Cromwell from the Tower in four days."

Tim stepped back, as if a snake had bitten him. "An—"

"Escape." Annie moved around him, toward the cavernous kitchen, where the kitchen servants were kneading dough, cutting up potatoes, unaware of the drama unfolding yards away from them. Tim caught her by the arm, pulled her back into the corner.

"Does the Duchess know?"

"It isn't meant for her to know."

"Are you—"

"Leave me be. I've told you more than I should."

Three days. Annie sat by a window, watching a bird peck among the gravel on the garden paths. Another woman? Jane had asked, desperately. Trust, said Annie. Are you well? Drink the tea.

Down the gravel path came Tim, no grin on that impudent face of his. What is wrong with Tim? one of the maidservants had asked just this morning. I have never known him to scowl so. Annie closed her eyes, waited, patiently. After a time, someone's hand touched her shoulder. Tim knelt down close to her, his face, for once, serious.

How many women love you? thought Annie. A dozen, at least.

"I want to help. I can't think of anything else but little Mrs.

Cromwell. Wood violet, the Duchess calls her, Tamworth's wood violet. Let me help, Annie. Please."

"I need a woman to go to the Tower with us, a woman who will wear an extra gown over her own. She has only to do that and then disappear. We've money for her. Do you know someone who doesn't mind seeing the last of London once she's done?"

Tim nodded. Annie had known he would.

"What else?" he asked.

"Someone to drive a carriage or cart. Sir John will drive one, the one with Gussy in it. Someone needs to drive another, with Jane and myself."

"Done."

"This is no game, footman."

He stood, looked down at her, impudent, bold, tall. No wonder the Duchess adores him, thought Annie. If I had a heart, I might, too.

"The Duchess will miss us."

"Leave that to me."

"Tim has a sweetheart," Annie said later to the Duchess. "He's been scowling like a singed cat in the kitchen for days. A lover's quarrel, the cook thinks." Annie coughed.

"I don't like the sound of that. Go and rest."

"I am fine."

"You are not. You are getting ill. I won't have it."

"I am fine. You fret like an old hen over her one chick."

"Bah. Go ahead and be ill. Little I care. No one listens to me anyway."

Three days.

"Well, now," Jane said, to the turnkey in the wardroom that led to Gussy's cell, "I have wonderful news. The King is going to accept my petition for mercy tomorrow night. I think that my husband will not die after all."

Jane smiled and handed the turnkey a small sack of coins.

"You and the other gentlemen here drink a toast to that. Will you?"

"God bless you, Mrs. Cromwell, that we will, with all our hearts."

She followed the turnkey up the short twisting staircase, and at its top, he unlocked the door of Gussy's cell. She and Gussy sat together on the bed.

"Tomorrow afternoon. Annie helps, and a woman Tim found."

"What woman?"

"A woman of the streets, who will be given enough to disappear from London. Tomorrow," whispered Jane, "my mother takes the children to Gravesend." Ships sailed from Gravesend, a village east of London. Barbara had sent word of a ship.

There was a knock at the door.

"Visitors," said the turnkey.

Jane went down the stairs, passing through the wardroom, where guards and their wives and children were gathered at one end by the fire, as was their habit. It was what had given her the idea in the first place: The guards paid more attention to their families than who came in and out. They expected nothing of her. No one did. She was too meek and quiet.

"God bless you," one of them called. "We'll drink to your husband's good fortune tomorrow."

Outside the wardroom was a long flight of stairs, at the end of which stood friends of Gussy, men he'd gone to school with.

"They allow only two inside his cell," she said to them. "So I may not go with you."

Later, going up the stairs to be with Gussy once his visit with his friends was ended, Jane paused a moment. She felt odd, had been feeling so since yesterday. She shook her head and walked into the cell. This was her last night with Gussy, if her plan failed. They lay together on the bed, holding each other, for hours.

WINTER

. . . CHARITY, THESE THREE

CHAPTER 60

December moved on frosty feet toward the birth of the Christ. . . .

The day.

"Drunk as ever I've seen him, over that sweetheart of his," said Annie. She put her hand to her head. "When he shows himself again, you'll need to punish him."

"Fever," said the Duchess. "Have you a fever? Does your head ache? I knew it. Go to bed."

"I am fine."

"You are ill."

The day.

The children were gone with Jane's mother to Gravesend. This is the last day of my old life, thought Jane. Farewell, Barbara.

Barbara sat in Walpole's office, a tiny cubicle near the chamber in which the House of Commons met. She could hear the shouting from where she sat. Roger's fine was the subject, and it was as if an unhealed wound had been touched, men shouting and bellowing about the South Sea Bubble, the trickery and treachery of His Majesty's ministers and stock jobbers.

The Tories had jumped on the question, and for two days now there had been long speeches and much posturing. All the old feeling against Walpole was up; Skreen, he was being called to his face and in the venomous little broadsheets. He'd chosen his time well, though, for many of the members were absent, already out of London, gone to their country homes for the season. Robin, thought Barbara, do you never misstep? What was happening with Jane? She did not know.

She heard a great shout. Today would be the vote, Robin told her. She went to the door, looked down the hall. What did it mean? The shouting continued, and then men were streaming from the chamber out into the lobby. She saw Wart and Tony, who had been watching the proceedings in the Commons since they began. A tall man beside Wart turned, and it was the Prince de Soissons.

Barbara became wary instantly. Philippe. He bowed to her.

When did you return? she thought, and then was distracted by Robin, coming out of the chamber, his face red. She walked to him.

"What I've put up with," he said to her, taking her hands, "you cannot imagine. The things said of me." And then, with a smile, "It's done. The fine is relented entirely."

Like that, one hundred thousand pounds of debt disappeared. She felt like fainting.

"Thank you, Robin."

He was leaving soon, to go to his country home, taking the boxes and boxes of notes about Rochester and the invasion, to see how he might proceed against a bishop. They were going to doom the Bishop to exile. His Majesty was pleased. He'd have rather had a headless body, but exile would do. Jane, thought Barbara, how do you do?

"Go and see my mother before you leave town, Robin."

"You're fretted for her, aren't you?"

"Yes."

"I'll do it."

Now here was Tony, a smile on his grave face.

"It's done," she said. "Walk me to my carriage, cousin."

Outside, as they waited for her carriage to be brought forward, someone called her name. She turned; there was Wart, and with him was Philippe.

"We wanted to congratulate you," Wart said. "Everyone who knows you is glad, Bab."

"I congratulate you, Barbara," Philippe said. "You have risen, like a phoenix, from ashes."

Which you did not expect, thought Barbara, and did not want.

Her carriage was here. Philippe held open the door for her before Tony could. She climbed inside without touching the hand he held out to help her.

"I will call upon you very soon," he said.

The carriage pulled away.

Wharton and Philippe walked down the street. Philippe stopped to buy a sprig of Christmas holly from a street vendor's basket. Carefully, fastidiously, he pushed it into his buttonhole, surveyed the scene before him: carriages and sedans, clerks from Whitehall walking to coffeehouses and taverns, someone selling fresh water to drink, someone selling herbs to bring good fortune.

"A pity she isn't a Jacobite," he said. "We must make her one."

In the carriage, Barbara felt numb. I've done it, she thought. I've survived Roger's debacle, triumphed over it. She closed her eyes, began to tremble. Someday, she thought, someday soon, I must grieve over all I've lost in this, but not today. Today I want to walk around Devane Square and say to myself, I've done it. I want to send love and blessings to Jane. Jane.

In her mind, Jane rehearsed the plan. This afternoon, she would bring friends yet again to see Gussy, as the guards had seen her do these last weeks. But this day Gussy would leave as one of them, if the guards and God allowed it. There was the carriage. Tim sat atop it. He grinned his broken-toothed grin at her, nodding his head. Dear Tim. Dear Annie. Their presence gave her strength, made her think she might succeed. There was no way ever, ever to repay them. Her father would try to give them coins, but Jane doubted they would take them. They did this for love of Tamworth and the Duchess and Ladybeth, all that they knew. They did it for love.

Inside the carriage, Jane said to the woman, "You understand everything? You are to go up to his cell with me, first."

Jane put her hand to her back, which was aching. Was it the child?

"What is it?" said Annie, sitting grim and sober beside the woman.

"Nothing; a little pain."

Tim pulled the carriage into the yard beside the Tower. Jane watched as he drove it back outside the gates. There was every possibility she would never see the other side of these walls again.

She and Annie and the woman walked across the yard, through the arch of Martin's Tower, under which was a bridge that crossed the moat. The afternoon was leaden, clouds like gray pillows. I am mad, thought Jane, completely mad to be doing this. It isn't going to work. They walked through yet another archway of yet another tower, down the path toward the entrance to all that was behind the walls, massive, thick walls.

My plan is too simple, thought Jane. I am a fool.

It was dark inside this last archway, an archway that would put them in the heart of all that was the Tower of London, like a small town behind its massive walls. The Tower held more buildings than Williamsburg, Barbara had said.

Jane stood a moment in the open space, breathing in air. I must not fail, she thought. I must be brave. But Barbara was the brave one, not she. Someone must stop this now, she thought, but who?

There, ahead, was the tower in which Gussy was jailed. Leaving Annie in the downstairs chamber, Jane walked with the woman up the stairs to the wardroom, and just before opening its door, took a deep breath that she felt all the way to her womb. Cramps in her womb. Something was happening. Annie knew. Courage.

She took Tim's woman by the hand and marched her into the wardroom, talking as fast as ever she had.

"I am to see the King tonight," she said to the woman, knowing the guards clustered by the fire would hear. "I am so beside myself I can hardly think. Where is the turnkey? Hurry, and open the door of my husband's cell."

Following the turnkey up the twisting stairs, Jane talked all the while, her heart pounding so hard she didn't know how her voice sounded over it.

"I must change my gown. My servant is coming here to help me change, turnkey. Let me know when she arrives, please. I can't go to the King in this gown."

Jane dropped a coin into the turnkey's hand; she and the woman went inside, and Jane continued to talk, to Gussy now, chattering on as the woman took off the hooded cloak she wore, took off the second cloak under that, and then began to take off her gown. Under it was another gown.

Jane picked up her skirts, and fetching out of a pocket in her undergown the wig and little bag of rouge and powder she had brought, she dropped these on the bed. As Gussy began to pull the gown over his head, Jane walked through his opened cell door and down the twisting stairs with the woman, saying to her as they crossed the wardroom, "My servant should be in the chamber below. Send her to me, or I will be late to see the King. Hurry. It will be dark soon."

She walked the woman out the door, walked halfway down the stairs to meet Annie.

"Thank you, God bless you," she whispered to the woman. "Be gone from London now." The woman nodded her head.

Annie had the hood of her cloak up over her head and a handkerchief to her face. She was weeping loudly.

"Never mind crying, my dear friend." Jane patted Annie's arm. "I am to give the King my petition tonight, and I know all will be well."

Annie climbed up the short, twisting stairs to the cell with Jane, Jane talking all the while, Annie crying behind the handkerchief as if her heart would break. Gussy had on the gown and wig.

Quickly, Annie pulled off her cloak, stepped out of the tall heeled shoes she had worn. Jane was still talking of this and that, whatever she could think of—one did not know if a guard or the turnkey might come up the stairs a step or two to listen.

The door must be kept open, for once closed it could be opened again only with a key. She brushed powder on Gussy's face, while Annie rouged him. Jane found she had to stand quite still for a moment. She saw Annie look sharply at the expression on her face.

Annie took hold of her arm, but Jane shook her off. "I am well. Put on the other cloak. Let us go now, before I lose my courage. Keep the hood of it down. If they don't notice you, Annie, we may have done it."

As Jane's foot touched the bottom stair, she moved quickly across the chamber yet again, saying to Annie, "My dear friend, go and see if my servant is below. She can't know how late it is. Has she forgotten I'm to give the King the petition? If I don't present it tonight, he will not receive it at all! Tell her to hurry. I shall be on pins and needles until she arrives. This is dreadful, that she should be so late."

A guard opened the door, and Jane walked to the top of the stairs with Annie, watched as Annie moved down the stairs. She put her hand to her back, the pain there deep, the cramp in her abdomen growing.

I must hurry, she thought. Half running across the wardroom, she went back up the stairs. Gussy wore the hood that Annie had pulled up over his head. In his hand was the handkerchief Annie had held to her face as she pretended to weep. If no one looked too closely, if they were all half blind, he just might be the weeping woman Annie had played.

Gussy and Jane held hands a moment.

"God fare you well," Jane whispered.

The moment of truth has arrived, she was thinking. Silly plan, foolish plan, now they catch us.

She took his hand, started down the stairs, chattering wildly, as it seemed she'd been doing for hours. "Well, there is just nothing for it! Come along! Come along! I cannot believe this has happened this night of all nights. Hurry, my dear, hurry!"

Behind her, Gussy had raised the handkerchief to his face, was making weeping sounds, false to Jane's ears; surely they were as false to the guards'. Jane put her arm through his as they crossed the wardroom, an eternal crossing, it seemed, but here they were at the door, and no one was stopping them.

"For the love of God, run quickly to my lodgings," she said. "You know where they are. Bring my maid to me. At once."

She walked with Gussy to the stairs, walked down with him. There was Annie in the downstairs chamber. Jane pushed Gussy toward Annie.

"Don't look back," she whispered.

She turned and walked back up, stopping once at the pain, which was bad now. Inside the wardroom, she brushed at tears. She couldn't help herself.

"The maid will come, Mrs. Cromwell," said one of the guards.

She stopped where she was, put her hands to her face.

"Don't weep, Mrs. Cromwell," said another.

"I'm just going up to say good-bye to my husband; then I must go. I have to give the King the petition."

She wiped at the tears running down her face, as they all watched. This cannot be happening, thought Jane. They believe me. Any moment one of them is going to say, You're caught, Mrs. Cromwell. Two women went up to your husband's cell, and three came down.

Expecting this, her whole body tensed for the words, she walked up the short flight of twisting steps into the cell, talking to Gussy as if he were still there. "There is nothing I can do but leave this moment. Give me a kiss, my darling. If the Tower is still open when I have finished with the King, I will return tonight. If not, I will see you in the morning."

A long cramp took hold of her and made her gasp. When it was passed, when she thought she could walk, she went to the stairs—

everything felt strange now, she felt as if she were moving through water—and shut the door of Gussy's cell. Now, only the turnkey could unlock it again. She walked down the stairs.

In the wardroom, she said to the turnkey, "I must go. If I finish in time, I'll return. My husband desires to pray awhile."

She put another coin in the turnkey's hand.

"I beg you, allow him quiet this evening. Never mind bringing up candles, later. I've shut the door. You can go and see, but I beg you, don't disturb him. I need his prayers this night."

"God bless you, Mrs. Cromwell, I hope all goes well for you this evening. You've my prayers, too."

The turnkey walked her to the door and opened it himself. Jane walked out to the stairs. Her head was dizzy. Had this happened? Did they sense nothing? Had she taken Gussy from the Tower? Was it this easy?

Three brown cloaks, a woman's gown and wig, was that all it took?

She waited a moment for a guard to open the door behind her and bellow out her name. It was a silly plan. What on earth had made her think it would succeed? The pain was bad.

Can I walk down these stairs? she thought after a time, when the door behind her remained closed. She did it, walking outside, into growing twilight, walking onto the grounds, as guards moved about lighting candles in the hanging lanterns. She walked through the entrance gate, nodding to the guard there, as always she did. How far away the bridge across the moat seemed; she leaned against the wall, considering it, but there was Annie, hurrying toward her, dear Annie, strong Annie, stern Annie, the Annie of her girlhood and Barbara's, glorious girlhood, apple blossoms and country charms, fairy cups on the hillock. . . .

"Is he—"

"Safe with your father. Already on his way to Gravesend."

"Annie—" The word was a sob, for the pain, for the cramp.

"I know," said Annie, holding her arm, catching her own through it. "Walk with me down this walk, through that arch, yes, keep going, then we will walk through the yard, and then Tim will be waiting for us. We have a carriage for you, my Jane, so that you may rest. Just a few steps. Think of your husband and children waiting, waiting for you in Gravesend, think of your triumph. You've snatched him away, yes, you have. Lean on me, and I will see to you, that I promise. Annie is here, Jane. We'll keep that baby if we can. And if not . . . well, there will be another one."

Yes, thought Jane. Annie is here.

In Devane Square, dusk had come. Barbara walked away from the garden. Philippe, she thought, shall I set you and Andreas against each other for the honor of building on Roger's square? Smiling at the idea, she walked up the stairs to the first townhouse, unlocked the door, walked up more stairs to the parlor with its windows along three sides. She would be in by Christmas Day. Some furniture was already here in the parlor, covered in cloth. There was a portrait leaning against a wall. She moved the cloth from it. Roger.

I thought I would not get over you, and now I have, she thought. Someone else has my heart, but you're in there, also. Nothing changes and everything does. It is nearly the New Year. Shall I give you a final gift, Roger, before we part forever?

"Tell us, thou clear and heavenly tongue, where is the Babe that lately sprung? Lies he the lily-banks among. . . ."

Her lovely contralto echoed in the chamber as she sang one of the beautiful carols of the season.

"Bravo."

It was Colonel Perry standing framed by the doorway. How long had he been there? In one hand was a bottle, in the other two goblets and winter violets from Saylor House's hothouse.

"Peach brandy," he said. "I waited at your mother's, but Bathsheba whispered she had a feeling you'd come here. These were sent you just before I left. Well?"

From Annie, violets for Tamworth's wood violet. Gussy was rescued. They were on their way to Virginia. Was it possible? Had the great and powerful Walpole been bested by a woman, a meek and quiet woman? Oh, it was too wonderful for words. She wanted to laugh. She wanted to weep.

"It's done. The fine is relented."

He poured brandy into the goblets and handed one to Barbara, seeing, as he did so, the uncovered portrait.

"Is that Lord Devane?"

"Yes."

"A handsome man." He lifted his goblet. "To triumph over adversity; to courage in the face of fear. The courageous person is not the one who does not feel fear. The courageous feels fear and proceeds in the direction of dreams anyway. To you." He drank the brandy.

She could feel them, the tears. If I begin weeping, she thought, I won't stop, but they were seeping out, running down her cheeks, betraying her.

"Tell me."

Gentle man. Dear friend. Angel. The words stuck in her throat. "Roger, my brother, my marriage, Hyacinthe, the dream, the dream I had."

Jane. Jane has triumphed. She has her husband and her children. Grandmama. Now you can't die, for Gussy isn't going to die.

"Yes. You've lost much. Let us drink to that before we leave. It is cold here, and we must go. You must rest from your labors, Barbara; rest is welcome and necessary. Come. Lift your glass, let us drink to all that is gone, all that you've lost."

It seemed to her she drank in more than sweet brandy. Her heart hurt. Life is never finished, said her grandmother, never. That is its terror and its beauty.

"Now," Colonel Perry said, "let us drink to all that is to come. So much, my dear, so very much."

Annie left Tim at the back garden gate of Saylor House, moved quickly down gravel paths, the hood of her cloak over her head so that no one should know her, past the stable, through a side door and up the back stairs to her chamber.

It was done. The last she'd seen of Ashfords and Cromwells, they were awaiting word from the captain to board ship. She boiled water, steeped tea leaves, strained a portion of them out, drank her tea. That done, she looked down at the tea leaves left.

They'd make it safely to Virginia. Mistress Barbara and the Duchess would survive the disgrace. Annie and Barbara were agreed; they'd tell the Duchess of their parts in the escape later, when some of the first noise about it died down. Mistress Barbara. Her life was a wonder. There'd be disgrace over this, but also triumph.

The tea leaves. Sometimes they told too much. A death had been in them just now. Whose? Annie's mind went moving over all those she'd seen go from this life, the Duchess's two sons from smallpox, Diana's children, too. Harry from suicide, the Duke, Richard, from his mind. What was it she remembered from one of the Duchess's letters, that Lady Mary Wortley Montagu said there was a cure for smallpox, a putting of the pox on a small, opened place on the skin. Then fever, a few spots, but nothing more, nothing of the horror and rotting flesh and almost certain death that was smallpox.

Had the cure always existed? Were there other cures existing, out there? Would there be a day when women did not die in childbed and men's minds did not make them break inside like dried-out twigs? Annie touched her face. Tears for Jane, there.

Mistress Barbara had told them the stories of the fierce Indians of that world across the sea, Indians who sang songs to proclaim their deeds, warriors' songs, Mistress Barbara had said, rising to the skies like hawks. Did Jane sing now, on the ship, sailing away from here? Sing loudly, thought Annie, proclaim yourself. What is my song? she thought. What is anybody's? There has to be a song, for us all. It was a round of years, wasn't it, an up and down, a lesson to be learned, then learned again, until we were spun pure as gold and like the angels themselves.

She touched her face, brushed away the tears, for Jane and Barbara, for two girls who had played at tea under Tamworth's oaks, girls using acorn tops for cups. Fairy cups, they said. Warriors, now, the both of them.

SPRING

. . . BUT THE GREATEST OF THESE IS
CHARITY.

CHAPTER 61

Barbara sat in Alexander Pope's grotto. I am mad to do this, she thought.

Walpole hanged poor Christopher Layer next month, May. The pitiful man sat in his cell with chains around his ankles. They said he howled like a wild dog in his cell, howling that he had been betrayed, that Walpole had promised life for testimony. But since Gussy's escape, Walpole had been like a demon. If he could have proved anything against Barbara, he would have. As it was, she knew she lived on borrowed time; somehow he was going to see her disgraced, removed from her office.

The truth was, she was ready to leave all the scheming and machination, except that she had a new love, tiny, only a month old. Her brother. Someone was waiting for her in France: one Lucius, Viscount Duncannon, who asked her to come and visit his mother.

The trial against Rochester was going on; it was all people talked of, as Rochester refuted each and every charge against himself. He'd be banished, however, that was certain.

No word yet from Jane. Lord Bolingbroke, the great traitor, had been pardoned. Ten thousand pounds made him traitor no more.

She sat in this amazing cave Pope had built in his garden along the Thames, pieces of shell and stone glittering into the twilight this grotto made, waiting to meet the one who was the new head of the

Jacobites. Life unfurled like a many-petaled flower. Which path did she take?

You have to do nothing but listen, Philippe had said. He was her ally now, because of Walpole. He schemed and planned for her as if she were his daughter. Don't leave the King's household, he said. We need you there. Barbara tossed her head. If you go, said Philippe, I will see you made lady-in-waiting to the new Queen of France. That will serve my purpose just as well.

The new leader of the Jacobites, Philippe said, was Rochester's chief adviser in all this, one of the original planners of the plot, a longtime ally whom King James could not do without.

She heard footsteps, bit her lip.

Her grandmother's last words to her before leaving for Tamworth had been to keep her heart. There was a rustle of skirts, the sound of bracelets jangling, ten bracelets if there was one. Startled, Barbara looked over to Philippe.

"Never mind looking like that, Bab," said Aunt Shrew. "You and I have talking to do. Go away now, Prince, and leave us be."

Quiet, waiting, Blackstone squatted, listening, the way the slaves had taught him. Even so, Kano heard before he did, and touched his arm with a finger. Blackstone stood and watched the man stepping out into the clearing. He was older, heavy, his face tired, haggard; there was quite a party of people with him, back in the trees: a woman his age, a younger woman great with child, a tall, stooped man, and at least four children, all of them travel worn, with that look that came from crossing over in a ship, landing in a strange land, a fierce and forested land.

"Jacobite," the letter this older man had brought to him yesterday said. Blackstone knew the writing at once. It was the same writing that had made him a freed man. "I send you my dearest friends . . . trial . . . escape . . . secrecy and care . . . settle them beyond the Huguenots."

I am Sir John Ashford, the man said, and my telling you that puts my life in your hands, or it will when ships with the news of the London Jacobite trials arrive, but Lady Devane told me I could trust you. We've been hiding since we arrived. It has taken us days to make our way to you. My daughter is near her childbirth. We are so tired. Can you help us?

"Help them," Lady Devane wrote.

Well, of course. That was what friends were for.

Blackstone stepped out from his hiding place, smiling, teeth bold in his wild beard.

"Well, now, Mr. John Ashford, just what is it I can do for you?"

Purge me with hyssop, and I shall be clean: wash me, and I shall be whiter than snow. Make me to hear joy and gladness; that the bones which thou hast broken may rejoice.

EPILOGUE

Two Years Later: 1725

The lines from the slave song flew in and out of Thérèse's head, with the same quickness, the same darting motion of the purple thread she drew in and through the fold of material in her hand. She was embroidering flowers, violets, dozens of them, all along a sleeve. I want violets, Thérèse, Madame had written, all along the hem and sleeve. She desired violets. She would have them. It was her wedding gown Thérèse made, with all the joy and skill her hands and mind could command.

The dead are not dead, went the slave song in her mind.

"Someone to see you." A fellow servant stood at the door.

Carefully, Thérèse set aside the folds of material, to follow the servant to the great kitchen of Leicester House. She was a favorite now, among the servants and with the Princess. But another year, perhaps two, and there would be the coins for her own shop. Come to Paris, Madame wrote. You can have a shop as easily in Paris as you can in London.

"Outside," said the servant. "He said he's been sent here by the Duke of Tamworth."

Thérèse peered out a window. A gaunt boy stood there, clothes ragged enough to belong to a beggar. It seemed to her that her heart stopped beating a moment, so that she hadn't the strength to pull open the door. But then strength came, and joy.

The Duchess sat dozing on her terrace. Leaning against a large stone vase, Tim watched over her. She was dreaming, a wonderful dream. June, thought the Duchess in her dream. She liked the month of June. Richard's roses bloomed like mad things. Down the avenue of limes came Sir John Ashford, in a cart, with a young woman and children beside him. The Duchess smiled. It was the only time she saw her friend, now, in dreams. There'd been a letter this year, from Virginia, from a Mr. John, who sent her a hogshead of his tobacco with his compliments.

"Look, Your Grace," said Tim, in the dream, "who is coming down the lane. It is Sir John and Mrs. Cromwell. Shall I tell Cook to put on the kettle?"

Long ago, Harry and Jane had courted in the apple orchard. They thought she did not know, she who knew everything that happened at Tamworth. They had been in love. Calf love. Coming to nothing. Harry was dead. And Jane now, too, Mr. John had written. How Barbara had grieved. They had all grieved; even Tony, colder than ever now, even Tony was touched. Did you help with the escape? he'd asked her in that month or two afterward when it was all any-one talked of, before Walpole had his trial of the Bishop, and talk shifted to that. No, she could say truthfully. Others did, she did not say, but he knew. How could he not?

Sir John and the occupants of the cart waved cheerfully to her as the cart and its horse rattled to a stop in the pebbled courtyard at the front of the house. What good things dreams were. Here, now, Jane was alive and well.

"He has brought his grandchildren," she said to Tim. They were as she remembered them the last time she saw them, the winter of Gussy's escape. "Have Perryman send them here. Children ought to be outside on a evening like this one."

The soft dusk and the smell of roses would bless them. She knew what children needed. Yes, she did. Once she had had three sons. And they had grown from little boys to young men who towered

over her, and now she watched over their graves the way she had
once watched over their cradles, and in the fullness of time, such no
longer seemed a curse, but rather a blessing. She had loved her sons.
That love was in her heart still. No death could take it away. Loss
made a body afraid to love again, but in the end there was nothing
else but love. . . . "Charity," wrote St. Paul, "beareth all things, believeth all things, hopeth all things, endureth all things. . . . When I
was a child, I spake as a child, I understood as a child, I thought as a
child: but when I became a man, I put away childish things."

She had thought she would die when they had died, but she had
not. . . . "For now we see through a glass, darkly; but then face to
face: now I know in part; but then shall I know even as also I am
known." . . . She visited the many graves of those gone and felt only
tenderness and gratitude to have had them for as long as she had. . . .
"And now abideth faith, hope, charity, these three; but the greatest
of these is charity." . . . Love.

"It will do you no good to close your eyes and pretend to doze,"
said John, her beloved friend. How she missed him. "I am here to
visit, and you cannot ignore me." He gave her a hearty smack on the
cheek. "Amelia, Thomas, Winifred, come and show Her Grace your
manners. Not that they have many."

She smiled at what was in his voice, and as Dulcinea leaped up and
away from her lap, the Duchess looked at the trio bowing and curtsying to her. Then Jane walked forward, Harry Augustus in her
arms. There was another, the one she'd borne in Virginia, but they
must have left it there. Jane looked all of fourteen—perhaps she *was*
fourteen. After all, this was a dream. Jane leaned down to kiss her.

"Your father wrote me you'd died," the Duchess said.

"Yes."

"I am so very sorry. Barbara was wild when she heard it. She left
the King's service, took herself off to France. She is marrying a
colonel in the French army, wants me to come to the wedding. I'm
too old, but she says she will come and fetch me herself, or send
Colonel Perry to do so."

Annie grieved, too, the Duchess did not say. It was one of the only times the Duchess had seen Annie weep, the day they received the letter from Virginia.

"A wedding; how lovely," said Jane. "Tell her I will be there, blessing her."

Yes, of course she would. Once the Duchess would never have believed such a thing, but now she knew it was true. Those we loved were all around us, blessing us.

Perryman and Tim were bringing armchairs out to the terrace, and another footman was carrying a small dark table. Annie came forward with a huge silver tray, and there was tea and milk and lemon tartlets and warm, freshly baked bread and Tamworth butter and honey and preserves. All became children and noisy confusion as Jane settled her three oldest ones onto the terrace, and Annie spread great white napkins into their laps.

When the children were finished, mounds of crumbs and spilled milk on the terrace, Tim offered to take them onto the lawn to play in the dusk.

"Tell me all your news." The Duchess served herself a huge lemon tartlet in spite of the look Annie gave her. You ought to have been dead years ago, Annie would say tonight, when the Duchess would suffer from wind. Bah. Annie was a stubborn old stick. Paris, said Annie. I'd like to see it. Ridiculous to think they could travel to Paris. Tony was going. Do you think I would miss Barbara's wedding? he said, but something in his face warned the Duchess. Family. They never behaved. Tony rose in the King's esteem. He was not a minister yet, but he would be. He allied himself with those who opposed Walpole, open in his disdain of the man.

"I farm beyond the falls, beyond the Huguenot settlement. It is good, rich land. I had my first crop of tobacco last year," John said.

As well she knew. He'd sent her a hogshead. The tobacco was labeled "Friendship." It was the name of his farm.

From the lawn came screams of delighted horror, and everyone turned to see. Tim had become a monster and was pursuing the three children. But he was a monster with a broken leg, and he dragged it slowly behind him, and the children screeched with pleasure and ran around him in circles, and he waved his arms at them, coming so close, trying to catch them, but always missing.

The Duchess shivered under her light shawl. In the house, Perryman was lighting candles. I must go now, thought the Duchess, loath to give up her dream, her time with John and Jane. Tonight I will lie in my bed and think of this dream and remember the smell of Richard's roses, the bittersweetness of this moment as my friend's grandchildren play on my lawn, and his beloved daughter sits nearby.

"Me!" screamed Amelia, daring Tim. "You cannot catch me!"

Suddenly Tim's leg was well, and he grabbed her, and she pierced the air with her bloodcurdling shrieks as he picked her up and tossed her high before catching her again.

"They will sleep like logs tonight," Jane said. In her arms, the baby, Harry Augustus, began to cry at the sound of his sister's screams. Sir John stood up and held out his arms for him, and Jane gave the child to his grandfather, who walked down the wide steps of the terrace, patting the child's back and speaking softly to him.

"I did not want you to die," the Duchess said.

She died with us all around her, John had written. She was never alone, not a moment, in her dying, which is my only consolation. She could not get back her strength from the journey and the childbirth. She tried, but she could not. She was never strong.

On the contrary, thought the Duchess, she was the strongest of us all.

The baby was still crying a little, and he held to his grandfather's wig with one small, grim fist, and he seemed to be listening, his little round face concentrated, to what his grandfather was saying to soothe him.

"Do you know," said Jane, "I think Harry Augustus is Father's favorite," and she smiled at the Duchess; it was a lovely smile, just a hint of mischievousness to it. No, John had not liked Harry, had thought him a wild rogue who would break his daughter's heart. The Duchess remembered when Jane and Barbara and Harry had run wild over Tamworth and Ladybeth Farm. Not so long ago. It was good to have children running again on her lawn.

"I should have allowed Harry to marry you," she said.

"No. You were correct." Jane's voice was gentle.

Calf love, Diana had said.

"Harry would have broken my heart."

"He was a bad boy, wasn't he?"

"Yes."

"Then why did we love him?"

"We are fools."

"Well, come here and let this old fool kiss you." The Duchess kissed both Jane's cheeks. "Go and walk in Richard's rose garden awhile. The roses are in their finest blooming, and you need some roses of your own in those cheeks. Go on before the sun leaves us. Pick as many roses as you want. . . . Pick a bouquet to take to . . ." She stopped.

Pick a bouquet for yourself, Jane, and for Harry, and for your Jeremy and my Richard, for all of those gone on before us. . . . What did the psalm say? . . . "Have mercy upon me, O God, according to thy lovingkindness: according unto the multitude of thy tender mercies." . . . lovingkindness, tender mercies: the lime trees in the avenue, her roses, this dream of John and Jane, her old friend walking toward her in it with his small grandson gone to sleep in his arms, Dulcinea atop the table now, picking her way through the food to find and eat the last crumbs of lemon tartlets. In the end, there were great deeds, but there was also, most importantly, this. . . .

The door was open. Thérèse and the boy stared at each other before, finally, she was able to say his name.

"Hyacinthe."

They were in each other's arms now. He is as tall as I, thought Thérèse, and the tears streamed down her face.

"Where," he said—his eyes were dark, fierce, sad, as deep as an ocean; Old, thought Thérèse, he has old eyes now—"is Madame?"

The dead are not dead. . . . They are in the fire that is dying, in the grasses that weep . . . in the whimpering rocks. . . . The dead are not dead. . . . Listen . . . listen . . . listen.

Tim shook the Duchess hard by the shoulder, not liking the way her head lolled to one side. She wasn't . . . she couldn't be . . . it was what they all feared.

The Duchess opened one eye. "Things have come to a pretty pass when footmen behave as you do. I ought to have you beaten for the dream you have just waked me from."

"I thought you—"

"Dead? Bah!"

But which was the dream? That which she'd just left, or this, now? Paris. She was too old. . . .

Listen. Listen. Listen.

ABOUT THE AUTHOR

KARLEEN KOEN was an editor at *Houston Home and Garden* magazine when her interests in writing fiction and in the eighteenth century led her to write her first novel, *Through a Glass Darkly*. She lives in Houston, Texas.

ABOUT THE TYPE

The text of this book was set in Janson, a mis-
named typeface designed in about 1690 by
Nicholas Kis, a Hungarian in Amsterdam. In
1919 the matrices became the property of the
Stempel Foundry in Frankfurt. It is an old-style
book face of excellent clarity and sharpness. Janson serifs are concave and splayed; the contrast
between thick and thin strokes is marked.